Take The Strain

D V Canale

3

Thanks to my daughter, Donna, for all her help in getting this book published.

Vince Canale
2014

PROLOGUE

CYPRUS, 1990

It was a little after nine o'clock on a brilliantly clear June morning. On the many beaches of the sun drenched Mediterranean island of Cyprus, thousands of pale-skinned invaders had already claimed their part of the beach, staking sections of sand with towels, deck chairs and sun beds. Oil slicked backs and bosoms glistened along the water's edge like washed pearls as the early sun worshippers offered their sacrificial skins to their fiery god's ultra violet glare.

Not too far from one of those beaches, the British military base at RAF Episkopi was, despite rising temperatures functioning perfectly. Precisely as might be expected of a British military establishment on foreign soil. There was no sign of beach towels or sun blockers as a young WRAF corporal, a member of the Royal Military Police, left the guardroom.

Resplendent in her sand camouflaged uniform she climbed aboard a similarly marked Land Rover, started the engine then drove the short distance to the lowered gate pole barring exit from the camp. Here she paused as the pole was raised before easing out to the Limasol-Paphos junction. On the vehicle's nearside mudguard was a small, almost unobtrusive red white and blue roundel, whilst the other bore a similarly low profiled pink flamingo surrounded with a wreath of laurel leaves. The former the symbol of the Royal Air Force, the latter that of the Akrotiri base, some ten miles to the south on the tip of the island peninsula.

The road was quiet and the driver turned right en route to the last port of call: an outlying radio and observation post in the hills to the west. The woman sighed contentedly, anticipating the remaining miles of coast road, by far her favourite section of the mail run. The main part of the run was over with the delivery of documents, official papers, royal and internal mail etc. to Episkopi. Nothing of prime military substance, but paperwork including personal mail still required safe delivery. The pumping heart of RAF Akrotiri fed administrative paraphernalia through arteries to key organs all over the island. This morning she had just fed the Episkopi organ. All of which helped keep the military body on the island of Cyprus functioning.

Traffic was light, the heat bearable and the day perfect. The corporal relaxed, removed her white hat and visualized the cool Seven Up awaiting her in the tiny R. and O. post. Content with her lot she hummed a Greek tune popular in the clubs and Naafi bars.

She loved this most exquisite time of day. The air always seemed particularly clear as her keen blue eyes swept over the beautiful scenery surrounding her. All windows were lowered to their maximum allowing the cooled turbulent air to whir round the cabin, whipping her sun-bleached short hair around the girl's pretty face. Her cap on the seat beside her was an added bonus. She was on duty so it should be on her head but the sheer joy of the buffeting air cooling her head and frame was irresistible. Plus there was the added mystical human element of when biting into fruit that is forbidden, the flesh tastes that much sweeter.

Comfortably cruising, the tyres hissing on the tacky tar, she drove round a tight bend, anticipating the scene that would greet her. It was not the beautiful blue sea as one might think. That delight was still to come.

The sight that brought a smile was simply the view of the Happy Valley sports ground. Deep in the hill's cleavage to her left, set on the flat valley floor, was a splash of emerald green. It was so unexpected in the washed out dun coloured hills. It stung the eye with its sheer unexpected beauty. Happy Valley was protected on three sides with rolling hills, aglow with the course sandy soil peculiar to the Mediterranean. The scorched hills, all but infertile under the merciless sun, were saved marginally by the scant peppering of ancient carob and olive trees. Annually

8

through each dry summer, the precarious plant life clung to the feeble curve of the hills and existence, like starving infants to undernourished mothers' breasts. They had a long time to wait for sustenance as the winter rains were still four months away.

Running her eyes over the soccer sized sports field, she felt the therapeutic vibes the spread of colour and tranquillity instilled in her nervous system, loving the tingling charge she always felt up the back of her neck. It usually evoked a sigh. This morning however, an unusual movement snagged the sigh and her attention.

Initially she assumed the man was a groundsman, but noted the man was wearing a dark suit! Happy Valley leased to the British was looked after by the Ministry of Public Buildings and Works based in Akrotiri. MPBW employed local workers to care for the grounds and they wore civilian clothes, but a suit? Hardly the attire for a groundsman.

There was something unusual about this man. He was tall with a shock of white hair, athletic but old. He moved slowly or perhaps simply unhurried. What was he doing? The trained powers of observation having triggered her female sense of curiosity helped make the decision to pull over near an overhanging rock and stop. Applying the handbrake and switching off, she went to the rock's edge where she could see clearly the spread of Happy Valley below.

The man continued to walk slowly, but it was the unusual manner in which he walked that caught her attention. It was slow and solemn, as one would walk in an ancient cathedral. When he reached the area in front of the stand, he stopped and peered at the ground before crouching down. Then he did something strange! He placed his right hand palm down onto the ground, holding it there momentarily before moving it round in a semi-circle through the grass. Had he lost something? The crouching position became uncomfortable so he moved awkwardly to a sitting position, legs splayed out, arms straight behind, supporting the upper body.

The WAAF corporal was puzzled by the man's behaviour. Undecided on her next move, she watched the recumbent figure for some minutes. His head was moving now, from one side to the other in a slow mechanical sweep. Continually, with no other movement. Deciding he may be in need of assistance, the military policewoman returned to her vehicle and drove to the Derbyshire road entrance and into Happy Valley. Parking under a line of trees behind the stand and donning her hat she walked past the end of the stadium where the toilets were situated, down some steps, crossed the running track and approached the sitting man.

"Good morning sir, forgive my intrusion but I happened to see you from the road," she nodded towards her vantage point, "and I wondered perhaps, if I could be of assistance?"

The man raised his head as he did everything, slowly, and peered up at the uniformed woman.

He did not answer but the look he gave acknowledged her presence then continued to move his head round in the same manner. His eyes locking momentarily on the few landmarks.

About to repeat her question, the man spoke, "Corporal, I'm sorry I'm a little distracted, but to answer to your question, yes please, you can help me up, if you don't mind." He held up a hand which was ignored as the active woman moved smartly to the back of the sitting figure. "Try to rise when I ask you please," she said. Bending her knees she placed her arms round his chest, gave a slight rocking pull. "Up we go," she said, straightening her back and knees, and effortlessly lifting the man to his feet.

The man frowned, "Thank you, you've learned your training well." He paused then sighed heavily before going almost reluctantly on. "The last time I was here on this ground, was many years ago." Echoing his movements, his speech was slow, picking words from scenes rolling across his mind's eye. Shaking his head he went on, "It could have been so much better, all ... all so different really!" He stared again intently at the area around his feet.

"I see." The woman's inquisitive mind was sifting what he said. "Is that your car sir?" She had only noticed the car when entering the ground.

"Yes," he answered blinking rapidly, clearing cobwebs of memory. He pointed to the southern end of the ground. "I parked there, where the athlete's marquees are usually erected, or perhaps were erected, at one time?"

She was intrigued. Looking more searchingly, she put his age at around sixty. The shock of thinning white hair and slow movement initially caused her to think he was older. Marquees were erected near where the car was parked during sports meetings, confirming the man's familiar topography. Intriguing yes, but the man was doing no harm. She would take her leave.

"I've already intruded too much into your privacy sir ... and your meditative musing. I'll be off then, if there's nothing else?"

"No nothing, thank you, I'd rather be alone; I've waited years to come back here - a long time."

"Of course, I was concerned when you sat down, and just sat there! I just wondered ...."

"Don't worry about me, I am perfectly all right," he said starting again on what was now a rather irritating slow, miss nothing scan.

About to turn away the woman hesitated. She was finding it difficult to leave this man but could not understand why? He obviously wanted to be left alone yet she felt drawn. Something deep down she could not quite place. He broke her train of thought with another request. "The stand corporal, may I sit in the stand, just for a while. That shouldn't break any rules?"

"Sitting in the stand! No sir, it certainly won't."

The unlikely pair walked back across the track, up the dozen steps then into the stand. As they climbed the woman's nagging curiosity got the better of her. "Sir, you mentioned you were here, on this ground years ago, would you care to elaborate?"

There was no immediate response. Then when they reached the first row of seats, he repeated her last word almost indignantly. "Elaborate? There's no need to elaborate young lady, it's all true. It happened ... here, I can assure you, right here!" He waved an arm around, "It may have been a number of years ago, but that does not deter from the fact, it happened! Does it, does it corporal?" He spoke emphatically, staring into her eyes while feeling his way into a seat.

"No, of course not," she answered as the man stared once again onto the field, obviously ensnared in vivid memories of a world long past.

"I'm going sir, but if there's anyone I can telephone perhaps, let them know you're here?" She could not pin it down, but something about this man concerned her.

"Thank you for your consideration, but I have told you, I will be all right! I'm merely reliving some moments from my past, something I've been doing a lot of lately." He smiled crookedly, "Please, go about your duties corporal. I intend to sit here for some time."

"Then take care." The woman walked briskly to the Land Rover and ducked gratefully into its shade. Turning the vehicle and driving away, the figure in the stand did not respond to her wave. On impulse passing the man's hired car, distinctive due to the red number plates, she noted the registration number. 'Can't be too careful,' she thought.

The intruding, well-intentioned MP was quickly forgotten as the man gazed intently at the ground directly in front of the stand. The patch of grass where the last event brought military sports meetings to an end. The tug-of-war final.

"If only. Oh, if only." He mused. It was neither whisper nor thought, but something in between. If what the man said were words, the shapes tumbled from trembling lips in an exalted silence followed by a sad headshake. "Too many diversions in the forked roads of time," he hissed, the whisper again barely audible. "But there's no denying, at the end of the day ... what a team!" He sucked air, his chin lifted and his voice at last found timbre, with eyes sparkling he said, "How could they go on, year after year, dozens of different men yet still produce such teams?"

Down on the manicured green lawn of the sports field he clearly saw the unfamiliar yellow and black quartered shirts of the 103 Maintenance Unit tug-of-war team. They were lining up on the last sporting occasion he had been on that field, involved in a final all those years ago. The smell of the new hemp rope was strong in his nostrils; he could feel the nervous tension and adrenaline flush through his veins as his fists clenched tight. The noisy, expectant crowd hushed as the official raised both his arms. Clearly, he heard the umpire's stentorian words roll across the valley floor, "TAKE UP - THE - ROPE." A pause, "TAKE - THE - STRAIN."

The words echoed round the ground. Another pause. The man's stomach muscles tightened, he braced himself - wait - wait - then,

"PULL!"

Chapter 1

103 Maintenance Unit. 1953

On the east side of the Royal Air Force base at Akrotiri, Cyprus, on an area of ground allocated to 103 Maintenance Unit, two airmen were crossing the road bordering the main yard of the MU. They were leaving the yard pulling a low rubber tired trolley on which lay a heavy looking metal container plus a dozen or more scrap metal pieces, off-cuts etc. Every piece had its weight newly painted and stamped in two surfaces.

On the opposite side of the road, they made their way between a row of camouflaged marquees then down the slope to a shallow depression of rough ground, some fifty yards from the road, the training ground for the 103 Maintenance Unit tug-of-war team. There were two training tripods at each end of the depression. The larger team-training tripod was sixty yards to their right but it was at the small individual training tripod where the pair stopped. Dropping the 'T' handle on one of the three horizontal support bars of the rig, the two airmen sat gratefully on the trolley top.

"Your lob Phil, get them oot," the smaller of the two said leaning back enjoying the sun.

His compatriot dragged a packet of 'Benson and Hedges' from the breast pocket of his khaki drill working jacket, "You're like a bloody elephant Dougie!" he moaned, "Last time you lobbed me a fag was three weeks ago - in the Naafi! I'll never forget it, such an earth-shattering event. Did you mark it in your diary?"

"Aye we can do withoot the cheek, but ye're right! It was an unusual experience. That's mebbe why Ah've no' forgotten it so - it's your lob, git them oot!"

This was the airmen's second visit to the training rig that morning. Soon after roll call and starting work, they had been sent to disconnect the container from the small rig. In addition, they had to collect every lump of metal used in conjunction with the container and bring everything back to the workshops. They were then given the job to empty then weigh the steel container, then paint and stamp its weight around the outside. Every piece was then weighed, painted and stamped with its weight. Finally, the container was to be filled until it weighed 16 stones in total.

The small rig consisted of three poles poking fifteen feet into the blue sky were set in triangular formation. Three feet from the ground, were three support girders five feet apart, forming the horizontal base triangle. Two pulleys, one fixed at the apex of the three poles, the other on one of the three support bars around knee level. A half-inch steel cable ran between the pulleys. The bottom end ran through the bottom pulley where steel couplings attached it to a length of rope snaking along over the ground of the pulling area.

The other cable end ran over the top pulley where it was fixed to a shackle. The shackle was now snagged at the mouth of the pulley. This happened when Phil unscrewed the shackle pin to release the steel container. When both cable and shackle were let loose it had taken off like a live thing, snaking up over his shoulder to stop only when the shackle hit the top pulley at the apex.

When in use a training individual would attempt to raise the weighted container off the ground and hopefully continue to haul it fifteen feet to the top of the rig. The larger piece of equipment was exactly the same only much heavier used for team training. Both were used to simulate an 'end' in the sport of tug-of-war. The 'opposition' being the not quite unbeatable but never tiring force of gravity on the weighted containers, or 'buckets' as the participants preferred to call them.

The team coach, a Chief Technician carpenter complained he could never tell the precise weight in the buckets so over a pint in the Sergeant's Mess he mentioned his problem to a sergeant from the Blacksmith section. The outcome was the latter agreed to have everything weighed and marked. Nothing was too much trouble for the MU tug-of-war team. As it was the middle of the athletic season, they decided to start on the smaller rig and work piecemeal on the heavier bucket and therefore team training would not be interrupted.

"I can understand what the coach's moaning about," Phil flicked his cigarette butt cleanly into the container. "I mean how can he assess anyone if he doesn't know the weight in the bucket?"

"Aye," answered Dougie running his eyes around the solid gantry. "But Ah still think they're a daft shower o' bampots, they tug-o'-war blokes! Haulin' that fuckin' thing up an' doon, up an' doon aw day. Great way to spend yer time in' it? Anyway, better get wir fingers oot Phil, you've got yer dental appointment!"

Removing some of the heavier pieces from the container, which weighed two ounces over sixteen stones, they carried it to the circular hollow at the tripod centre, and then replaced the pieces. The bucket thumping on the same spot thousands of times had created the circular indentation. Finally, the few extra pieces they stacked at the side of the rig.

"Right get it connected up and we're offski. Get up and pull that shackle doon will ye Phil, ah'll never reach that." Being the taller of the two Phil climbed on to a crossbar and with a little trouble reached the shackle jammed at the pulley. He pulled it and the cable free, passing it to Dougie.

"Wait a minute Phil, where's the bolt?"

"What bolt?"

"For the shackle ya clown, the bolt that locks the loop inside the shackle. You unscrewed the fuckin' thing remember? When the cable twisted free and aw but took yer baws aff."

"Shit" Phil recalled how the cable had untwisted and whipped against his family jewels. "That's right; I tossed it in my tool bag in case I lost it. That's where it'll be.

"Up in the shop? You asshole!" Why no' screw it back intae the shackle, then it wid still be here, widn't it? Better git it afore they super fit tug-o-war guys come doon and use us as weights.
Phil nodded then, "I can't come back Dougie, I'll be late for the dentist. Just a minute." Phil dug into his pocket and pulled out a pencil stump. "Screw that in the holes, it'll keep the cable from shooting back up the top. You'd never reach it if it does that again would you?"

"Good thinkin' Batman. Ah gees, how ah wish ah'd been born bright instead o' beautiful?"

Dougie took the three-inch pencil, "Aw hey, can you spare it?" he laughed holding up the stump. Then as his mate suggested he pushed the stub through the larger hole of the shackle, through the eye of the cable then forcibly screwed the soft wood into the threaded hole of the steel shackle. "Right, that'll hold it for a wee while. The team's no' due for anither half oor yet so I've got time. But there's nae time tae hing aboot so c'mon ya great long streak o' piss."

The unburdened rubber wheeled trolley bounced over the ground as the pair attacked the slope. At the top end of the training ground, a young man dressed in training gear watched the two airmen pulling a trolley until the pair merged and disappeared into the shrubbery. He heard them laugh and shook his head at their inanity. Why did so many fools surround him? And what were those two clowns doing in the tug-of-war training area? Probably skiving but just in case he'd have a good look around before starting his training.

On the plus side, Junior Technician Bernard Cornelius Kowaleski was a gifted man in many ways, but contrarily on the minus side, he was a palpably unpopular loner. He didn't particularly like his own company but much preferred that to spending time with anyone, male or female. Bernhard loved his life in the RAF, but detested being surrounded with envious mediocre underlings jealous of his aptitude and his ability to learn quickly. Most of all, they wanted to fawn over him at his outstanding sporting abilities. Kiss ass when he won races or events, all of which he spurned. He wanted to win, most certainly but not for the morons that surrounded him. He needed that inner glow that comes from winning, the warmth that goes hand in hand with victory, proving he was above them, all of them. With no urge to share those feelings he showed no emotion, merely nodding keeping them at bay, hoping they'd go away. So they left him and so his reputation of being a loner grew. So much so his ever-on-guard instinct warned him lesser athletes may attempt to end his athletic dominance, if they could. Bring him down from his self-elevated perch.

This did not trouble the young man; his adult life had always been like this. He was used to snide remarks, to resentment, hate and all the offshoots. But nothing was ever said to his face, the cowards knew he was capable of looking after himself.

Bernard was a little over six feet tall, blessed with an athletic build and a head of thick black hair. Coal black eyes peered from deep sockets at a world that had robbed him of many things. Not least of all a normal childhood. As if regretting the rebuttal of a good, or indeed, a less than normal upbringing, 'Life' it seemed had tried to balance its own books by showering this young man with a plethora of sporting abilities. At twenty-three he was passably good looking with the classic square jaw and straight nose typical of eastern European characteristics. A born athlete in that he never really trained his body to reach its present condition. It had simply grown into a mould of perfection with muscular shoulders and narrow hips weighing in at eleven and a half stone. His image mirrored what he had achieved in athletics where Bernard was a phenomenon. He had at one time or another won every RAF track event he applied his mind to winning, and discovered with a modicum of proper training he could master most of those he chose to enter. The world outside was beginning to take notice.

However when anything comes easy, too easy, and human nature being what it is, the warm glow of facile victories tends to cool the very confrontation of challenge. His natural urge was still to win, but in winning, victories became commonplace. The warm glow was beginning to cool.

Sport, and athletics in particular were without doubt Bernard's whole life but he needed a different outlet, something new. It goes without saying one day in the not too distant future Bernard would return to track and field events, but the urge to turn his attention to communal or team sports was strange. Bearing in mind his well-known preference to work alone. The reason may have been the niggling but nevertheless persistent thought was he might be missing something. The deciding factor happened when he received information he was due to be posted overseas. This made up his mind. Aware his natural ability would shine in anything he tried he decided to end this boredom and look around.

It was a mistake. Not the sport he chose, for he was excellent in tug-of-war as he was in others. But it was at this point when everything was going well for Bernard that Fate was to wag her fickle finger at one she had blessed.

When J/T Kowaleski arrived at 103 Maintenance Unit on the island of Cyprus on November, 1952, his reputation preceded him. When it was assumed he would sweep the boards on the track, the newly arrived Junior Technician surprised everyone by joining the Unit's emerging tug-of-war team. The team's coach, initially overjoyed to acquire such a mighty asset into his squad, soon discovered the new arrival was having a detrimental effect on team spirit.

No one knew why Bernard chose one of the oldest forms of team sport. The coach curious to know asked the young man, who informed him he needed a season away from the track and would fit in perfectly into his squad for the oncoming season.

During some friendly pulls to his great satisfaction Bernard discovered, much to his surprise a deep love for the sport. It happened during his first friendly match against a military police team drawn from bases all over the island. When applying his quite considerable strength into a heave, he experienced what could only be described as a surge of warm gold course through his body. His entire nervous system was set aglow it seemed with flowing Herculean strength for as long as that first end lasted. When in that awe inspiring turning point the eight statuesque powerful men at the opposite extremity of the rope had initially been pulled over into a bent position, he felt a rush of adrenalin. Then much against their will, those proud figures had doubled, crumbled into eight crouching scrabbling figures, all caused through absolute pressure to eventually succumb. Bernard was disappointed when the whistle blew. He wanted to drag those beaten men like so many wriggling fish on a line. They were beaten and tired men, and Bernard Kowaleski truly believed their defeat was due to his own superior strength. The young athlete lay on the ground after the match exalting in the sweet orgasm of sheer physical power over others. The feeling so intoxicated Bernard it meant little that seven other men were literally alongside him. Their presence never scaled the walls of arrogance Bernard surrounded himself with. The track may have a long wait for his return.

Tug-of-war training took place on workdays between 11 am and 12.30 pm in the training area across the road from the General Engineering Flight offices of 103 Maintenance Unit. As the 1953 athletic season progressed Bernard's love for the sport had grown to near obsession and he took it upon himself to go training at 10.30, a full half hour before his team mates. Bernard was with this sport as with any other; he had to be the best and training would make him the best! Apart from his section NCO from whom Bernard gained permission, he told no one what he was doing. This was typical of the man; he never felt the need to explain what he was doing if they had no need to know. Bernard was a few minutes late the morning he saw two airmen hauling a trolley from the training ground. Hurrying into the dip to make up lost time he felt the energy build up as he approached the individual gantry. He regarded the bucket as an opponent and could not wait to come to grips with it. Clad in steel heeled training boots and PT kit he hurried over the tripod.

His keen eyes soon noticed and understood immediately. The clean bucket with its weight newly painted on the side and the similarly painted and stamped contents. Mute proof of the legitimate reason for their unusual appearance of the two giggling airmen to the training ground. Other pieces of steel, also painted and stamped with their weights, were stacked neatly at the base of the tripod. Bernard nodded, satisfied the coach had finally got the heavy steel bucket and contents weighed and marked.

Bernard knew he was unpopular. Positively disliked in some quarters though he cared little for opinions. It was because of their jealousy he was always on guard. Just in case, for jealousy hate and bitterness know no end. For all he knew one day they may try to harm him.

Tossing his towel under nearby trees, Bernard lifted out a piece of steel. 10 lb. 6 oz. was marked in still tacky paint. The same weight was clearly stamped into the metal.

"Must be fifteen, sixteen stones in there," Bernhard said testing the bucket's weight grasping the support bar with both hands, beneath the pencil held shackle. Feeling the delicious resistance of the dead weight he declared, "Let's see if we can bounce you off the floor then."

Almost scurrying in his eagerness to come to grips with the newly weighted 'opponent', Bernard went quickly over the hard baked earth and stopped a yard past the point where cable and rope were perfectly sliced together. With no more ado he spat on his hands, rubbed the spittle into the palms to enhance his grip, then in the time worn enthusiasts manner of the sport, lifted the rope with the toe of his boot into his waiting hands. With fire pumping in his veins he mentally pitted his strength against the sixteen stone upstart at the other end. He wanted to make this a really good drop and force the bucket to bounce at least twelve inches off the ground, then if possible, keep the momentum going and haul it, under control, always under control to the top of the gantry.

Gripping and twisting the rough sun heated rope in his strong hands he imagined he could hear the umpire's commands. Trying to dig and cut the steel heel of his right boot into a groove in the scarred, iron hard ground, he prepared his body for the backward lunge.

Roaring the word "YES" to the heavens he twisted and catapulted his superb body into a lunging backward leap on his mental command, "PULL!"

The unyielding ground crushed the young airman's right kneecap, broke his right arm, his shoulder and collarbone. A small stone ripped his right cheek to the bone and all but tore off his ear as the pencil holding the shackle exploded into a thousand pieces. The disintegrating soft wood and carbon brought to an end an unquestionably brilliant and gifted sporting career. In its place it installed a burning lifelong hatred, triggered an emerging madness and worst of all, an undying compulsion for revenge.

~~~

Junior Technician Kowaleski spent the next year and a half in various hospitals. There is no doubt at the end of that time he would have been medically discharged but for a number of reasons. The medical officers in whose hands the future of their patient lay deliberated long and sympathetically during the lengthy convalescence. The airman's record was exemplary and had been an above average sportsman though due to overzealous training, he may well have crippled himself in this unfortunate accident. If however, the doctors condemned the youngster back to civvy street in his condition, he would no doubt end up in some menial job. When the character of the man showed he was grossly endowed with leadership qualities. And leadership being a prime requirement in the Royal Air Force they were reluctant to give up on this man.

The main problem was the right leg and shattered kneecap. Time and treatment were the only factors that would tell if it would heal sufficiently for Kowaleski to remain in uniform. The young man had signed his future to the RAF therefore they would give him the benefit of any doubt. When he was ready, on release from hospital he would be assigned to light duties for two years, after which his position would be assessed.

For three months Bernard lay in an RAF hospital on the outskirts of Lincoln. Whilst under their care he travelled through various agony zones of pain and discomfort as they stitched and plastered him together again. This model patient impressed doctors and nurses. Quiet and reserved he made no complaint about his injuries or the painful treatment being administered. Beneath the calm surface of dark brooding eyes however, there burned a roaring furnace of hate and bitterness that charred the inner soul of the sombre faced airman. Retribution and acrid loathing seethed and boiled in the very pit of his being for those who had callously set the trap to so mutilate his body. He never dreamed those bastards in the Maintenance Unit would go to this length to cripple him, disfigure him to put an end to his only love in life - sport and athletics!

They would pay, they would be forced to pay - and dearly. Those responsible knew he trained on the individual gantry before the team arrived and thus informed had set their hellish trap so cunningly. It was no wonder the two fitters from the yard were laughing as they left the training area. They were all laughing at him now! The team, his section, the General Engineering Flight, the whole accursed MU. Laughing at him. As he lay quietly in his hospital bed, never allowing the bubbles of molten hate to rise to the surface he promised he'd get back at 103 Maintenance Unit. Somehow. Someday. NO! Not promised – vowed. VOWED with all his heart and every gene in his being. No matter how long it took, they would pay. They would not laugh at him then!

Staring at the ceiling Bernard might have been totally alone in the full hospital ward. He was allowed to do very little physically, so unfortunately there was plenty of time to think; plenty of time to look back on his life. But looking back on his past was akin to having a large hellish bird pecking at his innards. He tried desperately to push the suffering images back down, down deep into the black depths of dormant memory. He was denied even this. The thoughts were irrepressible corks in his acid pools of contemplation. They kept popping up! The bird would rip and wrench them free only to expose the squirming evils within. He could not escape them; even in troubled sleep they were more prominent and acerbically alive. The pre-accident avenue of escape to happy oblivion had been blessed slumber, but now sleep and the accompanying nightmares were somehow to be avoided. There was nowhere left for Bernard to hide!

He squirmed at one recurring vision of himself as a child. He was sitting with other children on steps somewhere in some forgotten location. The children were reminiscing on amusing events that happened in their homes, recalling familiar objects and happenings, events with mothers and fathers, brothers and sisters, cats and dogs. Everyone was laughing, each story sillier or funnier than the last. Then little Emily Parkes, who'd taken a shine to Bernard, turned to him. "C'mon Bernie," she said innocently, never dreaming she was about to carve another unhealing wound into the memory banks of a bruised child, "You must have a story to tell us?" she peered hopefully at him through expectant eyes.

Bernard sat for a moment immobile, aware he had nothing to tell. He stood in bewilderment before running away, hearing behind him, the horrible stunned silence quickly followed by the racking laughter of children. Emily's worried blue eyes followed him. She did not laugh.

The boy could not think of anything to tell the other children. He could not think of any place from his past he could call home. There was nothing nice to tell them, and what they might have found funny was certainly not nice either! They had until that moment been his friends, but they had laughed, turned on him. Just like those at 103 Maintenance Unit

Bernard Cornelius Kowaleski had grown from an unsettled and underprivileged background. He was born in Blackpool in the cold and windy December of 1930 to a German /Polish mother and Polish father. The boy had a dim and brief memory of his father who had been killed in a bar room brawl during a game of dominoes when the 'kitty' held the grand total of one shilling and six pence. This happened in a pub in Preston when Bernard was five years old.

His mother, left to fend for herself and small son when times were hard, found it necessary to move around the country to find work. Burdened by her child she took him to her sister's home in

Redcar where the youngster stayed for a year, seeing his mother at intervals. One day his mother brought him a new father, a Polish carpenter who appeared to be a decent man and treated young Bernard as his own son.

Bernard did not see much of his step-father until his mother came to take him to their new home in Manchester where his step-father had secured work and a highly sought after commodity of the times; a company house.

The excitement of a new abode in the big city soon quelled when the new home turned out to be a tiny flat in a dingy tenement consisting of one bedroom, a box room and kitchen with one cold water tap. It had the added luxury of a communal toilet in the stairwell. The living quarters were small but were somehow surprisingly adequate for the frugal needs of the times.

For the first time in his life Bernard had a room to himself. The box room was allocated to the boy and a bed bought for him from a second hand dealer in the area. For a very short spell in his short span of years, life was beginning to look good for the boy, but it was not to last! He was awakened one night as something was happening in his groin. He grew fully awake as he realized it was his stepfather who at first seemed to be nudging the boy out of bed. The man was not allowing this to happen however for he had an arm clamped across his middle while a course hand fondled the boy's genitals. But worse, as he came fully awake the boy gasped when he realized something unspeakably uncomfortable was being repeatedly pushed into his backside. He started to call his mother when the sweaty hand was quickly transferred from his groin and clamp over his mouth. The pain and nudging then continued unabated for more uncomfortable minutes until at last his stepfather seemed to hurt himself for he grunted and groaned in pain, all the while crushing the boy hard against himself.

Afterwards, his stepfather on leaving to return to his own bed slipped a shilling, more money than he had ever seen, into his hand with a hoarsely whispered, "Say nutting to your Mama!"

This practice had continued surreptitiously for four years until Bernard was eleven years old, at which point it came to an abrupt halt. His mother on feeling ill one evening, returned home from the bar where she was working and walked in on her beloved husband as he approached the climax strokes. The man was bent over her similarly bowed son whose startled face was peering round at his equally astounded mother. It was bad enough to have been caught at it, but her husband, at a point where he was incapable of stopping, had carried on, indifferent it seemed to her, and her presence. His interpretation of the situation was he had been caught with the lamb, he might as well be hung for the sheep.

Bernard did not particularly detest the degradation of his stepfather's practice over the years. Nor did he like it, but he did like the fee of half-a-crown. The remuneration having grown with the cost of living, and the lad's acceptance of two shillings and sixpence was a reasonable fee for a few minutes minor discomfort.

For his sins Bernard was bundled off to a boy's home in Derby, his mother claiming he was disturbed and she could no longer look after him. There Bernard stayed until he was sixteen dabbling during these formative years in the odd homosexual encounter with two tutors and other boys. The latter sniggering experiences were, or so it seemed at the time, merely adventurous bouts into the unknown; meaningless if somewhat pleasant acts in a world of unpleasantness. They were happening at a time when sex was rearing its bulbous head over the horizons of adolescence. These years were the influential stages in Bernard's tree of life where his growth and grain of malleable and fundamental roots were being formed.

From childhood Bernard had shown distinct signs of a budding athlete. Whilst in the home he excelled in every event he participated in. He was breaking records in many school sports, having been guided and taken under the wing of a caring PT instructor.

The nascent athlete grew proud of his achievements and of his growing body, muscling up nicely as he approached the initial stages of manhood. It was at this point in his life he began to shun the lesser beings that surrounded him. He had always preferred his own company, but it was only now he was developing the inner confidence needed to spurn others. At sixteen and with the PT instructor's prodding, Bernard decided to move on to where he could further develop his undoubted athletic talents.

Bernard joined the Boy's Service of the Royal Air Force. He was screened, medically checked and sent to RAF Honiton in Devon. As soon as he stepped off the bus, and for the first time ever Bernard felt his insides click and fall into place. At last he had a stable base, something solid on which he could build a life.

The whole concept of the RAF was to the youngster, akin to parents. They looked after him, supplied his every need, taught him, fed him, clothed and gave him comfortable living quarters. After providing all the basics for a decent life, they actually paid him for the honour of having him around! Most important of all, he felt something he never felt before - a strong sense of belonging!

Bernard could not pin down why he felt this deep sense of affinity to the RAF. Then one night as he lay in his billet bed he realised he was as a page in a massive book. A book where each page was categorised then placed in its best position, exactly the same as the page on either side, but different in interpretation and content. The pages may be the same but each had its own individual number and situation. Every page contributed an integral and important part to the structure of the entire book. Every passing day, more words of wisdom were added to his page and when complete, he would at last be slotted into the vast book of RAF life. It may not suit everyone, but the life, indeed everything, eminently suited Bernard Cornelius Kowaleski.

On his seventeenth birthday he transferred to the regular staff of the Royal Air Force, signing on until the age of fifty five. His first permanent posting was Brize Norton where he started his new life slowly but once loose on the world and absolutely free to roam in adult life for the first time, Bernard discovered yet another new world. He discovered girls. Boys were relegated to mere substitutes and promptly discarded. The opposite sex had so much more to offer a virile young man. But sadly, eventually even with girls Bernard realised something was missing.

Unfortunately the scars of his early life were cut too deep. Since that hellish night when he was seven years old, the night his stepfather first crept into his bed, his body had been abused and continued to be until reaching puberty. Now at this point in his life his position had literally reversed! Bernard became the abuser of younger boys. This seemed perfectly natural and normal to him in the continuation of a game he played and enjoyed, but did not fully understand! Bernard felt all along he was playing with less than a full pack. Something was missing.

His divergent tastes in sex nagged Bernard over the years for something more. The straight sex act with females he enjoyed, but only as a novelty, so as he grew older, so he grew increasingly unsatisfied. Males lost their attraction. Females had rounder softer bodies, were eminently more attractive; but finding a girl with whom he could make love as he did boys was proving difficult. He'd been told by a number of young ladies who suddenly turned from being friendly to distantly aloof, that his tastes were bizarre, unnatural. Confused, never being one to discuss it with anyone especially intimate feelings and wondering if he was a total freak, Bernard returned with his first love, sport! Here he could safely burn off these excess energies and in so doing gain a high degree of physical satisfaction. This diversion worked adequately for a while; carving a name for himself in many aspects of sport, eventually to hold no less than five RAF athletic records.

Despite his growing reputation, Bernard daily grew more reclusive losing himself in physical training and hard study. With the latter he wanted only to work his way through the ranks, for rank with the extra pay provided security. Something Bernard had never experienced. Security within the confines of the Royal Air Force was a basic need. By August 1952 when he was placed on the Preliminary Warning Role for an overseas posting, Bernard managed to ward off the few potential friends that had tried to break into his inner sanctuary. Latent and spurned mates wrote him off as a 'loner,' 'quirky,' and downright 'peculiar.'

A posting as a Fitter to 103 Maintenance Unit on the island of Cyprus came through. He would join the Unit on the 28th November 1952. For this outwardly confident but basically troubled young man, the posting came at the right time. He needed a change of surroundings. Regular transfers in the work place surroundings without altering his lifestyle were aspects of RAF life that suited Bernard abundantly.

Bernard's short sojourn on the exotic, sparsely populated non-commercial island of Cyprus in the fifties ended with his terrible accident on the training rig. The small military hospital had sewn and plastered the young airmen as best they could. But his injuries, especially the knee, resulted in evacuation to Britain where the long painful struggle began.

For Bernard physical fitness was not an option, it was an absolute necessity he must achieve to fight off the beckoning finger of medical discharge. He could not allow them to kick him out of the only decent life he'd ever known, and loved.

A year after the accident, Bernard still found walking painful. Two operations on the damaged knee had not worked the hoped for miracle. Medical discharge began to adopt demonic dimensions in the shadows of his nocturnal and daytime fantasies.

One day after an intensely painful hour of physiotherapy, he overheard a nursing sister and a Medical Officer conversing. Overheard may be stretching what he actually heard, but one word he heard clearly was; 'discharge.' Whether this referred to his case could not be determined but the indomitable fighting spirit he conjured up in competitive sport rose to the surface - and to Bernard's rescue. He fought with every ounce of his being to impress any doctor treating him he could still be a worthwhile asset to the RAF. Many stressful hours were to pass. Hours filled with agony and tension but as much as they were filled with pain they were met with an iron clad determination to rise above mortal boundaries of suffering.

Six months later the Medical Officer in charge of Bernard's treatment informed him of their decisions. He would be placed on Light Duties for two years, sent immediately on a clerking course and from there, attached for the remainder of the two years to a Recruitment Office. The doctors were satisfied he'd made sufficient recovery to warrant this decision and confidently predicted a return to normal station duties in due course. He would have periodical medical checks to determine if one day he may return to his trade of General Fitting. In the meantime he would remain in clerking for the purposes of recruitment.

Posted to RAF Northolt in March 1955, Bernard threw himself into his duties as a recruiting clerk working from an office in central London. Many airmen regarded Northolt a top posting due to its close proximity to the capitol but to Bernard it was merely a stopgap. He desperately wanted a return to Cyprus.

Although working as a clerk, Bernard took the Corporal trade test in General Fitting resulting in an 'A' pass and immediately applied for the Senior Technician trade test.

Wednesday afternoon in the RAF was officially 'Sports Afternoon' where airmen were allowed to participate in their chosen sport whatever it might be. However many a blind eye was turned to those who abused the privilege, as sport was not a top choice for some as a pastime. These unsporting worthies would write their chosen sport into the Guardroom roster then armed with tennis rackets, golf clubs etc. would sidle off to cinemas, snooker halls or pubs.

An older sergeant who worked alongside Bernard noted his chosen 'sport' in the roster as 'Swimming.' A most peculiar description for he spent his Sports Afternoons visiting a prostitute.

Bernard for that first year had burned his excess energy in the Northolt gymnasium, working toward complete fitness. But as his strength and confidence rose, so he grew bored and restless. Coupled with listening to the sergeant's boast of debatable conquests and sexual acrobatics with the prostitute, the younger man felt familiar aches assault his erstwhile dormant groin.

A curious Bernard accompanied the sergeant into town one Wednesday under the pretence he too was going to the swimming pool. However when the older man abandoned him abruptly in Soho with the remark, 'Don't know what you're here for Bennie but look around, there's plenty of everything'. His words were quite true. It did not take Bernard long to realise any pleasure of the flesh could be bought in this little community. Prostitutes advertised their wares on shop windows with notices. Bernard noted two such numbers. The accompanying messages, thinly disguised claimed 'rain wear would be supplied for a wet afternoon' etc.

The 'wet afternoon' however proved disappointing. To a corporal's pay sex was expensive, anything considered kinky was financially abortive. He could barely afford what these girls delicately phrased as 'a short time,' 'quickie,' or 'straight screw.' Bernard pointed out the latter was not quite what he wanted as that particular commodity could be obtained free of charge in any of the many London dance halls. He declined their services, much to the girl's vocal indignation; "Ye wants somat kinky ya pays for somat kinky boyo," and, "Bugger off you kinky bugger!" the latter being one of the most befitting in a bouquet of parting sentiments.

Life went aimlessly on. He met the occasional girl but none hung around when he tried but succeeded on only one abortive occasion in his odd coupling.

Medical checks went well. Apart from a barely detectable limp, he was categorized as A2 G2, removed from Light Duties and at last placed on the PWR list for overseas posting. For choice he listed Cyprus as No.1, El Adam No.2 and Malta No.3, all in the Mediterranean area.

In March 1957, Bernard would cheerfully have cut the throat of the clerk responsible for appointing one Corporal Technician Kowaleski B.C. to R.A.F. Changhi in Singapore.

Utterly deflated with hate fermenting on bitterness, Bernard could not be consoled until the prostitute visiting sergeant took him to one side, two weeks prior to embarkation.

"Listen son," the sergeant said quietly. "I know you're on the quiet side, likes to be left alone and all that, but a frienda mine tells me you 'ave peculiar tastes with the gels?" The man stared at Bernard, defying contradiction. Bernard's returning glare may have spoken volumes but he said nothing. The prostitute community was obviously a close-knit group.

"Right then," the man went on. "If you 'ave kinks in your personal taste that only female, or boys can take care off, so whawt?" he shrugged, "We all got different urges at times eh? Anyways Singapore is the place for people like you Bennie - an' me!" Again that sidelong stare, this time with the slightest suggestion of a conspirators grin. "I've spent two wonnerfull frantic tours out there and foocked as many gels as a retired milk maid 'as wanked cow's tits lad! You don't know it yet, but you're going t' paradise. Yeah, a paradise of 'airless legs and tight young fannies. They can't do enuff for you AND never say no eevah!"

Despite Bernard's resentment of this man's intrusion, he listened. When the sergeant saw the softening eyes he went on, "I see I've got your attention! First thing you'll 'ave to get is a marriage certificate. Nah don't warry, I'm not proposing to ya, but those that wants the good life out there, gets themselves a marriage cert - tif - i - cate, understand?" He spoke the word in separate syllables, emphasizing each one. He went on, "Nobody checks if you're living wif your wife or not, but you'd like a couple of nice chinkie slits wouldn't ya? And I'm not talking about their eyes! You'd like some extra cash too, wouldn't ya? Marriage allowance, yeah? Living out allowance yeah, yeah? Course ya would! Right, 'ere's what you do ...."

Bernard followed the instructions, got himself 'married,' then armed with the appropriate certificates flew off to Singapore. Within a day of his arrival on the southern end of the Malayan Peninsula, he was living in a 'hiring' flat in the centre of Singapore. Two days later two Chinese girls moved in with him. The girls kept house, cooked, cleaned and looked after his every need. On occasions they'd bring friends home, but no men, strictly girls only. Food was cheap and cash was plentiful. Through the forged certificates, bought and paid for in London's Soho, Bernard drew both marriage allowance and living-out allowance and for well over two years life was extremely pleasant. The girls living in his flat changed frequently. Some left, others were thrown out, but most were content to live with this man. There were not many places poor country girls could eat and sleep in safety. If he gave them money, which he sometimes did for clothes and other luxuries, this was a bonus for their services. They loved him for taking them off the streets, for the decent shelter he provided but their love and familiarity was shallow and temporary. The girls knew when this master returned to his own land then it would be time to seek another. These pale intruders were plentiful, some had different kinks with various twists in tastes and needs as this one, but generally he asked no more from the girls than other men.

Human nature is the most mercurial and peculiar aspect of man. If the brain lusts after an item that is rare, the brain accepts that shortage and the body will accustom itself to the unavailability and go without: If however that item suddenly becomes plentiful in gluttonous quantities, the brain will want to gorge itself rejoicing in the fulfilment of desperately sought after dreams and desires. It may well go on devouring these suddenly bounteous sweetmeats until completely satiated, at which point it will slow and cease gorging, take stock of its gluttony and very probably take a scunner, a sudden reversal and sickening prejudice against that for which it once craved, the too much of a good thing syndrome. The brain, like any organ in the body will turn away from that which it has revolted and seek other venues to satisfy the ever demanding needs of an ever changing, ever hungry body. It might, indeed probably will one day, in a whimsical whim, return, switch back and seek again the rejected item from which it once feasted, made such a pig of itself. The passage of time has a habit of lulling the memory banks into recalling only the best of the bad, so if the item upon which it once lusted, then sickened, becomes available again, and if the brain is in harmony with that upon which it once sickened, human nature being what it is, the body, and mind will return to eat again.

Two months before Bernard's tour in Singapore ended, he sat in a bar in the red light district, contemplating his unusual sluggishness. Wondering why he was uninterested in either of his girls or their friends for over two weeks. He shook his head irritably as a girl attempted to join him at his table but minutes later was approached by a young and very thin Chinaman. For a brief moment Bernard found himself recalling his youth. This man was unusually different, very effeminate and might be worth trying. He shivered inwardly as an irritated frown creased his face but paradoxically agreed when the dainty creature suggested they take a walk. However he had no wish to be seen in the company of such an obvious homosexual so Bernard insisted the man leave the bar first.

With an exaggerated wave Bernard dismissed the little man. Minutes later the silky Oriental after moving round the bar, shrugged expansively implying the lack of interest and left.

Bernard allowed some minutes to pass, finished his drink and unhurriedly he too left. Outside in the narrow street, Bernard look around, saw the slinky form and followed until the man turned into a dark alley. Conscious he could be in some danger of being robbed or worse. Bernard glanced round, saw no one then looking again up the alley was just in time to see the man enter a doorway. At this point Bernard realized he was growing strangely excited. Not the pre-sex buzz he usually felt; this was entirely new! Hurrying up the alley he was aware he did not want this sorry excuse for a man, or a woman, sexually, yet he was scurrying after him, like a dog in heat, and there was no denying the fierce urge in his groin had returned. This was all too strange and did not add up. He could not understand what he was doing here yet excitement was immense! His pace quickened.

Catching a glimpse of the man's shimmering silk shirt in the darkened doorway Bernard joined him in the shadows. Within seconds the smooth hands of the Chinaman took control. For some moments all was calm as Bernard, desperately trying to relax looked down on the smooth black head nuzzling his groin, knowing hands caressing his genitals.

This little man or whatever he was, knew what he was doing as sensations buzzed, and Bernard, lost in these swirling sensations, was unaware his breath was quickening, the back of his head pushed hard against the shop door. Suddenly he was gasping, felt enclosed, a lack of oxygen. A tightening tourniquet had looped around the Englishman's lungs. Then there was no air! And he was having trouble with his vision as his eyelids began to flicker furiously. Within five minutes of stepping into the doorway Bernard had lost control of his senses.

The little man was like an animal at the taller man's groin, picking and pecking at his genitals.

For a desperately worrying few seconds Bernard thought he was about to faint and in that short space of time another being took control of his movements.

Helpless, he gasped sucking for air then moaned as the kneeling figure engulfed his rampant manhood for the last time. The hot mouth was caressing and causing his mind to slip crazily out of gear into a fuzzy turmoil of gaudy lights and weightless instability. He tried to focus his rapidly flickering eyes, fighting desperately to stay on the ground but this grew increasingly difficult. The cause of his distress was in his groin, lifting his feet off the ground, hoisting him up, up into grotesque smothering clouds of uncertainty.

Bernard struggled to find something to hold on to. His hands were floating around like weightless objects in a bizarre dream until one descended to encircle the diminutive neck of the Chinaman. The suckling creature did not react initially, thinking perhaps the hand was a warm caress, which it could have been, at first. Without warning the caressing hand turned into a choking air blocking clamp round the tiny throat gripping hard, squeezing tighter, tighter! By the time either realized what was happening, it was too late for both Bernard and the Chinaman.

Deep, deep down in Bernard's body, a blowtorch burst into roaring cutting flame. Involuntarily he stood high on his tiptoes, pushing his groin forward. He could no more stop the burning than he could stop what his hand was doing to the hopping, kicking thing at the end of his arm. He was approaching a sexual climax of immense proportions as he hoisted the wriggling strip of humanity and stare fascinated at the grossly distorted face in front of him. The bulging slanted eyes. The blow torch was searing through the base of his groin. The spasmodic jerking and a lolling blue roll of meat, the man's tongue, which on impulse Bernard leaned over and sucked into his own mouth. As he did so, the flame cut and burned painfully like molten lava through the centre of his penis to explode in a volcanic burst of heat and flame, rapturous hellish pain, blinding flashes of euphoric ecstasy caught in a roaring mass of exploding stars. He was totally unaware his lower regions were humping madly against the death throes of the Chinaman.

Sometime later, it could have been minutes or hours, Bernard's hand slowly released the crushed windpipe. He spat out the thing from his mouth, the limp lolling tongue resembling so much a plump dark purple aubergine hanging on its stem from a maniacal grinning mouth. The white table tennis balls, the man's unseeing eyes stared at Bernard accusingly as his slackening hand allowed the lifeless body to slither from his grip. It dropped rumbling like a sack of potatoes on the concrete slab of the doorway, adopting as it crumpled around the splayed feet of its killer, a foetal position.

Gasping, dizzy, sweating profusely Bernard leaned heavily against the wall conscious only of one thought; he had experienced in those ferocious and volcanic few moments, the most explosive, satisfying and certainly the most fulfilling climax of his life.

Two months later Bernard returned to London and spent his disembarkation leave in the Union Jack Club. Late one evening he lay disconsolately staring at the ceiling of his room after spending the day with a very beautiful, very expensive but very co-operative prostitute. The reason for his contemplative mood was the woman had done everything in her vast repertoire to please him. He'd left her premises physically satiated yet there was little satisfaction from the encounter! It may be a temporary lull but there was a sexual void and he could not determine why.

In March 1960 Bernard reported to his new posting at RAF Kirkcross. The Singapore incident with the Chinaman was a distant but pleasant memory.

Settling in to his new camp and surroundings, Bernard with three years of debauchery and one murder behind him, realized at the age of thirty, his life was going nowhere. In a moment of clarity, he decided to lead a more stable, normal and if possible, fuller existence. He regretted nothing of his past life, indeed regarded all past experiences were his natural efforts to fulfil some nagging gaps in the flickering switchboard of his life. There remained however one minor problem; he must lose the fictional wife for which he had drawn marriage allowance. She was almost as easy to lose as she was to find.

On reporting to the Kirkcross orderly room for 'Arrival,' he informed the personnel clerk his wife had run off with an unknown man in Singapore and was filing for divorce. He therefore wished to live on the base and forthwith ceased to qualify for marriage allowances.

In R.A.F. Kirkcross he was trained as an instructor in his field of General Fitting. Once qualified he took intakes of fresh faced airmen straight from basic training, or 'square bashing' These students eventually qualified as General Fitters who were then posted out to every corner of the R.A.F. empire.

The nearby village of Kirkcross was a few miles from Blackpool, the major holiday resort on the North West coast of England. Despite the temptations and glittering lights of the Lancashire hot spot, Bernard led a blameless life for the first five years of his stay on the base. With only a candle burning at the back of his brain to retain the heat of a dormant loathing for 103 Maintenance Unit, he lived for the present for his work. With 98.8% of his intakes qualifying as first class General Fitters, Senior Technician Kowaleski was elevated in the ranks for tutorial purposes to acting unpaid Chief Technician.

Bernard worked, lived and loved the life on his new camp, taking part in many functions, even coaching tug-of-war teams in the annual Station sports. The transitory teams were made up from students en-route through the station. The experience nevertheless proved stimulating. They revived stirrings in his bowl of buried memories of his love for the sport, but the basic essence from the agitation inside the bowl was not allowed to surface. The stench of that mix was being saved for another time, another place.

As in everything with Bernard, the good life, or normal life was not to last. One June night in 1965 without warning, he all too easily slipped back into the mould he sincerely and until that night had effectively avoided. His developing problem re-emerged when he almost murdered a girl he met on his first visit to the Blackpool Tower ballroom. A young auburn haired girl with a slightly heavy figure appealed to him. They danced and chatted; she was from Ayr and he an airman from the local air base. After a few drinks, the Scots girl, whose friend had already gone off with a bloke, was keen for a holiday romance. Especially with such a handsome airman with the dark Slavic looks. She was prepared for a romantic and intimate encounter.

Not long after leaving the ballroom, they lay in a small park, and although past the point of being tipsy, the girl was certainly not inebriated enough to allow what this man was attempting.

At the delicate but as yet unexposed moment of truth, she allowed him to remove her underwear and obligingly and expectantly lay on her back. When he turned her over however, and pointedly ignored the normal point of entry, she contemptuously called a halt.

With a woman under him for the first time in many years, Bernard became agitated at her blunt refusal and his brain tripped into uncaring overdrive. Heedless he was hurting the girl the almost robotic man would calmly have killed her to achieve his aims. Indeed he was in the process of doing just that when two patrolling policemen heard the girl's bleating cries. They were cruising in their patrol car but stopped when the driver thought he heard a scream. Switching off they listened, then stared at each other when a man's voice and a muffled cry came from the small park on the elevated ground to their right. The policemen charged up the grassy bank and found, by stumbling over her, the semi-unconscious girl. Bernard on seeing their approach ran off, glancing back wondering what the fuss was all about.

Three days later Chief Tech. Kowaleski got word the local

police were at the main guardroom looking for an airman who allegedly attacked a girl in Blackpool at the weekend. The description they left was that of a man about six feet tall, approximately thirty years of age, dark hair and eyes, sporting a clipped moustache with an upright athletic figure. The description was fairly accurate but fortunately for Bernard, not all that uncommon on an RAF base such as Kirkcross. The camp had hundreds of new arrivals moving in with equal numbers moving out every week, on various courses both extensive and brief.

A week passed uneventfully then for the first time in his life, although they were minor, Bernard experienced the gut twisting pangs of panic. Because he fitted the description of a man the Blackpool constabulary were seeking, the guardroom informed him, he and five others from the base were summoned to attend an identity parade the following afternoon.

All six airmen dressed in civilian clothes as requested, lined up the next day. Fortunately the others were all strangers to Bernard so without being too obvious, he would attempt to fool the girl. Adopting a sheepish expression and drooping his normally square shoulders, he waited.

Still showing bruises around her face and neck the girl, nervously sat in the viewing area behind a glass wall having been assured the suspects could not see her. The men all fitted her damning description, right down to the clipped moustache, but there was no doubt she was staring long and hard at No.2.

Not completely certain for they were all similar under the bright lights, but the more she looked the more uncertain the girl became. His voice and an almost neutral accent was still ringing in her ears so she asked if it was possible to hear Nos.2, and perhaps 3 and 6 speak the words that burned deep into her mind on the night in question. The words were; "You'll fuck as I want you to fuck!"

As requested each of the three spoke the words in a threatening manner but Bernard in the No.2 slot raised his voice an octave and spoke in a refined accent, making the threat sound completely innocuous.

She had almost decided, but the accent and voice were definitely not that of the man she had lain with. The voice and accent of No. 3 sounded like her attacker but perhaps he was taller? No 6 was a Scotsman. Confused and upset and desperately worried she may point a finger at an innocent man, the girl broke down and lost all interest in the proceedings Once more Bernard shuddered at the thought of coming so close to being discharged and swore he must drop this kink in his life that inevitably led him into difficult situations. The trouble itself, reluctant girls to his peculiar tastes, he cared little about, but the RAF would not wear friction with the civil authorities. This last scrape was much too close for comfort.

Bernard reverted to the quiet life. In future Blackpool was off limits. He would use the Sergeant's Mess or perhaps venture occasionally down to the village pub.

~~~

Chapter 2

It was the middle of March 1965 and the Scottish winter was weeks away from easing its grip to the pitiful advances of the encroaching spring. The night was bitterly cold as the airman watched the snow swirl round the Leuchars station lights as they vainly strived to cast diluted glimmers into the boundless black night.

Conflicting thoughts were dancing through Junior Technician Frank Connolly's mind as he turned away from the biting north wind. "When the north wind doth blow, then we shall have fuckin' snow," he muttered. "Whoever said that got it fuckin' right!" he added miserably, giving the Anglo Saxon expletives extra emphasis into the folds of his heavy greatcoat.

He looked balefully towards the married quarters of R.A.F. Leuchars. Orange street lights could just be seen through the snow, and warm visions flashed through the airman's head; of his wife getting ready for bed; of his two daughters asleep and his many friends and workmates scattered willy-nilly in the houses under those warm twinkling lights. Many would be watching 'News at ten' or the ten o'clock play. Both due to start ten minutes after he left his quarter to get down here to this freezing God forsaken hole of a railway station. Others no doubt were climbing into electric blanket heated beds, slipping arms around their wives.... Frank shook his head and looked again at the station clock which must be frozen solid. He was sure it had not moved for fully five minutes. As though motivated by his thoughts the minute hand laboriously rocked and shook its way from 10.09 to 10.10.

"Jesus wept, where the hell is this bloody train?" Frank moaned, tearing his dark blue eyes from the clock's frozen face to again gaze north, seeking a sign and a minor miracle for the train was not due until 10.15.

He had tried to cheer up with thoughts of his eventual destination as the freezing wind again strove to drive the warm images from his head. J/T. Connolly F. was on his way to sunny Cyprus on a three year posting. Sounded good! Everyone congratulated him on landing such a plum. The Unit to which he was headed was alleged to be one of the prime postings anyone in the RAF could hope to get - 103 Maintenance Unit, Akrotiri, Cyprus. Sounded good! The MU had the reputation of a happy family environment, and as a bonus had a great tug-of-war team, which interested Frank immensely. Sounded great! So why was he so miserable?

The wind lashed the front flap of his greatcoat away from his knees and again he turned away, wondering why he was being so macho. The truth was he detested the cold and could not stand the winters in his own country. Bred and born twenty seven years ago in Montrose, brought up in the northerly town, and with three winters already behind him in bitterly cold Leuchars, one would think with those credentials under his belt, he might be a tiny bit more acclimatized.

He cursed again; macho or stupid, there was no way he would shelter in that smelly waiting room. It stunk of urine and stale cigarette smoke and no blending of two smells on earth could surpass that pair. It clung inside his nostrils for weeks. Perhaps he was being cruel to British Rail, perhaps the stink was stale steam from the trains but it certainly smelled like piss to him! He cursed again.

Frank regretted having allowed his neighbour Bill Croply, or rather his ex- next-door neighbour to take him to the station. The weather had been fairly good a week ago when Frank was about to ring the M.T. section to book transport for tonight. Cpl. Croply stopped him insisting he would take his Cyprus bound neighbour down to the station. Poor Bill, he'd not taken into consideration the fickle swings of Scottish weather. Bill had trudged a hundred yards to his lock-up, got in and drove his beloved Morris 1000 into this quite unbelievably foul weather to pick up one J/T. Connolly. Then deposit passenger and kit at railway station. Back in the lock-up, Bill no doubt would lovingly give his turquoise love a squeegee down and pat on the bonnet before slogging home.

"Well Frankie, off to the bloody Med. you lucky sod. Hell I wish I could change places with you. They tell me it's really be-yootifool over there." Bill seemed cheerful despite the two mile potentially horrendous journey from married quarters in Tudor Road to the station. If the thick flakes of falling snow bothered Bill, to his eternal credit he didn't show it.

"Aye, so they tell me Bill." Frank said, not really wanting to get snared in conversation but Bill rambled on, his words falling like the snow on the windscreen, soundlessly on Frank's ears.

Frank wondered how Bill could see where he was going but suddenly and all too soon the car stopped, the station lights winking weakly. Bill was still talking, "... you'll not get any of this crap where you're going," misinterpreting Frank's sightless gaze through the windscreen.

"Aye," Frank muttered in reply. Strangely he was reluctant to leave the snug warmth of the little car. At first he thought it was the weather then realised, once out of the car and Bill was off home, there would be no turning back. Not that he wanted to reverse the next step in his life, but an umbilical cord was about to be cut. His recent life at R.A.F. Leuchars was about to be severed, gone forever. All known familiarity would cease from this moment, and what of his friends?

Despite taking addresses and promises to write, they would remain as they were now, just pages in his book of memory. The only attachment he had with Leuchars now was his wife Lorna and his two daughters. This sweet comfort was nullified however, with the bitter pill of not seeing them for three months. He'd left them only minutes ago, in their married quarter lounge where good-byes had been made with hugs and kisses - no tears! Lorna was too strong a person for tears. If there were to be tears it would be when she was in bed, when the loneliness would strike. Frank felt a flush of warm gut feelings as visions of the previous night flashed through his mind. Lorna had clung to him and he to her as they tried to instil enough of themselves into each other. Enough love, enough warmth and feelings that would see them through the next three barren months. Suddenly Frank Connolly felt utterly alone.

Bill Croply was watching his deep in thought friend, but time was marching on. "Better make a move Frank or we'll have to dig ourselves out of here." he tried to sound light.

Bill's remark shook Frank from his reverie and was surprised to see how the snow was building up on the glass. "Sorry Bill, aye I'm dreamin', hope you can get home awright." Frank opened the door forcing himself and any lingering thoughts out into the night to be replaced immediately by swirling snow which invaded the sanctuary of his fleeting refuge. Bill bravely followed. A small suitcase and an R.A.F. grip were lifted from the boot and passed to Frank. Bill carefully closed the boot lid. Holding the handle, he pushed it until there was an audible 'click.'

Frank admired that. Another indication of Bill's love for his year old Morris 1000. Most people, on a night such as this, would've banged the lid shut and scampered to gain shelter inside the car, before scuttling off home. Not Bill! The car was a living loving entity to the man.

Bill stuck out a gloved hand, "Bon Voyage Frankie, behave yourself and don't do anything I wouldn't do, which gives you lots of scope," he chortled heartily at the time weary parting joke.

'I'd have to live like a bloody monk' Frank thought ungraciously as they shook hands. "Cheers Bill and thanks. I'll ah, I'll send you a postcard," he added wondering why on earth he'd uttered such a stupid statement. He wasn't going on bloody holiday.

Something was said but Bill's words were carried off in the wind. Frank didn't want to hear anyway, caring little for further chitchat. He merely nodded and turned away struggling with his kit. Bill watched him for a moment before ducking into his car.

Frank made his unsteady way up the station steps then regretting his bad manners, tried to repair any damage by giving a broad smile and nodding when Bill gave a final toot. The tail lights of the Morris disappeared quickly in a flurry of snow.

Not being able to wave hampered as he was with luggage, Frank suddenly felt stupid. He was nodding and smiling like an idiot at a wall of swirling whiteness. The nod sagged to a rueful head shake as he turned wending his way to the windy platform. His mounting isolation was creating lots of uncharacteristic behaviour.

The station clock had not stopped. It now read 10.23. Frank's wandering thoughts had nudged the mechanism to tick a little faster. Typically it had also made the train late! He was about to bemoan his luck again when the dormant public address system spluttered into life.

'The train arriving at platform two is the 10.15 to London, Kings Cross, stopping at Edinburgh, Newcastle, Doncaster, Peterborough and London.'

'Good,' thought Frank, 'not too many stops.' The PA system gave a noisy death rattle before perishing for the night, as Frank's spirit lifted for the second time in the same minute. He saw the lights of the engine eerily ghost into view and almost as quietly glide past the airman. It was one of the new diesel engines replacing the 'steamies' all over the country. 'The passin' of an era,' Frank reflected as the gleaming wet transport slowed to a smooth stop. He felt his luck was beginning to look up when a carriage door stopped directly in front of him. Opening it the welcoming heat rushed out to greet him. 'Definitely! Things are changin' for the better!'

The train was surprisingly busy. Leaving his luggage at the junction of the carriage, Frank walked down the central passageway. Halfway down he saw a sailor seated at a table. Opposite him sat a soldier, the seats adjacent to the two were empty. The soldier looked as if he'd just awoke so Frank spoke to the sailor, "Anybody sittin' here?"

"Jesus, an airman!" declared the sailor. "What did I tell you Jock?" He addressed the soldier, "Didn't I say we'd get an airman at this station? Right next to the RAF camp, Eh?" He grinned up at Frank. "It's all yours mate, park yourself down, or should I say, berth your bum here, or better still for the RAF, land your arse next to mine." He snickered happily, then still snickering at his attempted joke pointed to the seat, "Go on, sit yourself down man, all we need now is a bloody marine and we've got a full hand." He dissolved into another fit of giggles.

'Oh shit, end of good luck,' Frank thought. 'Don't know if I can handle this all the way.' Choice was severely restricted. There appeared to be no more vacant seats, and it was now obvious why these were unoccupied. He removed his hat and greatcoat, placing them in the overhead rack. "Gonna get my gear," he informed the sailor.

"Stuff your gear, it's all right where it is. So where are you off to? Let's see, you're dressed in your best, all brass buttons and gabardine, an' at this time of night, plus you've got your half ton o' kit down there! You're on a posting eh?"

"Aye" Frank nodded. "On my way to Cyprus."

"Are you now?" The sailor replied, then looked across the table at the soldier. "Jock. Jock," he shouted. "We're in big trouble mate! I thought we were going to London, but it seems we've set a new course. We're now on our way to Cyprus mate. What do you think of that eh?"

"Fickin' great," the soldier was having trouble focusing his eyes, mumbled sleepily then added, "Fickin' great," unsure if he had said anything the first time.

Frank smiled and sat beside the sailor. His first impression was wrong; already he was warming to these two. The night ahead may not hold much sleep but there was no way his mind would be allowed to dwell on the past. His miserable frame of mind had been left on the cold and windy railway station, and blown away with this instant camaraderie. The soldier however would not last the night. His lips were moving as were his eyebrows over closed lids. Whatever it was he'd been tippling that day was now easing him into a happy but unintelligible conversation with himself.

The night passed for Frank with a spectrum of illuminations accompanied by a cacophony of murmuring thuds from the small shrinkage gaps in the railway lines passing beneath his feet. They seemed to be tapping a message that try as he might, he could not quite grasp, 'Biddy-be-dum biddy-be-dum biddy-be-dum,' followed sharply with 'eedie-be-dee eedie-be-dee eedie-be-dee.' The rhythmic reverberations were aided with strange but friendly faces floating in front of his own, abetted with many a twinkling amber drink; a kaleidoscope of flashing lights, drink, cordial voices; another drink; a dawning love for British Rail for providing such affable companions on their lovely warm trains. More drink, adolescent antics, drink, hilarious laughter, drink, until at last, a most wonderful sumptuous feeling. A slipping away sensation like slowly sinking between the mountainous breasts of a huge but sensuous woman. Down - down - down into beautiful, blessed warm and soft oblivion. His last flashing recollection was, if this was death, he wanted only to live so that he may die over and over again.

Chapter 3

Harold Ross flicked the cigarette butt hard and watched it rocketing towards the indigo blue star strewn sky before gravity caught it and forced the spark trailing mini meteor earthwards, where it raced to extinction on the beach below.

Harold, not for the first time, was feeling pangs of guilt. He was experiencing the usual regret network of feelings and mild physical pains that filtered their way through his abdomen in the quiet aftermath of illicit sex. The spasms were part of him, and he accepted them as much as having sex with a girl other than his wife was part of him now. In Harold's mind these pains were in a way, an act of contrition and so alleviated somewhat the depth of guilt.

The girl beside him was coming to the end of her cigarette also, and like Harold, was very quiet. She too was deep in thought and like Harold's cigarette butt, was still floating earthward from the fiery peak they had reached some minutes before.

A dark grey blanket with a light blue stripe running down its entire length covered them, not as it would seem to keep out the encroaching chill of this mid-March evening. The military issue blanket served to cover their nakedness and perhaps preserve some warmth of their cooling ardour.

The couple had spent the afternoon swimming off the nearby Submarine Rock beach. The cigar shaped rock was a comfortable forty yards swim from the beach. Or that distance could be halved by the more ambitious with an exhilarating dive or jump from the cliff top. The leap, or dive into the deep pool between Submarine Rock and cliff face could not be described as too demanding. For the less venturesome the small sandy beach provided swimmers with easy entry into the sea and an effortless landing point. The area was an ideal meeting place for personnel living in the RAF base at Akrotiri, on the south coast of Cyprus.

Carol Cook stretched her body under the blanket. She noticed with growing awareness, with the throes of passion cooling and consciousness returning to normal levels the blanket was decidedly prickly against her bare skin. Funny it had been as smooth as spun silk only an hour ago!

She and Harold had met and spent the day on the beach. Later after swimming and sunbathing they had clambered up these gentle grass slopes to the cliff top overlooking the Mediterranean.

Harold had been seeing Carol, a Senior Air Craftswoman in the Women's Royal Air Force for two months. But both had reluctantly agreed today was to be their last meeting. After a three-month compulsory break Harold's wife Marion would join him the following evening, and stay with her husband for the next thirty three months.

Before leaving Marion in December Harold vowed he would stay faithful for the three unaccompanied months he would face in Cyprus. He had been successful for only the first month. Harold truly loved his wife of only nine months and tried dutifully to stay within the bounds of his marriage vows but Harold had two unique problems. Problems most men would sacrifice their mothers, fathers and first born child to be the proud owner of either one. Rarely did our creator bestow upon one man the riches he showered on Harold Ross. His problems; he was abnormally attractive to the opposite sex. Two, happily coinciding with the first, Harold's sex drive was unusually over active!

To say Harold was handsome would be as far off the mark as saying the sun was no more than a stone's throw from Earth, and physically flawless as a human being could be. He was six feet two inches of perfect manhood with wide muscular shoulders and narrow hips. His muscles were not over large but so well defined that Donatello would lovingly have chipped away at the finest marble to form each augmentation or sinew line with devoted care. Perfection is often flawed however and Harold although at a physical peak, was unaware of the annoying air secreting from his person that everything in his garden was not merely lovely, but ripe, pleasant, and without any effort from his good self, would always remain so. His face was nobly proud with a set jaw line. Lightly curled fair hair and wide set light blue eyes sat astride a nose that was slightly flattened at its tip, which surprisingly enhanced the well-favoured features. Harold kept reasonably fit but every muscle on his twenty four year old frame formed without effort of exercise or training. He had been cast it seemed, in a faultless mould.

An abnormally high sex drive for someone like Harold Ross, was as might be imagined, not an immediate problem. Indeed initially it was a gift that had been allowed to run amok among many that frankly had no answer to his attentions. With his heavy artillery Harold had met and loved every female he deemed to raise his blonde eyebrows at since being seduced at the tender age of thirteen in his home town of Nottingham. Even at that age he was noticed when a woman, browsing in the local library observed the schoolboy's covert glances at her breasts. She got chatting with the youngster and told him she was clearing out some books at home, would he like to check them before she disposed of them?

The books turned out to be pornographic magazines her husband collected and she had no intention of throwing them out. Harold had gone into her flat innocently as a boy and emerged two hours later guilty of being a man long before his time. Like a child learning to walk, the first step had been taken and Harold realized after that mind-boggling afternoon, the opposite sex wanted him more than he, at that stage wanted them. His strike rate with girls grew as he grew and eventually Harold did not waste time with the occasional female who played hard to get. There was always someone 'around the corner' who was more than willing to oblige.

Harold had happily strolled through life content with his lot until he met Marion. He could never understood why he went back to this graceful eighteen year old creature time and again when she knew he lusted after only her body, but always, always affably declining even his best advances. Eventually he began to doubt if it was only her pliant and wonderful body he wanted? She seemed to draw him with something he could never quite define, yet she would continually deny him and he would go, as it were, 'round the corner.'

This situation continued until eventually he got the feeling he was somehow missing out with other girls. They were lovely and warm, good companions but he couldn't stop thinking about that girl Marion. He had taken her out three times, three very platonic dates they turned out to be, so what was it about her that attracted him so. He fooled himself it was the challenge she presented to his punctured ego. All he had to do was meet the challenge. She would succumb in time, but Harold did not know Marion at all. She almost drove him mad but in the end he had to do her quiet, consoling bidding and wait. And like a lamb to the slaughter Harold waited until they were married.

Marion, strictly one of the old school, had been worth waiting for. Harold truly loved the dark haired beautiful young girl - in his own way! To others it may have seemed an immature love with his need for female companions in Marion's absence, but Harold's love for his doe eyed beauty filled his whole being. He loved her as much as he was capable of loving anyone. Being close to her, making love to Marion was not something that simply fulfilled his sexual drive. In their lovemaking they instilled something into each other that was intangible but intensely real. With Marion he felt absolutely complete, before, during and especially afterwards. If he had been a normal man, it would never have occurred to Harold that other women lived on the same planet as Marion, she would have been his whole world. But Harold was not a normal man.

For the first month after arrival on the island in December Harold lost himself in reading and the odd trip to the Naafi, fervently hoping he could see out the three months. It was a forlorn hope and for the first time his over active sexual drive emerged as a problem. He had never experienced such a gap in his sexual life, and being cut off from both sex and Marion so abruptly, it was inevitable. Like a camel seeking and finding water in a trackless desert he had no choice. The robust and energetic young airman could only go the way his instincts took him.

The bright spark of a flint ignited the wick of an old army issue lighter as Harold lit another cigarette. 'Well,' he thought recalling his monastic month and weak efforts when confronted with the full facial frontal of the delightful Carol, 'I couldn't have gone on like that, I would've blinded myself.' He grinned recalling the grim period spent denying himself visits to the strip joints and brothels of Limassol, or the classy all ranks Peninsula Club on the base where WAAFs, and unaccompanied wives and daughters could occasionally be found enjoying a night out. To his credit, however minor, he had not intentionally sought a sex partner but despite his efforts, it happened very simply.

An airman from Akrotiri Ground Equipment section was returning to the UK at the end of his tour. Departing airmen usually invited section colleagues for a farewell drink in the Peninsula Club. And so Harold and his workmates were into their third beer when two WAAFs, also friends of the UK bound airman joined the group. Harold soon picked up signals transmitting from the very pretty blonde girl of the duo. His resolve melted like butter in a very hot frying pan and pushing aside his nagging conscience, asked her out. Carol agreed and they became lovers that first night. Afterwards Harold choked with remorse, cursing his weakness but the aching hard held drive of his groin proved too strong. Easily pushing aside all resistance and celibate intentions.

From the outset they agreed their meetings were simply to use each other's bodies. Carol understood perfectly but it was such a long time since she had met such a lovely man AND one who knew how to satisfy her. A rare combination. Harold liked her quick wit, her natural blond hair and of course the stunningly endowed body.

Initially they were like a honeymoon couple and tried to meet every evening. It may only be for a drink, the cinema or a swim, but it always ended with sex, even Carol's time of the month proved no barrier for the inventive pair.

Although carnal sensations were naturally present, Harold knew what was taking place was very good, but it was very good physical sex. There was no mental fulfilment with this stand in lover. No feeling, as with Marion, of mental electronics engulfing his brain ricocheting down through his body as every nerve end was set aglow, leaving him until reality crept back, an amalgamated part of Marion's body.

With Carol tonight, after he climaxed yet again, he had simply rolled off her and lit his first cigarette. A job well done! Both were only dimly aware of the other, and for the moment, carnally sated and content with the mutual contortions of their sexual manoeuvres.

Harold flicked his second butt into the night sky as Carol snuggled close. "Now that you've satisfied yourself with one hunger, what're we going to do about the other. You know, the one necessary for survival?" she hissed against his chest.

Harold looped an arm round her and cupped her breast. "I think what we've just finished is very necessary for survival, but if you're referring to such mundane matters as the intake of victuals, I suppose we could get something at the café. They stay open 'til nine."

"Which gives us about an hour," Carol said slipping her hand down his groin.

"Piss off Carol; you know my missus arrives tomorrow. Have you no shame girl?" Harold said, moving lazily away from her hand.

"No, none whatsoever," she answered simply, moving her hand gently around the soft mound of dormant manhood. "Oh," he groaned, "don't you ever give up?"

"Not when I'm about to lose the sexiest screw I've ever had. In case you've forgotten, we agreed not to see each other after tonight." She smiled up at him before licking the hair around his nipple.

"Mmn," the thought of Marion's arrival distracted him from her tongue and soft roving hand.

Three months absence and guaranteed abstinence in Marion's case, was a long time. She would no doubt be prepared and happy for the expected onslaught from her husband to claim his conjugal rights. A picture flashed across his mind; a scene from their honeymoon when he first saw Marion nude. He had seen many a female body but with Marion it was like seeing a naked woman for the first time. He recalled his sudden intake of breath and gasped in wonder at her marble smooth classic beauty.

He gasped again as he realized while in deep thought, Carol had slipped her head under the blanket and working on him with her mouth. With his thoughts on Marion and now Carol performing on his overworked manhood, he felt a hardening in spite of himself. He could do little to stop her, indeed, as her mouth expertly brought him back to full erection, did he want to?

Carol's tousled blonde head reappeared as simultaneously he felt her leg slip over his body. She adjusted her hips slightly then her full weight settled on his groin as she sat up. Once again he felt the familiar wondrous warmth engulf his penis. She grinned.

"Comfy?" she teased.

"Fuck you Carol," he moaned as she started to move and do wonderful things with her hips.

"No," she said huskily, "it's my turn to fuck you!"

They missed the café closing time easily. It was almost ten o'clock as the tired pair wandered through the camp towards their billets. Passing the Airmen's Mess Harold disappeared inside seeking the duty cook, hoping to scrounge some food. He told the semi true story of falling asleep on the beach and missing the evening meal. The cook, spying the shapely Carol in tight shorts and T-shirt standing in the bright moonlight, made a wild guess why Harold had missed the evening meal. 'I'd starve for a month,' he thought, 'for just a little piece o' that.'

The couple ate the solicited sandwiches as they ambled slowly towards Carol's barrack block set back off the road. A short distance from the entrance they stopped and placed their folded blankets on the grass. She turned taking both his hands into hers.

"Harry I've got something to say. I'm not going to be silly and ask for a commitment, but we are good for each other, aren't we?" Carol stared up into his eyes, "But - our -well - our - unions. Oh shit, there's no other way of saying this. The sex is fucking brilliant! Let's not finish like we planned, hmn. Even if we meet once or twice a month? There's duties, Fire Picket and others you could apply for. So, we could still see each other ... occasionally?"

"I don't want to make promises I can't keep, besides we agreed when we started it would end when Marion came out." He was saying the right words but they sounded less than convincing.

"Thought I'd give it a try. Can't blame me for that. And don't worry I won't cause any trouble but, well, if you ever feel like a fling, like you're missing me? Give me a ring, Air Traffic Control, S.A.C.W. Cook, at your service, any time!" Carol smiled ironically, "Sweet Jesus Harry, I know blokes who'd happily walk barefoot over miles of broken glass to hear me say anything like that. So just for you, I repeat, service you, at any time."

"I appreciate that, I really do, and I can't say it's not been great. I've really enjoyed ... you," he smiled squeezing her hands. "Look, if things were different, I'd never walk away from you. You are, if you'll pardon the expression, a spine cracking screw. Happily you're also a nice person, but I never made it a secret all I was after was your body and that lovely little crack of yours! It's true, Carol, your body drives me nuts. The only difference between you and Marion is, I love Marion, I really love her."

"Well now bully for her, but you Harry, you don't know the meaning of that word," Carol said as she bent over to gather up both blankets. Whether it was intentional or otherwise, she presented a parting view of one of the most perfect, sexiest bottoms he was ever likely to see. Irresistible to a man like Harold Ross, he could not stop reaching out and gently squeezing the area where the soft flesh of her inner thigh ended and the shorts began.

"Carol," he said as she straightened, "you're a conniving little bitch! I know that bum of yours so well, it's going to haunt my dreams. Maybe, just maybe I will give ATC a ring."

"You'd better, you big horny bastard," she said, "you big weak horny bastard. You know, you should've been an Arab Sheik Harry. Can you imagine your own harem with both Marion and me in there, at your convenience?" She shook her head almost sadly, "You and me, we can't get enough of each other, can we? And like you, I love sex, good sex and yeah, I do live for it, especially with someone who knows what they're doing. Someone like you." She laughed in her dry raucous way. "But you, with both your misses and me at your beck and call in that old harem ... you'd fuck yourself to death."

They pecked rather than kissed then Harold whispered, "There is one thing about you I am going to miss Carol."

"Fuck sake only one, and what's that?" she asked, handing him his blanket.

"In tender moments such as these, I'm really going to miss your very delicate turn of phrase."

The Following Morning, Kings Cross station, London.

Junior Technician Frank Connolly's journey to London was to register in his memory as an epic. Frank was not a great drinker, nor did he suffer fools lightly and he certainly did not normally get involved in childish drinking games. All that changed when Frank accepted a large whisky, one quiet drink, but unknown to him, he was joining with people who turned out to be deranged travelling companions.

The soldier, who had given a very good impression of dying, came back to life after a fifteen minute sojourn with his Maker, and suggested a game between the three servicemen, 'to while away the time.'

The game was a three-way contest that saw the loser down a whisky at the end of each round. A pleasant enough task one might imagine, but when one considers each round lasts, even if contestants took their time, no more than three minutes, then it is not hard to picture the condition of a consistent loser. The game was a silly test of skill as most drinking games are, but some efforts were hilarious therefore in that vein the pastime had gone on to its comatose and oblivious end.

The game was simple, or deemed to be so in a sober condition. One had only to find their own ear hole with the end of a pencil, first time, no second chances! The judge's decision - the judges being the other two participants - being final. The pencil was held between thumb and forefinger with the non-sharpened end offered to the ear. If the pencil end did not enter the ear hole cleanly, the pencil was gleefully exchanged for a measure of whisky. The drink was not to be sipped or heaven forbid, enjoyed! The drinker was a loser after all so the fiery liquor had to be downed in one swallow.

The soldier was not very good at the game, losing the first five rounds, whether by design or otherwise will never be known. He withdrew from the game a few rounds later when he actually managed to centre the pencil perfectly. However on losing once more and downing a sixth whisky after pushing the pencil into his eye, he decided wisely to retire. The method of informing his co-contestants he wished to stop playing was by laying his head on the table, breaking wind rather noisily before emitting a long heavy sigh.

"Poor old Jock, he's been at it all day," volunteered the sailor.

It was not long afterwards Frank noticed finding his mouth was a lot easier than locating his ear hole, then after countless whiskies, it was difficult to find either. When the score was somewhere in the region of 19-16 arguably in favour of the sailor, Frank's last recollection before he passed into that senseless void of nothingness, was the pencil was growing increasingly heavy and slippery. Because of this, he was finding it laborious to hold in his hand, let alone between two fingers.

Opening his eyes with an uneasy feeling he was in a strange place, Frank found he was not alone in a train carriage in London's King's Cross. A conductor was shaking him vigorously.

"Come now lad, can't sleep here all day, what would the Group Captain say about this eh?"

Frank shook his head immediately regretting the rash action as sharp edged broken crockery rattled in what felt like an empty tin bucket serving as his skull. He squinted at his watch catching a glimpse of both hands in a vertical line, "Six a.m. Jesus!" he groaned.

"By the way, your sailor mate said you were to keep this, and hopes the rest of your trip is as pleasant as the first leg." The conductor held up a bottle of amber liquid, less than half full.

Frank's stomach lurched, "Jesus! Is that all we drank? I feel bloody hellish."

"Don't know, but the cleaners haven't been so I imagine you had a hand in that lot." The man nodded to a corner and Frank saw bottle necks protruding from a brown paper bag. "Jesus," he groaned a third time. Struggling to sit up he faced the conductor,

"Keep it," he muttered looking at the bottle, not trusting a nod of his head.

"Thanks lad, don't drink it myself you unnerstan', but the wife she likes a drop 'casionally. By the way, that's your kit there," the conductor indicated the end of the carriage. "The sailor put it on the table for you. Couldn't waken you he reckons."

"Cheers," Frank muttered then asked, "Tell me where do I catch my connection to Swindon?"

Two and a half hours later Frank waited miserably at Swindon railway station having phoned RAF Lyneham for transport. He'd never felt so hellishly tired but the cheering thought occurred to him, in just over two hours he would be on his way to Cyprus, the sun and blessed sleep.

"Lyneham mate?" A voice cut through the pleasant haze of drink induced coma Frank was finding it difficult not to slip into.

The driver was chatty and thoughtfully placed the kit marked 'Connolly. F.,' into the Land Rover for the owner could barely stand. Grunts was all Frank could manage to questions so the driver gave up, glancing at his passenger occasionally. 'Piss artist,' he thought, 'suffering from S. double I.' He'd seen the condition of Self Inflicted Injury often and his nose wrinkled as the sickly stale and off sweet smell that emanates from 'morning after the night before' revellers.

"Right mate, 'Movements'. Through those doors, okay. You're on your own now pal. I've taken your kit to the doors for you, over there, see?"

Frank had fallen asleep in the heat of the Land Rover. He was being gently propelled towards a double door entrance. He mumbled something and the driver took his leave. Frank sucked the freezing air, steadied himself then launched his weary body towards the last lap of his trip.

Doing his best to appear presentable, Frank somehow managed the double doors and headed across the floor towards the distant Movements counter. His legs were doing their own thing as his RAF holdall and suitcase bumped against them. To make matters worse the blinding winter sunlight ricocheting off the highly polished floor, was flashing his eyes as he floundered over the sea of light. 'Shades of the ancient bloody mariner with his dead bloody albatross,' he thought as his holdall twisted uncontrollably at the end of a dead arm.

At the Movements counter a matronly WRAF corporal watched the scruffy airman's progress. She'd seen it all before of course. Some airmen, because they were posted overseas felt, for whatever reason they had to down a few stiff drinks to send them merrily on their way. This one was merrily stiffer than most.

"J/T Connolly, corporal, for Flight 6532. Akrotiri, 1100 hours." Frank handed the woman his documents with the best smile he could manage. The smile was to fade.

"Sorry Connelly, afraid your flight has been delayed," the corporal stated blandly.

The information was not well received. Frank stared but as the woman did not offer anything further whilst stamping his papers, he felt compelled to say, "That only happens on civil airlines. The RAF never delay their flights. How can you say the flight's delayed when it hasn't taken off yet?" It was a daft response but he had an awful feeling of sinking.

"Departure time, I was referring to when your flight would actually take off, that's 'Departure time' sonny, as I'm sure you were aware. And it's R - A -F, not RAF, as I'm sure you are also well aware. And for your information we, that's you and me, we are, unbelievably, on the same team, we DO delay our flights, just like civil airlines, and unfortunately not immune to gremlins either. You were just having an early morning joke with me, weren't you airman, hmn? Oh, I nearly forgot, your flight has been rescheduled. It will now take off at 19.30 hours, and that I'm sure you know, being in this man's Royal Air Force, is 7.30 this evening. If, and I do stress the IF, we get rid of our gremlins." She grimaced but to be fair, it may have been a grin, even a smile, it was difficult to tell.

Frank gave a watery smile in return before looking at his watch, 8.45 am and for the hundredth time in the last hour the word "Jesus" crept out between tight lips. "Corps," he said in a strangled voice, "Jesus that's nearly eleven hours away an' I've been travellin' since early yesterday mornin'," he lied. "I'm totally whacked, I'm dead."

"Airman!" she said as if he were at the back of a classroom, "According to your travel documents, you travelled from Leuchars last night, LATE last night, and if you made the correct connection as these documents clearly instruct you to do, travelling time, including waiting time, would have been eight and a half hours. IF, as you tell me you left early yesterday morning, then I can only assume you saved the British taxpayer the price of your travel warrant, and walked all the way here, as I might add, the sorry state of your condition indicates!"

"Jesus!" Frank stared at the impenetrable round face. "Movement clerks, should've known."

He decided to strike out in a more passive direction. "Look, can we start again, I've had a really bad night?" the corporal sighed and nodded knowingly. Frank battled on, "An' I was lookin' forward to gettin' my head down on the plane. Now there's a helluva difference between my scheduled 11 am and 7.30 pm flight. An' I have been travellin' since last night, LATE last night on a train so busy I couldn't get a seat so I tried to sleep sittin' on that!" He pointed to his holdall, adding a tiny white lie just to try her out. The woman's features and eyes had not moved. He carried on, "So come on, help me out. Point me in the right direction where I can grab a few hours kip."

She gave him a long hard look. "Connolly!" she said as he cringed. "It is a quarter to nine in the morning, a little late to be greeting a day that's half gone, and you want to go back to bed!" Frank was about to question the 'back to bed' comment but wisely decided against such recklessness. She went on, "However I can see you've had a draining time doing whatever it is you people do with yourselves when posted overseas. Now then, if you look over there." She pointed with her whole arm extended more towards the roof than the back of the hall. Frank turned hopefully and saw two overstuffed settees. They could not have been more inviting if they had been king sized silk covered beds with both Bridget Bardot and Racquel Welsh waving madly for him to join them. The corporal dragged him back to reality. "No one will trouble you on those. If anyone asks about your untidy person, I will truthfully pass on your predicament. We do have dormitories you understand and we do send people to them, but at night time, you know, when normal people sleep through the night?" she grimace grinned again.

"Thanks corp, you're all heart." Frank said feeling utterly stupid as the ridiculous emotion rose within him that urged him to hug the woman. Wondering if he was coming down with something, he gathered his belongings and staggered over to the settees with their open welcoming arms.

Using his RAF holdall as a footrest he sank gratefully into the soft somewhat smelly mock leather upholstery that blended perfectly with their accompanying fusillade of farting noises. Frank imagined many a stranded airman had probably left pockets of trapped gas within the confines of the sponge cushions. Hence their unwelcome attentions to his nostrils as the crushing weight of his reclining body set them free. They would disappear soon enough when he fell asleep. He glanced quickly around before finally settling down.

A young woman, slim, very beautiful with smooth ivory white skin and long black hair wearing a dark suit was watching him, then looked quickly away. She looked lonely. Frank stifled the inclination to go to her and strike up a conversation. But damsels in distress were not his immediate concern. He covered his eyes with his round hat, stuck his gloved hands into his greatcoat pockets and almost immediately fell asleep. It was not the sleep of the innocent but fitful, broken and uncomfortable, but very welcome to J/T. Frank Connolly.

The young woman watched the airman settle down. She noticed he wore a similar badge of crossed rifles her husband Harold wore on his uniform. Harry had been so pleased to qualify for the badge, which indicated he was a registered 'marksman' and took great care sewing the badge above the cuff of his uniforms. To demonstrate the complexity of achieving the badge Harry, proud as a peacock had drawn the precise five hole pattern he'd shot through the top half of a bisected one-inch circle.

Marion Ross was weary. She'd been told at Movements her flight to Cyprus would not be leaving until seven thirty that evening. Not eleven o'clock this morning, as notified by the RAF people who sent her all that baffling paperwork she did not understand. Her dad sorted it out and he and mum had put Marion on the train in Edinburgh the previous night. With a chaotic change in London she somehow got here in good time for the eleven hundred hour Flight 6532 to Akrotiri, as directed in the RAF paperwork. And why all these hundreds of hours? Marion was confused enough without throwing all this hundreds of hours business at her. Eleven hundred hours must be about a month! Did that mean she would be flying around in the sky for a month? 'course not, so why confuse everybody? Couldn't they just say eleven o'clock like normal people? And now, for all their military lingo, they couldn't stop the 'eleven hundred hours' flight being put back to nineteen thirty hours? She wasn't even born in 1930! Just as well the big lady behind the counter told her nineteen thirty hours was half past seven this evening. Otherwise she might have just got right back on the train and gone home to Kirkaldy. This was 1965 after all, why did they muddle everyone about with Victorian hours and years?

Marion sighed deeply. Of course she knew it was all to do with adding twelve or subtracting the first number you thought of, or whatever. She never quite grasped what Harold had tried so patiently to explain. They had been in bed at the time and no self-respecting girl should concentrate on anything other than the man she loved when snuggled up in bed with him.

Again she sighed and pushed thoughts of Harry to the edge of her brain, not wishing to throw him out completely, but direct thoughts about him at the moment were much too painful. Her eyes wandered to the settees again where the airman with the marksman's badge was already sound asleep. 'I wish I could join him,' she thought then giggled inwardly. 'I mean, I wish I could join him on a settee. No, no,' this time she had to stifle a throaty laugh. 'I mean, I MEAN let's get it RIGHT girl. I wish I had a settee to MYSELF. Not to sleep. Perhaps snooze a little, after all, what am I going to do for the next eleven hours?' The magazine on her lap had been opened, flipped through but nothing penetrated her beleaguered brain. Making a determined effort to read something, she again opened the magazine.

No good! Excitement and worry still blinded her. Her mind kept drifting from the printed page back to her husband of nine months, Harold Ross. Among the many thoughts were the questions, 'Had he or would he be told her flight was delayed? How would he learn of her new arrival time? Would he meet her and what would she do if he wasn't there?' Again she drove away these irritating thoughts with the comforting words, 'This must have happened before, the RAF know what they're doing. Oh, I do hope so.'

All Marion's precious plans revolved around seeing Harry that night. She'd spent a lot of money on herself buying perfume and a nightdress in preparation for their first meeting in three months. If her flight had not been delayed she would have arrived in Akrotiri around seven in the evening! Now it was uncertain at what time of day, or night she would arrive! She allowed herself a little smile, 'I suppose it'll be sometime tomorrow morning. Poor Harry. This will just make him all the more anxious,' she thought warmly.

Last September, all of six months ago when Harry came home for the weekend, he brought with him the news they would soon be on their way for a three year tour of Cyprus. Her first question had been, 'How can they call it a tour Harry, I thought you were going over there to work?' She smiled at the memory. They were staying with her parents, in their two bedroom Kirkaldy council house. Marion was apprehensive about Cyprus. The Edinburgh zoo had been the farthest she had ever travelled in her life; and certainly never realised a three month separation from her husband could last so long! Harold informed her, because of some troubles or other with terrorists (which had quietened down, he hastily added) he must spend that short spell alone prior to her joining him. "Three months," she shrugged, "That's not so long." That 'short spell' felt like a year now, and still she was not with him.

The first six of their nine month marriage had been blissful, even though Marion felt at least half of that time had been spent mostly on her back. Harry was insatiable and hardly ever left her alone. A smile crossed her face as she recalled she'd been almost as bad. But she did welcome Monday mornings when Harry returned to Leuchars. For no other reason than to give her body time to recover. Come the following Friday however she could not wait for him to come home. The three nights that followed were lost in what was a dreamlike ethereal state. What her parents must have thought she could only guess, but Marion didn't care; she loved her Harold and the only thing that ever mattered to her was her husband. She still blushed at the movements and noise they made in that little upstairs room. The all too recognisable rhythmic sounds would not be lost on her folks, although her mother one evening asked her father, "What on earth can they be doing up there George?" Thus displaying the eternal maternal instinct that no daughter of hers could actually perform the same act she herself had performed in producing that same daughter! Across the room the only thoughts the very realistic George had were, 'Get on with it lass, get me a grandson!'

Marion clasped her hands and tried not to sigh yet again. 'To think I could have been in Harry's bed, our bed tonight! Now I'll be millions of feet up in the air? All right, maybe not millions of feet, whatever Air Force planes fly at then.' The young woman leaned forward and pressed her thighs together as warm visions flashed across her mind. "Damn, damn, DAMN!" She muttered then castigated herself immediately for swearing, allowing her emotions to surface in such a public place. She snapped the magazine shut.

Thirty feet away the action drew the attention of the uniformed lady behind the Movements counter. They exchanged smiles and Marion guessed she had probably seen this scene many times; that of the frustrated wife anxious to join her husband. 'Is that what I am, God? A frustrated wife?" Her mind could not accept this so she counted back. Harry left on the 8th. December, 1964, and today is the 16th March. 'So,' she thought ruefully, 'it is over three months! It's three months, one week and one day! Goodness—I've every right to be frustrated!' This time she could not suppress the giggle gurgling up her throat.

Harold Ross had written to his beautiful and naive young wife bi-weekly letters, never failing to say how he loved and missed her dearly, how he could not wait for her to join him to restart their life. In one of his last letters he told her of the house he had rented in Limassol. It sounded like a mansion. Two bedrooms, large lounge, fitted kitchen, bathroom with fitted shower and large hallway. No garage but it had a carport. Carport? Was Harry thinking of buying a car if he mentions a carport? Even her dad, after all his working life could never aspire to owning a car! 'Oh,' she thought for the hundredth time, 'why my 'plane?'

If the reason was sound Marion could accept any waiting period, tolerate long stretches of boredom. What she found morally exhausting was the abrupt halt to the start of her new life. She had been so looking forward to it and now stifled excitement and budding anxiety sat like a heavy yolk across her aching shoulders. 'If I could just unwind,' she thought making an intense effort to relax her shoulders and melt into her seat. Mercifully she felt an immediate over all easing of her uptight frame. 'Hhmnn, nice, now if I can just close my eyes, just for a minute.'

The God of sleep and dreams was at last kind for Marion was unaware of slowly allowing her chin to sink to her chest. All conscious thought left her as Morpheus swept her off. She slept.

Three and a half hours later, Frank Connolly for the second time that day felt someone shake him. He was sitting in his Ford Popular with Lorna and their kids. They were discussing how exciting it was to be going in an aeroplane to Cyprus. The two girls in their excitement were jumping around on the back seat, the car started rocking. Frank was yelling at them, "Stop that, stop that!" Then Lorna shouted at him, "No I won't. I WON'T, wake up, wake UP!"

Frank opened his eyes uncertainly. It was certainly not Lorna looking at him. It was a face he did not recognize, not at first. As his vision cleared he looked again at the commanding figure standing over him. "Jesus," he said, making an immediate mental note never to utter that word ever again. "Jes ... it's you! When did they start lettin' Nazis into our Air Force?"

The woman bending over him was talking over his mumblings. "... goodness sake, waken UP!"

"I'm awake, I'm awake for God's sake."

"Good!" she said, "I'm off duty in half an hour but I'll have you know airman, I do not do this for every scallywag that comes through here."

"I'm sure you don't," Frank mumbled, then added hurriedly, "Do what?"

"You are obviously in need of a meal, a proper meal, not any of that take-away rubbish but you'll need to hurry. Let me say right away this is not entirely for your benefit." She turned her gaze towards the rows of seats and the girl Frank noticed earlier.

"You see that young lady?"

Frank grunted.

"She is also a passenger from your delayed flight and exhausted too but not as lucky as you. She cannot spread herself out as men can and sleep comfortably until boarding time. Now then! There's a wash room over there. You'll find everything you'll need, you see, over there?" Again her arm elevated towards the roof but at least indicated the general direction. "You have half an hour before the mess closes. The mess is that way." Her pointing arm suggested Frank and the girl might be eating with the pigeons in the roof.

"You know corps, I was in a deep sleep and would probably have slept until flight time."

"Nonsense!" she bellowed. "You and that young lady have missed breakfast and you are now on the verge of causing her to miss lunch! Is there no gallantry left in this world? Get yourself over to that wash-room, NOW. I will speak to the lady," she added kindly.

A number of other travellers were watching the pair, grinning at Frank's discomfort.

'This can't be true, I'm still dreamin',' Frank thought, struggling to get up. The corporal placed a hand under his elbow and was lifted effortlessly to his feet. For the first time Frank scrutinised his benefactor. She would be around the 35 mark and weigh in around eleven stone. 'Aye,' he thought, 'she'd make a good anchor in any tug-of-war team.' Despite his unkind thoughts the matronly figure was a good egg who obviously had taken him under her wing. She was not quite finished. "Take anything you might need for the flight. I'll check the rest of your luggage onto the aircraft. You won't see it until you arrive in Akrotiri." She was already lifting his grip onto a trolley.

"Where have you been all my life?" Frank said lifting his small pack before she ran off with it. "And don't say hiding from me!"

She smiled properly for the first time, "Get on with you," she said pushing and knocking him back into the settee. "Speak to the girl when you've completed your ablutions. Now move!"

The wash-room was well equipped. Turning a shower on, he undressed. Adjusting the cold to where the surprisingly hot water would not scald the skin from his back, he gingerly stepped inside.

After a few seconds allowing the jets to run over his cold body, Frank shuddered with sheer ecstasy as the cold was driven from his bones. The water felt like ripples of liquid gold coursing down his back and totally immersed in the pleasure it gave him. He stood for five minutes, not moving, relishing the physical well being it stimulated. He then washed and carried out the rest of his ablutions in double quick time.

Tying his shoelaces he realized he was indeed hungry, very hungry. The WRAF corporal knew his needs better than he did. He felt almost new and after a meal he could tackle the world again.

The girl in a dark blue figure hugging suit was still sitting alone, doing her best not to look miserable. Frank approached her.

"A little bird told me you're going to Cyprus," he said brightly to the top of the bowed head.

The head lifted to look up at him and offer a tentative half smile. But the half smile confirmed Frank's initial opinion before dropping off to sleep. About eighteen or nineteen, this girl was a classic beauty. Her shining black hair highlighted exquisite china blue eyes and her oval face was blessed with the most delicate unblemished skin that lifted neatly at the corners of her mouth when she smiled. "Yes, that lady did mention you were also going to Cyprus." Her lips were full, slightly quivering and her voice was throaty, yet light and soft.

If Frank had not been armoured with a deep love for his wife Lorna, the arrows from this young lady's formidable arsenal would surely have pierced his heart. Nevertheless his eyes had no defence against her beauty and at her question he could only nod. He didn't trust his voice.

Marion, unaware of the inflicted damage went on, "Yes, well I hope I'm going to Cyprus. I should be on my way to meet my husband. He's stationed at Akrotiri but my flight's been put ...."

Frank recovering from her initial visual onslaught picked out her Scottish accent. She was trying to speak precise English, nervously rambling, trying to tell Frank her life story in her initial homily. He had to put the apprehensive lass at her ease so thickening his own accent he said, "Sorry tae interrupt ye miss," then remembered she mentioned her husband and the gold ring was in plain view, "oh sorry, it's Mrs ...?"

"Ro-Ross?" Marion stammered, "That's my name, Ross, that is, ah, Mrs. Ross. Funny, it still sounds strange for me to say it like that. Misses, I mean ... and, you're Scottish too? Isn't - "

Frank knew the name but there was little time for social talk. He had to interrupt again, "Look I'm really sorry Mrs. Ross - "

"Marion, you can call me Marion ... if ye like? What's your name?" Her accent was easing back.

"Eh, Frank, Frank Connolly, now we only have - "

"Connolly? I think I've heard my husband mention that - "

"Are you hungry?" Frank cut her off brutally but it worked. She went quiet staring at him. Frank tried again, more gently this time. "Marion, do you fancy some grub?"

"Oh I'm famished. Oh aye ... I mean, yes, I was beginning to wonder where I might ... the lady mentioned some - "

"Okay, we've five minutes to get to the mess, the mess is our canteen by the way, where we eat, but we have to move! If you want to eat, we'll have to go now!"

Marion hesitated, "I want to eat, yes but I'm not in the Air Force, I mean, am I allowed?"

Frank took her hand, "Come on," he eased her to her feet. "Don't worry about that now, let's eat first and if they want you to wash up afterwards, well ... I'll dry." She laughed. It was a husky sexy sound, not at all what Frank imagined her laugh would sound like. It should have been light tinkling bells to suit her unblemished image, not this throaty chuckle that strummed the basic chords of man's reproduction system. The girl's husband was a lucky man.

They hurried towards the Mess, Frank striding out, she doing her best to keep up as he dragged her along. Safely inside the building, Frank paused to point out the various trays of food, two thirds empty after the lunchtime rush. "Just follow me, do as I do but make your own selections."

Sitting at a table little was said for the next ten minutes as they ate. Frank was first to finish and sat back. "Phew, I needed that. I think I could've eaten a horse, which on reflection, is probably what I've just done," he smiled. "Enjoying it?" he asked.

"I didn't have the horse," she smiled, "but the fish was lovely."

Marion started on her sweet so Frank went for the coffees.

"Thanks Frank. I must say, that was tasty, not at all what I expected after all the stories."

"It's all a front, they knew you were coming," Frank laughed then relented. "Aye, they can work the odd miracle. I don't normally eat in the Mess being married but when I do, I enjoy it."

"I'm still learning to cook," Marion volunteered, "but I've learned a couple of dishes which I think I've perfected. I'm hoping to make them for Harry."

"Harry Ross! Your husband's big Harry Ross? ex-Leuchars?"

She smiled, properly this time as the whole of her face lit up. Frank blinked at her simple beauty. The full lips pulled wide and set free the glow of shining white teeth that were childlike in their innocent beauty. Two black manicured eyebrows that had never seen tweezers sat above the half closed delicate blue eyes melting him with their warmth. She was a doll, a fragile porcelain doll. Frank sucked air as he thought, 'No, not Harry Ross, she's too good for that big bastard.' Despite twinges of jealousy, which was natural for any man who stood in the blaze of Marion's smile, he said, "No need to answer that Marion, you're Harry's wife right enough!"

She nodded happily.

'Big Harry Ross,' Frank thought as the last hope this girl was not connected with the person he knew, disappeared with her nod. The man he knew did not deserve a girl like this, certainly not for a wife. Trying to contain his disappointment he asked, "How is he?"

Suddenly Marion seemed a different person as she talked and if half of what she said was true then Harry was a changed person. Frank knew him from the Leuchars tug-of-war team; a well set up man who had every female in the camp sending him signals, not to mention many more in the surrounding area. A renowned womaniser. Frank just caught Marion's last words. "... he enjoyed the tug-o'-war at Leuchars, did you play?"

"Play? Oh you mean was I in the team? I was, aye, we had a good side."

"So Harry told me, you won a few games, didn't you?"

'Won a few games!' Marion's terminology made the sport sound like rounds at dominoes. "We won everythin' 'cept the Braemar Highland games, and RAF championship. Got beat in both by the best team in Britain, and eventual winners, St. Athens."

"That's what Harry said. They must be very good, the team that beat you."

"The best like I said, now enough about tug-of-war. Where is Harry, is he on 103 MU?"

"I don't think so, I've never heard of one oh three. What was it?

"M, U, it's short for Maintenance Unit, where I'm posted, 103 MU. Can you remember where you address his letters, where he's working?" Frank asked hopefully. Harry's morals may be in the gutter but a good man to have on the rope.

"Yes ... three letters, G-E-F, that's it," she beamed, "it's Ground Equipment Flight, Akrotiri."

Akrotiri's gain was the MU's loss. Frank was headed for a similarly initialled section, General Engineering Flight but on the Maintenance Unit.

In somewhat meditative mood, they quietly sipped their coffees when Marion asked, "Frank, you know our flight's been put back, well something's worrying me."

"What's that?"

"Will Harry be told about the delay and new arrival time and, well, just everything?"

"No doubt. Movements are over there too, just like here, so Harry'll be in touch with them. Don't worry, if I know Harry, he'll be cursin' the delay just as much as we are.

~~~

Chapter 4

"Thank God!" Harold Ross sighed with a blend of relief and regret as he replaced the heavy black telephone into its twin cradles. "The wife's flight's been delayed."

"Has it?" Chief Technician Ray Price frowned, not entirely surprised at his airman's reaction. Most unaccompanied married men would regard that as bad news. "What's her ETA now?"

"They're not sure."

It was shortly after Naafi break when SAC Ross was summoned to Ch/Tech. Price's office. It was to take a call from Movements informing him of at least a ten hour delay with Lyneham Flt. 6532. They had no ETA at present but if he contacted Movements section around midnight they would have more information.

"Not too anxious to see your misses then ... after three months?" Ray asked dryly.

"Course I am Chief but I still have lots to do. I need time to organise some details in the house, you know what it's like?" Harold did indeed need time, but not for the house. His body was not at its peak, needed time so he could welcome Marion, as she would naturally expect him to. The undeniable facts were physical reservoirs, like everything else needed topping up when great demands were made upon them, and only time could perform that minor miracle. A few hours respite had been divinely granted so Harold was confident now he would be in perfect working order when the situation arose with his young wife. Of course he was anxious to see Marion, but he couldn't help what had happened the previous night. Carol was like a sensation sucking leech from which he simply could not cut free. And besides, he had loved every fiery moment! Sexual opportunities to Harold Ross were similar to fruit that was ripe - it had to be devoured at that precise moment or wasted and lost forever. Now with Marion's flight delayed Providence had provided yet again. Already a warm exciting flush was spreading through him as he thought of Marion. He'd go down to Limassol that afternoon, collect the hire car, buy flowers, she'd like that, and more groceries. He might even manage a couple of hour's kip before returning to camp around midnight refreshed and recharged.

Harold left the office door open as he had found it and returned to his work bay. Through the door, Chief Tech. Price wistfully gazed at Ross crossing the workshop floor. The airman wore only a pair of KD shorts and Ray understood why females were mesmerised. This young man arrived on the base three months ago on the crest of a rakish reputation. And it was common knowledge a month later he was knocking off the best bit of skirt on the camp; that cracking crumpet from Air Traffic Control. SACW Cook. 'Little Carol Cook. Hmn, not so little,' he mused, 'five two or three and a real blonde, so I'm reliably informed. What's a female like that doing in the RAF and not pregnant? Shame on you lot!' Ray smiled wistfully denouncing every airman on the base. Ross had been seen with the little sexpot and for a married man he was hardly discreet. 'Am I jealous?' Ray asked himself, 'bloody right I am! Some people have all the luck. That lass could warm the cockles of any man's heart, especially mine!' From the grains of information gathered from the fertile fields of the Workshops floor, it seemed Ross could not give that little WAAF enough! The forty four year old Chief Technician shook his head rapidly, blew through clenched teeth, picked up his pen and exclaimed to the empty office, "Why is life so bloody unfair?" then went back to work.

Harold finished setting the points on the generator he was servicing then entered the soul destroying worksheet details before hurrying off to find Alf Morris, his team corporal. He found Alf in the crew room checking the Duty Roster.

"Just had a call from Movements Alf. Seems the wife's aircraft won't get in 'til the middle of the night. I've still to pick up the car, get more grub and stuff. Something to welcome her, you know. Okay if I piss off now?"

"Sure but check with Paddy at what stage you're at on that 'jenny'."

"Cheers," Harold said experiencing prickles of excitement.

69

"You've booked your 'Settling In' leave Harry?" Alf asked, still looking at the roster.

There was something about Alf's tone. "Yeah, you won't see me until Monday. It'll be difficult for you with me away, but you'll manage." Harold said lightly. Three days leave was granted to help airmen help their wives and families get settled in to their new environment.

"I'm sure we will." Alf paused, then, "They have you down for Fire Picket a week Friday."

"You're joking!" he growled staring at his corporal. The seed of doubt he carried for three months burst into full flower. "You must be fucking joking!" He grabbed the roster from Alf's hands and searched the pages. "Where?" he said, followed by, "Oh fuck! They can't put me on Fire Picket. My misses is new here. She's never been on her own. And for a week!"

"I'll keep her company if you like," volunteered the suddenly helpful Alf Morris, but quickly added when he saw Harold's black look. "It's not so bad, get someone to stand in for you, but it'll cost you." Alf rubbed his thumb and forefinger together.

Harold threw the roster on to the table, "The bastards knew my wife was due about now, they could've put me back a couple of months."

"D'you think they're watching when every airman's wife is due to arrive? Besides you've only yourself to blame. We've been warning you to volunteer for weeks. Get it over and done with but you couldn't take time off from screwing around."

The growing flower from the tiny seed of doubt, planted in his first week on the base was climbing up Harold's throat choking him. It was true; he'd been advised to volunteer for the duty, get it completed before his wife arrived. Fire Picket lasted from midday Friday to the same time the following Friday. For single men as Harold basically was living on the base prior to his wife's arrival, the duty was usually undemanding. Airmen simply changed billets and beds, from their billet to the Fire Station and were expected to help out in any emergency. For married men living out off base, it meant separation for a week.

Harry was fuming at himself for not volunteering. Around two thirds of all airmen arriving for permanent duty under the rank of corporal would be called to perform this duty. Harold had gambled on not being called and lost. "I'll see the Station

Warrant Officer Alf, he'll put it back, long enough for the misses to get acclimatized at least. As it is I'll barely get back from leave then go straight on this duty."

"Wish you luck Harry, but you've as much chance of the SWO man switching it as I've got of getting my leg over Marilyn Monroe. Or maybe that blonde WAAF from Air Traffic Control. She'd make a good second best." It took great effort by Cpl. Morris not to smile, 'Serves you right, you dirty lucky bastard,' he thought as SAC Ross stomped off.

Less than an hour later Harold caught the eleven thirty bus from the Akrotiri main gate to Limassol. He got off outside 'Nick's Garage' on the Bypass. Crossing the garage forecourt he passed a collection of cars for sale then three hire cars. Harold noted among them, the gleaming Ford Cortina he had booked with a hefty deposit the previous month. Hurrying into the office with warming excitement he completed the final arrangements. From now until Sunday, the new 1965 Ford Cortina belonged to him.

'God, wait 'till Marion sees this,' he thought sliding behind the wheel. Starting the engine and savouring the wonderful surge of power, he rolled the car slowly across the forecourt and eased onto the Bypass, knowing Nick the garage owner was watching his every move. 'Probably worried about me driving his latest acquisition, and if I was him I'd be worried too.' Harold grinned as he cruised along wanting to get a feel for the car.

The garage owner need not have worried. Harold Ross was competent and surprisingly careful for a young driver. His progress on the fairly quiet Bypass was interrupted when he stopped at the chicane of three military checkpoints on the town's outskirts. The first checkpoint was manned by Greek-Cypriot Police, the middle by U.N. soldiers and the third by Turkish-Cypriot Police. They did not delay him long and soon he left the town behind speeding down the open road. Harold had never owned a car and the simple fact this engine started immediately thrilled him. The few cars he knew always coughed and spluttered in slow reluctance to offer a manifestation of life.

Today Harold and this car were full of life, one charging the other, each contributing to the many facets of this wonderful day! Marion was on her way, he had money in his pocket and the rest of the week with the woman he loved stretched ahead into glorious oblivion. The car purred happily under him, responding to his every touch, as he knew the beautiful woman he adored would soon be. The sun was beating down on the shining blue paintwork of this lovely flying machine. Electricity crackled through his veins as he floored the accelerator in elated exhilaration. The car took off with a squeal of tyres and Harold turned his face to the sky and roared in sheer exultation. This wonderful day was his, and the world really did belong to him.

An hour later having burnt a load of rubber and petrol on the coast road to Paphos, Harold's joy ride ended as he drove back into Limassol. It may have been his day but it did not deter the hands of the clock. His good intentions had been to buy last minute items for the house, top of the list being a huge bunch of flowers to welcome Marion. Trouble was it was now a few minutes after one o'clock. Every shop closed at that bewitching hour for a midday sleep, a Mediterranean siesta and would not re-open until four. Miffed at his lack of ability to coordinate his time, he toyed with the idea of going to the Twiga bar for a beer. Bars thankfully were immune to siesta time. Suddenly on impulse he decided to go to Pappachristos street, to the house that would be his and Marion's first real home. He'd look around, note items he may have forgotten, then buy them after four o'clock when everything opened up again. And, he recalled happily pointing a mental finger to the heavens the other day he'd put six beers in the refrigerator on his last visit .They would be ice cold now, plus he could join the locals and grab a couple of hours kip too. The hot embers of excitement that had dampened a fraction glowed again at the thought of doing something - anything - just to fill in the long waiting hours.

He drove down the quiet street and parked outside the house, resisting the urge to park in the driveway. There was something too ostentatious about parking a car like this in his driveway, a reluctance perhaps to set a precedent he could not live up to.

Unlocking the front door he entered the large bright hallway. The very presence of the house energized him. Their first real home, where they could live and love together without distraction of prying eyes, or ears of anyone. Harold signed the contract in February, and paid rent from March 1st, over two weeks ago. His two boxes of household goods were delivered from Akrotiri storage the previous week and he'd visited the house on two occasions to unpack them. These two boxes he and Marion had lovingly packed all their worldly goods whilst he was on embarkation leave in early December. Most were wedding presents they had not had the chance to use.

He unpacked everything carefully, including his precious new record player which thankfully was intact, placing everything where he thought it should go. Marion no doubt would change it around to suit her tastes. He, a mere man, knew nothing about arranging ornaments and furniture.

The furniture that came with the house was dated but serviceable. All Harold need supply for everyday living was towels and bed linen. The landlady Helena and her husband Andreus, were the proud owners of an unpronounceable surname that Harold immediately forgot on hearing it. They also owned the semi-detached house next door, which was at present unoccupied. Harold had questioned Helena if the adjoining house was in any way superior but she swore both were the same. Helena and Andreus lived with their two daughters in a small house to the rear.

Harold walked through the hall and kitchen to the kitchen's back door. Searching through the keys Helena gave him he unlocked the door. A low railing divided the long covered patio shared by Helena's two houses. Glancing round cautiously but with the comforting knowledge Helena and her family would be enjoying their siesta, he decided on impulse to have a look at the adjoining unoccupied house. He was curious and wanted to dispel lingering doubts that, as Helena had assured him, the empty house was no better than the one he rented.

Stepping over the rail, he tried the back door expecting it to be unlocked as these people were so trusting they never seemed to lock anything up. It was as he expected. Slipping inside he gently closed the door and leaned against it. In line with next door he was in the kitchen. There was no difference at all. Same cupboards, fridge, cooker and scrubbed clean surfaces. He shook his head. 'Why am I feeling guilty?' he asked himself. 'I just wanted proof.' However a definite feeling of intrusion lingered. 'Okay, quick look round, satisfy my curiosity then leave.' He padded into the passageway and turned left towards the lounge and front hall. Again, similar lounge furniture but the hallway was empty, whereas he had three cast iron garden chairs and table for use in his hall or veranda. Harold smiled, he was fractionally ahead with the furniture. That alone made this impromptu inspection worthwhile. Turning towards the bedrooms he froze! There was a sound, which Harold had often heard, but it was out of place or rather context here. What he heard was a giggle! A stifled titter tinkling from the back bedroom.

'Holy shit! I haven't gone and gate crashed Helena and Andreus. Maybe seeking a little privacy from their young daughters!' Harold felt much as a burglar might feel on being discovered. 'Fuck sake, let me out of here.'

Stealthily creeping towards the kitchen, retracing his steps that unavoidably led him towards the main bedroom's half open door, he heard it again. This time there was not one, but two snickering sounds, two distinct and different FEMALE giggles!

Relaxing slightly but intrigued yet fully aware he was an intruder, Harold contemplated but for only a moment for the unmistakable scent of female bouquet was in the air. The hairs in the young man's nostrils were catching unmistakable scents and signals sending primal messages to his ever receptive brain. He was trapped but it was a contented trap. Even if he imagined otherwise, nothing on earth could turn him back now. 'Oh well,' he thought, 'I'm here and they, whoever 'they' are, know I'm here. Might as well be hung for a sheep as a lamb. Let's see what's going on.' Sucking a chest full of air he crept to the door and peered around the jamb.

Sitting up in a double bed were Giga and Nina, the landlady's daughters. He'd met them when discussing the rent and entry date with Helena. Giga, the oldest at sixteen had brought coffee and some sort of sticky doughnut that day. The doughnut having been soaked in syrup was so sweet it was almost inedible. Nina had sat quietly watching the proceedings.
The sisters were coyly holding the sheet under their chins. Harold quickly noted the bundle of clothes and underwear on an adjoining chair and did not have to be an Einstein to work out they wore little if anything under the screening sheet.

In those first few seconds a multitude of warnings flashed through his brain; He must keep his head and neither touch nor harm them. They could cause mountains of trouble with Marion, their parents and he could and probably would be reported to the RAF.

Harold knew, but pushed the annoying thought aside. He should turn and walk away. But when it came to the lure of something new, daring and so positively innocent this strong young man was as weak and helpless as a rabbit caught in the glare of twin headlights, and like that mesmerised rabbit, had little chance of escaping. Harold actually believed he could leave; the drawbridge had not yet been raised! Nothing could have been farther from reality. He was trapped in that merciless twin dazzle of escalating femininity, totally unaware he was awaiting their move, which would determine his. This came when Giga gave her sister a sidelong glance, which sparked them both into a sustained fit of nervous giggling. It was this spark, which could have been anything from a falling leaf to a shooting star that set off the scenario that followed.

Smiling reassuringly Harold approached and sat near Giga on her side of the bed. "And what are you two doing here?" he asked, a smile playing round the corners of his mouth.

"We are having, ah ... you know ... siesta ... sleep, the afternoon sleep? Giga said hesitantly, trying her school taught English.

"But, you are not ... sleeping." Harold sang the last word, inevitably gaining confidence.

"But yes, we sleep. Nina, she wake, hear keetchen door, it open," Giga gave a delicate shrug of her shoulders, "She wake me," then nudged her sister for support. Nina nodded agreement, her wide eyes gleaming.

"I don't think you were sleeping at all" Harold said in a schoolmaster, mock threatening manner, "I think you two were lying there, discussing boyfriends." He imagined most girls in their age group talked about little else.
Another glance at each other followed with more giggles and staring apprehensive smiles.

Harold laughed inwardly, 'Bull's eye!' He could see from the profile of her drawn up knees, Giga had her feet crossed, one on top of the other. Without warning he reached under the sheet and poked a finger into the instep of her left foot. Giga let out a stifled shriek and reached for her mouth with one hand and feet with the other. For a fleeting second Harold caught delightful if

75

brief glimpse of breasts and thighs before Giga recovered, composed herself pulling her knees up to her chest. She was however smiling broadly, nervous eyes flashing, tempting, inviting his next move?

"You musta behave, Mista Harry, Mama, she hear!" Giga indicated the shuttered window that overlooked the small house where Helena and Adrieus were hopefully sleeping soundly.

"You're the one making all the noise," Harold chided, thoroughly enjoying this bawdy but playful interlude.

"Yes, but you must not make so queek the move," she wrinkled her brow impishly.

Harold held up his right hand, "I swear, no more the 'queek move.'. Whatever I do now I will do much more slooowly." As he spoke he was little by little 'spidering' his right hand towards the edge of the sheet and Giga's legs. "See," he said, "no more the 'queek move.'"

Giga was fearfully following the progress of the spider like hand, edging away but her encroaching smile would not be denied. It spread across her face as yet another chirp of a chuckle pipped from her lips. Nina, on Giga's left decided to join in and laughingly would not budge as Giga pushed against her in an effort to escape the advancing 'spider.' They were all laughing quietly now as Harold's five-fingered marauder started to dive under then out of the sheet continually brushing against soft thighs and velvet skin.

Strange as it may seem, at this point, there was no real lust in Harold's advances. His guilt lay in his surprising but immense naivety to think he could horse around with two naked and nubile females and imagine the situation would progress no farther. They really were too young so he was or so he imagined playing around, having a laugh in a cosy situation that had presented itself.

Perhaps deep deep down Harold did know. If so then they were too deep. His relevant train of thought informed him this was just a bit of fun. Not perfectly innocent but nevertheless, good fun! He could and would walk away anytime with no deep sexual involvement. What his relevant train of thought was not telling him was, Harold being Harold, already it had gone too far.

Just as Harold made a playful grab at the soft inside of Giga's right thigh, Nina jumped out of bed and padded across to the shuttered window. She peered between the slats that kept out the afternoon heat then turned to face the couple. Harold froze. Initially he thought Nina heard something, that the parents had been aroused. But there was no panic with either of the girls. It was then he noticed Nina's body. He was astounded and for a moment speechless. She was the younger by perhaps a year yet fully developed and perfectly formed. Her skin bore an even tan except where her underwear had shielded her tender areas from the sun's rays. Dragging his eyes from the scant pubic hair as Nina turned back to the slats, he looked at Giga.

For a man like Harold, he had been in similar situations before, but never with girls so young, or with parents nearby, also this situation was potentially all round dangerous and dangerous situations were best avoided.

"What's she doing?" he whispered, aware that Nina appeared to have taken up sentry duty at the shutter, that his hand was merely resting now on the soft velvet inside of her thigh. Coincidentally he couldn't help but notice, the girl was making no move to remove either her thigh or his hand.

"Nina, she make sure Mama, Papa no come, no look for ass, no see what we do ... weeth you!"

Harold looked at her, then at Nina who was smiling over her shoulder at him.

"Just a minute," he said, suddenly for the first time in years unsure of himself. "I can't ... you know. You're too young! Besides, aren't you people supposed to be ..." he paused at the word, "untouched ... virgins when you get married, or at least when you get engaged?"

Giga laughed heartily this time, "Me? I am not the vergin," then winking at her sister, went on, "And Nina too? She like me, you know ... ahhh ... wanna learn, cure-you-us ... yes correct word ... yes? She ... ah ... like to try thees thing." Giga gave a delicate nod and shrug of a shoulder.

Two beautiful girls, demanding his attention! Even for Harold this was a unique but the timing so terrible. After last night and approximately twelve hours before he was due to meet his wife after a separation of three months! His initial attraction to the girls was to play around, to lustily enjoy their nakedness,

77

yes, and matching vulnerability, certainly, but not a Bacchanalian binge. He had not entered the room with a feast of fornication in mind. Or had he? He wasn't sure but felt with a real effort he could still laugh it off. Make an honourable withdrawal. They were very young after all, repercussions could be drastic.

Giga sensed the hesitation and crossed her left thigh over her right, enclosing Harold's hand, trapping it in firm folds of cool flesh. In the process, she presented him with a delightful glimpse of a tiny inverted triangle of black pubic hair. Any doubts that may have lingered about his rising to the occasion disappeared when he felt the growing bulge in his groin try to drive painfully free from the folds of his shorts and his fragile resolve weaken farther, 'God, how can I walk away from this?' he asked his Maker.

Without waiting for a bolt of lightning, Harold, easing his hand slowly out from the closed gates of heaven, stood up. "Keep watching Nina," he said unbuckling his belt, simultaneously, accompanied with a touch of mounting impatience, he wriggled and kicked his feet free of the flip-flop sandals.

~~~

R.A.F. Flight 6532 for Akrotiri, Cyprus eventually took off from R.A.F. Lyneham at 23.30 hours on Tuesday, 17th March. The aircraft, a Viscount from Transport Command, was fully loaded with Royal Air Force personnel plus wives and families of personnel already in Cyprus.

Prior to take off, passengers gathered in the Departure Hall and despite the late hour and lengthy wait, excitement that had waned began to surface again.

When a board displaying seat numbers lit up above the exit doorway Marion and Frank saw they would not sit close to each other. Marion had seat D4 and Frank N2. The arrangement actually suited them although Marion would disagree. She did not relish being separated from her new found friend but they needed sleep. Frank certainly did. Had they been seated together Marion would keep them both awake with her reborn excitement, plus she was about to board an aircraft for the first time. Frank liked this girl very much; her absolute innocence in everything she talked about endeared her to him. He hoped Lorna and Marion would become friends though it was not certain he and Harry Ross could hit it off. They had worked in Leuchars Station Workshops but in separate sections. Frank knew Ross but only as a tug-of-war team mate.

Frank was exhausted; his journey had started in Scotland over twenty-four hours ago and was still six hours plus from completion. But if Frank was tired to the point of dropping dead, there was little sign of languor with Marion. She was still talking, excitement the fuel feeding her motivated tongue. "Once we get settled you will come visit the house Harry's got for ... us!" She paused. "Funny, it's difficult to say 'our house,' or 'our home.' I've not seen it so it doesn't seem appropriate to call it 'ours', know what Ah mean? Not yet, it's still a figment of my imagination. Anyway when you come, and you better make it soon Frank Connolly, I'll make you a nice plate of Scotch broth!" She was trying to refine her accent, and succeeding. The Scottish lilt was still clearly there, but her words were more rounded and full. Regarding her culinary delights she had in those last few words given Frank a complete list of what she could prepare unassisted. A week ago, Marion's mother had shown her daughter the best way to prepare the old Scottish favourite of savoury mince and potatoes. Marion had prepared the dish only once, with a fair degree of success, but she could not confidently list it as a dish she could prepare. Not yet. Hence the positive offer of Scotch broth, something she made often since mastering it the first time in her school kitchen.

"Thanks Marion, I love Scotch broth, I'll take you up on that."

"And see that you do," Marion said firmly, "I hate getting stood up on promises." As she spoke the tannoy announced the first list of names to board, Mrs. M. Ross was among them.

"Oh, oh that's me!" she cried in surprise, her mood plummeting from light hearted firmness to uncertain meekness.

"Do I go ... get on that ... now?" she asked with wide-eyed hesitation.

"Aye lass, off you go. Just follow the others. I'll try to see you for a chat once we're airborne." Frank took and squeezed her hands giving her a reassuring grin.

The worried look cleared at the hand squeeze and she returned his grin with one of her wonderful smiles, lighting up the whole of her face. She was so wholesome Frank was about to lean over and plant a platonic kiss on the lovely girl's cheek. Unaware of his impulse she disengaged her hands and with a nervous flutter, lifted her bag then hurried to catch the passengers leaving the hall.

Frank watched her with a degree of sadness. He wanted to stop her, turn her round, send her back home. To protect her. So wonderfully naive and at the end of her journey waited Harry Ross! 'If the leopard has truly changed its spots then Harry'll be pawin' the ground waitin' for her to get off that plane. I hope he is, as any man would be. But a leopard has as much chance of changing its spots as Harry has of going without for three months. Hope I'm wrong.' The tannoy blared, Frank heard his name. Shouldering his small pack he soon boarded. Sidling down the passageway to his seat he passed Marion talking animatedly to a smiling WRAF girl.

Blissfully he got settled and muscles and bones sagged as tiredness pushed him into every corner of his seat. When the passengers settled it wouldn't take him long to nod off. Sinking fast Frank did not regret the previous night's indulgences for now they were responsible for melting the marrow in his bones and pouring them into the warm folds of a heavy golden and satisfying slumber.

It was a strange coincidence that both men in Marion Ross's current life; her husband and this new temporary companion who took her under his protective wing, should both be suffering the agonies of fatigue. One self-inflicted with over indulgences of drink. The other? Also over indulgence but his drinking was from a different cup.

~~~

Harold awoke at 9 pm. The sheet that had recently shrouded the girl's bodies was tangled around him. Yawning then stretching luxuriously on the soft down mattress, he caught the unmistakable sweet musty scent of the sisters and smiled, recalling their frantic involvement with himself a few hours ago.

80

He tried to lazily roll on to his back but the effort was so heavy, so sluggish he felt the blood had been removed from his veins and replaced with lead!

Giga and Nina left at four o'clock as their parents were rousing. They intentionally locked the kitchen door behind them, which would force Harold to leave by the front door. They could not take the chance he might be seen leaving the same house where the sisters had spent the afternoon.

As always Harold regretted, afterwards, always afterwards what he had done. If only he could feel this intense guilt before competing in sexual Olympics, then it would be so easy to walk away.

Rolling off the bed like a man three times his age, he rummaged around in the semi darkness; searching for the five items of clothing he'd thrown off earlier in less than that many seconds. 'Two flip-flops, shorts, okay, my shirt, now where's my drawers?' Strange, there was no sign of them! "Shit where ARE they?" he whispered. He dare not switch on the light, for muted voices ghosted in the night air. He could easily drive to camp wearing no underwear but how would Giga explain a pair of Y-fronts in the bedroom she and her sister had spent the afternoon? He must find them! In the dim half-light filtering through the room's shutters from Helena's house, he could just make out the light switch by the door. Dare he chance it? No, no course not. Much too bloody risky! What a stupid idea. Glancing up at the light fitting above his head as if willing it to shed just a glimmer, he frowned. 'Oh yes, what do we have here?'

"The little pair of bastards!" he muttered. His underpants were draped around the lamp fitting. He could not help grinning as cautiously standing on the bed he unravelled the pants. With his apparel now complete he quickly dressed. He badly needed a shower. The faint musky smell of the girls, so sweet and intoxicating a few hours ago, but now mixed with his own stale sweat was pungent. A shower would be top priority when he got back next door.

Quietly making his way to the front door he eased out. A warm breeze welcomed him as he slipped across the mutual front patio. The hired Cortina was still parked on the road as another pang of conscience stung him; a mute reminder of all his good intentions. "Where the fuck am I going to get a bunch of flowers now?" he groaned.

Opening his front door, he went straight to the bathroom, switched on the light and urinated loudly into the bowl, the act somehow signifying he was safe. He showered and while dressing there was a knock on the kitchen door. Buttoning his shirt and with tentative feelings he opened the door. Helena was looking at him enquiringly. "Hello Masta Harree. I wonda what happen you? You sleep? I see car from thees afternoon, but no see Harree, you sleep yes?"

Harold's mind raced, his guilt was exposed like his fly was open, or there was lipstick around his mouth. Here was the mother of the two young girls he'd been having carnal relations with all afternoon, and she was staring, scrutinizing him. She went on, "Dis car, ees car you tell me you book from Neek's Garage, yes? I see Neek's stickah but, no Harree! I reeng bell and knock door but no Harree! You sleep yes, Harree! You okay? You no' look so good?"

'God, she's been at the door! Holy shit!' His panicking brain was searching then suddenly came up with an answer, "Yes, yes I'm all right Helena and yes you're right, I was asleep. I just come off a night shift duty you see, that's why. I'm so tired." Harold gave his best apologetic look.

"And your wife ... she no come today, yes?

"Later, delayed flight, arrive later."

"Ah! Later, sorree, night shift eh, that why you so tired Harree! You no' eat?" Helena shook her head, then, "You eat?" This time she nodded. The woman's negative-positive method of questioning always confused Harold. He never knew how to answer her. Helena however came up with her own affirmation.

"You come, eat, come!" She placed a hand behind his elbow and half led half pushed him across the patio and down steps to a table beneath the iniquitous window through which Nina had peered. Andreus seated at the littered table, blithely drinking coffee, stood and welcomed Harold, He offered the freshly groomed but obviously tired man a cigarette which was gratefully accepted,

"Mama, geta cognac for our guest. You lika the cognac Harree?"

Helena berated Andreus in Greek which ended only when she stormed into her small kitchen.

"Sorry Harree, I no know you no eat. Mama she say you musta eat before the dreenk, neh?" Andreus shrugged his shoulders, "But no worry, the food she ees ready, we, my famlee," he waved an arm towards the house behind him. "We no long finish to eat."

Harold was ravenous. When Helena brought out what resembled a steaming cow patty, despite his reservations, he picked up a fork and tentatively tasted it, hoping against hope it tasted better than it looked. To his utter amazement the dish was delicious. Harold ate the mixture of black-eyed beans, ham, garlic, eggs, and mixed herbs, with hearty relish, much to Helena's delight. The young Englishman was a big eater but surprisingly just managed to clear his plate of the very filling food. He had no difficulty however in downing the bottle of beer Helena placed in front of him. Sighing he sat back contentedly. The incident with Helena's daughters and danger of discovery was over. His receding guilt had sunk like a mere pebble in his pebble strewn stream of shortcomings.

"Thank you Helena, I've never tasted anything quite like that. Whatever it was, it was delicious."

"You like!" Helena stated rather than asked, nodding to Andreus who had never paid such a compliment as to clear a healthy helping of her food in so short a sitting. She whipped Harold's plate away only to return seconds later with another steaming cow patty.

"No, no, I couldn't!" protested Harold, patting his stomach, "Full, too much, honestly."

"You eat, eat Harree, no worry, plenty, plenty," Helena jerked a thumb towards her kitchen.

To hurt the generous woman's feelings was the last thing Harold wanted, but could not force down another morsel. "Helena it was lovely, really tasty but I can't eat any more," he pleaded.

"No be shy Harree, you eat, make a you strong for you wife." Helena clenched a fist then bent her arm at the elbow, vibrating the fist into her shoulder It had to be an innocent gesture but after the physical hammering his body had taken, his guilty conscience and now her phallic forearm may have suggested something else! He had no idea if what it looked like was what this simple Greek lady was suggesting. The doubt dispelled when Helena touched her biceps and smiled. "Strong Harree, neh?"

Harold shuddered, 'God help me,' he thought picking up his spoon and started to eat.

Giga suddenly appeared from the house and placed a second beer in front of Harold. She neither spoke nor smiled, but gave an inclined nod of her head, acknowledging his presence. Harold sat back, "I'm sorry Helena, this is excellent but I cannot eat any more. I hope you're not offended. It was so tasty I got greedy but I've eaten twice what I normally eat."

"Okay, okay Harree. No warry, you eat good. Now dreenk you beer. I know you Eengleesh you lika beer betta than you lika the cognac, yes? Dreenk Harree." She turned to her daughter, "Take take," she indicated Harold's plate. Giga nodded then leaned over Harold to lift the plate.

Screened from the others by the young girl's head, he took the chance of whispering in her ear, "Covered any lamp shades lately?"

Giving no indication she heard him, on straightening Giga said, "I go bed now, goodnight Mama, Papa." She faced Harold continuing, "Goodnight Masta Harold, I hope your wife, she lika the house, and I ah, hope you have no the problem of ah, how you say ah, getting her up," she stared directly into Harold's eyes.

"Ich ich ich," Andreus spluttered. "You Eenglish Giga, she no good. You musta say, 'Peek her up, peek her up! No 'getteeng her up,' ich ich ich."

"Don't worry Andreus, I understand perfectly what Giga's trying to tell me," Harold interrupted not taking his eyes from those of the girl's. "Thank you for your good wishes Giga and," he held up his beer, "for everything else." Tipping it slightly towards her, he went on, "I feel for you. Strange English subjects can be very hard for young Greek girls and I am really surprised you managed to take it all in." He grinned before carrying on, "I myself have entered and got through two Greek subjects recently. It was very hard for me too," he paused, "for a while. Sometimes they got on top of me, other times I was on top of them. It was really hard for a long time but I thoroughly enjoyed what I was doing. My hard times are over for the moment, having a little rest now." Giga nodded understandingly before he went on, "But don't despair, in your case I've no doubt no matter how hard it gets, you'll handle it well. You may gag and choke occasionally on your English, as I did with my Greek subjects, but you're young, adaptable and clever. I know eventually you'll take it in, and what's more, really enjoy doing it. Goodnight Giga, sleep well."

"Thank you, I am happy for you, that your hard times are over ... for the present? The performance was satisfactory with the ... Greek subjects?" She was trying hard not to smile.

"Yes, oh yes, full marks for both. I was really amazed with the overall performance."

"Full marks!" Giga clapped her hands, "Oh so happy. Full marks Mama, Papa, we have a very clever Eenglishman I theenk." Turning back she shot Harold a waggish look before mincing away.

Andreus watched her go, "Keeds Harree, I don't know what they are going from these days."

Harold was taking a drink when he spluttered and sat forward choking.

"You awright, you awright Harree?" Andreus tried to help Harold but noticed the Englishman was laughing then choking intermittently. The Greek-Cypriot smiled, "I wrong Harree?" he joined in the laughing as Harold tried to control himself. "Iz troo. I say wrong, neh?"

Harold nodded, speechless for the moment. When he at last gained control he corrected the smiling Andreus's statement before making his apologies, explaining he must return to camp for information on Marion's flight.

Andreus was still chuckling as Harold was about to drive off. "'Coming to' ha ha, I say wrong, 'Coming to.' My Eenglish eh, like Giga, ees sheet eh Harree? Bye Harree bye."

Harold drove up Pappachristos street, still trying to cough clear the gaseous beer from his throat, still sniggering. "Bloody hell that was funny," he muttered wiping his eyes.

At the Main Guardroom Harold registered the car then drove to Movements. "Yes," he was told, "Mrs. M. Ross is a passenger aboard Lyneham flight 6532. The ETA ... your wife will arrive at 06.00 hours ..." the clerk looked up, "... or thereabouts. It's unusual but this one seems to have had more than its fair share of problems, sorry, better get some sleep mate."

The clerk's words were most welcome. Yet again he had been granted a few hours bittersweet grace. Although desperate to see Marion, his eyes felt full of grit; he was wrecked, totally drained due to those crazy sisters. He needed time and rest. The latter could not be gained without the former so this time, he would spend this God given gift safely in his billet bed.

Back in his billet the other airmen were asleep as he quietly packed what remained of his gear into the already bulging holdall. At last he slipped into bed and drifted off easily knowing he'd waken with the usual noises made by the other lads rising.

Next morning Al 'Midnight' Johnson who had the adjacent bed was surprised to see SAC Ross sound asleep. Al was sure Harry was to have met his wife yesterday. She was due in from Lyneham last night! So what was he doing here in the billet, still in bed - was he ill? He checked out of the billet yesterday, hadn't he? Or was he due to check out today? Al was confused and worried. But of one thing he was certain, his mate Harry Ross shouldn't be here!

Al was nicknamed 'Midnight.' Not simply because he was West Indian for Al's skin was not just dark! His sooty mat hide had no shine whatsoever and as such, was extremely difficult to see in the dark; hence the perennial 'Midnight' suited him perfectly. He also took lots of ribbing with his real name Al Johnson, near enough Al Jolson the popular American singer, who coincidentally blackened his face while impersonating a black man! Al Johnson could not escape the wags on learning his name, prodded and coaxed him to sing an Al Jolson song. On the odd occasion the genial Al, with enough ale inside him, had obliged with 'California here I come,' leaving the wags to solemnly doubt their wisdom at having asked for a song in the first place.

Al cast a worried glance at Ross sleeping peacefully. It was 6.10 am and he was now sure Harry should have moved out of the billet the day before. Something was wrong! He moved closer, calling his name, "Harry, Harry!" The call was no louder than a whisper but not a flicker of an eyelash from SAC Ross. Al shook the exposed cold shoulder. Still no response! Bending over, Al peered at the chalky face. Dark grey swellings under the eyes, cheeks sunken. 'Christ he looks ghastly, so cold 'n' white. Oh shit, maybe he is dead. That'd explain why he's not with his wife!' Al shook the chilled shoulder again.

"Harry!" Nothing, absolutely no response! "Oh Christ. He's COLD, he IS dead!" Al starting to fluster flicked his wide eyes round the room but the others had gone to the ablutions. His eyes fluttered in uncertainty. "What to do?" He was rocking on his heels, on the verge of blind panic. Looking again at his friend's slack, immobile face, rising panic erupted. "HELP-HELP!"

Al's shout did indeed produce a miracle of waking the dead for Harold's dead eyes popped wide open. The black man staggered, toppling onto his own bed as he involuntarily stepped backwards.

"Good grief Al, what time is it?" Without waiting for an answer from the staring and for the moment dumbstruck man, Harold glanced at his watch. "Shit and corruption," he roared, "I'm supposed to be at Movements!" Grabbing his toiletries he dashed off to the ablutions.

He was back in five minutes, dressed quickly and rushed out, only to stumble back into the room.

"Al, give the Bedding Store a ring for me, tell them I'll hand in my bedding when I get back, and could you tidy up my bed space please, I'm so bloody late."

Despite his skin colour, Al was looking decidedly ashen. He had moved very little since waking Harold but managed to nod to his bed space neighbour's request.

Parking the car in the shadow of a hanger, Harold laid his head on the driving wheel for a moment and sighed deeply. Knots of airmen were standing at the fence surrounding the low building that served as the Arrivals Hall. By their presence it was safe to assume this almost mythical aircraft bearing his wife had not yet landed. Bracing himself he joined the nearest group and tossed the question among the waiting men, "Lyneham flight's not in yet then?"

"It's in circuit," came the answer.

Harold grunted his thanks. He was so tired the very act of walking back to the car was ponderous. He felt like an elephant plodding across the road one heavy leg swinging with its own weight in front of the other. And the way that crazy bastard Johnson woke him could well have initiated a heart attack. He lit a cigarette and sat back pushing away the worry that Marion would expect him to rush her off to bed, as he would have loved to do, as he had threatened to do in every letter. 'What a bloody fool,' he moaned. The way he felt at the moment it would take a week to rise to any occasion after his most recent orgy. His groin felt abnormally heavy, as if a particularly angry horse had kicked it. 'What an idiot! What a fucking arsehole!' Before he could berate himself farther a flash glinted between the gap of two hangers, a quick blast of noise like a gust of wind; Marion's aircraft had landed.

Fifteen minutes later, buses started delivering the most recent arrivals to Cyprus, disgorging their contents outside the Arrivals Hall. Harold noticed something familiar about a Junior Technician who stepped from the fifth bus. The man removed his hat, ran a hand through a shock of black hair that had to be tucked back under the hat. Harold watched the JT who was fairly tall with a slightly stooped gait. "That's Connolly," he muttered as Frank turned back to the bus to lift out a dark bag. A female stepped from the bus and Frank handed her the bag.

"Marion!" It was an involuntary outburst, Harold was waving madly, "Marion, MARION!"

The slim girl in a dark well fitting suit stood blinking in the bright sunshine but she heard Harold. Marion saw him immediately then that well loved smile spread across her face outshining the morning sunlight. She waved then dropping her bag, waved both her hands. Resisting the urge to run to him she pointed apologetically towards the Arrivals Hall.

Harold watched his wife and Connolly disappear through the doors. "God, she looks gorgeous," he exclaimed loudly, proudly, not caring who heard. His stomach was dancing after seeing her then realised she was wearing something new. Harold always noticed what his wife wore and had never seen the dark suit before. 'She looks great, that suit really accentuates her figure. Fuck it!' he cursed inwardly, 'Think I'll go see the doc. Get one of my fucking balls cut off. How can I fuck around with every bitch that crosses my path when I've got such a prize as Marion? Something's got to be wrong with me.'

Twenty minutes later Marion shielded her eyes as she at last exited the Arrivals Hall. With a quick search she found what she sought then she broke into a run. "Harry, oh Harry," she cried wrapping her arms around her strangely immobile husband. Harold was almost fainting with emotion. He hugged and squeezed this wonderful person. She was so much part of him and was on the point of sobbing as multitudes of feelings coursed through his body. He could not speak as Marion cried over and over, "I've missed you, oh how I missed you." They kissed and held each other and kissed until breathlessly Marion broke away, holding him at arm's length. "Harry, I've never known a longer three months in my whole life."

"Marion, I ... I ... love you so much!" Harold's emotions were running amok, with guilt leaving a bitter taste. Suddenly he wanted to tell her everything but stopped. This was not the time. With the realisation came the doubt; was there ever going to be a time? The sour guilty bile frothing to the fore of his conscience would yet again, have to be swallowed.

Attempting to draw her close again aware she was studying him but she held him off, concern creasing her brow. His face was tanned but the skin had an ashen sheen, circles under his eyes were black "Harry," she paused, "Harry, are you ... well?"

Harold tried to stop his mind racing. He'd dreaded this inevitable moment but comeuppance time was here. He had to come up with a believable answer. In turmoil of guilt and shame he could think of nothing better than what he'd told Helena. "I'm okay darling, I've just come off a week's night shift. And ... and I'm only now getting over a ... a bad cold," he added for good measure. "Don't worry, a few hours sleep, I'll be fine."

"What, you mean you've been on night shift ... for a week? They put you on night duty knowing you were meeting me? Today? Why that's heartless Harry, and what would they have done if I had arrived last night ... as I should have done?"

'Shit,' he'd forgotten that minor detail but like the true trooper he was, he squirmed clear.

"Well Mari, there's a seven day duty here, actually it's a night duty that's got to be completed prior to your arrival darling. We can do it one night at a time if we want to, or all seven in one go," he ad-libbed brilliantly. "As soon as we get seven nights in, it's over, I won't have to do that duty again. By yesterday morning, I had only managed six straight nights, so I still owed them one shift. Then they told me about your delayed flight!" He shrugged, "I thought it was a good chance to get the last one completed - so I volunteered. That duty's out of the way now. They let me away at six this morning to meet you! So, no more of those night duties!" It sounded convincing.

"Oh Harry, you shouldn't have done it! You look, tired. Really tired like you've had no sleep for weeks. What sort of duty was it?" she asked gazing fretfully into his face.

"Look, it IS finished so we can forget it," he smiled, feeling he was breaking free from an excruciatingly tight spot, "You're here, that's all that matters, I just want to take you home."

Leading her to the car through the hugging reunited family groups he skilfully steered the conversation from himself, when Marion stopped and looked back at the Arrivals Hall.

"Just a minute. I must say goodbye to a friend of yours."
Frank had just put his holdall on the RAF transport when he saw Marion with Harold. She turned, saw him and waved for him to join them.

With one glance Frank knew the tall Englishman had been messing around, and very recently. They shook hands and Frank's standard greeting of 'Nice to see you, you're looking well,' stuck in his throat. He settled for "Hullo Harry."

The next few minutes were spent on mutual queries; Harold about news from Leuchars and Frank on Akrotiri and the island. Harold concluded with, "You'll love it here, make no mistake about that! Just remember, roundabout a month from today, get down to Limassol to look for a house. Speak to the taxi drivers, they act as commission agents for the house owners. They'll drive you around, show you lots of houses up for rent. Book one you like then apply to live out from, let's see, June, your misses will arrive sometime in June. It's like a three year holiday here according to the older hands, a different life." Harry may look half dead but excitement fluttered around the edges of his voice. Frank was already missing his family.

"Sounds fantastic," Frank said but it was time to go. He was intruding in a very special moment of Marion's life. "Look, there's no point in the pair o' you hangin' about here. I know Marion's dyin' to see her new home. I'll see you both, soon enough."

"Leave it for a few days Frank," Harold said, as Marion stood back, a picture of happiness, content to let her husband organise her life. "Then get yourself down to our place. I'm on leave until Monday then come down to the Ground Equipment Flight, you'll find me there. We'll talk, give you my address, right?"

"Okay," Frank said adding, "You're with Akrotiri GEF? Not the MU?"

"GEF Akrotiri. I was hoping to join the MU team, I actually went to see them but I'm not with the MU so ..." he shrugged, "they couldn't take me. But don't worry, one of these days Station GEF will get a team together and beat you lot."

"Look Harry, we'll talk about your daydreams another time. Your patient wife's still waitin' for two bad mannered idiots to stop rantin' on. So take her now to this wonderful house you have for her. Sorry Marion." Frank smiled at the calmly waiting girl.

Harold placed an arm round Marion's slim waist, "It's not such a wonderful house," he said tugging her in close, "but it will be now she's here. Let's go my little beauty, if you're ready?"

"Yes I'm ready," she smiled up at him then, "Oh I nearly forgot! I still have to collect my case Harry, that nice blue one we bought?"

"I'll get it, back in a minute." he said kissing her cheek.

Marion watched him wistfully as he walked wearily away. "Poor Harry, imagine," she said as haughtily as she could muster. "They put him on night duty all these past seven nights. I didn't think they did things like that in the RAF. You know ... in these situations?"

"Is that what he said?"

She nodded pushing up her lower lip.

"Well lass, a duty's a duty and by its very name, has to be done whether we like it or not. It is after all, our duty to do what we're told, comes with the job." Frank tried to sound convincing but had his own ideas on exactly what night duties had exhausted 'Poor Harry'.

As soon Harold appeared carrying the suitcase, Marion turned to Frank, "Now remember, come visit us whenever you feel like a nice plate of Scotch broth, or mince and tatties?" She laughed, "or even if you're a wee bit lonely. But you come and see us ... I like you Frank," she said suddenly and innocently. "You're a nice man, an awfy nice man, and remember, I'm really looking forward to meeting Lorna, and your children."

"I will ... honestly, now go on home Marion or you'll make me miss my bus." Frank had never met such an open-hearted girl and her sudden declaration of fondness surprised him almost closing his throat with emotion. A warm feeling surged through him on this early bright morning in a strange new land.

Marion glanced anxiously towards the blue bus filled with air force personnel but as it showed no signs of moving she laughed, "Oh I see!" she said, "'Here's your hat, what's your hurry,' is that it? I'm very quick you know. I can always tell when I'm not wanted."

"Oh that could never happen, Marion, never in a million years," Frank said fondly causing Harold's head to turn towards him.

"Ooh you men!" Marion said coyly. "Right then, see you soon." Leaning forward, she kissed Frank on the cheek then with a smile, rubbed the slightest smudge of fresh lipstick.

Frank glanced at Harold to get his reaction at the impulsive kiss but the tired features only creased into a grin, "She does things like that ALL the time Junior Technician Connolly, I'll have to put her on a leash. She kisses the strangest people."

"But ... but, Frank's not ... ooh Harry," she chided.

Frank walked with them to the car and watched as they drove off with Harold's hand waving from the driver's window. 'There go I in three months,' he thought with an added 'I hope.' He was never one to tempt providence into doing anything nasty.

Marion's excitement was bubbling over as they left Akrotiri. After clearance from the Main Guardroom Harold pointed towards the area's annual visitors; thousands of flamingos wintering on the salt lake, forming a pink haze a mile to their right.

"Isn't it beautiful," she murmured repeatedly. A statement rather than a question. Turning her restless head, trying to take everything in at once, her repeated statement was soon followed by, "Isn't it hot!" Again not a question. The latter challenged for the most frequently used as the journey progressed, then finally a question, "It's awfully dry Harry, isn't it?"

Harold, keen to impart some of what he'd learned about the island, answered, "It probably is drying now but this is the end of the wet season. There's lots of green growth out there, trouble is, it hasn't rained for a couple of weeks so everything gets covered in that yellowish dust. It rained a lot in December and January. It only rains in the winter by the way, so when it rains everything turned green, washes off the dust, see?"

Marion's brows lowered questioningly. Something he said caught her curiosity. She was unsure if Harry was dangling a baited hook waiting for her to bite, as he tended to do, preying on her naïve nature. "No rain," she said quietly, "no rain in the summer, only in winter?" This was unbelievable to a person who had lived all her life in Scotland.

"That's right, no rain from March to October!"

'He's not trying to trick me' she thought happily but said nothing, just in case. Harold went on, "Great isn't it, no rain in the summer, enough in winter which fills the reservoirs. At the end of the dry summer when reserves are running low, mid October whoosh, down it comes. Over the winter months rain falls regularly, fills the reservoirs and off we go again. What a climate!"

"That's very convenient," Marion said, "but what happens if it doesn't rain?"

Harold considered then glanced at her, "There's one helluva panic! How the hell do I know?"

They both laughed then Harold said, "And how come my wife asks questions I never thought of asking? Now you've blown my cover as the clued up island guide. I'm not so bright after all."

Marion dizzy with happiness leaned over and whispered, nuzzling his ear, "You'll always be the brightest star in my life, my wonderful Harry. I love you so very, very much."

A warm flush ran through him as he picked up the huskiness in Marion's hissed tones.

'She needs me as I need her. Oh God.' Guilt dampened the warmth. How could he ever explain? Change the subject, he had to cool the moment, but carefully. "And I love you my sweet little pet, so much so I've made plans for us this morning."

"I sort of guessed you might have," she smiled happily relaxing back in her seat.

"Let me tell you what I had in mind. I thought it would be nice if I take you home, you get unpacked then I'll take you to out to one of the bars for a lovely breakfast they do."

"Bars! You eat breakfast in bars?" she asked incredulously. Marion's image of a bar was a long wooden, highly polished counter top that men leaned on, drinking beer.

"The bars here are not like those in Britain! Just wait, you'll see."

"But Harry, I'd like a bath and ... well, I've been travelling for what seems like a week."

"Sure darling, have your bath and whatever. I'm just dying to show you round the place, and ... and show you off," Harold said plaintively, desperate to steer his loving wife away from the bedroom. After three long months she could never comprehend his problem. To Marion it would appear he did not want her. He'd been tired before, often, but it never stopped him.

Marion looked hard at Harold. Was it her imagination? Was he trying to divert, postpone the union he had guaranteed in every letter? This was not like her Harold at all! She fully expected to be fighting him off even now, begging him to wait until they got to their new home. Yet here he was talking about leaving the house to go for breakfast, when he had her alone and all to himself! His face told it all. He'd taken on too much over the past week. Obviously he'd overdone it. Never in a million years would she have guessed how close she was to the truth.

"Harry I can't understand why they put you on that duty when they knew I was coming out."

"I volunteered Marion, I wanted to get the duty finished before you arrived. Unfortunately it was just too close to your arrival! It's my own fault." He could not keep the sharpness from his voice.

Marion smiled. She did not consider herself the brightest of females but now she understood why the duty was so important to him. He simply did not want to leave her alone in a strange place, with him away on night duty. She had not fully grasped his reasons in the first place. "I understand now Harry. Oh how I love you," she said simply.

Harold glanced at her. Marion was looking at him with a tender smile. He could never determine what prompted her words but his guilt growled response was, "And I, I do love you."

They drove on wordlessly through Limassol, turned into Pappachristos street and stopped at the house. Opening the gates

94

he drove serenely into the drive. "Here we are," he said proudly. The carport under which he parked was festooned with budding jasmine flowers, the trapped air heavy with scent of the most enchanting natural perfume known to man. Marion closed her eyes and sat still breathing in the heady fragrance. Totally captivated she had never experienced anything like it.

"What is it?" Harold asked. Marion was sitting very still, eyes closed and breathing deeply!

"Oh, you never mentioned this, the wonderful flowers, and this perfume!"

Harold, not entirely beguiled with the botanical properties of the small garden, sniffed. "Yeah, it is nice isn't it."

Smiling wryly, shaking her head, Marion said, "Well done, that must be the understatement of the year Harry or maybe the century!" She slipped out of the car.

Harold had promised himself to do something at this precise moment. This was their first real home, he was physically at a low but surely he could lift a slip of a girl like his wife. Opening the front door he placed the luggage inside then before Marion knew what was happening, he slipped an arm round her back, the other behind her knees and lifted her off her feet. She gave a squeal of delight as he carried her into the airy hall then into the lounge where he gently set her down.

"Welcome to our first real home Marion." They kissed and clung to each other intimately. Marion was first to break away. The simple effort to lift and carry her a few feet had caused Harold to breathe heavily but Marion misunderstood. "Harry," she said looking mischievously into his eyes like a child about to unwrap a present, "I'm dying to see the rest of our home, please, my lovely man?" She patted his cheek then turned and walked slowly, inquisitively through the house.

Harold followed, watching her open cupboards, look out windows, then in the kitchen, open the refrigerator. "Oh, I see we're organized. Everything in its place, and goodness there's even some food alongside the beer. Apart from this my darling ..." she leaned inside and withdrew a carton of salt, "I'm really impressed." She giggled.

Harold shook his head, "Don't know how that got in there."

Marion was peering inside the refrigerator again, "As long as you've not put the bacon in the cutlery drawer or some other daft place, we should be fine. You do have bacon, eggs? Yes it's all here. Good." Taking off her jacket she said, "I'm going to change, I want you to run a bath for yourself. When you're all nice and clean, get into bed and I'll bring your breakfast. How's that?"

"Wonderful, but wouldn't you like to have a bath first?

"Harry my sweet hunk of a man." How wonderful it was to throw her arms around him, hug him. She squeezed his solid frame, "I'm not saying you're smelly, I wouldn't care if you were, but you need a bath to make you feel a wee bit better. I'll cook your breakfast," she pointed to the cooker, "then I'll hop in the bath. Right off you go!" She playfully turned him and patted his bottom.

Harold deposited the abandoned luggage from hall to bedroom then ran his bath. Marion seemed to have changed since carrying her into the house. Perhaps demonstrating to him she was capable of organising their lives? He could not recall his demure little wife ever giving an order; 'Run a bath for yourself' indeed, followed by 'get into bed' and the final indignity, 'you need a bath!' It was only the previous night he had showered in that same bathroom, 'I can't be that bad,' he thought sniffing under his arm, 'Mnn maybe she's right! But I'll put my foot down on that bossy little madam. Can't let her away with that!" he grinned happily.

Twenty minutes later soaking in blissful relaxation, Harold heard pots and plates clattering. Suddenly, Marion popped her head round the door, "Harry ...." she began but stopped when Harold quickly covered his shrivelled manhood. "Harry," she started again ignoring the coy movement, "there's no gas?"

Harold sat up hands still in his lap, "Oh sorry, forget to tell you, it's bottled. Hang on."

Marion turned away, aware of the unusual air of self-consciousness between them.

"Be with you in a minute" He called, fussing around, embarrassed and uncomfortable.

Marion having changed into a dressing gown went to the bedroom to finish unpacking. 'Why had he covered himself like that? He was never bashful before. Quite the opposite! He's so proud of himself in that department,' she recalled with a smile. 'Not to worry, my poor Harry, I won't hold you to your promises.'

"Marion, the bottles are in here," Harold called from the kitchen. She hurried through, "Oh, I'd never have guessed that was a cupboard!" Harold, a towel round his midriff was holding a door open at the end of the units. Reaching inside he turned a lever on the bottle to 'ON.' Marion gave a small cry then dashed to the stove where she hurriedly closed the hissing switches she'd opened.

Harold stepped behind her and slipped his arms round her waist, caressing her flat stomach.

Nuzzling her ear he whispered, "Marion, you know I want you so much, so much, but sweet, I'm ... I'm ..." He paused, his intention was to say 'not up to it,' but to his utter amazement, he was suddenly on the point of confessing, everything!

It was Marion who stopped his confessional words when she turned to face him. "Darling, I know how badly you want me, and me you, but my body has been unkind to us," she lied.

He pulled back for a moment uncomprehending. Then enlightenment dawned in his eyes.

"Yes, I'm sorry."

Stuck for words, Harold kissed her gently then whispered, "You mustn't be sorry for a natural occurrence pet. Besides, I don't know if I could have loved you as I wanted and dreamed of loving you Mari dearest. I'm so tired, but we have time. We have the rest of our lives."

"Yes, yes we have, and I'm so privileged I can spend it with you." She placed her head on his broad chest and held him close. It would never occur to Marion Harold's condition was due to over indulgence with another female. Her love was so complete, it was inconceivable she could go with another man, so for her it was an automatic equation; Harold could never go with another woman.

She stepped away rather breathless, "As for the rest of our lives Harold my sweet, that starts right here. Off to bed now, I can manage a fry up breakfast. Go on, shoo, off you go."

Like a good little boy Harold did as he was told. In the bedroom he slipped blissfully between cool sheets, the refreshing effect of the linen on his nakedness drawing a sigh of contentment. The bath had worked wonders as once again he relaxed completely. His tender feelings for Marion were scarred with his too recent escapades; the constant guilt a heavy burden. So heavy it was like a weight on his chest. He would do anything, try anything to stop this wanton lusting for the female form. Maybe now with Marion in daily close proximity, his mind and body would settle into a normal routine. He would try. Definitely ... have to try ... to try ...

Harold was in that that never-never land between being awake and asleep when Marion brought his simple breakfast of bacon, eggs and fried bread. "Eat that Harry. I'll have my bath then join you. Won't be long" As she turned Harold asked, "Aren't you eating?"

"I've eaten, pinched some of your bacon for a sandwich. That's plenty, besides I'm still excited with all this." She waved her hand around.

She ran a lukewarm bath and soaked for half an hour. On returning to the bedroom she was not surprised to see her dear tired husband sound asleep. Taking the tray she washed up then made a fresh cup of coffee. Sipping at the steaming brew she sauntered round the house a second time. Voices echoed from the rear and she drew her housecoat together, recalling Harold's warning of the close proximity of the landlady's house in his last letter.

'What a funny language. It's all Greek to me,' she smiled at her witticism on entering the hall. 'It's so nice, so bright, and all these tiles. I've never seen so many, not in a house anyway!' Placing her cup on the table she spread her arms wide and slowly spun in a circle, "I cannot fail to be happy here," she spoke to the plain painted ceiling, then wrapping her arms round her middle, hugged herself in sheer contentment.

Opening the bedroom door, she dropped her housecoat and slipped into bed. Resting her head on the pillow she studied Harold's face. In repose he did not look so tired but there was an unusual slackness of the skin that surely indicated exhaustion. 'Despite that slight, but oh so temporary blemish,' she thought, 'what a good looking man I've got.' She was so proud of him, her feelings like strands of electric prickles driving her happiness to near emotion. She simply had to get closer to her slumbering giant. Snuggling her nakedness against his sleeping frame she whispered, "Not to worry my dearest sweet Harry. I will build you back to complete fitness again, or my name in not Marion

Ross!" She spoke across his chest in a barely audible but happy voice. Then a little louder, bolder, "Marion Ross you're a lucky son of a bitch." It sounded so good! Running her hand through the golden chest hair she impulsively reached to kiss his nipple. There was a delicious feeling of wickedness in the action, but if she could not be wicked. Well, perhaps not wicked. Mischievous? Yes, if she could not be sexually mischievous with her husband, who could she be mischievous with? No one! Simply no one but her adorable Harry. "Marion Ross," she growled, "you are such a bloody lucky son of a bitch!" Closing her eyes thankful no one could hear, smiled at her profanity.

~~~

Chapter 5

The bus carrying the most recent personnel to arrive on RAF Akrotiri made its first stop. The occupants taking in their new surroundings noted the nearby blocks. Built in the shape of the letter H, these buildings were unusual. In the UK 'H' blocks were double storied, the buildings outside consisted of one single storey only. They were the quarters for permanent single personnel, who for better or worse would live here for the duration of their tours.

A wide quarry tiled veranda extended along the outer legs of the H. The middle connecting bar was a short passage leading to central ablutions block. On either side of the passage there were five rooms, each room capable of housing ten airmen

The rooms identical in shape and furniture had ten of each; single beds with mattress, single wardrobes, bedside lockers and bedside mats. Additionally there were four kitchen type chairs and one table in the centre of each room. Above each bed was the added luxury of wall fitted lamps and suspended from the ceiling was a huge four bladed fan. There were two windows on either side of the room and finally a tannoy speaker with one gauzed eye watched from its perch above the door.

A sergeant from the Movements section stood and faced the crowded bus. "These quarters on my right are for 103 Maintenance Unit personnel only. Those of you posted to the MU collect your kit and alight here. Find yourself a bed in any of those billets which you will find pleasant and comfortable. You will report to your Orderly Room by 10.00 hours, which gives you approximately three hours to see to your ablutions, unpacking, etcetera. If you want breakfast, the Mess serves late breakfasts until 9.30 am." The sergeant went on to give directions where the Orderly Room and the airmen's Mess were situated before going on, "Within the next few days you will be notified to attend an induction meeting. Good luck, welcome to RAF Akrotiri and 103 Maintenance Unit."

Seven weary men left the bus. Five were single airmen who unless their status changed would live here for the next three years. Frank Connolly would live a single man's life here but only until his family joined him in three months.

"Not exactly the Ritz." The voice came from an SAC walking beside Frank.

"Wasn't expectin' the Ritz"

"Colourful mind you, pretty in a chocolaty box kind of way, colonial probably."

"Aye, well Cyprus was a colony not so long ago." Frank said glancing at the suddenly talkative airman. He was tall with fair hair and walked, despite his holdall, with a swinging gait. Fairly good looking in an unobtrusive way and apart from one feature there was nothing particularly noticeable about him. Plain blue eyes, a straight angular nose on a face that was somewhere between round and long. But as if to compensate for the man's anonymity, nature had provided him with extremely large ears. They spread like the wings of an osprey about to pluck an unsuspecting trout from the water.

"I know we're strangers but we won't be for long," he said suddenly, "do you fancy finding a room where we can bunk together?"

Frank shrugged, "Fine by me, but I'll have you to know I'm married and I intend to stay true!"

"I'm married too but I'm always open to suggestions," the man laughed. "Now we've declared our feelings must forever remain platonic, let's go this way, for no other reason than the others all seem to have gone that way."

Frank nodded; the other five were checking the rooms to the right of a central passage.

He followed his new found friend along the covered veranda. He stopped at the fourth room with the number '2' above the door. "There's three in here," he called.

The spare beds gave the room an unoccupied look despite the fact the others were made up. There were folded used sheets at the bottom of each bed. Also some personal bric-a-brac pictures etc. on locker tops. The unclaimed beds appeared naked with nothing to garnish their presence, openly announcing availability with their bare mattress's folded over exposing scrawny bottoms, scrawny legs, wire mesh and bed springs.

There were two beds in the far left corner; the SAC took the one in the corner, Frank the one next to it. Dropping his gear Frank sighed, "Home at last".

"Yep, or until the wife comes ... and that usually takes her two minutes," the blue eyes twinkled. My name's Buckley, Ray Buckley and I intend to make these three months unaccompanied as I am of baggage and baggage, the best three months of my depraved, and may I add, deprived life! Wot say you?"

Frank chuckled as they shook hands, "Frank Connolly, pleased to meet you Ray."

Ray unfolded his mattress then sat on it. "Smoke?"

"No I don't smoke." Frank answered beginning to unpack.

"Good for you!" Ray lit an unfiltered cigarette, "These things are getting bloody expensive in the UK." He held up the cigarette to blow on the red tip, "But I'm told they're dirt cheap here. Imagine that! Cheap fags and even cheaper booze, what a posting. Wonder if they provide cheap women?"

Their conversation continued as they filled in their backgrounds; Ray from London was married to a girl named, Babs. Like the Connolly's, the Buckley's had two daughters of similar ages. Ray dabbled in rally driving and happily described how on two occasions came near to killing himself. It had only been his quick thinking and even quicker reactions it seemed, that saved his life. Frank found himself relaxing, talking about his recent background; of playing soccer for years but gave it up when joining the Leuchars tug-of -war team. "I'm lookin' forward to gettin' involved with this crowd's team, they're supposed to be very good."

"Who are?"

"The MU, their tug-of-war team, got quite a reputation!"

"Yeah? Well I've never heard of them," Ray said ungraciously, then added when surprise registered on Frank's face, "But then, having never participated, it's not surprising is it? Being unaware ... of their reputation I mean!" Ray dragged on his cigarette before contemplatively going on, "I'm a big strong boy, maybe I'll have a go at that."

Ray crushed his cigarette into a makeshift ashtray, a discarded boot polish tin. Frank despite his long journey was surprisingly restless. After unpacking he sat down but excitement of the new surroundings was firing his blood. He stood up, "Right, I'm for a quick shower, then breakfast?"

"I suppose," Ray said apathetically.

They showered and shaved in the well-equipped ablutions. On returning they found an SAC collecting the soiled linen from the bottom of the beds. He looked up as they entered, "Good morning," he said pleasantly, "Moving in?"

Ray, placing his toilet bag into his bedside locker answered flippantly, "Very observant of you mate! But you're right, two very tired, very new to this very wonderful island reporting."

The SAC smiled. He was about five feet eight inches tall, of slender build with abundant fair hair that must have been longer than regulation length. "I'm Julian Cantwell, as you see, I am Room Orderly this morning." His voice was soft and friendly. Ray extended a hand, "Pleased to meet you Julian. And now, you have the honour of meeting, and the distinction of shaking the hand of one Ray Buckley, a moment you will no doubt treasure for the rest of your natural life. And this, this is my life-long friend, Wing Commander Connolly. Frank, VD and scar, currently reduced in the ranks you understand, while they search for his spitfire." They shook hands.

Frank extending a hand said, "I've just met him Julian," he nodded at Ray, "and it looks like our 'life-long friendship' is going to be the shortest friendship on record. Pleased to meet you." As their hands clasped Frank was immediately aware of the flaccidity of the hand he held. There was no firm grip, as men tend to do when greeting one another. Unaccountably he could not help staring at smooth well-defined soft features. Light blue eyes penetrated unashamedly into his. In a matter of measured time it was two seconds their vision locked but it felt like minutes to Frank. He dropped the hand and hurriedly turned away. He was slightly disorientated so to disguise his discomfort he went to his locker in the pretence of tidying up. Something disturbed him about Julian and the message was buzzing loud and clear inside his head. But after his exhausting journey Frank's brain was not up to accepting the clear communication chasing round his brain. It did not imprint itself into conscious understanding until Ray spoke again; "Can you tell us where the

Mess is ducky?" Frank's head spun to look hard at Julian who was not in the least offended at the intonation in Ray's voice. Nor was he aware of Frank's expression as the latter's mental clockwork cranked into motion. 'Jeezus! How could I have missed that?'

"The airmen's mess? Yes, just a little way down that road over there, the same road that leads to the MU by the way ... that way." To say Julian held out an arm would be an exaggeration. He did indeed indicate with an extended arm but the limb looked tired with the first finger curved and slack. Again Frank turned to his locker, again too hurriedly, as if witnessing something private. Julian noticed the movement and grinned.

Dressing hurriedly into the serge trousers, blouse and beret of their working blue uniforms they collected their knife, fork, spoon and white pint pot, the standard 'eating irons' issue. On leaving the room, Ray called "See you later Julian."

When safely out of earshot Frank almost burst, "How the fuck did he get into the RAF?"

"I thenk he mutht haf kithed the recrooting thargeant" Ray laughed lisping the words in the standard demeaning manner presumed to impersonate homosexuals.

Frank ignored the jibe. He was feeling strange, "He's the first ... first I've ever met."

"The thecond!" Ray said giving a lewd wink.

Frank scowled, "Seriously Ray, there's fuckin' rules about that sort o' thing?"

Ray somewhat miffed at not even a smile for what he considered two worthwhile cracks on a subject begging buffoonery, answered "Definitely, but try and prove he's queer. I mean if he doesn't make advances to anyone, if he's never actually been caught being fucked, well ... who's to prove he's not just a very nithe bloke?

Frank shivered, "Like I say, he's the first I've ever met, I ... I just can't handle these guys."

"No, no Frankie boy, you got it all wrong. You don't handle them, it's the other way round laddie, they handle you!" Ray crumpled over laughing uproariously.

"For Christ's sake!" Frank felt he was walking on a mattress, unstable, unsure. "Look Ray, I'm gonna need time to get used to this ... guy. Maybe I've been livin' a sheltered life, I don't know, but truly he's the first ... fuck it! He might be a very nice bloke but, but I don't want him comin' anywhere near me just at the present time, no' until I get used to him anyway!"

Amused at Frank Ray couldn't resist another dig, "You don't like him near you? You've still got it wrong Frank. He's the effeminate type, so he will most definitely not approach you, but if you fancy getting your leg over, you will most definitely have to approach him!"

"Piss off!"

In the Mess they ate a large breakfast washing it down with a mug of hot sweet coffee.

Walking back to the billet, which was now empty, Frank suggested they find another room but Ray persuaded him to stay put. "Don't be daft, the bloke's all right. He can only add colour to the place, besides what can he do? He can't rape you, but then again, if you get smitten with a bad case of the rampants you can-" Ray had to dodge a low flying shoe before he could finish.

Sitting on his bed Frank removed his remaining shoe, "There's still an hour before we report to the Orderly Room Ray, I'm goin' to have a wee lie down. Half an hour'll see me right."

Ray agreed and both stretched out on the bare mattresses. After only a few minutes of rare peace and quiet, Ray whose mind would not settle disturbed the tranquillity with, "Frankie in a few weeks, it'll be Easter weekend. How about hiring us a car, we could tour the island?"

"Aye, sure, I'd like that," Frank answered, "as long as it's no' too pricey."

"Typical Scotsman," Ray muttered, then warming to his dream he added thoughtfully, "Maybe we can cut our costs and ask a couple of blokes to go with us, or better still, find us two nice WAAFs. There must be plenty crumpet on a camp this size."

"A couple of blokes'll pay their way," Frank was a normal red-blooded male well aware of the dangers of tangling with the opposite sex. The image of Marion flashed across his vision. If he met a girl anything like Marion there was no knowing how it would end up.

"WAAFs can pay their own way, or even two local girls. They can pay too, if not in cash I'm sure there must be some way they could pay ... in kind?" Ray tried to sound innocent.

"Dirty old man!" muttered Frank, still flat on his back, eyes closed.

"No I'm not! What I was thinking was maybe they could do a bit of cooking for us."

"Cookin'?" Frank queried, "Aye, an' what sort of cookin' did you have in mind?"

"Well now, let me see, I know you're a Scotsman and like all Scots, you're a wee touch on the slow side but you ARE aware you're in a strange land?"

There was no movement from Frank apart from a raised hand showing two stiff fingers.

"Good, that's out of the way" Ray said warming up, "Well now, when in a strange land, any well travelled adventurer knows in order to survive we must find one, sorry two, one for me, one for you, two seasoned campaigners who know what they're doing and -"

"I thought we were lookin' for cooks?" Frank interrupted.

"You're not paying attention! Now lie quiet and listen carefully. Didn't you hear me say 'seasoned campaigners'? Seasoned cooks if you like! But seasoned! As in spicy?

Frank moaned, "And what are we goin' to do with our 'spicy cooks' as if I didn't know?"

"To continue," Ray went on, "and stop interrupting otherwise I won't tell you the end of this story! Now be a good boy. Right! In strange countries as the one we currently find ourselves in, you just cannot go charging up mountains giving a yodel, oh - he - doo, or whatever they give in this place. No-no-no! You must take your seasoned spicy cooks with you for you don't know what you're going to eat in a strange country, now do you?"

"No."

"Of course, now then you take your seasoned cooks up into the mountains on a cold night, and before you interrupt again, it gets cold in ANY mountains in ANY country, believe me! Right we have two seasoned cooks and two horny bastards, sorry, sorry ... two adventurers up in the mountains and we erect our tent."

"Tent?" enquired Frank.

"Shut up! Erect our tent and once erected we sit inside and leave it to them. They do the rest."

"The rest? What does that mean?"

"Well, being good local girls, they'll get the fire going and once it's going nice and hot they will sit in front of the fire and warm up their individual cooking pots, right? And when their pots are all nice and piping hot, they'll come to the tent and tell us their pots are ready! And we must act quickly! The pots must not be allowed to grow cold. We take them in immediately, while their pots are piping hot and we quickly place our cold sausages inside their hot cooking pots ...."

"I don't fuckin' believe it!" Frank groaned placing an arm across his eyes.

"You don't believe what? Which part? The cooking po-"

"You keep me awake for half an hour. All that crap with saucy cooks."

"Five minutes that's all and it's seasoned cooks Frank, *seasoned*."

"And you come up with a crap story like that! Jesus." Frank moaned.

Ray looked pained, "I thought it was quite good, considering. All right, but just tell me, which part of the plan you didn't like?" He smirked as laughter lines flitted across the corners of his mouth then a giggle, which triggered Frank into a spluttering laugh forcing him to sit up, "I've never heard so much twaddle in my life" he choked, "God, you're a fuckin' idiot!"

"Oh I don't know, it wasn't all that bad." Ray mumbled, "You can never please some people. So, after all that I take it WAAFs are out?"

"Aye."

"And seasoned cooks?"

"Aye."

"Stick in the mud! Right, okay that's women out of the way for the next three months. So what do you suggest we do meanwhile, chat up our new found friend?" Ray nodded to where they had last seen Julian.

"Give over Ray, I'm beginnin' to think you might just be a wee bit bent yourself."

"A wee bit? Don't insult me! Tell you what" Ray smiled, "I don't do things by 'wee bits' and I am certainly not 'bent,' but I have to add, not yet! However after three months without the wife, or better still a real woman, I'll be so fed up clapping it with my hand, that piece of arse over there will be ever so very inviting. You know what they say, don't you?"

"I've the strongest suspicion I'm about to find out."

"Yes you are! They say 'Any port in a storm! And that's ANY fucking port in a storm! You know what that means?"

"I assume it means when a storm threatens a ship, it'll seek any nook or cranny for shelter."

"No, well yeah, but not in the context I'm talking ab-"

"Och!" Frank twisted off the bed, "I've had enough. C'mon, let's get to the Orderly Room and start Arrivin'. The quicker we're start, the quicker we'll be finished."

Ray nodded his reluctant agreement. They made themselves presentable, squared away berets, locked lockers and left the billet. After a ten minute walk they found the 103 Orderly Room.

Handing in their travel documents the pair completed the necessary forms for arrival on a new base. Minutes later they were issued 'Arrival' forms. These were blue postcard sized cards printed similarly on both sides, but with one main difference. The heading on each side bore the antonyms, 'ARRIVAL.' and 'DEPARTURE.'

Beneath the headings, the card was sub divided into four columns. Every section on the base was printed down the first and third columns; 'Sick Quarters,' 'Station Library,' 'Armoury' etc. Alongside each section title, was space for a signature. An NCO from each corresponding section would register the new arrival into his sections records. Once the new arrival's number, rank and name was recorded, the NCO signed the allotted space, certifying the airman had officially presented himself and 'arrived' at that particular section. There were thirty such sections on Akrotiri and 103 MU and every section must show a signature! The card was then returned to the Orderly Room. The next time the airman, or airwoman, saw their 'Blue Chit,' would normally be at the end of their tour. They would then be required to repeat the process, filling the 'Departure' side with signatures.

By four o'clock that afternoon the two weary airmen had criss-crossed the Akrotiri base a dozen times. Finally at the Bedding Store they gained their last signature, which allowed them to draw four blankets, two sheets, two pillows and two pillowcases. With instructions on when to change sheets etc. they carried their bedding to Room No. 2 of block No.1. Quietly they set about the final task that would transform their bed space into a home; making up their beds. A picture and an ash tray on the locker top would complete the set up.

Almost solemnly they walked to the Mess for an early evening meal, having intentionally missed lunch. Afterwards they wandered even more slowly back to the billet to collapse on the newly made beds. Only a few quiet minutes passed before the irrepressible Ray asked, "Would you care to take in the local night club tonight? Better known to the natives as 'Naafi' for a couple of beers?"

Frank sighed, "Much as I fancy a beer I'm not goin' out. I'm gonna write the wife then an early night. You won't have noticed but I'm absolutely cattled."

"Cattled? Now there's a word! Why don't you Scottish illiterates just say 'fucked' like normal people? But yeah. I'd like an early night too but the strangeness of this place winds me up. I mean it's not like other RAF camps, billets like these, corrugated iron all over the place. Reminds me of a holiday camp I went to in my horrible youth. And like the girls in that camp, maybe this Naafi can produce some topless dancing girls, who'll dip their tits into your beer for lonely airmen to savour? I say that only with the fondest, but weakest hope"

"Oh we're not goin' on about women and their cookin' pots again." Frank groaned.

"Not at the moment," Ray smiled reminiscently, "but maybe I should have a look at the establishment that's to supply us, certainly me, with alcoholic beverages for the next three months! You're against WAAFs, hate poofs, don't smoke, God! I've a feeling the next quarter may not be the most exhilarating period of my young life! If you don't like beer, divorce looms squire."

Frank folded an arm over his eyes, "I told you, I'd love a beer but I'm ... och ..." he broke off. "I'm not goin' to repeat myself."

Ray lit a cigarette and undaunted by the Scot's rebuff, carried on, "It's early yet Frankie. Have your nap. Later you might feel better."

"Maybe." Frank mumbled sleepily, then, "Sorry Ray, I'm not usually so grumpy."
Picking up the novel he started on the flight, Ray lay back. Despite his over active brain, reading lulled his diminishing

excitement. It was not too long before his eyelids began to feel the weight of his recent travels and the book fell slowly over his face.

The other room occupants having finished work, noted the new arrivals. They filed quietly in then out for a quick wash, returned to gather eating irons then off to the Mess. The movement in the room although subdued woke Ray. He stirred and when the room was empty, he reluctantly and noisily rose to stretch and yawn.

"I'm sure a herd of matin' armadillos at the height of their passion make less noise than you, you noisy bastard" Frank complained swinging his legs off the bed.

"And good morning, good evening or good fucking night to you too! I'm so disorientated I don't know what time it is." Ray peered at his watch, "Five fifteen, is that all? I feel this day's a year old already but it's only teatime old buddy."

Frank took a writing pad from his locker and started to write. Ray lay back and tried to lose himself in his book.

The room gradually filled as the established residents filtered back. Julian Cantwell, their earlier subject of discussion greeted the newcomers then went to his corner bed and began to strip off his working blue uniform. Normally, men would leave their underpants on for whatever reason, but this young man started to peel these off too! Slipping his thumbs into the waistband he pushed the pants down a few inches at a time, first the left, then the right, moving a hip with each push. When he reached the fullest extent of his arms, he bent at the hips and slid the Y-fronts down and off, lifting one foot daintily, then the other. Shaking the garment he walked around his bed space and placed them in a linen-washing bag. A white RAF issue towel with a blue stripe hung across the bottom rail of his bed. This he slowly wrapped around his middle. Gathering a toilet bag from his locker he sauntered from the room.

On his bed directly opposite, the book lay flat and forgotten on Ray's chest. With his back propped against the headboard having watched and been fascinated by the Julian's little show he noticed the room had gone quiet. It was quite a performance. Men stripped all the time, no one noticed. When Julian stripped as he did that evening, everyone noticed.

"Well now, don't care if the wife never comes out here. My

Babs could never put on a show like that! By fuck, I've got a hard on already!" Ray growled rubbing his groin kindling a round of subdued laughter.

Frank had looked up as Julian stripped and caught no more than a glimpse of the naked form. He had looked away, again hurriedly, embarrassed. Head down, he tried to get back to his letter. The man on the corner bed to Frank's right, noticed the quick diverted look of his new neighbour. His skin was a light coffee colour while piercing black eyes suggested an Indian bloodline. When he spoke his voice was richly deep. "I see Julian has caught your interest," he said with a smile.

Frank looked up, "I don't think so. Are we to expect a performance like that every night?"

"He only gives a show like that for newcomers, he is harmless, really," the man rumbled.

"It was fuckin' disgustin," Frank said with more feeling than he actually felt.

"Oh, I don't know," Ray trilled which made the Scot's head swing round to face him.

"I'm gettin' really worried about you!" Frank snapped evoking open laughter from Ray.

"I've told you," Ray said between chuckles, "wait a couple of months, we'll be fighting to get into the shower with him. Holy shit, I wouldn't mind getting in with him now!"
Frank's expression suggested he was about to be sick, "He made me feel uncomfortable this mornin' but that! That display gave me the willies!"

"Jesus, Frankie boy," Ray interrupted delightedly, "will you never get it right? It's the other way round! He doesn't want to give you his willie, HE wants YOU to give him yours!"

"RAY!" Frank exploded glaring at him. Undaunted at the outburst Ray raised a quizzical eyebrow. The coffee skinned airman intervened picking up the tenseness in the Scotsman's voice. "So you have met Julian?" he offered a divertive crumb.

Frank swung on him, "Either you've no' been hearin ' what I've been sayin' pal, or you're no' very bright. Aye, we met this mornin' when he ... or she or whatever you call it ... was Room Orderly." Frank wanted to bite his tongue. His anger gave him no right to be insultin. The man let the verbal slap hang in the air for the moment then started to unbutton his working blue tunic

111

causing minor tension ripples but this dissipated when laying it carefully on his bed he growled, "This would be playing right up Julian's street. To find us squabbling over him."

Frank sheepishly spread his hands, "Look, I'm really sorry, it's just these queers give me the wil- heebie fuckin' jeebies," he finished glancing at Ray, "Sorry, I'm probably over reactin'."

The man smiled again showing two rows of perfect white teeth, contrasting with his light brown skin. He was of average height, five foot ten or eleven, but big and solid boned with the square look of a wrestler. "Let's start again shall we? My name is Clarke, Arthur Rowland Clarke, and yes they call me Nobby. Can't for the life of me think why. Oh, and by the way, the word is 'Queer.' Maybe he is what the word suggests but whatever else he might be, he is, genuinely a nice bloke and ah...one of us!"

"Nice to meet you Nobby and aye, I am out of order. A bundle of apologies to everyone," he looked around the room, "I rarely get hot under the collar, but sometimes ...." Frank shrugged. "Look, this is an unusual situation for me, I've never ...." he stopped. "Right Nobby, clean slate, start again. I'm Frank Connolly," he wagged a thumb at Ray, "but I don't want the responsibility of introducin' this arse hole to anyone!"

"Thank you Frank, thank you for being so kind, trouble is I'm not sure if I can live up to the high standards you set for me but I will try!" Ray turned to Nobby, "I assume they call you 'Nobby' because of your surname and not I imagine does it refer to a part of your anatomy! If it is indeed the latter then I can only repeat what my granny said to me many years ago!"

"And, what was that?" Nobby asked warily.

"With absolutely no disrespect Nobby, you are obviously from Indian descent. My granny grew up in Bombay so she knew a lot about your country! The poor old dear sent for me when she was dying and as she lay dying she said, 'Raymond' she said, she always called me Raymond,

'Raymond,' she said; 'There is a tribe in India that stand for hours upside down under cold showers especially after eating Vin da loo specials.' That's what my old granny said! Is that true Nobby?"

Puzzled, Nobby thought about this then looked at Frank inquisitively.

"Oh don't look at me," Frank shook his head, "you should hear him when he warms up!"

"My comments must not be taken lightly," said Ray, "I'll have you know my quotations are read extensively on the best toilet walls, and my name, if you're interested?" He paused but hurried on when his captive audience began to turn away, "My name, Raymond Kenneth Buckley, a noble title is it not? Lesser beings, such as the previous speaker addresses me by rather more imaginative titles, but you my Indian friend, you can openly address me as Ray, as in ray of sunshine which has just entered and shall forever brighten your life."

Nobby grinned widely, "Cyprus will never be the same. Nice to meet you Sunshine, and you too Frank." They exchanged handshakes. "Just to fill you in, my father is Scottish, hence my name, my mother is as you guessed, a lovely Indian lady. Now about Julie." Nobby went on, "Were all fairly new but I've noticed, he comes on heavy with newcomers, God knows why but once he sees there are no takers he settles down. Mind you I don't know what he'd do if he got a taker," he laughed, "but we all like him, a very nice guy."

"Are you serious?" asked Frank.

"Yes," Nobby said emphatically, "I truly think he is a very frustrated young man who does not understand his own situation. I doubt very much if he has ever been, you know ... with a man."

"Well there's your answer," said Ray, "that's why he's so bloody frustrated!"

Ignoring Ray; much to the latter's chagrin Nobby carried on, "When he returns he'll probably do the same routine. Ignore him; say nothing and he'll settle back to his usual self, his effeminate self you understand. He cannot help that, but he'll stop coming on to you."

Frank and Ray nodded. "Okay, good," Ray said, "Now, tell us more about yourself, about this place, where you work, how long you've been here and whatever else you might have of interest skulking in that old head of yours?"

Nobby was in the process of removing his socks and shoes. He completed the task then sat back. "I was posted to the MU two months ago; I'm a fitter in Ground Equipment section. It's a great place to work and I love it. You will find it a little different from the RAF back in the UK. It's still the Royal Air Force of course, but different, slightly laid back, probably because of the situation of the island, bang in the middle of the Med. The wonderful weather, totally different atmosphere, surrounded by exotic beauty. Good hours, better money. In a couple of weeks we go onto summer working time, only six hours a day!" He shrugged, "There is more, but it is better I think to find out some things for yourself. What is good for me may not be good for you. Most of the guys love it, as I do. Others, well the heat, mosquitoes, dust you know. Where are you going to work?" he asked.

"I'm an M T S and O said Frank, "so I expect -"

"A WHAT?" Ray bellowed.

"For the benefit of the ignoramuses among us Nobby," Frank went on loftily, "I am a Machine Tool Setter and Operator. One of the top trades you know? And as I was saying before being so crudely interrupted, I'll be in Workshops or machine shop, whatever they have here."

"It's a machine shop, well equipped too, and you Ray?"

"Me?" Ray sang, "Well, it just so happens I am one of the elite, the haute monde of the Royal Air Force." He pouted, pursing his lips as if about to kiss an unfortunate child.

"Oh shit!" Frank groaned.

Ray was about to let loose with yet another oratory when a corporal and an airmen entered the room. Greetings were exchanged as they went to their bed spaces. The corporal to the corner bed across from Nobby, the airman next to him. The corporal was at least six feet tall and very slim. The striking features about this man were his pale blue eyes, and in tandem with their washed out colour was his hair. It could not be described as red yet neither was it blonde. A female blessed with such colour would probably be described as strawberry or honey blonde. These were the only points about this man that might be described as attractive. His features were plain but rough, almost gnarled. The slight stoop of his lean twenty five year old body might give the impression he was aware of his height, self-conscious about it. Neither impression could be farther from the truth. The stoop drove every square bashing Drill Instructor in RAF Padgate crazy, trying to get this man to straighten his back, but after eight weeks of soul-destroying effort the DIs lost the battle.

The other airman, an SAC was not quite as tall as the corporal but because of the latter's slim figure, the broad shoulders of the SAC appeared accentuated. Apart from his large frame, he had dark hair, brown eyes and sharp clean-cut features. He was smiling at Ray, "Don't let us put you off your stroke mate," he said, "don't mind us."

"Thank you, but introductions first, then you can listen to me and rejoice in our addition to your humble abode. My name is Raymond Kenneth Buckley and oh, before I ramble on, this is, for what it's worth, Junior Technician Connolly Frank. He had the honour of arriving with me."

Frank managed a quick nod before Ray went on, "Enough familiarities; I was about to say when you entered, that I am of the breed of Armourers, the highest and most regarded of trades in this Royal Air Force. A three month course for intellectuals such as myself, a course of high precision and delicate touch which ensures our pilots can blow up -"

"Their rubber fuckin' dolls!" Frank interrupted. "Now give over Ray, they'll be throwin' us out if you keep on with this crap!" He turned to the others, "I've had this all day, just say the word and we can throw him out now, before he has time to take roots."

"I had the same trouble wi' this one." The tall corporal said nodding towards the SAC, reclining on his bed. "Invited me out for a meal one night in town when I was skint. But when it's time to pay I find myself followin' him, at great speed, climbin' over a ten foot wire fence at the rear o' the restaurant. People like him embarrass innocents like myself. I'm Callum McAlpine from Edinburgh, that object sprawled on his bed is Josh Munroe." The words were said clearly and precisely in the rolling drawl of the Scottish lowlands.

Introductions and backgrounds were being more finely explored when a towel clad Julian sauntered into the room. Ray, who was doing most of the talking, stopped mid sentence. No one else spoke. Frank who had wandered from his bed space, turned back, sat on his bed and resumed writing the letter on his locker top. Nobby, sensing the awkwardness broke the silence.

"What do you say we go up to the Naafi tonight?"

"We'll all get better acquainted over a couple of drinks?"

"I could kiss you Nobby!" Ray cried.

The others agreed and Nobby looked at the scribbling Frank, "You Frank?"

"I'd like to finish this then maybe get an early night. It's like months since I slept in a bed."

"Of course." Nobby said in his growling tone. He turned to Julian, "What about you Julie?"

"No, I don't think so, I have a little washing to do and I too would appreciate an early night."

Frank, still writing, said, "Listen, I'm just thinkin' I might as well see what this place's got to offer. A couple of beers might be just what I need."

Julian suppressed a smile. He dropped his towel exposing small genitals and wandered languidly around his bed, fished a pair of underpants from his locker and keeping his back towards the others, lethargically pulled them on, almost reluctantly covering his bottom.

"Nobby," he said turning round, tucking the edges into his crotch with his thumbs, "maybe I'll finish my washing and join you, later?"

"Of course Julie. Whenever you're ready."

Julian Cantwell was an enigmatic man. He knew he was effeminate, attracted to men but he had never crossed the line, never got close to a man. In the RAF he was protected from venturing into such an ordeal. Homosexuality was not tolerated in civvy street, and meant instant discharge in the forces, which was not on Julian's current wanted list. In his teens with a growing awareness of his lack of interest in girls, he took the massive and brave step of trying normal sex with Susan, a girl he'd known since childhood. Susan, aware of his problem hoped dearly she could instil into him an interest in her, for her feelings were deep towards this quite beautiful young man.

For Julian it was a time when he was trying to find himself. Struggling to live a normal life, with friends who were nibbling round the edges of giggling girl's skirts, boasting experiences. Julian had tried to tap into that mysterious vein, plumb the depths of what were for others primal urges, but for him they simply didn't exist. To fiddle around with a girl's private parts, which seemed the 'In' thing to do, was to Julian abhorrent. But he had a friend Susan, had liked her since childhood. Perhaps once started on this hellish enterprise, it all might change for him, kick start his motor as it were, discover what it was other boys found to their obvious delight.

The experiment with Susan, Julian found repulsive. The act in itself he could not complete despite Susan's gentle coaxing. It had been the 'little experiment,' that confirmed his inner fear that he was, 'different.' Girls, the rage of his age, meant nothing to him sexually, but could be exceptionally good friends. At the age of nineteen still trying to come to terms with what was a unique problem he joined the Royal Air Force. That was three years ago, but nothing changed! In those three years he'd taken stock of himself, he understood now and accepted his situation.

He knew within his male hormones were slowly losing way to their female counterparts. His genitals never developed properly; his buttocks were growing rounder and softer and apart from his scalp, he was almost entirely hairless. He never needed to shave and was still waiting for his voice to drop. The last thing he wanted was to approach the medics. They would have no choice other than discharge him, thus he'd escape the occasional remarks and sporadic antagonism. But he could never escape the changes taking place within. Julian yearned to be one or the other; this balancing in the middle of nowhere was draining. He was happy in male company but for all the wrong reasons; and happy in female company, again for all the wrong reasons, which equated to overall misery. He was trapped in a world that was upside down, inverted to him, yet he had no choice but to ride out the howling storm of quiet physical change taking place every day of his life.

Eyebrows were raised when Julian applied to help Flt. Lt. Barrymore with his tug-of-war team. In response, Mr Barrymore elucidated there was little he could offer unless Julian cared to look after the kit. This included seeing to the laundering of jerseys and socks, which Mr. Barrymore explained farther; the blue and white hoops were actually the Akrotiri station colours. As 103 MU continually won the Akrotiri station sports over the years, they were obliged to represent Akrotiri and wear their colours in the many sporting events round the island. The dormant colours of 103 Maintenance Unit were yellow and black diagonal squares.

Julian also tended to the steel heels on the team's boots. The conventional 'U' shaped heel plates were removed from standard issue boots, and replaced with full tempered steel plates. These constantly required removing and sharpening as the edges invariably dulled in the course sandy soil. Julian travelled with the team helping where he could. Strangely, the job was newly created, just to give Julian something to do. Now everyone involved wondered how they managed before his arrival. As for Julian, he enjoyed the set up, loved their success's and revelled in the reflected glory, not minding in the least the lewd comments directed at him in training. On rope climbing, 'Fastest to the top gets to jump Julie,' or 'If Julie holds your nuts you'll raise that bucket soon enough.' He was now an established member of the 103 MU tug-of-war organisation.

The evening chores of domesticity never bothered Julian. He stepped daintily into blue shorts, hitched them up to his hips then from his locker fished out his washing and a small packet of soap powder. Thus armed he returned to the ablutions.

Frank disconsolately watched Julian's exit. Perhaps he was making the proverbial mountain out of a molehill. This was after all, just another element in life he knew existed but never had to face. He shook his head. 'I just don't know, should've moved rooms.'

Nobby noticed the Scot's head shake, "He's a very nice bloke, really, once you get to know him."

"Aye, I suppose he is Nobby. I'm just so bloody uncomfortable in his presence."

"Listen ...." started Ray.

"Oooh, oh" growled Frank.

"Will you stop your bitching, you're fooling no one! You'll be after his bum like the rest of us ... in time. Now will you shut up, finish that letter and get up the road for that lovely pint!"

"The only thing I'll be holding before the night's out will be your scrawny neck!" Frank could not suppress a grin at his new and unsinkable friend. "Right, as you say," he went on, "I'll just add a couple of lines. Explain the C.O. requires my presence in the Officers Mess ... two minutes."

"I've just had a thought," said Nobby.

"See the MO right away," Ray said earnestly.

Nobby ignored him, "Let's go to the Pen Club!"

There was general agreement but Ray, suddenly serious at the mention of yet another possible provider of sustenance to the exclusion of a definite source said, "The what?"

"The Pen Club, or Peninsula Club, an all ranks club here on the camp. Bit more expensive but classier." Callum offered.

"What d'you think?" Ray was not convinced. .

"Aye, why not?" Frank was sealing an envelope. "Sounds fine."

There was a seriousness now about their preparations laying out civilian clothes before leaving noisily for the ablutions. When they came back, Julian had returned and still in a state of undress. "New venue Julie," Nobby informed him. "It's the Pen Club now."

Julian merely nodded.

The Peninsula Club was approximately three hundred yards from their billet if following the road, but considerably shorter if crossing the 'bondoo,' a word used mostly by personnel on camp to describe rough ground. The drying vegetation had caught fire that afternoon, so it was unanimously decided, it would be prudent to walk on the road rather than cut time and risk soiling trousers from the blackened stumps of cremated plant life.

Arriving at the club Frank and Ray were impressed with the one story building and lush surroundings. The large lounge had a thick pile carpet, the furniture modern and comfortable. The bar was exceptionally well stocked with wines and spirits but beer selection was conversely limited as Nobby informed his new room mates.

"We'll get a kitty going but we have agreed, as this is your first visit and have yet to draw pay, tonight's on us. So! They serve lots of fancy spirit drinks but only three beers; Double Diamond draught, Tennant lager in cans and the local brew Keo, which comes in both bottle and draught so, pick your poison."

"Thanks to all of you lads, but," Frank hesitated then, "What are you drinkin' Nobby?"

"I don't drink beer, but their brandy sours are nice so yes, that's what I'll have."

"If you prefer beer," Callum offered, "try the local stuff, I've been on the island a couple o' months and for what it's worth, I think it's not bad. A lot of the guy's drink it and we've no' had a fatality yet." His craggy face spread into a grin.

"That's as good a recommendation as a beer ever had. I'll have a pint of that." Frank said.

"I drink it with just a wee spot o' lemonade."

"Lemonade? That'll make it a shandy!"

"No no, just a teaspoon, that's all," Callum laughed, "The reason I tell you that is some o' the blokes after a night on the stuff, have heart attacks when they go for a crap next mornin'. On perusal of their newly exited works of art, they saw not the usual friendly brown turd curled and ready for dispatch. At the bottom of the bowl lie jet black polished objects. Shinin' as though freshly varnished! I'm not sayin' it is the beer, but on learnin' the trick with the lemonade, the spit and polish disappeared and the friendly wee dull brown chappies were back again."

"Fair enough, a pint of Keo then, aye an' wi' just a touch of the lemonade." Frank grinned.

Josh collected a kitty of ten shillings a head, missing out the two 'guests', ordered the first round and soon the banter was buzzing. Frank noticed Josh was offering little in the line of chat and tried to draw him into the conversation. "You been out here long Josh?"

Josh raised his dark brooding eyes that crinkled warmly on the Scot, "No, not too long, but I'm the veteran among this lot. Arrived last October." He nodded his head in friendly fashion.

"October, five months. So we're all relatively new. You're not married then Josh." Frank assumed Josh was unmarried, knowing the separation period for couples to be three months.

The raised friendly eyebrows that awaited Frank's questions slowly fell. The expression on Josh's face slowly changed as he raised his glass and swallowed a large draught of beer. "No," he answered simply. Replacing his glass he stood up and excused himself.

Frank frowned as the broad shouldered figure made towards the toilets. He turned to see Callum looking at him. "Hit a sore spot?"

The red head nodded, "Aye. I made the same mistake a while back. Don't know what it is.
Mention women and Josh goes into his shell."

"He's not ...?"

"Him? Naw!" Callum said scornfully. "Not him, but he's got

120

a problem, just won't talk about it.

He's just no' interested in ... puttin' it delicately, fanny, and there's plenty about. Hundreds of WAAFs on the base, dozens o' young skirt from married quarters workin' in offices round camp. A good lookin' bloke like Josh, he could take his pick." Callum shrugged, "I dunno."

Callum failed to mention that he himself had not yet taken advantage of the 'young skirt' around the huge Akrotiri base. The angular Scot appreciated females as the other half of the human race and as such provided the logical requirement for his natural needs. He was strict with himself in this department allowing such delicacies to surface twice or perhaps three times a year, depending on his situation. Rather than abuse himself, the twenty five year old had no qualms in approaching a prostitute at these times, if female acquaintances were proving virginal in pursuit. He'd then proceed to drain his pent up reservoirs with an overnight session, leaving the girl next morning sore but well paid. His love life he preferred to keep simple, with neither attachment nor comebacks.

Frank tasted his beer. It wasn't bad, slightly bitter even with the lemonade Callum dribbled into the glass. The conversation had lulled when Josh went to the toilet so hoping to clear the prickling thoughts he was having about Julian, Frank asked Callum. "You've been here long enough to form an opinion. What do you reckon on this Julian character?"

"Ah he's a good lad. Aye a bit on the fairy side mebbe but so what, I like him."

Frank sighed, "Look I'm not writin' him off, you all seem to like him, so okay, fine! My problem is, he's a new phenomenon to me, my first ... queer!" He laughed then added, "To my knowledge! I must've met others but he's so obvious. It's a wee bit disturbin', to me anyway, d'you understand what I'm stugglin' to say? He's the first I've met, ye know, like face to face!" Frank shrugged resignedly. Finding the right words was proving difficult.

Sitting next to Callum, Ray leaned forward, "You thick Scotsman," he was shaking his head lamentably. "Will you never get it right? It's not 'face to face' with these people." He raised his eyes in mock frustration, then through a chortling giggle. "It's face to back, or back to face if you like, or even the very popular arse about face, whatever takes your fancy." He could not help himself and folded over with laughter.

"Aye, you'll be speakin' from experience I suppose." Frank suppressed a rising chuckle.

"Oooooh" wailed Ray and was about to reply when Nobby intervened in the verbal horseplay,

"Give the bloke a chance you two. You know, if he really was ... for the want of a better word, available for what you're suggesting, the blokes in the tug-of-war team would chase him."

"How do you know they aren't?" Ray managed to splutter.

"I mean chase him from helping out with the team. For goodness sake! Where do you come from Ray. Don't you know homosexuality is taboo? If he was being, you know, it would be common knowledge, for goodness sake!" His voice and darkening colour might suggest Nobby was growing weary of the verbal mutilation of the defenceless Julian.

"All right Nobby, all right! I'm sorry I brought it up. Can we just let it drop? Besides you mentioned tug-of-war Nobby, now that's a subject very near to my heart. At the risk of disturbin' that sleepin' dog I've just put to rest, what's Julian got to do with tug-of-war?"

Nobby blew a sigh before answering, then as Josh rejoined the group, the Indian said, "He told me what he does a few days ago. He looks after the kit, gets it laundered, takes care of the boots. He arranges transport for away matches. Organizes grub and beers for visiting teams, all with Barrymore's approval ..." Nobby paused as the waiter arrived with the second round of drinks.

"Sorry sir, the barman," the waiter nodded towards the bar, "he say he changing the new barrel for the Keo beer. It will be few minutes."

"Good," said Josh, "in that case bring us a round of brandy sours and five, no, four plates of pigs trotters, none for you Nobby, right? It's time these guys were introduced to the real pleasures of this establishment." There was no sign of the sullen Josh now. Swallowing the last of his abandoned and almost flat beer he continued, "I don't see why we should wait for the Keo, who's for a Double Diamond? I'll fetch them myself." He wagged his empty glass. "I am as you see, at critical levels." He took money from the kitty jar before loping off to the bar.

Callum gave a shrug at Frank's quizzical glance but it was Ray who spoke, "Quite a different chappie since his visit to the piss house. They don't have topless waitresses in there performing quick blow jobs by any chance?" He nodded optimistically towards the toilets.

The evening passed pleasantly, apart from when Frank felt his usually dependable stomach rumble. He had eaten but not enjoyed the supposed delicacy of pig's trotters,. Fearing the worst he made his way to the toilets. Once inside an exceptionally clean cubicle, the recently devoured trotters were, with the aid of a probing finger, spewed into the toilet bowl. Frank was not feeling ill or upset as a result of the episode; it was merely the mechanical act of emptying out something not sitting comfortably in his gut. The images of the trotters, which, when attached to their owners wallowing in all kinds of mud, excrement and urine, had been the prime mover of his upset. He'd eaten them to be sociable but his churning brain could not blot out the after thoughts. Returning to the group he found Julian had joined them in his absence. It was he who asked, "Feeling better?"

"I'm fine!" Frank said brusquely and to prove his point downed the double brandy sour laid at his place on the table, then half the accompanying pint. There was also another untouched pint in his place, probably the Keo ordered earlier. 'Hey ho,' he thought, 'here we go again, but at least it's beer, I can handle that.'

With a dubious parting glance at Frank who had interrupted their conversation, Julian said, "Please go on Callum, I didn't know you were a tug-of-war coach!"

"I'm not really, I just coached a Workshops team on my last station's sports day. Must have done somethin' right for we won. Thoroughly enjoyed it though. But I did something daft."

"What was that?" asked Ray.

"Well, for prizes we were presented with these fancy pint pots. Pewter, you know the type o' thing. And of course we had to have a piss up in the Naafi, to celebrate. I got so pissed, left my pot on the table when we all staggered back to the billet. Never saw it again! An' I really miss that pot considerin' the short time it was in my possession."

Julian leaned over and patted the Scot's knee in a purely conciliatory gesture.

"Never mind Callum, you'll soon replace it when you get involved with the MU team. One of the team told me they won five tankards last season, or was it six?"

"Huh, fat chance I've got of gettin' into the team. I'm like a jockey's whip wi' the wood scraped off, but I wouldn't mind gettin' into the coachin' side. I wrote that on my arrival slip."

Frank, fully entangled in the myth of the MU team had to ask. "How good are they Julian?"

"The best! There is absolutely no doubt about that Frank. Can't tell you why, but they are simply the best one hundred stone tug-of-war team this side of the world." The statement was said with quiet but absolute conviction.

Ray looked closely at the young man and for once was serious, "A sweeping statement."

"Yes Ray, I know, and your remark is very apt, for they swept the boards last year, unbeaten for the second year in succession. That includes pulls against catch weight teams who were here on NATO duty, the New Zealand police and a similarly long unbeaten team, the Danish army champions. We did come close to losing, giving the New Zealanders about eight stones. It was only our experience that got us through to win two pulls to one.

"Been here a while Julian?" Frank asked, suddenly aware he could actually speak to this ... man.

"Since July. I'd heard of the team's reputation so I went to watch them. Got hooked and followed them round the island like a devoted puppy. I wanted so much to be part of the set up, so I applied and was delighted when Mr. Barrymore gave me the job of looking after the kit."

"What will you have Julian?" Nobby was ordering with the waiter standing attentively at his shoulder. 'Surely he can't be ordering again?' Frank wondered looking at his beer and amazed to see his glasses were empty. Were both empty glasses his? He would have to watch carefully, someone was surely drinking his beer!

Julian was grinning mischievously, "What would I like?" Julian said thoughtfully. "I think I would like something long ... yes a nice long screw ... driver." He smiled into the timorous eyes of the newly arrived Frank who was not at all sure of his ground. Julian dearly wanted to purse his lips into a kiss, but decided not to. This man may just run from the club.

Frank who was totally taken in by Julian's spurious, yet strangely genuine flirtatious display, was thinking 'If I was to have taken bets on what drink this ravin' queer ordered, a Screwdriver would've been the red hot favourite!' He shook his head at the thought.

"Why do you shake your head Frank?" It was Julian, all innocence and concern.

"Pardon?"

"You shook your head, why?" Julian smiled, his face friendly.

"Julian, you're gonna have to give me time." Frank spoke firmly but quietly. He had no wish to hurt but he had to come to terms with his own feelings. "Please try to understand I've never met anyone like you before, and frankly I'm bewildered. At the moment I don't like what I'm feelin'."

Everyone was talking so no one noticed his hushed words. Frank leaned forward and impetuously finished his third, or was it his fourth brandy sour? Whatever! They tasted good and the beer was proving more than palatable.

Julian's head had dropped at Frank's words and for a fraction of a second his expression was of crestfallen sadness. But in that minuscule particle of time before Julian's eyes had pulled sadly away and into his lap there had been a fleeting flashing blip of something! As if a door had been thrown open and Frank had involuntarily snatched a glimpse into its depths. What Frank saw in the grim darkness and in those soft blue eyes, eyes that were desperately trying to close the door, desperately trying to replace a semblance of normality, endowed Frank with a profusion of understanding about this person's unique and displaced life. It was this shock comprehension of Julian's position that made Frank hurriedly reach and swallow his drink. What he saw in those depths was a tangled web of confusion in a cauldron of writhing impotent convictions. The image brought with it the insight that Julian was more to be pitied than feared.

The waiter appeared again, like a ghost it seemed and Ray applauded the fact. More money was going into the kitty jar, within seconds tumbling out again. The atmosphere was pleasant with conversation swinging from one subject to another before

Frank heard Nobby ask, "Julian, what do think the chances are of getting into the team?" Suddenly Frank perked up, pushing back the encroaching stupor.

"If you're as strong as you look Nobby, make yourself available for training, and everything else being equal, I should think your chance of a team place would be pretty good."

"And me?" Frank could not resist growling. His build was average tipping the scales a little over eleven stone. With not an ounce of fat on his five feet eleven gangling frame he gave the impression of being on the thin side. But appearances were notoriously deceptive.

Julian's answer was diplomatic, "Frank, I can only tell you what Mr. Barrymore says. Anyone who can pull his own weight up our training gantry can theoretically find a place in his team, but believe it or not, it's in this area where Mr. Barrymore struggles. You have no idea how many hopefuls cannot do that. Flt. Lt. Barrymore is the team coach just in case you don't know that already. You won't know of course but on Station Routine Orders last week he has called his team and anyone interested to come along to the first meeting of the new season. It's on Monday morning. Why don't you come?"

"Try and stop me!" The frosty edges of Frank's attitude were thawing by the minute.

The waiter appeared yet again. Frank glanced at his glass. Someone was definitely drinking his beer. It was disappearing at an alarming rate! The glass was empty and so too was the fancy short Ray had insisted he must try; an Atom Bomb or some such daft name. Well the Atom Bomb had not dropped down his throat that was certain, or had it? God Almighty, he could not remember from one moment to the next! He was growing very tired, but it certainly was not the drink, for he was not drinking it, was he? Or was he? Oh shit! Frank was finding it hard now to concentrate on the air borne conversation flying and rumbling about his ears. His mind kept drifting off to Lorna and his daughters, five year old Caroline and Dawn, who was three. He reached for his glass, or was he replacing it on to the table? The glass was half empty! How the hell did that happen? Or was it half full? He tittered. "Fuckin' amazin' this beer."

Julian was watching, well aware the Scot was no longer taking part in the heated discussion on the shape of medals. The wet tabletop was the sketchpad and fingers the pens. Ray was asking if anyone would like another drink. There seemed to be no takers so Julian tried to call a halt to the evening, "Don't you think it's time we retired gentlemen. I for one am ready for bed, and obviously Frank agrees." The Scot was unknowingly nodding in agreement.

Ray stood up, "I suppose you're right," he agreed watching Frank's eyes blinking in a losing battle to stay open. "But if nobody else fancies a nightcap, I shall proceed to the bar where one more tot will ensure my night's sweet repose. Nobody joining me ... sure?"

Ray crossed to the bar as steadily as his feet would allow and the eager Greek Cypriot barman took his order for a double brandy. Ray exchanged the drink for a one pound note. By the time the barman turned to the cash register and back with the change, Ray's glass was empty. The smiling airman tipped the man a half crown. He was feeling good, the booze was wonderfully cheap, the company welcoming and he had three years with extra pay just to live in this wonderful climate. He was going to enjoy every minute of his time on this island.

Nobby watched the downing of the double brandy with thoughtful raised eyebrows. Also he couldn't help wondering how anyone could eat the feet of pigs. When joining the RAF, having spent half his life in Scotland and India, he decided to ignore all mixed and confused religious callings of his upbringing and eat and drink whatever was being served to the rest of the men. There had been many pleasant surprises, but pig's feet? No, no. That was something he could never ever try. And sometimes, watching Ray, the drinking was overdone. Why did some men had to have that extra drink at the end of an already alcohol saturated evening. He had seen it many times.

Dismissing his wandering thoughts as they stood to leave, he steadied Frank then, after a visit to the toilets the group made their unsteady exit from the club.

The night was crystal clear with not a breath of wind but Frank appeared to be on the deck of a heavily rolling ship and making heavy weather of simply walking. His feet persistently refused to go precisely where he tried to place them. Defiantly and determinedly, sticking his hands into his pockets he walked unaided, if unsteadily, but under his own steam.

Julian watched him closely. In their inebriated state it was decided the road back to the billet was much too long. Nobby was elected leader of the newly organised 'Search for Home' expedition. It would be his job as leader to guide the stricken party through the uncharted territory of wasteland known as 'Bondoo' to discover the territory and safe haven known as 'Home / Billet!' The leader set off with a warning called over his shoulder to watch out for snakes and scorpions which had an immediate if short lived effect of sobriety in the exhibition, especially Ray.

Making good headway considering their condition, they reached the area where the dried undergrowth had been on fire that afternoon at which point progress slowed considerably. On a command from their leader all stopped to roll up trouser bottoms in an attempt to keep clear of the minefield of sooty stumps. All that is, except Frank to the rear of the column. He could not bend over, as he was having trouble keeping himself upright. It was Julian who helped Frank roll up his trouser bottoms, then complained as they resumed their progress. "We should have stuck to the road Nobby, it'll take us all night at this rate"

Nobby realizing his mistake, agreed. Treading carefully through the scattered mounds of soot was indeed time consuming for the unsteady bunch. To turn back now was pointless however, as the billet lights were just ahead. There was another call from Ray at the rear.

"Look, will you just look at those stars! They're so close we can touch them!"

Everyone was gazing skyward so Nobby followed suit to witness a spectacular sight. The wonderful array of bright silver stars spread across the indigo blue of the Mediterranean sky was breathtaking. The various groups were easy to spot as eager arms pointed towards each newly recognized galaxy.

Julian too was caught up in the magic of the celestial display. He had seen it before of course. In quiet moments alone when creeping from the billet on nights when sleep was reluctant to join him and relieve his troubled brain. Suddenly nearby, a heavy thud and Julian immediately lamented his moment of self-indulgence, mindful from where the noise originated. He looked down and was not surprised to see Frank spread-eagled on the blackened ground, still and quiet.

"Frank?" Julian knelt beside the prone figure. "Frank!" He cried again, anxiety flooding his voice. The Scot was on his back out cold. He had gazed skywards with the others, tipping his head far back and past his point of balance. The message in his befuddled state of mind was slow to register in his alcohol sodden system. When his brain issued the message 'Beware! You are about to fall!' Frank was already falling backwards, like a tree, straight, unbending and gathering speed. The back of his head made contact with the hard ground first, and for an ethereal tantalizing instant, Frank was amazed to see the stars, those same stars he had struggled to see, suddenly come flying down at him in a swooping rush, and into his eyes! He lost consciousness.

A concerned Julian cradled the injured man's head yelling for the others. "Help me," he yelled, "Frank's knocked his head, he's out cold!"

Nobby arrived and bent over the pair, for a moment nonplussed. "What do we do Julie?"

"I don't know, revive him somehow." Julian leaned down peering close into Frank's face.

Ray, flippant as ever and presuming Frank was not seriously injured, decided this was too good a chance to miss. "If you're thinking about the kiss of life Julie, I'd think twice. If he's not dead now he'll die of fright if he wakes up and you're sticking one on him!"

Ray was disappointed at the negative response his attempted witticism received as only Callum graced him with a grin.

Nobby successfully ignoring the asinine comments of the too ludicrous Ray, tried to recall the first aid course he attended years ago. Now that he needed it he could not remember a thing! There was something about tight clothing! Loosen it? Yes loosen all tight clothing! The big Indian, surprisingly gentle, loosened Frank's tie, undid the top three shirt buttons, unbuttoned cuffs and trouser belt. 'What next, what next?' his mind was racing.

"Try rubbing his hands Julian," he growled while he began to massage the neck and shoulders with gentle slaps on the inert cheek. "Come on Frank, can you hear me? Waken up Frank, come on."

Swimming in a sea of darkness and rising up through a long tunnel of heavy sleep, Frank moaned. His eyes opened, much to the onlookers relief. "What's goin' on, where am I?"

"You took a knock on the head. How do you feel?" Nobby asked anxiously.

Frank did not answer. He felt he had just awoke from the deepest of deep slumber. Julian switched from rubbing Frank's hands to reaching, as best he could his neck abandoned by Nobby. Frank relaxed allowing the soft hands to push back the shadows clouding his eyes. Breathing deeply through his mouth, the fresh night air was clearing the clinging mists. He tried to sit up, to pull away from these hands that were soothing, not comprehending why he wished to be free of them. "Wait, wait a minute," cried Julian. "Lie still, until you have your bearings!"

"I'm all right now," Frank's voice was shaky. "Just help me up."

Nobby was peering at him, "You sure?"

'Where did he come from?' Frank thought drowsily then it all started to come back as his brain cleared. He blinked rapidly then, "Aye aye, I'm fine now, just get me on my feet."

His legs felt wobbly as Nobby and Julian partly hauled, partly supported him. "Here lean on me," Julian offered as the small party hesitantly resumed down the slope less concerned now about the blackened stumps.

Reaching the lights of the first billet Frank looked down at himself, "Shit, look at the good trews, they're covered in that bloody soot!"

"Your shirt's covered in that crap too Frankie," said Ray,

"Yes I'm afraid it is," confirmed Julian starting to flick his hands lightly over Frank's back.

"Fuck it!" Frank groaned, annoyed with himself, at his stupidity and his silly adolescent drinking started only minutes after leaving Lorna, "Jesus Christ, what a fuckin' idiot!"

Julian thinking Frank's initial anger was directed at his sorry state and condition, tried to help, "Don't worry Frank, the laundry will make short work of getting your shirt and trousers clean, the soot washes out quite easily."

"How the fuck would you know, you regularly roll around in that shit, do you?" The irate Scot, still loose tongued with alcohol, immediately regretted his outburst. The recipient of his outburst had done nothing to gain his wrath; if anything he was a big help. 'Another fuck-up! I'm makin' fuck-ups hand over fist! But it stops here, right here, now.' Frank mentally vowed.

130

"Sorry Julian." Frank said to the young man who had momentarily frozen, "Look I'm really sorry. You didn't deserve that. I've been makin' a right numpty o' myself these past two days but it's over. What you've seen up to now is not me! And I can assure you there'll be no more open demonstrations of how big an arsehole I can be."

There was only the slightest pause before Julian smiled, "I understand completely. You've had a lot to drink Frank. So let's see, do you think you can reach our billet?" He held out his arm.

"Yes I think I can, I'm fine now, thanks Julian," The short blackout had a surprisingly sobering effect. He was still unsteady but Frank put that down to the bump on his head. When they reached their billet Frank was disgusted when he viewed himself in the full-length mirror in his wardrobe locker. Soot was everywhere; even his face had black smears. Reaching delicately into his small locker, not wishing to soil anything, he withdrew his toilet bag and towel. "I'm goin' for a shower Ray, I'd appreciate it if you'd keep any comments to yourself." Frank started to undress.

"You're talking to the wrong bloke old son, I'm not the type to give you anything funny, can't speak for the others though."

"RAY, it's wearin' thin! I'm callin' time on that line o' patter. No more! D'ye hear? No fuckin' more!"

"Okay, okay, hint taken," Ray grinned then shrugged apologetically towards Julian.

"That was more than a hint Ray." laughed Nobby,

"Yeah," Ray agreed, "just goes to show I can be pretty thick at times."

"I give up," Frank said quickly removing the rest of his clothes. Clad only in underpants, he gathered his toiletries and stalked out. Ray was really not his point of anger. He was boiling within at his so unusual recent behaviour. Since leaving Leuchars, perhaps because he did not have the steadying effect of his family round him, he had made a first class effort of demonstrating what a buffoon he could be. The latest in front of men he was to spend a lengthy period of time with! This was an unrecognisable Frank Connolly, known in Leuchars for his stable and dependable nature.

He marched along the veranda and turned up the central corridor to the deserted ablutions. Frank selected a shower unit turned on the cold water first then the hot a fraction. Once under the powerful spray he turned the hot off completely only to find the cold water was tepid. He wanted a really cold shower in the hope the chill would blast away the last vestiges and cloying mushiness that went hand in hand with the drunken state still clouding his brain. He washed quickly then allowed the fairly strong jets to caress the back of his head that had struck the ground.

His mind wandered back to yesterday morning where again he was showering and trying to ease away the pain and suffering, inflicted on his body through his own stupidity, aided and abetted with the over consumption of drink. Was he then, when let loose, out of Lorna's sight, such an easy led individual who could not resist the well trampled avenues of escape from loneliness that alcohol offered? Rubbish! It was simply circumstance and coincidence. He should've and would've been sound asleep by now if he had not been such a snivelling coward in the presence of Julian! Who it turned out, by his own brief précis and as testified by others who knew him, a genuinely nice person. If he was 'queer,' so what! It made no difference. He could handle Julian now.

Steppin from the shower, Frank dried off quickly then wrapped the thick issue towel round his middle. Gathering his belongings he walked out of the ablutions, feeling a whole lot better than when he walked in.

Approaching the end of the central corridor he looked up sharply when someone retreated hurriedly back round the corner of the veranda. He knew instinctively who it was. Turning at the corner he saw the sad figure under the shaded lights presenting a sorrowful impression of someone caught with his hand in the money box.

Frank had made his mind up. The only way to handle this Julian situation was to treat him no different than the rest of the blokes. Keeping this firmly in mind he simply nodded with a mumbled 'Lo Julian' and made to pass. Julian with head lowered appeared uncertain, fidgety and apparently caught in two minds. He was about to move on again when Frank heard his name hissed across the cool air, followed by, "Please, may I have a word?"

Frank stopped. "Look Julie, my head's poundin' an' I really

want to hit the sack. If what you've got to say is not of world shatterin' importance, could it wait until tomorrow?"

"Frank!" Julian said plaintively as he looked deep into the Scotsman's eyes then turned away and stared out into the lunar blue darkness, "What I've got to say won't knock the world off its axis." A sad attempt at humour, then soft words that hit Frank like a blow to the stomach. "But I've got to talk to someone."

Something in the tone stopped Frank from speaking or walking on which a simple 'Yes' answer from the other would have permitted. Now with those words there was a morose and disconcerted medium hanging between them. Frank, concerned and despite recent affirmations, uncertainty showed when he asked, "What? What is it Julian, what's wrong?" Even as he spoke he felt utterly inadequate.

Julian's head lifted, the troubled expression highlighted with eyes that licked over Frank's face. "I've got to talk to someone, soon. Very soon or I'll ... I'll go crazy!"

The words were said quietly with icy conviction and with them Frank saw this cocktail of a human being for the first time, all pretences and fronts cast aside. He was wounded, utterly vulnerable. "Look, ah, I don't know if I'm the one for you to talk to, but I'll help if ... if I can?"

Still with that feeling he was standing on an unstable deck, Frank went on, "But Julian, I must make one thing clear before I ... we ... go on. I am not ...." The damn word still would not come. A word he had used many times in the past but to cast and spread it like a net over Julian seemed crude and grossly cruel. Before the word could stumble from his mouth Julian finished the sentence for him.

"Homosexual Frank, the word you are looking for, is 'homosexual.'

Frank nodded more than embarrassed; the offensive term he was searching for was 'Queer.'

"That IS my problem Frank, I can't speak to anyone on the subject. It's taboo to everyone and I don't know what's happening to me. I swear this is not an approach on my part to solicit you for anything other than help, I swear! If I go to the medics they'll kick me out. I don't want that! I'm worried sick and can't find a corner to hide in until this goes away, or settles down. Which way to turn Frank? I'm not one of the boys though

I try to be, but I'm not one of the girls either. I feel so utterly alone ... so isolated!"

Frank felt a rush of sympathy for this forlorn figure standing like a thief in the shadows, and for a surprising moment he felt the need to put his arm around the effeminate shoulders and hug him. As he would have done for Lorna, or any female, even a man in a moment of crisis! It was simply the stigma involved with people like Julian that stopped Frank. All the other restraints may be washing away like a block of salt in the lapping waters of understanding, but he stopped short at physical contact, even friendly contact was taboo, not yet! It was too soon for Frank, but with the gelling empathy he felt the need to offer some sort of succour.

"Look Julian. I don't know you too well, but you're a decent bloke and ... and it's painfully obvious, you ... you have a problem." He paused and Julian's head sank again. Frank hurried on, "If I can help in any way, then I will. I'm not sure how exactly, but when my wife and I have a problem, we talk!"

The fair hair, almost yellow in the lights lining the veranda, lifted to show the glimmer of a smile on the worried face. The reflected specks dancing in the quite beautiful blue eyes. "That's all I want Frank. Oh God, believe me, someone to talk to. That's all I want! Even these few words, knowing there is someone prepared to listen has helped." Julian's voice was cracking and Frank found he was nodding in sympathetic understanding though the awkwardness remained. This situation would take some getting used to, but strangely, as his initial distaste abated Frank felt he could help this lost waif. If all he was looking for was a friend, Frank could be, would be his friend.

They stood for some seconds without another word passing between them, an acceptance period almost, then mutually turned to walk back to their room. After a dozen paces Julian said, "You go on Frank. I want some fresh air."

Frank understood and welcomed Julian's ploy to stop them being seen together. He was all bravado in front of the others but confronted with a situation where he could be seen returning from the ablutions with a half naked man? Julian's facade crumbled. Seeds of wavering indecision could be cast into the spurious minds of those already in doubt about him but real life facts were another matter. Better that Frank returned alone. As the solitary figure of the Scot walked over the red quarry tiled veranda his mind was recalling earlier scenes when Julian had dropped his towel, twice, in full view of the others! What was that? A rebellious act in the face of his own abnormality? Indeed was it an abnormality? This condition, if again, was a 'condition' Julian was floundering in? It certainly wasn't accepted nor was it normal by today's standards, therefore if it was not normal did that make it abnormal? Frank shook his head, his confusion complete.

How could he possibly hope to help someone when their condition, abnormality, or whatever it was, was foreign to him,? How could he help with something that he himself did not understand?

~~~

Chapter 6

The following morning J/T Connolly and SAC Buckley reported to No.103 Maintenance Unit. They soon discovered the distance between their respective sections, Machine Shop and Armoury was a mere fifty paces so there was no doubt the pair were going to see a lot more of each other. Not that they were joined at the hip but a certain rapport had gelled between them and could just about stand each other's company.

In the machine shop Frank was bombarded with questions about Britain; "Are the Beatles as popular as the Stones - What was that business about Mick Jagger and a Mars bar - What about this mini skirt, we've only seen pictures - Yeah, do they really wear them that short?" Suddenly all questions locked on to the same subject. The short skirt, popular in the UK was seen only when worn by newly arrived wives or daughters of older airmen. However these females after settling into domestic life and noting the staid dress of the island women and shocked looks from the reserved natives, most but not all British girls condemned the titillating garments back to their wardrobes.

"They say it's six inches above the knee?" Irishman J/T. Steve Power said doubtfully.

"That's right," laughed Frank at the unbelieving expressions. "Some o' the young things are really darin'. It's quite common to see some o' the younger fifteen, sixteen year olds wear them an inch below their whatsits." He couldn't help laughing, "Just enough to cover their crotches."

This comment produced incredulous "You're fucking joking!" - "Whew!" - "Can't believe that!" One in the group, another junior tech. had a thoughtful look on his face. He said, "Wait a minute! Are you saying females back home are walking around flashing suspender belts and stocking tops?" This was greeted with roars of laughter.

"No no, some don't wear stockin's. But those that do wear these new things they're callin' 'tights.' They're like stockin's and pants all in one. They had to invent somethin' like that to protect their modesty, stop us gettin' too excited."

"Speak for yourself man, hell I'm boiling at the thought." Steve Power turned away, "I hope it never comes here. Fucking hell! Fifteen and sixteen year olds running around flashing their fannies, they'd have to lock me up!" He made a fuss of adjusting his trousers provoking another round of laughter. An older corporal technician, Jim Clarkeson, shook his head, "I'd brain my missus before I'd let her parade around, flashing her arse to every Tom, Dick 'n 'arry."

"Must be chilly on the old knees, this time of year," Frank's roommate Callum McAlpine said. Frank discovered only that morning the slim Scot was a fellow M.T.S & O.

"To say nothing of another place I can't stop thinkin' about!" Steve Power added.

"Right you lot, enough of this dirty talk. You'll be catching your balls in the lead screws if you're not careful," called Senior Technician Pat Sawyer, the NCO in charge of the machine shop.

"Cpl. McAlpine, a minute please," he added as the group broke up, still discussing the latest exciting events from swinging Britain.

Senior Tech Sawyer, inevitably nicknamed 'Tom', spoke to Callum, "Would you give Connolly a quick tour, show him where everything's kept, give him a locker, denims, you know, the works. I'm going over to the office."

The mini factory was well equipped as Callum ambled round with Frank pointing out various machines. Frank noticed a stack of brass plates stacked alongside an engraving machine, each about the size of a playing card, all buffed to a high polished finish. "What're those?" he asked.

"That's the worst job in the place Frank, each of us does a month on the engravin' machine, and those, they're coffin plates!"

"Coffin plates, there won't be much call for them, surely!"

Callum looked at him, mildly surprised, "D'you know how many British personnel are on this island, how many wives and children, includin' the army bases?"

"Oh I don't know, ten thousand?"

Callum shook his head. "The figures are not broadcast you understand, but we reckon there must be over thirty thousand

British people here. And every death has to have one of those little beauties cut, polished and engraved in here. We get orders every week, mainly children."

"Don't tell me any more. Children, for God's sake!" Frank stated sadly.

"You're gonna see it anyway. Aye kids are dyin' all the time, at birth, drownin' acci-"

"Where am I goin' to work?" Frank changed the subject.

"Anywhere, wherever. Pick a machine! Tom gives us a job and we produce whatever's on the drawing. Material's over there, brass, steel, aluminium. We can make almost anythin' here." There was a note of pride in the words, then it was Callum who abruptly changed the subject. "Oh by the way, a strong rumour doin' the rounds that Barrymore'll be sendin' for us this mornin'. You know that form you filled in asking what sports you were interested in?"

Frank nodded. "The idiots that wrote 'tug-o'-war, like you and me, he's been callin' them in since Monday."

Excitement stirred the butterflies in Frank's stomach. "Do you know exactly when?"

"Why, you got somethin' more important to do?" Callum smiled.

The phone in the nearby glass enclosed office rang cutting off any reply Frank may have had. Callum hurried over in his long crouching stride. Frank watched him lift the instrument and his lips move in silent speech behind the conversion tables and chart laden glass. With a nod Callum held up his thumb, a grin transforming his rugged features. He replaced the instrument.

"Wants to see us both," Callum said, joining Frank, his blue eyes dancing. "Shit," he went on, "I only wrote that I'd like t' coach, don't know why he wants to see me! Coachin's his job!"

"When?" Frank asked.

"When what? Oh, nine thirty. I'm a wee bit rattled. Don't know what to say to the man!"

"Tell him just that! You'd like to coach, maybe you'll get the second team, who knows?

Anyway, nine thirty, that's in ..." Frank looked at his watch, "forty minutes."

"Aye, so if you fancy a Coke or an Alka Seltzer, whatever, you've plenty time. There's a wee stall round the end o' this buildin'. It's handy for mornin' afters. You'll find Mustafa, our labourer in there." Callum smiled, "An' there's no rush to start work."

Frank nodded. His head still ached from the previous night. However what he'd seen so far was promising. He could grow to like the carefree atmosphere that permeated throughout the small yard of the MU Engineering Flight. Taking his leave he walked to the small metal wicket door that allowed exit and entry without the need to open the large sliding machine shop door. Frank ducked through and into the bright sunlight. Facing him across the fifty foot square yard was the section headquarters building. A notice board on the roof declared boldly this was the domain of 'General Engineering Flight'. The title had pride of place on the top line. '103 ' was central straddled by two R.A.F. crests, one bearing the Akrotiri flamingo, the other the M.U badge, a pair of callipers. Underneath these was the simple legend 'Maintenance Unit.'

Frank soon found the stall tucked behind the carpenter's shop in the corner of the square. It was a converted field office, fitted with counter, double door refrigerator, tables and benches. A small dark civilian with cheery blue eyes and a ready smile greeted Frank with a nod of his head that was not all grey. Some of the brown curly hair had not yet succumbed to the invading signs of age. The man spoke with a rasping but pleasant throaty voice. "You noo, eh? You noo, I know what you want, what I get you. Alka Seltzer … eh … eh?"

Frank's eyes that were scanning the shelves whipped back to the smiling innocent blue eyes. "Why do you ask if I want Alka Seltzer?" Frank wondered if he was looking under the weather bearing in mind his forthcoming interview with the tug-of-war coach.

"You no wahnt?" blue eyes shot back.

"YES, yes I wahnt ... want," Frank answered hastily, conscious of his involuntary mimicking the vernacular of the Turk's mangled English; simultaneously anxious the magic pain removers might be denied him. He went on, "What I'm tryin' to establish is, how did you know what I wanted. You asked if I wanted Alka Seltzer, how did you know that's what I came for?"

"You NOO sah! All noo peepel, they eet the Alka Seltzer! They come Cyproos, drinka tha brandy, get too much the peesed, next morning they come see Mustafa, eat Alka Seltzer. You sah, you noo, yes? You getta peesed, you come here, see me, you eat Alka Seltzer! Yes?"

Frank grinned. The earthy little character was tilting his head at an angle in a questioning manner. "Aye, you're right, I'm new. My name's Frank Connolly, you're Mustapha I gather?"

"Me? Yes, my name he ees Mustafa!" The man spoke the name proudly. "You still wahnt?" Not standing on ceremony he was holding up two of the butterfly wrapped pain killers.

"Aye, I mean, yes I do."

"Two piastres please," said the busy bustling little man as if he had a shop full of customers awaiting his attention. He handed Frank a glass of water with the pills, "You dreenk weeth the watah, you know, eh?"

"Yes," answered Frank, handing over the money. "Mustafa," Frank dwelled on the name, then, "You're Turkish!"

The blue eyes went wide with an even wider smile. Drawing himself up to his full five feet with back ramrod straight and face deadly serious, he said, "Sah. I Toork. Ferra good man. I wok here twenny year - maybe? I luv zee Breeteesh. Queen Victoria - ferra good man!" With that he threw up a vibrating salute of sorts.

Frank did not see the salute, nor did he see much in the next few seconds. At the Turk's comment about the long dead queen, he had been in the unfortunate position of drinking the effervescent mixture when half the drink shot up his nose and down the 'wrong way' in his throat. He erupted into a coughing and spluttering paroxysm with tears cascading from his eyes. Mustafa was happily surprised. He had said the line about the old queen many times before, knowing it was good for a smile or even a laugh or two, but never to such a spectacular effect as someone choking or even expiring! He must remember to say it again while someone was drinking the fizzy drink.

When Frank controlled himself sufficiently and cleared his eyes, Mustafa was holding out another glass of water and in the other hand, two Alka Seltzers. "On de house!" he announced.

"Ya wee bastard! You nearly choked me! Jesus. The queen's no' a man, ya soft prick, she's a wumman, an' she's deed an' been deed for sixty odd years. We've got another queen now. Och, never mind!" Frank stopped, aware his accent was

140

thickening in frustration. Also he had the feeling he was not getting through to the grinning little figure offering the peace offering. Resignedly Frank accepted them, popping the large pink pills into the water and drank the wildly effervescing mixture.

"The queen ... she deed?" Mustafa asked, hoping to keep the fun going.

Frank lowered the glass to glower at the dark handsome face, which quickly adopted a pained expression. "I'll have to watch you, won't I?"

The pained expression disappeared immediately replaced by the broad smiling mouth, topped by the expectantly wide humorous eyes. "Yeser," he answered happily.

Mustafa was one of those rare men God, or in Mustafa's case, Mohammed smiled upon. He was instantly familiar with a nature strangers and friends alike warmed to. Mustafa, over his fifty-five years had long ago recognised this ability and played upon it. For all his years he was still a boy at heart and people recognised this youthful, almost childish air. They liked him because of his perpetually happy and mischievous nature.

"This your permanent job Mustafa?" Frank asked regaining his composure.

"Part time sah! Onlee the part time. Me, my job, I wok mahsheenshop."

"The Machine shop?" Frank repeated in a mock display of dismay. Callum had mentioned Mustapha was manning the kiosk stall. He was about to go on when the little Turk cut in. "Yah, mahsheenshop! Wassa wrong? You no' unnerstan' deed queen's her Eengaleesh?"

Frank made a grab for him and Mustafa yelped, ducking behind the counter. The sudden movement had its repercussions however as waves of pain shoot up the back of Frank's head.

"Hey, I'm not in the mood for this," he groaned pulling back gingerly from the cowering figure.

No sooner were the words said when Mustafa popped up smiling widely. He was enjoying taunting this new 'Eengleeshman.' Everyone from Britain was English to Mustafa.

Turning to leave Frank said, "I'll catch you in 'Mahsheenshop' Mustafa, when I'm feelin' better, for surprise, surprise. 'Me I wok Mahsheenshop' too you little rat."

"Bye sah," called the malapert little Turk as he rinsed the glass with a flourish and flash of white teeth. He was not finished, "You catch thees rat in shop eh Eengaleesh Frank? I theenk only pussycats catch the rats sah. You a puss, you a big pussy ser?"

Frank was stepping outside as Mustafa shot his parting jibe. The best he could do in response was shake a fist at the grinning Turk. This in turn received a blown kiss.

"You can't win wi' that wee bastard," Frank chuckled. "The place is chock fu' o' characters."

The impish Mustafa had happily diverted his growing headache. He placed a hand on his forehead. "Whew," he muttered squeezing hard gaining only a modicum of relief. On removing his hand he saw Julian approaching, smiling at Frank's obvious efforts to ease an aching head. "Never again, Julian," he said.

"I wish I had a pound for every time I've heard that," Julian laughed. "But understandable. You did take a terrible bang on your head. That wouldn't help an impending hangover."

"Aye, back o' my head's very tender which only proves I've got to pack in one of my two favourite pastimes. One, stop bangin' my head on the ground or two, stop drinkin'. One or the other has to go!" He grinned.

"You were out cold, you know that don't you?"

"Oh aye," answered Frank, "an' thanks again for lookin' after me. I don't know what's happenin' to me with all this drinkin' but that's gonna stop."

Julian looked down at his feet and kicked a pebble. There was a short awkward pause before he said, "You recall our discussion?" Without waiting he went on, "I don't want you to feel obliged to anything that was said. We both had a lot to drink and perhaps ..." he paused, "maybe I spoke out of turn ... did I?"

Frank looked closely at the fine featured young man. Could God, or nature or whoever responsible for creating the human race be held accountable for allowing such a travesty? To sanction and nurture the genes of a female inside a man's body? Indeed apart from the small genitals was this person's body, that of a man? Did they realize too late their biological blunder? If so the realisation would not help this blighted man/woman. Cursed to spend its misbegotten life forever trying to merge, live, grow

142

up normally in fields of contradiction and doubt, while the dominant female genes struggled to surface?

Frank saw the misery ingrained in what could only be described as a lovely face. Was Julian regretting having opened his closet of personnel feelings, allowing one of his many skeletons to escape? His total reversal of feelings towards Julian surprised even himself and was therefore amazed he felt the need to comfort this troubled soul that had bared itself to him so profoundly.

"Look Julie, I don't feel obliged to anythin' that was said. For what it's worth, what I said last night still goes, unless of course you want to change somethin'. I can only repeat what I said. I'll help you, any way I can, but I know nothin' about ..." he paused awkwardly then, "The only way I think I can help is to be your friend, your confidante. Now there's a good word." Frank laughed, attempting to lighten the tone.

Julian was staring at Frank. For the moment he could say nothing so the Scot went on, "I can understand how isolated you must feel at times, and ... well ... shit Julie, I don't know what else to say. I'm feelin' my way here too, you know? But there's somethin' I've got to say an' I must say it otherwise I'll never be comfortable. You and I can be friends, but a friend I can put my arm around when I feel like putting an arm round a friend. Shake his hand, pat his back, or even kick his arse if he deserves it, like I would do to someone I consider a friend." Frank looked openly into the blue eyes.

Julian looked down, then slowly up. He held out his hand,

"Friends, Frank. There's nothing more I want more on this earth than a friend, a true friend, oh yes please Frank, be my friend."

"You're on!" Frank gripped the extended hand gently, shaking it as he would a girl's.

"Hey you two!" Callum's long frame struggled through the Machine shop small door, "Hope you're not makin' advances on my first love, Junior Technician Connolly?"

"Our secrets out!" Julian smiled happily, "Right Frank, that's a date." He winked, spun around and trotted off towards Mustafa's stall.

Callum's piercing eyes searched Frank's face, "I've seen many about turns but him and you?"

"Don't knock it 'til you've tried it pal!" At the surprised look from the gangling Scot, Frank could not maintain the pretence. "Remember the dropped towel last night, and his ordering a Screw ... driver? He's still playin' games Callum, poor bugger."

"Aye well poor bugger or no', he's connected with the team which we'll certainly not be if we don't get over to see the coach like now, right now, it's nine thirty, c'mon!"

Across the yard from where they were standing, in the first office down the passageway of the GEF section headquarters sat a Flight Lieutenant. Although not quite six feet in height, because of his muscular body the image he presented was that of being thickset and not so tall. His facial features were sharp and handsome with thick wavy black hair although the black was now aristocratically silvered with strands of grey. The eyes were dark blue, penetrating and determined. Errol Barrymore had been scrutinizing new arrivals on the MU over the last three months. He was the coach of the renowned, certainly in military circles, 103 MU tug-of-war team, but to describe this man as simply 'coach' did him no justice. He lived, loved and breathed the sport, being manager, trainer, first aid man, scout, and kit attendant. Recently his tasks had been lightened somewhat when the latter task had been taken over by a capable volunteer, an SAC Cantwell.

The officer, in his early forties had been an active member in the sport since a lad of seventeen. He worked his way through the non-commissioned ranks then at the age of thirty, successfully applied for a commission. Two years later Pilot Officer Barrymore, in his last competitive pull, was a member of a team representing the Royal Air Force in an Inter Services Competition at Earl's Court, London. In the round robin contest, two teams managed to go through the competition unbeaten, and as luck would have it, these teams met in the last match. They were the Royal Marines and the Royal Air Force. The Marines took the first end in three and a half minutes. The RAF took the second in five and a half, and the third end in a brutally long nine minutes. No member from either team could walk after the third end, with two airmen suffering temporary blindness. The Medical Corps took a full half hour to get both teams fit enough to climb the rostrum to receive their trophies. Errol was proud to have been involved in that team and talked, some might say boasted, about his last match.

If Errol was a good man on the rope, he was even better off it! His ability to spot a good man, and if necessary correct any faults, then blend eight men into one coordinated unit, raised Errol into the master class of coaches. His current team was his finished product, an excellent side, but the ever-present problem of time erosion of everything on the face of the earth was working overtime on his squad. From his present eight he would lose five good men by the middle of the forthcoming season. The five having completed their tours of duty. The inescapable pruning left Errol with a major repair job. He must introduce five new members during the first half of the season, blending them into the team in easier matches. Therein lay the danger! There was no easy match for the 103 MU eight. Lesser teams, knowing their reputation, gave their all hoping to lower the MU colours. To take just one end of three would be a major achievement! Something to boast about in the NAAFI and bars. 'We took an end off the MU!' The odd end had indeed been lost to Errol Barrymore's team during his term, one end but never the match.

Besides five team members returning to Britain, Errol himself would bid the lovely island a fond farewell towards the end of July, only four months away. He had won everything there was to win, there were no more targets to chase, except perhaps one where there was no prize! To complete his dream Errol wanted something intangible, and wanted it more than anything. That was to get through these last months with a clean sheet, to preserve his three years unbeaten record. Cutting his coaching teeth in Singapore Errol enjoyed similar success but had lost the odd match in the Far East. The challenge to achieve invincibility was greater in Cyprus for strong contingents of both RAF and Army teams existed on the island.

There would be a few hard fought matches but none worried the MU coach more than the final cherry from the top of the athletic cake: the Near East Air Force Championship. Nearly three years ago, in June 1963, Errol was keen to win his first NEAF final. A year later he quivered with concentration when winning his second final. Now three months away, a third NEAF championships loomed like some great Colossus. He desperately wanted to win the jewel in the Mediterranean sporting crown for a third and final time.

The Near East Air Force Championships was the pinnacle of the RAF athletic season.

Athletes trained, prepared and cherished the dream of winning at the zealously contested games. No athlete or team could normally dominate the games but the 103 MU tug-of-war team were the one exception. They had won the NEAF championships for the past eight years and Errol did not intend to let their crown slip.

His attention that morning was focused on the new arrivals list. Thirty three men had marked 'tug-of-war' as a sporting interest, only seven with experience. Regrettably two thirds of the thirty three would fall away or prove unsuitable.

An interesting item caught his eye earlier in the week when starting his interviews. It seemed there was a coach out there! Interesting, for a coach in any sport did not arrive on the MU unheralded. If he was a tug-of-war coach as this man claimed, and worth his salt, he should have received the red carpet treatment. He was young too Errol noted, twenty five years old. Usually coaches were, as he was, an ex-team member who had grown a little long in the tooth for this demanding sport. He had phoned this chap under an hour ago, a Cpl. McAlpine from the Machine shop and realised it must be nearly time for the interview. Errol glanced at his watch surprised to see it was already nine thirty. McAlpine and an experienced man from Leuchars, Connolly would be here shortly. Despite his curiosity in the coach, it was the Leuchars man he was most interested in.

There was a light knock on his door. It opened to Errol's "Come!"

"Cpl. McAlpine is it, and Connolly, Yes? Good, come in lads, let's have a look at you."

"Corporal McAlpine, Junior Technician Connolly, reporting as requested, sir." Callum threw up a salute, which for the gangling Scot was unusually smart. Frank did likewise.

The officer surveyed the pair standing at attention in front of him. Both looked healthy and fit. The tall thin corporal sported more of a tan than the recently arrived Connolly, other than that, thank God, there was nothing unusual about them. "At ease, please stand easy and thank you for being so sharp. My name is Flight Lieutenant Barrymore. My reason for sending for you is I am rather anxious to find replacements for members of my team

146

who are due for repatriation in the coming months. Unfortunately I must include myself in that group. Now ah, let me see." He ran a finger down the list. "Yes here we are, McAlpine, Callum ... with two Ls"

"Yes sir," Callum confirmed.

"And you're a coach. Tell me about yourself corporal, what experience do you have?"

Callum shuffled self consciously, "Sir, that may have been a wee bit presumptuous. I've no real trainin' in coachin' tug-of-war, or any skills in the sport. The only experience I can lay claim to was, I coached Workshops to win the Stradishall Station Championships last year an' I really enjoyed it, enjoyed the experience. When my posting came through sir, here to the MU, I got to hear about their reputation so I ...."

"Sorry corporal, 'their reputation'? Whose reputation would that be?" Errol asked.

"The MU sir, the 103 tug-o'-war team," Callum answered frowning slightly.

"Oh aye sir," Frank intervened. "There's only two teams in the forces, St. Athens in Wales, and 103 MU, currently based here."

"Really? Well there's a feather in the old cap." Errol smiled, "Thank you Connolly, perhaps one day a match can be arranged." His question had been superfluous for Errol knew the 103 MU name was well known in the RAF sporting world. Nevertheless it was nice to have clarification.

"Please continue corporal."

"Well sir, in the Orderly Room on Arrival, I thought it would do no harm to enter tug-of-war on that form. I'd like to learn more, maybe run the second or third team, whatever!" Callum shrugged, "Just to help out like, any way I can."

"I see," Errol said thoughtfully, "and how many pulls, or ends, altogether did your team have that day back in Stradishall?"

"Altogether?" Callum thought for a moment. "Seven sir, aye that's right, seven ends. We beat three teams in all. In two matches we won two nil, and two pulls to one in the final."

"Good, and tell me, as coach, what did you contribute to your team's success that day?"

Again Callum had to think back.

147

"Well sir, it was probably in the third end in the final. We'd won the first end, lost the second and were losin' ground in the third against the Armoury. I ran to each team member and shouted in his ear. Tried to make him think it was his strength we were dependin' on, or I might say somethin' else dependin' on the character of the man into whose ear I was shoutin'. One bloke I knew was a bit of a hard case so I shouted that he wasn't tryin'. He got angry an' redoubled his efforts." Callum smiled at the memory, "But generally I made the man think the others were relying just on him. The blokes said afterwards each of them thought he was Hercules, holding up the others, when in fact they were all doin' their bit! It worked anyway, once I'd stopped the rot, I got them to gather their last reserves, put in some concentrated heaves an' ... an' we won!" Callum shrugged.

"I see," Errol was aware this complete novice, had just given a brief but very conclusive summing up of the basics of what coaching in the sport was all about. "I see," he repeated, "and you never participated in any tug-of-war competition before that day, coaching or pulling?"

"No sir."

Errol nodded thoughtfully, he had a feeling about this thin young man, "Thank you corporal McAlpine, that's very interesting, and now?" His gaze turned to Frank whose eyes were locked on photographs on a board behind Barrymore's head. One showed a smiling King George X1 presenting a silver tankard to a slim and younger Barrymore at the unmistakable Braemar Highland games. Frank moved his eyes down into the dark blue orbs looking back at him. They were friendly and knowing eyes set in a handsome face. "You like my photograph collection?"

"Yes sir," Frank answered. "Very impressive. You've been around."

"Yes," the officer confirmed softly, almost sadly glancing over his shoulder. "They were good days." Turning back his voice strengthened, "And more to come, don't you agree?"

"Oh aye, I mean I'm sure there will be sir," stammered Frank.

"Of course," Barrymore cleared his throat, "As you are a very recent arrival Connolly, allow me to welcome you to 103 Maintenance Unit."

"Thank you," Frank answered dutifully.

"I believe you have some experience?"

"Yes sir, some. I pulled for Leuchars. We were doin' well in the UK Championships last year until we met St. Athens. Surprised them I think at first, took the first end but then lost the next two. They went on to win it, again." Frank smiled.

"Yes, they're an excellent side! I am very glad to have you here Connolly. I must confess I asked for and received some feedback from your Warrant Officer Upsall at Leuchars. Seems from what he tells me he's lost a very good man. Would you agree?"

Frank was surprised that this doyen of the tug-of-war world had taken the trouble to check his background and ability. The officer went on, "I'm sure you do. Mr Upsall described you in very flattering terms, the backbone of his team no less!"

"That's news. I didn't know that," Frank muttered, more than a little embarrassed.

"There's no need to be coy with me Connolly. If you are good, you are good, simple as that. Some have it and some don't. If I were to ask if you were good, or very good, what would you answer, truthfully, without girlish modesty. Come now Connolly, good, or very good?"

Frank glanced at Callum who was looking to his front. The thought suddenly crossed Frank's mind, was there a reason behind this officer's goading? Was he being urged to give more than just an answer, did Barrymore want something else?

"Good, or very good Connolly? Maybe you are very, very good! I don't know, and I won't know until Monday. I simply want you to tell me here and now, which are you?"

Frank looked deep into the unflinching eyes, "Sir, if you want me to give an estimation of my abilities on the rope, I'm afraid the three choices you've given me don't come close. If you'd said the word 'excellent,' even 'brilliant,' they might've been a wee bit nearer, but still a long way short of fully describin' the length and breadth of my abilities in the sport of tug-of-war!" 'See how that grabs you,' Frank thought.

Barrymore looked calmly at the Junior Technician. The face was expressionless but there was a determined gleam in his eyes, which were returning his look unflinchingly. Never had Errol heard a self appraisal to match this young Scot. For a number of years he had been using this gauge of self-assessment, which was simply to ask awkward questions about their own ability. Mainly to note their response and for the obvious reason it was extremely difficult to live up to a high evaluation. With this in mind, most would mumble a grudging, "I'm not bad," whereas the promising lads usually settled for, 'I think I'm pretty good.'

"That is quite an assessment Connolly. To be perfectly honest, I have never heard anyone burden themselves with such a high evaluation of their own ability. Can you live up to it?"

Errol felt a tinge of disappointment as Connolly paused, wondering if he'd overstepped the mark perhaps. The officer was wrong; Frank was merely casting his mind back to Leuchars. He had nothing to fear on a rope, knowing in this sport he was better than most. "Sir, why don't we wait until you can assess me for yourself." The words were said quietly and confidently.

Errol Barrymore was immensely pleased. This airman was exactly what he was looking for. Brimming with confidence, around eleven stone plus, and with the report received from the WO at Leuchars, he had landed a good man. Which was just as well. The new batch of arrivals had not yielded much of a catch.

"All right Connolly, we'll see on Monday. I apologize for my unusual interviewing methods and thank you for your patience." The coach turned back to Callum, "Now then corporal, unfortunately we do not have a recognized second team but we do have a clutch of reserves where you may acquire some basic knowledge as a coach. We could think about forming a second team? However I find these chaps most useful for practice pulls on the training ground."

"And who coaches, in the practice pulls?" Callum tried to sound less eager than he felt.

"Any one of the reserves. Anyone who for whatever reason is not pulling, he coaches in practice pulls. Now then," Errol sat back in his chair and looked speculatively at Callum. "Maybe you can help me in that department corporal. We won the Inter Services league last season, and purely for experience I entered these reserves as our 'B' side. I felt however at the end of the exercise, it was more trouble than it's worth. It did not produce the desired effect for I was not seeing them! I lost touch with them, and also they were losing lots of matches, which I dislike. Losing can develop into a nasty habit. Consequently I was not about to re-enter the 'B' team this season." He paused then, "Corporal, do you think you could run that team? I'm not looking for great achievements. All I want is appraisals, feedback on who is shaping well, I'm looking for replacements. Can you find some decent replacements for me?"

"If they're there sir, I'll find them!" Callum answered confidently.

A good firm answer, "I think you will, corporal McAlpine, I think you will. Thank you both and I'll look forward to seeing you on Monday. Dismiss!"

Both airmen came to attention, saluted and turned to leave. At the door Callum stopped and facing the coach felt compelled to ask, "Forgive me sir, just to clarify, am I actually the coach of the second ... the 'B' team?"

The officer chuckled, "It's yours corporal, but perhaps you'd best look at it this way. My team is the finished product. You're in charge of the factory! You receive raw material at one end, and the finished product comes out the other, like any factory. When I am ready, I will take, I hope, the finished product you produce. Understood?"

"Yes sir. I've got a feelin' in my bones you won't regret this," said a contented Callum.

"I tend to agree," Errol smiled. "See you on Monday."

The airmen left the building and crossed the square, both feeling a sense of jubilation. Frank sensed he was already in the team. Trying not to be pretentious or self glorifying, he could not escape the warm gut feeling. He knew his capabilities, and had he not just been informed, gaps were about to appear in the best tug-of-war team in this part of the world? "Roll on Monday," he muttered quietly.

Callum's frame of mind was slightly different, just as jubilant as his confident partner but why? He was after all only a newly appointed coach of a second-class second team. They had not done well in the Inter Services league, and reading between the lines of what Barrymore said, there was no one in the second team capable of filling the boots of the those going home. So why was he elated? He certainly was not about to win any tankards with this lot but his excitement was not rooted there! The turmoil in his stomach was fermenting from something said shortly after entering Barrymore's office; '... unfortunately I

151

must include myself in that group'! It had never entered Callum's head for one moment that Barrymore could be nearing the end of his tour And here he was, Callum McAlpine, the complete novice about to take over the running of the second team! And by the laws of simple deduction if, IF he made a decent job of coaching the second team, the distinct possibility was he could take over the reins of the first team when Barrymore flew back to dear old Blighty? Maybe he was shooting at the moon but Callum rubbed his hands and slapped a surprised Frank across the shoulders, "Oh aye man, roll on Monday!"

~~~

Monday morning, shortly before eleven o'clock, outside marquee No.7 in a row of dark green marquees, approximately forty airmen carrying PT kit and boots were gathered. Flt. LT. Errol Barrymore crossed the road from the MU yard noting the turn out. The numbers were misleading as most would fall away but the turnout was heartening nevertheless. Surely he could winkle out five good men from this noisier than usual gathering. Flipping the tent flap aside he went to the blackboard at back of the marquee. Hard on the officer's heels came Junior Technician Colin Drake, the current team captain, one of the men due to return to the UK early in June. Drake's eye lit up when he saw the team coach. "Good morning sir,"

Errol checked a table for chalk and pointer then turned, "Good morning Drake, would you mind calling the chaps in please?"

Had Colin Drake possessed a forelock he would have tugged it. As most of the hair at the front of his head was already lost he did something which was almost but not quite a curtsy; a quick slight bend from the waist and nod of the head. "Right sir!" Colin the epitome of the 'gentle giant' hurried to the entrance. He was big, solid, strong and harmless, completely at the beck and call of the man he idolised.

The airmen entered quickly after Colin's summons and soon milling around but settled immediately at Errol's signal.

"May I have your attention please." A nervous cough or two greeted Errol's words. "My name is Flt Lt. Errol Barrymore. I'd like to thank you all for this quite magnificent turn out to this our first meeting of the season. Some of you may be aware the MU or to give it it's proper name, 103 Maintenance Unit is a highly respected name, not only in the world of RAF engineering, but for its tradition of producing quite exceptional tug-of-war teams." He scanned the faces for signs of disinterest but saw none. "Tug-of-war is a vigorously competitive sport on this island where we have up to thirty RAF and Army teams from bases all over Cyprus. Most take part in league and knockout competitions held during the season. Also once a year we are invaded with teams from Malta, El Adam and others who come here with but one thought in mind, that is," he paused dramatically, "to lower the colours of the team from 103 Maintenance Unit, your team, my team! Every side we meet, whether based on this island or elsewhere, strive for that highly elusive honour!" He paused again looking over the faces before going on. "No team has been able to pull my eight men over their line in the best of three pulls for two seasons, and I not only want, but demand this season be equally successful. My men are dedicated to the sport and from each of those men, or future hopefuls I can accept nothing less."

Again he paused, allowing the point to sink in. "Once training starts I will not simply ask, I will demand total commitment. If I do not get it from any one individual, he will be asked to leave. I do not have time for, nor do I want, bad apples. That individual is not only letting himself down, he is letting me down, he is letting my team down, but worst of all he is letting   the proud name of 103 Maintenance Unit down! However on the other hand, I'd like to point out to any of you talented enough and worthy of selection, I promise you, you will experience nothing in your entire life that will give you greater satisfaction. When eight individuals under my command pick up the rope, they cease at that point to be individuals! They merge, gel into one power unit, mould to such an extent any one man feels he alone is holding or pulling the opposition by himself. The communicating factor for all eight men is the rope itself. Through that rope each individual will feel, will communicate with seven others. The rope tells a good man what's happening, he can feel through those twisted strands of hemp when the opposition is weakening, or winding up. To the seasoned campaigner the rope can signal what the opposition are thinking!"

Errol turned to the blackboard and drew a series of eight interlocking circles, as in a chain. Turning back he said, "You've all no doubt heard the saying, 'A chain's only as strong as its weakest link.' Nowhere does that adage have greater affinity than to a tug-of-war team." He rattled his pointer on the line of circles, "If each of those links were unbreakable, no amount of sustained pressure could fracture that chain!" A rumble of agreement as Errol went on, "And yet," he reached up and drew a finger through one circle, "if pressure were applied now?"

"The link you've broken sir, would open, break the chain," a voice called out.

"Exactly, yet seven are unbroken, but this one," he rubbed out the broken circle, "has made the others as weak as himself! No matter how strong the chain, or team, one weak link will break the chain, the team beaten! It is precisely for this reason I select my men very, very carefully. I cannot afford a weak link in my chain." He pointed to the board, "That is a very simple theory gentlemen, but effectively demonstrates my point. If any of you here today feel you may be a weak link, or could be, then already you're showing signs of imperfection. Anyone with such negative thoughts, please do me the honour of returning back to your sections. Leave quietly and in your own time. Please spare me the trouble of having to whittle you out later. Now, questions?"

A hand went up towards the back. "Yes," said Barrymore.

"What style do you use sir?"

"Style ... hmn?" Errol frowned. "The side pulling method like everyone else. We don't straddle the rope, four on each side as some favour. We simply face the opposition with the rope to our right. We turn onto our sides on the drop with the rope locked under our right arms. I try to use a speed drop and keep on the move. We are very regimented. Does that answer your question?"

"Yes sir. The reason I asked was the camp I've just left were starting to use a new square pulling technique. Apparently it's very effective."

"And which camp would that be, and your name please?" inquired Barrymore.

"Corporal Banks sir, from RAF Weeton," answered the fair

haired crew cut airmen.

Errol nodded, "Thank you corporal. Yes, I have heard what you describe, the 'square pulling style.' It is not as you say, entirely new, although it may have been refined, I don't know. What I do know is." He turned back to the board, rubbing out the circles. "I would like to demonstrate something if I may." Quickly he drew a tent and while sketching, carried on with his dialogue, "You are all aware a tent is rather a fragile fabric shelter, and yet this tent, or indeed this one," he directed his pointer first at his sketch then the marquee around them," can withstand the elements. Sometimes even gale force winds cannot dislodge these delicate structures. The reason for that is these little chaps here." He pointed to his sketched tent pegs. "These spikes are driven into the ground at an angle of approximately forty degrees and the tent secured on the spikes with guy ropes. If these spikes are driven deep enough into firm ground it would require a considerable force to propel them through an arc of fifty or sixty degrees in order to tear that peg out of the ground! I compare my men to those spikes, very difficult to uproot. On that theory my faith is rooted in side pulling! Always has been and right or wrong, always will be for me. Thank you for your observation and your update on the latest styles in the UK young man." Errol nodded towards the board at which Colin Drake approached and wiped it clean.

"A word about forthcoming competitions," Errol went on, "Next month we have the MU sports meeting which is little more than the season pipe opener. Two weeks later however we have our first real test, the Akrotiri Station Sports. Now let me explain a rather unusual position we have got ourselves into. The eventual tug-of-war winners at the station sports, are not only crowned Akrotiri champions, but claim the honour to represent the station and wear their blue and white hoops colours for the remainder of the season. Now we, that is 103 Maintenance Unit have won the Akrotiri Station sports for an unbroken period of eight years, therefore we have proudly represented Akrotiri in blue and white hoops, for all that time. Therefore 103 Maintenance Unit have become rather well known over the years and are instantly recognised by the distinctive blue and white hoops of Akrotiri, which is misleading as 103 M U has its own forgotten colours of yellow and black! That is the price we pay for winning our parent station's title I'm afraid."

Errol Barrymore chalked the words 'Near East Air Force,' on the board. "That gentlemen, is the most prestigious sports meeting in the Mediterranean. It is held in our own Happy Valley sports ground where they allow two teams to rip their rich turf for one match only, the final! I want, very badly, to win that again gentlemen. Each RAF base in the Near East send their champions here. The pull-offs take place the day prior to the main sports day to decide the finalists. We have won the NEAF crown for the past eight years, and every year it grows more competitive. Annually we meet unknown quantities from every base round the Med. baying for our blood. We are unbeaten on that hallowed turf at Happy Valley, and so it shall remain!" The officer thumped a fist into his palm, light of fire dancing in his eyes. For a moment he was quite breathless before gathering himself, reluctantly passing on from something he had set his mind and heart on winning.

"Interspersed throughout the season there are Inter Services league matches, in August, a Knock Out Cup. We have won these competitions since their inauguration three years ago. That may sound glib but the opposition is fierce I assure you, particularly with some Army teams who would love to win one or both of these trophies." He smiled, "We intend to deny them, or any team that pleasure. That concludes all planned official matches we have lined up. There may be others, invitations to open an army sports meeting, or an RAF station where they gather their best lads from all section teams and pitch them against us. It gets quite hairy at times." He glowed with pride. "Lastly gentlemen, but certainly not least, there is one ingredient that makes us, 103 Maintenance Unit, stand tall above all others in this sport. Many frustrated coaches must ask themselves, what is it that makes us different, so much better than their eight tried and trusted men sweating and hauling at the end of our rope? We are eight men, we weigh, like them one hundred stones or less! What magic ingredient gives us that extra ounce of whatever it is that year in, year out, wins our pulls? Do you know? Can you guess? Our opposition have copied our style, our drop, even to manufacture the same training gantries we use, but they'll never see the difference between the rest and us. Have any of you new arrivals, I refer to new arrivals only. The older hands know which direction I am heading. You new chaps, have you any idea to what I am referring?" Errol was greeted with blank faces, shaking heads.

"One word gentlemen, one word makes the difference between the men and the boys: 'DETERMINATION!' He was glaring now. "A team with determination, with dedicated, unrelenting determination will beat any eight men gifted with all other assets that make a good team. We are a good team, an excellent team, but without determination we would join the others in the lottery of good sides that are best 'on the day'. We are best EVERY day! The reason? We are a team with pride in our own ingrown tradition, and a team such as, 103 Maintenance Unit who have this embryonic tradition. We have found, when all else is equal, we can reach deep inside the pit of our beings, tap into the bone marrow reserves of determination and that will pull us through, as it has done, many times! I do not apologise for the pun!"

He searched through the crowd for first team members and was happy to see dogged conviction on their faces. The words 'If only I could keep this team,' flashed through his mind for the hundredth time. Pushing the impossible dream away, he concentrated on driving home this very important factor. "I cannot emphasize this point enough! If any man can instil into the very centre of his being, that far reaching dedication, they will find that will pull them through! When all strength, grip, foothold and mental grasp of physical surroundings have melted down through tiring hands into the rope, the one thing, the ONLY thing that stops them falling off is sheer determination. That and that alone is the difference between 103 Maintenance Unit and all those other well trained teams out there!" He continued to glare at the airmen most of whom were receiving a glimpse of the bedrock quartz, the basis of power behind his team.

Time as usual was flashing past on this the first morning of training. Errol was keen to get the men down to the training ground.

"Gentlemen, I always get carried away with that last point, but it is a point you must believe in. Sheer determination is more important than a good technique on the rope! Now then, my talking is done. Please change into your PT kit and boots then come down to our training ground directly behind this marquee. You'll find me at the individual training gantry."

Ten minutes later Flt. Lt. Barrymore scanned the group and soon found the eager face he was seeking. "Drake, would you gather the old hands for me? Start them on the team gantry, slowly, don't overdo it on our first day, ease them into it." As Drake rose Barrymore said, "Hold on for one minute please." Glancing around he found the light ginger hair. "Corporal McAlpine!" Callum, studying the small gantry answered sharply surprised his name was called.

"Corporal, during training sessions I intend to address you informally. I find it easier just to use names. There is no rank in sport." Turning to the man next to him Errol went on, "This is my team captain Colin Drake. You will accompany him please, watch everything he does, perhaps you will learn something."

"Thank you sir," Callum was about to introduce himself to the team captain but stopped when Colin shouted, "Newcomers stand fast. The rest to the team gantry."

Feeling a little out of place Callum followed Colin, the established team and reserves.

Errol split the remainder into two groups; beginners on his left, experienced to his right. "What we have here," the officer explained pointing to the bucket on the individual training gantry, "is a motley collection of steel pieces. Each piece has been carefully weighed so we know at any given time the precise weight in the bucket. There is fourteen stones in there at the moment, I would like a volunteer from the experienced men please, to try their hand."

No one moved. A mistake at this early stage would take forever to erase. Frank Connolly was considering the bold step, as the gantry was a replica of the one he knew so well at Leuchars. Fourteen stone held no terrors for him. The coach interrupted his deliberation.

"I understand your reluctance but faint heart never won anything gentlemen. Connolly, would you give us an insight to what RAF Leuchars can do?" Errol's exuberance for once knew no bounds, he had to see if this man measured up to requirements.

Frank stepped forward confidently, pleased at being selected. He placed both palms on the dusty ground, rubbed them together then picked up the rope. He stared down its short length to where it spliced with the steel cable as the latter wound its way up and down through pulleys to where the cable finally connected to the bucket by a solid steel shackle. When Frank pulled the rope the bucket should rise off the ground and travel vertically up the centre of the steel tripod for what he guessed was over twelve feet to the top. He locked the rope under his right armpit, looping the excess across his back and up over his left shoulder.

"In your own time Connolly, don't break any records," Errol smiled, "or anything else!"

At the moment of truth Frank grew uneasy. Back in Leuchars twelve stone was regularly kept in the individual training bucket. Could he manage two extra stone? 'Too late now bullock-brains,' he thought taking a deep breath then throwing his body backwards into the drop. The bucket bounced two feet of the ground and stayed there. Perfect! Lying at an angle of around thirty degrees with the rope running across his abdomen, his back ramrod straight. With barely a pause, Frank drew up his right knee and chopped the boot into the rock like surface simultaneously pulling with back and arms whilst pushing down on the right leg to straighten it. The bucket rose six inches. Repeating the action he worked into a rhythm and was mildly surprised and pleased when the weighted container rattled the top of the gantry. He locked his body along the rope in the straight position.

"Hold it there Connolly, two minutes please." Errol could hardly believe his eyes. Connolly would be a little over eleven stone yet the bucket had flown skyward like a champagne cork. He knew the fourteen stone inside the bucket was a conservative estimate for Drake invariably added more. 'Must have the weight checked,' the officer thought, but everything else was right, even if the weight was incorrect! His chopping, slicing right boot creating the levering point to push on. The straightening back as he pulled apparently with ease, without the bucket dropping an inch indicating no loss of pressure. And there he remained - still - showing no strain after two minutes. But it was time. Pity, he looked so comfortable.

"Thank you Connolly, slowly and under control please, let it down."

Frank's heart was bursting. This was his first pull in six

months and his hands were growing numb. 'I'm not going to bugger this up now,' he thought managing to lower the bucket slowly, under control as Barrymore requested, using the same movements in reverse.

Errol sighed with relief scribbling on his clipboard. 'Connolly, replacement for Endicott.'

He turned to the group, "Banks, how about you, would you like to have a go?" Then to Frank,

"Well done Connolly, please would you join the others at the team gantry."

"Right sir," Frank was satisfied. He knew his performance was near perfect and being shunted up to the team group, must mean he was at least on the replacement short list!

Errol had to concentrate hard on the others but as the last of the experienced men dropped the bucket on the dusty ground, he added only one more name into his clipboard list of probables; that of Cpl. Banks, who had followed Connolly but with less aplomb. He was however, the best of the rest. The note read, 'Banks, possible/probable No.7 or anchorman?' The rest he wrote off. They may have pulled for other teams but were not the material required for 103 MU.

The second group, the newcomers to the sport were keen. After instruction with some practice drops and pulls, each tried a full blooded effort on the individual gantry. Errol was more than pleased with the endeavour shown by an Indian chap who rejoiced in the un-Indian name of Clarke. Finesse was naturally lacking but the man was strong and well balanced. With training and guidance he could be another find. Clarke went into the clipboard, 'inexperienced, strong, needs work, definite probable.'

The last name to be added was Munroe. It read, 'Strong, worked hard, keen, bad hands?' Munroe had pleased Errol. A good athletic build, on his first attempt had managed without much of a struggle to raise the bucket to the top, which was more than many of the others had accomplished. It was on the return journey when lowering the bucket under control, Munroe's hands began to lose their grip. He did not manage to pass the halfway mark on his second and third attempts before the rope again slid through his hands. Munroe was good raw material but the hands needed work. Errol would issue squeegees immediately. These were 'U' shaped spring steel implements which when squeezed between fingers and palm incessantly, worked wonders with weak hands. Errol fully expected they would help Munroe. This sullen six footer had potential.

The party at the larger, more robust team gantry were having a break when Barrymore and his newcomers joined them. "Well lads," pride rippled through the officer's words, "I can't have you lot hanging around here doing nothing. You'll be giving these new chaps the wrong idea entirely." Glancing over the faces, "Do we have the full team?" Doing a quick head count he went on, "Yes I think we do." Raising his voice the coach went on, "Would the recognised first team line up on the gantry, please." It was obvious the level of Errol's hard held excitement had risen in the presence of his team. He faced the main group, eyes glittering as he addressed them in a lofty voice.

"I want you to watch this. What you are about to witness is the result of tug-of-war training and the application of that training at its very best. The lads are a little rusty but what I want you to pay particular attention to is my commands. They are exactly the same commands you will receive in competitive pulls. That bucket," he pointed to the forty-five gallon drum, the top of which could just be seen protruding from a hole in the ground at the centre of the tripod, "is the opposition, backed by the unrelenting force of gravity. Watch it carefully. If it drops other than when we allow it to do so, that indicates we are losing ground. Please pay attention."

Errol joined his men and spoke quietly, "I want you to show these fellows what you have learned in your time here. I want you to imagine at the other end of the rope is the St. Athens team and you are pulling for the RAF Championship. Put on a show lads." He stepped nearer to the tripod and raised his left hand. "Take up the rope," he called in a loud clear voice.

The group sitting in the shade of nearby trees saw the eight men slip their right toecaps under the rope, bend their right knee thus lifting the rope into waiting hands. The movement, though simple was executed with the precision of a drill manoeuvre. "Take the strain," called the coach and the rope snapped level and taught. Frank watched the eight men, running his eyes up and down the line; they were perfect statues, all cast in the same mould. The image flashed across his mind of a Jack Russell terrier he had as a boy. The dog used to quiver in poised frigidity as it waited for Frank to toss the ball. These men were Jack Russells poised and waiting. They had the rope locked under their right arms, both hands gripping it. The left hand immediately in front of the right; elbows slightly bent as were the knees. Frank looked at their eyes. These were locked on Barrymore's mouth, just like his long dead terrier, waiting for the earliest indication of movement.

"Pull!" As Barrymore yelled the command eight bodies were already catapulting backwards, twisting onto their right sides in the same fluid movement. Eight right boots smacked into the ground and simultaneously the word "YES," roared across the ground, the watching group of airmen recoiling as the phonetic wave crashed around their ears. In the mini second it took the eight to push with their right legs and straighten their bodies, Barrymore had pounded towards them shouting the word, "And." To this the team chorused back a roared "Yes," as they went through the routine of chopping, pulling and pushing. In a matter of seconds the beat gathered momentum, similar to the cadence of marching men, 'Left - Right - Left - Right' differing only with the words, 'And - Yes - And - Yes.'

The experienced hands in the watching group were impressed, the newcomers, awestruck. The harsh chorused shouts of 'Yes' corresponding with the smooth ascent of the one hundred and ten stone bucket held them enthralled. The bucket clattered as it hit the stop at the end of its thirteen feet travel and swung lazily in a circular clockwise motion.

Barrymore steadied and settled them in for two long minutes. Nothing moved. From the command, 'Pull' it had taken these semi fit men twelve seconds to pull the bucket to the top of the gantry. Quite an achievement considering they had not pulled together for almost five months. There were no signs of fatigue as they lay poker faced and straight backed. Every man looked exactly right in his position, as in other sports some men were better in one position than another. The Nos. 1 and 2 men, those at the front of the rope, nearest to the opposition, were the 'feelers.' These two are best placed to 'feel' the opposition, test their strength and stabilize any sway. The middle men, 3, 4, 5, and 6 are the engine room of the team, the heavy pullers, the pressure builders and stamina men. When everyone else was finished, had given their all, these four must remain strong. The 7 and 8 men are similar to Nos. 1 and 2 but heavier to provide weight and balance at the end of the rope. Although the last two men cannot feel the opposition, they can feel their own men and can inform the coach if his team is still strong or beginning to crack. Lastly and most important, all eight must be as strong mentally as they are physically and able to channel their full blooded efforts down the rope as one unit

Frank nodded in admiration. 'Aye, they could give old Leuchars a hard time.'

Barrymore broke the deadlock, "Okay lads, let her down, slowly please, Slowly."

Like the well trained dog allowing the coveted ball to drop from its mouth, the team eased the pressure as the bucket slowly moved earthwards under the tightest control. Each right boot chopping into the dusty ground followed by similar action of the left. Frank watched the bucket drop smoothly like the mercury on a freezing day. The demonstration was all but over when suddenly Barrymore roared "HOLD - HOLD IT!"

The bucket did not stop immediately but dropped another foot disobeying Errol's order. He stared at the container, wishing it to pause, willing it. The suspended weight did stop with a grinding effort from the tiring eight and another minute passed before Errol screamed "AND," punching a fist into his palm again and again. The response was not quite immediate though the answering "YES," was emphatic. The static bucket however, hardly moved.

"AND," the call came again. The bucket inched upwards with the "YES." The third "AND," got it moving, the cadence picked up, growing regular until the bucket rattled the top stop.

'Shit,' thought Frank, 'we get the message. He's showing off, killing them!'

Errol loved to display his talented team; he also knew their capabilities. Another minute passed in immobile exposition then,

"All right lads, this time all the way, under control."

The bucket eased down, perhaps faster than Errol would prefer but under control. Frank watched the return journey as it slowly and evenly eased its way into the deep hole, hardly causing a stir of dust.

"Well done gentlemen, excellent!" Errol called. For your first

163

pull together in five months that was quite outstanding. I'm sorry if I pushed you farther than I intended but you were looking so good I rather indulged myself!"

Frank watched the faces of the eight. Only a minute ago they were near to exhaustion through this man 'indulging himself.' Now they were rapt, he was heaping praise yet apologising for causing such pain and their faces were spellbound! All traces of fatigue magically wiped with a few words of back slapping patter. If he asked them to repeat the effort they would do so immediately. 'He's got them brainwashed,' Frank grinned, gaining an insight to their dedication.

A few minutes passed as Errol and Drake chatted then the officer walked towards the group. He beckoned Callum McAlpine to join him. "I have asked Drake to organise a pull between the second team members and some of the new chaps McAlpine. It's a start and will give you some coaching practice. I have one or two things I wish to discuss with my chaps who are due to go home. I'll join you in a few minutes." To his captain he said, "Mix them evenly Drake."

A little piqued that he was landed with the bunch of newcomers when he could be at his master's side, Drake gathered the second team and split them, giving Callum the 1, 3, 5 and 7 men, Colin taking the even numbers. "Pick any four newcomers Callum, it's just a practice."

Having nothing to go on, Callum chose Connolly, Clarke, Munroe and Banks. The first three were seriously interested, looked the part and he knew them. The bloke with the crew cut who asked about 'square pulling,' if he could ask that question, he knew something about the sport.

Colin selected his four newcomers and the sixteen men walked towards the individual gantry where a training rope lay under the trees. Markers were already on the rope and Colin went on to explain their significance.

"You've all seen a tug-of-war rope I'm sure, but briefly." He pointed, "There are three equally spaced markers on the rope, and three corresponding marks on the ground just there," he pointed to three barely visible lines cut into the hard earth. "Each team has to pull the marker farthest away on the rope, over the line nearest to them on the ground. Nothing simpler, eh?"

Josh scratched his head, "Eh , would you go over that again, slower this time?"

"I'll kick your arse for you, that's what I'll do," Colin laughed. "Okay then, let's get started."

Unfortunately Flt. Lt. Barrymore did not watch the pulls. Errol was in his element talking to the team he had modelled and shaped into as perfect a machine as eight human beings could possibly be. Had he watched the pulls he would have seen Colin's team take the first end. More significantly during the two minute break between ends, he would have seen Callum speak to one or two of his team then behold the transformation as Callum took the second and third ends. As for Colin Drake, he was surprised to lose! Not that a training pull meant anything, but never the less he was puzzled. Colin knew he had in his eight, four men regarded to be the best from the second team. All four had been called at one time or another into Errol's best eight! The 1, 3, 5, and 7 men in Callum's eight had never made the first team.

The coach wound the meeting up informing everyone training took place daily at eleven, adding ominously missing faces would be noted. This threat was unnecessary; those interested would never miss training. Even those with little chance of making either team were happy to make up numbers, help out where they could.

Errol saw the dusty figure of his captain rejoining the group. Colin, ever tuned to his coach, glanced in Errol's direction and caught a slight nod indicating he was required.

"Finished already Drake, that was quick. Sorry I got caught up with the chaps. Not many more days like this I'm afraid. How did they go, see anything interesting?"

"Yes, think I did sir!" answered Colin.

Errol's head swung to face his captain. Colin saw the questioning light in the officer's eyes and was happy in a condescending way. He had something to pass on; something the coach would have missed had it not been for his keen eye. Colin made the most of it. "If I told you I had Barton, Bert Smith, Grazman and Miller with four experienced newcomers against a mixed bag in a practice match a few minutes ago, which team do you think would have won sir?"

"With those chaps I should say you probably won, I imagine by - two ends to one?"

"Strangely enough sir, we were beaten by that score, and I can assure you, we were trying."

"It's my guess McAlpine's four newcomers must be fairly good." Colin beamed.

Errol was annoyed with himself, indulging in a whim. Spending time with his team was understandable but his first duty should have been to watch the newcomers. He was slipping. Never before would he have allowed himself such luxuries. Although annoyed, he was pleased with the report and knew before asking what the answer would be. "Tell me Drake, did McAlpine's newcomers include Connolly and Clarke?"

"Yes sir," Colin frowned, "along with Munroe and Banks."

The coach nodded his handsome head. "Connolly and Clarke could just about make it into our team right away, Connolly certainly. They seem ready made replacements for Endicott and yourself when you leave us. We need only tune them up a little, show them some of our tricks,"

Colin Drake preened himself at the confirmation Barrymore thought enough of him to forecast he would be in the team until 'you leave us.' "I think you might consider Banks as an anchorman sir, he caught my eye too." Colin clung to the last shred of the coach's attention.

"Thank you, yes I'll do that, and thank you for your observations." Errol turned back to the group all mixed now, talking in little knots. "Just before you return to your sections gentlemen, one last thing. Those of you intending to take up the sport seriously must have two pairs of boots, one immediately for training and eventually a match pair. We have a Senior Aircraftsman Cantwell from the Fabric shop, who will undertake to get your boots heeled. I insist on full steel plates, hardened and ground, which this chap will attend to." The coach glanced at his clip board, "I think that's all. Those of you who want to come back, we'll see you tomorrow." He knew as he spoke most of the faces would not be seen pulling a rope again. Which was just as well, there was far too much dead wood anyway. Once he pruned that away he could look forward to training the new young shoots that were bound to spring up. It was the law of nature. Whether the new shoots were as strong and enduring as the branches they were replacing, only time would tell.

Corporal Callum McAlpine watched a thoughtful Flt. Lt -

Barrymore climb the slope. For his part in the proceedings the red haired Scot was exhilarated having enjoyed every minute. The more time spent in this atmosphere, the more he felt comfortable channelling the strength of eight men into one parcel of power and stamina. The feelings he experienced in winning the training pulls had been inordinately tremendous. The hour and a half had flashed by. Joining Josh and Nobby in the throng of conversing men trudging up the slope he declared, "Wasn't that just fuckin' great?" he addressed them enthusiastically.

"Maybe but I've a feeling old Barry wasn't impressed with my performance," Josh moaned.

"Don't be daft man, it was your first time. He wasn't lookin' for miracles!" Callum snapped.

"And he didn't get any, not from me anyway, but did you see his old sparklers light up when Frankie boy got on the rope?" Josh asked.

"What was that," cried Frank joining the trio, "my name's bein' taken in vain."

"Oh no it's not, you lucky bastard," smiled Josh at the beaming Frank who like Callum had obviously enjoyed the session. "We were saying you were a hard act to follow down there."

It was not the first time Frank was pleased yet embarrassed at his own ability. "Look lads, I've got a head start on you lot. I was only doin' down there what I've been doin' at Leuchars for the past couple o' years. They've got exactly the same training routine over there."

Josh shook his head, "I wish you'd told old Barrymore that. Everyone that followed after you were made to look like pregnant WAAFs!"

A round of chuckles greeted the rhetorical comment before Callum said, "Never mind Josh, when I'm finished with you, you'll be every bit as good as that bag o' haggis, just you wait!"

The friendly dark eyes of the ambling Josh looked at Callum, "Funnily enough Cal, I have no doubt about that, no doubt about that at all my old fruit," he placed an arm around the sloping Scot's shoulders. Callum looked at the hand hanging over his shoulder, "Careful who you're callin' an 'old fruit,' aye and talkin' of fruits, I never saw Julian."

"Aw come on," Frank snorted, "I'm the last one who should be defendin' him after all I've said. But I realise now he's got a problem, a problem none of us would care to be addicted with. Must be hellish hung over the threshold between the Ladies and Gents like he is!"

"Ooooooh aye, you have changed your tune!" chided Callum.

"No I've not," Frank stated only to rapidly change when he recalled the outright disgust he felt on his first day. "Well I suppose I maybe have. It's just that I'm beginnin' to know him better and understand his ... call it what you like, affliction? Whatever it is, he's got to live with it." Changing the subject he went on, "Besides, Julian's no' the only one missin'. What's happened to the redoubtable Ray, he was supposed to be comin' this mornin'?"

"Knowin' Ray," said Callum, "he never knows if it's arsehole or breakfast time. If we want him here tomorrow, we'll have to lead him by the hand if he's in anythin' like the condition he was in last night" Callum had awakened in the early hours with Ray mumbling and stumbling around in the dark.

~~~

Ray knew very well what time it was! He knew it was time to rush over to the ablutions yet again. His bowels had been burbling and gurgling since breakfast, which he declined, settling only for a cup of coffee. The previous evening he had decided quite suddenly to reconnoitre the nearby town, and unwisely spent the night drinking in various bars in Limassol. He made up his mind at the outset to make this a 'local' evening. By Ray's reckoning a 'local' evening would be spent sampling as many of the local alcoholic creations as possible.

Starting with the Cypriot wines which he found delightfully smooth the natural progression led to brandies with the occasional Keo beer thrown in for good measure. Ray feeling rather like a wealthy child in a ridiculously cheap sweet shop had thoroughly enjoyed himself but could not recall how he got back to camp. Or at what time he'd clambered into bed at the end of his Sunday night/Monday morning jaunt.

He was as quiet as a church mouse that morning in the billet when everyone was going on about the tug-of-war meeting. No one noticed him galloping off to the toilets when his stomach noises proved to be more than mere rumblings. He just managed to slap his bottom onto the well smacked toilet seat in time. During the course of the morning the locality of ablutions may have changed from billet toilets to those behind the GEF headquarters, but the surroundings were the same. He'd spent most of the morning squatting on the bowl, wishing he could take it with him when he left. To make his misery complete he was decidedly queasy and nauseous.

Chief Tech. Jock McKinley inquired earlier if Ray was feeling all right as he looked very pale. Ray informed the old Chief his stomach was feeling somewhat fragile, which gave an entirely new meaning to the word, understatement. The Senior Non Commissioned Officer had been assured by the stricken airman the condition would pass. It had clearly not, the only thing to have passed that morning were the contents of the new arrival's stomach.

Ray cursed himself for missing the tug-of-war meeting as he sat staring at the colourfully decorated toilet door. He wondered idly during his enforced encampment how misguided artists could sketch their impressions of the female anatomy on of all places, lavatory doors and walls! Other similarly gifted literal creations accompanied the drawings with collections of flowery verse indicating the best uses for those grossly exaggerated womanly parts.

He cursed the crap wine which he blamed for this dose of the trots or in his case desperate gallops. But neither wine, beer or brandy was to blame for this attack of diarrhoea verging on dysentery. Taken individually or even collectively to an acceptable level, none of the beverages would have harmed the young man. Taken as Ray had downed the multiple alcoholic cocktails, some in large quantities, his system had been knocked for six and he was paying for his over indulgence. Ray knew he had only himself to blame; nobody forced the wonderful fluid down his throat. "Getting greedy," he mumbled miserably, placing his head between his knees, then raised it immediately with both his reek and lancing pang of pain that ripped through his innards.

Chief Tech. McKinley was well aware his latest charge from the UK had spent most of the morning in the 'bogs.' When Colin Drake had called into the Armoury for anyone interested in their tug-of-war meeting, Buckley had been firmly ensconced in his powder room.

It was now reaching a point of concern for the old chief. 'If he spends any more time in that fucking shithouse,' thought Jock, 'he'll have to sit in a bucket of iced water for a week. His arse must be red raw by now!' McKinley dropped his chin onto his chest, forcing his eyes to look over the top of his glasses as the wan figure of SAC Buckley entered the Armoury.

"Buckley!" called the chief. "Over here lad."

The older man shook his head sadly at the airman's sluggish response, "You know Buckley, you've not been with us five minutes in this land of sunshine and shit and already you look like death warmed up! That usually takes three or four weeks even with hardcore alcoholics!" He tilted his head and looked over the sad figure from top to bottom. "My God, I've seen more fibre in a wee boy's willie than in your entire frame. Get yourself over to Sick Quarters! D'you hear? I don't know if you're clamping your cheeks or in a coma. Get the MO to give you a dose of that wonderful pink cement to bung up that arse hole of yours. On your way now!"

Ray had a fleeting glimpse of the billet and his lovely bed beckoning, but the enchanting thought of some blessed sleep disappeared when the streetwise McKinley said, as if reading Buckley's mind, "I'll phone Sick Quarters and tell them you're on your way, to look out for a white washed zombie, okay?" As he finished the old timer lowered his head once again in his favourite mannerism; peering over his glasses to give Ray the warmest of smiles.

"Any chance of a lift up to Sick Quarters Chief?" Ray asked hopefully.

"This is not the MT section, Buckley, I haven't got any transport unless you fancy our bike but in your condition that's not an option. You'll walk laddie, it's not so bleedin' far. They might have to change your nappie when you get there but that's part of the excitement in this life, isn't it? This could be deemed 'Self Inflicted Injury' Buckley, a chargeable offence, that is! So get on with you before I plug up that leaking vent myself with the toe of my boot. I'm beginning to think you're a wee bit of a skiver son." Jock did not mean the last remark. Most newcomers to any overseas posting hit the cheap booze for the first few months and sooner or later got a taste of what he knew as 'Gypo gut.' Here in Cyprus it was probably 'Greeko gut.' Whatever it was, Buckley had it, exactly the same thing; a breath holding, anus locking, knee knocking trot to the nearest toilet, tripping along with lips sucked into the mouth and eyes popping, bent in silent prayer with only one thought in mind, to get there in time. This lad Buckley wasn't any worse than others, but in the few days in his section, Jock suspected his latest arrival may just have a touch of the drinking problem. The stale smell on the man's breath this morning had nearly knocked the age hardened veteran over. 'Christ, we've all had a taste of that magic fountain,' thought Jock. Learning to control it was by far the bigger mountain to climb. "I'll have to keep a fatherly eye on our Mr. Buckley," he said quietly as he watched the wretched airman duck out yet again through the small wicket door, then disappear in the flash of bright sunlight.

~~~

Chapter 7

Marion and Harold were ecstatically happy. Being the man he was Harold speedily recovered his libido, but Marion being the woman she was knew if she allowed her husband a free hand he could do himself an injury. Although exactly what type of injury she had no idea!

Before leaving home her mother vaguely hinted; 'Don't overdo anythin' Mari', followed with, 'Three months is a long time - for a man! Don't let Harry do himself to death now, will you Love?' Each advisory pearl had been offered with that maddening knowing smile. Then the totally perspicacious observation, 'Remember, your Harry is a man. He's different from you!'

'Oh Mum, of course he's different!' Marion was the tiniest bit peeved at her mother's innuendoes. Why could she not come straight out with what she had to say instead of leaving her bewildered daughter guessing?' Harry would be with her every night now, not 'weekends only' that was for six months the only married life they had known prior to Cyprus. So how was Marion to know if Harry was overdoing anything? Other than the obvious of course, but surely her mother was meaning that?

Although there had never been any suggestion of 'rationing' her husband in their love making, there was a slight hint of better timing. Marion truly believed the dizzy heights of their deep feelings and the inexhaustible pleasure gained from each other's bodies, could if abused, burn out their blistering passion. Impossible as it may seem knowing the extent of their love, she felt no flame could burn so bright forever and their lovemaking was much too precious to be allowed to diminish or contemplate losing. Consequently under her delicate control, when lovemaking did take place it was eagerly anticipated by both parties, and proved to be always deep, warm and tender. Harold noticed Marion was coquettishly avoiding his advances at times, never allowing the gaps between their sometimes extremely tender and at other times recklessly frantic unions to become too frequent. With this growing awareness of how she was controlling the gaps, he did not complain. What she was doing was for them both, for their mutual pleasure and he was grateful. He also knew if it was left to him, he would make love to his lovely Marion in the morning when she opened her eyes, at noon when she looked at him kindly over lunch, and at night, especially at night and if possible, twice in between these times! She knew what she was doing and he loved her all the more for her control. His goddess of love allowed him to drink from the cup of Venus whenever he felt the need, not simply the want! For he wanted this heavenly creature whenever he laid eyes on her, every minute of every day. Harold, well aware of his weakness knew it was up to him to maintain the relationship he had with this wonderful person he had been lucky enough to claim as his own. To be taken under her gossamer wing where she could touch his soul whilst soothing his burning breast and groin. This slip of a girl understood Harold Ross better than he did himself.

Their affinity was not all one sided. Marion was happy at the way their life pattern was taking shape. The first two days of their renewed life together was spent rediscovering each other, but remembering the 'advice' from her mother, Marion worried that Harold might indeed injure himself. At the end of their first week, the young wife skilfully slowed the physical side of their love. Harry, bless him, had meekly complied. She was not sure but it seemed he might even be welcoming the restraint.

The few days leave had flown. Harold drove her over half the island but there were areas where Turkish troops would not allow tourists so they never got to the 'Panhandle', the north eastern part of the island. Marion swam in the sea for the first time at Famagusta, where Harold likened the episode as 'splashing about in warm soup.' Marion's retort to his comment was he was talking rubbish, which resulted in her being half drowned by her playful whale of a man.

Whilst in Famagusta Harold took his wide eyed young wife to see the Roman ruins at Salamis and suitably impressed, drove back along the coast road, through Limassol and on to Paphos where extensive archaeological diggings were taking place. Marion was fascinated with the pipe work of the ancient baths and intricate mosaics being recovered and pieced together like a massive jig-saw puzzle.

The next day they discovered Mount Olympus was very cold which was not surprising as it was still spring and the warm sun of summer had not yet penetrated the snow laden crests of the Troodos mountains. The views, when the clouds parted enough to allow such privileges, were breathtaking, as were the scary narrow mountain roads. Harold booked into a chalet in an almost deserted retreat among tall majestic pines near the village of Troodos. They walked in the evening on a deep carpet of pine needles, confirming Marion's feeling she was walking on air. Even more ethereal was their night cloaked in shimmering blackness, which they spent wrapped in blankets in front of a roaring log fire making whispered plans for their future.

If the drive up to Troodos was frightening, the route down the north side on Friday morning with tight S-bends and winding roads cut in the rock face of the mountain was exhilarating.

Harold drove to the northern seaport of Kyrenia and due to a cancellation was fortunate to find a room in the extremely busy Bristol Hotel. They had lunch then retired to their room for a nap after which the couple walked around the small picturesque harbour. Seeing rowing boats bobbing by the pier, Harold spoke to a man repairing fishing nets. He rejoined Marion, "That bloke said we could hire a boat and fishing tackle. Do you fancy catching us our supper?"

"I don't know," Marion said dubiously, eyeing the tiny insignificant boats in so much water.

Harold caught the indecisive glance, "Don't worry pet, I spent my childhood in rowing boats," he lied happily. Though not entirely without experience, he managed with little trouble to convince a very reticent wife everything was quite safe then spent more impatient minutes shepherding Marion into the boat. Once safely aboard, he rowed confidently, trying to inspire the same feeling into Marion as the boat cut its way over the quiet water of the harbour.

Harold baited the hooks, much to Marion's disgust and they fished and rowed around feeling tugs but nothing significant before Marion's line suddenly went taught. Harold transformed back to his schooldays, gleefully helped pull the wriggling fish from the water.

Marion, on seeing the pitiful efforts of the creature, no bigger than her hand desperately trying to wriggle free from the cruel barb imbedded in its tiny lip, shrieked and threw her hands over her face. The action caused her to drop the rod. The fish and line plopped back over the side. Harold with a shout grabbed for the rod but the fish was gone. Marion saw the crestfallen look and whispered, "You wouldn't have wanted to harm the wee thing, would you Harry?"

Harold looked up from gazing into the black depths and stared at the white face encased in thick tresses of luscious black hair, "Dear sweet woman, what do you think we're fishing for. Think very carefully! The word 'fishing' might give you a clue?"

"Oh I know," she said, "but we don't want to actually kill the fish! Poor wee thing, having its dinner when suddenly he's yanked out of his environment, by a nasty hook... in his mouth! Well I mean, how would you like that Harry?" she asked sadly.

"Marion, tell me something," said her bewildered husband, "do you think the fish you buy from the fish and chip shop comes out of the water ready battered and fried. Or maybe the man in the shop goes out and picks fish out of the trees?"

"Oooooh," she cried, "you're just trying to put me off eating fish! Well Harry Ross, I'll never be able to enjoy a nice fish again." She daintily folded her arms and shrugged dramatically

Harold sighed, "Marion, see those long pieces of wood beside you? They're called oars."

"I know that!" she tried unsuccessfully to sound indignant.

"Good, I want you to pick up those oars and row around the edge of the harbour wall there," Harold pointed out to sea. "So the people in the bars and cafes on the wharf can't see us."

"Why Harry?" Marion asked raising her eyebrows.

"Why? I'll tell you for why! I'm going to drop you in among your beloved fish. You know love, I'm just a simple man, so when I asked if you wanted to go fishing, I naturally assume you knew we were going to, hopefully, catch fish? And having caught the bloody fish, kill them!"

Marion dropped her eyes, "I thought we were going to catch fish and sort of ..." she paused then lifted her face, gazing up into Harold's blue eyes, "look at them and well, put them back again," she whispered then smiled. "You, big strong man that you are, you wouldn't really kill those tiny wee creatures, now would you Harry?"

"No," he answered readily, "not the 'tiny wee' ones," he mimicked her voice, "but if I was lucky enough to catch a big one, well now. I'd get the priest and smash its bloody head in." He reached into the bag of fishing tackle supplied by the boat hirer.

"Oh Harry!" Marion wailed. "Now you're showing a side of you I've never seen! Kill the poor wee fish if you must but there's no need to drag the church into this!"

"Church?" Harold repeated nonplussed, then looked at the small club taken from the bag. "You mean this? THIS is a priest, it's part of the tackle the bloke put in the bag. What other reason do you think he put a club into the bag?" He leered wickedly. "Unless it's for clubbing wives who throw fish back into the water."

"Oh Harry, if that's true, then it's a terrible name for something that sole purpose is to kill defenceless fish."

"Oh, God!" Harold cried in mock anguish placing his head between his knees shaking it sadly. Slowly he straightened up and smiled at the slightly bewildered girl opposite him. "You're a nut," he laughed, "but a truly delicious very edible nut." Stowing the fishing rods he tipped the tin of bait over the side. "Watch the little sods take it now there's no hooks in it." Leaning over he shouted at the water's surface, "Eat up! No nasty hooks NOW." He watched the last of the fish and meat cuttings sink, hoping at this late moment he might catch at least a glimpse of the elusive denizens of the deep. He was out of luck there again.

Moving carefully he sat beside Marion, "I think the fish you put back warned the others off," he moaned moving an arm around her waist.

"I'm glad Harry, now isn't this better than killing fish?" she asked moving closer and looking up into the brooding face.

Harold could not help smiling at her. One look from this girl could right the wrongs of the world. "I'm reserving judgement," he said, the smile staying firmly in place. "I don't know about any new sides of me you are seeing for the first time," he paused, "but the more sides I see of you, the more I find to love you."

Marion nearly fainted with pleasure as his unexpected words melted her heart. She slipped her arms round him and hugged hard. "Let's go to bed," she murmured, surprising herself. Within her body her rising reciprocal feelings erupted, showing more than anything in the world, she wanted to please him, love him.

"You wanton wench," he laughed, pleased her thoughts matched his own.

"I'm not!" she shot back, "but when you say things like that I just want to hold you. Anything else that follows is your fault." She smiled coyly.

"If someone is to blame for what happens between you and I, then yes, I am guilty as charged and accept the censure absolutely. I truly am at fault when it comes to wanting you."

Marion pulled away, "Oh Harry, there you go again. If you go on like that we're going to end up in the bottom of the boat," she giggled.

"Yeah better cool it but, no need to pull away." They moved close and embraced then sat in their awkward embrace until the hard uncomfortable seat forced them to move. "Marion," Harold said looking at the brightly lit bars ringing the quayside, "what do you say, I'll take the boat back then maybe we can buy some bread and wine in one of those little cafés?"

The girl looked towards the lights that were now beginning to twinkle inside the diminutive shops and cafes lining the waterfront as evening approached. "If you like Harry, but I'm not sure about the wine, it goes to my head."

"Just have a glass or two and see how you feel," Harold pleaded. "If that's all you can manage then I'll come happily to your rescue to get rid of the nasty wine you can't handle!"

"Oh I'm sure you will."

Harold took the oars and rowed strongly with long easy pulls. Marvelling at his strength, Marion felt the surge of each stroke and soon saw the boatman awaiting their return as dusk was falling fast. Because of the semi-darkness, stepping out of the boat proved a trickier task for Marion than she had getting in, afraid the little craft might move away when she hopped between bobbing boat and rigid pier. Eventually the boatman held the stern hard against the jetty so the lady could see no water. Even then Harold, at yet another moment of indecision, had to physically yank her onto the solid wooden landing.

"Don't be so rough," Marion complained brushing her ruffled feathers into place whilst Harold paid the grinning boatman.

"Tell me," he asked the man, "is there a nice bar here, along the waterfront, get something to eat?"

"Aff caws," answered the man, "Demetria's, der, der!" He pointed. "Demetria's fera nahs, fera goo food, you lahk fera mash." The man's mangled English was accompanied by his vigorously nodding head.

Harold tipped the boatman the same amount as the cost of the boat, which made both men feel very good. The big Englishman placed a huge arm around the tiny waist of his wife and they strolled in search of the highly recommended Demetria's.

Like everything else on this wonderful day, Demetria's Bar turned out to be a pleasant little open fronted tavern with a dozen tables, half of which were inside the establishment. The rest outside on the cobbled street, all covered with bright tablecloths. What appealed most to the young couple was the place exuded cleanliness with a kaleidoscope of light ricocheting through the massed glasses on the bar top and a floor clean enough to eat off. It was still early, the only customers were two men at an outside table playing baccarat. A third man idly watched whilst passing prayer beads between his fingers.

Harold chose a table inside the door and ordered a bottle of muscatel from the barman. Minutes later a huge woman in her middle fifties waddled over to their table carrying a bottle. "You on holiday?" she asked inserting and twisting a corkscrew with a massive ham of a hand.

"Yes," Harold answered.

"From where?" she shot as the cork popped free with minimal effort from the woman.

"The UK," he answered. Marion gave her husband a curious look.

"Ah-ha!" a smile spread across the expansive face. "Me, I am Demetria, I own thees place," she waved a hand lazily. "The UK eh? I leev in Lawndawn ten year already! Lovely ceetee but the weather she sheet, yes?" the smile grew wider.

"Yes," Harold echoed the fat lady and Marion tittered which

drew Demetria's eyes towards the girl and her ringed hand. "You just married, yes?"

Before Marion could answer, Harold said, "Yes, we're on honeymoon."

"Ah yee! hawneeymoon!" screeched Demetria making the baccarat players jump and look round. The woman was now rattling in Greek and the men nodded sagely towards the couple, causing Marion to writhe uncomfortably. "Harry, why did you say that?" she whispered.

"Sssh," he hissed leaning towards her, "watch the service we get now!"

Demetria held up the muscatel bottle, "You like dees?" she asked with a grimace, then, "You wahnt champan-ya?"

Harold shrugged spreading his hands giving a perfect indigenous impression of someone unprepared for such hospitality.

"Champan-ya, yes!" the woman yelled. She almost ripped the cork from the corkscrew, popped it back into the muscatel bottle and with a whack of the mighty fist the cork vanished into its recently vacated neck. With bottle in hand she waddled away and disappeared through a door behind the bar, only to very quickly re-emerge with two dripping bottles of champagne in one fist, a clutch of glasses in the other.

Marion was astounded at the difference in the sudden buzzing atmosphere. Five minutes ago they had wandered into this quiet little bar where the only noise was the clicking and rattle of dice of prayer beads. Suddenly a mountain of a woman was popping champagne corks and pouring the frothing liquid into long glasses. At the woman's command the three customers crossed the room and collected a glass of the bubbly liquid. Wearing wide smiles, they held them out towards the couple. The woman was speaking, "Congratulations to you! May thee cheeldren be strong and money plenty," she paused frowning. "Naw, maybe it should be the cheeldren, they be plenty and the money eet be strong, neh?" She guffawed and slapped Harold on the back nearly making him swallow the glass raised to his mouth. Reaching for a napkin he winked at Marion and chuckled at the massive woman and her obvious zest for life.

Marion managed to stifle a laugh at Demetria back slap and the resultant champagne shower everyone in the vicinity received but could not hold back her giggle at Harold's mischievous wink. She had no wish to be unsociable but felt a little out of her depth at the deception and was the only one who had not lifted a glass.

"You no' dreenk?" Demetria, completely unaware of the discomfort she caused Harold, was addressing Marion, "You no' lika champan-ya?" The black concerned eyes were staring.

'My God,' Marion thought, 'what's he got us into?' "Yes, yes," she managed to blurt out at which the warm face broke into a wide smile. "I love it," Marion added a tiny lie wanting only to please this woman. The only time she'd tasted champagne was at her own wedding reception where she dutifully sipped a glass.

"Then you most dreenk!" Demetria grabbed a chair and with one hand swung the cast iron seat easily in a semi circle, clunking it down beside Marion. "You no' wahry, Demetria," she slapped an enormous hand against an equally massive bosom. "She look afta you, yes? But now we have the pahty!"

"How nice," said Marion trying to catch Harold's eye around her baulking blocking form but Harold was engrossed in hand waving conversation. Marion picked up her glass and drank.

"No, no, NO," cried Demetria. "You no' dreenk the champan-ya lika dat. You dreenk slowly, yes?" Demetria refilled the glass with one well practiced tilt of a wrist, the liquid rising to the rim of the glass, not daring to spill a driblet over the side.

"Whassa your name?" Demetria asked plopping the bottle into the ice bucket a second after the barman placed it beside the table.

"Oh I'm sorry for being so rude," Marion stammered. "My name is Marion, Marion Ross and my husband is Harold, that is, Harold Ross," she added timidly and unnecessarily.

Demetria sensing the girl nervousness said, "Ah Mar-ee-yawn, it ees the loverly name, and you come here forza honeymoon. 'Stoo beautifool here, yes?" The warm smile never left the large moon face.

"It is," answered Marion still worrying this friendly woman might guess they were not really on honeymoon. Demetria misunderstood the younger woman's caution for shyness. Not wishing to further embarrass her, the Greek Cypriot woman was happy to talk about herself.

"Me?" she said as if Marion had asked a question pertaining

to her background, "me, I marry Charlee, the Breetish soldjah, here," she pointed to the floor. "The soldjah een thee Breetish army!" she repeated. The eyes fluttered as she recalled her Charlie then went on, "When he feenish army we go Lawndawn and open feesh and cheep shop, 'twas good for us. Charlee, he good man but after nine year he 'poof.'" She made a puffing noise and snapped her fingers. "Maybe I too much thee woman for Charlee eh?" She guffawed and slapped her thigh, making Marion look away in embarrassment. It was also to hide her smile at the image conjured up in her mind of the departed Charlie. Somehow she imagined Charlie to be a small man, and her vision was of a suffocating man trapped deep in the cleavage of Demetria's massive breasts.

"But even when Charlee die he good to me, yeh!" Demetria affirmed with a nod. "For I get the beeg insurance. I sell shop in Lawndawn, come back, buy dis place," she swung both arms around her head conveying a waft of body odour from under the pendulous arms. "Nice yes?" Demetria concluded her little discourse with yet another wide smile.

"Yes, very nice," Marion agreed nodding looking around the bar, seeing it in a different light.

The conversation between the two continued and before long Marion found a fond affection flowering for this large woman with the booming voice and motherly protection. With the champagne flowing freely Marion was suddenly talking about Kirkaldy. Strange, there was nothing spectacular about her home, but since her short departure from the small Scottish town, Marion found herself thinking and now talking about her birthplace.

The large lady disappeared into the kitchen again and Harold was filling her glass for the fourth, or was it the fifth time? It didn't matter for Marion was embarking upon a wonderful and new mellow world of brightness where the edges of timidity were melting her reserves. She was deeply engrossed in her own thoughts for a few minutes gazing at the many reflected strips of dancing lights across the harbour water. Demetria, who was placing bowl after bowl of food on the tables, caught the faraway look in the young girls eyes. "Eat!" the bar owner commanded. "You musta eat. When you dreenk you musta eat, neh Maree-yawn?"

The voice Marion thought initially so harsh was softer now, more tender.

Marion ate. She was pleasantly surprised at the delicious taste of what looked in the main, oily unappetizing fare, though this did not include the chicken which tasted as it looked, delicious. 'Demetria's right,' thought Marion, 'eefa you dreenk,' she giggled as her brain reproduced the wonderful lady's accent, 'you musta eat,' or was it 'eefa you eat you musta dreenk?' Marion took no chances. She did both.

Marion did not recall leaving her table to dance! But here she was doing the same side stepping dance the men were doing, arms around the shoulders of strange men on either side of her. Everyone was going round in circles and the circles were going faster. How she managed to keep her feet she had no idea, but why should she fall? She was sailing, floating like a feather caught in a wonderful revolving swirl of friendly faces whirlwind.

Snatches of conversation were penetrating her bemused brain, "You take care Harree," and "Too much wine, she's not used ...." and lastly, "You come back, see us, enytam hokay?"

"Ghoonuch," Marion tried desperately to bid 'goodnight' to the smiling faces swimming around, but her mouth felt as it did after a visit to the dentist. Her lips were sluggish. Safer to close her mouth and eyes but as she did so a whole spectrum of lights flashed across her inner vision. She gently sighed as strong familiar arms lifted her, floating her off into a world amid shimmering vibrations and brilliantly bright yet gentle calming colours.

When next she opened her eyes her surroundings had changed; they were in the hotel room. She was lying on her back and Harry was removing her clothes. He seemed to have a problem as he kept rolling over. Both were laughing hysterically. Snatches of her sitting on the toilet; how long had she sat there in a state of fluid immobility? Did she have the strength to stand up? Then Harry appeared at last, her beautiful strong shining knight. He carried her off to bed.

Oblivion! Total oblivion. Deep deep sleep. How long Marion slept she could not tell but the wonderful velvety blankness was being pushed aside as impressions of sounds, movement and feelings were forcing the heavy sludge of stupor aside. She could feel Harry driving himself into her! Was she dreaming? It seemed not; the rhythmic action of his heavy body driving into her groin was forcing her head painfully against the headboard. Only half awake she squirmed her head and shoulders to a more comfortable position which in no way interrupted the grinding motion of her husband.

Despite what was taking place Marion wanted to return to the quiet oblivion of slumber but the regular movements were driving the last shreds of sleep from her alcohol drugged brain. It was a few minutes before she surfaced completely and realized what was actually taking place. Harry was indeed inside her, making love to her body. He must be conscious of the fact she was, or had been asleep, taking no part in his lovemaking. That hurt! That he could just use her body for what could be nothing more than base sexual gratification. Before she could settle in her mind what action to take, if any, Harold's action grew grossly erratic as he reached climax. Moaning passionately, mumbling something in her ear, his loins jerked spasmodically, heavily as finally his erection drove hard, deep and remained vibrating for some seconds Finally a deep sigh soughed through her hair then he lay still.

With his dead weight Marion could not move then abruptly felt the bile of revulsion rising.

"Harry move, I'm going to be sick." She felt the sluggish dead weight begin to slide off her trapped body and somehow gaining her feet, staggered unsteadily to the toilet where she was painfully and violently sick for many minutes.

The thought of what Harry had been doing to her non responding body nauseated her further as she reached deep inside, retching torturously. She stayed cowered by the bowl until feeling only slightly better, rose to her feet. She washed then gargled her grossly acidic mouth. Finally Marion douched herself, a chore she normally did not mind, carried out as it was, in the afterglow of love. Tonight the action was gross.

Steadying her swaying frame against the cool basin, she waited for her stomach to settle. A further five minutes passed before eventually like a wraith she crossed the room and slipped into bed. Harold was lying on his side with his back to her. Marion did not snuggle into him as she always did, but lay looking at the wide unresponsive form. "How could you Harry?"

she whispered. The deep resonant breathing went on without a pause. Marion repeated the question but the heavy breathing continued rhythmically, blissfully unaware of her disgust. He was in a deep sleep, or that was how it seemed as Marion turned away, hoping she could settle her mind and join him in deep repose though in her present frame of mind sleep did not seem possible.

Harold was awake. But he was doing his best to make Marion think he was asleep. If Marion was disgusted at her husband's actions it was nothing to what he himself felt at his despicable, unexplainable performance. What had just taken place happened in a wonderful dreamlike state. He was in the deepest of drunken sleep, enjoying the most beautiful lovemaking session. He had no idea his body was actually making love to a sleeping Marion. He was using...no! He wasn't just using, he was defiling the one person he would never shame, never debase. Ashamed he may well be but his innards cringed painfully as the mists of his too vivid dream cleared. Like a breeze blowing through his recalling brain cells, in his abstract condition, he saw his lover was not Marion - his dream partner had been Carol Cook!

Why had his mind fooled him like this? Why do this when he loved Marion so very much? And had he in his dream state inadvertently speak Carol's name? The thought made him break into a sweat and a low moan escaped softly from his lips.

Marion heard the groan and wondered again if a man could possibly be asleep and still carry out an act so intimate as to make love? Harold was certainly sound asleep now, dreaming of dragons and witches judging by the sounds he was making. As if seeking justification for what had taken place Marion's mind had without conscious bidding, started to seek a reason, any reason in the hope of absolving Harold. The act in itself, although unwelcome and disgusting, was vaguely understandable as both had been very drunk when they got back to the hotel room.

Something else was itching her, tugging at the strands of reflection, like a fly caught in a web in her deepest semi conscious faculty of thought. It was somewhere close to the moment when she came fully awake, when slowly surfacing through the last veils of sleep, at the point of time when Harry's thrusting weight had grown erratic in climax. He had called out, spoken her name as he often did when they made love. Was that it? Could this be the flaw in the fragment of translucent memory, snagged in her lace of recollection and because it somehow did not fit, was fighting to be free?

Suddenly, that ... that foreign body ensnared in the fretwork of her mind, that entrenched flaw so recently implanted where it did not belong, broke free, flew clear and unfettered. Her mind recoiled in shock. It was not her name uttered at the height of thrusting passion as she again heard Harry's guttural moans, 'Carol ... oh God ... Carol."

~~~

At five o'clock the following Monday evening an ancient Austin bus that once did the London central route stopped at the top of Pappachristos street. Harold with three other airmen got off and he walked the short distance down the dusty street. His first day back at work had passed quietly enough but try as he might he could find no one to do his Fire Picket. The best he could manage was a short postponement. A Safety Equipment bloke due to do an FP duty at the end of April agreed to swap and do Harold's upcoming stint. Had this Safety Equipment chappie not popped out of the mire, how on earth was Harold to explain another week long duty after supposedly coming off one only last week? Marion was perhaps naive in the ways of the RAF but she was not stupid.

Marion had been noticeably subdued since their return from Kyrenia. Not cool or distant but unusually quiet. He assumed her reticence was wholly due to his sickening nocturnal behaviour on their last night in the Kyrenia hotel. It rankled him too as to why he had done such a thing. It was certainly not because he desperately needed sex! They'd made love that afternoon before their walk and turn in the rowing boat. It must have been the gallons of wines, spirits and beer that wonderfully dangerous woman Demetria had poured down his gullet. People did funny things under the influence of the evil brew, and he had been without doubt under a tremendous amount of influence. Harold had been trying to ease his guilty conscience but high-quality excuses were hard to come by. 'Men did far worse things than make love to their wives when in an inebriated state, didn't they?' However deep down he was worried. Well aware of his deep love for Marion, and his needs, but was he turning into some sort of over sexed fiend who could and indeed would prey on her when she was unconscious? This wonderful woman who would deny him nothing! The thought made him chill and shaking the images from his head he ran up the steps to the little veranda.

Marion was in the kitchen stirring some concoction in one of her gleaming wedding gift pots.

They kissed and Harold peered into the pot, "Soup?" he asked surprised.

"It's Scotch broth," Marion answered proudly.

"Isn't it just a little hot for soup love?" Harold asked as delicately as possible.

"I suppose it is," she answered disconsolately, her stirring hand slowing. "But it's what I make best. I've made mince and potatoes too but I'm not sure if the mince has turned out right. As a back up, I thought I'd make something I'm good at, just in case," she said glancing at him, still unsure of herself in the mysteries of the kitchen.

The meal turned out a success despite the heat. They washed up and while Marion put the dishes away, Harold settled down on the front veranda with the Sunday newspaper and a cigarette. A few minutes later Marion joined him and started a letter to her parents. Harold opened his day old newspaper at the sports section. The RAF flew the newspapers to Akrotiri with the mail and distributed both the following day. 'Better late than never', was the general opinion of the servicemen who ordered the papers. Preparing to catch up on all recent events back in the UK Harold felt suddenly uncomfortable. Lowering his paper, he was surprised to look into the dark sad eyes of his wife staring at him. "Marion?" he asked questioningly.

Marion looked down, "Harry," her voice hesitant. Then after a long pause "Something's been bothering me. It's probably nothing but it is worrying so I've got to clear the air." She looked up and deep into his eyes with just a trace of a frown.

Harold braced himself.

"On Friday night Harry, you woke me, and it wasn't the normal way a husband … would. You were … were making love, no, you were using me." Her voice broke as tears began to swell.

"That wasn't me Mari," Harold blurted out. He was going to deny anything and everything but seeing tears in her hurt eyes his heart melted. "I wasn't even awake when I ... no, deep in the recesses of my brain, I knew I was doing something ... something unnatural. I'm so ashamed. Dearest Mari I'm so sorry and can't offer an explanation for I don't know how it happened."

Marion did not want to go on. She saw how regretful he was and in turn felt sorry for him, but she could never rest if the main burning question was left unanswered. "That was bad enough Harry, just the thought of being used, but under the circumstances, the party and all the drink, I've managed to put that at the back of my mind, but oh God Harry, There was something else!"

An icy finger traced its way down Harold's spine, he shivered as Marion paused again. She was feeling increasingly, as each painful second ticked by, she should not have started this and had to force the hated words from her mouth, "Who is ... Carol? Who is Carol, Harry?"

"Carol?" His head was spinning as if it had received a blow, "Carol?" he repeated, frowning.

"Harry, as I awoke, you were making love to me, to ME Harold Ross, but when ... just as you finished ... you called me ... CAROL!" her voice was shaking with emotion.

"You must be mistaken," Harold's mind was racing, "I don't know any Carol," he lied.

"I'm not mistaken! I can hear you saying it now, it's branded into my brain. I've hardly slept since that terrible night!" Marion was growing more distraught.

"I wonder?" said Harold, his mind scampering, searching for possibilities faster than any rat seeking escape from this tight corner.

"Darling," he started, not quite sure of the unformed story taking shape in his brain. "You know, I'm only guessing but there's a Carol who works in our Orderly Room. I didn't think of her until now, and yes she is good looking with a nice figure. While you were in the UK she used to come on heavy, I wouldn't be a man if I said she wasn't attractive. She's very sexy and flaunts it but I stayed clear of her, I swear. Maybe you should know, when I was in my teens I used to have some really erotic dreams about girls like Carol. In fact, during our separation I did dream about this Carol, but it was only a dream Mari. An unbidden dream." He looked into her sad but responsive hopeful eyes, that were hanging on his words. He went on, "I just wonder if during my drunken coma, did my mind switch to that Carol and try to live latent thoughts I am honestly not aware of?"

Marion sat quiet for a minute then, "You never made love to this Carol?" she asked timidly.

"Carol from our Orderly Room?" he tried to sound surprised and held up his right hand, "No, I swear to God my dearest pet, I've never touched her, in any way" he answered truthfully.

"Oh put your hand down, don't be over dramatic Harry, but honestly," she sighed, "I've gone through agonies. I can understand how other girls are attracted to you and how you can be attracted to them but I don't know how I would react if you were going, you know ... doing ... oh ... with another woman!"

Harold stood and crossed the short distance between them, pulled her into his arms and hugged her tightly. Conflicting thoughts and feelings were coursing through him. "I love you Mari,' he whispered sincerely in her ear as troubled guilt stung his eyes. If time could be frozen at that very moment, the purity of Harold's sincerity was insurmountable but of course time cannot be stilled and neither could Harold in his disingenuous ensemble, veer from his rail guided path. Earlier that day when re-organising his Fire Picket duty he'd thought about Carol Cook. He had spent time thinking how he could arrange to take her to some quiet place, be alone with her, make love to her. No that was wrong! There lay the crux of his feelings! He did not want to make love to Carol! He wanted to fuck her, as brutally and as freely as her whimpering body would allow. Not always, but occasionally she liked to be mishandled, abused, even occasionally hurt! It all added to the magic spice of their love fucking. He could do things to Carol he would never dream of doing with his precious Marion. Somewhere in the mix was the fatal attraction. Harold detested this weakness and his less than feeble attempts to stop thinking of Carol. He had tried, but deep down Harold knew he was two people, one who wanted to live within recognised guide lines controlled by a good woman and true love. The other was weak, selfish and wanton that lived only

188

for the pleasures of the flesh. At some point, and it would have to be soon, he had to decide which route he must take.

A worried Harold was still holding Marion tightly. She eased away to wipe her tears and looked up into his anxious blue eyes, "Harry, if you tell me there is no Carol then I believe you, but if you ever feel I am not woman enough for you, then you must tell me that too. If you have any feelings for me at all, please, please tell me."

"Mari, you're all I shall ever want. If you're in pain, I'm in agony. I can't scratch you without mortally wounding myself. Please forget that incident dearest, let's get on with our life."
Marion pulled away from his encircling arms, "I'll try Harry, of course I'll try but it's left a scar inside, no matter how innocent it was." She wiped a hand over her eyes again, "I'm just going to wash my face," she said turning to go inside. At the door she turned back, "Harry?"

Harold looked into those warm but worry ridden dark eyes, "Yes?" he said feeling the frosty prickle dance along his spine yet again. "I want to get on with our life too, our life Harry, that's all I live for, I wouldn't have a life if you didn't love me." She disappeared through the dark doorway leaving Harold gazing at the space where she'd stood, imagining through a trick of the light he could still see her.

~~~

Chapter 8

The taxi was driving at speed towards Limassol. It was Saturday afternoon and Frank Connolly the only passenger wondered if he should have waited for the hourly bus as the old Mercedes rocked and rolled doing over 70 mph. He had given the address of Marion and Harry Ross to the driver but even now was doubtful if he wanted to see too much of Harold Ross, although the lovely Marion was a different person altogether.

Frank met Harry Ross the previous Tuesday, a day after the latter returned from leave. Normally introverted, Harry unusually spoke excitedly of his island tour, especially about an impromptu party in Kyrenia. All of which sharpened Frank's impatience for his family to join him. It was only when they were about to part Harry said, "Oh, nearly forgot, Marion's keen for you to spend a weekend with us, OK? There's a spare room. How about this weekend?"

There was a short delay as the taxi stopped at the first of three checkpoints on the outskirts of Limassol. The Turkish Police manned the outer post, then the UN, then the Cypriot Police. Each policeman had taken Frank's RAF 1250 ID card, gave both the card and Frank a quick scan, asked if he carried any weapons or ammunition then was allowed to continue hurtling along the Limassol Bypass. The road may have been a bypass when originally built but new shops and buildings had swept along the road and up a hill to Frank's left. So much so it was now the main road through the new town.

The taxi turned down a side street and stopped outside a neat semi-detached house. An abundance of flowers surrounded the steps leading up to a small veranda. As Frank paid the driver a glass door enclosed in wrought ironwork opened. Marion was first to emerge wearing the smile that had locked itself forever in the vaults of Frank's heart. Their mutual fondness obvious in their genial greetings. Harold stood back smiling as his wife displayed her natural warmth, as contagious to others as it was to him. He watched them hug then said, "Come inside you two, you'll give the place a bad name."

Ushering Frank inside Marion's movements demonstrated how excited she was to show their first ever visitor around their first home. Also of her rediscovered baking skills flaunting a majestic unbaked pie in her kitchen. "I'm still learning," she said lightly with a modest tinge of pride, "and that's my first attempt at pastry since school. I'm praying it'll turn out all right. It's mince Frankie!" She looked doubtfully at her visitor, "You do like savoury mince pies?"

"You couldn't have picked anything better. Mince pie's my favourite, especially homemade."

"Oh good, I'm so pleased," she cried and looked at Harold who smiled indulgently, "It's also beginning to come out of my ears. If I eat any more mince I'll turn into a hamburger," He laughed, placing an arm round his wife's shoulders, squeezing her.

"Harry you told me you liked mince!" Marion complained, then seeing his expression cried "Oh, I can never tell when you're joking."

"Who's joking?" Harold said. "Did you ever make the mistake of telling your missus you liked something Frank? I told this little piece of crumpet I liked the way she made mince. Fatal mistake! Now I'm getting it with toast at breakfast, spuds at lunchtime and my cocoa at night."

"Oh you are not!" Marion tried to punch the solid mass of humanity, which resulted in her ending up in a bear hug to her obvious giggling delight.

Frank was glad to see they were happy. Big Harry Ross certainly was a changed man. Or appeared so. Perhaps Marion, and marriage had worked the oracle after all.

They returned to the coolness of the veranda and sat for the remainder of the afternoon, chatting and drinking beer. Later Marion went inside to see to the meal.

Marion was nervous for other than Harold, Frank was the first non-family member she'd ever prepared a meal for. When they eventually sat down to eat, she need not have worried. The pie, indeed the meal was excellent. Her visitor however, was a poor yardstick if she was hoping to gain some measure of her

191

gastronomic capabilities as cook and hostess from him. In deference to his delightful young hostess, Frank would have licked his plate clean no matter how good or bad the food tasted. Fortunately no such demonstrations were necessary.

There was no doubt in Frank's mind Lorna and Marion could be great friends but he was still unsure how his wife would take to Harold. Lorna, who had met the strikingly good looking man only once, at a Leuchars dance, could never take to the flamboyant type. And what was it about Harold that stuck in the craw with most men? Whatever it was Frank would have to swallow it for sitting opposite him was an amiable likable man striving to make Frank comfortable. Yet despite his mental reaching, Frank could not shake off his initial vacillation. It was like looking at a Goya in the British Museum but somehow feeling the genuine article was absent, reclining somewhere in the dark recesses of the building.

Marion's smiling face crossed Frank's view. She was placing the used dishes onto a tray.

"If I had been a Casanova Harry," Frank mused, " I could've grabbed my chance in Lyneham, right Marion? I should've whipped you off to climes unknown. We could be reclining on some faraway beach at this very minute, living off the fruits of love, or maybe mince pies."

Marion laughed happily shaking her head whilst peering warmly into Frank's eyes.

"Listen pal," said Harold, "she was on her way to climes unknown when you met her."

"Missed my chance, missed my chance," Frank groaned, much to Marion's delight.

"Well now, you'll get your chance tonight if you fancy a bit of skirt while you're on the loose. We, that is my wife and I, are taking you to our local den of inequity, the fabulous nightclub known to loose women and scrubbers alike as the 'Gold Fish Bowl', where all the debatable talent hang out. Maybe you'll land lucky."

"Stop that Harry," Marion sprang to her guest's aid, "You're not interested in other women, are you Frank?"

"Only in one, Marion, and she's married," he groaned.

"Oh Frank," she giggled turning towards the kitchen with the tray, "you're worse than him."

"Oh thanks very much, now you've really hurt my feelin's. Nobody's as bad as Big Harry."

Marion's face turned back slowly, soft dark eyes probing, her smile momentarily frozen.

Frank's statement made in the light banter of the moment but from the look on the girl's face he'd struck a chord that had gouged something sore inside her. From the gist of his comment it was not hard for Frank to adjust his mental digits to see clearly. Harold had already slipped up. Marion's eyes, although doubtful, carried the tinge of lingering doubt.

With difficulty Frank kept smiling, trying to mask his thoughts. He was fooling no one. Marion saw from his sudden wooden expression her friend was valiantly hiding something. She understood his position. There was no denying the trace of intelligible concept that flashed between them and that spark ignited the faggots of doubt in her mind, reflecting fire in her eyes. Her overriding love for Harold hemmed in by her own insecurity could not accept what she had just witnessed in Frank's eyes. But human nature being what it is with women in love, doubts breached her defences to invade her conscience. Doubts however, being no more than what they were, she automatically sought clarification, and was now in the process of channelling questions into her imagination. Perhaps she was forcing the issue here, not thinking straight? Was she compromising Frank? Twisting something into his statement that did not exist?

For a few seconds, confusion reigned then Marion smiled, releasing all trapped images. If nothing else, she was happy for Frank when immediate relief slid over his face. Harold didn't appear to have noticed Frank's blunder. Marion continued on her way to the kitchen so Frank took the opportunity to change the subject. "So where is this legalised knockin' shop you're so intent on takin' me?"

"It's hardly that," Harold replied, "but not far off I suppose. It's just along the Bypass, frequented mostly by British. Not too bad a place," then added quickly "so I'm told." He had better be careful for he had visited the 'Bowl' with Carol. He cleared the way earlier with Marion telling her the chaps at work highly recommended the club, well worth a visit to see the budding Limassol night life.

"The Bypass? Is it out of town then?" Frank asked.

"The Bypass, no," Harold said. "It's in the middle of town. You'll find there's no road sign anywhere with the word 'bypass' on it. I believe it was to be named after Archbishop Makarios, a boulevard actually but they took so long to put a name anywhere, the British blokes just named it 'the Bypass.' Appears to have stuck."

Two hours later, the men changed and ready waited on the veranda for the lady of the house to apply the never ending touches to her appearance.

The cooler night air was pleasant as Harold lit a cigarette. Frank was looking at the twinkling lights of the quiet town, not particularly keen to go out. He was experiencing his first night in a Greek Cypriot suburban area and finding the occasion mildly exhilarating. He couldn't stop his mind reaching out to when Lorna would joined him, which made him glance towards the house, "You've got yourself first prize wi' that lass Harry."

"I know," Harold blew a long stream of smoke into the still air. He seemed preoccupied.

A quiet moment passed. "Harry?" Frank said quietly across the short distance. There was no reaction. Frank knew the signs, "Harry, you're not messin' around are you?"

There could be little doubt Harold heard the question but there was no answer. The blue eyes staring into the flowers under the veranda were deep in thought. Frank was losing his patience, "Christ almighty Harry, you're a married man now. Surely you're no' messin' around?"

The question was unnecessary in Harold's case but Frank was hoping for Marion's sake.

The handsome head turned slowly and looked at Frank before he crossed to sit on the small enclosing veranda wall. In a voice matching his quiet mood he said, "Frankie, you know me. I was out here for three months on my own and ... it got very bad for me. I didn't want to fuck around but if it's on offer, I just cannot refuse." He raised his head and looked almost pleading for understanding. "I tried to ignore it, I swear I did. But you're a man. You know the feeling. How would you react when you're dying of thirst and suddenly a pint of best bitter appears in front of you? I stayed away from them for a month, honestly, I swear, then I met this fucking WAAF." He sighed heavily, "The only

194

way I can describe it is I was like a pressure valve about to explode. And she was more than keen, I couldn't help myself!" He looked up again, a pained expression making the handsome features appear hard in the half light, "I hate myself Frank, disgusted with myself but when an opportunity presents itself I just cannot walk away, especially in the circumstances I was under."

Frank was dumfounded at the outpouring of what was obviously pent up guilty nibbles and before he could say anything, Harold went on, "But she ... this WAAF means nothing to me Frank, someone I used. She didn't mind, in fact admitted she was happy just to get a good screw, I mean it was reciprocal. Oh shit! This is not sounding the way I want it to sound! Do you understand? We emptied each other's tanks. Just used each other! Frank ... I love Marion."

Frank was disgusted, not at the confession itself but at its tone. The inference was Harold had some God given right to use another woman in the absence of the woman he loved.

"And of course being the Casanova you imagine yourself to be, you must get plenty pints of bitter." Frank hissed, shaking his head in frustration, "Bastard," he muttered then asked, "Was there any others, apart from this cream of bitter WAAF?" It was none of his business but felt he had a right as Harold was using him as a piss pot to empty his bad feelings. Frank could not understand how a man could claim to love one woman yet in her absence, calmly seek out and screw others. "Were there others?" he asked again.

"Frank, drop this, it's not a subject I'm particularly happy about, but I'm working on it."

Frank blinked rapidly, "There were others?" he said incredulously, and again shook his head. "Jesus Christ Harry, have ye no' got any feelin's at all for that lassie in there?" He wanted to smash his fist into the square jaw of the face that was anxiously glancing up the passageway for signs of Marion. "I love her Frank," Harold said soberly, "I do with all my heart, but like I say, I am working on this other thing, I need time. I'm no different from any other man. You wait until you've been out here a month or two, you'll see. Anything in a skirt is going to look sexy and attractive." Harold emphasised his point by flicking his cigarette hard into the flowers.

"Maybe so," said Frank, "but that's all they'll be, sexy and attractive. You don't try to bed everything that's sexy and attractive! At least I don't, and Harry, there's plenty like me."

Harold shrugged, "Like I said, I'm working on it, it's my problem."

There was a movement in the passageway and Marion clicked her way towards them, high heel shoes announcing her arrival. She wore a tight black skirt and white blouse, her groomed hair perfectly framing her lovely oval face. She stopped and stood in the doorway smiling at her two admirers. If she planned it, it was brilliant but Marion being the girl she was could never have exploited her figure the way she did. Her silhouette outlined in the doorway, with the passageway light behind her, displayed the perfect hour glass shape. Frank felt his breath grow short. "Gees Marion, you look gorgeous".

Harold, spurred by Frank's words added, "Yes, you do Darling."

"Thank you kind sirs," she preened happily running her hands over her hips, "I'm sorry I kept you waiting so long."

"The wait was worth it Mari,' Harold said, conscious he was behind in the complimentary stakes. He locked the door then took Marion's outstretched hand. "Let's go," he said, "The Bypass is just up the road, Frank we'll catch a taxi there."
Some fifteen minutes later they entered the Gold Fish Bowl nightclub. To give the title 'Night Club' to the establishment was being abundantly charitable. The entrance was gained through the doorway of an empty shop on street level then down a flight of stairs to a fairly large room, probably the storeroom for the empty shop above. With no windows two extractor fans battled valiantly to suck off the cigarette smoke hanging in layers across the dancing patrons like floating ghosts through the blue haze. For decor Frank could just about see the rough brick walls had at some time received a half-hearted wash of whitewash.

There was a motley selection of tables and chairs, some plastic, others wood or wrought iron, all spread round a circular dance floor. The bobbing mass of heaving humanity rippled on the tight little floor to a group of four musicians who fashioned as best they could, button up suits and mop hairstyles to that of the Beatles. They were belting out "Can't buy me love," at which point all similarity with the Fab Four ended. Harold led the way through the milling crowd and managed to secure a small wrought iron garden table near the back of the room. Frank following Marion was surprised the place was so popular. It was not until later he understood why.

A waiter appeared and Frank ordered. He could not see a bar anywhere but within minutes the drinks arrived along with bowls of nuts and crisps. If nothing else the service was excellent.

The evening passed pleasantly. Harold and Marion danced a few times before Frank, not the best of dancers hesitantly asked the beaming Marion if he might trip the light fantastic with her, the "emphasis being on the trip." The experience proved highly gratifying for the girl was so light and agile, despite his floundering steps. So successful was their dance, some time later Frank was keen to take Harold's offer and give the big man a break. Frank happily discovered the evening turning into a haze of effervescent gaiety.

Leading Marion back to the table after yet another dance floor excursion, they found Harry talking to a young West Indian man with the darkest of black skin. He was sitting on Marion's chair. When they reached the table, the man who was clean cut, solidly built and good looking, jumped up and faced Marion flashing an excellent set of gleaming white teeth.

"Marion, this chap's a good friend of mine," said Harold. "We were in the same room during my sojourn in the billets. Marion, Frank meet Al Johnson, or 'Midnight' to his friends.

The smile grew even broader on the friendly face as he shook Marion's hand. "I'm really glad to meet you Mrs. Ross. Harry, he spoke about you all the time." The voice was rumbling rich.

"It's very nice to meet you, Al ..." she paused, then, "Harry might very well kill me for this, but all these nicknames! Please, forgive my ignorance Al, but why 'Midnight'?"

The black face erupted with laughter triggering off the other two.

"Mrs. Ross ...." Al began trying to control his spasmodic chortling.

"Please, my name is Marion."

"Okay, Marion it is," smiled Al, looking keenly and unashamedly deep into the eyes of the slightly frowning girl. "First of all Mrs. ... sorry, Marion, now Ah is sho yo'd nevah try t' fool a simple black boy lak me, nah would ya Ma'am, Hmmnnn?" Al asked in his mangled version of a south American Negro accent.

"Of course not," Marion replied, regretting her simple question.

"Right Marion, I believe you, okay," Al said dropping the accent before drawing a deep breath indicating he had a lot to explain. "Now I want you to imagine you're sittin' in a windowless room at dead of night, okay? And someone who don't much like you, switches off the only light in the room, okay? Now, what do you see?"

Marion looked at Harold uncertainly, wondering what was required of her. Harold shrugged.

"Look round, windowless room, no light, what can you see?" Midnight persisted.

"Nothing," a delicate eyebrow dipped. "If it's dark I won't be able to see anything."

"Why?" Midnight asked.

"Because there's no windows, the room will be in darkness," she answered plaintively.

"How dark?" the smiling black man persevered.

"Very … it would be very dark, pitch black I suppose."

Al grinned, opened his eyes wide, spread his hands palms upward, "As black as midnight?"

"Oooh," Marion cried, covering her mouth to stifle the embarrassing laughter that threatened, although everyone else seemed to be laughing including the genial West Indian. Between fits of giggling Marion managed, "Well Mr. Johnson, if you don't mind, I will call you Al,"

"You call me anything you like Love, why don't you just call me 'Anytime,'" he chortled.

"Won't you join us?" Harold asked.

"Thanks Harry, but I'm sitting with friends. Over there," Al indicated the dance floor. "Maybe got a thing going, you know?" his deep voice purred giving an exaggerated wink.

With a cheery wave Midnight left them ambling back to his table where two men were sitting. As he re-joined his group, a blonde girl dressed in a very short black mini skirt and red chiffon top, tapped him on the shoulder. Showing his beaming and seemingly permanent smile, Al led the girl to the dance floor.

Frank watched the pair but lost them as they merged with the other dancers. Glancing around the edges of the floor, it struck him then why this sleazy run down dive was so popular. Young British girls were using the Gold Fish Bowl as a meeting point. The tables bordering the dance floor had groups of girls, laughing, chatting in high spirits. The young women had one mien in common, something still foreign to Cyprus; they were dressed in the latest sexy gear from Britain, and all screamed availability.

Harold leaned over to Frank, "I see you're selecting a victim?"

Slightly embarrassed to think he presented such a picture, Frank shook his head. "No Harry I'm not, but I can't help wonderin' lookin' over there, if we men haven't lost the place. I could be wrong but there are more females in heat and on the prowl than there are men."

Harold nodded, "That's what makes this place so fascinating -" he stopped abruptly. "Jesus," he laughed, staring over Frank's shoulder, "look at Midnight!"

On the dance floor the blonde girl was gyrating her hips slowly, pressing her groin hard against that of her partner. Her thrusting hips keeping time with the heavy beat of the music.

Midnight's squeezing hands cupped her buttocks whilst she in turn had a firm grip of his hips. Their eyes were locked together unaware of anyone around them.

Scenes such as these were seldom witnessed on a dance floor in the sixties, and Frank was more surprised than shocked. There was no doubt about Marion's reaction, "That's shameless, Harry! Carrying on like that on a dance floor."

Harold was smiling at the performance, "Just thank your lucky stars it's not a rumba or a samba they're playing, then it could get really embarrassing," he joked. "I'll have to speak to Midnight, didn't know he was such an exhibitionist," he said then signalled a waiter.

"No Harry please, no, I think I'd like to go," Marion said, her eyes darting to the dance floor.

"Go?" Harold cried looking at his watch. "It's just after eleven, it's far too early, the night is barely out of its womb my little darling. This place stays open until the last customer leaves, which will probably be around this time tomorrow morning. You don't want to go just yet."

Marion looked crestfallen, "I do Harry please, I don't want to spoil the night, but I think I'd like to go home now, besides we've all had a lot to drink."

"A lot to drink?" Harold was beginning to sound edgy. "There's been more drink spilt on the barman's apron than what we've had tonight!"

Signs of distress showed on Marion's face. She fluttered then lowered her eyes, clasping her hands in her lap, trying unsuccessfully to hide her discomfort.

"Y'know Harry, this place is smoky and noisy, an' I'm a bit tired, maybe Marion is too, after all I've been tramplin' on her feet all night," volunteered Frank. "If you like, we could maybe have a drink in one of those bars along the Bypass. Let's call it a day here?" Frank tried diplomatically to please both parties.

"Right Frank, it's a day!" Harold reluctantly agreed. He peered at Marion, "You tired Mari?"

"Yes I am, and I feel we've enjoyed ourselves but I'm embarrassed at what's going on over there. I'm worried about what comes next. No Harry, I'd like to go ... please."

"Mari Doll, when you put it like that," he leaned over, took her face in his hands and said, "how can I, who loves you so dearly, refuse?" He kissed her gently on the lips. "Okay, let's go, but just one minute. You said just now you were worried about what comes? Well Sweetie, from the look on Al's face I should think it could well be him!" He sniggered then openly laughed when the image hit him. Frank could not hold back a chuckle either when he stole a glance at Midnight.

"Oh you two," Marion said punching Harold's shoulder. "You really do embarrass me Harry. Why say things like that?"

They made their way to the exit passing the dance floor where Midnight and the girl were still in seventh heaven. Frank glancing at the pair as the threesome passed, saw the girl was pretty in the classic blonde mould. Her long drop earrings were swinging erratically, out of time with her hip movements, which only helped emphasize the overall sensual scene. Midnight's expression was that of a man no longer on the planet.

Harold suggested they walk the short distance to the Twiga Bar. It was he pointed out a favourite meeting point on the

Bypass for British personnel in Limassol. The bright without being garish Twiga was surprisingly quiet for a Saturday night, with less than a dozen patrons quietly chatting in the square room. Harold wanted to sit outside but Marion vetoed this as a cool breeze flicked the tablecloths edges. They settled for a table near the bar. Harold ordered brandy sours and again Marion intervened. "Just a coffee for me please Harry."

"Of course," Harold changed the order then said, "There's two reasons why I brought you to this bar Mari. One is a record I'm about to play, just for you, Pet. You'll love this." Crossing to the jukebox he inserted a coin then made the selection.

The beautiful strains of a topical Greek song, 'Kai Moss' floated smoothly around the bar. When the hoarse voice of the Greek vocalist started to sing, Marion listened entranced, "Harry, that is so beautiful, so typical of this island. Such a rough voice, but it's so warm, so romantic."

The waiter brought the drinks and placed a bowl of oddly shaped salt encrusted objects on the table. "Second reason! Both of you must try these." Harold picked one of the objects resembling a fat white root. He crushed it and two huge peanuts appeared among the broken white shells. "You see," he explained proudly, "they're monkey nuts. The nuts, still in their shells are soaked in water, rolled in coarse salt then allowed to dry. The salt impregnates the nut with the flavour but no salt actually gets to the nut, clever isn't it. Here, try them," he held out the bowl.

Despite her initial rejection of visiting another bar, Marion's insides began to settle. First the music then the revelation of the nuts Harry obviously felt he had discovered. Their night out was closing in a pleasing atmosphere.

Across the room an untidy rat faced man in his middle twenties with brown greasy hair and narrow set eyes, rose and made unsteady progress towards the threesome. Dressed in a shirt and shorts that gave the strong impression they'd been worn as pyjamas for at least a week, he approached their table. "Hello Harry," the man said brightly. "This the wife, then?" He placed an arm round Marion's shoulders with an accompanying waft of rancid sweat. "If you're not Harry's wife then whose wife are you?" He laughed heartily into the girl's face, adding whisky fumes to the other odours.

Harold answered with undisguised disgust. "'lo Fred, who let you out of your cage?"

"The wife, who do you think, she lets me out sometimes you know? She's doing her own thing t'night, or somebody's doing it for her," he laughed coarsely, "so I'm out doing mine." He leered down at Marion, "So you're Mrs. Ross? You really ARE Mrs. Ross?"

A slight nod from Marion.

"Aha, so you really are the wife of 'Harold the fu- oops, Great!' Surprise, surprise." Why Marion should be the wife of Harold was a surprise only to the intruder. "Ha, your husband I see does not wish to introduce us so I will do the honours for you my pretty. Fred Parrott Ma'am, at your service," he bowed nearly losing his balance. "Oh shit," he grabbed the back of a chair, "an' anytime you want servicing Mrs. Ross, Fred Parrott will supply ... the red carrot." The man broke into a staggering bout of coughing and raucous laughter.

Harold watched the man, anger glittering in his eyes.

Fred Parrot, recovering from his coughing, laid a hand on Marion's shoulder and squeezed hard. "And as your Harry knows -" Fred stopped abruptly as Harold had him by the shirt collar and seat of his grubby shorts. He was lifted clear off his feet, then half marched, half dragged across the room where a bewildered Mr. Parrott was unceremoniously dumped into a seat at a vacant table. Harold's orders were heard clearly around the bar. "You do not come near us in that condition, nor speak to or handle my wife. One more time and you will be, I firmly promise, dumped outside in the gutter where you belong!"

One of three men seated at a nearby table for an uncomfortable moment was about to retaliate but thought better of it as Harold returned to his table.

Joe Costalides, the bar owner called to Harold, "Please sir, no want no trahble een my bar, please, awright?"

Harold held his hands up in a gesture of surrender.

"What was all that about?" Marion asked as her husband downed half his drink.

"I hate that dirty little bastard. Don't want him talking dirty and pawing you. You don't know what you could catch off a little turd like that. He's not going ...." Harold stopped when Frank said, "Watch it, here he comes!"

202

"Oh no," cried Marion staring fearfully into her lap. Harold was already on his feet.

Halfway across the room Fred started shouting, "Who the fuck d'you think you are, up on your high horse, what gives you the -" Quick as a cat Harold had grabbed a handful of shirt front then with his free hand gave Fred a hefty back handed slap. He then preceded to frog march the struggling man outside.

Marion watched with staring, uncomprehending eyes. She swung round to face Frank, "What's wrong with him Frank, why is he so angry?" her face screwed up in consternation.

"Don't know. The bloke's a bit on the seedy side but Harry's bein' a wee bit hard on him."

Frank was watching the three men who were taking an agitated interest. He had no wish to become entangled in this fracas but if those three moved towards the door he would have no option. Clenching his teeth he saw first one then the others rise.

'Whoops, here we go,' he thought. 'this could turn into a right barny.'

"Sit here Marion. Do not move!" he said. Before she could react Frank followed the three men outside.

As promised, Harold was depositing the luckless Fred in the gutter when the first of the latter's cohorts reached him. Harold heard rather than saw the man coming and twisted away from the clubbing right fist, catching the blow on his shoulder. The attacker was on Harold's left, so the big Englishman holding Fred with his right hand, dropped him and swung the clenched right fist in a swinging arc to crash heavily into the attacker's face. The man dropped in an untidy silent heap. A second man hesitated when he saw his friend fall, then he too came on clambering over his crumpled mate.

Everything was happening with the speed of light but Harold somehow seemed to be seeing what was taking place through the lens of a slow motion camera. As he dropped the first of his attackers, two others were coming at him. He clearly saw Frank catch the shoulder of the man farthest from himself so Harold had only the chap stepping over his fallen comrade to deal with. Harold bore none of these men any animosity; it was now merely a matter of defending himself, to stop them doing any harm in their misguided bid to help Fred. He was confident he could have handled all three without too much damage but something happened which caused his attitude to change.

Just as Frank dragged one man away, the other caught Harold with a clumsy glancing blow across the left cheek. There was little pain but Harold felt the skin tear as the man's silver identity bracelet ripped across his face. Up to this point, Harold had not lost his temper. He was actually in total control and enjoying the rough and tumble, until now! He wiped a hand across his cheek, saw the blood, and with it scars and worse, future disfigurement.

Assuming the man had used a knife or blade, all reasoning left Harold. A flood of red clouded his eyes as he focused on his armed attacker who on carrying through with the impetus of his misplaced swing, was facing him only inches away.

The fist Harold had downed the first man with, came up behind the staring face and locked on the back of the man's neck in a vice like grip. Harold had a glimpse of wild eyes glaring into his before he crashed his forehead into the face, again and again. The man would have fallen but Harold, on automatic drive now, held him firm, crashing his forehead repeatedly into what was very soon a mushy bloody mess.

"Harry, for Christ's sake! You're gonna kill him, stop it, stop it man!" Frank's words had little effect but slowly, Harold was dimly aware of his friend separating him from whatever it was he was holding in his right hand before laying it on the ground. He blinked repeatedly, vision returned but not comprehension. The man on the ground looked like a dozen ripe tomatoes had been squashed over his face.

Harold raised his hands to his own face to find them covered in blood. Suddenly he felt his stomach jolt, he had caused this carnage. "He cut me," the words hissed from tight lips. Frank was walking him, leading him away. Marion spoke in the background.

"Oh that poor man, Harry," she cried, "that poor, poor man."

Holding a handkerchief to his blood soaked cheek, Frank had him walking fast now, clearing his head. "Keep goin' Harry, don't want to get involved wi' the police, keep walkin', need t'get a taxi!"

Marion had come down a notch from hysterical to highly emotional, "That man Harry, did you see what you did to that poor man, oh Harry. Harry? Oh what's happened?" Marion's tone dropped to a more reasonable level when she saw the bloodied handkerchief Harold was holding to his cheek. "Oh my God, your face Harry?" She was trotting alongside as Frank propelled them from the scene. "Don' care where we go but we've got to get away from that bar." Frank muttered.

"I'm all right Mari," Harold mumbled through the sodden handkerchief. "Just lost the place a bit. Calm down, I'm okay but the bastard cut me, used a blade on me."

A taxi rolled to a stop thanks to Frank's frantic waving and minutes later were outside their Pappachristos Street home. Frank paid the driver then followed the couple into the house. He ushered the big man into the bathroom, ran hot water into the wash hand basin, then said,

"Let's have a look Harry. I'll need to clean all that crap on your face first."

"I'll do it Frank," Marion stated quietly, "please, let me wash him." Her voice was soft yet firm. Frank stepped away casting a sidelong glance at Marion. She had regained her normal grace, was removing her husband's jacket and shirt.

"There's a first aid box in that cupboard Frank, will you get it for me please?" She was very calm. Frank marvelled at the change from the frantic female outside the bar to this controlled nurse figure tending the injured man. She dropped the bloodied handkerchief into a bucket.

Carefully she washed the blood and congealed mess from Harold's face holding his head low over the basin. The water changed from red to dark maroon then slowly she raised his head, fearing the worst. Holding the cloth against the injury she saw the apprehension in Harold's eyes. Steeling herself she eased the cloth away and stared at his cheek.

Harold saw the look on her face. "Is it bad?"

Marion held up a hand mirror, "You might have killed a man for that Harry!"

Harold looked at the glass and for a moment wondered if he was looking at the injured cheek. He switched to the right side of his face then back to the left. A small drop of blood swelled slowly about two inches under the left eye. He noticed another and yet another then saw the scratch. It was not a cut but a the shallow furrow of broken and slightly swollen skin.

"I thought ... it felt like a knife or something! Oh Jesus, the poor bastard!" Harold moaned. He was reeling with feelings ranging from relief to deep remorse. "Oh Christ all mighty, Marion!"

Frank standing at the bathroom door said with more confidence than he felt, "He'll be fine, a bloody nose made it look worse than it was. Now come on, I've put the kettle on."

"He got more than a bloody nose Frank," Harold murmured, recalling the first crashing blow as his forehead crunched into the close face feeling the nose bone collapse with the resilience of an egg shell. "Why the fuck did he come outside anyway, it was none of his business?"

"Please don't swear Harry, swearing doesn't help matters!" Marion's composure had fully returned as they sat down at the kitchen table. "Besides Harry, what started all the trouble? That seedy Fred character was disgusting, but surely he didn't deserve a hiding?"

"I over reacted," Harold muttered lighting a cigarette. To Marion and Frank it certainly looked that way, but Harold had his reasons for keeping the little weasel of a man quiet.

Harold had been in Akrotiri for three weeks, spending his free time in the Naafi, playing darts and snooker with the usual accompaniment of a half dozen beers. That may have been a pleasant pastime but there was nothing fulfilling about it, certainly not for three months. To break the monotony Harold decided one night to have a look around Limassol. Semi inebriated but still carrying the banner of celibacy, he met another airman from the base, Fred Parrott in one of the many bars in Hero's Square. Not a man fitting Harold's taste, but similarly alone and with a good line of cheerful patter, they both proceeded to down more of the fiery local brandy. They visited a selection of bars where dancing girls tripped in and out of dance routines, barmen and waiters fiddled the airmen's change until eventually they arrived at a brothel, thinly disguised as a bar. The women had pawed and plied drinks from the pair until Fred happily capitulated to their advances and staggered off with a woman to a room at the rear of the bar.

Harold had not taken the other 'ladies' very intimate offers, explaining he was merely waiting on his companion. How Harold would have behaved had there been a girl under thirty and had taken his fancy, is anyone's guess. The best that could be said about this bar was the ladies were 'experienced,' their looks fading and charms drooping. Being ultra selective, the young man was not attracted to their frayed appearances or doubtful offered delights.

Fifteen long minutes later, as the dreadful Fred had not surfaced and continually bothered by these creatures that had once been women, Harold left the bar.

Dragging deeply on his cigarette, Harold was afraid Fred Parrott might mention the night in the brothel. Fred whilst absent and partaking in the fruits of the establishment had not known his erstwhile drinking partner had left the bar with honour intact. Harold had simply taken the precaution to nip Fred in the bud, before he mentioned brothels or anything else.

Marion was looking at him, "Well, what did he do Harry, to deserve you dragging him outside? If you ignored him he would probably have gone back to his table."

"Pet," he said, "you saw him! He was poking his nose in where it was not wanted. That little bastard, sorry. Fred Parrott got off lightly with a couple of slaps compared to his mate. It was that greasy little shit that got me so angry and started all the trouble." Harold turned at Frank, "Remember the sexy blonde number giving Midnight such a hot time in the Gold Fish Bowl?"

"Me, I don't remember any sexy blonde," Frank laughed.

"Of course you don't, well that little whore happens to be the little scumbag's wife!"

Marion stared in undisguised shock, "You shouldn't talk about the girl like that. And you're wrong Harry, that girl in the club wasn't married!" she said indignantly.

Harold raised on eyebrow, "You noticed did you, don't miss much do you, Mari? No, she wasn't wearing a wedding ring, that doesn't mean she's not married? The truth is, the first thing that slut removes when entering a night club is her wedding ring, and the first thing she removes when leaving is her drawers!"

Frank although aware of Marion's tender presence could not help joining Harold's laughter at his lurid description of the fair Mrs. Parrott. Marion of course was shocked. "Oh Harry, don't talk like that, please, it's disgusting and besides, how do you know so much about this girl?"

Parrott's wife had made a move on him on one occasion but wasted no time moving on when Harold ignored her. Mrs. Parrott had plenty of takers.

Harold did not hesitate with his answer, had he done so Marion would notice immediately

"It's common knowledge on the base," Harold answered, "everyone knows she's the camp bike. Fred's brought her up to the Pen Club a couple of times when I was there. On both occasions he did not take his wife home. Somebody else did with Fred's approval! Both their morals are in the gutter Mari, where he ended up tonight!

Marion was silent for a moment then said, "Harry, I proved earlier tonight how naive I am, but these nick names and expressions everyone uses here. First it was Midnight, now 'camp bike.' What are you talking about?"

"You don't want to know!" Harold said, glancing at Frank.

"I DO want to know, I'm fed up! You use these terms all the time then fall over laughing and I'm left wondering what's so funny. What do you mean by 'camp bike'?"

"If you think about it, it's self explanatory Mari," he said placating her, trying to wriggle out of the corner. She was terribly naïve having lived 'the sheltered life' but Marion was a terrier! An innocent terrier certainly, but when she got her teeth into something she would not let go.

"Tell me!" she said in her soft but firm tone.

"Okay," he all but shouted, "all right!" Dragging deeply on his cigarette, giving himself time to think he started uncertainly. "Most sections on the base are issued with a bicycle. The reason for that is, first of all, there's no means of transport on camp like buses etc. So if someone wants to go from one section to another, deliver, collect paperwork for instance, because of the distance and time wasted walking between sections, he'll jump on the section bike and ride over to where he's going. Anyone from section 'A' for instance, can ride section 'As' bike. People from section 'B' can ride section 'Bs' bike and so on, well," he started to laugh, "if it's a camp bike, not belonging to any particular section, then anybody can ride it ...." he couldn't continue trying unsuccessfully to stifle his laughter.

Marion helped him when she said, "And she ..." she stared at her husband, "... she is the camp bike so any airman in the camp can ... oh Harry don't be ridiculous."

"You've got it, I'm afraid the sweet Pat Parrott is the camp bike," Harold stated emphatically.

"I don't believe you! They warned me I'd get my eyes opened out here and they were right! Anyway, I don't care as long as you were not one of her conquests?" She gave him a sidelong quizzical stare.

"Give me a break Mari! I've never, and never will, have anything to do with that slut. She's worse than a bitch in heat!" Harold looked into her eyes, "But it's entirely up to you my pet, you must make sure I never get that desperate." He meant what he said, Patricia Parrott, although a perfectly shaped and sexy young woman, had too many bunnies visiting her burrow, there was no challenge there.

Marion embarrassed at Harold's comment in front of Frank was not quite ready to drop the subject of the fascinating Pat Parrott, "She's such a bonnie girl Harry, how could she go with lots of men. And lots of men she doesn't know?" asked a wistful and thoughtful Marion.

"Being married to Fred could have a lot to do with it, that's bound to drive any woman daft!"

Frank smiled at Harold's words but he was growing tired, it had been a long day. "Don' know about you two but I'm about ready for my bed, sorry your, stroke, my bed. I'm so tired I don't think I'll be dreamin' about the erotic Mrs. Parrott tonight." He stood and stretched.

"I've shown you our bedroom Frank ... no, "Marion laughed, "I mean I've shown you your bedroom" She stifled a yawn, "and I agree I think I'll join you ... my goodness!" she giggled. "That's the second time you've done this to me ...." She stopped at the surprised look on the men's faces. "I'm sorry Frank, I'm so tired I'm talking in circles but I think I better explain. When I first saw you asleep on that nice big settee in Lyneham, you looked so comfortable and the settee so inviting I wanted to join you ... no, not you ... I mean when I saw you stretched out I thought 'Now that there is exactly what I need! No, not ..." She frowned, shook her head, then said plaintively, "Good night Harry, good night Frank, see you in the morning."

The men smiled as Marion left the kitchen."Just another reason why I love her," Harold said.

Frank nodded knowingly, bid Harold "Goodnight," then he too went to his room.

Harold strolled out to the veranda for a last cigarette in the hope it might calm his still jangled nerves. His mind went to the sickly Fred Parrott. 'Perhaps he was not as bad as the picture he presented, and what a life he must be leading, poor bastard, married to a bitch like Patricia Parrott. Maybe one had driven the other to lead such unsavoury lives, who knows? And who knows if Al 'Midnight' Johnson at this very moment is getting his leg over the lovely if utterly available Mrs. Parrott? Good luck to you Al. No doubt Harold would hear in technicolor detail from Al soon enough, and soon enough would be on Monday.'

On Monday morning Harold did not hear if Al 'Midnight' Johnson had bedded the wanton Mrs. Parrott. What he did hear at work was the chap on the receiving end of his vicious assault was a British army private who nearly died from his injuries. A particle of bone had lodged in the man's nasal channels and he was choking on his own blood. He was also bleeding from mouth cuts and teeth lost from the front of his mouth. The hospital had worked wonders and just got the injured man to the operating theatre in time. The minor injuries, like cracked cheekbones and lacerated eyebrows would mend without too much trouble, as the man was young and strong. The nose would require major plastic surgery.

The worry that plagued Harold was pushed aside, at least the man was alive. The purveyor of these ghastly details was no other than Fred Parrott. He had sought and found the dealer of the damage in the Akrotiri Station Workshops. Harold was working alone on a generator.

"Police are looking for you Harry, they want to lay a charge for assault and battery." Fred's black beady eyes were searching Harold's face, "But you don't have to worry. The police asked around the bar if anyone knew you, but the strangest thing Harry! Nobody knows you. They asked Bob McAleer too, that's the guy you beat up by the way. Once he regained consciousness they had the neck to ask him! Do you know what he told them? He said he had never seen you before in his life, which was absolutely true, but Bob could have referred them back to me, couldn't he Harry, for Bob knows you and I are 'big buddies,' don't he?" Fred's rat face and black glittering eyes looked up at Harold with a twisted sardonic smile.

"And what did you say when they asked you?" asked Harold, more than a little uneasy.

"What did I say?" sang Fred, "Do you know what I said?" He pushed his rat mouth so close Harold could almost feel the whiskers bristle. His breath was fetid as he hissed, "I said I didn't know you. Told them in so many words, 'I wouldn't want to know a cunt like you!' Don't you find that strange Harold fucking Ross, a low life degenerate fuck like me, he don't want to be associated with a high flying bastard fuck like yourself?"

~~~

Chapter 9

Harold yawned expansively. He stretched and tried to refocus but his eyes kept skipping off the page. Wednesday evening, there had been no call outs, no fires, nothing to break the monotony. Only two days left but this duty was driving him crazy with boredom. Fortunately the monotony would be relieved somewhat tonight, as it was his turn for cinema duty. The highlight of the Fire Picket week was two visits to the Astra. Harold had given his first cinema duty on Saturday to another picket, but wanted to see tonight's film. It was something called "Darling," with that sexy bitch Julie Christie starring and Julie was certainly Harold's darling.

Try as he might Harold had not found someone to stand in for his Fire Picket duty. This puzzled him for it was unusual not to find at least one airman who wanted to make some easy money. Harold made it clear he was prepared to pay over the top but still no takers. What the big man did not know was; word had spread from his own section that SAC Ross felt the lowly Fire Picket duty was below his station! That he, Harold Ross should not be subjected to such menial tasks. In addition to the rumour was the persistent projected atmosphere of discomfort, jealousy and mistrust emanating from Harold that made everyone in his close proximity feel inferior. Top grudge among the men and perhaps related to the green god of envy was the knowledge he was screwing the sexiest WAAF on the station. Many airmen would normally stand in for any duty for a fee but this time his call was universally ignored. This man somehow, without effort, always managed to claim the cream from the top of the milk. In any walk of life this was resented. He could do his own duty.

Separated from Marion for seven days and nights was hard work but the week, as he almost hourly reminded himself, was nearly over; two more nights then off home after work Friday. Marion had not taken it kindly when eventually he got round to informing her he would have to do 'another' week long duty.

Early on the morning he was to report for the duty, they lay in the quiet aftermath of making love. A point in time when Marion was at her softest, he again tried to explain - and lie.

She had to accept in his job, he told her, there was always the possibility he could be ordered to do two, or even more duties during his tour. The majority he emphasised, would do it only once, he had been unlucky! Simple as that. And other than emergencies he would do no more such duties. He went on to explain, truthfully, other trades could be heavily weighed down with shift work and duties, indeed, he was very lucky. Attached to a squadron he could be away for weeks on end. It was just unfortunate the Fire Picket had come so quickly after his last duty.

"I didn't know that" she had whispered in his ear.

"What part didn't you know pet?"

"The squadron bit. That men could be away for weeks."

Harold smiled into her sumptuously thick black hair that smelled of lemons and the wonderful essence of Marion herself, "It is the Air Force I have sworn allegiance to my hot little bundle of innocence, they do have first call on my services you know?"

"Ooh, why didn't you warn me about nasty duties? Nobody has first call on you but me!"

"Yes my sweet, I know that, but my boss the queen doesn't agree."

Marion looked deep in his eyes, "She may be your boss, my lovely sweet Harry, but I am your wife, your lover and I love you so very much."

Harold rolled off the bed in the Fire Picket billet and stood up. Whenever he thought of Marion arousal came hard and uncomfortably fast. Five days was a long time for an extremely healthy and vibrant young man.

He sighed heavily as through the barred window he saw a WAAF crossing the road. She entered the Main Guardroom and disappeared. Just seeing her made him congratulate himself on his stout refusal to contact Carol Cook. He could certainly use her right now. Pushing a hand into his pocket he adjusted his non issue Y-fronts around his painfully hard erection, 'Two more days that's all, just two more fucking days.'

SAC Jimmy Walsh, Harold's partner for the cinema duty came

213

Harold might have fared better for a partner for Walsh was a dour deadpan character. Harold felt if the cinema burst into a roaring inferno round them tonight he would have to dig Jimmy in the ribs to inform him the place was going up in flames.

Walsh sat on his bed and stared off into space. It was time to go but typically he said nothing waiting for Harold to make the first move. Harold checked the clock, put his book into the locker and pulled on his tunic. "Time we went sport," he said to the inert figure.

Walsh followed Harold into the office where they signed for the cinema duty, pulled on red arm bands with the word 'Fire' emblazoned in black letters. Both set out on the ten minute walk to the Astra.

They reported to the manager then proceeded to check fire appliances and the satisfactory operation of the fire escape doors. It was a cursory inspection, a facile part of the duty. Having completed their tour the two seated themselves in their reserved seats. These were the first two in the back row on the right of the entrance. The reason for this arrangement was so the manager knew exactly where to find the duty pickets if required.

The cinema was empty a good twenty minutes before the 7.00 start. Harold lit a cigarette, not offering or bothering to apologise to the zombie next to him it was his last one.

Despite the size of the fairly large cinema, it filled quickly. The lights dimmed with the last patrons queuing at the ticket office and a cartoon initiated the evening performance. Ten minutes after Harry had crushed out his cigarette in the small ash tray and just as the cartoon started Jimmy Walsh elaborately opened a full pack of Players and lit one. Raising his elbow high he pushed the pack into his breast pocket, making a show of reciprocating the ill manners shown by his partner. The little act in itself did not bother Harold but it occurred to him it might be best to buy a pack before the main feature started. Leaning over he informed Walsh he was nipping out to get some smokes and swung out into the isle. In so doing he blocked a couple just entering the cinema.

"Sorry," Harold said before looking into the girl's ice blue eyes. "Carol!" The word slipped from his mouth. No one could explain Harold's feelings as they simultaneously dropped to his boots and shot through the roof. "Harry!" Carol said at the same time he spoke her name, staring at one another in surprise, she taking in at a glance his arm band and working blue uniform. They stood awkward and silent for some seconds, a point not missed by a watching Jimmy Walsh or Carol's partner who eventually said, "Would you mind?"

A thousand signals had flashed between the two in that short space of time. Harold stepped aside allowing Carol and her partner to pass with a prolonged look from the man. Harold ignored him as he watched the shapely Carol pick her way down the darkened isle. He could not move, his breath knocked from him. He waited until the couple merged into s row of seated patrons. Only then did he force himself to turn and push through the exit curtains out into the bright foyer. He stood sucking air feeling he was surfacing from a deep underwater dive.

'God, that's a fucking woman,' he thought, his body on fire. 'Why do I fool myself I don't want her. It's bad enough trying to keep her out of my mind when she's not around but walking straight into her like that! Jesus, it's worse than a kick in the balls.' Muttering under his breath he battled to compose himself. Forget Carol, besides there was no way he could contact her with that suspicious escort glued to her side. He caught himself staring at his image in the long hall mirror whilst collecting his scattered thoughts. The first thing he needed was unfortunately unattainable, the second most certainly was! He needed to suck smoke deep inside his body almost as bad as his body needed to be deep inside that of the luscious Carol Cook.

He bought a pack of cigarettes at the machine and lit one immediately with trembling hands. All thoughts of Marion were gone, not gone precisely but the door to her compartment in his brain was firmly closed. He could not allow Marion's image to mangle the machinery of his central nervous system when all combinations were locked on this representative from the goddess Venus. This girl who had within her body the blissful power to lift his mortal being into the heights of pleasurable heaven. This conductor of fusible delights was this very minute sitting only a few yards away yet he could not reach out and tap into her reservoir of rapture.

He pushed his cigarette uncharacteristically into the sand of the fire bucket and returned to his seat. A travelogue was showing which he forced himself to watch. After a few seconds he could not stop his eyes sliding over the dozen rows to rest on the blonde head. His right eyebrow lowered and gnawed his lips in frustration.

The main feature started and even the delectable Julie Christie could not hold Harold's attention. His eyes and thoughts firmly locked on the back of Carol's head.

Twenty uneventful minutes passed then he saw Carol lean over and whisper in her partner's ear. She wended her way along the row into the isle, then turned towards the exit. As she approached he could vaguely make out her face in the dim light from the exit lamp above the doorway. As he knew they would be, Carol's eyes were searching then looking directly into his, then flicked towards the exit, back to his eyes, then back to the exit.

His stomach contracted with the wild surge of excitement. She could give no clearer signal.

Forcing himself to sit for what seemed much longer than the actual two minutes, Harold turned to Walsh, "This is a boring film, Jimmy, I'm going to take a walk around."

Walsh gave no indication of having heard. Harold couldn't care less. His groin was burning. Jimmy glanced over his shoulder at the flapping black curtains after Harold's hurried exit, "I'll bet you're going for a fucking walk!" Walsh worked for Air Traffic Control in the same office as Carol and knew she'd been seeing the bozo he was partnering on the Fire Picket. Their clandestine affair may have been under that title initially but it was now common knowledge. With a girl like Carol it would have been nigh impossible to keep her movements under wraps. 'Lucky bastard,' he thought sliding lower in his seat.

Harold entered the deserted foyer and looked around. Where could she be. Where, where, where? There was simply no place to go other than the toilets! He looked warily at the 'Ladies' sign. In his line of duty he had legal license to go anywhere if he suspected fire. There could be a fire in the Ladies toilet, couldn't there?

Again a quick glance around; nothing, nobody. He must hurry, time was short and his need was great. Everyone was in the cinema watching the delightful Julie being screwed by Lawrence Harvey or some other thespian. He hurried to the toilet and pushed the door open. A row of six cubicles and a waft of chemical fragrance greeted him. Lots of mirrors and wash hand basins but no Carol! He stepped inside, heart thudding at the back of his mouth but the place was unoccupied and dead quiet, apart from tinkling of a leaking water valve somewhere.

She had to be in here, she had to be. Then his heart leapt! The fourth cubicle door had the red 'occupied' sign in the slot. A glance at the others verified all showed 'vacant.' Surely the crazy wench would not hide in the cubicle when she must know he'd be looking for her. How would he know if it was Carol and not some other female in there? He was getting desperate, it had to be her. "Carol!" His rasping voice sounded strange echoing in resonance off the tiled walls.

The 'occupied' sign snapped to 'vacant,' the door opened. Carol smiled at him. "What took you so long?" she hissed.

Harold stepped inside pushing the girl against the wall and locked the door. He was kissing her and reaching under her skirt all in one frantic movement. Carol, ever the thoughtful, had removed her panties and Harold hurried to enter her, almost climaxing before he did so, then suddenly it was over. His thrusting, heaving hips continued for a minute then stilled but he held his shrinking manhood hard against the softness of her groin.

Harold gasped for air his face in the crook of her neck. "Jesus Christ Harry, talk about 'wham bam, thank you ma'am' and it's nice to see you again too!" she whispered huskily in his ear.

"Carol," he said taking time now to note the perfumed hair and smooth creamy neck, rubbing his mouth and nose into both, "I don't know what comes over me when I'm with you. I catch your scent then I'm like a stallion covering a mare, a dog with a bitch in heat, a ..." he stopped as Carol wriggled around. "Oh thank you very much, that's really nice, a bitch in heat am I? A bitch in fucking heat? Geez! It must be your slow build up and romantic foreplay that gets this bitch worked up. Give over." She tried to pull away from him.

He smiled into her neck pulling her buttocks firmly against him as his shrinking penis slipped from her, "Yes, you're a bitch and I'm a big randy dog but hang on. Your dog's just like a pot of boiling milk, too much heat and he boils over, but he's back to simmering slowly over a gentle glow now. Soon he'll be back on full heat. Don't you dare go away."

In the cinema the film played relentlessly on, extolling the life of a London model in the modern sixties. Carol's escort having long since lost the gist of the story, was growing increasingly agitated. She had been gone for half an hour and still no sign of her.

Jimmy Walsh watched the boyfriend grow restless, looking over his shoulder repeatedly at the exit door.

Jimmy went out to the foyer, not at all surprised to find there was no sign of the pair. He didn't exactly expect to find them rutting on the lobby floor so there was only two places they could be. The 'Ladies' or the 'Gents.' 'Christ, some people couldn't care less where they fuck! They say love is blind but their noses must be blocked up too if they can happily screw in shithouses.' Jimmy mulled miserably as he tried the Ladies toilet first. He saw the 'occupied' sign on the fourth cubicle right away then heard the diminutive but distinctive noises of fornication. Down on his knees, he peered under the six inch gap at the bottom of the door. He frowned when all he saw was the side on view of a pair of RAF issue black shoes whilst around the ankles the crumpled legs of working blue trousers. As he watched the heels were lifting in unison accompanied by small grunting sounds. Jimmy scowled.

Walsh stood up and knocked at the door, "Harry! I'd return that honey pot you've got in there to its rightful owner, before the angry bee comes and stings your bare arse!" He smiled, a rare event, and smiling at his own wit, an even rarer event. Walsh was not given to joking; then again it was not often he had the pleasure of interrupting people having sexual intercourse. He was of that peculiar breed who acquired a cruel form of delight when hurting people or interrupting pleasure of any sort.

"Who was that?" Carol whispered, blinking rapidly, unwinding her legs from Harold's hips.

She came back to earth with a bump as Harold set her unceremoniously back on her feet. "My partner, he's trying in his own sweet way to tell me your boyfriend's looking for you." They heard the outer toilet door close as Walsh left.

"Christ it's been ages Harry, what do I say?" asked Carol teetering on unsteady legs as she pulled on her panties then fluttered in alarm straightening her rumpled skirt.

218

"Just tell him you've got women's trouble, you don't have to go into details."

"I can't say that, he knows I came off last week!" Carol moaned.

Harold looked at her, "You're screwing around!" he stated, scowling at her.

Carol raised her eyebrows and shoulders simultaneously in a mute answer to his question.

"Tell him you're constipated or got the runs, whatever!" Harold said, piqued at her.

Carol nodded, understanding the edge in his voice. "Sorry Harry, but you know me," she smiled. "You can have your share like I told you before, anytime, and you can jump the queue like tonight, anytime, but don't expect me to hang around waiting for you to call."

"You won't wait after tonight but get rid of that bastard out there, I'm on duty. He could cause trouble for me." He kissed her quickly, "You go first, if the foyer's clear, knock on the door. I'll give you a few minutes to get settled before I make my appearance. But you get rid of him ... hear me? I'll be in touch."

She slipped out, followed by an almost immediate knock on the outer door. He checked his clothing before following. Entering the foyer again he was just in time to see Carol push through the dark curtains of the cinema. Near the kiosk there was a settee. Harold sat down gratefully, his leg muscles quivering after their recent exertions. Lighting a cigarette he sat back and meditated on what had just happened. There was something deliciously sexily evil about Carol; in complete contrast to Marion and he was unequivocally attracted to the base and gross debauchery this gorgeous creature offered. Just as paradoxically, he adored the pure clean love of his wife. Strangely he was not experiencing the guilt trauma as he had when Marion was in Scotland. His guilty conscience was replaced now by sorrow, yet the remorse was not for his wife Marion, but for his own weakness! He knew now he could never change, had known it all along. There was nothing he could do to control the wants and needs of his groin. He genuinely had tried, twice, and failed. These burning desires ever ruled his head. He wanted Marion near him, needed her extrasensory vibrations, her telepathic warmth and her tender lovemaking. It was because of all her

219

inherent wonders he could not, would never, abuse her and use her as he had Carol tonight. Against the wall in a ladies toilet? Marion? The very thought appalled him as it would his genteel wife. Yet Carol loved it, and so had he! The excitement, the degradation and fear of discovery all added to the exquisite mix of licentiousness. When this lethal concoction was injected into the bloodstream, every vein in the body caught fire, vastly more intoxicating than any drug.

Half an hour later the dark curtains swished noisily along their rail and snapped Harold from his musing. Jimmy Walsh after a cursory glance at Harold hooked back the heavy curtains. They waited for the National Anthem to reach its mournful end then the foyer filled with emerging patrons. Carol's blonde head appeared, a quick word to her boyfriend then made her way to the toilets. In so doing she had to pass the settee where Harold was now standing.

"Phone me!" she hissed, raising her eyebrows. Harold did not respond but glancing towards the boyfriend crashed straight into smouldering eyes watching him closely. Carol's escort understandably was not amused. Not wishing a confrontation Harold passed him and entered the cinema ignoring the burning glare. Whatever excuse Carol used to explain her absence, it obviously involved Harold. Fair enough, he couldn't care less.

Jimmy had already started down the right side of the theatre so Harold took the left. They checked for burning cigarettes etc. Some minutes later the pickets met in the foyer, reported to the cinema manager all points had been checked and found to be safe. Their duty done, they left to return to the Fire Station.

Harold, aware he was morally in debt to this dour man who had probably averted at the very least a dispute with Carol's escort, broke the silence. "Thanks mate," he said simply.

Walsh glanced at Harold with that typical baleful look, shook his head but said nothing.

Not sure what the shake of the head indicated Harold decided to ignore it, "How did you know where to find us?" he asked trying to ease open the conversational clam.

Again the sideways look and this time a slower head shake. This could become annoying.

"Look Jimmy," he began, exasperation spilling over the rims

of patience, "if you're trying to tell me something, feel free. Just don't give me any more of that shaking head!"

Walsh stopped, facing his partner belligerently, "I knew you were screwing that bitch!"

"I gathered that when you knocked the toilet door Sherlock, that's why I thanked you."

Walsh clearly did not care for Harold. Jealous and verbally outgunned, he slowly shook his head again.

"I asked you not to do that!" Harold said menacingly.

It appeared the threat went unheard. The head went on shaking accompanied with a glance at the heavens, then Walsh drawled, "I'm not talking about screwing her tonight." he smirked. "That cow works in my section where it's a well known fact you've been knocking the arse off her for months. It's only the past month she's been spreading her legs and allowing others to drink from her furry cup. I'm just waiting my turn." He grinned lasciviously enjoying the hurt he hoped he was inflicting.

The irrational thought scampered across Harold's mind that some men simply begged to catch a smack across the mouth, and Jimmy Walsh had just elevated himself to the top of that crazy people pile. With one last restraining strand on his temper he growled, "What do you mean, 'this past month?'"

"You've not been giving her enough, sport!" he spat out the term.

The strand snapped, Harold swung at him, but Walsh well warned by the flint struck glint in his partner's eyes, stepped back only just avoiding the clubbing fist. "Hit me pal and you're in big shit. Remember! We're on duty!" Jimmy Walsh was yelling now, trying to cool the fire he had been fanning.

The words were enough to restrain and choke back Harold's anger. Although shouting in panic, Walsh's words were true. Harold would be in deep trouble for attacking a colleague especially on duty.

Jimmy seeing the big man was controllable, was not finished, "Here's something else you might want to chew on pal. Before that twat started going out with you, she was very fussy who she handed her knickers to. Now," he laughed, "she's throwing them at anybody who wants to catch them!" He held up two fingers and wagged them in Harold's face, "So fuck you pal, you're not the only prick having the pleasure of dipping the delectable SACW fucking Cook!"

Harold fought to control himself. He could not allow this bright green with envy worm to antagonize him into raising his hands again. That most certainly would be risking a charge and no doubt a week or so of Confined to Barracks, plus when giving evidence Walsh would no doubt bring up the name of a certain S.A.C.W. Cook. C. Possible repercussions were endless. Then Walsh had to say something that broke through the limits of Harold's tightly held control, the literal straw that broke the sagging back of Harold's camel. "You're married sport, so does wifey know you're humping Cooky, or does she sometimes join in kinky threeso-"

A grabbing fist had Walsh before he stopped speaking. Then two hands were gripping his tunic and lifting him off his feet. The breath gushed from his body as Harold unceremoniously dumped him heavily on the ground. Flat on his back he lay, winded and surprised.

Straddling the prostrate figure, pinning his arms to the ground with his knees Harold proceeded to slap the unprotected face soundly across the cheeks in a swinging pendulum motion. He stopped after the eighth resounding smack and bent over nearer the cringing face. Resisting the strong urge to butt his head into the obsequious scowl beneath him for fear of breaking the skin, Harold hissed, "Listen you fucking turd! Don't you ever talk about my wife, EVER! Do you understand? Report me for this and you're the one who'll catch the shit for insulting my wife!" Gripping the unfortunate man's ears, he banged the head on the ground. "Do you fucking HEAR me?"

Walsh was nobody's fool. In the short time spent being slapped around, he realised the man sitting on his chest was not about to inflict any real damage to his person. The thought changed his flinching expression to that of defiance. Deciding not to answer the bellowed question, he adopted his usual belligerence, staring obstinately back at the figure on top of him.

Harold noted the change and realised he must get away otherwise he was going to smash those staring eyes into oblivion. Pushing away from the inert creature he stood and brushed himself down. Scooping up his beret he turned and stalked off.

Some minutes later he stopped and waited for his reptilian partner in the shadow of the Fire Station. Harold could not report back from a dual duty alone.

Halfway down a cigarette he saw the shambling figure come into view. Stepping from the shadows he entered the building. Jimmy watched the well set up figure of his partner precede him and the very explosive mix of hate and jealously burned in the craw of the bitter Walsh. Nobody had laid a finger on the form of Jimmy Walsh since his schooldays and his face still glowed from that bastard's neck wrenching slaps. 'I had to land that fucker for film duty,' he thought ruefully, but he could not mention the assault. He had let the big bastard off the hook with his comments about his twatting wife. Jimmy cursed himself for being so silly. He had indeed presented the big prick with the opportunity to hand out a few belts and each stinging slap had all but torn the head from his shoulders. 'But I'll get him,' he vowed sullenly, 'He'll step in his own shite one day, then I'll make him eat it.'

Next morning back at work, Harold quickly crossed the Ground Equipment Workshops floor and slipped into Ray Price's office after he saw the Chief taking his newspaper to the toilet. This meant a ten to fifteen minute free period for Harold to call Carol in private. He dialled Air Traffic Control and asked the girl who answered if he could speak to SACW Cook. After a couple of minutes of impatient waiting the instrument was picked up, "SACW Cook, hello?"

"Carol listen, there's a prick who works in your section with you -"

"Harry?" Carol cut in.

"Yeah," he said, "listen, I haven't much time. There's a creep who works in your section -"

"The place is full of creeps," she laughed.

"Will you listen! This one goes by the title of Walsh, Jimmy Walsh. He was my partner on the cinema duty last night."

"Yeah I didn't know it was him until after the show finished Yeah, so it must've been him that came into the toilets ... oh shit!"

"Never mind that, I had a bust up with him on our way back to the Fire Station, tried to tell me in great detail how you were screwing around."

"Screwing around?" she hissed in his ear.

"Yes, said you were screwing around but we covered that. What's worrying me is he knows about us, says it's common knowledge Carol. I'm worried in case this gets back to Marion and that little bastard is just the one to pass it on."

"I've not been screwing around!" she said indignantly, "I've been out with two blokes since I saw you last and one of them was the guy you saw me with last night. And he out of the two is the only one to have reached the promised land, besides I'm not a nun! You know I -"

"Okay okay, I understand. What I want to know is, do you know this little shite-hawk. Is he likely to do anything dangerous?"

"Yes I know him and 'shite-hawk' is the perfect description. Always bumping against me, trying to touch me up, but dangerous? I don't know, he's a classic wanker and wimp I'd say, frightened of his own shadow."

"Yes, thought as much, anyway I thought it best to warn you, he thinks he's next in line."

"What? Next in line! You mean with me? The only fucking thing he's in line for is a swift kick in the balls, and that's what he'll get if he says anything else about me!" she bristled.

"Like I once told you, you have the most delicate turn of phrase for a young lady," Harold chuckled at the image of an angry Carol. "Okay, drop him. I just wanted to tell you I've got to see you again, but be patient until I get my own car and get organised. I'll work something out."

"Car!" Carol sounded pleasantly surprised, "You're buying a car?"

"Yeah, something to get us out of the way, and some privacy."

"Harry," she breathed huskily down the mouthpiece. "See if you can get a van."

"A van, why a van?"

"Use your imagination," she whispered. "A friend back in Essex told me her boyfriend had a van and God, the antics they got up to. See if you can get a van with a bed in the ba-"

"Sorry Carol," Harold cut her off. "Have to go, Price is on his way back. I'll be in touch."

Telephone calls were not banned but Harold could hardly

224

call Carol openly and discuss the things they had to talk about with the envious old Chief listening to the conversation. Harold had donned the cap of respectability since Marion domiciled herself in their Limassol home so had no wish to feed scraps of scandal to the gossip hungry Chief Tech. Ray Price.

Harold returned to the Workshops floor with Carol's words ringing in his ears. 'The randy bitch,' he thought, 'buy a van with a bed in the back! Mnn, not bad, not a bad idea at all.'

~~~

Chapter 10

In the two weeks since their arrival at 103 Maintenance Unit Frank Connolly and Ray Buckley quickly settled into camp routine. Being competent tradesmen work was similar in their new environment and both attended daily tug-of-war training with the onset of the new season only weeks away. There was always plenty to keep them occupied. In the evenings there was the occasional visit to Limassol for meals and a few drinks, but most nights the NAAFI took care of their social needs. Frank, a fair snooker player, usually managed to beat Ray at the table game but the Londoner was in a league of his own at darts. He had the uncanny habit of hitting his target if not with one out of two, certainly with one out of three darts. The dizzy heights of Frank's experience in throwing the little arrows were for a social pint in his local 'Commie Bar' in Leuchars village. The Scot could never hope to beat Ray without the latter's help in bending the rules. In '301' the player must score that amount of points precisely, must start and finish with a 'double.' Ray would allow Frank a 'straight start,' in other words to start scoring without hitting a 'double.' This turned out to be no real handicap for the flap eared joker. With his first dart Ray normally hit double sixteen, then proceeded to score freely. The handicap was increased; the Scot was given one hundred points plus the straight start, which brought the two closer but Frank's inability to finish, to land a dart in a closing 'double,' inevitably cost him the game. However playing with the much better Ray, Frank's throwing arm improved marginally with every game.

The Naafi was as usual fairly busy on the Wednesday prior to the fortnightly payday Thursday. These bi-monthly Wednesday nights, were openly labelled penniless, or 'skint' nights when most airmen had too much week left at the end of their pay. Contrariwise pre-payday nights had the ability for airmen to lick around every nook and cranny of their pockets, seeking every last mil and piastre to buy a last whiskey or beer. Every airman on the base knew the revered Golden Eagle would the following day defecate into their outstretched palms, a golden egg in the form of a fortnight's wages. And it was every airmen's dream and heartfelt prayer that one day the afore mentioned bird might develop a bad case of diarrhoea.

Those who still had a few bob left on a pre payday Wednesday night would rather spend it in the Naafi thus saving the taxi fare to and from Limassol. Beer, smokes and food were cheaper in the Naafi, facilities plentiful, which included the rare pleasure of chatting up British girls that tended the various bars. These die hard airmen chose to ignore the quite horrendous odds of around a hundred to one in the girls favour.

Girls were the last things on the minds of Frank Connolly and Julian Cantwell however as they sat at a table, waiting for a board to become available in the area set up for playing darts. All five boards were in use whilst those waiting their turn chalked their name on the bottom of a list beside each board. Ray Buckley who had left the pair to add his name at board No.2, rejoined them. "Fifteen minutes I reckon before we get a game," Ray moaned then supping his beer reverted to their subject of discussion, "It can't be long before the MU sports day Julie, will that be our first competitive pull?"

Julian nodded, "Yes, but I don't know if it's all that competitive Ray, it's only section teams."

"Then Barrymore's MU team, it must get broken up for that day," Frank stated.

"Yes of course. Clarkeson and Gaskew will be pulling for us in our GEF team, along with you Frank, you too Ray - and I assume Josh. You'll have to pick three other blokes from the GEF yard to make up the team. The Motor Transport section have three chaps from the MU team so they'll represent the MT section. It is the MU sports day after all, so the meeting is only for athletes and teams from sections within the Maintenance Unit." Julian shrugged, "It's more a pipe opener for our athletes whose main targets are the bigger events later in the season. You can't compare our tiny sporting 'get together' on the MU with the main Akrotiri sports meeting. We are after all, only one little tree in their forest."

Frank smiled at the comparison, "Do many sections enter

tug-o'-war teams?"

"No not many, three or four. The finalists are usually our yard and the MT. If you look back over the records it's either the Motor Transport or us that win. As I say it's more a fun day."

"Does Barrymore pick our GEF team?" Ray asked thoughtfully.

"No no, he's already told Callum to pick a team. It will be good experience for him."

"I heard talk the league might be startin' in a couple of weeks. Anythin' on that score Julie?"

"I know nothing about the league yet. We're waiting for a Royal Corps of Transport sergeant in Dhekelia to send the fixture list. The Army organises league fixtures and draw for the knock out cup. Don't worry Frank you'll cut your teeth in Mr. Barrymore's team soon enough."

"And me Julie, I suppose I'll lose my teeth before I get into his team?" Ray growled.

Julian laughed, "You're on his short list Ray, I know that for a fact. Twice I've seen him write something on that board he always carries when watching you and the other possibles. What he writes however only the boss knows. He doesn't tell me everything!"

Ray scratched an ear, "I know what he writes. It's my fucking ankles, they keep bending, losing strength after a couple of minutes on the rope. But pull! I can pull as well as any bastard," he glanced at Frank. "Including you, you Scottish twat! I just don't know what it is with them," he rubbed an ankle. "They just start to bend and I start to slide, not much but enough for me to slip and chop around. Of course old 'hawk eye' doesn't miss these things and writes me off!"

There was a slight pause after Ray's outpouring before Julian said, "Ray, Mr. Barrymore has not written you off. I know because he would not waste time if he thought you had nothing to offer. You know Jim Clarkeson, works alongside Frank in the Machine shop?" A slight nod as Julian went on, "He is thirty six years old, used to slip all the time, angle of pulling too high or too low, his knees were too straight or too bent. Whatever it was, only the boss saw potential in Jim. He spent a year and a half under Errol's scrutiny before Jim got his chance. Now there is no better man in the team apart from perhaps Colin Drake. But

Clarkeson is the rock in the middle, and Errol moulded that rock!"

Ray looked at Julian for a long spell then smiled, "If nobody else loves ya cuddles, Ah fuckin' loves ya!" he growled. "If evah in da future Ah shows doubts, yo' just preach dat whole sermon on me agin."

Frank smiled at his crazy friend but was surprised to see tinges of red creep up Julian's neck. The irrepressible Ray saw it too, "And don' yo go blushin' on me now, yo captivatin' slut!" Julian tittered then said, "Much as I hate to stop you, I see your board is vacant."

"D'you fancy a game Julie?" Ray asked.

"Please specify Ray, exactly what game am I being invited to play?" Julian asked delicately.

"Later, later," Ray made an exaggerated wide eyed sweep round the tables then bending over whispered, "Darts me little beauty, for the moment anyway."

"I don't play darts as you well know, but I can count. From what I hear you can throw a lovely dart Ray but you cannot count, therefore I am almost certain once we have mixed our talents we will make the perfect couple together. So, lead me to the dartboard please, if you have no intention of leading me elsewhere." Julian winked at Ray, "You bastard Julie, you're going to get the surprise of your life when you bend over to pick up the ten bob note I'm about to drop at your feet."

"At last, a firm promise," Julian clasped his hands, "and it seems I'm to get ten bob too!"

With Julian taking his stance dutifully by the marking board and after some warm up throws, Frank noticed Ray's darts were not landing in the double sixteen slot. In nine throws he hit the double only once! Frank looked at him questionably to which Ray just shrugged.

"Off your game pal?" Frank said confidently, "Happens to us all. An' I've a feelin' in my water, even before I saw you throwin' like an old wumman I'm goin' to thump you tonight, so no handicap, okay?"

"Suit yourself. Middle for diddle?" Ray said throwing a dart to decide who would throw first.

The game started but Ray was much too casual, not throwing anything like his normal game.

Frank laboriously chipped away at his score but was stuck, having missed his finishing double with six darts. Ray was in no man's land having twice burst on double one. Taking careful aim Frank held the dart in line with his eye and his elusive double five bed. He threw. 'Shit, a gnats cock outside the wire.' Same procedure again followed by the most delicious of soft thuds. At the end of the five wedge in the narrow bed of the encircling outer ring nestled Frank's dart. He was elated, slapping his rather reserved friend on the back, "Got ye at last, ya big bugger!"

Ray nodded with an unusual comical grin. He was acting very strange, "Mugs away then!"

Frank's brow furrowed, his eyes narrowed. Ray was too calm, not in the least upset that Frank had finally beaten him. In the past Ray had kicked himself in frustration when narrowly missing yet here he was calmly throwing darts like a beginner! 'No,' Frank reasoned, 'something's no' quite gelling. He could never play this badly, so he's up to something.' The canny Scot looked around the immediate area. Everything seemed normal; airmen throwing darts at the other boards, a little noisy but nothing unusual; groups waiting their turn, others sitting at tables drinking, voices mixing in the general hubbub of acceptable background noises. Ray was throwing again but Frank was not interested where they landed. The train of curiosity had taken off in his brain and was searching for something amiss, something out of step. Again he looked around; the next two airmen waiting for a game, who had been casually talking to Julian a few seconds ago, were watching Ray's darts. Were they watching too closely? 'No I'm dreamin',' he thought squeezing his eyes shut in frustration, yet nothing else seemed to snag his searching brain. 'Could that be it?'

"Ray," Frank caught his partner's attention on his return from the board after another futile attempt at a double. "Why are you playin' so badly?"

For an answer Frank again received a comical grin and a flick of the eyebrows.

"I have a funny feelin' Ray. I just hope to God you're not tryin' what I think you're tryin'?"

This time a covert wink. "Don't worry, they're shysters, I've seen them at it in town."

"Oh shit! Don't like this," Frank said unbuttoning his shirt

230

giving his hands something to do.

"Look just go along with me for a laugh. See how it turns out," Ray whispered.

"Don't like this, I mean we don't know these guys, for fuck sake," Frank mumbled.

"We couldn't do it if we knew them. Come on you're being a wet fart. Let's have a laugh."

Somehow they got through the second game, which Ray 'won,' and in the third Frank pulled himself together and played what was for him, a very good winning game. He was under no illusions had Ray been trying it would have been no contest. With their best of three games completed, they moved aside and rejoined Julian.

One of the two men stroked a line through the name 'Tighe' then pushed around Julian to get to the board, "'scuse me" he said, then stopped in front of Frank. Before the man uttered a word Frank knew the trap had sprung. "You lads wouldn't like to play a foursome now would ya?" The accent was broad Irish.

"No, not me, I don't -" Frank started but the Irishman cut him off.

"Shoar you wait an hour an' then you're on the board for what, five minutes. A foursome we could get t' best of t'ree games, ye know, an' we could do dat twice, whadya say?"

Ray stepped in looking at his watch, "Why not Frank, we've got nothing better to do and plenty of time to do it in?" he flashed a wide smile. Frank said nothing but his concurrence seemed to be accepted.

The Irishman said, "Were all average players here, whar about mekkin' it interestin'. Whadya say we play forra small side bet, coupla bob, dat's all?"

"Side bet?" said Frank looking at Ray.

"Justa mek it interestin' ye unnerstan'. Whadya say, five bob then, is that better?"

Side bets were usually for drinks, usually a pint. Five shillings could buy four pints of beer at Naafi prices. Ray said, "Five shillings is high for a friendly game."

The man shrugged and Ray playing his hand as well as any professional hustler went on, "Well I'm fairly flush and the way you're scoring Frankie, five bob isn't too much of a gamble. What do you think, five shillings all right with you?" Before

Frank could answer Ray went on, "Right, okay then, middle for diddle?"

"Yeah, an' is it yer buddy there that's markin' t' board? He did a perfect job for you two?"

Julian nodded.

"Foine," the man said turning to his partner, "T'row for bull Pete," he said then added, "Oh forgive my ignorance. Dis one here is Pete, Pete Oldham, from Birmingham! Can ya believe dat? And I'm John Tighe, I t'ink ya kin guess where I'm from." He grinned broadly.

Ray did the introductions for his trio then after warming up they watched Pete throw just outside the outer bull. Ray's dart was marginally farther away. 'What's he playin' at,' Frank thought. 'I hope he knows what he's doin'.'

"It's 501 right, an' we'll extend the game a little. Start with a double, okay?" Pete asked.

Ray smiled inwardly. The pair had obviously been watching Frank and Ray. Ray hardly landed in a double all night and Frank was throwing slightly better than his usual mediocre darts. Pete wanted to open the new games with a double hoping to delay Ray and Frank's scoring. 'Yep, they've done this before.'

"I t'ink dat's foine?" John said. "We might as well mek use of t' board, you agree Ray?"

Twenty minutes later after excellent but clever throwing by Ray and some fairly steady scoring by Frank, they won the first set by two matches to one. Ray made a show of exuberance when retrieving his winning dart nestled tightly in the corner of the double sixteen. "You beauty!" He called giving Frank a slap on the back.

Pete threw his last dart, unnecessary as the game was over, but it landed in the double twenty, which would have won the game, had Ray missed. "You just got there mate," Pete said retrieving his dart.

"True," answered Ray jovially, "but we got there first old son, and to the victor, the spoils."

"Whoa boy, whoa, just a minute," John interrupted. "Shore we've another game t' play, haven't we, that was the agreement was it not. We were t' have two matches, isn't that right?"

"Yes that's right, but we won that game John, so we get our truly won gains," Ray smiled.

"Not a bit of it, not a bit of it man. Shore it's double or quits, a winner must surely give the loser a chance to get his money back, it's only ferr." His expression was quizzical but firm.

Frank always the middleman in matters of fair play, stepped in, "We agreed to play the best of three games. The losers were to pay the winners five shillins. Right? There was nothin' said about doublin' the stakes for the second set but ...." Frank glanced at Ray who gave a nod, "we'll give you the chance of gettin' your money back, which in truth John, we haven't seen the colour of yet."

"And you know what the actress said to the bishop, don't you John?" Ray volunteered.

"Oh that pore old fockin' actress, she's gettin' done again," said John, "No, what'd she say?"

"No pay, no play!" Ray grinned, "So if you'll kindly give Julian your ten shillings, which you will get back if you win, then we'll get on."

Pete was first to hand his money to Julian but John dug into each pocket a dozen times before producing a grubby ten shilling note, which Julian accepted delicately giving him Pete's two half crowns back in change.

The pattern of the games was as before only slightly more tense, more close, but as the games progressed, Frank's scoring rate dropped alarmingly. One game each and the deciding third game started with Pete getting off to a flyer. His first dart landing in double sixteen. Frank was unlucky in his attempt at a double then John scored one hundred. Ray got off with a double twenty and two singles, eighty, which kept the other pair in sight. However they were well behind, and Ray could not expose his talent too dramatically. He wondered as he stepped away after scoring one hundred, if he had let the game slip. It fell to Pete who followed Ray, with the first opportunity of a finish. He stepped up to the board with eighty three to close. With a quick calculation Pete decided on treble seventeen, double sixteen.

The match, as far as Pete was concerned was as good as over. Even if he only managed three seventeens, John would surely finish on the double sixteen before the big guy Ray got back to the board. The other bloke, Frank was moderate, half his darts were wild. Taking careful aim Pete threw at the treble seventeen then blinked as luck deserted him. The wire clicked as the dart slipped past the treble, stuck fast in single seventeen. Taking more than his usual time to line up on the double seventeen he carefully rocked his hand back and threw just as someone at the next board roared in delight when throwing his winning dart. Whether it was the ill-timed shout or the quality of the throw, the dart landed outside the double. Not in the least perturbed, Pete this time without pausing in his action threw again, landing plumb in the middle of the double seventeen.

"Darts partner," John said, appreciating the double sixteen finish Pete left him.

Frank's total was one hundred and five. Uncertain of the best way to reach that amount he stepped on the rubber mat and toed the line. Ray saw his uncertainty, "Knock off the odd number anywhere at the bottom of the board Frankie, get an odd number."

"C'mon Ray, no speech play," cried the Irishman.

"Sorry, but he's not sure of the scoring," answered Ray, who knew the set was lost anyway with John on an easy double.

"Makes no difference chappie, he's t'rowin' his darts, an' he kin count for himself. Leave the man be, will ya?" John retorted.

Frank meanwhile was studying the bottom half of the board. There was a clump of odd numbers. The wedge of the three was straddled on one side with nineteen whilst on the other was seventeen. Funny he had never noticed that before, and seven was next to nineteen. The nineteen looked the most inviting. Taking extra careful aim he threw.

"Och," he groaned. All that wide area of four numbers to land in and his dart nestled in the tiny outer strip of double nineteen. Thirty eight scored and still the odd number to knock off.

'Bastard,' Frank muttered bitterly at his bad luck and at the thought of letting Ray down. He threw carefully at the nineteen again. 'Sweet Jesus, I've balled this up.' His dart finished two wedges to the right in the single seventeen. Frank was still adding up, trying to deduct from the total when a watching airman at one of the tables shouted, "Go for the bull mate!"

Frank nodded when he realized his score of fifty five left him with a round fifty to finish, and a bull scored fifty exactly! But could he finish the game on a bull? He turned to Ray for confirmation and received a quick nod, then aware John was about to complain again, Frank said, "Look John, I'm not clued up on the rules, so I'm askin' you. Can I finish on a bull?"

John looked around expansively tilting his head sideways, "'Can Oi finish on a bull?' he sez." Turning back to Frank after his theatrics he went on, "Course ye can Frankie boy, now git on wit' it, an' if ye getit, not only can ye keep our ten shillin's, what say ye that I kiss yer arse for a bonus, how's dat?"

The comment brought ripples of laughter from the handful of spectators. John's effort at a joke bore the unmistakable stamp of trying to sidetrack the thrower, distract his concentration from the serious job in hand. In some cases it worked but John's comment did not register with Frank. He was thinking of only one thing; that little half inch circle in the centre of the board. He stared at it, knowing if he waited too long he wouldn't get anywhere near it. He was aligning the point of the dart with his own eye and the bull, when John called out, "I've jest the double sexteen to git, in't that right Pete?"

Frank never heard the words and certainly not the answer as he drew the dart back past his ear and threw. He did not see it land, his pent up excitement blinding him for that second. He had to blink; could it be? Sticking out of the board at a slight angle inside the circular wire of the bull was his dart! Ray was pumping his hand as Frank had taken an involuntary step closer to look at the result of his throw, peering at it unbelievably. "That is absolutely fuckin' incredible, I can't believe it!"

"Naw! Neither can I!" muttered the Irishman, "I just hope ye had a fockin' bath before yeh's come up here t'night." he added miserably.

Frank was jubilant, he laughed too heartily at the Irishman's comment and Julian was shaking his hand, "Beautiful finish Frank, well done!"

"Thanks Julie," he gave his friend's hand an extra squeeze, then turning back to the Irishman who was still shaking his head, "John I feel fantastic, I have never thrown darts like that in my life, I swear!"

"I don't suppose my ten bob had anythin' t'do wit' you comin' good t'night, now would it?"

"You're ten bob had everythin' to do with it John ma boy. But just to show you I'm not the mercenary you think I am, let me buy you and Pete a pint."

"Hey, der must still be a God in heaven!" cried John, "t'ought you would niver ask."

The five airmen made their way into the lounge area and Frank took the order, collected his winnings from Julian then walked over to the bar. "Two pints Double Diamond, two cans Tennant's lager and a brandy sour," he ordered from the girl behind the bar. Feeling he was floating on a cloud, Frank added, "An' maybe you'd like a wee lemonade for yourself?"

"Oh, I hope you are not trying to buy yourself into my favours, throwing your money around like that," the pert little redhead said as she pranced to and fro making up the drinks.

"Not tonight Josephine, but you'll go into the notebook for future reference," Frank smiled.

The girl raised her head as she dipped the glass rim into a sugar bowl for the brandy sour, "'ere! Oo you callin' Josephine then? Name's Linda, and if you want Linda nestling in your notebook or anywhere else, you better put a gin in that orange. Don't like lemonade, all right?"

"A gin it is Linda my little beauty, and what do I owe you?"

Linda totted up the total and handed him the slip, "Seeing it's you, a Scotsman throwing his money around, such an unusual sight," she grinned, "we'll make it a round eight shillin's if you please. And thanks for the drink Mr. Carnegie, there's not many that buys a girl a drink these days that don't expect a little rough and tumble to follow!" She winked and smiled, accepting the recently acquired note Frank fished from his pocket.

"Aye well your luck is in tonight lassie, for had I not been a happily married man I most certainly would be looking for more. Ah well easy come easy go. Here ye are, ya ravishing wee redhead, my hard earned winnins."

"Winnings?" Linda asked, her eyes giving him a sidelong stare.

"Aye, won it at the darts," Frank answered grandly.

Linda glanced past Frank in the direction of the tables, "Who'd you win it from?"

Frank followed her gaze, "That guy wi' the green shirt, an' his mate sitting beside him."

"Oh that's John Tighe, and Pete Oldham," she laughed. "They've been taking money off mugs at the darts for months! You must be good to take money off them!" Linda laughed again, "It's funny isn't it? Usually it's them buying me a drink with the money they've won, now you're buying and this time they're the chumps."

"Aye, either way you're still gettin' your drink Linda, see you later at the back door then!" He gave an exaggerated wink then carried the tray back to the table. "Just before we get into our beer I want to tell you two that we, Ray and I took you two, that's you Pete and you John, for a couple of mugs tonight." Frank took a long hard swallow at his pint. "And before I get told I'm talkin' through drink let me say, tonight I personally played out of my skin, but Ray was shit!" Frank looked first into Pete's, then John's eyes, "You see, there was two things I didn't know when we started; the first was that I would play so well, an' the second was that you two have been takin' money off blokes, mugs for months now."

John's eyes screwed up, "Look Frank, are you sayin' that you two are a pair o' shysters?"

Ray was about to speak but Frank cut him off, "Yes and no! No means we've never done it before, and yes, we did it tonight! I think you should know that Ray here, when he's on form, could give either of you a hundred start and beat the shit out o' the pair o' ye. Listen, I did it for a laugh, not for the money. As it turned out you two can play well anyway, but it rubs me the wrong way to think you've been beatin' blokes like me out o' their drinkin' money for it seems, quite a while now. I'm just chuffed that we took your money tonight. When you saw us settin' up our trap, throwin' darts all over the board, you thought you would cream us, another couple o' dafties to contribute to your drinkin' money. Well you fell short, I normally don't play so good but knew I had good backup. I've seen Ray finish a game of 301 in seven darts, double start and finish!" Frank nodded emphatically, his temper rising, "I don't like bein' taken for a mug Mick, I think you should both take your drinks and piss off out o' my sight!"

There was a becalmed stillness around the table. Julian shuffled uncomfortably. Ray looked on edge, his eyes flicking between Pete and John. Frank's voice had risen towards the end of his tirade. Everyone within hearing distance was hushed. John was looking up at Frank calmly, allowing a time gap to grow and the heat to cool before he spoke.

"I may, or I may not be a t'ick Oirishman, but if you have somet'in' to say, I wish t' fock you would come right out an' say it!"

Frank and the others stared at John, before he carried on, "An; if by dis little outburst you t'ink you are NOT gonna get your arse kissed, you are very, very wrong! John Tighe ALWAYS pays his debts, so if you would be so kind as to drap your keks, I will pucker up me lips!"

Frank's sense of humour dissolved the tension when he exploded in laughter along with the others. John smiled, reached over to Frank's tray for a beer and took a long drink allowing the laughter to subside. "Shore now, what were we gittin' uptight about? It's true Pete and meself have been playin' darts here, and in town, for a few beers but where's d'harm in dat? As for our ability, well now we reckon we're fairly good but just a bollocks hair above t' average pub player. Aye, an' it's true we've won more than we've lost, but we have lost, and paid up, just like t'night. If it's true what you tell me about Ray here, then it's you two that's been doin' the hustlin', not Pete an' meself. An' finally Jock," John leaned forward towards Frank, "me name's not Mick, it's John. I t'ought you knew dat."

There was another awkward silence. Frank who had never been the one to back off from a confrontation was also never slow to offer his apologies when the situation demanded it.

"What can I say John, maybe I put too much credit into somethin' I just heard. Anyway, I'm sorry for speakin' the way I did."

John looked at Pete, "Whadya say Pete, should we let these scoundrels off light?"

Pete who had actually said very little all evening, looked at no one in particular while slowly scratching his chin, then he picked up his glass and took a long drink of beer.

"Just when you're good and ready now, don't go brekin' your neck givin' us an answer."

Pete lit a cigarette, blew a blue trail of smoke before speaking, "After due consideration and having heard presentation from both parties, I'm in the process of weighing the pros and cons." John nodded his head enthusiastically, eyes wide and expectant. Pete went on, "I think the only route for these competitors to redeem themselves is for them to remunerate the aggrieved parties with a supplementary cycle of inebriating libations, after which, all demerits shall be wiped clean from the slate."

John stared at his friend, "Whatever it was our man said, I agree wit' him wholeheartedly."

It was amazing how in service life, a situation which had existed only minutes before with individuals set on a collision course, could be diverted with a few well chosen words. The quintet settled down to a chatting laughing group and after an hour the topic of conversation had covered a wide range of subjects from jaunting-cars in Ireland to rally driving in England, salmon fishing in Scotland peppered with snippets of soccer from Birmingham to Julian's wonders of London. The conversation inevitably swung to tug-of-war, for as it turned out John and Pete both worked in the Motor Transport section on the MU. Both were Senior Aircraftsmen Driver Mechanics and had been on the island for fourteen months, having arrived within days of each other. Strangely they claimed not to be enjoying their stay on the island. Pete had boxed for the RAF but gave it up since his arrival in Cyprus. He was now dedicating all his free time to blowing his wages in the Limassol clubs and pubs, wining and dining the girls and generally having a wild time with his Irish friend.

John Tighe was the ideal single man's accessory. He took nothing serious, loved the good life, was an easy come, easy go, happy go lucky character blessed with the patience of Job, and rarely got upset at anything. Life was too short to burn energy over the mundane aspects and problems of everyday life.

"As you both work on the MU have you never thought of giving it a try?" Julian asked, "After all you must be surrounded constantly with talk of tug-of-war."

"It seems such a waste of energy. We went one time, Pete and I, t'watch ye train. Ye put all that effort t' git that bloody big tin filled with mettle and t'ings up to the top o' dat tripod, den when you git it there, what do you do? You let the bloody t'ing down again, what's the point?"

"The point is John, that 'tin' as you call it, represents another, slightly heavier team, and pulling it up simulates a real pull. The blokes doing the pulling are perfecting styles, hardening hands, toning muscles, getting the correct chopping angles, pulling in unison. There's a dozen things the blokes learn on that gantry." Julian patiently explained.

John thought for a moment, "Yeah, t'ought there was more to it than met the eye."

"There is," Frank said, "and they're a great bunch o' blokes, you'd like them."

"There's another little item that might appeal to you two," Ray got into the act. "After every competition there's a piss up, free, and from what I hear, the MU, because of their reputation are treated like royalty."

"Dis is beginnin' t' sound better an' better, what d'ya t'ink Pete?"

"Yeah, sounds okay," the man of many words had spoken.

"Right, I'm convinced!" John said, "not, you understand that I'm in the least interested in this tug-o'-war lark, but darts an' the company," he nodded at Pete, "are gittin' a bitty tiresome. I've got to wind dis bastard up before we come out nights, you can see dat fur yourselves now. Look at 'im, he's beginnin' t' run down already, ye can see dat, can't ye?" He shook his head sadly.

Pete gave a benign smile indicating he was still grasping the edges of the conversation.

John turned to Julian, "Okay kiddo, tell me what we'll need, an' anythin' an' everythin' we'll have t' do t' get started. Niver mind Pete, I'll have t' repeat everythin' t' him in the mornin' anyway. He's not wit' us right now ye see, ye realize dat don't yes, he's off fockin' some burd somewhere in the back of his moind. Jaysus, what a memory he must have."

Julian was immensely pleased. The two latest recruits weighed in around the twelve stone mark, looked strong with athletic figures. Although claiming to have spent most of their free time in the NAAFI and Limassol bars, the pair looked surprisingly fit and did not appear to be carrying excess weight. "Okay John, tomorrow at eleven o'clock, behind a row of marquees."

~~~

Chapter 11

Callum watched the bucket jerk its unsteady way up the gantry. The eight men on the rope were a mixture of first team, reserves and newcomers who would represent the GEF section at the 103 Maintenance Unit sports meeting the following day. The smaller sections on the MU had sportingly made a few entries more in the spirit of the event rather than in the hope of winning. From larger sections, along with genuine athletes, they   added half dozen or more worthies in various events simply to make up numbers. So much so that one airman, having reluctantly entered to run in his first mile race, turned up at the track in an attempt to do some training. Casually joined by a bona fide athlete as the pair started to jog round the track, the athlete asked, "I'm also entered for the mile, I've managed four minutes 20 seconds, what's your best time?" Our reluctant hero gasped, "Don't know ... haven't got a calendar!"

There were however a modicum of established athletes on the MU who used the gathering to gauge fitness for the major meetings later the season. Included in this group were the tug-of-war fraternity who never took any match frivolously. These included the GEF and MT sections, which between them boasted the majority of the team that represented the Maintenance Unit.

Interesting inclusions to the MT team were the latest converts John Tighe and Pete Oldham.

~~~~

Callum's amalgamated team were uncoordinated in their heaves, their shouts a staccato disconnected rattle. Nevertheless, although not the finished article they were not far off. Callum watched his No.3 and the same thought that crossed Barrymore's mind, flashed through his, 'If only I had eight Connollys.' There was no doubt about the Scot's ability. If an onlooker who had never witnessed a tug-of-war team in action, he would easily pick out this man as the complete athlete. Strong, resolute, lithe and his precise well balanced hands re-gripping the rope. The bucket in its seventh vertical climb that morning was stationary halfway between its nadir and zenith but showing signs of strain, like a tense bird poised to take flight. They were into their third minute, and gravity with the assistance of time was winding on the pressure.

After holding the dead weight midway for a reasonable length of time, Callum wanted to see if they had the strength to take the bucket to the top. Crouching down, his back to the 'opposition' bucket Callum called, "To the top now lads, on my call."

With his "And," and their responsive "Yes," the coach got them moving, the bucket jerking fitfully upwards and soon the heavy steel container hit the gantry top. "Hold it, hold it," Callum roared noting the unsettling effect the sudden jolt had on the eight men. For a second the bucket hung suspended then slowly, silently it inched earthwards. Then suddenly as if a cord had been cut, it plummeted to the ground. Whether intentionally, or they couldn't let go, two or three of the men hung on to the rope and were dragged over the hard dry ground, whilst the others rolled clear. A resounding crump and the ground shook as the bucket bounced in its hole with some of the contents scattering.

Callum took it all in at a glance. No one was hurt, humiliated maybe but no injuries. He stepped among them. "Bloody awful," he said in disgust. "A dozen - no a half dozen pregnant waafs could've done better an' that's bein' very unkind to the poor old fuckin' waafs - comparin' them to you lot. What the hell happened?"

No one answered. "Josh?" Callum appealed to his friend.
Josh rubbed his hands, "Don't know, maybe it was because the bucket was halfway up before we really got started. Our momentum was just picking up when we hit the top, got the backlash maybe. The rope slid through my hands and if it happened to me, it happened to the others."

"I agree," Nobby Clarke added. "When we hit the top my feet slipped then I was hanging on to the back of a runaway truck." Nobby had been one of the few who had hung on to the rope. Others were nodding.

242

"Right," Callum said thoughtfully, "food for thought in there somewhere." Raising his voice he cried, "Done enough this morning lads, don't want to do too much today. Thanks very much, see you tomorrow. Oh one other thing! Do me a favour. Get to bed early an' stay off the nest tonight, those of you who have nests to get into. I'd like to win tomorrow."

"No chance of that Ginge," called Tom Muir, an 'A' team reserve who was pulling for the MT section the following day. He was sitting under the trees with some others.

"What," Callum laughed as he shouted back, "no chance of me stayin' off the nest?"

"No," Tom said derisively. "No chance of you winning. We'll murder you corps. We've won the past two years an' there'll be no change tomorrow, you'll see!"

"Can't agree Tam, but you got the last bit right. You'll see us tomorrow."

Callum's eight dusted themselves down and made their way up the slope, Callum falling in behind. He recalled earlier that morning some older hands in the yard told him the MU usually put up excellent trophies for their little sports meeting. Last year the MT section each received a half pint tankard. 'A half pint's better than no pot at all,' mused the coach as they crossed the road, the booted men's steel heels clipping like so many clopping horses into the GEF yard.

Callum noticed Josh clenching, unclenching his fists. "Josh," Callum caught up, "when the rope slides through your hands, why can't you grab it again?"

Josh stopped and faced him belligerently, "Are you joking?"

"No I'm not," Callum answered firmly, "I'm feelin' my way here, just like you, tryin' to get to the bottom to a couple o' things. I'm not blamin' you or anyone for the bucket droppin' the way it did, but it did drop didn't it? Like I said down there, it's given me somethin' to chew on. I'm just lookin' for feedback an' you've been selected so c'mon son, feed me."

Josh shrugged, "There's nothing more I can tell you Ginge. When you've been hanging on for ages, my hands go numb. It doesn't matter how many squeegees we play with they still go dead. I'm sure half the blokes are gripping it with their upper arms, jamming it against our ribs, look at this." Josh lifted his PT shirt. A red weal ran across his rib cage and under the right arm.

"Jesus!" Callum exclaimed, "Will you be all right for tomorrow?"

"Of course, it's only a rope burn. We've all got them, it's part of the game."

"Somethin' else I've learned," Callum kicked a stone, "I want to win tomorrow Josh, it's no great deal but I've got somethin' to prove. Besides I'm told they're puttin' up tankards! I'd like to win another one," he said hopefully.

A holiday atmosphere spread over the huge RAF Akrotiri sports field the following day. There were still vacant seats in the small stand but some families decided to sit in the shade of their own parasols. Others, the early arrivals had staked claims to areas under the trees partially surrounding the track. Children were emulating competitors whilst mothers were pestered for cool drinks, ice cream or sweets.

Callum and his team waited at the south end of the small stand as they prepared to take the field for the final. They had earlier beaten the Administrative Wing, if beaten be the correct term. The match had been an absolute burlesque show. When an edgy Callum in his first match lined his men up on the field he waited impatiently for the appearance of the as yet unknown Admin. team. When they did appear, marching round the end of the stand, all anxiety melted away. He and his team were confronted with a motley collection of men sporting women's brassieres, fishnet stockings, nightdresses and bloomers topped with wide brimmed hats, some complete with ostrich feathers. Clearly their intention was to provide a spectacle for the crowd.

Still undecided Callum told his team to ignore the burlesque, "Get the first end in lads, I don't give a fart what they look like, win the first end then we'll see," had been his harsh instructions. Despite their outrageous dress which at the extreme end of conceivability, could possibly be a front. The Admin team were all big men! And the inexperienced Cpl. Callum McAlpine intended to treat them as he would any team - at least for the first end. They'd lined up with the No.1 men looking down the rope at each other. Parker the GEF No.1 was smiling broadly for his opposite number, a squat round man wearing massive silk bloomers and a huge brassiere stuffed with balloons. Holding the rope with one hand the man licked a huge lollipop in the other. Farthest away from the lollipop sucking No.1, the Admin. No 8, or anchorman, had not the slightest idea about tug-of-war other than it was required from him to 'give the rope a bit of a pull.' The man, a Warrant Officer had been quietly coerced into the team by his section CO.

'We have only seven men Norman, make up the eight, there's a good chap.'

Norman, because of his girth had been stuck at the end of the rope, given a bell tent of a floral dress to wear and a huge floppy hat. The nearest to any instructions received, apart from 'give the rope a bit of a pull,' was 'It's only a bit of a giggle Norman, nobody will take us seriously.' These were the homily words of advice whispered into his ear by a winking C.O.

'That's all bloody very well,' thought the Warrant Officer who, unknown to him was about to be yanked off his feet at a ferocious and frightening speed. He bent over to pick up the rope when the man with the whistle ordered them to do so. 'Oh my Gawd,' he thought witnessing close up a tug-of-war rope for the first time in his life. 'What size of a bleeding rope is this, they could tie up the Queen bloody Mary with a rope half this thick. Barely get my hands round it.'

"Take the strain," called the umpire.

'What do I do now?' thought the bewildered Norman. 'All these blokes in front of me have someone behind to pass the rope to, there's no bugger behind me.'

The correct method for the anchorman to contain the end of the rope is under the right arm, across the back and up over the left shoulder where it can hang loose. Both hands are thus free to grip the rope to his front. No one had thought to inform Norman.

In haste now, for the Warrant Officer realized something was imminent, passed the rope under his right arm, once up and around his neck then once around his body. 'That shouldn't move,' he thought. He was wrong of course as the rope suddenly moved at frightening speed, taking the bewildered Norman with it.

Callum's team put everything into their fast drop on the command "Pull." The Admin Warrant Officer was all but horizontally hanged as the trained GEF team initially flew into a very untidy backward run and stumble due to the complete lack of resistance. Fortunately strangulation did not take place. This was prevented as the unlucky anchorman, realising the rope was tightening round his neck, managed to grab and hold on to the rope with both hands. The downside of hanging on meant he was dragged on his belly over sweet smelling grass, eating new dug mud and having the most wonderful worm's eye view of many flashing steel heel plates. The driving boots powering away like a pumping engine towing him along in their wake. Norman's team mates experienced pangs of guilt as the rope was, without warning wrenched from their hands and they stood to one side watching in amazement as their gallant WO went scudding past them ploughing a furrow with his chin, like a fallen skier towed along behind a speeding motor launch.

Bewildered at the speed of events, all seven of the stranded Admin team felt they too should have held on, put up a bit of a show as their plucky Warrant Officer was doing. All were guiltily rooted to the spot, all that is, except their anchorman, who instead of being behind them where he should be, was now a bouncing bundle of floral dress twenty yards to their front.

The abashed Administrative team recovered and rushed to attend an even more bemused Norman, who had no idea how on earth he ended up sitting among the green shirted opposition with his dress around his neck!

The crowd loved it of course, not quite sure if the comic turn had been put on especially for their entertainment, but they laughed, clapped and cheered as a much warier if wiser Norman took his place for the second end after given time to recover.

Callum trying to stifle his giggles joined in the fun. He apologized for his zeal informing the Admin coach he'd meet little resistance in the second end. His offer received cat calls and jeers. "Got you worried have we, just watch our style, we were only fooling around last time."

The second end got under way to more comical theatrics. Ray Buckley and Josh Munroe left their team and strolled along the straining Administrative eight offering advice. Eventually the pair joined the tiring clerks to help them 'win' the end, amid frenzied cheering from the crowd.

When the third end got under way the men from the Administrative Wing lifted the rope above their heads with one hand and swayed as if travelling on a bus. Callum's team turned their backs on them, put the rope over their right shoulders and trotted away, leading the 'bus' passengers over the line.

And now the last event and highlight of the meeting, the tug-of-war final always followed the mile relay which was in progress as Callum issued last instructions. "No messin' around lads, fast drop, take them quickly. Watch Priest's mouth when he gives the command. Drop on the puff o' his cheeks, Don't wait for the word . If you wait for him shouting you'll be too late. When his cheeks puff, that's the time to drop. Beat them to it, we gain the advantage!"

At one time the MU Commanding Officer had, in the tone of the overall light hearted meeting, acted as umpire in the tug-of-war final. In recent years, as the sport grew in stature, better, more competitive teams had entered so the CO had stood aside. Proper umpires were delegated to officiate but the CO, still keen to be seen partaking, at least in part insisted on claiming the privilege of starting the pulls. The qualified umpire would give all primary commands to ensure all was in order.

As the last of the relay runners crossed the finishing line the Field Controller immediately hailed the tug-of-war finalists over the tannoy system.

"I want this win lads, but I can't do it without you, nor can you without me!" Callum was stressed again, nervously punching his palm, "If you do your own thing out there, you'll be eight units workin' away on your own! Do as I tell you an' you'll be eight workin' components drivin' one powerful machine! Just listen - do as I say an' I'll win it! With your cooperation!"

The rope was lined up parallel to the stand where umpire and CO Wing Commander Priest waited.

Made of hemp the rope was two inches in diameter, one hundred and twenty feet in length. In the middle was the all important central marker, a two inch band of white tape. Six feet on either side of the central marker were two more markers and another three feet from these were similar symbols, only this time in red tape. These two red markers were where the leading man in each team, the Number One would stop when lining up on the rope. The red tape was the nearest both No. One's could get to the central marker. The first thing Umpires did was check the three diagonally painted white lines on the ground aligned perfectly with the central marker and those on either side, twelve feet apart.

Bill Parker led his team down the rope and stopped at the red marker. Always nervous before any pull he noted the fresh white lines running horizontally across his vision. Staring at the white central marker Bill muttered under his breath, "Come this way, come to me you little bastard, d'you hear?" he glared at the glistening new tape. "You must come this way for this end."

Men do strange things in sport; some talk to balls, some to bats, wickets, or boots, indeed to any accoutrement aligned to their sport. Bill talked to rope markers.

"Take up the rope!" called the umpire. The teams hooked the rope up into their waiting hands.

"Watch Priest's mouth!" urged Callum watching both CO and the umpire.

"Take the strain"

"His mouth, watch his mouth!" Callum spoke only loud enough for his team to hear.

"Give right," the umpire called. The MT team had to ease the excess slack back until all three markers were vertically in line with the ground lines. The umpire was rocking his right hand back and forth, eyes fixed on the central marker. The rope crept back to its alignment point.

Wing Commander Priest watched the umpire keenly. When the official had the markers precisely above the painted lines, the CO would receive a signal.

"Steady," called the umpire then flicked his eyes from the rope the Wing Commander.

"Pull!" shouted Priest.

The teams dropped as one with the psyched up GEF lads gaining two feet before cancelling each other out. "Steady, hold steady," Callum spoke tersely as he went up the line of men, glancing back all the while at the MT team. He saw immediately they were not into position. Their middle men were totally unsettled and as he looked the No.3 slipped, his feet scrabbling to gain a foothold.

"AND!" yelled Callum quick as a flash, hitting them with speed and strength in their moment of vulnerability. "YES," roared his team strong and frightening as they hauled a foot of rope.

"And!"

"YES," another foot.

The MT were trying to settle, to dig in but were not allowed the chance. Callum's men were on the move with each "AND," from the coach who had his team perfectly balanced from the drop. The red hair of the coach, almost orange in the bright sunshine, was punching down with his right fist as eight heels chopped into the ground with resounding "YES - YES - YES!"

The whistle sounded and Callum looked up, surprised that the end was over so quickly. His men had not broken sweat, the MT in complete disarray.

"Okay lads, well done indeed, but the fat lady's no' singin' yet, let's get the second end before we even begin to think anythin' daft." As he spoke, Callum saw the MT coach talking animatedly to his team, especially the No.3 man.

They changed ends, and lined up for a second time. Callum scrutinized the umpire as he gave the initial commands. As in the first end the MT team took too much slack on the 'Take the strain' order. "Give left," the patient official called as his left hand waved slowly, watching the marker inch back to the central line. As the rope marker lined up with the central of the three white lines on the grass, the umpire raised his eyes towards the Wing Commander.

"PULL!" the CO shouted in a tone not used for years, trying to inject a modicum of power into its timbre. He failed in that it sounded more like a squawk. The effect on the two teams however was immediate and no different had he bawled at them for some misdemeanour. The teams dropped but this time the MT grabbed the initiative taking a foot or so.

It was too early for Callum to worry but he was disappointed at not gaining the advantage.

What was lost had to be won back just to return to level pegging, but his men were steady, looking good and well dug in. Glancing along the rope to his right, the MT were rock solid still. 'They've got it right this time.' There was little for Callum to do at this point other than verbally encourage his straining men, offering compliments and reassurance.

There was no movement anywhere. Sixteen men were testing each other. Callum could feel the delicious flow of adrenaline flow down the lifeline between the teams. His stomach tightening with each pulse of pressure. He continually glanced up the line at the opposition only to see the depressing sight of eight straight athletic bodies lying side on They were alike, the rope running up across their pelvic area, across their bellies and locked under their right armpit, all looking backward in the direction they were hoping to pull the rope. No movement, nothing! He would have to wait.

Time crept on, past the three minute mark. From facial expressions Callum could see heavy pressure was being applied by both teams. They were burning themselves out. No sooner had the thought crossed his mind when he caught movement in his team. It was Buckley.

"Steady Ray, hold steady pal, this is ours if we can hold steady, just don't move."

Ray managed to hold firm for another thirty seconds but he was battling. His feet began to lose purchase, flattening out. Worse, one up from Ray, Josh felt his hands begin to slip. Callum was quick to spot the movement, "Get a grip on that rope Josh, c'mon mate, you can do it!"

From a long way off Callum heard "HEAVE!" It was so far away surely it had nothing to do with his current surroundings. Suddenly his team bent over, losing footholds. "Hold it lads, steady for a counter!" he yelled, "steady up." Callum had to act quickly. Another heave like the last would surely dislodge his tiring eight. With Ray's ankles and Josh's hands gone, they had no chance in another lengthy layout. Movement was their only hope.

"One heave, all you've got," he glanced up the line. The MT were immobile, surprisingly not following up their advantage. Callum had no option he had to try. "AND," he yelled.

The expected "YES," came but it was weak although they did take enough rope to straighten up to their best positions. Movement was the best remedy for tiredness as they had just proved. Callum tried again. "And," - "Yes," another six inches. "And," - "Yes," - twelve inches.

It was coming, under great pressure but it was coming. "C'mon lads, you've got them," Callum tried more encouragement. "And," - "Yes." It was a hard slog and Callum saw how tired they were, but the initiative was still theirs and amazingly taking rope. Then it stopped!

Callum looked at the markers. "Two feet, two feet an' you've won. A couple of good heaves!"

It might as well have been two miles. The GEF team were a spent force. The opposition though little better, had enough left for one last heave, hauling the pendulum back all the way in their favour. After four and a half minutes the GEF marker crept over the Motor Transport line.

The whistle blew and Cpl. Callum McAlpine knew he'd need a minor miracle if he were to offer any resistance for the final end. Munroe's hands, after the stipulated two minute break, would last a minute or two. And Ray, too, after all the work he had put into strengthening his ankles. Callum shook his head ridding it of negative thoughts. If there was a way, he'd find it.

"Okay lads, heads up! You've lost an end but you're not beaten, they're more knackered than you are, believe me! This is not over. You made them work bloody hard. Straighten up when you pass them changin' ends. Show them you're fit, strong, for you ARE fit and strong. C'mon now!"

"He's looking for fucking miracles," someone muttered. Callum heard it and sprang in the direction it came from, "You're bloody right I am!" he roared at the sweating faces in front of him. "Remember, we're NOT beaten until that whistle blows and I swear I'll kick the first gutless weaklin' I see not givin' me his all." He glared at Ray and Josh.

"Think we better change ends Ginge," said Frank Connolly. Callum had not heard the umpire's call and nodded. The team followed the smartly marching Parker not only in single file but in example. The sweating, almost spent men gave a near perfect impersonation they were fresh from the shower.

Callum's mind was racing. He knew both teams were drained after a hard fought five minute end. He was equally certain if either team could muster enough strength for one really good heave, that team would win. Neither side had much left in their reserve locker. With Ray and Josh near the end of their tether he could not allow the end to develop. If he was to win this, the end would have to be won quickly.

Desperately seeking some sort of solution, Callum barely heard the words. "Take up the rope!" Then his head turned, his eyes locked on the umpire. 'That's it!' he thought, 'that's it!

He darted forward and ran up the team, "Don't watch Priest! Drop when I say 'Pull,' when I SAY pull!" One or two faces were confused as they looked at him. "Watch me, ME, watch

251

MY lips, watch THESE!" he pointed to his mouth. Still a couple of frowning expressions.

"Take the strain," rang out behind Callum. Some eyes were already locked on their coach, others unsure, flickering back and forth in uncertainty.

"Watch ME," he implored, "ignore Priest, watch me, my lips!" At last eight sets of eyes locked on Callum's mouth, some still apprehensively. In turn Callum could not tell now if they were doing as he beseeched them to do, for his eyes were fixed on those of the umpire.

The MT were again guilty of taking too much slack. "Give right," called the umpire, "give - give - give right!" The official turned in frustration and addressed the MT coach, "Please, give back slack when I call for it. I cannot start until the markers are in line." A tiny head shake then raised his arms again. "Give right," he called, flipping his right hand slowly.

The GEF team were as taught as piano wires. Callum had not missed his chance during the reprimand. He implored them with the same message, keep their eyes on his mouth, act only on his command. They did not know precisely what their coach had in mind but sensed some sort of a plan. Every man in the GEF team watched the mouth of the coach.

The central marker lined up. Callum saw the umpire's eyes and head start to lift towards Wing Commander Priest. "PULL," yelled Callum, half a second before the C.O. called the same word.

For the briefest fraction of time the umpire was unsure if the team on his left had anticipated the call, which would mean a restart. It was desperately close but the side judge had not signalled any unlawful advantage so he allowed the green GEF team their marvellous start. They'd been very fast in the first two ends anyway and were now in full flight. Their choruses of "Yes - Yes - Yes," were surprisingly loud and strong for a team that looked beaten. The coach had them moving in perfect rhythm and balance. The chopping right boots were thudding in perfect unison deep into the green turf, like oars of a well trained rowing eight cutting into still water.

Josh at No. 4, was grunting with each dig of his right boot into the ground, trying to keep in time with 'This - grunt - YES - fucking - grunt - YES - robot - grunt - YES,' in front of him.

Frank at No.3 was indeed moving like clockwork as he methodically worked backwards. Ray from somewhere got the strength to dig his right boot in with everything going into his heaves. He was desperate to get the end won and when the whistle shrilled, he could not believe it.

The umpire's whistle did indeed blow, long and hard as some of the winning team seemed not to hear his blast. "Well now," the official exclaimed gazing at his stopwatch, "nine seconds! They had me fooled. I'd have wagered a month's salary they were finished after that second end."

The jubilant eight gathered round their grinning coach, "Don't know what or how you did it," gasped Jim Clarkeson, "but I wouldn't have given tuppence for our chances. Well done lad."

"How did you get the jump on them?" asked Josh ruffling the coach's red hair.

"I'm a very fast laddie," answered an elated Callum.

A figure in the crowd dressed in a dazzling white shirt and shorts had watched the whole performance. Barrymore smiled, he was not the type to miss anything and had caught the way the heads of the GEF team had turned to face their coach at the start of the third end, and not as in the established manner, towards the umpire.

"Capitol, Cpl. McAlpine," Errol nodded. "Chancy but yes, quite brilliant. It appears this needle sharp Scottish chap we have happily inherited, could possibly teach us all a few tricks."

~~~

"Still no pissin' pot!" Callum cursed as he held the large bronze medallion he received from the wife of Wing Commander Priest at the presentation ceremony following the final.

"You didn't expect a tankard for winning at the MU sports did you? We were lucky to get such a fancy medallion," Josh said proudly holding up his trophy.

Frank pushed another drink over to Callum, "For what you did today Ginge, you should have got the DSM, the DCM, the VC, VD and scar, and as many medals and pots as you could carry. We should all club together and buy you a bloody pot!"

"No no no," Callum shook his head vehemently, "it's got to be won! It's got to be presented to me after I've won it! Beer tastes ten times better when you drink from a pot that's been won. Back in Stradishall, when I drank from the pot I won, and subsequently lost there, I experienced all the elation, euphoria and jubilation I felt when the pot was actually bein' bloody won. It was a wee bit o' magic" Callum was so pleased the way it all turned out. He had not really expected a tankard, but still it would have been nice. The only mug he ever won languished on some thief's sideboard back in England. The lovely hard fought pot Callum had so carelessly left on the Naafi table in Stradishall. "I'll win another pot, an' I'll win it before I leave this island, you'll see,"

"You will Ginge, you will for sure if you can produce miracles as you did today, you'll probably win dozens," Jim Clarkeson, veteran of hundreds of matches said.

"Aye so I keep gettin' told Jim, I'm just impatient to replace the one I stupidly lost, that's all."

The group, made up from various team members, wives, girl friends and friends, were having drinks in the Peninsula Club. They were seated in a corner of the club lounge that over the years had grown to be known as the 'MU corner.' All were soaking in the atmosphere and camaraderie that was invariably present in the Maintenance Unit tug-of-war community. The main topic of conversation was not the fact the GEF team had taken the spoils earlier that day, but the method on how the coach had achieved the smash and grab win.

Merging with the GEF section were different groups from other sections on the Maintenance Unit. The jovial crowd having been blooded into the sport with the achievements of the main team under Barrymore enjoyed the quite unique ambiance that apparently exuded from the winning team. It didn't matter if the winning team was only a section team like today's GEF side or the full blooded 103 MU team.

A hubbub of noise reverberated round the tables. Everyone was talking, reliving that third end. Josh and Ray were overjoyed with the win, amplified by their mutual feelings that neither could contribute a lengthy contribution towards winning the third end. Yet when the adrenaline started pumping, floods of energy had poured through their limbs. For nine pulsating seconds they had the strength of Hercules. "When this twat said," Josh pointed at Callum, "'Watch me,' I thought he'd flipped, I really did, but when he said it, no, growled it quietly a second and third time, I knew then he was on to something!"

"And by the bloody centre, was he not absolutely bloody right!" Ray was within a decibel of shouting. He turned to Callum, "You rascal, you cheated, didn't you, just a tiny little bit, eh?"

"No, I don't think so! But I knew you lot had to fly out of the starting gate first if we were to have any chance. We just got the drop of them, that's all!" Callum gave a tiny shrug.

"But the question remains," said Frank Connolly, "how did you manage to get us down so fast and within the framework of the rules. When we hit the rope for a fraction of a second there was no resistance, nothin'. We took three or four feet before we felt them. By then they were a shambles."

"What a great feeling it was," Ray's eyes were gleaming. "After that second end my balls felt they weighed a ton, each! Oh what an experience to feel that rope coming and coming. When the umpire blew his whistle I could gladly have kissed his ... both cheeks!" This was greeted with an explosion of laughter.

"Yes, it was wonderful, very well done indeed Callum, if I may say so!" The voice came from the back of the group. Everyone turned to see the powerful figure of Errol Barrymore.

"Thank you sir," Callum said with a wry grin as others scrambled to find the officer a chair.

"It's a brandy sour sir, I think?" asked Clarkeson.

"No sirs or corporals tonight if you please, this is a celebration after all. And please, allow me to contribute to your bank." Errol placed a £5 note in the 'kitty' glass.

Callum promptly returned the note, "For all you drink eh ... Errol," he hesitated as airmen sometimes found it difficult to address an officer informally. "There's no need," he finished.

"If you don't mind, I would like to buy you all a drink," the officer said again poking the note into the pint pot. "Not only to celebrate the GEF success, but also to commiserate with the MT section." Errol smiled to the Motor Transport team and section workers scattered around. "And with that drink I would like you all to toast one of the finest pieces of opportunism I have ever witnessed in the sport of tug-of-war." He looked at his reserve coach. "I hope I am not embarrassing you Callum, but the truth is, your team was beaten today after that long second end.

You knew that at the time, didn't you? They had very little left in the locker yet you managed to conjure up a drop right out of the top drawer. A drop that had your men moving in perfect unison over those first few crucial feet. A drop that reduced the opposition to eight struggling units. I can only assume your timing was the quintessence, the very pith of perfection. Or ..." Errol paused, "perhaps you anticipated the call?" The officer looked deep into Callum's blue eyes.

The slim relaxing figure with the light ginger hair did not answer. He merely smiled.

"Either way Cpl. Callum McAlpine," Errol went on, "I would just like to add, I think the Gods that look over our little Unit, has been very kind to us. We seem to have unearthed a natural, and if I may say so, a worthy successor to my good self when I sadly depart this island at the end of next month."

~~~

Chapter 12

Frank was packing toiletries into his small pack when Josh Munroe and Callum McAlpine entered the billet. "Has Ray gone to fetch the car?" Callum asked looking round.

Frank nodded, "Left about an hour ago. Old McKinley let him off early."

Josh rubbed his palms together, "I'm so bloody excited. Three and a half days all to ourselves to tour this beautiful island ... shit," the scrubbing of his hands quickened, "I can't wait!"

Callum placed an arm round his friend's shoulder, "C'mon now son, we mustn't get our knickers into the proverbial twist, we might do ourselves a wee injury. Just sit down and play with yourself, there's a good lad."

The congenial and generally tranquil Josh smiled broadly, "So what's the plan Frank?"

"No change Josh, it's still Paphos first stop. Then we head for the hills and Troodos. Hopefully we'll find the Raf camp Ray reckons is up there somewhere. We'll stay there overnight then Kyrenia next if all goes well. Maybe try the 'Panhandle' after that, we'll see. It's a fair old trip. I hope you've packed enough gear for three days."

"Of course," said Josh, "I've got three bottles of brandy and a pair of, I think, clean drawers."

Callum shook his head, "He doesn't half fancy himself," turning to Josh he went on, "Three bottles of brandy would kill you, you soft turd."

"Maybe," Josh agreed, "but what a way to go! To drift off on a golden cloud of alcoholic buoyancy. That's the way I'd like to go, yeah, with maybe a nice woman on top of me. That would be a bonus!"

Frank glanced at Callum. With the Scot's miniscule frown, it was obvious neither had missed the unusual comment. It was the first sexual reference Josh had made towards the fair sex,

257

certainly in their company. During the silence that followed, footsteps slapped across the red quarry veranda tiles and Ray exploded into the room, "Git along you lot, git your asses into them thar saddles, I gotta Lancia Flavia snortin' ana kickin' hatside, just a'rarin' t'go.!" He headed for his locker from where he yanked out his gear. Throwing his bag round his shoulder he shouted, "Git along you dogies, y'all still hyah?" He shouted before galloping out the door.

"Sorry about that," Frank said, "We went to see a John Wayne western in the Astra last night. Poor bastard, he'll never be the same."

The relationship between the four airmen had grown close during the nine weeks since Frank and Ray first wandered into their billet, not exactly fresh but certainly neoteric arrivals from the UK. It was Ray who first suggested a tour of the island over the Easter weekend. The planned trip, as so often happens with the best of well laid plans, had gone slightly astray.

By the time Ray had got round to making inquiries about a hire car every available vehicle on the island had been booked for Easter. Undaunted the genial joker had booked a car for the next holiday weekend at Whitsun, seven weeks after Easter. The weeks had flown for Frank and Ray, merging quickly and easily into the magical influence of life on the MU and sorties down to the quaint town of Limassol. It was quiet now but the seaport still bore scars from the recent troubles between the Greek and Turkish communities.

The newly arrived pair, taking older hands advice had both applied to do Fire Picket duty and two weeks afterwards their names appeared on the duty list. Reporting after work on the Friday to sign on at the Fire Station, Frank met Harold Ross signing off. They exchanged pleasantries before Harold hurried off anxious to see Marion. Frank and Ray were settling into the Fire Station billet when a very pretty waaf came looking for Harold. Disappointed to have missed him the blonde girl who did wonders for the Air Force uniform, left. Ray understood but said nothing at his friend's muttered, "The stupid big bastard!"

The sporty Flavia, gleaming white in the afternoon sun rocked on its springs as Callum and Josh clambered into the back while Frank joined Ray in front. Keen to demonstrate his driving skills Ray gunned the engine a number of times, then with the wheel at full lock, using the hand brake he danced the powerful car in a tight circle spraying dirt and stones from its arcing perimeter. With a flurry of hands, feet and thrumming tyres as he gained traction, Ray scrabbled the car onto the tar road and raced towards the Guardroom. The occupants were reduced to cheering waving schoolboys.

"Paphos here we come!" roared Ray the holiday spirit building to a crescendo now they were finally on their way. Callum was the first to settle down approaching the Guardroom and as the car passed through the gates he said, "I hate to dampen the atmosphere girls, but we've neither food nor drink aboard this flyin' machine. Food, obviously is of no great concern, but in order to get our little excursion off on the right foot, the lack of booze on board ... now that IS critical!"

Ray said, "Do you take me for the village idiot, I've -"

"Yes we do"! Three voices said in almost perfect unison.

"Yeah, yeah," Ray gave Frank a sidelong look, "Well bright sparks, did any of you think of vitals and perhaps a drop of the magic juice. No I bet you didn't." He paused whilst overtaking a bus, "To continue, I thought we might travel to that tavern of dubious delights, known to idiots and intellectuals alike, even down to the likes of us as 'Twiga Bar.'" He paused briefly, then, "Where once ensconced in their welcoming interior, we may partake in consumption of aforesaid vitals, accompanied with a glass or perhaps two of their delicious beverage, known to the natives and ourselves as the dreaded Keo. Having supped and dined for one hour only, ONE HOUR ONLY," he raised his voice dramatically, then went on, "we will then pursue our pilgrimage to the far distant Paphos. "

Completing his soliloquy amid a stunned silence, Ray placed a shading hand above his eyes.

Sweet Jesus," said Callum, "he makes it sound like we're off on a biblical expedition."

Leaning forward he drilled a finger into Ray's shoulder, "Listen son, 'the distant Paphos' as you so quaintly put it, is but an hour down yonder road! So enough theatrics, a bit more reality, put your boot down and let's get to this wonderful Twiga Bar, I'm dyin' o' fuckin' thirst."

~~~

259

Frank surfaced very slowly, trying to push back the encroaching light and fight off this aching awakening. His conscience self was trying desperately to pull back into the depths of sleep, but the more he tried, the more awake he became. To compliment this totally foreign sick feeling in his gut, he could only suppose someone had obviously taken a great dislike to him, and stuffed a pair of unwashed underpants, worn for a month by a constant diarrhoea and incontinent sufferer, down the back of his throat. The disgusting act of breathing through this mess of concentrated camel dung was urging the contents of his stomach to demonstrate their repugnance to their present surroundings and all were gathering to make a voluminous exit. To keep the nauseous feelings company there was a steady thumping at the back of his head and with each thump he felt his face being driven harder and deeper into the malodorous crook of his arm.

Deep down he felt a bubble of bile begin to fight and bobble upwards towards the surface. With a moan he kicked free of whatever it was that covered him and rolling over, sat up on the edge of the bed. Looking down he wore only underpants, not pyjamas, and the garment he had fought free from which covered his head was his shirt! Puzzled he looked around. He was in a billet room; not his own billet but similar. Perhaps Ray had found a military base in Paphos?

Frank could not remember a thing. The previous night was a complete blank. He looked round the room again. Ray, Josh and Callum were spread-eagled on other beds, lying as he had been, on top of bare mattresses. Ray as usual was snoring loudly.
Frank lowered his head gently into his hands and tried to remember. Slowly, very slowly it was coming back.

They started off at the Twiga Bar before going off to Paphos. He could remember eating a meal. Each one of the quartet had ordered their own bottle of wine. There were sketchy pictures of the foursome eating, drinking, laughing then at some stage other members of the tug-of-war crowd joined them. Dreamlike visions were sliding into place. He remembered having a good time, drinking pints of beer then brandy sour chasers. 'Stupid bastard,' he cursed. Mixing his drinks! Would he never learn? The bile bubbled, growing impatient, fermenting upwards.

Suddenly Frank found his body had overtaken his slow thinking brain and was mildly surprised to discover he was running towards the door on rubber legs. He was a puppet and an amateur puppeteer was controlling him towards the open door. He was being propelled with flaying arms and legs out through the door and across the tiled veranda onto the patchy grass. At this point the puppeteer lost interest and he fell on hands and knees just in time to start retching and heaving out the contents of a furnace burning stomach. For ten painful minutes nothing else existed in the world except this mechanical jettisoning of everything inside him. When at last nothing was left to come up, he continued to retch for ten more excruciatingly painful minutes. His throat was being torn apart and burned from the inside with a blowtorch.

Kneeling, gasping in air only to curse, 'Stupidbastard, stupidbastard, stupidbastard' over and over. Rising anger replaced what he had just ejected then hated and cursed himself repeatedly again.

Trying to wipe his streaming eyes, embarrassed at his situation he muttered, 'Here I am like a dog, feelin' like shit an' I don't even know where the fuck I am? Aw Jesus! I only just made it over the veranda to this waste ground ... veranda??" Drawing his forearm across his eyes he peered more closely at the covered walkway. It was certainly similar, maybe it was the quarry tiles ... but all RAF camps were made exactly the same, weren't they? So it would look similar, wouldn't it ... they. Oh fuck!"

A door opened two doors down from the one Frank had staggered from. A man emerged then stopped when he saw Frank on the grass, kneeling in his own spew.

"Frank, God's sake, what are you doing out here. I thought you were off on a trip?"

Frank could not keep his eyes clear of water as he frantically wiped them with his wrist. He didn't want to look at the mess on his hands. "This must be a fuckin' nightmare," he blurted as the figure approached. Staggering to his feet, attempting as he did so to wipe the cloying mess from his legs, he peered at the man. "Julian?" he said in bewilderment then looking round saw to his total amazement he was standing outside his own barrack block! He had spent the night in a billet only two doors from his room, so blind drunk he could not find his way to his own bed!

Frank washed as best he could under a garden water tap before

261

tottering towards the room where the three sleeping beauties still lay sound asleep. Unintentionally he ignored Julian, his senses having not yet caught up with his confused brain. Crashing through the doorway he went straight to Ray's slumbering form, his snoring reverberating round the otherwise quiet room.

Frank placed his mouth close to Ray's ear. "YOU STUPID BASTARD," he roared as loud as he could, hurting his vocal chords in the process. "YOU STUPID BASTAAAAARD!" Again hurting his throat, starting to cough and choke as the recipient of Frank's vocal blast cringed away grimacing painfully, bringing a hand up to protect his ringing ear.

"Hey. Agh, what the fuck?" Ray battled to sit upright flaying his other arm wildly but suddenly felt his forehead slip forward. Hurriedly he transferred the hand protecting his injured ear to catch his falling forehead. "Oh sweet Jesus, what's happening?" he moaned as both hands were now firmly clasped to a reeling head.

Frank meanwhile had recovered sufficiently to carry on the tirade. "Aye, what's happenin' ya stupid prick, ye managed to find a fuckin' bed but ye could nae find Paphos, could ye. Rally driver? Rally driver ma arse! You'd have difficulty findin' yer way oot o' a one way street!" On the rare occasions Frank lost his temper his accent broadened and this morning he was very angry, raging mainly at himself for getting so badly inebriated, again. For a bonus he, like Ray was suffering the mother and father of a hangover.

Julian followed Frank into the room and tried to quieten him down. "Wait a minute Frank, keep it down please. You've obviously all had a rough night but shouting won't help matters."

Frank rounded on him, "Well what d'ye expect? This idiot here was supposed to take us to Paphos last night and do you know where we are now Julie. Saviour of the downtrodden. Do you know where we are? Just in case ye've no' noticed, we're back in fuckin' camp, that's where this rovin' Romeo's brought us, back to our fuckin' startin' point!"

Callum was watching the bizarre goings on through half open eyes under a sheltering forearm. He sat up painfully. "That's right," he declared scratching the back of his head with both hands.

"That's right?" Frank repeated, unconsciously raising his voice again.

"Yes," Callum calmly returned his fellow Scot's stare, "and what's more pal, it was your idea!"

Frank's eyes blinked, "Me," he said incredulously. "My idea?"

"All yours Sunny Jim. When we came out of the Twiga last night, Josh, me, an' Goldilocks there," he nodded at Ray, "wanted to carry on to Paphos or wherever the fuck we were supposed to be goin'. We were all bombed, pissed out of our minds remember, but you ...."

At this point Ray, who had ponderously been trying to follow Callum's portrayal of the previous nights heroics, gave up and flopped backwards on the bed with a grunting sigh.

"You Frankie," Callum carried on, "had the sense, against heavy opposition mind you, to come back here, pointing out Ray was too drunk. In truth we were all too drunk, to drive anywhere."

Frank could only stare at Callum as the latter carried on as though reading a monologue. "We listened and you changed our minds, that is Josh and me but Ray still wanted to go on."

An agonized "No," escaped Frank's mouth, then "You're no' gonna tell me this is my fault?"

"It's nobody's fault! Fuck me, at the end of the night we were lucky to get back here. What happened was, we all sort of agreed with you that it would be a bit dodgy travellin' in our condition an' we weren't' sure where we would spend the night, even if we reached Paphos. We hummed and hawed a wee bit outside the Twiga then decided unanimously it would be better if we hummed and hawed inside the Twiga, so we all trooped back in. That was fatal for I don't remember anything at all after that but," he looked around, "to be honest I'm surprised Ray got us back here in one piece." Callum finished his summing up of the previous night's chronicle of events, then with a final "I'm for a shower," he left the room.

Frank was feeling worse with each passing minute, mentally now as well as physically. He stealthily glanced at Ray who resembled a beached white whale wearing underpants.

Quietly he sat at the bottom of the bed. "Ray," he started uneasily, "Ray, I'm sorry pal! Jesus, I'm awfu' sorry for shoutin' at you, I can't remember a thing honestly, But geez how I'm sufferin'. I feel like I spent the night at the bottom of a Turkish army's shit barrel, honest!"

The mass stirred slightly but the arm covering his eyes remained in place, "If you are really sorry Frankie, you'll do one last thing for me ... before I expire!" the voice croaked.

"Aye, of course, anythin' Ray," said a contrite Frank, thinking he was about to be sent to the mess for tea. "What can I do for you?"

Ray rolled on to his stomach, pushed his underpants down and said, "You can kiss my arse."

The action brought smiles all round and when Frank gave the exposed buttocks a resounding backhanded whack there was more laughter. Ray hastily covered the smitten area rubbing it hard, showing a remarkable return to life. Frank tried for the last word, "If you were so fuckin' clever last night, how come we ended up in the wrong room, answer me that?"

"You're lucky I found the right island and dear old Akrotiri! The state I was in I'm just hoping the car's all right. Haven't a clue where the fucking thing might be!"

The car when they found it was indeed in better condition than the four occupants, although parked rather dramatically with one front wheel resting on a high kerb stone.

By lunchtime the four would be travellers had bathed, rested and eaten and as youth does seem to spring eternal, their eagerness to see the island had made a marvellous recovery.

Paphos, when they eventually arrived at the seaside town, after a very short and wary stop at the Twiga bar to buy a case of wine, was disappointing. The town was small with very few facilities. Ray and Callum went in search of whatever adventure could be gleaned from whatever source they could find, whilst Josh and Frank were enthralled with the ancient castle on the waterfront. All four eventually met at the geographical diggings going on at the Roman ruins a short distance from the town.

Whilst having a meal in a small cafe it was unanimously decided to push on to the RAF camp at Troodos. With little or no night life in Paphos the idea of familiar surroundings and a bed sounded better that curled up in a car in drunken oblivion. With that picture in mind Frank took his spell at the wheel heading north east for the Troodos mountains. The surprisingly good road was serenely quiet allowing Frank to drive comfortably, enjoying the dusk and eventual darkness.

After an hour the road entered the thickly wooded mountainous area of central Cyprus. Like entering a tunnel it cut a pathway through the thick forest of pine trees giving a silvery green luminescent sheen to the silent surroundings. Only the lulling of the powerful engine concurring with its pleasant low growl to the silence of the night. With his passengers asleep, Frank was enjoying the solitude of the moment when he saw at the extreme edge of the headlights, a figure on the road carrying something on one arm, waving what looked like a red flag with the other.

Frank nudged Ray awake, told him to waken the others. Slowing down Frank to his dismay, saw what the figure was carrying other than the red flag was a sub machine gun.

The car stopped a few yards from the man when another, similarly clad in camouflage uniform   bearing no insignia, stepped from the shadows. He knocked on Frank's window.

Frank lowered the window. "Eengleesh?" the man asked peering inside.

"Yes."

"May I see identification please."

The man out front lowered the sub machine gun menacingly as Frank and the others reached for their RAF 1250s; the official identification cards all Royal Air Force personnel carry.

A curt command from the hawk nosed man collecting the 1250s and the gun was again raised skywards much to the car occupant's relief. "Where you go sir?" The voice and question was polite, as the figure produced a torch then scrutinized the plastic enclosed I.D. cards.

"We're on our way to RAF Troodos," As Frank answered Ray leaned over and growled, "What's it got to do with you. You've got no right to do this, who the fuck are you lot anyway?"

The greasy face frowned and glittering black eyes peered beyond Frank as the man switched the torch beam. "Your name sir?" he asked unperturbed it seemed at Ray's hostility.

Ray was not in the best of moods after a bottle of wine and this rude awakening. Moreover he was grossly uncomfortable at the situation they were in. Paphos had turned out to be a dead hole, Troodos could be on the moon, and the night ahead held no promises. His stomach was churning with nerves; was it fear? No, his rally training taught him never to hesitate in the face of fear.

"You have my ID, can't you read? Enough of this nonsense man, tell that clown to move over and let us go on our way," Ray shouted defiantly at Hawknose.

The beam stayed firmly on Ray for what seemed an age then switched back to the 1250s.

"You are Buckley sir?"

Callum were urging Ray to answer the man's questions. Stirring up trouble could mean they might be detained, perhaps all night. Ray was reluctant to see reason and patently ignored the man at Frank's shoulder who continued to shine the torch in his face

"You are Buckley sir?" the man asked again, more sternly this time.

"YES!" snapped Ray, "and take that damned light out of my eyes."

The light lingered on the glowering features moments longer then flicked to Josh and Callum in the back of the car, where they were compared to their ID cards. "Thank you, now I look in rear of car please." It was a curt statement, not a request.

"Why?" asked Frank. "What, may I ask are you lookin' for? You've established who we are but we know nothin' of you."

"I look in rear of car, please!" It was a guttural command. The man was losing his patience.

Frank turned to the three occupants, "What do I do, I'm not sure what this wee man's after?"

"For fuck's sake," said Callum, "we've got nothin' to hide! Don't you start messin' him about. Show him the fuckin' boot an' let's get out o' here!"

Frank stepped out of the car aware Ray was not the only one on edge. He moved to the back of the car and watched warily as the dark figure bearing the weapon followed with levelled barrel. Hawknose shone the torch into the opened boot, scanning slowly over the untidy luggage and case of wine bottles. "You like Cyproos wine sir?" he asked.

"Yes, yes we do," answered Frank noting a more civil tone.

"Look, I don't want to prolong this any longer than necessary, but it would help if you told me what you're lookin' for?"

The man though small had a proud upright bearing. He smiled for the first time, white teeth flashing in the dark face,

"No sir, you no have what we look for. Please to be on your way. Thank you!" The camouflaged figure turned sharply and walked into the darkness of the surrounding trees. Frank closed the lid then returned to the car. As he did so he caught a glimpse of another man kneeling in the roadside shrubbery, holding something he could barely make out.

"My God," he muttered easing into gear, "I think that's a fuckin' bazooka in the bushes. Christ an' I was toyin' with the idea of drivin' straight through. These guys mean business."

"Well, it's none o' our fuckin' business, so move! Get out o' here." Callum said from the back.

There was silence for a few minutes while distance and time lengthened the gap from what had been a nerve-racking experience. Frank, suddenly realizing he was hammering along on a tight little road at 70 mph eased back on the accelerator.

"Who were they?" he asked.

"God knows," Josh spoke for the first time since leaving Paphos.

"I think they were Turks," Ray said morosely.

"Wonder what they were lookin' for?" Frank said.

Again Josh said, "God knows," as Callum went on, "They wouldn't be EOKA would they?" He named the Greek guerrilla group that had been a thorn in the British government's side, responsible for the deaths of a number of British servicemen in the struggle for independence.

"I doubt if they were Eoka," said Frank, "if they were why are we still sittin' here, freely drivin' along? We are RAF you know, British servicemen?"

"Mind you," Callum's voice floated from the rear, "Eoka have signed a peace agreement so when you think about it, they were probably after weapons. If so then Ray's right, they were Turkish Cypriots. Turks have no dispute with the British, but their dispute with Greek Cypriots continues. An' that's why we're still here."

"Yeah probably but we can't be sure" Ray said still annoyed at the blunt invasion of privacy. "There's still a lot of infighting going on between the Greek and Turkish Cypriots that we know nothing about. But either way the bastard's got a fucking cheek stopping us."

They were a much subdued group when sometime later all eyes were searching for directional signs to the tiny RAF Troodos camp as the road grew narrow and the curves tight. "Do you want me to drive?" Ray asked suddenly. He was an excellent driver but a nervous passenger.

"Sit tight, it can't be far now," Frank answered staring into the blackness.

Ray did exactly that. He sat taught, almost rigid tensely watching the headlights float off ghost like into endless space as the car swung round yet another tight curve of the unfenced road hacked out of the mountain face. His toes began to curl with the waiting, waiting for the lights to pick up on the white vertical cliff face, then relief as the solid hewed out mountain magically reappeared yet again in their swinging searching lights. When he felt Frank must ram the car into the harsh rock face, the road took another long swing outwards, the headlights would float off again into a void of nothingness. At this point he would glue his eyes on the tiny strip of road that resembled a mottled revolving wheel with the periphery persistently flying under the car bonnet. The repetitive cliff face threatened to chew them up, the impenetrable depth of space wanted to swallow them. Ray shut his eyes. After twenty minutes of sweating, at times almost crying out in terror he was about to show his hand as the world's worst passenger when the friendliest sign he had ever seen preserved his image; 'R.A.F. Troodos. 1 mile.'

Frank slowed as he approached the guardroom and stopped under the glaring lights. The duty corporal checked 1250s then apologetically explained the small camp's transit accommodation had only was four beds and was already full. The best he could offer was four biscuit mattresses and as the mountain air was cold, they could doss down in the 'Drying Room.' This room was kept at a constant seventy degrees where airmen dried their washing. They wouldn't be cold.

And so it proved, using their small packs for pillows they spent a surprisingly comfortable night. Next morning after ablutions they breakfasted as soon as the Mess opened then anxious to be on their way, returned the thin mattresses then drove to Troodos. They found in the quaint village of wooden houses and shops the first signs of commercialism, which clashed brassily with original surroundings. This did not stop them buying souvenirs, trinkets and soft rounds of goat cheese.

The northern seaport of Kyrenia beckoned Ray with a heavy hand. The big Londoner loved the sea so was glad when at last he got behind the wheel for the run to the coast. He revelled in the exhilaration of driving but offered a silent prayer of thanks for the previous nights velvet black darkness when he saw in broad daylight the road snaking down the north side of the mountain.

The paradoxical side of Ray's nature and his quite brilliant driving skills were both clearly apparent when he drove at breakneck speed with squealing tyres round the many tight curves and U shaped bends under superb control whilst his adrenaline pumping passengers goaded him on to even greater feats. After half an hour of taught stomachs and clenched fists the purring Lancia rolled onto the valley floor where a long flat road stretched ahead. The passengers though suitably impressed breathed a collective sigh of relief. With the valley spread out before them Ray suddenly pulled over. "Take over Josh," he laughed, "I'm drained after that little romp." In truth, Ray hated a long flat road where there was no challenge.

Josh took his turn, driving the rest of the way to Kyrenia. It was a beautiful little town where every house gleamed white, topped with red tiled roofs. Comments were made on the blinding light that seemed to reflect from the houses and their surrounding walls, stinging the eyes somewhat as Josh cruised through the quiet hilly streets. All four had RAF issue sunglasses but typically these were in the boot with the rest of their gear.

Josh breasted the brow of a hill to be greeted with the most wonderful expanse of the Mediterranean. The shock of sparkling aqua blue after floods of red and blinding white was awesome. "Oh my aunt Fanny's fanny, will you look at that," Ray uttered reverently. Frank felt the same way, as his breath was sucked from his lungs at the sight.

There were plenty of bars along the harbour and quayside but they decided to spend the day on the deserted beach. Whilst the others cavorted in the water, Josh industriously wandered among the rocks. He was searching initially for a container that might serve as a pot. This he found with a whoop of delight. His prize was an empty five-gallon olive oil drum complete with lid.

Obviously it had not been on the beach long as it was entirely rust free. Pleased with his find Josh removed the lid and washed the inside thoroughly then partly filled it with fresh water from a convenient bathers shower. Gathering some large rocks and driftwood he built a fireplace and soon had a fire going. Carefully he set the drum astride the rocks. The flames from the crackling fire soon blackened the shining exterior of the corrugated drum.

The others watched quietly as Josh went happily about his business gathering a wide selection of shellfish along the beach. Most were dropped into his blue small pack, others he discarded. Eventually with his bag overflowing he returned to the now blazing fire. With his white RAF issue pint pot, Josh scooped some of the boiling water from the drum, replacing each mug of water with the same measure of shellfish, much to the unsavoury comments from his bemused audience. When the last of the shellfish had been added to the drum, Josh went to the car and returned carrying the box of a dozen bottles of white wines. With his mug he scooped out some water then opened a bottle and poured the contents into the drum amid further exclamations from the watchers, pertaining to the waste of good wine. The drum was allowed to simmer with Josh occasionally stirring the mix. In minutes the surface was covered with the creatures that lived in the shells and the more Josh stirred, the more mussels, periwinkles and other molluscs floated to the surface. "Go get your mugs," he said to the now inquisitive threesome then proceeded to open and hand a bottle of wine to each of his bemused watchers. He took Ray's mug, dipped it into the stew and offered the steaming mug to Ray.

"Oh I don't know Josh," Ray said doubtfully taking the pot warily.

Frank wore a slight frown so Josh filled Callum's mug. With a broad grin the flame haired Scot said. "Cheers Josh, okay, let's give a wee taste to your concoction." He blew across the surface then supped at the edge, sucking in some of the soft shellfish. Chewing slowly he nodded and grinned, then reached into his small pack for a spoon. Ray shrugged, tasted the brew and nodded.

"As none of you have dropped dead, let's try some o' that," Frank said thrusting his mug at Josh.

The makeshift meal was an amazing success. Ray, on finishing his second serving exclaimed wiping a hand across his mouth, "Pure magic Josh, you conjured that meal out of nothing! I've been known to fall in love with people who could do that. Pity my missus can't cook," he mused with a faraway look in his eyes. "But to her eternal credit, she did the next best thing, she dropped her drawers!" Ray sniggered happily at his derogatory remark, then asked, "Too late now but I suppose that, whatever it was, was safe to eat? I mean we're not likely to shit through the eye of an needle at ten yards, are we?"

"Not at all, but I wouldn't bet on catching anything if you shit through a tea strainer!"

The three erupted in laughter at the unexpected return from Josh who was showing a whole new side of himself. However when Frank inquired how he managed to cook such a meal from what could be gathered at the water's edge all he would say was, "I learned to do that years ago."

The wine flowed and the fire crackled as scouting trips along the beach ensured there was enough fuel to keep the comforting flames dancing through the night. With the aid of blankets from their Akrotiri beds and more wine they slept, if not like babes, certainly like bottle fed men.

Next morning they experienced the cool freshness of a new day that sleeping in the open air can magically conjure up to house bound society. Showering quickly under the cold water of the swimmers shower and whooping with excitement in the raw air, they quickly cleared the site.

In the nearby Bristol Hotel, owned they discovered by an English couple, all four ordered and demolished a huge English breakfast. Savouring the last of his second coffee Frank sat back comfortably. "Where to next?" he asked, wondering if he could manage another slice of toast.

"There's only Nicosia left, but I thought we would save that for another day." said Callum.

"Leaving out Nicosia there's only small villages between here and Limassol," offered Josh.

"I've just had the most wonderful idea," said Ray.

"Oh fuck!" Callum moaned.

"Listen, you'll like it," Ray said confidently. "Today's Sunday, we return the car tomorrow evening, right. What do you say we drive leisurely back to camp, get there for the evening meal, then do the town in the car tonight? We might even get lucky and snatch a couple of females?" he smiled. "On reflection, if we can't find any real skirt, we could offer our services to some Waafs. How does that sound, tomorrow early we can drive up to Famagusta, it's only an hour or so from Limassol. Spend the day there, return the car in nice time and finish up in the Twiga?"

Frank ignored Ray slamming the Waafs and fantasizing about the opposite sex. Flights of fancy in that department were thankfully all the whimsical Ray ever amounted to, despite his threats, and 'doing the town tonight' with Ray sounded ominous. Frank felt they could still see more of the island so he tried once more, "I fancied a run up the coast, maybe see how far up the 'Panhandle' we get before the Turks stop us. We could visit Famagusta and Larnaca on our way home." On maps the long eastern strip of land looked like a handle to the island's pot and rumour had it Turkish troops occupied most of the 'Panhandle'. Frank glanced at the others but they weren't keen on his suggestion. Perhaps the possibility of another brush with Turkish activists was not flavour of the week, or maybe the attraction of familiar surroundings were too strong. And so it proved..

They trooped out to the car. Ray took the wheel, and drove smoothly out of Kyrenia for the run that would take them from the most northern town to the one nestling farthest to the south. The terrain was mainly flat and Ray intent in racing back to Akrotiri made excellent time.

Some thirty minutes later cruising at around seventy mph, Ray breasted a small rise. An exceptionally long stretch of straight road bisecting fields on either side of the road loomed ahead melting into the far distant haze. "There's plenty left under my foot," he called. "Let's see if this thing can do the ton."

"Go for it Ray, I've never travelled in a car doing over a hundred," Josh shouted.

"Aye go on," Callum called from the back, "but don't kill the fuckin' thing, will ye?"

"Or anythin' else," Frank said warily watching the speed build up.

The engine noise that had been relatively quiet, took on a deeper more portentous sounding purr that built quickly into a growl as the speedometer needle climbed past the eighty mark. It seemed to settle for a moment at that speed then the growl grew into a roar as the ninety miles per hour registered.

"Jesus, this thing can go," Ray shouted, his bright eyes fixed dead ahead. "Ninety five and still trying!" Three other sets of eyes joined Ray's, constantly flicking from the road to speedometer.

Initially no one saw it. Off in the indistinguishable heat hazed distance, something moved. It was too far to recognise in the tantalizing shimmer, but something was moving from the field on the right side of the road creating a cloud of dust as it left a dirt track. It was big and dark brown. Ray saw it at the same time as the others, as his foot floored the accelerator.

"I want to get over the ton!" he yelled at the unspoken question bombarding his ears. The object ahead was barely discernible now, but the details were growing sharper with each passing second. On their left side of the road was an ancient open sparred truck. Livestock was jammed in the back, pressing against the wooden spar supports. Easing out a little Ray saw the road ahead of the truck was clear with enough of room to pass the lumbering vehicle.

"Careful Ray," Frank watched the swaying vehicle and it's unsteady load. The gap between dawdling truck and car was closing rapidly.

"There's plenty room and I want the ton!" Ray said determinedly forcing his eyes beyond the swollen sides of the truck for oncoming traffic. He need not have worried, the road was clear for miles. The only transport they'd laid eyes on since leaving Kyrenia was this dilapidated truck and as the car approached its swaying rear, the occupants could clearly pick out the details.

The load was cattle, held in by the fragile looking spars running parallel along the sides and back. The weight of the animals had flattened the springs at the rear end of the truck.

Ray was already in the overtaking position a good half mile from the truck when he yelled, "That's it, we're over the ton!"

Frank was dimly aware of the excited call as his eyes were locked on the ramshackle abortion that looked like it might fall apart at any moment as pieces of straw and rubbish rushed past the car in its wake.

Suddenly the attitude of the truck changed. There was no signal; no mechanical indication of the driver's intentions, but the vehicle was clearly beginning to turn right, and across their path into a dirt road!

Frank saw many things in the millions of micro seconds that followed; the wide and if not fearful, definitely apprehensive cow's eyes staring balefully down at the car as it sped towards them; the greasy wooden spars bent outwards due to the pressure of the packed animals. Worst of all, the huge right front tyre crunching terribly on the road surface as it turned into their path. The driver of the truck was blissfully unaware of his impending doom whilst cranking and turning the heavy steering wheel clockwise. As the truck started to cross the right lane he casually glanced out through the space in his door where the window used to be. He saw much to his surprise, a white car. It was travelling faster than he had seen anything travel in his entire life and knew at that moment he was finished. He closed his eyes then calmly raised both hands from the wheel in an attitude of prayer. This in itself was a major achievement for the driver had never done anything calmly in a life that was about to end. And it was too late even for prayers.

In the front of the car Frank actually saw the driver close his eyes and felt obliged to follow suit. He felt a light lurch to the left, then to the right and seconds later opened his eyes. The road ahead was clear, they were flying along unimpeded, their speed unabated. He turned to look at Ray. His eyes were staring to the front, robot like as the car arrowed down the road. There was no indication he had just missed certain mutilating death. The bat eared Londoner still sat in the classic driving position; straight back, arms slightly bent, hands lightly holding the wheel.

"How the fuck!?" Frank exclaimed as he craned round to look out the rear window. Josh and Callum in the back were doing the same. The truck had stalled. It was broadside off the road with no movement apart from the cattle. They were showing minute signs of life, continuing to look baleful, the only difference being they were now watching the car speed away from them.

"What happened, how in God's name did you miss it?" Frank was in minor shock, only seconds ago he was facing what appeared certain death, now it might never have happened.

Ray was slowing down, "I don't know," he answered in a sober voice tinged with wonder, "I saw that bloody great front wheel turning across my front," he slightly raised his shoulders, "and I flicked, at least I think I flicked the wheel. We went into the dirt at the side of the road and I thought we must skid so I flicked it again, the other way this time and we were back on the road. If you're asking me how I missed that stupid ... I don't know, I can only say it must have been divine intervention, that's why at the moment, I am not cursing that stupid fu- ... man back there!" He was driving now at a sedate sixty and after what had just happened, it seemed they were moving at walking pace.

Frank continued to study Ray, "Listen my wee cherub, I don't know what you did or how you did it, but that was indeed some sort of a miracle, and to my dyin' day, I'll never understand how you got past that truck on a road such as this, with all that gravel an' stuff at the side."

Ray nodded, "I know. I've come close a few times, but I must admit, that has to be the most hair raising. I hope I never come that close again. I'm using up all my good luck coupons."

"I honestly thought we were kissing our bums good-bye," Josh spoke quietly from the back.

"I know what happened," offered Callum, "I know exactly what happened back there."

"What, what happened Callum?" Frank asked his fellow Scot starting to relax.

"We're bein' saved for better things! The man upstairs has plans for us in the future. I saw it all from back here. It was like bein' at the pictures, and if ever there was a case where we should have been wiped out, oh that was surely it! But ye see, the big finger in the sky wasn't beckonin'. Don't ye see? Somebody up there definitely has plans for us, it just wasn't our time."

"Maybe His plans are just for one of us," said Ray, "and I was driving," he smirked.

"Aye you could be right Ray, But it could be he has plans for just one of us, so maybe that's why you were drivin'! To make sure one of us got through?"

Chapter 13

The change over from the heavy serge of working blue uniforms to the lightweight and more comfortable Khaki Drill, or 'KD,' usually took place over the third weekend in April. The 'old timers', that is those with at least one summer behind them, happily accepted the switch to the lightweight uniform. And most first timers tried to be ready and prepared. But for some, the transformation of the initial wearing of khaki shirts and shorts could prove to be hilarious.

Most newcomers took the 'old timers' advice and had their KD issue tailored before that metamorphic Spring day. But the indelible dyed in the wool military types ignored the well intentioned counsel, deciding to stick with the original garments, afraid with the unauthorised alterations, they may contravene one or more of 'QRs.' Queen's Regulations, the forces bible.

The problem was, all Khaki Drill uniforms had been made in the early thirties to a standard pattern. These had been churned out in their hundreds of thousands over the years with the proviso that if the uniform was too big, which they inevitably were, they could always be altered. Unfortunately initial contracts had been placed and machinists all over Britain were kept in steady employment for many years producing khaki uniforms to a pattern they now knew by heart. This being the case with millions of KD uniforms stockpiled before their production could be halted, the upper echelons of the Royal Air Force turned a blind eye to airmen having their KD issue tailored and re-styled to a more conventional cut. Although the powers that be ignored this exercise, there are many traditionalists in the RAF and to these men the very thought of altering a uniform was sacrilege. It was these dedicated but red faced airmen who turned out at work that April morning with massive baggy shorts down to their sallow knees, and sleeves rolled up to their proportionately chalky white elbows. The legs of the shorts were so wide a good gust of wind could quite easily carry the wearers off over the rooftops of the nearest buildings, or so the jibing wearers of tailored versions claimed.

The wonderful Mediterranean weather was warming up and recent arrivals were reaping in the harvest of the ideal climate. Cars were being bought to tour the many beauty spots and visit otherwise inaccessible exotic beaches, or travel to work, take the kids to school or do the weekly shopping. A car made it easy and convenient to visit the Astra cinemas in Akrotiri or in the married quarters camp at Berengaria on the north fringes of Limassol. Single men bought cars to carry girl friends off in; to make love in at deserted exotic locations far from prying eyes and suspicious parents. Some were buying their first car, others their best car, and some sadly, their last car. After purchasing their vehicles for whatever reason, the new owners wondered how they had previously got by without the convenience of the four wheeled conveyance.

On the Maintenance Unit, the tug of war team started their season with their usual flourish. Callum McAlpine's reformed second team were also doing well having lost only the once to their 'elders.' Their momentum slowed somewhat when Flt. Lt. Barrymore claimed first Connolly and two weeks later Clarke to plug gaps of his UK bound team members. This sparked a jockeying around in the 'B' team for more positions due to arise in the 'A' team. Errol Barrymore was suffering with a paradoxical problem two months ago he could never have foreseen. Five men in the 'B' team could fill the three imminent gaps but all five had flaws; some were as good as they would ever be but not in the Connolly or Clarke class; others would eventually be as good as the Scot or Indian but the flaws were proving obstinate, and Time, the great enemy was short.

The first sports meeting of the new season had already taken place in May. From this a brilliant if inexperienced prospect to replace the departing Flt. Lt. Barrymore. Corporal McAlpine had demonstrated a quite extra ordinary dexterity in winning the humble Maintenance Unit final.

The major Akrotiri sports meeting was now only ten days away when the young coach elect visited the camp gymnasium. He wanted to ask the Physical Training sergeant if he could help with problems he had with two of his team, Josh Munroe and Ray Buckley. For Josh's hands the sergeant produced two heavy-duty squeegees and swore with regular use they would induce the desired results. For Ray's ankles however he came up with an unusual winner. The PT instructor produced two huge toecaps from which extended a rod of steel. If used diligently and faithfully worked on for at least an hour daily, he guaranteed the man's ankles would strengthen up in time for the Akrotiri meeting.

The exercises involved swivelling the ankles to their extremes whilst wearing the contraptions strapped to the toe of each boot. Adjustable weights were attached to the rod extended from the toecap. Callum saw the potential immediately. When signing for the equipment the sergeant added a word of warning.

"Just remember corporal, the MU isn't the only team on the base. I've issued lots of similar gear to a number of other sections."

"Thanks sarge, but if that's the case, they are having problems too."

He took the equipment to Buckley and Munroe insisting they start exercising right away. And to their credit the two airmen unhesitatingly did as their probing coach requested. A strong bond of belief and trust had grown around the red headed Scot.

After only a week Ray's ankles verified vast improvement. He used the equipment at every opportunity and together with Josh working for hours on his hand exercises, the pair were overjoyed at their progress..

Errol experimented with different line-ups in the league matches prior to the Akrotiri and Near East Air Force Championships, searching for the perfect blend. Whether it was due to his single mindedness or blind concentration on the forthcoming events, he was to make a decision which was for Errol a rare and unusual mistake.

A week before the Akrotiri Station Championships, Errol still seeking the perfect eight, picked two men from Callum's 'B' team and put them into his 'A' side for a league match against the HLI. He was hoping this would be his final eight for the remaining matches under his control.

The Highland Light Infantry were based in Cyprus on United Nations duty. The Highlanders, on arrival had learned of the existence of an Inter Services league and being keen on the sport, entered an experienced team. From the fixture list, they saw they were due to meet the previous year's winners, 103 Maintenance Unit 'A' on the 4th June at Episkopi.

If Errol had been more relaxed, his usual clear thinking self, he would have done something he always did when meeting an unknown quantity. That was, look into their background, check their previous form, especially an army team of which he had no previous knowledge.

Errol's team won the match against the HLI that day in early June by two ends to one but was disappointed in his team's performance. They had struggled to win the third and final end which lasted over six murderous minutes. Pleased with their obvious staying power the only missing ingredient needed now to wrap up his perfect team was more muscle, a little injection of strength.

At this point in time, circumstance and fate linked their very considerable powers to work against Errol. Had he taken a few minutes to telephone St. Athens in Wales, which he had done on countless occasions to gain background knowledge on individuals or teams, he would have been entirely satisfied with his team's performance on the 4th of June. He would have learned the same Highland Light Infantry team had met St. Athens in the final of the unofficial UK Inter Services championships the previous August at Braemar in Scotland. The soldiers took an end off the current UK and RAF champions that day also, and fought dourly in the third, only losing out after six long minutes!

Therefore strictly on form Errol's team were on a par with the UK and RAF champions. But Errol, due to the lack of his usual reconnaissance was unaware his best eight had produced a similar result against the doughty Highlanders. And so a tiny fragment of doubt clouded Errol's judgment. He had one remaining league match left against RAF Nicosia. This would decide his team for the NEAF Championships. The previous season, the Nicosia lads were an excellent side so Errol at least had a good yardstick. He dropped the two newly elected men from the close HLI match and chose two from the 'B' team, going for strength and speed against RAF Nicosia.

His new eight literally murdered the RAF men from the island's capitol in a very short one sided match. The first end lasted eleven seconds, the next thirteen! What no one told the

103 MU coach, or indeed what he had never taken the trouble to find out, was the RAF base in Nicosia was in the process of running down prior to closure at the end of the year. Their tug-of-war team from the previous year no longer existed! The men Errol met were simply turning up to fulfil league fixtures with the added attraction of free beers after the match. Errol it has to be said in grossly unusual manner, never questioned the runaway win. Perhaps in his growing desperation to find the absolute cream from what he had available he subconsciously ignored his usual pernickety digging and fooled himself this was the best eight for the forthcoming meetings. The two he dropped from the team that just managed to win against the HLI were Ray Buckley and Josh Munroe. His replacements that did the demolition job in Nicosia were John Tighe and Pete Oldham.

~~~

"Take up ... the rope!" The umpire called raising his arms level on either side of his body.

Errol had been watching the green shirts and white shorts of the RAF Regiment, their co-finalists in the RAF Akrotiri station final. They appeared massive young men but obviously as all had been weighed on the Station Sick Quarters scales, they must be within the 100 stone limit. Funny how the opposition at times appeared bigger, heavier, more formidable prior to a match.

"Take the strain!" The words rolled across the flat field over spectators and participants alike.

The previous afternoon on an adjoining field these finalists had pulled their way through two preliminary rounds, gaining the right to meet for the prestigious title of Akrotiri champions. It was a glorious afternoon; the large crowd had seen lots of competitive sport with a number of records broken in the process. The Station sports day was always well attended and the crowd waited eagerly for the last event of the meeting, the tug-of-war final. The youngsters in the crowd were rooting for the blue and white hooped 103 MU team. The glamour side, reigning champs, the very name carried the charisma of being unbeatable. They looked and carried themselves like winners with the added element of their handsome officer figurehead Errol Barrymore. His clean and sharp good looks guaranteed to sway every neutral in the vicinity. Everyone loves a winner in sport and this tug-of-war team were proven and popular champions.

Conversely, the RAF Regiment team had managed to reach this final twice in the last five years, losing to the MU on each occasion. They were under no illusions of their immense task.

"PULL!" yelled the umpire, simultaneously dropping his arms, bending at the waist.

The drop was equal, neither team gaining an advantage. Errol calmly walked up the rope slightly bent as he looked at each of his men. They were all in perfect position. "Good, well done," was all he said. A minute passed in silence and absolute stillness, then Errol as ever, watchful of the opposing team, knew from the body movements of the opposing coach, a heave was due any second. "Brace yourself lads," he called tersely, "they are about to try and hit you!"

There was a long drawn out "H-E-A-V-E," a sound that always carried with it an echo of threat, of evil intentions, that your opponents are fully intent, if you cannot resist their strength, then they are going to drag you, unceremoniously feet or head first through the dirt.

Errol watched mildly surprised as Connolly's heels ploughed deep grooves in the grass.

"Laus Deo," muttered the officer, "not only do they look strong, they are very strong!"

Another heave and more furrows from the heels of his men. Errol was not worried at this show of brute strength. He knew any eight men foolish enough to expend a great deal of energy dragging a trained, well dug in team would burn themselves out quickly. His team were merely holding, offering resistance but using little energy. It would take an extremely strong team to pull his men through the ground over twelve feet.

The Regiment took the first end. The MU offered only equal resistance but the churned and furrowed ground bore witness to the terrible price the team in green had paid for the opening end. Errol did not attempt a counter heave, his men were applying enough resistance thus sapping the opposition's strength. He did not believe in wasting energy in lost causes.

The crowd warmed to the Regiment, feeling they may be witnessing an upset and cheered the underdogs as the teams changed ends. "Fickle turncoats," Errol grinned as the teams lined up. Nevertheless, he was surprised at the sheer power shown by his opponents.

The MU coach's convictions were well founded as his team took the second end but not without an unexpected and prolonged three minute battle. The officer noticed again, as after the first end the Regiment team could barely stand on rubbery legs, taking time to line the rope.

Errol was confidant as the third and final end got under way. The drop was even. 'They have certainly done their training,' the MU coach noted a little uncomfortably. 'If they look spent why are they proving so stubbornly strong,' He settled down to wait.

A minute passed uneventfully. 'Strange,' thought Errol. He expected a similar assault as in the first end but the opposing coach could now be heard steadying his men.

Furrowed eyebrows hooded Errol's black probing eyes as he looked along the rope. The eight men he could see at the opposite end of the rope were not in any way comfortable; they were ragged, out of position and looking decidedly vulnerable, yet they were holding his team. There could be only one reason why the opposing coach was steadying his men, he was regrouping, gathering their strength! Initially the Regiment had been stronger, they were certainly heavier than his comparatively light 95 stone line up, so the longer this non action went on, the more the heavier side were tapping the reserves of his team. It was a fine balance and Errol was caught in two minds; he had every confidence he would win a prolonged pull, but how strong would the heavier Regiment team be if given time to recover, and how weak his team if he allowed the opposition to sap their strength? He decided to act quickly. Crouching down he called only loud enough for his men to hear, "Prepare for a heave." A surge of authority flowed through Errol as he saw his men tense like the cord of a bowstring awaiting him to loose his arrow of power. "AND!" he yelled into Connolly's face.

"YES!" the roar washed over Errol as the drilled men of the MU team, confidence flowing with pent up patience took five feet but the glow was tempered with the feeling they were pulling an anchor through deep mud. Errol was amazed, as were the men in his team. This feeling was depressing and for lesser teams could be foreboding. Errol tried again, "AND!" once more his team started to move sweetly only to grind to a halt after three feet. The pride of the MU were actually looking tired!

Trying to retain his decorum, Errol looked again at the opposition. The Regiment team were a shambles yet stubbornly resistant to defeat, metaphorically as well as physically digging in. Their very attitudes glowed with defiance. His pride and joy was ragged round the edges as the end crept into its fifth minute. How much did the Regiment have left? Errol had to find out though it would mean gambling with his dwindling vestiges of reserves.

"AND!" he yelled.

The rope crept, resisting the MU team for another three agonising feet but despite all his urging and the team's straining efforts, the last few inches required to win would not come.

Incredibly, as Errol gathered his thoughts, whilst trying to restore confidence into his sagging men, he heard, as threatening as the hissing slide of a dropping guillotine blade, "Heeeave!"

"Brace yourselves," he roared but could do nothing as his beloved team eased over into the bent position then started to lose ground. Slowly and at first under perfect control their authority was reduced to a scrambling shuffle, then stumbling out of control as each man tried to dig in and hold before tumbling forward. They lost all ground so hard won and were three feet from defeat when Errol tossed a trump into the game.

"Prepare to jump ... JUMP!" Errol roared as he sidestepped alongside his disorganised and scrabbling men. Gathering their last ounces of strength for this last attack, and like the well trained team they were, all eight men simultaneously lifted both feet and jumped forward as best they could, digging their heels into new positions as hard as possible.

It was not picturesque, it was not fully coordinated, but all eight men did the one thing they had been taught to do under such circumstances, concurrently. They somehow threw their bodies into a twisting leap like so many salmon and forced their heels deep into the turf together.

The effect was amazing, especially so on the Regiment team. Some of the green shirted team glanced down the rope in confusion thinking the rope had snagged. It had been coming so easily. By some miracle the MU team were back in solid position!

283

Errol glanced at the marker, knowing he had cut his escape route to the finest hair. His team had come to within an inch of losing the crown the MU had held for so many years, HIS team!

This situation was unthinkable! In a flash he was down staring into the face of his No.3 man.

"We've stopped the rot. How do feel Connolly, think we can take them?"

"In a minute, they feel strong. You'll have to get us all together."

Errol nodded then raised his voice but spoke calmly, "We're right on the line gentlemen, don't do anything silly." Despite his tense situation the officer did not betray his inner turmoil.

Standing in the crowd, Callum McAlpine, Ray Buckley and Josh Munroe watched the intriguing final, wondering what was going wrong. It seemed whenever the Regiment put in a heave their team lost ground, which was unheard of! The MU never lost ground so easily. "They must be a helluva strong lot that Raf Regiment mob," Callum muttered, "or somethin's far wrong wi' our lads."

Josh and Ray nodded, speechless at the unexpected turn of events. Callum's eyes flicked along each member of the MU team he knew so well. Searching for anything that might snag his attention then, "Why did I not see that before!" he whispered as his gaze stopped at Tighe and Oldham, "Those two worthies are completely knackered!" Again his words were hissed but Josh replied,." What ... what did you say?"

Callum could not answer as he watched in deep concentration. Nos. 5 and 7 were giving wonderful imitations of how to take position in a tug-of-war team and appear to be contributing as much as everyone else, but in fact were giving very little. As he watched the MU staggered backwards as they somehow took the marker away perhaps three feet from the danger zone and settled down again. How long could six very tired men hold out against eight equally exhausted opponents? Surely numbers must tell in the end. Callum cupped his hand round his mouth, "Give us a bucket the MU, give us a bucket!"

Errol had indeed been contemplating the move. His men had very little left. Connolly had muttered words to the effect when taking those last few feet. If his top man was finished, in what condition was the rest of his team? 'The 'Bucket Throw,' like the

'Jump' was another manoeuvre practiced in training but unproven in a match. He had only seen it used once in Singapore but with devastating effect. His team knew the move perfectly, had practiced it many times but Errol hesitated to use it. He felt he should win without resorting to such a tactic, but he could lose!

As the 103 MU coach deliberated, the RAF Regiment gathered themselves for one last effort. They knew from their coach's urgings, there was three feet of ground to be won that would gain them an acclaimed victory. Their legs felt like lead, hands like lumps of dough but their hearts were huge. "One last heave lads, that's all it'll take, one good un!" cried the coach.

Errol heard the appeal and all indecision left him, "Prepare for a bucket," he roared, not caring who heard the call. His team gathered themselves, knowing if this did not work they were surely beaten.

"BUCKET - BUCKET - THROW!"

The blue and white hooped team, lying on their sides at angles of around thirty degrees with their hands grasping the rope in their groin area suddenly changed shape. All in one movement they bent their knees. As their knees bent, every man in the MU team simultaneously threw their arms and rope straight out to their right. The effect this had on the Regiment team was that rope suddenly came quickly, too quickly and threw them off balance. As they fell backwards, their falling weight pulled the outstretched arms of the MU team round in line again and bent their backs into a cramped sitting position. With their knees and backs bent and the gripped rope between their knees, they were like eight coiled springs! Without any more commands from their coach, for the manoeuvre was carried out in one flowing movement, they threw every last ounce into straightening their backs and knees and literally yanked the unbalanced men at the other end off their feet. It was over in seconds.

Errol was aware of the wildly cheering crowd but he felt the victory was hollow. The MU had won the match but the Regiment were the true winners. He felt bitter! Such gallant resistance should be better rewarded than with loser tags. Where had they got such resilience and strength?

In the crowd a few feet down from where McAlpine, Buckley

and Munroe were standing, two tug-of-war enthusiasts shook their heads in amazement at the versatility of the 103 MU team. They were two airmen on detachment from RAF El Adam in North Africa. Having heard of the team's reputation they watched the final and were totally in awe of what they had just witnessed. "That was amazin'! Shit Tod, the Regiment's a good side, but that MU lot, they really are somethin' else, eh, when they can pull lost ends out of the fire, an' do things like that!" one said appreciating the way the moves had been carried out.

Tod, the other airman, a man of West Indian origin, nodded. "They are very good indeed," he agreed still a little bewildered. "I've never seen anything like that!" He watched admiringly as the MU coach congratulated the Regiment coach, then made his way down the green shirted team who were lying in heaps on the ground. "Yeah," the black man said, "that guy certainly knows what he's doin'"

~~~

In the Peninsula Club that night the usual celebrations were taking place. The active members and followers of the 103 Maintenance Unit tug-of-war team turned out in their numbers and the MU corner was crowded. Every end and move was chewed over, swallowed, regurgitated and picked clean over and over again. Each bone of contention was gnawed upon and sucked until every fibre of recollection was laid out, re-examined then at last stored away in personal vaults under the title of 'Treasured Items' in the memory banks of time.

The bone of contention that was sticking in Frank Connolly's craw was why his team had been towed by admittedly a strong team, but even an extremely strong side could not pull a well organised, well dug in eight men over the distance - twice! Certainly not a team of the MUs calibre. Any team trying to do that should have burned themselves out long before the third end, yet the RAF Regiment were still hauling away well into the third end. It was anyone's guess whether they could have pulled the MU over the retrieved three feet before Barrymore hit them with the Bucket Throw. Whether they could or couldn't the Regiment had produced reserves of staying power in unparalleled proportions that amazed everyone, not least Errol Barrymore himself. 'It seems our team's not all it's cracked up to be, that's the only answer,' thought Frank, 'I'm convinced no eight men could have been that strong.'

"I thought we'd lost it today sir," Callum McAlpine's words cut across Frank's thoughts.

"When the lads went tumblin' arse over tit in that third end I truly thought it was curtains."

"Yes, I agree, perhaps not so colourfully as you describe but I'm so pleased we had that jump move to stop the quite uncharacteristic shambles we somehow got into. If I looked up the rope once, I must have looked a thousand times. I was convinced they had more than the stipulated eight men on the rope. A very strong team indeed."

"They looked heavy too, could they have been over the hundred stone?" asked Nobby Clarke.

"No, I checked the official weight list. They were a few ounces under the limit, which meant we were giving them around five stone. That's quite a lot."

Frank was shaking his head, "They felt like two hundred stone at times."

"Did they? Stronger than you've experienced before Frank?" asked the officer.

"Oh aye, without a doubt. I suppose they could have been a bit stronger than the norm, but then we're no' exactly weaklin's, are we? Somethin'," Frank shook his head, "I don't know, maybe one of our blokes was off colour. We just didn't feel right today somehow."

"Perhaps, but I truly believe everyone of you were heroes today," Errol said thoughtfully before going on, "But I do agree, there was an intangible element I think we were aware of but difficult to determine!"

"I've seen those Regiment guys train on their keep fit programme," said Colin Drake, "and believe me they are all extremely fit. They run for miles in full kit. Their strength and staying power nearly saw us off."

"Yes, those chaps are put to the sword when it comes to keeping fit, but might I remind you," Errol said with a wry smile, "they've trained in that same manner for years, and presented us with no problem last year. We met them and won in two straight pulls. There was something else today however that transformed the whole team. Has anyone any idea what it might have been?"

Blank looks greeted his question then Drake offered, "They really wanted to beat us sir."

"Yes, that was painfully obvious Colin," Errol laughed but his captain was not to be so easily sidetracked. "No, what I mean is they desperately wanted to beat us. US, sir, the 103 MU team. They would have died out there today to have beaten 103 Maintenance Unit."

Errol was nodding, "You are close, so what word sums up their desperation to beat us?"

Callum recalled Errol's first meeting in the marquee, "Determination will beat the best of teams," he said, "they were determined to beat us today."

"Precisely Callum. Some of you may think I have been hammering a dead horse with that word, but today after the final whistle, I went immediately to offer my congratulations to the coach on their splendid performance. He reciprocated on our display of course then said something to me that totally gratified me and explained the essence of their resistance. His precise words were, 'Yes sir, I was a little surprised at their efforts myself. They've been working hard for weeks and were determined to beat you today, the renowned one-oh-three-m-u team, absolutely determined they were sir!'"

Nods and frowns moved around the gathered heads then Callum said, "I think, although I hope it doesn't happen in my time, but surely it's just a matter of time before someone, some camp with a very good team, comes along with that same determination we saw today, and beats us. Now that team, whoever they are, are goin' to take some catchin'."

The same agreeing nods and frowns were seasoned with comments, "Never," and "No way!"

Callum was not finished, "When you think about today's match, the Regiment were not such a good side. They had strength and determination sure, but that was all, they weren't a great team."

Errol cast his junior coach a quizzical glance, "What exactly are you saying Callum?"

"In your own words sir, any team that beats us would have to be, first and foremost, an exceptionally good side. I agree with that, but let's assume, theoretically, just for argument's sake, in

288

today's final, if determination was equal in both sides, then we were nearly beaten by a poor team!"

This time Errol's brows met in the middle, "Are you implying our team lacks determination?"

"No no sir, I said if determination was equal - on both sides"

"Then please, I understand what you are saying but your point eludes me," said the officer beginning to wonder if the observant young Scot had seen something he himself had missed.

"Well sir, the Regiment lads were stronger than us from the word go, our team had no answer, we gave way on their first heave!" Callum shook his head, "That's not like our blokes."

The surrounding group of men and women went quiet, but Errol stared intently into the unflinching blue eyes. He felt a slight note of discord strum across the tightening chords of his belly. He did not want to, was hoping not to find fault with this team, not now, it was too close to the NEAF championships. Then again, this young man did not express his views lightly and Errol felt sure his disciple had more to offer. "Tell me Callum," Errol spoke quietly and slowly, "did you perhaps pick up any faults in my team today?"

Callum remembered Tighe and Oldham but why had no one else witnessed their if not feigned, certainly less than wholehearted efforts? Was it possible he was mistaken? On that theory he was not prepared to expose the two in front of a group gathered to celebrate the team's win. He would speak to the coach at a later date. "Sir, today I saw eight tired men, some worse than others. They appeared to be givin' their all, again some more than others. A man can only give his best, but sometimes his best is not enough."

"You should have been a politician Cpl. McAlpine, you speak a lot of words but say nothing that we do not already know," Errol smiled trying to hide the doubts that had taken flight in his head. He had been content with his team's performance. They had after all beaten a very strong, and the magic word, determined side today. Or did the Regiment appear strong because of a weakness in his own team? There was nothing wrong with his men's fighting abilities or the way they had worked so precisely with the Bucket Throw. The concentrated Jump Stop was not so pretty or precise in its execution, yet worked perfectly, but then these manoeuvres were last minute escape moves, to get out of trouble. So why were they in trouble in the first place?

Niggling productive and counter productive thoughts were digging at the pedestal foundations he had placed his final eight men upon. He wanted to relax his mind, ease it away from the worry of the one remaining hurdle that barred his way to complete perfection. Every match, up to and including the final in the NEAF championships would inevitably be a hard fought contest. Could they be harder than today's match? Errol sighed, should he take the word of a raw young man with little experience in the sport yet had a natural eye and talent as he had displayed many times? The coach collected every clue and scrap of information and stored them in yet another pocket reserved in his brain for later scrutiny. He wanted to enjoy the night with his wonderful team. There were not many left.

The party began to break up as the 11 o'clock closing time approached. Errol left early as usual knowing his presence would stifle any boisterous feelings that may erupt later. Before leaving he drew Frank Connolly aside, "I hear your wife and family are to join you in the next few days. I'm very happy for you Frank. I hope they like it here."

"Thank you sir, I'm sure they'll love it."

The officer looked hesitant for a moment then said, "I hope you won't think I'm interfering with your personal life Frank, but you haven't seen your wife for three months. As you know we face the pinnacle of our year in two weeks and frankly, I am building my plans, my team around you. You are aware of that?"

"No sir," Frank was surprised, "around me? I didn't know that sir."

"You're the No.3 man, and a very good one, but your position carries a lot of responsibility, so I hope you won't overdo anything in the next two weeks, that's all I ask. Goodnight Frank."

Frank watched the officer wend his way through the tables, smiling, shaking hands. 'Hope he's no' askin' what I think he's askin',' thought the Scot. 'I think he's just asked me to stay away from Lorna until after NEAF. Aye well, that's all very well, but will Lorna stay away from me!'

Groups broke up as they went their separate ways with John

Tighe and Pete Oldham bidding goodnight to their GEF team mates as they reached the MT billets. They were laughing as both stumbled down a small slope still in high spirits. The combined efforts of both men to the teams success that afternoon was too harsh to be described as minimal, but fell short of their normal full blooded efforts. Their contribution to the evening's party had been much higher with their good natured and quick-witted repartee. They were still giggling like a couple of errant school boys sneaking back to their dormitory as Pete steadied himself after nearly falling. He clasped the little plinth mounted chrome statuette and held it out at arm's length. "I'm so chuffed with this trophy John," he exclaimed.

"Why's dat?"

"Well, back home I've got trophies for soccer, cricket, darts and boxing. This little beauty is the first I've won at the noble art of tug-of-war," answered Pete, holding up and silhouetting the figure against the pale moon.

"We were fockin' lucky t'win the bloddy t'ings," said John, thinking back to the afternoons exertions. "Oi swear t' God, nivver bin so knackered in me fockin' loife."

Pete nodded, "Shouldn't have gone to Limassol last night, it wasn't fair on the lads."

"Sshhush up your fockin' mouth man," said John looking round furtively. "Shore we weren't t' know we were gonna git involved wit' dat bitch, now isn't dat so?"

Pete did not answer. He saw again the woman on the beach, waiting for him as John rolled off her. "We shouldn't have gone to town knowing we had the final today," he said, his guilt rising.

"Fock you Pete, we only went for a coupla drinks, where's d' harm in dat?"

"Yeah," Pete said sarcastically, "a couple of drinks."

The mindless pair had ordered their tenth double brandy in a small bar at the far end of the Bypass. They had played darts all evening and in the process, chased away all opposition. It was midnight anyway and about to declare the night's action was over when a woman in her late twenties walked into the bar.

The airmen gave each other a sidelong glance at this bizarre opportunity for as John said later, 'A woman walks inta a bar at midnoight, alone, shore she's only lookin' for the one t'ing, and it most certainly is not a game a darts or a fockin' drink!'

The attractive woman with flaming red hair wearing an expensive light summer dress ordered a double whiskey which saw John leave his seat. He ambled over to her, paid for her drink and immediately started a conversation. The fairly tall and sharp aristocratic featured woman was easy to talk to and when Pete joined them, she explained without preamble. She was the wife of an army officer who she had left only minutes ago. As he undressed for bed, she noticed, not for the first time, smudged lipstick and sperm on his underwear. She was now hell bent on getting laid for the first time by someone other than her husband. If she had not met the airmen she would have offered herself to the man behind the bar or to the first taxi driver. Indeed anyone who would have her. The woman told her story in monotonic sophisticated speech, as if taking a test. "Well now missus," John said, "you don't want to be goin' off wi' these nasty local chappies, you could end up in a bloddy harem, and ye know what them places are loike. You could wait yares for what me an' me mate here are prepared to give ye, when ye'r ready."

The woman took them in her car to Ladies Mile beach. Once there she stripped off and lay down on a blanket she brought from the car, then calmly waited legs apart, arms behind her head.

It was cold and brutally callous but this did not worry either of the young men. They spun a coin and as always Pete lost to John's call of, "Heads Oi win, tails you lose,"

Pete sat on the sand and smoked waiting his turn. He was not particularly excited about having sex, perhaps slightly uneasy about being able to perform after all the drink. His feelings did change however as he watched John throw the woman around like a rag doll in a myriad of sexual contortions for over an hour. By the time an exhausted John detached himself from his partner and twisted blanket Pete was more than ready.

The woman looked much better than John; indeed she was surprisingly fresh, as if she had not taken part in anything tiring, let alone sexual convulsions. As Pete approached he felt this female looked grossly out of place. She should not be on a beach in the middle of the night screwing two strangers. Whilst removing his clothes the woman stood up, shook then spread out the blanket. He was mildly surprised again as she calmly got down, roll over onto her back, then supporting her upper body on her elbows beckon him over like an experienced whore.

When Pete finished John joined them and they formed a threesome until the sun streaked its golden rays across the eastern sky. At this point the woman thoughtfully smoked a cigarette, walked naked to the sea, had a short swim, then dressed and gave the two airmen a lift back to Akrotiri. She dropped them, and without a word, turned the car round and drove off.

John watched the car's twist of trailing dust with a philosophical look on his face. After a few minutes when the engine sound and dust had subsided, he turned to his friend who was smoking his last cigarette. "You know Pete, dis is the forst toime in me fockin' loife, in a situation such as dis, Oi'm the one that feels Oi've been focked. It's a strange feelin'."

They fell into bed half an hour before the others rose for work. This was not the first time the pair had returned to their billet in such a condition. It happened a number of times after visits to bars, brothels or homes of prostitutes in the seedier parts of Limassol. They were young and their bodies would slowly recover during the course of the day.

The difference was they had never faced a tug-of-war final the following day on previous excursions to the sea port town of Limassol.

When Tighe and Oldham lined up that afternoon, they believed the RAF Regiment might be a problem initially, but one that would be overcome, as always.

By the third end the marrow in their bones had turned to the consistency of water and although trying their best, were barely hanging on, reacting only by instinct to the commands.

The moonlight cast a silvery blue sheen over the roofs of the MT billets as the two friends staggered towards them. They had gone quiet on the last stretch as both were feeling their guilt but they were happy too for nothing was lost. Their team had won despite their watered down contributions so the world had not been knocked off its axis with their irresponsible actions.

John broke the silence, "When you t'ink about it Pete. you know, we got t'best o' both worlds you an' me! We got our ends away did we not, wit' a sophisticated an' beeyootifool bit a skirt an' we won the bloddy trophy too. We done our little bit didn't

293

we, in fact we did our bit Oi don' know how many toimes," he guffawed, "an' no harm done."

"We came damn near to losing this," Pete said wagging the small statuette under the bleary eyes of the Irishman. "We can always get our ends away any day of the week John. But it's not every day we can win one of these little beauties with the best team you and I are ever likely or lucky enough to be part of ever again. We let them down John, we could have lost it for them."

John was silent as he eyed Pete's trophy. "Oi suppose you're roight, we were fockin' stupid, still Oi wonder," he paused with a thoughtful look on his boyish face gazing up at the moon,

"Oi wonder if we could find dat lovely laydee again t'noight if we went lookin' for her. Y'never know, shore she coulda found lipstick on her old man's drawers again, ye know ... an' there's no final t'morrah!"

Chapter 14

Frank stood at the fence where thousands of airmen had stood before anxiously watching the buses as they stopped at the Arrivals point. It was hard to believe only three months had passed since he and Marion had met Harry Ross at this very spot. In that relatively short time he had made many friends, saw a fair part of the island and seen to the business of renting a lovely house. Yet despite his crammed life, it was all curiously empty without Lorna and the girls.

A friendship had grown between himself and the Ross's. Due mainly to Marion and her fixation that Frank needed looking after. He had spent a sprinkling of weekends in their Limassol home and was persistently reminded after his family landed on the island, Frank must bring them to visit. "Now you remember Frankie Connolly, the very first chance you get, you bring them here for their dinner. I won't chance anything new with them, just in case, so you bring them or I'll be awful angry with you!"

The quicker Lorna arrived the better. Frank recalled Marion's mind boggling smile and her warm nature. 'A lassie like that could very easily get under a man's skin.' He inwardly admitted he loved Marion, but not in the groin burning physical need for her. That special feeling he reserved only for Lorna. His feelings for Marion were deep but being the man he was, Frank only allowed them to lean no farther than platonic warmth and brotherly protection.

Suddenly Lorna stepped off the bus turning immediately to help five-year-old Caroline down the high step. Frank called and waved but Lorna appeared not to hear as she lifted three-year-old Dawn down, the child nearly falling over in her excitement. As they walked to the building Lorna turned and looked directly into Frank's eyes. He waved. She saw him but turned away.

Frank frowned, "She must be gettin' short sighted in her old age - and deaf," he mumbled as Lorna herded her girls into the

Arrivals Hall. An impatient twenty minutes later Lorna holding the children's hands, emerged and again his wife not a dozen paces away, looked at him only to look away. Caroline looked at her father, then at her mother doubtfully.

'This is ridiculous,' thought Frank, 'what are they playin' at?'

Dawn looked at Frank and he smiled at her. She squealed and galloped straight into his arms which seemed to set Lorna and Caroline free from their trance. Suddenly Frank was surrounded with arms and heads and kissing squealing mouths. After a few minutes when the welcoming embraces settled down, Frank asked "What was wrong with you, I know you saw me but you didn't let on, what were ye playin' at?"

Lorna was staring at him with round eyes, "I didn't fancy throwing my arms round one of the locals, and that my dearest darlin' man, is what I thought you were!"

Frank's brow furrowed, "What ...?" he spluttered.

"Think about it, the last time I saw you, you had a full head of hair and light skinned. Now you're nearly bald and dark as treacle toffee," she giggled.

Frank drew a hand over his short crew cut forgetting he had followed the cult of short haircuts. Reaching for her he drew her close, "Oh how I've missed you," he whispered in her ear.

Lorna pushed him away, much too coy to show her feelings in public, "Me too," she smiled up at him, "now let's go to this new home you've been so proud of in your letters. You can show me there how much you've missed me. Mind you Frank, I'm not sure I like the crew cut."

Frank felt a surge in his throat, she was all the woman he would ever want but his feelings were diverted when his trouser leg was tugged. Caroline and Dawn were looking up at him, the latter still clinging to his trousers. He bent down, "What is it my wee beauties?" he asked the round questioning, and very pale faces.

"Dad," Dawn sang, gazing into his face intently, "why ARE you so dark?"

"It's the sun darlin', it makes everybody's skin dark. Anybody who spends lots of time in the open, the darker their skin will get. I've spent some time in the sun the past three months."

296

Dawn seemed to accept his explanation. After collecting the luggage Frank led them to the hired Cortina Estate. "Ours?" Lorna asked hopefully as Frank placed the luggage in the boot.

"Yes and no. Ours until Sunday night, it goes back Monday."

"Thought it was too good to be true," Lorna said settling into her seat as Frank helped the girls clamber into the back bubbling with excitement.

Frank drove through the heart of the camp and passing the entrance of the Maintenance Unit said loudly, "That's where I work, 103 MU, it's a little camp within a camp," he explained.

A open topped Land Rover driven by Midnight Johnson stopped at a junction on the road ahead. Frank saw him and waved. Midnight seeing Frank and his passengers, waved exuberantly showing a slash of white teeth. Dawn turned and watched the first black person she had ever seen recede in the distance. "Dad?" she said, her tone already asking the question, "Dad, that man! He must've spent lots and LOTS of time in the sun?"

Lorna looked at Frank, both smiling at her innocence, "I'll explain later," her mum said.

The next three days were spent in idyllic bliss for the Connollys. Frank drove them to the main places of interest around Limassol. Roman sites abounded along the roadsides overlooking the deserted golden beaches skirted with white fringes of frothy foam. The sea varying in patches of colour from the lightest opal to deep blue. The children wandered among the ruins of a site known as 'Apollo's Temple' until a snake skated quickly from one mound of square cut stones to another. After that they never left their father's side.

Saturday was spent on Ladies Mile beach where Frank erected a tent he had made in the Fabric section for the sum of three pounds. It was an ingeniously simple structure perfectly adequate for the beach. Made from calico it formed a six feet square box tent with one side of the cube that opened up to form an awning. There were six poles, one for each corner and two for the awning.

Ladies Mile was deserted and Lorna, Frank and the kids spent their first day together at a Mediterranean haven, swimming. Later they stopped and ate spaghetti at a restaurant Frank spotted on the way home. When retiring after a long satisfying day, the couple made love for the third night in a row, unheard off since their honeymoon. Their lovemaking on this third night was by far the most fulfilling. The first two nights had been greedy, bordering on the edges of desperation for each other, whereas on the Saturday, their union was warm relaxed and totally fulfilling. The separation highlighted their awareness of each other but now they took their time. It happened again on Sunday morning and as they lay in each other's arms Frank gasped into Lorna's neck, "We should separate more often."

"Don't you dare believe it," Lorna shot back, "I don't care where Mr. Connolly F. is posted in future, Mrs. Connolly L. goes with him from the word go, even if I go in his holdall!"

Frank smiled at the thought of packing her into his RAF grip. "That would be nice," he whispered, "bet the blokes in my billet wouldn't complain either."

One of the children went to the toilet and Frank eased back to his own side of the bed just as Dawn burst into the room. "Are we goin' to the beach Dad?" she shouted.

"Not today ye wee demon, we're goin' to see a friend of mine and I want your mum to meet a very nice lady," Frank said grabbing the wild bundle of young life.

"Can we meet the nice lady too," she yelled in his ear.

"Aye of course. The lady's lookin' forward to meetin' all three of you."

They spent a lazy morning in their new home and Frank introduced three very wary females to a basking chameleon. He placed it on a green paper bag and everyone watched fascinated as the reptile changed from a drab grey to bright green. Dawn immediately claimed it as a pet. Frank sat back happily watching all three chatter excitedly as the chameleon held their undivided attention. Life for Frank Connolly was full again.

~~~

A little after two o'clock Frank turned into Pappachristos street, an area he had grown familiar with over the past three months. As he neared the house Frank saw a green Ford van in the driveway. Sitting on the veranda Harold looked up as Frank parked and gave a quick wave.

The children went quiet as their father helped them out of the car and Lorna in an unguarded moment, opened her door to get out. To her horror she discovered the kerb was high on her side. Realising too late she should have waited for Frank but it was too late now as she struggled to lift her bum out of the seat. In the process her very much in fashion mini skirt hitched even higher up her thighs. Harold from his veranda vantage point smiled appreciatively down at her.

Lorna knew she had an excellent figure, especially her legs which she'd always been proud of though it was never in her nature to flaunt. She looked after her twenty four year old body and even after two children her figure could still slip perfectly into a size ten dress. 'Still the same old Harry,' she thought recalling their introduction at a Leuchars dance. He had danced and held her far too close that night; his whole demeanour suggesting all females should fawn and melt in his presence. None of these things went down well with Lorna. She did not particularly like Harold, nor did she dislike him. Her feelings towards the man were neutral.

"Thank God for the cavalry," she said lightly as Frank arrived to drag her out of her predicament, "better late than never I suppose," she added pulling her skirt into place.

"I would have helped you but I never do anything to spoil a good show," laughed Harold, "besides you've got nothing to be ashamed off."

Lorna smiled despite herself, gaining an early glimpse of Harold's perennial patter. He just could not resist the challenge of a female in close proximity, whatever her availability.

An extremely beautiful, dark haired girl emerged from the front door and Harold smiled warmly at her. As he did so Lorna saw immediately Harold was in love with this girl. The moment she appeared he was transformed, the outer cloak of pretentiousness dropped away and his bared soul gelled with this lovely girl's aura. The girl's appearance brought with it a moment of indecision; who would make the introductions? Lorna recognising the younger girl's hesitancy, stretched out her hand. "Hello, I'm Lorna Connolly, you must be Marion, my ignorant husband's second love. He talks about you all the time. I'm so pleased to meet you."

Marion's eyes flashed towards Frank, her lovely smile spreading across her face, "Oh Frank Connolly, I thought that was our little secret," she laughed happily, "Yes Lorna, you're right, I'm Marion. Please bring the children inside, I've got Fanta and Seven Up in the 'fridge. We'll ignore these bores, let them see to themselves. Oh, I've been so looking forward to meeting you ...."

"Well, how's that for a 'How's yer father,'" said Frank as the females retreated into the house, "women like that drive men to drink."

"Thought you would never ask," Harold said as he too followed the women inside only to emerge seconds later with two beers. Handing one to Frank he said, "Nice Cortina, is it hired?"

"Aye, afraid so, but I intend to get me a car as soon as the 'Livin' Out' allowance goes into my pay. Can't live in a terrific place like this without a motor."

Harold nodded, "And lots of nice cars to chose from. Saabs seem popular with that Carlson bloke winning those rallies. I fancied one but five and a half hundred's a little out of my range."

They sat down discussing the plus and minuses of which car was the best buy in the tax free zone enjoyed by British servicemen serving abroad. As they spoke, Frank's attention was again drawn to the new Ford van in the driveway. "Does that belong to the landlord?"

Harold shook his head, "I've been wondering if you noticed it. No it's mine."

"Yours," said Frank in surprise, "a van! What do you want a van for?"

"Couldn't refuse it, it was such a bargain," Harold said emphatically. "I was looking for a car in the showrooms along the Bypass and saw that," he nodded towards the van. "Some British bloke working for MPBW had ordered it, paid the deposit then for some reason was recalled back to the UK They were only asking two hundred with no deposit. They're three seventy five brand new." Harold hoped it sounded convincing.

Only two days previously Harold had bought the van for the full price, to be paid in instalments over the remainder of his stay. Vans were universally cheaper than cars but it was not for that purpose Harold had invested in such a vehicle.

"That is a bargain Harry," said the Scot stepping down into the driveway and walking round the van, "I suppose it is a good idea for you and Marion with no kids. You can stash all your gear in the back and get away for weekends. Fit it out properly you could even sleep in it, do a bit o' campin'. Was that the plan?"

"That's exactly what I was thinking," Harold answered as Frank unconsciously presented him with the avenue of escape he needed. "Marion wants to put curtains on the back windows and a mattress for weekends in the mountains," he winked.

"Aye, well knowin' you Harry, as long as the mattress is for Marion an no' for the other bits o' stuff you tend to gather." Frank returned the wink to the golden tanned figure. The dour Scot had already breached his plans as he spotted something rolled up at the back of the van.

"It's only one of those three inch thick foam things I scrounged from the gym, not a bloody great big Dunlopillow Frank. You make it sound like I'm fitting up a travelling knocking shop."

Frank said nothing but raised his eyebrows and nodded his head slowly.

"It was Mari's idea to get a mattress for Christ's sake," Harold lied, pangs of guilt nipping the edges of his voice. He changed the subject. "Anyway, how goes it with this fucking tug-of-war team of yours, you've got the big one this week haven't you, the NEAF?"

"Aye, the big one, the Nee-aff championships," Frank confirmed saying the four letters as a word, "and Barrymore's havin' kittens pickin' his team."

"Can the MU win it again?"

"Oh I think so, we should win it but there's a wee flaw somewhere. We haven't been properly tested since the Regiment nearly buggered us up at the Station sports. There's lots of unknown teams comin' from all points in the Med., all hell bent on liftin' our scalps."

"The Regiment had you beat. If it was not for that bloody move Barrymore hit them with, they would have won, and I'm not sure if throwing the rope at them like you did was legal."

"It must've been otherwise we would've been disqualified. But it should never have come so close. In truth Harry, on a normal day we should have won without all that trouble, honestly."

"Well you won that's all that matters, even if you had to use that manoeuvre to clinch it."

"That's the trouble, the boss didn't want to use the Jump or Bucket Throw. He wanted to save them, in case we get into difficulties elsewhere, you never know." Frank sounded concerned.

"You can still use it. If you say it's legal what's to stop you?"

"Nothin', but the element of surprise has gone hasn't it? That counts for a lot in this game."

"In any game Frankie boy," said Harold thoughtfully.

~~~

On the day prior to the Near East Air Force championships, to be held at the beautiful sports ground in Happy Valley, Flt. Lt. Barrymore faced a dilemma he had never come across before. At this very late stage as he waited for the last of his team and probables to gather at the training area, he still had slight misgivings about his final selection. This team if successful would project his name throughout the Air Force as the coach who had gone unbeaten for three years against the strongest of opposition. His gut feeling had always seen him through in the past when in doubt about selections, but it was the same twisting cords in his belly that were now telling him something was wrong. Since the Station final and the diplomatic words of doubt expressed by his second team coach, he had mentally juggled with six names from which he may, or may not, use to improve his team. He was so lucky in getting Connolly, Clarke and Banks who slotted sweetly into the side but the last two positions were proving a massive headache.

Was it only a little over two weeks ago excitement had run riot when Errol felt he had at last found his final team selection? The eight men had moved sweetly and made what he thought was a very good team from Nicosia look like beginners. Then as he had done after the Akrotiri final, Cpl. McAlpine had discovered only the other day, the base in Nicosia were winding down! The team they put out for their league match actually were beginners! 'Why did I not have that information before the Nicosia match?' Errol reproached himself. 'I'm letting it slip, I once made it my business to know when the opposition laundered their shirts or changed heel plates. There was nothing I did not know about the opposition a week in advance, yet I did not know Nicosia and their 'team' were a few blokes out for free beers. I should have known, I should have KNOWN!' He was growing angry with himself again. 'Pull yourself together man,' he mentally tightened up, 'one more championship, one more team selection to make so don't balls it up my boy. Pull your head out of the sand, stick to the well trodden path that's served so well in the past.' He blinked rapidly and cast his eyes over the group.

"Gentlemen, this afternoon we stand at the threshold of a unique opportunity. No military tug-of-war team has gone three years unbeaten in every competition it has participated in. We, that is 103 Maintenance Unit stand on the brink of that achievement. It will be our privilege to maintain that proud record this afternoon when we take part in the pull-off matches to decide tomorrow's finalists. I have no doubt I could pick any eight men from your midst and I would have a very good team, but I do not want a very good team, nor will I settle for an excellent team. What I want gentlemen, is the best team!" Errol looked from face to each immobile face, before going on, "I am not about to tell you all how important this competition is to me personally, you are all well aware of that. However, before my final selection I want to appeal to you to be brutally truthful in this one request I make to you all. If any one of you feel for one reason or another that he cannot do himself or the MU justice this afternoon, I humbly ask you to raise your hand, or indicate in any manner you see fit, that you do not wish to be considered for selection. It will never be held against you. Rather, I will think the best of any man who is honest with me on this point!" The thought suddenly crossed the officer's mind it was not beyond the realms of possibility that Connolly might raise his hand! Had not this young man, and also Buckley's wife and family arrived on the island very recently - after a three month separation? Errol felt an unusual tinge of sweat flush across his forehead and suddenly a trickle run down under his arm. His whole person was reacting most peculiarly. With a huge intake of breath he saw only one hand raised. It was corporal Jim Miller, one of the six on Errol's short list.

"Miller, you're not available?" the coach asked.

"No sir, I don't think so. I've had a bad gut these past few days and feel a bit washed out."

"Thank you, I'm sorry to hear that but I appreciate you telling me. You were on my short list.. Stomach upsets can be most debilitating, thank you again. Anyone else?"

Errol waited. Apart from one or two who took a sudden interest in clouds or feet, the men could have been carved in stone. They all wanted a place in his team, which pleased the coach, but apart from Miller vetoing himself, his final team selection was made only marginally easier.

'Why,' the coach asked himself, 'am I messing about? Three quarters of the team picks itself! I still have three from last year plus the addition of Connolly, Clarke and Banks. I simply have to decide which of Muir, Oldham, Tighe, Buckley or Munroe will slot in the last two places.' The last two names entered his calculations solely on Cpl. McAlpine's recommendation. He made up his mind. It was simple really. All of his five prospective team members were so close in every respect his decision would rest on a physical inspection!

At the end of the minute of dead silence Errol said, "All right gentlemen, I can safely assume I can select any eight men from among you and I will end up with a team of hale and hearty individuals?" He nodded, "Good, then in that case I wish to inspect your hands please."

There were some questioning glances but the men dutifully held their hands out for inspection as the coach passed down the line. Errol was giving the upturned palms only cursory glances. He was scrutizing facial features for tired or baggy eyes, slack or puffy faces; anything that indicated over indulgence in any form.

Every face Errol passed abounded with health and vigour; suntanned features, clear eyes and tight glowing skin. Every set of hands, Errol noted with satisfaction, showed the tell tale thick leather pad at the base of each finger and round the heel of the palm. His spirits had started to climb again when they were brought to a halt as he looked into the face of Ray Buckley.

"Hello Buckley, how does your wife like Cyprus?" Errol asked conversationally.

"Loves the weather but hasn't had the chance to see much of

the island as yet. She only arrived yesterday morning sir." Ray replied.

"And are you all right?" Errol was peering at the haggard eyes sitting in their heavy dark cups.

"One of the kids had a toothache last night, kept us up for a while but I'm fit sir, feeling good."

"I'm sure you are, thank you," the officer said passing on to the next man, but his thoughts were written plainly across his face. Buckley's slack features and puffy skin had been noted.

Ray did not miss the look and after dismissal as he joined the others in the shade of the trees he moaned, "I've not got a chance of getting into the team, not now, not after last night!"

"Don't talk crap Ray, everyone's got a chance," Frank said glancing at the disconsolate figure.

Ray shook his head. He was thinking how ironic it was; how he had trained hard for weeks with the ankle weights given to him by Callum, how he had proved his ability on the rope with the second team. When Babs and his family arrived, he tentatively explained to his wife he was in full training, in excellent prime condition and had a good chance of getting into the team. He hoped she would understand for the next few days he had to stay at his physical peak. Babs had laughed at her cowed husband. "Great!" she cried, "I was expecting a physical onslaught, but if you're trying to tell me I have gained a few days reprieve – great. Besides, I'm in the middle of my period so it's worked out well for both of us, hasn't it?" Babs spoke lightly, "You know I never time that properly anyway," she laughed.

Babs knew from his letters how keen he was to make the team for some big games or other, but as luck would have it, their oldest daughter, four year Shirley had a nagging toothache which started the day they left home. The previous night Babs attended to Shirley as best she could, but Ray could get no sleep as the apple of his eye fretted through the small hours. He joined Babs and did what little they could until morning when mysteriously, the toothache disappeared!

On reporting to the Armoury, Chief Tech, McKinley took one glance at the airman who was a constant source of good-natured banter in the section and made the obvious assumption regarding his haggard looks. "I take it Buckley you kept your promise; when you got your wife home. The second thing she would be allowed to do was put down her suitcase?" McKinley had snickered as the sorry looking sight of the airman. The well used traditional comment brought no response from Buckley, maintaining the crusty old Chief's lurid vision of what had taken place in the Buckley household the previous night.

Ray could have taken two days compassionate leave allowed to airmen for family arrivals, but he did not apply, knowing Flt Lt Barrymore was selecting his team this morning. He had to be present if he hoped to be picked. Now the young Londoner sat disconsolately knowing the coach had peered closely, too closely at him and like everyone else had misinterpreted why he looked so drained. Ray glanced up and saw Callum looking at him, "I never touched her!" he declared as Frank joined the pair. "I swear to God I never laid a finger on her, we agreed ...." he said vehemently. "It was Shirley, poor little bugger had the toothache." He threw the pebble he had been turning nervously in his hands, hard into the sand at his feet. "Why does he not put me on the rope, one against one to see who's strongest," he turned to see Frank shaking his head, "I'd back myself to out pull you or anyone!" he glowered at the Scot.

Frank merely nodded his head in sympathy, "He doesn't believe in one against one Ray."

Callum believed Ray would be a good addition to the team and was not convinced Barrymore would not pick him. "Look Ray, I'll have a word with the boss before he makes his selection. Don't write yourself off, no' just yet."

Callum crossed the dusty ground to the coach who was scribbling almost agitatedly on his clipboard. "Sir, may I have a word?" he asked.

"Of course, what can I do for you?" the officer looked up, his usual smile was somehow taut.

"It's about Buckley sir, he -"

"McAlpine!" Errol cut him off, "I've made my selections. I found it extremely difficult but ...."

"If you have not included Buckley sir, with respect, you're makin' a terrible mistake."

Callum emulated Errol by cutting off the officer's words as he blurted out what he had to say. In so doing he stepped into an area where he had never previously ventured. He was made aware of his unsound footing by the glare from the officer.

No one had ever spoke to Errol in this manner, nor had anyone questioned his judgment, therefore the coach himself was on new ground. "I hear what you are saying and I understand your feelings perfectly." His voice was tight. "This is an entirely new situation for me. Usually my teams pick themselves and are proven and tested long before they reach this crucial stage prior to a competition. However, be that as it may I have picked what I consider my best eight. My selection methods have worked perfectly in times gone by. Whether by good fortune or otherwise I cannot truthfully say but I rely heavily on my experience and intuition. Corporal ... Callum," the officer's voice softened, "your day will come. Today is my day and be it on my head I feel through the methods I have just explained, I have picked my best eight men from this group."

His manner suggested the conversation was over but Callum was not finished.

"Sir," he said in a respectful tone, trying one last time, "I promise you, Buckley's ankles are stronger than Connolly's, his hands stronger than -"

"McAlpine!" Errol snapped, barking out the name as he would a command, "must I repeat myself. I have made my selection. Thank you!"

For the second time Errol was to experience a mood that committed in any other sphere of the Royal Air Force would surely amount to stubborn insubordination. Callum spoke slowly and deliberately. "Sir, if Buckley is not among your eight names, you're weakenin' your team and makin' a big mistake."

"Then so be it corporal! I stand and if necessary shall fall by my selection. Now if you do not mind I would like to get on. My being questioned like this is most unusual but I feel it is for the good of the Unit that is causing you to act this way. That in itself is most commendable and overlooks your dissension. But don't worry, I know what I am doing." With that he pushed past the unusually aggressive figure of his outspoken subordinate. The coach of the 103 tug-of-war team strode away. He was not angry but unsettled. The fiery Scot was only speaking out for the good of the MU. No one could blame him for that, it simply displayed where the man's heart lay. Equally Errol could only place his faith in what he thought was his best and his best today he felt sure, would win him the Near East Air Force championship. He approached the expectant group under the trees.

~~~

Chapter 15

On a lush piece of turfed land adjacent to the Happy Valley sports ground, fifteen teams waited to take part in the pull-off matches. At the end of the day only two of those fifteen would emerge unbeaten, winning the right to meet in the morrow's final, which would decide the overall Near East Air Force tug-of-war champions.

It was necessary to stage the pull-off matches on a spare piece of ground as it was doubtful if plough shares could inflict more damage to turf than vast numbers of driving heel chopping boots could do in the space of one afternoon. Thus the hallowed green turf immediately in front of the stand was reserved for the two teams left after this afternoon's efforts. These two groups of men would be allowed, in the sacred name of sport, to tear and hack the bowling green surface for a short spell of time in order to decide who would wear the mythical winners crown. Afterwards grounds men would repair the damage, roll the ground back to its pristine condition where it would lie in wait for the heel plates of next year's marauders.

The draw had been made and as luck would have it the MU drew the only bye in the first round. It meant a long wait as the seven first round matches had to be decided before the name of 103 MU could go back into the hat for the second round draw. Errol told his men to walk around in plimsolls, not to sit and go stiff. Also they would learn something by watching the opposition. As he observed the matches the officer recalled how bitter Senior Air Craftsman Buckley had taken the news of non selection. When Errol read out the list of eight names, Buckley stood up making himself terribly conspicuous, and momentarily the coach thought by the man's expression was about to commit himself to some vocal utterance. However, the airman had glared at him for a moment, turned his back on the officer and roared "FUUCKKIT" to the skies. After expressing his opinion to the heavens, the airman had stomped off in stamping disgust.

Errol had mixed feelings as he watched the dejected figure climb the slight slope. He was surprised at the outburst, another first; no man had ever expressed his feelings so openly. But if this was the depths of Buckley's feelings, such a fiery individual did indeed deserve a place ... but, he could not put nine men into an eight man team! For better or for worse, Errol had made his selection, just as he had throughout his life - as for instance when marrying his wife. For better or for worse! If his selection was wrong today, he would suffer for the rest of his life, just as he would by choosing the wrong wife. But Errol's wife nor his previous team selections had ever let him down, nor would they today.

The first round ties were over and soon Errol was leading his team out to meet RAF Pergamos, emphatic winners of their first match. No more than four minutes after the commands were given for the start of the first end, the MU team were sitting down again under the trees having completely outclassed the bemused airmen from the Pergamos base. Errol's team took the first end in thirteen seconds, and the second in similar time.

The lingering doubts Flt Lt Barrymore had were fast dissolving. His men performed magnificently, especially the two question marks Oldham and Tighe. They had executed their moves perfectly like the athletes he knew them to be. 'Thank God,' the officer offered his thanks. He had expected more of a tussle from a fairly good RAF team. 'Pergamos were certainly not as bad as my lads made them look, I've got my team.'

When the draw was made for the semi-finals, Errol wondered if he would draw one of the better teams he singled out from the earlier matches. El Adam and Malta looked good although the all in white El Adam team appeared disjointed and moved awkwardly though they did win with a little in hand. To Errol's chagrin he was drawn against old friends RAF Episkopi, well known opponents from the Inter Services league. Episkopi had never managed to take an end off the MU although today they proved more resilient but in the end could not cope with the power and stamina of the reigning champions. Errol was, as expected, in the final!

Malta were a doughty stubborn team but the lads from El Adam eventually got the upper hand in two hard fought ends. Errol noted in an earlier match the peculiar line up of the team from North Africa. Most teams lined up with their 'Shortest to the front, tallest to the rear,' mode. It was not a rule but generally felt weight was best at the rear of the team. The peculiarity with the El Adam eight however, they all seemed to have come out of the same mould; not one man looked taller than another and all appeared to weigh around the required twelve and a half stone. If there was one member of their team who looked fractionally taller, it was a man of West Indian origin who pulled at No.1. The whole set up intrigued Errol and when the whistle blew at the end of their match, he walked over to congratulate the El Adam coach.

"Flight Lieutenant Barrymore," Errol said offering his hand to the coach who had done very little in his team's victory. "Congratulations, you have a very good side there."

"Thank you, Warrant Officer Bould, and to you too. I must add the reputation of yourself and your team preludes you sir," said the WO who clearly was overjoyed to have reached the final.

"Really? Thank you mister Bould. So we'll be seeing you again, in tomorrow's final."

"Looks like it yes, I thought we might make the final if the draw was kind and we could avoid you lot. Happily we made it, though I imagine the real job lies in wait for us tomorrow."

"From what I've just witnessed I think we both have a match on our hands," Errol countered then went on as he watched the El Adam team pull off their boots to replace them with plimsolls. "Tell me Mr. Bould, your line up is so unusual. How did you manage to find so many young men all around the same height and build and I imagine the perfect twelve and a half stone. Only your No.1 man seems a few pounds heavier yet you have him near the front of your team, rather than at the back. Did you plan it this way?"

The answer came quick and sharp, "No sir, not at all. It just happens these lads were the best of the bunch that turned up for training," smiled the Warrant Officer, "and as for the black chap, our No.1, that's Baillie, yes he is a few pounds heavier. You have a good eye sir, but," the WO shrugged, "there's nothing devious in his pulling at No.1. That's the position he prefers so I let him have his way. He's a good strong lad, so well balanced, I could place him anywhere in the line-up." Mr. Bould was sending signals he was now anxious to rejoin his men.

"He looks good as do the others, Mr. Bould. Till tomorrow then and the very best of luck."

"And the same to you sir, although I seriously doubt if you will need any luck. If luck is on the go I think it will most likely be my lot that's going to need it," smiled the coach of the last obstacle that stood firmly in the path of the Flight Lieutenant's dream. Both men shook hands again, more robustly this time before returning to their teams.

Errol clapped his hands to claim their attention. "Well done lads, once more you have done me proud. One more win tomorrow and we will be the Near East Air Force champions – again - for another year. You have done everything right today, let us hope you will do the same tomorrow, and lastly, need I say it? Nothing in excess tonight - NOTHING! There is far too much to be lost by doing anything silly."

~~~

The Mess had closed its doors after the serving of the evening meal and airmen in their billets were settling down to their chores and pastimes. In an MU billet John Tighe pushed a piastre with the heel of his hand along the wooden table top trying to make it stop as near to the far edge as possible. Sometimes the coin fell to the floor followed by a disgruntled grunt from John. "Ach man, Oi'm fed up. How d'hell can Mr. Barrymore ask us t' stay in t'noight. Oi swear t' God the boredom'll kill me, swear t' God it will," he muttered slumping back into his chair after retrieving the errant coin yet again.

"The man didn't say we must stay in John, he just said we mustn't overdo anything," countered Pete Oldham who was lying on his bed trying to read between the Irishman's complaints.

"An' how, may Oi ask, can we overdo anythin' wit' only a coupla pounds between us?"

"It would be difficult I agree, but if I know you, you'd find a way," Pete said forcing himself to start at the top of the page he had read three times already but had taken in not a word.

A half hour passed. The picture of domestic bliss unaltered until the piastre clattered yet again to the floor. As if having suffered enough maltreatment, the coin rolled over the polished linoleum covered floor, out through the door, across the veranda and disappeared into the grass.

John watched its progress laconically. "Y'know Pete, dat piastre is tryin' t'tell us somethin'. D'ye know dat?" he said.

"Oh I'm sure it is, absolutely," parried Pete.

"That fockin' piastre's got more sense than we got! It's just focked off out the door an' disappeared into the bondoo," John was staring at the area where the wayward coin vanished.

Pete closed his book and stared at the ceiling fan rotating on its medium setting. "What do you suggest we do regarding that very clever runaway piece of copper?" He knew full well what John was angling at. He also knew he would get no peace until the Irishman had his say.

John's face broke into a wide grin, "Dat clever little piece of copper has indeed given us a soign. Don't you believe in soigns Pete?" he asked emotionally.

"Yes John, I do believe in signs."

"Then let's do what that clever little piastre is tellin' us t' do. I didn't tell it t' jump off the table, it did dat all by itself, now didn't it? Went clean across floor an' out the door and got itself lost in t' scrub. Not that we'll get ourselves lost ye unnerstan', we're not daft like dat stoopid fockin' piastre!"

Pete laughed as he reached into his locker for a clean shirt and pair of trousers. He knew there was not enough cash between the pair of hard drinkers to get a proper glow on. By the time they paid the taxi to the Twiga Bar, and deducted the return fare from their remaining funds, they would have just enough cash to buy a pack of smokes and maybe four pints each. Quite sufficient to pass the remainder of the evening quietly and contentedly, and that amount of beer would do neither of them any harm.

It was just after eight when they settled down at a table in the popular Twiga Bar and Michael the waiter was quick with their pints and bowl of nuts. "Now isn't dis better than mopin' away in our soddin' sacks?" asked John as he laid his already half empty glass on the table.

"Yes John but why do we do it? We must be the original class A idiots. I mean last night we had only two beers in the Naafi knowing we had the pull-offs today so we took it easy.

Tomorrow we've got the big one and here we are in Limassol which almost ensures a late night, and we're about to consume four pints of the local poison - why John?" Pete shook his head in frustration at the grinning Irishman.

"Now you're runnin' away wit' yoursel' Pete. We are NOT gonna be late t'noight I swear by my auntie's balls on dat. Look it's just after eight," he pointed at his watch, "an' by the toime we've sank our four pints, if we take it nice an' easy it should be nine t'irty or even ten, roight. We get a taxi back t' camp an' we're all safely tucked up in bed by ten t'irty! Now, what is wrong wit' dat, I ask ya?"

"Nothing," replied Pete, "so long as we don't bump into any wife who's fallen out with her ...."

"But sure that wasn't out fault now was it? No red blooded man could turn his back on a pretty little girl that was cryin' out fer help!" John interrupted. "T'ink about it Pete, a chance like dat does not come along wit' every corporation bus, does it?"

Pete nodded as he watched John swallow the last half of his first pint, "Better ease up on the way you're gulping down that Keo, at the rate you're going you'll be finished your fourth pint long before nine o'clock."

"Shore you're roight but the first one always goes down loike warm butter over hot toast. We'll slow up wit' the rest, nivver fear." With that John wagged his empty glass at Michael The waiter arrived with the drinks, "You thirsty tonight sir, yes?" said the smiling Greek Cypriot.

"Shore and begorrah," John said to the beaming Michael. "Shore and begorrah," was repeated for the waiter's benefit who loved and was mesmerized by the Irishman's broad accent. John rolled on in his inimitable manner, "Isn't it every Oirishman's roight t'be t'irsty after a hard day's graft, Michael?" He was laying it thick. The smiling waiter stood nodding but understanding very little.

With a flourish John handed over the one and only five hundred mil note, drawn from the vaults of the pairs meagre treasury and the waiter bobbed happily away.

Pete noticed a young man by the entrance look up sharply when John exaggerated his accent. The man, gazing intently at John, rose and made his way through the tables.

When he reached the table the man spoke quietly, "Excuse me, Oi hope Oi'm not interruptin' here but Oi have the strangest feelin' Oi know you."

John looked at the fresh faced stranger hardly out of his teens for a short spell before speaking. "Oh sweet Jaysus, an' Oi know you ... just a minute now," then in less than the requested time he said triumphantly, "Oi've got it. You wouldn't be Molly Moran's little brother now?" He placed a hand over his mouth and could be heard to mumble, "What the fock was 'is name again?"

"Danny," offered the smiling man.

"Wait a minute, I'll get it ... oh fock," he stared at the man, "Danny! Danny Moran of course!" exploded John, "What the hell are ye doin' here ye little prick ... yer in the forces aren't ye, ye must be?" John was pumping the man's hand.

"Oi'm in the Raf," answered Danny, "just bin posted here, to Episkopi. Only arrived yesterday an' someone told me about dis place," he nodded at the surroundings. "Said it was the place t' meet British people. Shore Oi've bin sittin' over der an hour an' you're the first fockin' voice Oi've unnerstood," he smiled.

"Jaysus," said John staring at the youngster then snapped out of his stupor and looked around at the almost empty bar, "Aye well shore enough, the place is a bit quiet t'night. Anyway sit yersel down an' give us some o' the crack from home."

"A minute." Danny returned to his table and brought back an almost full glass of Keo. "Oi don't know how in hell ye kin drink dis stuff," he said in his lilting accent whilst settling in a chair, "it's turrible. We use stuff like this back home for descalin' pub toilets, dat's if it don't melt the porcelain furst!"

"Ach it's not bad, you'll develop a taste for it after a while, you'll see. It's amazin' how the palate adjusts even under the most adverse conditions. Only one t'ing you moight want t' look out for. Tomorrow when ye go for a crap you might discover ye're shittin' the highest grade o' black ivory. Don't worry about dat, a drap o' the lemonade gets ya okay an normal again."

Turning to Pete, John continued, "Pete Oi wants ye t' meet a little fart Oi used t' know ... Jaysus, it must be eight, ten years ago!" he stared at Danny

"Must be," the small wiry Danny agreed grinning widely.

"Yeah, an while he's sittin' engrossed watchin' tele in the lounge," the irrepressible John went on, "Oi used t' screw 'is sister in the bedroom, then we'd nip back inta lounge while dis one's eyes had never left the screen. He wasn't even aware we'd left the room!"

Danny's eyes went wide, "Ye nivver did!" he said with just a trace of a smile.

"Bloddy did! Manys a toime. We'd wait for one o' your favourite programmes t' come on, 'Gunsmoke' or was it 'Wagon Train?' One o' them daft westerns you were crazy about. As soon as it started and you slid into yer trance, Molly would give me the wink an' away we'd go. Five minutes before the programme finished we'd slip back on the settee. The titles would roll then you'd turn t' me an' say, "Wasn't that smashin'?" an of course not wishin' t' offend Molly, my comment was somethin' loike, 'It was fockin' great!" John chuckled.

"Ya randy old bastard," Danny laughed, "an that bloddy sister o' mine used t' tell me she couldn't wait for Wagon Train t' come on telly. Jaysus, now Oi know why!"

John's face bore the traces of a melancholy smile as he recalled the memory, "She was a good old girl was Molly. How is she these days?"

"Foine, she's foine, married wit' t'ree kids, livin' in Dublin," answered the agreeable Irishman.

"Good, Oi'm glad t' hear dat. Now let me finish what Oi started." John turned back to his abandoned friend, "Sorry Pete, we got carried away in the waters that have long ago passed under the bridge. Pete, meet Daniel Moran, and Danny, this is my good ol' mate Pete Oldham."

The conversation moved from one subject to another but as always with young unattached men the talk inevitably drifted towards the fair sex. As they spoke and laughed at past experiences John noticed Danny was not touching his glass,

"You don't loike the Keo, do ye Danny?"

"Nah, not at all, don't they sell anythin' else? Can't stomach this lot honest," Danny said miserably, "sure Oi'd loike t' get a round in but Oi don't know what to ask for meself?"

Pete caught a glimpse of what lay ahead, "Danny listen, we're not too flush tonight, you know, so just get your own and we'll buy for ourselves, all right?" He spoke politely but Pete was not the strongest of persons in such situations, besides he was outnumbered.

"Not a bit of it!" Danny said emphatically as he reached into his back pocket. With difficulty he tugged and jerked out a fat wallet "Oi've got over fifty quid here! Didn't fancy arrivin' at a new camp skint ye unnerstan' so Oi brought plenty o' the ready wit me. Don't worry about money t'noight, it's on me."

John's expression was of wide-eyed surprise as he stared at the notes fighting to escape from the wallet. He raised his eyes towards Pete and asked an unspoken question.

"No no, the big one John, it's tomorrow remember? I'm taking it easy. We both should!"

"What are ye talkin' about man, d'ye take me for a man wit'out responsibility. BUT, Oi cannot allow an old friend an countryman to wander the streets of Limassol alone in his furst noight on the town, now can Oi? Look, look, look," he forced his way into holding the floor as Pete tried to interrupt. "We don't have to actually DO anythin', just take him downtown, Heroes Square, the Rivoli Bar, show him the soights ye know." A pair of white thighs flashed across John's vision as he recalled the normal routine of strippers in the Rivoli. 'Jaysus, it's loike years since Oi had me a bit a skirt, Oi'm seein' t'ings.' He blinked, "Lissen, we have a coupla drinks in a coupla bars and still be back in camp fur ten t'irty. C'mon man, what ye worried about?"

"That sounds good t' me," Danny enthused, "but what's this 'Big One' yer talkin' about?"

"Later, later Dan," John said not wishing to present Pete with the only lever he had.

"There's no harm in doing what you say, but come ten thirty, I'm leaving for camp. I hope you come with me. Let's not fuck up our chances of a winners medal tomorrow!" Pete said firmly.

"Foine foine, so what are we waitin' for, our glasses are empty so let's go." Turning to Danny John said, "Look little brother of moi very furst love, ye unnerstan', dis may be on you t'noight, but next toime it's on me, us, roight, OK?" He meant every drink laden word with all his heart but deep down he knew in that same heart, the chances of meeting Daniel Moran again, under similar circumstances with financial positions reversed, was highly unlikely. Living in separate camps was similar to living in different towns. Communication was not impossible but with no access to telephones real effort was necessary, therefore casual meetings rarely blossomed into friendships. Future meetings had to be arranged. Danny was young but he was not fooled.

"If we do this again," Danny said, "we do it again, an' we won't ever talk about dat turrible subject money either. It only causes problems ... and ... shore it meks good people tell fockin' loies."

"Dere's a good Oirish boy, fock you make me wish Oi had married your sister." Picking up Daniel's glass of Keo, John went on, "Now ye're sure ye don't want dis?" Before the younger Irishman could answer John put the glass to his lips and swallowed the contents.

They hailed a cruising Mercedes taxi, conspicuous by the horizontal yellow band painted along both sides of the car. The driver dropped them in Heroes Square, so named after a monolith had been erected dedicated to EOKA terrorists executed by the British.

John pointed out the list of names to Danny then hurried him across to the popular Rivoli Bar but found the bar packed. The trio were spoilt for choice however for the area abounded with restaurants, bars and thinly disguised brothels. Not surprisingly it was in one of the latter establishments the trio settled at a table. John in his element, rubbed his hands gleefully.

Their seats had not had time to warm before a woman in her middle thirties swivel hipped her way to their table. Obviously from Arab stock bearing all the characteristics of black eyes, hair and a sharp nose and wearing her best false smile she sat next to Pete. The girl was not beautiful nor ugly but something was cruelly attractive about her. Danny was immediately fascinated.

"Hello," the latest addition to the party said in a deep and practised voice. She was speaking to all three, throwing her bait to all and sundry to see who dared bite. The one who did wouldbe easy meat. Resting her hand on Pete's thigh she said,

318

"You like to buy a lonely gel a dreenk?"

"Certainly!" Danny called, delighted at the appearance of such a lovely woman of the world.

"He doesn't need any coachin' this one," John said proudly as the woman beamed a wide grin at the youngest of the trio, meanwhile moving her hand up Pete's hard and muscular thigh. "Thank you good sir, I would like vodka and orange please. You lonely boys yes? You like for me to eenvite some other gels to seet weeth us, perhaps?"

"No!" Pete jumped and shouted simultaneously as the woman's hand gently closed round his genitals. "No, no thank you," this in a normal voice but just as firmly. "Look love, me and my mate," he indicated John, "we're not looking for girls tonight ... not tonight some other night definitely, but not tonight. Now this lad after a couple of drinks, he will most certainly be looking for company." Pete was happy to focus her attention on Danny. In his opinion she was ugly and hard, even for a brothel. Make up was layered like chocolate over an old cake and each eyelash reminded him of coarse black bristles protruding from the pink cushion of a cheap hairbrush.

"Dalling," the woman's attention now switched to Danny, giving him what she imagined was her best smile, "maybe you'd lak me to seet beside you, mn?"

Pete was happy to stand and make way, for despite his jump she had not abandoned the work on his buttoned fly. The undoubted skill in her hand had started to arouse him and she knew it. One abandoned and reluctant sex victim was happily replaced by a willing and young adventurer as the raven haired woman slid along between the table and bench type seat covered in cheap red leatherette. She snuggled against Danny and his cherubic face broke into a wide grin. "Oh come here you bloddy beautiful nymph," he mumbled before clumsily kissing her upturned mouth.

'Jesus, it truly takes all kinds,' thought Pete as the pair's initial grappling gave the impression they were fighting each other.

John who was making verbal noises but had said nothing of consequence, took his chance when the waiter appeared, "Look Danny, while you fock around let me do the orderin'. They're dirt cheap in dis place and you can ..." he hesitated, "at least Oi can, get blind drunk for a quid in here." Turning to the waiter he said, "Give us t'ree triple brandy sours an' a vodka an' orange. Now lissen good. Ye know me don't ya, so make sure they're triples of the good stuff, for if they're not, ye won't get paid like last toime we wiz here! Ye remember the rumpus we caused, an no water, hear? Oi know when moi fockin' drink has bin watered. So good stuff an' no water! Keep them comin' an' keep them regular lad, there's money t' be made from dis table t'noight!"

"Yes sir, no warry, we no water the feerst dreenks," the waiter winked and hurried away.

"Fock me, a waiter wit' a sense of humour, wonders'll never cease," John said smiling happily.

"John, why order only a single vodka for this beautiful lady?" Danny asked as the 'beautiful lady' massaged his groin.

"Because," said a sagely and supremely wise John, "dis lovely bitch here will be gettin' a watered down orange, der won't be a snip o' vodka in it. Ye kin bet on dat!"

"Hey, why you talk like dat, I am no thee beetch," the woman squawked haughtily squeezing Danny's private parts causing him to grimace and jerk his thighs together.

"Love, I'm sorry, don't lissen t' me, just the way Oi talk ye unnerstan'. No harm meant Darlin'"

The woman nodded her head once, her honour restored. Turning back to Danny, "Me, I Rita, what your name ees Daleeng?".

"Danny, my name ees ... is ... Danny, Rita, but lissen, much as Oi love whit yer doin' down there, ye'd better stop. If ye carry on like dat, Oi'm gonna lose interest in goin' t' yer room."

Laughter echoed round the table. Rita who surprisingly had a tinkling pleasant laugh contrasting sharply with her dark looks, raised her hands and held Danny's cheeks. "Oooooh," she said, "I am going to enjoy thees babee!"

The waiter brought the drinks. In his wake came a buxom redhead also wearing her professional smile. "We seem to be having fun here, mind if I join in?" She stood at the table for a moment then sat delicately next to Pete on the seat vacated by Rita. "My name ees Angela."

John looked across the table at Angela hungrily. She had a pleasant round face with clear blue eyes and full lips. Her low blouse exposed bottomless cleavage. Pete found he too was gazing into their creamy depths. 'Oh sweet Jesus,' he thought, his resistance crumbling.

"You like?" the girl, still on the right side of thirty whispered huskily.

"I like very much sweetheart but I'm married," Pete said not very convincingly, "My friend and I only stepped in for a couple of drinks. We're showing Danny round Limassol."

"Oi'm not fockin' married," John growled at the full figured girl. "Git yer lovely fat arse over here Angie an' what are ye drinkin' me flame haired beauty." He grabbed the waiter's arm who had only just placed the last glass of the first order on the table, "Hey Bob Hope, bring dis ravishing wench whatever she wants t' drink."

"A double gin and lime Christo," Angela smiled at John and gave a quick flip of her eyebrows before turning back to Pete who's eyes were still having trouble vacating the deep line of her cleavage. She placed a hand at the back of the Englishman's neck and gently pulled his unresisting head, placing his nose deep in the cleft of her breasts. After some seconds she bent her head and said into his uppermost ear, "These," she pushed the face from one massive mound to the other, "are angels wings and they could have flown you to the gates of heaven tonight married man, but now they fly away."

The redhead stood, patted Pete's head and followed the same route as Rita her fellow prostitute, sitting beside John who was now rubbing his hands again in boyish excitement.

Staring in effervescent joy at the girls chest and full figure he declared, "By fock Angie, Oi won't have t' do any o' the work lyin' on top o' you. One jump on them tits and Oi'll be bouncin' up and down all fockin' noight!"

Pete laughed with the others but could not gel with the night's high jinks. Any other time and he'd be sifting through the girls, making the most of Danny's generous offer. But not tonight!

The waiter had been to their table three times already. Three trays full of drinks and as far as he could tell, they were undiluted. But if Pete could have stood back as a neutral and surveyed his situation, he would have seen the battle was already lost. He was not the brightest of individuals but he was most certainly a healthy red blooded male animal and the last woman he'd been with was the almost robotic army officer's young wife on the beach. That was two weeks ago and the blood was beginning to boil in his veins. Most of the girls in the bar were not his type, although Angela was the most eligible in a fluffy, soft and pretty way. He could and probably would have got lost in her charms tonight if it weren't for the damn final tomorrow. Pete sighed and looked at his watch. Ten fifteen, time to go.

Rita saw the man look at his watch. She looked fixedly at a barman and raising her eyebrows nodded at Pete. The barman caught the signal and called a girl who had just entered the bar. "Becky, there's a spare John in Rita's group. You go, take care of heem."

"You joking Mike, I just got back," the girl said tossing three one pound notes into a tray behind the counter then proceeded to write the amount in a book.

Mike looked with suspicion at the money, "Three pounds, how much you charge heem?"

"It was a quickie Mike, right?"
He glowered but let it go, the girl was a good earner, "Okay, but get over there with Rita. There ees money there, they are buying treeples."

"Are they now," the girl showed more interest.
Money always caught Becky's attention. She had charged her last client six pounds, one pound more than the 'quickie' going rate. "Pay," she told the man whose hand was between her locked thighs, "or I swear, I am returning to the bar."

Over in the booth there was a sombre guy Rita was talking to. He looked like he was about to leave. "Okay Mike, I'm busy."

Becky walked slowly towards the group lightly swaying her hips, nothing too exaggerated. She was cool, confident. In the year she had been working no man had ever turned her away.

Pete looked up when Rita said, "Hey, here comes our Rebecca, our Queen of the night!"

Pete saw the shapely girl dressed in a white sheath dress walking slowly towards him. He could not see her face but clearly saw the black G-string and the two rose buttons of her breasts through the thin cotton dress. "Oh fuck!" he heard himself say as the girl stopped in front of him and bent slowly at the knees until her face was level with his.

Pete turned to John, "C'mon John, let's go, now, NOW!" It was a last wailing effort to get out of the place but John's reply was typical, "Pete, you can go an' get focked!"

"And that is precisely what I would like to do to you," said the girl who was resting her hands on her knees and talking into Pete's ear as he looked balefully across the table at John.

Pete felt trapped but could not resist turning his head to look at the girl. Her face was small and round, a diminutive nose and even white teeth. Under the light of the booth her eyes were somewhere between green and blue and her soft and full blonde hair shook as she smiled at him. "Would you like that?" she asked pertly. She could be asking him if he would like a cup of tea.

Pete's mind was telling him this girl should not be talking dirty, she did not belong in this place.

"Well, would you?" she asked again, broadening her bubbly smile, her eyes laughing.

"I'm married," he heard himself say.

"And so are most of the men in this room," she countered, the smile still in full bloom. "And I could pick any one of them, but I'm offering you the first dance. Would you like to lock our loins in a love tango, or must I seek another partner?" This ploy never failed, it would not fail here.

"Wait." Pete's insides were in turmoil as he stared into those smiling, beckoning eyes. She really shouldn't be in a place like this. He was weakening but he had one last hope, "I'll have to check if my bandleader can play a tango!" Pete turned to Danny, "Can you pay for this?"

"If it's gonna take somethin' like her t' move yer arse, course Oi can." Danny was smiling lopsidedly and tried to wink unsuccessfully as both eyes closed.

Becky sat down and introductions made, a drink arrived for her. She picked up the glass and held it out to Pete, "You're my first and last this evening I'll have you know," she lied prettily, "so ... you can stay with me? Tonight?"

"Stay with you?" Pete almost cried, "Look, you're a sweetheart and I appreciate you giving me first option, but we've got a really big match on tomorrow and ... shit ... why am I telling you that?" The end of every nerve in his body was tingling but he could not deny his feelings. He'd never seen this girl before, she was something else, and despite his pledge, he badly wanted her. Equally he did not want to damage his performance the following day. And the body being the fine balanced machine it is, it was impossible to have both.

Becky wanted this perfect male specimen, and she was in the profession where, being a pretty girl, she could pick any man she desired. But not always and business always came first.

"All right," she said, "let's start at the beginning where all negotiations start. First, I have the most beautiful and very special merchandise that you would like to buy. Secondly, you must have the cash with which to buy otherwise you would not be here. It's a simple straight deal. Before we clinch ..." she smiled prettily, "the deal I would like to relax with you and have a few drinks. Afterwards we go home to my bed where we exchange our commodities, I promise to give you everything my body and mind can give. For this service, you will give me twelve pounds."

There were surprised gasps from the other girls. They had already agreed to a price of eight pounds with John and Danny. John was the first to challenge the girl on her high price,

"Hey Sweetie, what you got between your legs that's so different from moi lovely Angie, eh, what you got down there gal?"

Becky gave John her widest smile, "Without putting too fine an edge on things, just look at me," she stood and twirled bending both arms at the elbows and one leg at the knee, presenting a pretty picture. Brimming with confidence she sat down, facing them on the very edge of her seat. "I have nothing different, just better." Looking at Pete she asked,. "Are you fond of animals?"

"Me ... animals? I suppose I am, in fact yeah definitely, I love animals, why?"

"I'm so happy you do, for in answer to the question, I have something to show you." Still on the edge of her seat, Becky opened her knees wide apart. In so doing she forced the soft cotton of her white dress to sidle up her thighs until the black gusset of her panties could clearly be seen. Pointing to her crotch she said, "You see, I also love animals very much, and this little animal helps me make a living. She is my pussy." She could not suppress a small giggle as John almost upset the table in his haste to get out of his seat and round the table for an unobstructed view of the proceedings.

Smiling brazenly and certainly needing no encouragement from John's prompting, Becky went on, "This tight little pussy has not eaten today." Casually but tantalizingly slowly she pulled aside the gusset, "And it is hungry. It would very much like to eat but if you are not the one who is going to feed it, then I must go looking for the special food it needs, elsewhere!" With those words she closed her knees and pulled down her dress.

After a moment's silence, Becky nuzzled her face into Pete's, "See anything you want to buy?"

"Oh yes," Pete sighed, "oh fuck ... yes," he was breathless. "I would gladly pay a hundred pounds for that little pink and golden patch, but I haven't got a hundred pounds - and nor do I have twelve pounds. You're just too expensive for me tonight and I'm not talking about money. If it were any other night I would gladly give you a month's wages - honestly, that's the truth. I'll just have to catch you some other time."

Becky could not believe it. She had assumed these three men were loaded and had chanced on the price of twelve pounds knowing it was high. In the classier nightclubs downtown patrons would pay that price for a bottle of whiskey but with the added rider they would spend the night with their pick of the dancing girls from the cabaret. Becky had no bottle of whiskey to offer him. Men it seemed did have limits and she'd been a little ambitious. She had never been turned down and the other girls would love to see her crown slip the merest fraction.

"Sir, you must believe me when I tell you I have taken a strong fancy to you. You are very good looking and made of steel!" Becky squeezed the rock hard thigh. "But a girl has got to eat you know? And I know you want me," Becky would die if he said no this time, "So have you got ten, no, nine pounds, just for you, but I will not lower my price anymore?"

The man from Birmingham was on a tightrope, tipping one way then the next as he looked into the light blue/green eyes that looked back at him slightly worried. "It's not the money ..." he whispered, but before he could say more his indecision was made when Danny shouted. "For fock sake, how many times are we gonna dance round the price, of course he can afford it. Now quit it you two and get some drinks in. Hey John what's up, you've gone very quiet!"

"Aye well, no fockin' wonder loike," John answered, his eyes locked on Becky's groin. "It's not often ye see soights loike dat." There was a distant look on his face. "Becky me love, Oi'm just t'inkin' t' meself, it's gonna take a coupla weeks t' find the money for me t' feed that cat o' yours. Ye don't t'ink it could maybe starve in dat toime, an' if dat be d'case, Oi would be very, VERY happy to come and feed it tit-bits y'know, just enough t' keep us both goin' loike?"

"That is very sweet of you, but it will still be here when you have the money, and because you are so nice, maybe I will serve you something special, like I will serve this lovely man, tonight." John clambered back on the bench seat beside Angela, "Angie me love, at this very moment you are just a kick in the arse off being the most beautiful girl in the world, but I am a wizard, did ye know dat? Yeah, a fockin' Merlin I am, for after one more drink, Oi guarantee you are goin' t' change into the most gorgeous creature Oi've ever laid." he paused then faced the others "Me fockin' eyes on!" he added laughing uproariously.

Danny called a halt to the party at 2 am not because he was running short of cash or the bar was closing. He paid for the last round of drinks himself as John was now talking to fairies under the table. He gave Christo a pound note then peered into his wallet to check his money. He counted out £25 for the girls, which left him with £11. He was still rich and tossed another pound note at Christo. He was very drunk, very tired and very randy. There was nothing more attractive to him than snuggling up to his lovely Rita in her big bed as soon as possible, preferably before he dropped dead. Rita was the walkin', talkin', spittin' image of the last school teacher Daniel had in his secondary school, Miss MacIntee. By the sweet wings of the Archangel Gabrielle, Danny had a crush as long as a liars tongue for the lovely English teacher. At the school leavin' dance two of his mates had put somethin' into her drink and got his lovely Miss MacIntee stottin' drunk. When she complained of needing some fresh air they led the poor woman into the science classroom where he and his pals had not done anythin' really outrageous you understand, unless stickin' their evil young hands up her dress is in that category. That in itself was bad enough but when that daft Shaun O'Reilly placed her limp hand on young Danny's boiling organ, her hand came alive and she did to him something young schoolteachers should know nothing about! Well now, where did the sweet Miss MacIntee learn such secrets? Only adolescent males should know such t'ings that should be performed alone and in private! Daniel Moran had fantasized about his English teacher ever since that disturbing night.

John too was weary. He had just surfaced from under the table where he could get no sense from the fairies at all. For the past few minutes his head had been resting on Angela's ample bosom while she stroked his cheek and quietly hummed some Greek song.

Pete had not laid a hand on Becky, or Rebecca as she preferred, nor she on him. They had spent their time talking. He was fascinated with her, as he always tended to do with any female. She was such a good looking girl, as finally the persistent question fell from his mouth, "What was she doing working in a brothel?" Rebecca explained quite unashamedly she really liked her 'work'. One day she hoped to open a high class house with the best girls commanding the highest prices. There was no other business like it she claimed, for as long as there were men the demand would never fall. If she could keep a supply of good clean girls there would always be custom. Pete smiled at her logic. He was tired and glad when Danny called a halt. It was a few minutes after 2 am and forlornly still carried a hope he could do justice on the rope tomorrow ... no, today, in less than a day! In only thirteen hours or so he would be going through all sorts of hell for his sins tonight. Was he having a good time? Yes he was and surely the best was yet to come! He fervently hoped so, for he was so drunk! He glanced across at John who was resting comfortably between the ample breasts of Angela. Rebecca followed his gaze then looked into his eyes, "You want to go? I think we are ready yes, for bed yes?"

Pete looked into the light blue, or were they green eyes, and again he could not decide on their colour. "Oh yes, let's go." He drained his glass and replaced it heavily on the table.

Rebecca noted the action and turned to the others, "We're going now, I think my lover boy's in danger of passing out and I certainly don't want that, I want me to get his money's worth," she laughed and looked at Danny. "You are paying?" she asked lightly.

"Oh sorry Becky gel," Danny said withdrawing £9 from the £25 in a separate part of his wallet.

"You must come see me Danny, there are not many men who spend their cash on other men for nothing."

"Oh Oi'm comin t' see you all right Becky me girl, dat's a promise."

Rebecca took Pete's arm but he shook it free nearly falling over. "G'night lads and you too ladies." He'd forgotten the girl's names and was too drunk to remember. He had to speak to John before he left. "John," he shouted, "John!" louder this time.

The Irishman's eyes battled to open, "Wot?"

"You'll be up there tomorrow, won't you, to Happy Valley?"

"Course Oi fockin' am. What d'ye t'ink, mebbe ye t'ink Oi'm gonna fock off back t' Oireland! Oi'll see ye back in billet, don' worry yersel." John eyes were acting individually to each other as they fought to focus on Pete. They gave up the fight as the lids closed slowly.

Pete nodded and placed an arm around Rebecca, the first personal touch he had made towards the girl all night. Suddenly he was aware of the slim waist and firm rise of her buttocks. "C'mon Rebecca lass, you know what, I think ... now don't get carried away but I really like you."

He allowed the girl to guide him. His chin rested on his chest whilst intermittently opening his eyes to watch his shoes pacing unsteadily over the ground for what seemed a long time. He was enjoying the walk, the fresh air was steadying his whirling head when the shoes suddenly stopped. He had to climb some stairs now. This was more difficult as there was no supporting arm around him. The stairs were narrow, it was dark and he kept stumbling. He discovered the best way to overcome this was to lean forward and feel for the stairs with his hands, then climb as a dog would, only much slower.

He found himself in a room with little else in it but a double bed. Hands assisted him to fall out of his clothes before lying down gratefully. After a few minutes Pete opened his eyes. An oil lamp burning but he was alone! Shouldn't the someone who brought him, Rebecca, that was her name, shouldn't she be here?

Rebecca sailed into the room from wherever she had been,

328

wonderfully naked. She adjusted the lamp killing most of the light then clambered onto the bed. Now she was whispering something in his ear, something very romantic, "The john's through that door over there. You're not gonna be sick or piss the bed are you Pete my sweet?"

"Don't be daft ... but I might need a little help ... here." He was aware his manhood, normally so alert on occasions such as this, was showing little if any interest in the proceedings.

"Oh, don't you worry about that."

Her voice floated in the darkness which had a milky lunar depth and the ghostly walls of the room were coated in fleecy luminescent cotton wool. Pete drifted off into a world where he found himself rolling and flying, floating and falling. The last quite literally when he fell off the bed. Within seconds of heaving his heavy body back into the warmth of the girls clinging arms and the wonderful suffocating folds of her exquisitely supple body, he was lost once more, flying through a void inside each other's weightless bodies in the dizzying swaying motion of their hallucinatory coupling.

This went on for a long time. Pete never knew when they stopped, if they climaxed, when they fell asleep. He would never forget the wonderful self contentment he felt when he did at last open his eyes to reality and the beautiful new morning His lasting impression for many years was that Danny Moran's money was well spent.

Pete went to see Rebecca often after that night, trying to relive the quite unique experience. But like any beautiful dream, the lingering enchantment was a fairy-tale twinkling in time, never to be recalled nor relived. Years later in many of his waking moments Pete realised he was so very fortunate to have lived through the real life dream sequence once, if indeed he had lived through it at all.

~~~

Chapter 16

Happy Valley, Cyprus June 1965, Near East Air Force Championships. The annual sports meeting where athletes representing every RAF base in the Levant assembled. These men and women, having won at Station level were gathered in the comparatively lush surroundings to meet and compete, hoping to claim the highest athletic honours of the region.

All afternoon eagle eyed officials adjudicated and the atmosphere if not tense, was certainly more strained than the congenial ambience present at station level sport meetings.

The long hot afternoon was drawing to a close, only two events still to be decided; the one mile relay and tug-of-war final. As the relay runners prepared themselves, the brass band from the Akrotiri base marched onto the field whilst in a large marquee at the south end of the ground the umpire was briefing the tug-of-war finalists. It was rare that an umpire deemed it necessary to address two experienced teams before a final but as this was the last event and regarded as the meeting highlight it had to be presented correctly.

Julian Cantwell revelled in the crackling atmosphere; he felt it first when handing out the boots with their sharpened heel plates and much-prized blue and white hooped strips. On top of the jerseys and boots were matching stockings and white shorts. Distributing the pristinely prepared kit Julian wished each team member, "Good luck," but no one spoke. All had mutely accepted their bundle, not a 'thank you' from anyone! Julian understood; the occasion was too much. Even seasoned campaigners had allowed the moment to get to them.

The eight men changed soberly and quietly, each harbouring his private thoughts and those who had them, paid full attention to their good luck fetishes. Nobby Clarke put his head through the jersey neck first, his left arm next then his right - in that precise order. George Banks always put his left boot on first;

Frank Connolly had to push his fist down into the end of a stocking then lightly punch the palm of his hand three times before pulling it on.

The umpire, a huge man dressed all in white with matching bushy hair called their attention.

"Gentlemen," the man's voice matched his frame, "I am Flight Sergeant Flowers, your umpire this afternoon Although you are all seasoned campaigners there are a number of things I must point out to you all. Firstly, I will not tolerate laying on the ground. My side judge are armed with these," he held up a short cane. "Your heels must be the only part of your anatomy in contact with the ground. Side judge will pass these canes under anyone he suspects of touching the ground with any part of your lower regions. And I assure you I WILL disqualify anyone for persistent laying, therefore his team will lose that end,"

The starting pistol sounded for the mile relay as Flt. Sgt. Flowers was talking. This spurred him into quicker speech.

"Okay, there's no need to go into rules and regulations. You've got this far so I assume you know the basics, and it's too late now if you don't." A nervous ripple of laughter rumbled from the assembled group. Flowers cut it short. "The last thing is we had a heck of a job finding prizes, but managed to get some decent memorabilia for you, for the last time I fear with our budget and the way prices are going these days." He turned to face Flt. Lt. Barrymore and his team, "For the winners, we have lovely half pint, silver plated tankards embossed with the NEAF crest. And for the runner's up ..." he turned quite blatantly to face the El Adam side, "we have lovely mounted barometers. Good luck to you all and may the best team win. May I have the coaches please."

While the officials tossed for ends, Frank nudged Nobby,

"What did you think o' that?"

"Diabolical!" answered Nobby. "He's got us down as winners already, not that he's far wrong I hope!" the Indian winked but the smile was distinctly nervous.

"All right lads, gather round," Flt Lt. Barrymore called quietly, rejoining them, "I don't have to tell you how important this is, unfortunately we are required to present a bit of a show before we can get started. The two teams will march out together side by side and follow Flt. Sgt. ..."

Both teams heard their coaches words but all sixteen men were aching to get started. There was too much pomp and pageantry. They heard the band strike up and someone was heard to remark in a heavy Irish accent, "Sweet Jaysus, they're gonna be lookin' fur tridents and nets out there. They're playin' 'Entry of the gladiators!"

A tremendous roar greeted the teams and John Tighe and Pete Oldham perked up with the vocal support. Despite their overnight revelry, both were feeling fairly fit. Hot baths followed by huge breakfasts and lunches had gone a long way to recharging their batteries.

The teams took the field together splitting only as they neared the stand. They veered away from each other then followed their coaches to march to opposite ends of the rope then turned inward to face each other. Suddenly it was time; all plans, training, dreams and hopes were on the verge of happening. The band stopped playing and Errol was imploring his team with last minute instructions. Time did not exist anymore. The umpire had already given the first command with a stentorian voice and the crowd hushed. Each man lost in his own world had switched from mortal beings to robots. Two sets of men bent on applying their vast communal power into pulling the farthest rope marker over the nearest white line on the ground. Somewhere in the surrounding hills in the dry scrub that passed as vegetation a bird chirped. Flt Sgt. Flowers heard it clearly just as he called,

"Take ... the straaaaiin!" he levelled his arms.

The El Adam team stood calmly. They were ready and trained but well aware they were the probable lambs awaiting slaughter. Their three day break on the lush island had been enjoyable. They had actually seen grass again, were actually standing in the green stuff at this very minute. The only time airmen from the North African base experienced the succulent grass of the Cyprus bases, and other goods the huge base at Akrotiri could offer, was when sent on detachment to one of the many camps on the beautiful island. Or as now, to a sports meeting. Two members of this El Adam team had been on the Akrotiri base only three weeks ago on a ten day work detachment and watched in wonder when the coach and the MU team produced a manoeuvre that had literally uprooted the opposition in the Station final.

"Do they have any other tricks?" wondered SAC Baillie, the menacing thirteen stone West Indian El Adam No.1. He was not watching the umpire's mouth! He looked towards the team at the other end of the rope. The instant they flinched, so would he.

"PULL!" the umpire's roar triggered sixteen human robots into action. The eight in blue and white hoops took the drop, taking six feet of rope before the team in white stopped them.

"Wonderful, well done lads," enthused Errol who thought for a moment his men were about to take it all the way with a wonderful drop. "Settle down now, feel them out ... settle down ... hold!" The rope was creaking with pressure as the MU settled in comfortably. Errol was pleased as he crabbed up the line. They looked strong and confident. "Just about halfway there lads. How do they feel Connolly?" Errol was impatient but well aware he must not act until he knew they could take ground. The officer's brow wrinkled as his No.3 man did not, could not, answer. Extreme pressure registered on Connolly's face as he fought to hold position. Looking to his right to at the opposition, Errol was greeted with a strange sight! El Adam had changed their style from the previous day and looking a much better, solid side. All eight men were facing him, looking straight down the rope. For a moment, Errol stared at the full frontal face of the No.1. The black chap's broad front seemed to block out all seven behind with his impressive frame. Eight sets of bent legs like the letter M reminded the officer of a centipede, one on either side of the rope and they were still, unyielding, motionless. He swung back at his men, all were straining madly, sapping their energy, losing their straight backed positions - and ground. "Connolly, what's going on? They're not heaving. We're losing ground?"

Frank could not answer. Every ounce of his strength was pouring down his limbs in an effort to hold position. The pressure was incredible. He knew to maintain full resistance he would soon be forced to commit the cardinal sin and move his feet.

Errol saw the muscles and sinews stand out like steel cables on Connolly's legs and arms. A quick glance, the others were under similar pressure. "Prepare for a Bucket," he called.

'Good,' thought Frank, 'I can't believe this pressure.' He felt he was being reeled in with the relentlessness of a mechanical winch only marginally stronger than he was. Presumably, the others were feeling as he did. There were only ounces in pressure difference but it was enough to tip the balance. He hoped the 'Bucket throw' would unsettle them.

"Bucket - bucket - THROW!" The highly trained103 team reacted to their coach's command viciously, throwing loose rope at the opposition with the confidence of proven champions.

WO Bould had listened carefully to Baillie when his No.1 returned from detachment. He had brought glowing reports of the invincible MU and of their method of 'throwing rope' when under pressure. Bould knew if he wanted to win the NEAF championship, he would have to beat 103 Maintenance Unit. El Adam being the No.2 seeds had kept them apart in the pull-off rounds thus keeping his 'square pulling' method under wraps. The situation was at hand now where he must produce his second but unproven counter move, devised strictly on what Baillie described. It worked in practice, but he had no idea if it would work against a force like the MU!

Bould heard the command float down to him from the opposition coach. He was dreading this moment but the reigning champions had thrown down the gauntlet, there was no turning back. He had to act, "Take rope. TAKE ROPE - NOW!" he bellowed at his team.

El Adam were crouched like waiting cats. With their crouched bodies facing the opposition, the rope between their spread knees, as the slack came at them the men simply straightened their knees and backs without moving their entrenched heels. They took between two and three feet of rope with no effort. With a quick double chop of their heels, they were back in their crouched positions. Their confidence soared.

On Errol's command Frank Connolly threw the rope out to the right towards his coach, simultaneously bending his knees. He felt the whole team being pulled round sweetly into the coiled position. "Heave!" the confident roar blanketed the area as the MU team swung into their well rehearsed routine. The rope came less than a foot, they pulled and hauled but with no avail. They'd thrown nearly three feet and regained less than one, worse they'd lost their positions. 'They were waiting for us!' Frank realised, 'they knew what was comin'!' There was an empty feeling at the pit of his stomach when another cold shock bit deep. He realised the pressure had never faltered, and was mounting! Yet no commands were being given, no heaves, just the menacing pressure Frank could feel through the live artery of rope. Keeping his chin tucked in, Frank slowly turned his head from staring at the grass below his right shoulder to along the line of shuddering rope. What he saw was strange. The opposition resembled a crab like insect. Their faces and bodies were facing him, all exactly the same, coiled, crouching, holding the rope between bent knees that acted like springs. Bending and straightening with no loss of feet position. The iron bar of rope continued over their groins and under their right arms. The eight El Adam white clad men, so similar in build, bent and straightened, rocking, nibbling and creeping along relentlessly in a slow reverse crawl.

"Prepare to jump," Frank heard his coach. Perhaps sacrificing more ground for a new solid position was the correct move. The pressure El Adam was exerting must surely be costing them dearly, in both strength and stamina.

"Jump!" roared Errol. Like a clockwork toy the MU team hopped forward burying their heels into solid earth, locking their bodies into their classic straight side on positions.

All movement stopped with the El Adam team within three feet of taking the first end. They had tired it seemed for the MU at last were holding comfortably. The stilled voices in the crowd started to chatter with mutterings of advice as the stalemate crept over two minutes. Then as Barrymore went from one man to another to talk, to coax, he read again as facial expressions started to tell the tale of mounting pressure. From expressionless almost calm faces, they changed dramatically to furrowed foreheads, gritted teeth and mouths, grinning in demonic grimaces, eyes closing as if in ecstatic pain. Errol started to insult his men, trying to get them angry which could dredge up reserves of energy even they did not know they had. "By God don't go to bloody sleep No.2," and "Tighe show me some effort man, Clarke, some endeavour for God's sake." The final jibe at Nobby worked. The rope stopped and backs slowly started to straighten. Errol sighed inwardly, he'd stopped the rot, but he must win back some rope, "AND!" he yelled followed by the chorused if strained, "Yes."

They took two feet but Frank knew it was not right; it was the same heavy feeling of a tired, though not necessarily a beaten team. He felt he was dragging a heavy anchor through deep mud again. Hellishly sluggish but it was coming. Another "And," from Errol and the team with their responsive "Yes," sounded more like their confident selves but still straining to haul back another foot. Their next heave took nothing. Errol settled them for what he hoped would be a long lay out. He must try to drain some of the opposition strength.

A long layout was all that remained in Errol's box of tricks. If they could hold for two or three minutes his strong point was stamina. His men were trained to last up to seven minutes of heavy pressure. But on this day they were to be denied even this. Gradually like watching the minute hand of a clock his team were slowly bent over and pulled again into cramped positions. Errol tried everything he could think off over the last few feet, as did his fighting team but the whistle sounded. The coach frowned in black despair.

His team stood and stared down the rope in puzzlement, hands on hips in arrogant anger at these upstarts who had made them look second rate in a time of three minutes fifty seconds.

Errol at a loss approached his No.3. "What do you think Connolly?"

"Can't understand it. Their pressure's so regular, strong and steady. Feels for all the world like we're bein' reeled in by a slow turnin' winch, an' they're in positions I've never seen before! Only chance we have is try to hold them if we can. Try an' tire them out. If we can hold them long enough then we've got a chance. But it's a big 'if' sir."

"Thank you Connolly." Errol nodded lightly. He was worried.

Umpire Flowers had the teams change over and got the second end started quickly. Both teams settled with the MU digging well in establishing a good foothold. Within seconds, Frank again felt the now familiar pressure, it was tremendous but their backs were straight and the team solid. They were holding!

The end was less eventual as the minutes ticked by. It was well into the third minute Frank noted with some misgiving, the pressure was not easing as it should be after all this time, rather it was increasing.

Frank suspected but no one knew it at the time the difference in the teams lay in the styles. The MU were wasting energy in just holding the opposition in their side pulling positions, whereas the square pulling El Adam eight were apparently at their ease in their crouched and comfortable postures. Somewhere towards the end of the match, something deep inside Errol Barrymore started to rise through his entrails. It was cold and gnawing and when it passed up the back of his neck it made his eyelids flutter, his forehead layer with cold sweat. Even when he found himself screaming at his team he never realised, and it did not penetrate through his protective shield of consciousness what it was. Errol had reached a state of panic. His team, the icon of the tug-of-war world were being beaten! And beaten comprehensively in the last final he had lived and dreamed about for months. His lions were going out like lambs, his high flying eagles were plummeting to the lush green grass of Happy Valley. He had never lost a match in three years and here he was losing two ends to nil. It was too much for him. Errol did not hear the whistle blast. As the marker moved lazily over the line he yelled, "Bucket - bucket - THROW!"

Strange, his team had not responded. "Connolly, give me all you've got lad!"

His exhausted No.3 was standing up, "Connolly, what're you doing ... good God what's go ...?"

"It's over sir, it's over." Frank gasped looking closely at the coach. The fact the match was lost was nothing compared to the sadness he felt for the officer. "You all right, sir?"

Errol felt for a second he had been asleep, that he had just awoken from a long deep slumber. He blinked his eyes rapidly to see Connolly peering intently into his face.

"Of course, yes, yes I'm fine ... thank you." A little unsteadily, he turned and looked around. The crowd were strangely subdued, his shattered team were rising from their prone positions on the ground. All were looking at him, some apprehensively, some questionably, all miserably.

Well it had happened, the unthinkable. He had lost out on the big one. 'The Big One.' The very words were burned into the back of his brain. He had said it so often to his team, to himself. Three years! All the planning and work gone for nothing. Errol dropped his head on to his chest.

The stunned crowd started to clap the new champions. Their old champions had been no match on the day for the underdogs!

Indeed the underlings were their new champions who they started to cheer if a little uncertainly.

El Adam seemed reluctant to accept their new crown standing uncertainly, some still sitting on their hard fought battleground. Warrant Officer Bould had shaken every hand, congratulated each man for his excellent performance. He himself was uncertain of the protocol; was it his place to offer condolences, or should the losing coach approach to offer his congratulations? Bould glanced towards Flt. Lt. Barrymore. The man seemed to have actually physically shrunk! He was shaking hands with his team in a half-hearted manner, gone was the upright proud walk as he almost shuffled from one man to the next. 'Poor bastard,' thought the WO experiencing the slivers of guilt the victor feels when instrumental in the bringing down of a long and proven champion. "Line up the rope lads, shake hands with those lads, congratulate them. They've been at the top for many years and chased by pretenders all that time. Today we had the honour of catching them. Off you go!"

The Warrant Officer approached Errol, "I am truly sorry sir, yet at the same time proud it was my team that managed to do what dozens have failed to achieve for many years. I'm aware this result has denied you the 100% record you so richly deserve.

That's the reason for my apology. However your record as it stands Mr. Barrymore will surely never be bettered."
Errol's innards felt they had been kicked by a wild horse but his face registered only warmth as he shook Bould's hand.

"Thank you and well done! My heartiest congratulations. I must tell you Mr.Bould, although we have lost, I have to say never have I been so comprehensively beaten in all my years involved in this wonderful sport, neither when on the rope myself or since I started coaching. I feel no disgrace today for you have a truly magnificent eight. They'll take a great deal of beating." Errol meant every word. The moment of weakness when he exposed his miserable feelings, he deeply regretted. A better team had beaten him on the day, there was an end to it.

"Thank you sir, that's very kind coming from a man such as yourself, but may I offer a word?"

"Certainly Mr. Bould, today may I remind you, it is I who stands in your shadow. Please, I'd be most interested in anything you have to say." Errol looked into the lined red face of the WO.

"I believe you are Blighty bound sir, within the next few weeks?" Mr. Bould started uncertainly. He carried on at the officer's nod, "You will find on your return, side pulling has given way to the square pulling method we used today. You will also find, with respect, a good square pulling team will usually get the better of an equally good side pulling eight."

"On today's evidence, I have to agree," Errol thought about this for a moment, then his brow furrowed, "Mr. Bould, you were side pulling yesterday. I recall at the time you did not appear to be such a good team. I presume you had your reasons ... subterfuge perhaps?"

"Once again I apologise for that small deception, though perhaps I am being a little hard on myself. It was strategy yes, playing my cards close to my chest if you like. I was posted to El Adam last October though I'd heard of the MU's reputation. When young Baillie returned from detachment he told me the MU were still pulling side style, I knew then if I could get eight good men together and train them in the square style, I might be in with a slender chance of beating you sir. I just didn't want to show my hand yesterday unless it was necessary Mr. Barrymore, that's all." smiled the foxy Warrant Officer.

Errol shook his head, "You know," he said placing an arm around the older man's shoulders as they started to walk towards the presentation podium, "I will always regret losing this afternoon, always. But in a way I am glad. A mythological element has grown around the MU tug-of-war team, a ridiculous parable that we could not be beaten. Try living with that burden on your shoulders for a number of years. As for yesterday Mr. Bould, I could have watched a dozen square pulling teams and would never have given a thought to change our style. It was much too late anyway. I have always had it fixed in my head side pulling was pure and true tug-of-war. Maybe it is? You may have still won today Mr. Bould without adopting the square pulling style, who knows. However I do know one fact I am certain about. If the team from 103 Maintenance Unit of the future hope to beat you, or your counterparts, my form of purism must be put aside, laid to rest for the time being along with the myth that was so surely laid to rest this afternoon."

~~~

Frank and Lorna Connolly, Ray and Babs Buckley, Nobby Clarke and Julian Cantwell found a table and seated themselves in the MU corner of the Peninsula Club. At a next table Callum McAlpine sat with Josh Munroe, John Tighe and Pete Oldham. Despite the team's loss earlier the lounge was filling quickly as everyone connected with the sport wanted to show their respect and support for the departing coach. The officer had not yet arrived and the mood subdued. For many in the large room this was the first time they had come to an MU tug-of-war gathering after their team had been beaten. It was strange; no one knew quite how to react. Even the ebullient John Tighe and Ray Buckley could do little to raise the spirits of the group as they awaited the 'Boss'.

Babs Buckley, a plain girl with dyed blonde hair and sad brown eyes looked around the room dolefully. It was her first night in the Peninsula Club and she was not impressed. "I don't know if it was such a good idea, coming here tonight Ray. You can see everyone's down, and no wonder, the team losing their last big match!"

"Yeah, well give it a chance, it'll pick up when old Errol arrives," Ray said hopefully.

It was a little after 9 o'clock when 'Old Errol' stopped at the red and white crossbar gate outside the Main Guard Room. He had gone for a short drive along the Pathos coast road in the hope it might clear the disappointment that still clung like a shroud over his brain. Winding his window down he greeted the duty policeman.

"Good evening, may I see your ID please," the corporal asked in his toneless official voice. Then, "Oh it's you sir," he said recognising Errol. Taking and glancing at the card with the plastic entombed photograph, he nodded and returned it to the rather reticent officer.

"Your team put up a good show today sir ... considering." the policeman offered quietly.

Errol slowly slid the card into his wallet, "Yes," he said listlessly, then for no reason the word used didn't seem to fit. "Considering! That's a strange choice of word corporal, in what way considering, considering what?" The officer merely asked the question conversationally as the word had snagged his interest. He glanced up at the face under the peak of the white-topped hat as he spoke and was surprised to see a minor recoil. A slight but definite reaction from the man, and by his actions made it clear he was reluctant to answer.

Feeling his way gingerly, aware this policeman had made an involuntary slip of the tongue but in what aspect he had no way of knowing! Errol's probing intelligence drove him on. It may be nothing at all, but then again why use the word? He tried again, "I too, thought my team put up a splendid show but you mentioned the word 'considering,' I'd like to know, considering what?"

The corporal was very uncomfortable. He had not intended to drop the two blokes in the shit but with his big mouth that's precisely what he may have done. "I didn't mean anything sir, I only meant considering El Adam's a very good side."

Errol was nobody's fool and it was now abundantly clear from the man's body language he was trying to hide something. What it might be, he had no idea but Errol may have stumbled across a misdemeanour, transgression, perhaps nothing more than a minor act of misbehaviour? Whatever it was, the tip had partially surfaced. He must try to force it out and into the open.

"That's very interesting corporal. You see, Warrant Officer Bould, the El Adam coach did not know how good a team he had until today's final." Errol put the car into gear, drove through the gate and parked at the side of the Guard Room. He was not going to let this go. Obviously the MP was lying. He walked back, "Corporal, I am in no mood for fencing. If you have something to tell me, do so. Do not lie for I will certainly know and let me warn you, I will not let this rest until you explain what you are at present so blatantly trying to keep from me."

The corporal sighed, "I was standing in for my mate on the last shift this morning sir ...."

Fifteen minutes later Errol drove his Austin Cambridge into the car park of the Peninsula Club. He switched off the engine and sat for two or three minutes considering his mood and wondering if he should join the group he knew were waiting for him inside. He decided he would but at all costs, he must avoid confrontation. The water under the bridge could not be brought back.

The MU corner was strangely subdued as he approached the tight knot in the centre. There was none of the customary

341

laughing and raised friendly voices that usually flowed so freely. The muted hubbub went even quieter as he joined them. Nodding and smiling at the many greetings he weaved through the throng then as a seat was pushed forward, he suddenly regretted his decision to join them. His association with the team had been severed when the whistle blew that afternoon, not only ending the match, but his term as coach of the best overall tug-of war team he was ever likely to be associated with. And last but certainly not least, an impossible dream.

"Would you like a drink sir?"

"No, no thank you," it was Connolly, "I can't stay Frank but I would like to say a few words, if I may." His voice was tight, conflicting emotions churning at his innards. Someone at another table stood. It was Callum McAlpine. He banged his pint pot on the table for attention.

The reserved murmur in the room went deathly silent as Errol thanked Callum, the man who would take his place in just a few minutes time. In return he received a series of smiling nods from the yellowish red head, and noted the pale blue eyes studying him minutely. The officer raised his voice.

"You will all be aware by now, today we were removed from the high pedestal we have over the years made our very own. In addition, before we get the chance to regain our rightful place back on top we, that is, you, must wait a painful year. I have no doubt whatsoever you will achieve this ..." His words were interrupted by a frenzied outburst of cheering. He smiled and waved for order. "Unfortunately, I will not be on the island to see that day," he went on, "as I return to the United Kingdom at the end of the month. Initially I came here tonight to spend the last few hours with the chaps who have done all of us proud. Those chaps who did everything I asked of them and under normal circumstances it would have been a privilege to spend this last social evening with them and all of you." He paused knowing he was approaching the danger area, but like water trickling through a crack in a dam wall, it was difficult to stop.

"Regrettably I now find myself in a position because of a slip of the tongue, I feel at this point it best I sever all ties with my team now. I am no more than a figurehead anyway." He spoke slowly, feeling his way but what he wanted to say was eking out. Suddenly he had had enough: enough of the team; of the

342

training; of the men; of the remaining league pulls; of the whole damn set up. It was sad, all the warm familiar feelings connected with the tug-of-war scene were washed away. He had been let down as never before, that left him in a state of shock. Errol looked around the dozens of faces. Everybody was here, the entire first and second team members, wives, girlfriends and many faces from the GEF yard including the crusty old war-horse from the Armoury, Chief Tech. McKinley. The officer's eyes lingered on Tighe and Oldham, but he hurried on to Callum McAlpine where he stopped.

"Ladies and gentlemen, I will not take much more of your time. In the three years I have been here I have made many friends and in those years, endeavoured to keep the good name of 103 Maintenance Unit to the forefront of the tug-of-war world. We are, and I feel as long as we are in existence, will always be a team to be reckoned with. That lofty position we enjoy comes from maximum effort and much hard work. It comes through good management, training and team selection but above all, loyalty. Loyalty and dedication to 103 Maintenance Unit. Now I feel it is time to pass the controls, leadership, the buck if you like, and with it the traditions and responsibilities that go hand in hand with the running of any successful team. All these things I place into the very capable hands of Corporal Callum McAlpine." The outgoing coach clapped his hands, triggering noisy applause.

"Y've gat a hard act t' fallah there Ginge," called John Tighe.

Errol looked at the Irishman not with malice, but long and lingering, interrupted only when Frank held up a glass, "I know you said no before sir but maybe you could use a drink now."

"Thank you, Frank, yes of course, how silly of me." The officer took a long slow pull swallowing half the contents then stared sombrely at the glass, swilling the fiery liquid round his mouth. He was preoccupied, stepping on and off wandering trains of thought that strangely had no connection with his immediate surroundings. "I learned something today," Errol spoke loudly, suddenly snapping out of his reverie. "A number of things actually. I'm afraid I have been like the dear old ostrich. My head has been buried in the sand, happy with my lot, content to allow the world to pass by unnoticed, stupidly thinking the changes happening all around could never affect our safe little cocoon here, on this island. My way has proven to be best in the past, why should it not be so for the future? Something I was warned about many months ago emerged today like a skeleton from my cupboard and it will haunt me for the rest of my life." Errol scanned around the packed tables and stopped when he found the face he was searching for. "Ah, Banks, there you are. I believe it was you who mentioned the square pulling method was the current style in the United Kingdom?"

George Banks nodded, "Yes sir, in March on that first day in the marquee."

"Then this is a classic case of 'You cannot teach an old dog new tricks?'" Errol's voice dropped almost talking to himself. Visibly gathering himself, he again addressed the group, "To those of you in my team today, I want to apologise to each and every one you. I apologise because I cannot understand why, over the past few weeks, I have not sustained my usual high standards. Why have I allowed a number of things to slip? Those of you who knew me prior to my paltry efforts this year, must have wondered why I allowed the debacle of the Station final to pass, without delving into the reason why we came so close to losing? Tonight I may have stumbled across the reason for our poor show against the RAF Regiment, and subsequently, because of my inexcusable tardiness, our loss today. That is why I apologise to my present team and to you all for letting you down, and the MU down. I should have listened! Had I done so and adopted the square pulling method there's no doubt we would be NEAF champions tonight."

The large room was still. Everyone present felt a mutual sadness for the popular coach. He was a shadow of his former self. Gone was the square cut confident and commanding figure of the Flt. Lt. Errol Barrymore they knew and loved.

John Tighe also regretted that Errol had missed out on the last final he wanted so badly to win. John should have remained quiet but sadly he expressed his feelings, "Shore sir, even the best of teams get beat, it's got t' happen sooner or later."

"Yes, I am aware of that, thank you, Tighe." Errol did not want to hear the man's voice much less speak to him.

John should have stopped but didn't. Hoping to raise the tempo he blundered on, "Sir, Oi wouldn't feel too bad, even old Oirland's rugby team get beat on the odd occasion!" he laughed.

"I'm sure they do Tighe, I'm sure they do," Errol said but tonight he was not in the mood to be placated by one of the prime movers of his team's defeat. His reserves dipped. "But what would happen at Lansdowne Road if two players knew they were not at their best physical condition, would they declare themselves unfit Tighe. Have you any idea?"

The Irishman did not answer. His face froze in a half smile.

"Tell me Tighe," persisted Errol, "what would happen before an International match if two players were unfit. If two players knew they were not one hundred per cent fit, would they do the decent thing and declare themselves unavailable for selection, would they?" The Officer's voice was rising. "Oh come now Tighe, would they do the decent thing man. Surely it is obvious even to an Irishman! Would they disqualify themselves?" Errol was shouting now, the last few words rising into a roar and the uncalled for jibe at Tighe's nationality completely out of character.

"They would be drapped, sur," John spat out the last word.

"Yes ... correct. They would be dropped from the team! If the two men in question spent the night carousing and drinking until three or four in the morning, it stands to reason they could not give off their best. Could they, Tighe? It would be unreasonable to expect two men who had been expending their energies in directions detrimental to their well being to be at their physical peak only a few hours later, now would it John? WOULD IT JOHN?" The last words were roared at a defiant John Tighe who could only stare back at the darkening face of the officer. John was about to rise from his chair when Pete Oldham seated nearby said, "Sit still John and shut up!"

Errol swung on Pete, "And what do you think Mr. Oldham, do you think these two should have been dropped. Or perhaps you think the honourable option would have been for them to have dropped themselves?"

Errol Barrymore was looking ill. His face dark, his eyes wide.

"If they considered themselves unfit for selection they should have withdrawn from the pool of available players sir." Pete answered in a cool even voice.

"Well, well, well, well, well," the officer said, "do we have a pricking conscience here. Let me ask you Mr. Oldham. Did you think today, that is, this afternoon, that you were fit? And your friend here, was he fit after the two of you somehow managed to get to bed between four and five am, that is AM this morning Oldham? The day of a major tug-of-war final that we, that is all of us here in this room, have been aiming at, working towards, gearing ourselves up. TRAINING ALL YEAR FOR. Were you fit for THAT?" Veins were standing out on Errol's forehead and neck as his voice cracked with rage, "You let me down!" he gritted, "Do you hear me, you let me and you let my team down, and the MU and of course you let YOURSELVES DOWN! Although I should imagine you do the latter often. Airmen ... the pair of you are untrustworthy, unreliable, dishonest, deceitful, utterly contemptible, disloyal human beings," he fumed, "I am going to see to it, personally see to it airmen Tighe and Oldham, that this goes in your records. I will see you are never allowed to take part in any sporting event while you remain in the Royal Air Force. I will do my level best to see you are barred from taking part in any event worthy of the name. Apart from arm wrestling in the bar rooms and brothels you so obviously frequent."

Frank and Callum stood on either side of the officer as he ended his tirade, his voice growing hoarse which made his condemnation much more damning. "Sir please, you'll injure yourself." Frank had tried to intervene but his words were lost as Errol finished his outburst. In the meantime, Callum approached the unfortunate twosome. "Listen, get yourselves out o' here quick, he could have a stroke any minute, just disappear until this blows over, c'mon lads out!"

Pete responded immediately and for a second John hesitated then he too rose miserably, bitterly following his mate heading towards the exit.

The minute the two airmen went out the door, Errol slumped into a chair and rested his head in his hands. Nobby Clarke pushed his way through to the officer's side, "Here sir, drink this."

Errol looked up, saw the offered glass and reached for it, "Thank you," he said simply and tipped the drink over in one fluid movement. He gulped and bared his teeth as the alcohol burned down through his innards settling the jangled nerves as oil on troubled waters. Errol looked at the glass, "Whatever it was Nobby, it was exactly what I needed."

"It was a neat double brandy sir."

With a slight nod Errol stood up, "I sincerely apologise to you all for such an unseemly display," the clipped words and sharp tone were back. "Unfortunately, what is done is done. I have never lost control before and I regret having done so here tonight. However, most of what was said needed saying, although perhaps I could have selected a more suitable venue. Such a pity it has spoiled my last evening with you. Goodnight and may God bless you all." Errol caught Callum's eye as he turned to leave. "Walk me to the door, will you please?" he had to speak into the ear of the Scot with the clapping and calls of good luck echoing round the room.

Once through the main throng the retiring coach said, "I must say I feel a lot better since I got that off my chest and having done so, hope I have cleared all the worms and bugs that were in the air. With luck you can now start with a clean sheet." They stopped near the exit, "One last word of advice to you, if I may. You're a natural coach Callum, you see things before they happen and react quickly. You'll do well but it seems you must make the change over to the square pulling style, and perhaps the sooner the better."

"Aye, eh, yes sir, I intend to start as soon as I can find someone who's familiar with the technique," Callum answered noting Errol's strained face. The man had taken the day badly.

"Good lad." A wry smile worked its way across the tired but handsome features, "One regret Callum, only the one. I should have listened. I should have listened to you and to others, but," he nodded towards the main lounge, "my head was in the sand I'm afraid. I missed so much. Not like me. Why was I so blind, why refuse just to listen?" He remembered the Scot's impassioned plea to include Buckley. "It's academic now of course, but as a matter of interest, who would you have taken out to make way for Buckley?"

Callum considered a moment going through the team in his mind, "Without hindsight, for what you said in there about those two is unbelievable. But aye, it would probably be Tighe sir. John's very good on the rope mind you, but even with eight good lads, one has to be the weakest" he paused, "but a place for Buckley just had to be found. For what it's worth he is now almost the equal of Clarke or even Connolly, so aye, it would've been Tighe that lost his place in my team."

"Yes, yes," Errol said reflectively. "Ah well I did not listen did I? No one is infallible, most of all, me." He was gazing into the night as they reached the club exit, "This one time, the worst of all times, my selection methods let me down, should've listened ..." his voice fell away gradually.

"It probably would've made no difference to the result sir, with El Adam pullin' square," Callum offered a crumb.

"Perhaps, but we most certainly would have given a better account of ourselves," Errol frowned before going on, "Life is so very difficult to understand isn't it. Why is the apple at the top of the tree the one apple we want most yet seldom reach? Why are the things we want most the hardest to attain? Life is like a woman Callum, so bloody unpredictable, maybe that is why we love them both so dearly."

Both men stood at the top of the stairs outside the main building looking out at the indigo blue moonlit night where everything seemed to be sprinkled in silver dust. Finally, Errol brought their athletic association to an end. "Well Corporal Callum McAlpine," Errol held out his hand, "I expect to hear in the future that you have taken our team on to bigger and better things. If you can breed true determination into your lads you'll find that extra ounce or two when you need it. Today was only a hiccup in what is a magnificent tradition for such a small Unit, caught as we are in the wide network of the Royal Air Force."

Callum did not respond at that precise moment for although the officer had paused, the Scot felt he was not yet finished. Barrymore was staring out over the luminescent topped trees then after a deep sigh he went on, "I honestly feel you have it within your power to go on from here and do very well. Corporal I wish you all the best of the very best, here's strength to you and to the arm of 103 MU. Good luck and good night. Oh wait, I almost forgot. I am taking some leave as from tomorrow so I doubt if I'll see you again, not on this tour anyway. So not only is it good luck and good night, it's goodbye, Callum."

Callum tried to speak but words stuck in his throat as the officer turned quickly and trotted down the stairs to his car. It was only as the Austin Cambridge purred out of sight and the car lights dimmed did Callum return inside the club.

"Well that's it, the Boss has gone," he said sitting down and reaching for his beer, "I only hope I don't bugger the whole thing up."

"The king is dead, long live the king!" Ray Buckley shouted, then turning to his wife he said, "I'm never wrong am I? Remember what I said earlier, 'things will perk when old Errol arrives.'"

"Yes, things did get a little hot," Babs said recalling the roasting the airmen received from the dark oh so good looking officer. "But answer this, what's going to happen now he's gone?"

Taking hold of his wife's chin Ray gazed into her eyes, "I do not want to overwork my crystal ball but," in a theatrical raised voice he called out, "I see clearly ... I see 103 MU with their new star, a young good looking ex-rally driver from London with slightly protruding ears. He will lead them to new heights."

"I wonder who that could be?" Callum called from his nearby table.

"You wonder who?" Ray turned and looked quizzically at the new coach. Then turning back to stare deep into Babs' brown eyes his voice went up an octave, "This new star has a beautiful wife named Barbara, and this gorgeous creature is prepared to do anything, that's ANYTHING AT ALL to help her flap eared husband get into the team. This beautiful and obedient girl is at this very moment, sitting not too far from the wonderful newly elected coach ... is prepared to do wonderful things to the new coach! PLUS her husband ... who is SITTING NEXT TO HER is about to buy him drinks all night. That's ALLLLL NIGHT."

~~~

Chapter 17

The shock defeat of the 103 Maintenance Unit tug-of-war team caused many raised eyebrows on every service base around the Levant. The forces newspapers, usually starved of surprises on their sporting pages, had a field day. The main army paper the 'Lion' roared from its lair in the Dhekelia base, 'MU humbled by underdogs.' The Akrotiri Sun lit the headlines with, 'El Adam claim MUs crown,' and the unanticipated result reached the dizzy heights of the Royal Air Force News with, 'Long time tug-of-war Med. champs finalised 2-0.'

Life on the MU carried on as normal, on the surface. Only the regular observer would note heads were not held quite so high, or their team's step as jaunty when they took the field for the remaining league matches. The new coach tried the square pulling style in practice but it was experimental as there was no one on the MU to advise him on technique. This being the case Callum McAlpine decided for the remainder of the season he would stick with the familiar side pulling mode before attempting something foreign to him and his team.

Over the remainder of the season, the team regained some of its shattered confidence winning all their remaining matches. The league was wound up in October with a very solid win against the Highland Light Infantry, followed in November with the Inter Services Knockout Cup at the massive Dhekelia army base. Eighteen teams gathered for this event, all hoping to repeat what El Adam had managed, but the MU reaper cut down the opposition clinically. Tying up and disposing of each team almost disdainfully, never once looking in danger. In the final Callum's rejuvenated men beat the reigning army champions, 33 Field Squadron in two straight pulls before many hundreds of appreciative spectators.

Looking back to that day in June and the El Adam defeat, everyone involved with the team grew aware of a budding record; not only were 103 MU unbeaten but they had not lost an end since Callum took over! The new coach was more than pleased with his situation. He had an excellent team for the following year and if the changeover to square pulling went smoothly, as expected, then although the new season was four months away, he couldn't wait for it to begin.

To help pass the time between seasons, in October Limassol held an annual wine festival in the zoo gardens. It was an impressive and much anticipated affair where wine makers from all over Cyprus set up as many as twenty stalls. With between eight and ten barrels in each stall of the very best wine Cyprus could produce, and free tasting from any or every barrel, it's not difficult to understand why the Limassol wine festival was so popular.

The entry fee into the gardens was the princely sum of 75 mils, or one shilling and sixpence. But immediately inside the gate each visitor bought for the same price two very necessary items, a wine glass and bottle. Armed with these, one was free to wander around the stalls and taste any of the hundreds of wines on offer. It was impossible to taste every wine of course, although some hardies did try but failed miserably without reaching the halfway mark.

For the more responsible connoisseurs or indeed amateur, the recognised practice was merely hand the stall minder the glass and point to a barrel. The glass was filled with the selected wine and tasted. This could be done with as many wines as it took the glass owner to find a wine that pleased his palate. When this no easy feat was achieved, the glass owner then handed the stall minder his bottle, which was filled with the chosen wine. And this could be repeated as often as the bottle owner could empty it. To a dedicated drinker of fine wine the situation was heaven.

Lots of service people, especially those from the MU tug-of-war organization, let loose after a long season, spent three or four nights per week in the zoo gardens over the two week festival. Not only was there an abundance of drink, there was food too! In the centre of the gardens fresh barbecued meat could be bought at huge charcoal pits along with salads and fruit. British families joined locals in long blissful evenings eating and drinking in the congenial atmosphere, tasting and falling in love with the delights of a Mediterranean life most were experiencing for the first time.

Ray Buckley and his family were one of the groups that were completely enamoured with the subdued warm nights to say nothing of trying to drink a particular chardonnay barrel dry. Wine could be bought ridiculously cheap and rumours abounded the Buckleys were entering the export business as nightly they left laden with demi-johns of their favourite wine.

The constitution of the pair was legendary for they never showed signs of over indulgence. This was demonstrated one evening when Ray and Babs invited George Banks and his wife Sue to their home for a drink after meeting in a restaurant. The Londoner had invested in a cocktail kit and wanted to try some of his mixes on victims other than on himself and Babs.

Ray's cabinet was stocked with every imaginable alcoholic drink along with fruit, fruit juices, cordials and creams necessary to mix the concoctions from his magical recipe book of cocktail miracles. George Banks remembers his visit to the Buckley home. They started slowly, sipping the wonderful aperitifs Ray conjured up amid much laughter. To the best of George's recall, the night melted away after wading into Ray's version of Harvey Wallbangers. Sometime later, he was shaken awake by Ray who informed him Sue was being sick in the bathroom. His host went on to say he and Babs were off to bed but George and Sue were welcome to stay for what remained of the night, if they so wished. Apparently Ray forgot there was nowhere to sleep in the two bed roomed dwelling with the Buckley children occupying the second bedroom.

It was 4.am when the taxi dropped the Banks outside their home and George found it impossible to report to work that morning. He phoned in sick, complaining not surprisingly of a stomach bug. Ray however was waiting for his bus at 6.30 am bright eyed and bushy tailed after eating a hearty breakfast. He had left Babs happily buzzing around her kitchen.

As the season closed around Callum McAlpine, time, for the first time in his life began to weigh heavily on his hands. Since he was twenty years old, at least once a year, or three times at the most, Callum solicited the services of a prostitute. The number of times he did this depended on whether he was lucky enough to meet a girl who thought and felt as he did. But females such as these were thin on the ground. It was easier and less messy to go to a professional girl, ask her price and go to her room. He needed to purge the disturbing and distracting thoughts that bedevilled all healthy young men. If females were so minded, life would be so much easier and no one would get hurt in the exchange. In his teens he, like all young men, had chased and caught some of the girls who had not run too fast, but Callum realised he was not being fair to the girls. In exchange for sexual relationships they wanted commitment and Callum would not lie, nor commit himself to a permanent association. He felt it morally wrong to show interest in a girl, to wine and dine her when his interest was only to bed her. So one night when a young prostitute approached him when leaving a Manchester pub, he felt, until he was ready to start a long term relationship, this type of situation would suit him. He accepted her terms.

The encounter was both educational and satisfying, proving if no one was to suffer this was the route to go for his occasional but very necessary physical demands. Depending on his needs, and his predilection for the girl, he would stay an hour or all night. If it were the latter, the girl would be sore for a week for Callum's appetite was usually ravenous and prolonged. After such a visit however, a naked nun offering entry into heaven could not turn him on. He was totally switched off to the female of the species for at least three months when the prickling nibbling would annoy his groin again. The gritty Scot was an unusual man in that he enjoyed his own company yet a welcome individual when with a group of either or mixed sex.

On Saturdays Callum and Josh Munroe visited the Twiga Bar on the Bypass where they would quietly drink and meet with others on the same mission; to get slightly, half, or totally inebriated. Later depending in condition, they'd take in the sights of the old town.

In the sixties the old town of Limassol near Hero's Square abounded with night clubs thinly disguised as bars and brothels. Only on the very odd occasion would a member of Callum's group take a girl to the 'back room' as it was known. Their visits leaned more towards the light hearted side where a favourite pastime was to ply a younger less experienced girl with drinks, urging her to reveal lascivious, lewd and sometimes hair raising stories about their clients.

Only once whilst with Josh, had Callum gone off with a girl and not reappeared. Josh did not mind. He and his friends trooped off to the Rivolli Bar, one of the slightly better establishments where they watched the floor show and flicked peanuts off their palms at the strippers. But not Josh, he would never degrade the girls. He watched quietly, sipping his drink and smiling at the dancers antics, which at its worst in the Rivolli, was suggestive but tame strip tease. To see the real thing in the Bunty Bar a private viewing could be arranged. Dancing girls could be bought by informing the waiter, "I'll have the dark girl third from the left with the hole in her mesh tights." The waiter would pass the message the girl had an admirer. The fee was £12 for a 'bottle of whiskey' which the admirer never saw. The girl would come to his table, have a few overpriced drinks then both would go to a 'back room.' Half an hour later the girl was bouncing back kicking her holey tights as high as she could again. This may have been enough, some sort of release for some men, but never Josh! To his high spirited mates Josh was neutered. If he was ever turned on by what was going on around him he gave no indication.

The first rainfall came late that year, one week after the Dhekelia Knockout cup held on the fifth of November, Guy Fawkes day. Day turned into night just prior to the first weighty drops when the cloudburst broke. Even the web footed Britons welcomed the refreshing downpour. It lasted an hour and hammered down in great long silver drops exploding in the running rivers the streets had turned into in seconds. Just when it seemed flooding was inevitable, it stopped as if some great cock was turned off in the heavens. The afternoon sun shone amazingly clean again, the dusty air purified. Everything was bright and sparkling but most dazzling of all was the smiles on the faces of the local people, happy the God given rain was at last replenishing their diminishing reservoirs.

Marion and Harold Ross had settled into a contented happy life. The young wife daily sank deeper into a mind absorbing love for her husband where nothing else mattered but her man. For his part, Harold showed his love in many different ways. He had developed into a very caring and sensitive spouse who saw to her every need and took great pleasure supplying it.

Marion was now getting the hang of how important sex was in their relationship. Initially whenever they kissed they would end up making love, and because of this, Marion found she was beginning to avoid kissing Harry and she did not want that situation! It came to a head one night as they gathered papers, glasses and cigarettes from the table on the veranda to go inside, Harry impulsively leaned over and kissed her. Within seconds he was pulling her shorts down, laying her on the cold tiles. It was so embarrassing. He was inside her immediately but she could not participate, worrying all the while if anyone could see them hidden only by their small veranda wall. Later in bed she had mildly complained, explaining love was not to be snatched at, she was not about to run away! Harold apologised, deeply sorry for treating her so mindlessly. That night, just to keep their lovemaking within the bounds of respectability, she suggested and he agreed to try a lovemaking timetable and always in the bedroom. Of course with Harry it could never be strict, but try it as a guideline. Marion was pleased with her dearest love's reaction. Her 'timetable' was working well with only the odd impetuous 'mistake'!

Harold preferred to know beforehand if they were to make love. He would have sex literally at any given moment, but he did not want to make the approach if he thought Marion was unhappy about it. To Harry this was rejection, and he could not handle a rebuff! So it was agreed without being clinical, they would make love every Friday, Saturday and Sunday nights and one night, a Tuesday in the week.

When natural cycles interrupted their routine Harold accepted the break, he was a happy man, his life full. Perhaps the reason Harold was satisfied was he had something else to occupy his mind; he started to play darts twice a week for his GEF Akrotiri, his section team. They played every Monday and Thursday night in the Limassol league. On these nights he'd drive to various match venues, normally bars and arrive home well after midnight. For Harold dart nights served a double purpose. To Marion it was a night out for her husband with 'the boys'. Sadly, this was only partly true. 'The boys' got a couple of those hours, the rest he spent with Carol Cook. On match nights, Harold would drive to camp, pick Carol up then drive back to the Limassol bar where the match was to be held. For appearances sake the pair initially arrived separately, as much as one walking in to the bar a few minutes before the other could be called 'separately.' Carol was ostensibly a spectator but eventually they

355

both tired of the subterfuge that was fooling no one. Caution was cast on to the viscous tongues of scandalmongers as she graduated to brazenly arrive and leave with Harold. Carol was soon tagged as 'Ross's girlfriend,' although it was common knowledge he was married, nevertheless she grew popular in the darts circle. Her good looks, rough tongue and course sense of humour served her well, nor did she mind the odd bottom pinch or lewd suggestion. She welcomed the attention but her guidelines were down and Carol was known to deliver a hefty right hook, or driving knee to the lower regions to dissuade the more daring gropers. This made her even more popular with both the male and female community of dart throwers.

The two nights in the week Carol spent with Harold were more than she had originally hoped. They were having a night out and a few beers, enjoying the chat and patter of a cheerful crowd. Sometimes they managed a meal together before driving to a quiet spot where they would clamber into the back of the van and get comfortable on the mattress and pillows. All the comforts of home that Marion had lovingly set up but used only twice prior to the weather in the Troodos Mountains growing too cold as the winter chills set in. The van heater could not run all night so Marion had opted for the comfort of her own warm bed at least for the course of the short winter.

The cool nights around Limassol never bothered Carol and Harold as they stripped for their bi-weekly romps. Afterwards Harold drove Carol back to Akrotiri then return home where he would collapse into bed beside his sleeping wife. She would snuggle into him thinking he was worse the wear through drink, paying little attention to the odd musky fragrance that regularly invaded her nostrils.

Many teams from Akrotiri entered into the Limassol darts league. It was a pleasant way to spend a social evening and Julian Cantwell was another who took advantage of the night out, doing the scoring or just enjoying the company. On other occasions because he was such a harmless and lonely soul, he would get an invite to spend weekends with married members of the tug-of-war team in their Limassol homes. For the briefest period the gentle young female trapped in an ostensibly male body was seen as a square peg trying to fit into a round hole. Frank Connolly explained the delicate situation of the Julian

Cantwell state of affairs to his wife, and Lorna, grasping the despondency of Julian's problem, told Frank to bring him to their home that very weekend.

This proved a happy union for all concerned. Julian was grateful to the Connolly's for providing this venue to escape the boredom and worrying thoughts that tended to entwine, almost strangle him at weekends. Weekends when everyone else seemed to have somewhere to go or something to do. Julian fitted perfectly into the Connolly's lifestyle. Caroline and Dawn loved the elegant and intelligent creature that understood, read them stories and took care of their many whims.

Lorna liked Julian. His presence was comparable to having another female in the house. He worked alongside her in the kitchen and insisted on a Sunday morning to rise and make breakfast for the family. Then much to the surprise and delight to everyone, one Saturday morning Julian bought a guitar in a music shop in St. Andrew Street. It was years since he played but soon he was playing dozens of songs made popular by Burl Ives the American folk singer, songs the Connolly kids loved. And was obliged thereafter to give repeat performances before the girls would consider sleep. Afterwards he would join Lorna and Frank on the veranda for sundowners where he'd sing, unabashed and confidently in a pleasant gentle voice. His repertoire of songs was limitless it seemed, but preferred gentle folk and country music.

Only once during a visit did Julian's homosexuality rise into the open. Frank had asked Julian to demonstrate the basic chords on the guitar so he might practice as Julian left the guitar with the Connolly's. Frank, seated on a straight backed kitchen chair with Julian standing behind, slid his arms over Frank's shoulders. He placed the fingers of his left hand over his pupil's on the strings of a chord. With his right hand Julian lightly held Frank's hand which in turn held the plectrum, then strummed the strings. Frank, aware Julian could have removed his hand after a couple of strumming strokes, said nothing, allowing his friend, if it was anything, this small privilege. On removing his hand, Julian trailed his fingers over the back of Frank's hand with a warm smile. "Now, will you remember that?

"I'll never forget it!" answered Frank gently rubbing the back of his hand against his cheek and winked lasciviously. They both laughed uproariously, Julian heartiest of all.

And so the Cypriot winter came and went almost unnoticed by the most recent arrivals of the British contingent living on the island. The hours of darkness were certainly cooler, sometimes dropping as low as freezing, but as soon as the sun showed itself on the horizon temperatures climbed rapidly. Some brave servicemen and women made their way down to the deserted beaches on Christmas day and swam in the sea. Not for the sheer joy of it or for the exhilaration no doubt gained from the experience. Their reason was mainly to boast to the folks back home in a shivering Britain, and relate to children and grandchildren, no doubt over a Yuletide fire, that in their prime, they had swam in the sea on Christmas day, neglecting to mention in which sea and off which island!

The Cypriot winter was a little damp and cold at nights and the early mornings, compared to the hot dry summers, but reservoirs filled with the regular rains that fell in the catchment areas. Most people watched 'Peyton Place' in English with Greek sub-titles on television. Started later but worked slightly longer hours with no afternoon siesta. Listened to and watched the Beatles in the cinema, and gasped with shock when Ian Smith declared unilateral independence in Southern Rhodesia. Just as some swimmers no doubt gasped with shock at the unexpected cold when swimming in the Mediterranean Sea on Christmas day.

Generally, not all, but most of the island's impermanent inhabitants were unmoved by world events, cocooned as they were in a world of their own, puppets dancing to piped music, awaiting their master's call, but all, every single one, anticipated another golden summer.

Among the many airmen to arrive at Akrotiri in the year of 1966, two were to have a significant effect on the lives of the people they were involved with, and in the fortunes of two tug-of-war teams based within the confines of the base. The first arrived in the second month of the New Year.

What Flight Lieutenant Errol Barrymore said in the Peninsula Club about 'Gods looking after our little Unit' proved extremely prophetic when on to the Maintenance Unit straight from St. Athen in Wales, marched Flight Sergeant Terence Michael Craig. Terry, as he was known, had spent the past six years on the station that so proudly held the United Kingdom Royal Air Force tug-of-war champions title for many years. He was not a coach nor at the age of 43 was he interested in taking up the sport again. However, there was one department in which Terry was an expert! He and the present St. Athens coach, a Warrant Officer Taylor had initiated the St. Athens team to make the change over from side pulling to square! He was a Godsend!

Terry blessed the MU with his presence, for his arrival, as the watching Gods had obviously instructed, coincided in perfect time for the start of training for the new season. The new Flt. Sgt. had not had time to warm his desk seat when a rather thin corporal with rugged looks and bright yellow red hair approached him. Obviously some checking up on Terry's background had taken place when the gangling corporal asked if the new Flt. Sgt. could possibly help his MU team make the change over from side to square pulling as he had done with St. Athens. Flt. Sgt. Terry Craig was flattered and took the young Scottish coach under his wing.

The new style was quickly embraced by the adaptable men and the method made an already very good team, practically unbeatable. The new style 103 MU steam rolled through the 1966 season crushing everything in its path. In the NEAF final they outstayed the gallant El Adam, regaining the crown lent to the North African side precisely a year ago.

The season stretched into the cooling month of November and the last matches of the year took place. The Inter Services league wound up with a win against the Military Police. In Dhekelia the MU again took the James Inter Services Knock-out cup and the crowd gave the RAF team a standing ovation. Their feat of going through the season without losing an end could be equalled but never bettered and the knowledgeable crowd showed their appreciation.

With the resurgence of the team from the Maintenance Unit the sports pages of the service newspapers paid homage to the reinstated champions with photographs of their Dhekelia win.

A further honour was also bestowed when the Station colours were presented to the entire team and coach. An unheard of honour, which heralded a massive write up in the centre pages of the 'Akrotiri Sun,' detailing their achievements for the past year. The newspaper write up coincided with the arrival on Akrotiri's

Ground Equipment Flight of the second airman. As Flight Sergeant Craig had changed the style of the MU tug-of-war team, and through his knowledge, made them virtually invincible, this second airman who arrived in the penultimate month of the year was Chief Technician Bernard Cornelius Kowaleski. He was not only about to be responsible for changing a number of lives, but to end some of them.

~~~

After nearly killing the young girl he met in the Blackpool Tower ballroom and the subsequent brush with the law in June 1965, Chief Tech. Kowaleski had not wandered, apart from one occasion, farther than the Sergeants Mess for his occasional drink. Bernard was not a social animal and avoided his fellow instructors in the Mess, which again tagged him as a loner. No one cared too much that he preferred his own company. The man was good at his job but like other studious types, was quiet and uninteresting. He could never fit into the sometimes boisterous antics of the senior NCOs.

Bernard had walked the three miles down to the village pub once, for no other reason than the welcome change of surroundings. He had gone to the bar and somehow got inveigled into taking part in a darts match. Nothing unusual really and another man may have enjoyed the experience but Bernard was uncomfortable and decided never to return to the bar.

A quiet year passed, it was early June 1966, about the same day 103 Maintenance Unit were reclaiming their tug-of-war crown in Happy Valley. Bernard dressed casually and wandered towards the Sgt.'s Mess for a beer. Lots of cars were in the car park and it was only then he remembered there was games night. A 'Sergeants versus Corporals' evening. The place was in uproar so the Chief, glowering at the disruption, deliberated before he set out for the village. He would try the lounge bar where the drink may be a few coppers extra but at least he would not be troubled by dart throwing idiots.

To his dismay, the lounge was fairly crowded but the noise subdued. It was almost pleasant as the gentle murmur of voices floated over the many heads locked in the maelstrom of smoke, laughter and background music.

Within a minute of his entry Bernard met a girl. She was sitting alone at a small table, an isolated island to the side of the crowded room. She seemed out of place, alone yet encircled with this milling mass of humanity. Her lone image struck a mental chord with Bernard. He found an empty chair, placed it opposite the girl then sat down.

When he cared to turn on the charm Bernard could touch any maiden's heart, but this girl turned out to be not so much an untouched maid. She had a three year old son with no husband. Initially she was cold to Bernard's approaches but her heart did melt a little to allow this very pleasant man to buy her a drink. Then after two hours of pleasant chat, it had warmed enough to permit him to walk her home. He was the perfect gentleman and she was surprised at her own boldness when accepting his invitation to go out the following evening.

Their meetings became regular over the next month but never did she allow liberties. This modesty caused Bernard to fondly imagine perhaps an air of respectability might batten down the hatch of his latent sex drive that apparently took a back seat when he was with her. He did not love this girl, Yvonne Preston, a curvy and pretty little thing with light brown hair and dark eyes who had lived in the area all her life. He was incapable of love but he did like Yvonne, which for Bernard was the pinnacle of feelings he could muster for anyone, nevertheless, he surprised himself when his thoughts turned to marriage.

Yvonne did not particularly like, or dislike Bernard. He was cold and insensitive but she was attracted to his looks, quiet good manners and her body needed a man. It was almost four years ago when Yvonne foolishly thought, when informing the father of her unborn child about her pregnant condition that marriage would automatically follow. Something had died within her after that. How young she had been, how stupid, naive and inexperienced. Her lover, the one man she thought she truly loved, had disappeared into thin air, like steam from a boiling kettle on a hot day.

Since the birth of her son, she had allowed only a few men to touch her, not because of any moral aspect, for Yvonne enjoyed sex as much as the next girl. It was the fear of falling pregnant again, which outgunned any physical yearnings that wracked her awoken body.

The younger of two children, Yvonne lived in a small narrow-minded village community where her name was never brought up in conversations discussed in the best of circles. She was a fallen woman. One or two of the best men in the best of circles had tried their luck with the fallen woman but unfortunately, for the men, Yvonne had not fallen far enough.

She was treated like a slave by her father who detested the way people stopped talking when joining their company, especially the men, his mates! His daughter's bastard had not only ruined her social life in Kirkcross, but his too! Yvonne's mother died the year after her grandson was born; her father also blamed this on Yvonne. Since his wife's death, Fred Preston started to drink heavily, something his wife had always controlled. Now that she was gone, the brakes were off on his good behaviour cart and Preston lost control on his downhill run. It culminated one night when Yvonne, experiencing an erotic dream portraying herself in the arms of her long departed lover, awoke to find her father on top of her. He was fumbling around in the darkness making clumsy love to her dream betrayed body.

Disgusted and distraught at the incident Yvonne started to desperately look for a way out of her predicament. Two nights after the encounter with her father she had gone to the lounge of the village pub alone, for the first time in her life, caring little for her already damaged reputation, seeking solace as so many before her, in drink. Bernard had sat down at her table when she was halfway down her first gin and orange, and to the man's unawareness, she began to look on him as perhaps a God sent avenue of escape. She regarded Bernard not exactly as a beach blown wind of fresh air, but at least he provided a small bore airline in a situation where she was smothering.

After six years at Kirkcross Bernard was promoted from the rank of acting Chief Technician to full rank and because of the strong rumour of imminent camp closure, the new Chief Tech. was placed on PWRs. Excited at the prospect of perhaps a new life with Yvonne who he had now been seeing for three months, and another overseas tour, he experienced a degree of happiness for the first time ever with a woman. He mentioned his placement on the Provisional Warning Role for overseas, and on impulse, asked Yvonne to marry him. Whilst in her company Bernard felt relaxed, and the need for sex was not the monster that transpired within him when with other women. He knew she wanted him and the promise of sex with Yvonne had tranquillised his troubled and unstable passions. This was something new! To respect and be attracted ... normally, to a girl with the intangible feeling there was something more fulfilling in the offing! There was no doubt, had Bernard been perfectly normal and a permanently rational man, he would at this stage be on the verge of falling in love. But his ego and hapless intrinsic background could never allow such a thing to happen. The young man was fooled - for the moment!

When he asked Yvonne to marry him he expected an immediate response, but his feelings plunged when she demurred for some minutes. The closest Bernard ever came to knowing the full blast of true happiness was when Yvonne lifted her bowed head, smiled and said, "Yes, all right, let's do it!"

Bernard momentarily wanted to run away and at the same time was flushed with a strange feeling that urged him to hug the girl, neither of which he did.

"What's PWRs?" Yvonne asked when he mentioned his probable posting.

"It's the Preliminary Warning Role for an overseas posting. They're warning me, no, us, they're warning us, if it's an accompanied posting, we're due to be posted overseas soon."

Suddenly the thought of getting away from her tight restricting environment stimulated her.

"How long will it take for your posting to come through?"

"Two, three months, depends when a suitable posting comes up."

"Then let's get married, soon as possible!" She surprised him with her sudden enthusiasm.

The itch of leaving Kirkcross had bitten deep and so they married a month later. The only people attending the Registrar Office wedding were Yvonne's older sister Jean and her husband Joe Morton who lived in a little semi-detached villa in Manchester. The Mortons were childless after five years of marriage so they naturally doted on Yvonne's three year old son Allan.

Bernard whisked his new wife off to a hotel in Fleetwood for a week's honeymoon, leaving Allan happy in the tender care of Jean and Joe. The boy despite his tender years, knew the

Mortons and well aware he was about to be spoilt silly in his Aunt Jean and Uncle Joe's home.

Bernard was pleasantly surprised by the zest Yvonne displayed in her lovemaking so his deviations from the accepted path of the norm never surfaced. His wife in her furious efforts to satisfy herself and replenish her own grievously empty reservoirs, tried to find in Bernard's body, a replacement for the wonderful something she had been denied four years earlier.

On his return to camp in early September, Chief Tech. Kowaleski learned he was to be posted to RAF Akrotiri, Cyprus, on November 25th. Tiny needles pricked the back of his eyes.

Because of the close proximity to embarkation it was pointless applying for a married quarter in Kirkcross. Bernard however, was mildly surprised to learn they were not welcome in his wife's home for the short spell. Yvonne's father had not condoned her marriage to a 'Polack,' nor attended the simple ceremony and would not allow the 'Polack' over the threshold of his home.

The Chief Tech. made no comment, but took his young bride and stepson to Blackpool where boarding houses were now emptying after the rush of the holiday season. He arranged rooms for the three of them in one of the better houses for the remaining weeks before they flew off to the Mediterranean island.

One night as they watched TV in the lounge of the boarding house, Bernard made the excuse he must return to the base and report for a duty in the Sergeant's Mess. He caught the Kirkcross bus and went to the village bar where he knew Yvonne's father spent his nights. Bernard approached him and proceeded to buy his initially reticent new father-in-law double after double of his favourite Bells Scotch whiskey. After the second drink, Mr. Preston was putty in Bernard's hands. It was not often anyone bough Preston a drink and doubles were unheard of.

Five minutes before closing time and with a last double whiskey, Bernard bade the older man goodnight, claiming he must leave in order to catch the last bus back to Blackpool. Returning to the holiday resort however was the last thing on Bernard's mind. On leaving the bar, he walked quickly to his father-in-law's house. At the rear of the terraced row of buildings, he smashed a small pane of glass in the back door and leaning through, reached the iron key that was always left in the ancient lock. With a surprisingly gentle click the key turned and he opened the door.

Mr. Preston must have had met someone before heading home for he did not arrive until after midnight, by which time Bernard was in a foul mood at being kept waiting. There was not much in the terraced dwelling but he did find something to keep himself amused while he waited.

The front door of the house opened and Mr. Preston who was lurching and staggering whilst humming an unknown tune, pulled out a newspaper wrapped fish and chip supper from inside his jacket. Struggling to stay upright and unwrap the food, he called for the only thing that still loved him; Queenie, his beloved cat.

"Here Queenie, coom get yer fish lass." Reverting back to his humming he staggered into the scullery cum kitchen to find the cat's dish where he stopped and blinked. Unable and uncertain he could not take in what he saw in the bright moonlight filtering through the small scullery window.

On the wooden bunker top beside the ancient stone sink lay a rabbit, skinned, gutted and headless, ready for the pot.

In his befuddled mind he could not remember buying a rabbit. But stewed rabbit was his favourite meal! "Yvonne!" he mumbled happily, "she's brought her old man a rabbit! Good lass, good lass, wants t' coom 'ome eh Queenie lass?" He spoke to the darkened room then resumed his song and search for the dish. Casting his rheumy eyes into the darkness around his feet where the dish was kept and where Queenie should be mewing and rubbing herself around his legs by now, he located the wayward dish. It was indeed at his feet but as his eyes grew accustomed to the darkness and with the help of the pale moonlight, he could see something was already in the dish. Something soft and squishy which he had marginally stood on. Made his foot slip from under him, forcing him to reach out and grab the solidness of the stone sink. Frowning he scrabbled behind the door and his claw like hands crawled and slid around as he searched then at last found the light switch.

The parcel of fish and chips fell from his hands and scattered across the linoleum covered floor like a hoard of disturbed cockroaches. Queenie's head, still attached to her empty skin, was resting over the edge of her dish. Her mouth was wide open and the thin black lips were drawn back, exposing her sharp pointed teeth in a painful silent scream. Her skin had been laid out flat, as one would see a trappers pelt spread in the sun to dry, with both pair of legs laid out on either side of the main hide. The beloved furry tail that had wrapped so many times around old Preston's legs still had the bone inside and was carefully aligned with the empty fur where the spine had been.

Mr. Preston found the last whiskey he had drank begin to fight its way back up his throat as he tore his eyes away from those hellish sightless glass orbs. They appeared to be staring accusingly up at him from the edge of the pink plastic bowl. He could not help but look fearfully at the rabbit on the bunker top with horror. Dawning comprehension spread over the haggard face.

"Aww Queenie," he moaned, "who could ... aw Christ almighty who could 'ave doon that to you ma loovely?" He could say no more as the bile frothed from his mouth. Staggering over to the sink he retched painfully, spewing out the steaming contents of his stomach.

When the retching subsided he splashed water on his face from the solitary cold water tap then turned to enter the lounge groaning and crying piteously. With his second step he stood squarely on the cat's fur. If he had stepped on a roller skate the effect would have been exactly the same; his foot shot from under him and Mr. Preston pitched heavily into the darkened lounge.

Bernard watched the haggard figure as it spectacularly crashed onto the polished linoleum.

Coolly he leaned around the door and switched off the scullery light. The man at his feet lay dazed, sobbing and moaning. Bernard, taking careful aim, kicked the unprotected face as hard as he could. Slowly and methodically like a lady searching through vegetables for the pick of the bunch, Bernard picked his spots and remembering to favour his right knee, kicked his selected areas with every ounce he could muster. Delighted in his sick mind the squishy smacking noises produced with each blow. When his legs tired, he picked up the body and threw it onto the solid round table in the centre of the room, causing an enormous Christmas cactus plant to skate off the table where it had resided for years. The green and gold plant holder crashed into a glass fronted display cabinet, full of dishes and mementos covering a lifetime.

The noise of the shattering glass should have snapped Bernard's frame of mind back to reality but it had no effect whatsoever. He leaned over the broken man trying to ascertain if his victim was alive. "It's impossible," he muttered staring at the mess that had been Mr. Preston's face. "Fucking old reprobate's still here," he said as he listened and heard the laboured breathing. Leaning over he lashed down with his fist into the bubbling mouth before hurrying back to the scullery and the kitchen table looking for something that could inflict more damage than his fists could administer. Pulling open the drawer under the tabletop he searched hurriedly for the implement he had carefully washed and replaced. It was an unusual knife in that it had been made to look like a rather thick six inch rule. The handle or rule part of the knife was made of bone and when the sides of the 'rule' were pressed, a five inch blade shot out from one end as did two brass guards pop out from the sides of the handle. To retract the blade the guards were pressed down into their respective sides and the action pulled the blade back into its housing. A delicate 'click' could be heard when the guards locked into place, securing the blade inside the beautifully engraved handle. He used this to butcher the cat, discovering it while searching, looking for something to skin the damn animal that kept bothering him as he sat awaiting the old man. Bernard nearly jumped out of his own skin when pressing the sides of what he thought was nothing more than an unusually thick six inch rule when the exquisite blade had shot out.

Lifting the knife out and acknowledging again the fine workmanship that had gone into producing such a knife, he puzzled why he had replaced this exquisite item back into the hated old bastards kitchen drawer. A man such as Mr. Fred Preston did not deserve such a rare trinket.

Bernard pressed the sides and the mechanism ejected the blade with a precise 'tick' like a Swiss watch. Holding it out in the subdued light he turned it slowly, fascinated by the smoky gleam from the mirror surface of polished steel. For a moment his eyes glazed as he recalled how easily the blade had sliced through the skin of the living cat. The sensations that burned through his body as he laid the knife flat between the teats of the cat's underbelly and pushed upwards towards the head. He watched entranced as the slight lump of the blade travelled smoothly just under the skin surface until the point poked through and emerged at the throat. He had paused at this point then like an impatient lover he pushed on, up through the lower jaw and up, with a little more pressure and final thrust, through the cat's head. It was only then the animal had stopped squirming. It was a good cat, had given him lots of pleasure, his uncontrollable ejaculation had completed his enjoyment.

Bernard placed the cold metal on his tongue, revelling in the almost sexual experience he derived in its smooth coolness. Although he had washed the knife thoroughly he could still smell the hot smoggy wetness he had inhaled when cutting into the fine and wetting fur. Despite his earlier ejaculation, a massive erection was raging inside his trousers and had to adjust himself before he could move.

A sound from the lounge disturbed him and hurrying through was thinking, 'Can't believe the old bastard's coming round,' but on entering he saw Mr. Preston was still. No movement came from the figure sprawled across the heavy oak table. Glancing quickly around he saw a movement at one of the small lounge windows looking on to the main street. Scrabbling back into the shadows, Bernard saw two heads, that of a man and a woman. Both peering inside.

The woman was calling, "Mr. Preston, Fred! You awright loov?" Turning to the man she said, "Not lak him t' mek sooch racket. What think ye John?"

The man shielding his eyes pressed against the window, "Dunno Maggie, but Ah do thenk eet best you get youself dan t' corner. The bobby crossed junction dan there not long since. Ah'm pretty shore there's soombody still in t'ere an' eet's not Freddie Preston!"

There was a surprised "Oh!" before the woman's shadow and footsteps hurried away.

Bernard was experiencing a feeling he had felt a number of times before. He was being pulled, almost akin to being physically lifted and borne back to reality. He knew what he had done, there was never any doubt he did not know and enjoy what he was doing with not the slightest of regrets. Yet when he saw again Mr. Preston on the table he was shocked at the physical state of the man. Self-preservation suddenly prevailed as he glanced around at his surroundings, blinking as if seeing them for the first time. Hurrying back to the kitchen, pocketing the knife as he did so, he quickly washed his hands and face in the laundry sink adjacent to the back door through which he entered. Carefully he wiped the brass door handles and key before hurrying off into the darkness.

Mr. Preston was in hospital for three weeks during which time Yvonne and Bernard moved into her father's house, ostensibly to look after him when they brought him home. Yvonne performed the daily household duties but had no hesitation leaving her father to his own devices when the time came to leave for Cyprus. Bernard lived happily in his father-in-law's house as the bed ridden older man was in no condition to disagree. He was the perfect son-in-law, caring for the semi-invalid's every need, smiling at every opportunity into the distrustful glowering eyes as they crackled at the bottom of their swollen pits.

Yvonne enquired at the police station if they had any information on the assault and was told her father had disturbed burglars. There had been a number of break-ins in the area recently, but rest assured, they were looking into it. Bernard who accompanied his wife said "It's a terrible situation when an old man can't walk into his own home nowadays without getting beaten up!"

"Yes sir, that's true," replied the sergeant, "but fortunately Mr. Preston is not so old, he's only fifty one you know? And he put up a good show before they got to him!" said the slightly piqued policeman, a year younger than the 'old man' Mr. Preston.

The Kowaleski family embarked for Cyprus in the third week of November 1966. The restrictions where airmen precede their families by three months had been uplifted with the winding down of hostilities since 1960. The peaceful situation existed at least on the surface between the dormant EOKA guerrillas and British forces. Cyprus was now regarded as a trouble free zone, but still required the presence of NATO forces because of the continuing friction between Turkish and Greek Cypriots.

The newly married couple found a house in Christos Street on the higher slopes of the more contemporary part of Limassol. The house was unusual, almost unique in that it had a garage. Most houses had driveways and carports but few owners had foreseen, or indeed had the extra funds when building their houses that one day they would own such a magnificent possession as a motor car. Should that happy event ever occur then a car port, with the splendid Mediterranean climate, was surely all that was necessary.

The garage had been the deciding factor from the houses shown to Bernard, all of which were more or less the same. Taxi drivers acted as unofficial 'estate agents,' ferrying couples around the many houses up for rent then collected commission if they found tenants. The Christos street house was furnished with old serviceable furniture and it was clean and well maintained.

Bernard hired a car and collected bedding from the SSAFA, The Soldiers', Sailors' & Airmen's Families' Association, conveniently situated next to the Twiga Bar on the Bypass.

The RAF gave married arrivals two days compassionate leave to settle into their new homes and the Kowaleskis used the hired car to familiarise themselves with the surrounding area.

The trouble between the couple began on the night prior to the day Bernard was due to report for duty. Yvonne started her period that day and when Bernard got into bed unaware of her condition, he wanted to make love as they had the previous night. They kissed and caressed and he got naturally excited but when he wanted to go further than light fondling Yvonne informed him lovemaking was impossible because of her condition.

Bernard grew unreasonably angry, much to her surprise for he had previously accepted this natural suspension in their short married life. She could not understand the change in him but just as her body was undergoing its temporary monthly cycle, so the damage to Bernard's brain was forcing a confrontation with normality. The scars of his childhood and youth had lain dormant too long and were forcing up through the recent layers of normality to the surface. The difference was his mutation was permanent, and it was to get worse.

At her denial to his advances, he grew rough and bitter. Uppermost in his pounding head was he wanted, needed, sex and had to have her that night with or without her approval. Yvonne was confused and not at all experienced in the various games of lovemaking. She had heard of oral sex but that was something she could never begin to contemplate. Somewhat out of her depth she offered the poor substitute of hand relief. This had been coarsely cast aside when he informed her; "There are other ways to fuck!" He turned her unresisting body on to her stomach and straddled her, pulling apart straps and obstructions of her sanitary ware. He was beginning to force entry into her anus when Yvonne, realising with shock his intentions, swung a bent arm and drove her elbow hard and painfully into his ribs.

Bernard gasped in agony and toppled heavily on to the parquet wooden floor as Yvonne scrabbled free and ran through to the room where her son Allan was sleeping. She locked the door expecting him to come after her but strangely, Bernard did not follow her.

Next morning Yvonne heard Bernard moving noisily about, then leave for work. At the window she watched the Ford reverse down the driveway then drive off with a squeal of tyres. Frowning fretfully she recalled the brutal force he had used the previous night and shuddered to think what would have happened if she had not connected with her wild swinging elbow. 'Disgusting kinky bastard,' she thought, 'men do that to each other don't they? But not with women surely when we have the proper ...' her thoughts paused realising where her thoughts were going. 'Well there's no way he'll ever do that to me thank you very much.'

"Never mind, he's never tried that before so hopefully it was a one off." These words she spoke aloud, trying to convince herself that indeed it was.

Her voice penetrated the folds of light morning sleep her young son was emerging from and Yvonne smiled at the one bright light in her life. "If it wasn't a one off, then that bugger's in for a rude awakening. Isn't he Allan my boy?"

~~~

371

Chapter 18

The new NCO i/c of RAF Akrotiri Station Workshops, Ground Equipment Section, Chief Technetium Kowaleski walked into his office. He had completed his introductory interview with his section commander followed with his obligatory short tour of his new domain. Taking a deep breath as he rounded the desk he sat down on the swivel chair. They had cleaned everything in the room as requested. His predecessor, a Chief Technician Price, R. had not been the tidiest of men. Somewhere in his dim distant past, Bernhard had been taught, 'Cleanliness is next to Godliness' and it stuck. He could not stand disorder, especially other people's.

Three days earlier after Bernard reported on the base, and before he had gone off on the break of two days familiarisation leave, he requested the office be scrubbed out from top to bottom and anything not required for his job, removed before his return. Two local labourers employed by the Akrotiri based Ministry of Public Buildings and Works had done a thorough job. He could still smell ammonia. They even found time to give the room a coat of paint

He swung his chair round and gazed through the newly cleaned window. It looked over the surrounding fence and across the rough ground - the bondoo? That's what it used to be called! He sighed, at last! At long last he was back on the same land mass and within a stone's throw of the despised Maintenance Unit. It had taken many years but, just as fine wine matures, retribution after all that time would taste that much sweeter. He had three years; time enough to inflict his own form of retribution on those bastards in the MU. On those who ruined his body, his sporting career, his life! But he must not waste any of that time. Today he would start laying the foundations.

The unfortunate incident with Yvonne the previous night kept interrupting his train of thought. He was not ashamed. A woman had many entries to her body that would please a man, and many women! It was simply a matter of preferences and sooner or later she would learn of his preference. It now appeared to be sooner after last night! So be it! He had waited long enough, she simply needed tutoring.

Bernard set about his work. He had to read mounds of paperwork, must familiarise himself with Station Standing Orders, look over inventory sheets, sign and read up on duties.

The day passed pleasantly and Bernard was surprised when he realised his first day had almost flown when one of his clerks placed a cup of coffee on his desk at 3 o'clock. Thanking the man he stood and stretched, then taking his coffee, crossed to the opposite side of his office to stand by the window. The first thing to strike him as he looked into the Ground Equipment Servicing bay was his office was not the only place that needed sorting out. Since walking through Workshops that morning, the work area had degenerated into a shambles. Equipment was scattered everywhere and no one seemed to be working as small groups were engrossed in casual discussion all around the workshop floor. Tools and apparatus lay unattended, abandoned. "Maybe I should have seen to that lot first," he murmured picking up his beret, "time to go walkabout."

The entry of the new Chief on the workshop floor caused a minor flurry as the groups broke up, returning to the specific pieces of ground equipment they were servicing. Bernard strolled casually round making mental notes of people he would talk to and recognising some faces that had passed through his training course in Kirkcross. He noticed 'Crew Room' on a door and made towards it. Woe betide anyone in the rest room with the break period well past.

The room was empty but the sight sickened him. Chairs were scattered all over, unwashed cups, overflowing ashtrays festooned the two tabletops. Newspapers and magazines lay in heaps over chairs and tables. On another small table by the window was a tea urn, a bespattered chrome canister rising from the midst of abandoned cups, milk bottles and tins of sugar. Spilt milk and sugar provided a crusty formation round the base of the urn that would have done credit to a Christmas card. Cigarette ends and ash were everywhere and overall hung a rancid smell of stale tea and trapped smoke. As his eyes ranged over the litter, a photograph in one of the papers caught his attention. He reached into the rack of pages and pulled it out. It was the central spread from the 'Akrotiri Sun.' The headline across the top read, '103 MU Sweep The Boards, Awarded Station colours!' The naked words drew his eyes like a woman's breasts but without the warm significance. The whole middle section sang the praises of the tug-of-war team who had gone unbeaten since the previous year's NEAF final. There were photographs both in action and posed and another of the team receiving their Station Colours from the OC. Bernard could not read the blurb concerning the considerable list of achievements as his sight began to blur. Slowly he crushed the page, squeezing harder and painfully harder until it was reduced to a solid ball. This he dropped then placed his heel on it, pressing, twisting, grinding. His eyes glazed as he saw again that day when he lay writhing in pain, cursing and damning them forever for setting him up, cutting dead his whole life with the removal of the link pin. He blinked hurriedly as he had done so often washing away the incessant images.

"CORPORAL!" Bernard roared from the door of the rest room. He could not remember any of his junior NCO's names but three came trotting forward.

"Which of you is most senior?"

The three faces frowned before one stepped forward, "I suppose that must be me Chief."

"I suppose that must be me Chief," Bernard mimicked, "Good God man, don't you know. What's your name and who's in charge of this section?" Bernard barked.

"Alf ... sorry, Chief, I am Cpl. Morris. Sgt. Jones is i/c but he's on compassionate leave in Blighty. His mother died a couple of days ago."

"Then that leaves you corporal, you are from this moment i/c Crew Room." Bernard stabbed a thumb over his shoulder, "The animals that use and live in that behind me could teach pigs lessons on how to muck up a farmyard. That restroom is a disgrace. I want it cleaned by the end of work today, that floor ...." Bernard stopped when Cpl. Morris quickly looked at his watch.

"I know what time it is corporal, and well aware of all implications involved here with buses to town, meals and so forth, but that is not my department corporal Morris. My job is to delegate and I am delegating you! You, in case you are unaware of the lineage of authority here, must delegate enough people to clean this room as I have asked, no, ordered you to do. I want that floor shining so I can see your face in it, the table clean enough to at least eat off and the windows clean enough to see Blighty. Everything else in there will be washed and put away out of sight and if you have no storage, will be laid out neat and tidy. I don't want to see one particle of a tea leaf or a grain of sugar. That, I don't think is asking too much and, corporal," the new chief stopped threateningly, "if I find a speck of spittle anywhere in there, I swear that brush over there," he pointed to a long shafted sweeping brush, "the sweeping head will resemble a moustache on your arse!"

There was no mirth in the remark. Corporal Alf Morris felt if he let this man down the brush was no empty threat. He watched the Chief storm away, then stop and turn, his glare similar to physical assault. "Corporal Morris, tomorrow I want you to arrange a meeting in the Fitting Bay with all personnel under my command. I want them all here, everyone! Ten o'clock. Now get that room cleaned by a team or do it yourself, I don't care. Get on with it."

"Shit, fucks and double shit, where the fuck am I to get blokes for this? They've all got jobs! I'm going to be very fucking popular." Alf moaned looking around the suddenly very busy fitting bay.

The following morning at 10am every airmen of the Ground Equipment Flight, Akrotiri, who fell under the jurisdiction of the new Chief Technician gathered in the Fitting Bay of Station Workshops. Speculation was rife as to why the incoming Chief had called a meeting. It was an unusual way to introduce himself or perhaps he wanted to rattle his sabre a little.

"Morning everyone," Bernard called out, not so much a greeting but to quieten the rabble down. He was standing on a toolbox which put his tall frame a full head and shoulders above the assembly. "I am your new i/c Workshops, Chief Technician Kowaleski and I have a couple of things I want to talk to you people about. The first is in line of duty, the second recreational, but I will demand total commitment for both," he paused scanning the attentive faces.

"The first point I wish to address is the disgraceful condition of this section. I am amazed my predecessor allowed such filth and grime to accumulate to such an extent ... but no more! From tomorrow there will be, to start with, daily inspections, which, with the expected improvement, I will extend to weekly inspections then finally to the odd spot check. I can assure you, ALL of you, any section that allows shoddy housekeeping to continue, the man in charge of that department will be answerable to me! Not a pleasant prospect if that man values peace and contentment in his workplace." Bernard stopped again allowing his words to sink in.

That morning when he walked into the Crew Room before the start of work, he had found it as he expected to find it. Clean and spotless. He had ran his fingers along the conduit piping above shoulder height and was not surprised to find his fingers dust free. He'd commented to the dozen airmen changing into denim overalls, "Plenty room for improvement."

The faces of the men looking up at him expectantly reflected the brass badges in their berets as the morning sun flashed at the perfect angle. "The second and equally important point I wish to make is this; I intend to take over the tug-of-war training. For this purpose I want every fit man, whether he is sports minded or not to be at the training rig at eleven o'clock this morning. There is something I must impress upon you now, especially to any sceptics, make no mistake, when I am finished and have the eight men I want, when I have them honed to my satisfaction, the Akrotiri Ground Equipment Flight will have the best tug-of-war team in this Near East Air Force Command."

A hand shot up from the middle of the crowded central area.

"Yes," Bernard looked hard at the man.

"With all respect, you are new here Chief, you are perhaps not aware there is an excellent team in that sport on the station. The Maintenance Unit are unbeaten for over a year now. If you're interested there was a write up about them in the 'Akrotiri Sun' last week."

Bernard glowered at the man, "Perhaps you are not aware airman, 103 Maintenance Unit is NOT part of RAF Akrotiri! They are a parasite on the main underbelly of this base. Don't you think it's about time a team from Akrotiri took them down a peg or two? And I promise, no I swear, it will be my team that will lower the colours of that rabble down the road."

There was a rustle of movement at the vehemence of the new

Chief's words. Like a light wind had rippled through taut bulrushes. The airman raised his eyebrows, then a quick shrug.

"Do you doubt me ... airman?"

"Chief, It's not so much a question of whether I doubt what you say, but the MU have had every other team in the Med. snapping at their heels for years, but they always come out on top. It's a tradition with them and commands a huge following. They won't be easy to beat Chief, as a matter of fact, everyone at station level are quite proud of the tiny MU and their achievements."

"I see," Bernard said coolly, "I see! What's your name?"

"Clive, Chief, SAC Clive."

"Clive, I do not need defeatists such as yourself. Do me the honour of excusing yourself from attending my eleven o'clock meeting. I said I intend to have the best tug-of-war team on the island and I WILL HAVE IT, believe me. As for the rest of you," he swung away from the discarded SAC Clive. "I want every fit man at the gantry, as I've said, at eleven o'clock. Do not prejudge me or try to decide for yourself if you are tug-of-war material, leave that to me. If you're fit and strong I want to see you. Thank you for your attention. Return to your sections."

Harold Ross standing alongside Alf Morris said, "I don't know if I like our replacement for Chiefy Price Alf, this one seems a hard bastard."

"Yeah, he's a right shithouse. I've already had a taste of his nonsense. Have you seen the Crew Room this morning?"

"I have. When I walked in I thought I must be in the wrong bay. The Crew Room's never been that tidy, I couldn't find a thing. He's accountable I gather?"

"Well he gave the orders, old muggin's here and some of the lads got stuck in washin' an' scrubbing it last night. Windows too. Swore he'd have my arse in a sling if he wasn't happy with it." Alf muttered.

"Mind you, it was getting out of hand," laughed Harold, "but I'll tell you what I do like. He reckons he can get a good tug-of-war team out of this lot. If he can do that I'll be happy no matter how big a shithouse he turns out to be. It is, like he says about time someone knocked the MU out of their stride. Somebody's bound to sooner or later," he slapped Alf on the back, "and it might as well be us!"

"That's true! Why shouldn't it be us. We've been complaining for ages about how the MU get all the good coaches," said the stocky corporal who had pulled for the Akrotiri GEF team in the past two Station Championships,

"Let's see what this guy has to offer!"

~~~

Two matters of great interest and excitement were crowding Harold Ross's head as he stared ahead into the magical luminescent darkness. He was driving at breakneck speed back towards Limassol after picking Carol up outside the Guardroom. She sat in the only passenger seat, quiet and totally ignored.

The least important but nibbling all the while round the edges of his thoughts was the latest arrival and replacement for the section i/c Ray Price, was one Chief Tech. Kowaleski. The new Chief Technician, a powerfully compelling man, had among other things, wasted no time in announcing he was the new tug-of-war coach and had picked sixteen hopefuls from a fairly large group of men at the training gantry. The Senior NCO definitely knew his business and had a drive about him that rubbed off on the men. Also the towering athletic figure engendered a question no one could quite confirm - did the man have the merest suggestion of a limp, or was it simply an uneven gait? Whatever it was it made little difference to the man for he literally crackled with enthusiasm. At the end of the session he made a strange but exciting statement; he solemnly promised if he could not beat the 103 MU team in the forthcoming season, with eight men from the chosen sixteen, he would leave the Air Force. The only life he knew and loved. Harold was right to be excited; he was one of the sixteen!

The second and by far, most important incident to ever happen to Harold, second only to marrying Marion, occurred less than an hour ago. He was shaving in the bathroom when Marion asked, "Who are you playing tonight?" The question was unusual in that she did not know one dart team from another, had never previously shown an interest. Harold noticed she was a little pale. "Are you feeling all right Mari?" he asked.

Marion did not answer but picked at a non-existent piece of fluff from a towel.

"What's wrong, something's bugging you. I've noticed it since I came home. Don't you want me to go out? Just say the word, I'll stay home." Harold meant what he said, but his words sent a question scampering through his head on how he could get word to Carol. She would be waiting outside the Main Guardroom. He need not have worried.

"Don't be silly, Harry, you can't let the team down. Of course you must go to your darts."

Trying not to sound too relieved, but genuinely concerned he asked, "Then what is it?"

Marion glanced at him, turned away, then back to look him straight in the eye, "I don't know how to tell you this, I hope you're not going to be angry, but it seems I've gone and got myself pregnant!"

"Pregnant?" he repeated the word but in a tone as if a barman had informed him there was no beer in the bar, he could not comprehend the situation. "Pregnant," his brows creased as he said the word again, slowly this time, "You? You are pregnant ... with our child?"

Marion watched him, trying to determine his feelings but she couldn't tell. His face was puzzled, his eyes widening.

"With OUR child?" Harold said again.

"Well I don't know, it could conceivably be that pound of seedless grapes I ate. Could I get pregnant eating seedless grapes?" A slight pause, "No?" She went on as Harold stood open mouthed. "Then I'm afraid Harry, you'll have to accept responsibility, it is, or should I say, he is, as I am, all yours!"

Harold smiled recalling how Marion had literally pushed him out the door with the words,

"Off you go, I'm not likely to have wee Harry Ross tonight, next July probably, like the nice wee doctor said."

Harold could not wipe the idiotic grin from his face as images danced across his imagination.

From the passenger seat Carol watched him. He had not said a word. Not even when she got into the van and greeted him. He was in another world, totally gone, preoccupied. She decided to break the silence, "Harry, remember me?" It had been an attempt at a conversation breaker but the big oaf, he did not hear her! It might have been the noise from the engine, the rattle inside the unlined van was considerable. Carol sat forward and said,

"Harry, hello, remember me?"Carol couldn't believe it, he was actually grinning at the windscreen, staring straight ahead and ignoring her! Her patience snapped, "What the fuck's wrong with you Harry, you got a hair up your arse?" she shouted.

Harold blinked, "What do you mean?" he growled.

"Well," she railed, "no greeting like 'Hello fuckface'. Nothing! You ignore me completely and you're driving like a fucking maniac!"

Harold slowed to a sedate 50 mph., crushed out his cigarette, lit two more and passed one to Carol. He drew long and hard, inhaled and with great satisfaction blew the smoke at the windscreen. "I was told something tonight that made me very happy Carol. I was beginning to wonder but the news chased those doubts away. It's the one thing I have needed in my life." He spoke quietly, glassy eyes glistening.

"Well if that's you happy, I don't ever want to see you miserable. So what's the good news, you've grown another cock? If you have that's good news for both of us," she said flippantly.

"I wish," he smiled in the darkness, "Marion's pregnant!"

Carol blinked, she had to think for a minute. Had he struck her? She blinked again repeatedly and dropped her cigarette onto the rubber mat flooring where it produced a shower of sparks.

"Hey stand on that Carol, don't burn the bloody rubber." Harold snapped.

The blonde head bobbed down and reached for the cigarette. She was glad of the opportunity to do something. It give her a moment to regain her poise. "Sorry," she murmured, her mind still shaken as she settled in her seat. How could he calmly sit there and tell her his wife was pregnant? The cold bloody fish, did he have no feelings at all? Oh my God was that it? Did he really have no feelings? For her? Apart from the sex, had no bond grown between them?

Carol watched the trees and shrubs as they turned from shadows into silver as the probing headlights picked them out before flashing past her left shoulder. The trees and shrubs were images of things that were really there, outside the car they were actually solid and real. But when they slipped past the van lights they were gone, lost in the darkness! When she looked back over her shoulder, she couldn't see them. Carol for an instant felt related to those shrubs and trees. Back there somewhere they still existed but only an instant ago, they were bright and shining in the glare of Harold's light. She looked at the face beside her caught in the dim green dash light. He could have been on another planet. Was what she felt for this man imaginary? Certainly they had always made it clear their communion was only for the fantastic sex that come from God knows where, but it was fantastic, like a drug. She'd got used to it and could not give up. But, she despaired, even if it was just sex, surely there must be some other deeper feelings for the partner providing the high powered physical sensations transferring from one to the other? With a minor shock, Carol realised until a couple of minutes ago, she had actually been in love with Harold.

With those two words, Carol felt, like those trees outside, she had slid out of Harold's light and into the darkness. Harold had stopped and dallied at her 'tree' or was she something smaller to him, a 'shrub' perhaps? Was he now passing on without a backward glance, leaving her in the darkness? She always thought she could handle this situation as it was bound to happen sooner or later, but those words, 'Marion's pregnant,' pulled her up, made her realise if Harry had a permanent side, it was all sewn up and taken care of. When about to finish he always used a rubber with her, always! Did that not expose the transient situation that existed between herself and Harry? She thought she knew. Thought she had accepted their short term union must end throughout their relationship too, but it was this sudden finality! A baby for fuck's sake. It changed everything. With a baby went a wife, a home, a lifetime ... and her Harry! It was a shock, but yes, she had loved Harry Ross.

The remainder of the journey was silent and it was only when they saw the dozens of cars parked outside the 'White Rose' bar did Harold recall it was not the usual league match. It was a knock-out competition and he just managed to get his name on the long list before entries closed at 8.pm.

The huge lounge was jammed with bodies. Harold took Carol's hand and pushed his way through the crush. Four dartboards had been set up on the dais where the band usually played and Harold wanting to get as close to the dais as possible, threaded his way through the crowd.

"Harry," someone shouted, then again, "Harry, over here!"

Frank Connolly was seated at a table with a group from the MU. Glad of a familiar hand extended in this teeming sea of humanity, Harold hauled Carol in his wake through the heaving male masses. She was puffing and complaining but loving the attention and smiles as she bumped her breasts and rump against every male extension she could reach, twisting and tripping in Harold's wake.

Harold raised his voice to be heard, "What are you doing here, you playing?" he asked Frank.

Frank shook his head, "No, just came out for a quiet pint wi' the boys an' this is where they brought me, I've had quieter moments watchin' the steam hammer at Fords Press Shop."

Frank fell silent when Harold pulled Carol in front of him. She was an extremely pretty girl in a sexy if tartish mould. He recalled when she came to the Fire Picket billet looking for Harry. How she had filled her uniform that day and wondered why she stuck with a married man. As she took of her jacket every male in the vicinity was ogling her, dressed as she was in a white mini skirt, showing to the best advantage her well shaped bottom and legs. The blue T-shirt displayed clearly that there was nothing between the T-shirt and Carol.

Harold introduced her to the table with a brief, "This is Carol everyone, I don't know all your names, perhaps someone could do the honours."

The man Harold knew to be the MU coach stood up, "Hello Carol Everyone, that's a damn unusual name for such a bonnie wee lass. Allow me to do the honours." He pointed out and named each individual in the group ending with "and me, I am Callum, Callum McAlpine. And I'd like to add, all those I have just introduced to you are ALL married," he lied. "whereas I myself, am not in that matrimonial state of harmony but then, I've never been asked," he winked and smiled, a smile which transformed the hard craggy face. Callum was obviously on the happy road to alcoholic heaven but a long way from intoxication. He went on, "Now then, to find you a seat Carol Everyone. There doesn't seem to be many of those around, except maybe this," he patted his thigh, "but if I'm rushin' things. You can have this, an' it's all warmed up for your lovely wee bum." He stood aside, his open palm indicated his own chair.

Carol looked at the angular features of the red haired bloke and smiled at the frank blue eyes that were openly looking deep into her own. He was thin, thinner than she preferred her men but his demeanour exuded strength and confidence. "Thank you," she said squeezing past him to the offered seat, looking up as she did so, giving what she knew was a warm smile.

Callum for his part received the furnace blast of her 'warm' smile and his reservations regarding females melted somewhat in its heat.

Harold ignored the flash of communication between the pair. He had seen it a dozen times on dart nights. Tonight was no different. Carol he thought callously, tossed her arse around from one hopeful to another, and curiously he couldn't care less on this evening when he felt he should have been home with Marion. He shook her face from his head and digging into his pocket asked, "How much is the kitty?"

"Ten shillings ... eh, ten shillings a head," Julian Cantwell corrected himself glancing at Carol.

Harold dropped a pound note into the glass then, as Carol was in an obviously hilarious conversation with the MU coach, he crouched down between Carol and Frank Connolly's chairs. Turning to Frank he found his friend shaking his head.

"I've never known anybody like you in my whole bloody life Harry," Frank said glancing at Carol giggling at something Callum said.

Harold gave nonchalant shrug. "Don't worry about her," he declared, "besides, I've got good news for you Frank, AND," he raised his voice, "I have much more important news for you lot from the M U!"

Most of the people round the table were connected in one way or another with the MU team. It was Julian who asked, "Is it good news or bad Harold? If it's bad we don't want to hear it."

"Sorry Julian, Julian is it? He went on at the confirming nod. "For you, and your team, it is very bad! If you don't want to hear it now, you'll find out soon enough anyway. You see, as from today the supremacy of the 103 tug-of-war team is over, finished, kaput, end of story!"

"Oh aye," laughed Frank.

"Oh aye," mimicked Harold emphatically. "We've got ourselves a real firebrand of a coach in the section. Swears your days are numbered, so help me! It's like he has a vendetta against you lot. His name's Kowaleski, a chief tech. Ever heard of him?"

"Yes, didn't he father the Wicked Witch of the West? Anything else to tell us Harry, my kids love fairy stories?" Ray Buckley called from the opposite side of the table.

Harold laughed at the perennial wise cracking Londoner he had met a number of times. "Don't say I didn't warn you. I swear the Station GEF team are going to be very good."

"I'm pleased for you son, truly I am, now if you're finished wi' the pipe dreams, what was the good news ye had for me?" Frank asked, smiling at this unusual show of enthusiasm.

"Marion's pregnant!" Harold said it quick, his smile widening.

"Pregnant?" Frank hoped his face registered surprise. He didn't want to let Harold know his wife Lorna had that morning taken Marion to the clinic for the results of her pregnancy test. Lorna had been sworn to secrecy when Marion in her excitement exploded with the news she was expecting a baby in July.

"Please Lorna, you must tell no one for I want to make sure it's me that tells Harry first!"

Lorna had sworn wild horses could not drag the information from her lips.

When Frank came home earlier that evening from work he asked innocently, "What's new?"

The wild horses had obviously gone berserk for they ran right through Lorna's open mouth, hauling with them the exciting news that no self respecting woman could possibly keep secret. Marion would have been safer entrusting her secret to the Reuters news agency.

"Terrific, fantastic Harry, we'll certainly have a drink on that!" Frank went to stand up when Harold pushed him back into his seat. "Later Frankie, just a minute, there's something else I want to tell you," his voice dropped. "And you'll be equally pleased."

Frank's brow furrowed. He had no idea what was coming next.

"After tonight Carol and I are finished. We haven't actually said as much but we both want a break ... and this news with Marion has just ... I don't know, kicked the shit out of me I suppose. I have to stop screwing around sometime," he sighed.

"It's just that she ..." Harold nodded towards Carol accepting a drink from Julian who somehow managed to get a tray of drinks. "It's just that she is such a good fuck. Sorry Frank there's no other way of putting it, she really is, there's nothing she won't do. She's had me, literally by the short and curlies for so long now. I really don't want to let her go, but tonight when I told her about Mari, she went quiet. And I felt it too. We both ... we both let go I think. I fucking hope so!"

Frank stared at the man he had got to know fairly well and could at a stretch accept now as a friend, but his association with Carol would always be the stumbling block, a barrier between them. He seemed at last to be coming of age. Both accepted a pint Julian handed them.

Harold gazed into his beer. Already his brain was issuing signals; some self congratulating and warming his innards. He was actually cutting the bonds of sexual attraction, or was it addiction binding him to Carol. Flashing beacons were igniting regretting his words as he realised the possibility of no more stolen nights in the van. Visions of erotic and rousing sexual gymnastics flashed across his mind's eye. Perhaps, perhaps once more, just one last time tonight? Even now in his strongest moment his heart and head was telling him 'end it now,' but his groin was reluctant to let go!

"That's the best news Harry! It's even better than that of your son busy growing in Marion's belly." Frank looked at the sumptuous Carol, "Aye Harry, if she's as good as you say, I can understand why it's such a hard decision, but you shouldn't have tried her in the first place!

Carol was oblivious that she was the kernel of conversation Frank and Harold was chewing over. She was deep in the entangling intensity of heart warming chat and laughing like a schoolgirl at the verbally meandering Scot.

The Scot himself found all of a sudden his tongue had started wagging like the tail of an overjoyed puppy and talking such a load of unrecognisable garbage. Had the same balderdash fallen from another's lips, Callum would have written the poor imbecile off as a crap shooter, bent only on impressing a female and making a very poor job of it! Strangely, this creature, this extremely easy on the eye creature, seemed to be hanging on to his every idiotic syllable. Callum was also aware, he was receiving the odd quizzical glance from his friends but he himself did not feel in the least silly. He was quite happy treading the trappy path into welcoming oblivion. The drink was getting to him, but was it the drink? Being at the receiving end of this girl's eyes, smile and laugh was enough to make any man light-headed.

The night passed noisily although pleasantly. With the clock nearing midnight, interest in the competition grew as the field was whittled down to the last four. Frank's table was well represented as both Ray Buckley and Nobby Clarke were in both legs of the semi-finals. A stocky army sergeant surprisingly beat Ray the hot favourite as the beer and long night impeded Ray's throwing arm. Nobby on the other hand surprised everyone throwing steady darts all night and won his semi-final. Half an hour later he went on to beat the army sergeant who by this stage had lost his touch. Nobby kept his head and threw the winning double to an explosive roar of approval from the inebriated crowd.

The square set Indian showing his gleaming white teeth accepted the £20 cheque, but his smile widened when the main prize, a magnificent half pint gold plated tankard was brought into view.

"Shit and corruption," Callum exclaimed when the grinning Nobby came back to the table with his gleaming trophy, "I should've taken up bloody darts. Hells bells, that's a terrific pot!"

Overjoyed at his win, Nobby bought a bottle of champagne for the table then a second bottle arrived from the White Rose manager to fill and pass the tankard round the winner's friends. When the tankard reached Callum, the Scot held it out and shook his head. For a moment everyone was forgotten as he gazed at the beautifully shaped prize. He took a long drink and reluctantly passed it on. Nobby leaned over and ruffled the red hair, "Never mind, Ginge, our agreement still stands. We'll get you a pot as good as this one day, I promise!"

Callum nodded happily at Nobby before he got swept away in the wave of popularity.

"He's such a lovely bloke but, what did he mean?" asked Carol.

"He's referrin' to a wee promise we made each other a while back. If by some miracle we do not manage to win a pot at the tug-o'-war, we're gonna present one to each other. I'd really like to win one. Ye know pots were the standard prizes for tug-o'war teams at one time but they're either too pricey now or just out of fashion." Callum looked again at the tankard as it passed from hand to hand, "Now that one, that's a real beauty." He dragged his gaze reluctantly away and looked into Carol's blue eyes, "My God," he sighed heavily, "and so are they."

For the second time in as many minutes everything around Callum was forgotten. He could have looked into those deep pools of light blue for the rest of his life, well at least as long as he could keep his own eyes open. Callum had been drinking since going with Josh to the Peninsula Club earlier that evening. He had eaten only crisps and nuts to stimulate his thirst, which was nothing new but Callum had no idea on this special night he was going to meet someone as captivating as Carol Cook.

His eyelids were heavy and he was not sure, but had the slightest suspicion his speech was slurring. He had no wish to appear stupid in the eyes of this girl so with the last of his diminishing perception of his surroundings he went for the safe ground. "Carol, there's an awfu' lot of stories and background an' well, just everythin' that I would really, really love to tell you about myself, that I'm sure you're just dyin' t' hear about," he grinned at the girl. "But tonight, is just no' the night! I've had a wee bit too much. I'm sorry, I really am for I had no idea I was goin' t' meet," he stopped and sighed deeply, "God, the likes o' you!"

"Would you have stayed stone cold sober had you known?" she asked mischievously.

"Don't you go makin' a liar out o' me before you even know me," he answered sleepily.

Carol smiled. It was unusual to meet someone, drunk or sober who was in no hurry to get her on her back as soon as possible. Someone who talked to her, not at her. "If you ever feel like telling me your stories or anything at all, give me a ring at Air Traffic Control. I'll bring a towel if the stories are really sad."

Callum's half closed lids lifted, his blue eyes peering, probing into hers, "Do you mean that?"

"What, about bringing the towel?"

Callum grinned and mumbled, "Aye, Better bring two. Our time's short, lass, I'm being dragged off into fluffy white clouds."

"Of course I meant it, Callum."

"Then I will most certainly be givin' you a call in the very near future, but as for now, I fear I will shortly be restin' in the arms of that Greek queer Moseffus ... Morphus. Shit! Forgive me, I don't do this often." Callum placed his forearms on the beer soaked tabletop and laid his head on them.

A man sitting on their right got up and stood behind Callum. He nodded at Carol then proceeded to lift Callum back into his seat, away from the wet table "Hello Carol, this sleeping beauty and I are mates," he said, "but I've never seen him crash out like this before. It's probably because he's been mixing his drinks with the champagne. I'm Josh Munroe."

"I'm sure he'll appreciate what you've just did for him Josh." Carol leaned over and spoke softly, "Look I doubt if he'll remember our conversation tonight, but he said he'd phone me. Would you remind him, please, ask him to phone me, SAC Cook at Air Traffic Control?"

Josh nodded, "Sure I'll do that," He looked down at Callum, "At the risk of repeating myself, I've known this guy for two years but I've never seen him flake out like this!"

"He told me a few minutes ago I knocked him for six, I didn't believe him at the time." She gave his hand a quick squeeze, "You will remind him to phone me?" Carol smiled and stood up.

Harold was still talking to Frank but she wanted to leave. If she had not met Callum, the night would have been a complete loss. Harold had barely spoken to her, something that may have been a major discussion point between them before tonight, but now it hardly bothered at all. "Harry I'd like to go now," she cut across the pair's never ending conversation.

Harold nodded and held up his hand indicating he would not be long. She waited two long minutes then said, "Harry, I'm going!" As she turned to leave Josh grabbed her arm.

"Hang on, wait just a minute Carol. If you're going back to camp, come with us. It'll be a bit of a squeeze with the rest of the blokes but they won't mind," he grinned.

"Thanks Josh, I don't think I'd have much room to complain either," she laughed, "but unfortunately I have to go back with Harry. We've got some serious talking to do."

"Oh ... I see," Josh nodded, acknowledging her situation.

Carol made her way towards the exit. Before she reached the door, Harold caught up with her. They walked silently to the van and got in. Carol swivelled into the passenger seat, not caring as she did so her short skirt would sidle up her thighs. On other nights, this little action sparked the titillation, igniting their fuses, but tonight she raised her rump out of the seat and shimmied as best she could to pull the skirt back into place.

If Harold noticed he showed no sign picking his way through the crowd exiting from the White Rose. Once clear, he drove fast out of town, frustrated and annoyed at himself. No matter how many recently erected barriers were in his brain, they were now in the process of being scaled. He could not shake off the image of Carol's legs as she prepared for him joining her in the back of the van. Legs he knew every inch of, legs his hands had stroked up the inner smoothness hundreds of times and met the hot warmth at the top.

He could not stop his hand reaching out and slipping slowly between the well known thighs.

Carol sighed deeply, slowly shaking her head from side to side, a wry smile on her face. She had not expected this. She was so sure they were not going to 'perform' tonight. Yes, 'perform' was the perfect word for no one in their right minds could call it 'making love.' Fornicating, screwing, copulating and of course good old fashioned fucking! What was the difference between fucking and making love? Why did men make love to their wives, yet fornicate, screw, copulate and fuck girlfriends, casual acquaintances and prostitutes? Were they not all doing the same thing? Enjoying sex, performing a pleasurable sexual act to be enjoyed with a chosen partner? Yes, 'Perform,' Harold and she had never made love! It had always been 'perform' with her and Harry but she had known that! Why had she fooled herself into thinking there was ever anything between them other than sheer animal lust? Initially yes, she had actually wanted their association, YES, to be based strictly on what pleasure one could glean from each other's body. So in truth, YES it was she that had changed. Harry was still the cold hearted fish he had always been but now with his obvious joy of his wife's pregnancy, Carol felt left out. Why? Initially she never wanted to be part of that scene. Fuck, she was back where she started! "FUCK!" she exclaimed at her own frustration whilst dragging his hand from her crotch.

Harold said nothing at her first ever rejection. He breathed deeply and drove on, his macho mechanism forcing him to head for their usual place overlooking the sea, off the Paphos road. The beautiful girl's body sitting next to him was just a habit, but a very difficult one to break.

Carol watched the Akrotiri signpost flash by. She used to wait for that fork in the road, anticipating the moment. It was like foreplay to her, a turn on. How she had squirmed as they drove up into the mottled hills. Round the bend to pass the musty intangible blue haze that hung over the Happy Valley sports ground. Along the winding road until the breathtaking beauty of the shimmering silver and black moonlit sea hit them like a soft velvet blow. On past the ancient ruins of Courion and the Sanctuary of Apollo.

She drew in her breath as Harold slowed and eased the van through the bushes at the side of the road to the spot only they knew, their secret rendezvous where the van had lightly trembled on its springs on many a night in the past.

Normally Carol would be half undressed as Harold switched off the engine and before he had applied the hand brake she would be in the rear calling out in her urgency for him. But not tonight. "This is no use Harry, please take me back to camp."

Harold merely looked at her.

"You once told me there was nothing you hated more than a cold fish supper. Believe me Harry that's all your going to get here tonight, I don't want to do this!" she said firmly.

"Get in the back," Harold said in a quiet even voice. There was no menace; he could have been saying 'Good morning' to the milkman, but it was the best tone he could have adopted to speak to Carol at that precise moment. Had he been forceful she would have fought with every spark of her being. Had he begged her she would have spat in his face. As it was she returned his stare for a full minute then transferred her look over her right shoulder at the mattress and pillows behind her. With one last glance at Harold she shrugged then squeezed between the seats to roll over on to her back. Mechanically she unhooked and unzipped her skirt, then with practised ease hooked her thumbs into the waistband of her skirt and panties and wriggled free of both. She had a point to prove with Harry and this was the only way she knew of making it.

"This isn't fun anymore," she said as he crawled between her thighs.

"Tell me that when we're finished," he whispered pulling up her T-shirt.

"We are finished!" she said solemnly.

Fifteen minutes later Harold sat sideways on the passenger seat with his feet on the ground. He was looking out at the deep purple sea. He flicked his cigarette butt as far as he could, out over the cliff and watched it swing away in the breeze as it careered on its way to destruction. How often had he done that before after a satisfying union with Carol? Tonight's session had hardly been satisfying. In truth he was disgusted with himself. Carol had lain as if dead and to a man like Harry, it had been an entirely new and sickening experience. Every girl he ever made love to had wanted him as much as he wanted their bodies, and they responded accordingly. Tonight Carol made him feel dirty. After ten minutes of driving himself into her unresponsive body and using every trick he knew, he felt for the first time in his life, his hard erection go soft inside her. He had not come near ejaculation. He crawled away from her like a rejected dog.

"You were right," he called into the rear of the van. There was no response, only the slight movement as Carol dressed. "I'm sorry," he added.

"I was annoyed at first Harry, but the way you and I are made, something like this had to happen for next week we would've been looking for each other. What we had going between us couldn't end with a handshake and a peck on the cheek or even a fight. But this ... this little non-action killed it stone dead. I've known all along you were a right bastard oh and me too. Like you I couldn't have cared less who I was hurting. So I'm just as big a turd as you Harry." Carol's voice floated from the dark rear of the van. He could barely see the blonde halo of hair, yet her blue eyes were luminescent in semi darkness.

"Yes." Harold turned and spoke towards the sea. She was

right of course. He just couldn't let go. It wasn't in his nature to release anything that gave him the intense pleasure that Carol provided and promised with her every mincing step. He was grateful to her in a peculiar way for her action, or more precisely, as she had described it, her non-action in his disgusting little romp tonight. Her non-participation had driven any feelings that might conceivably be incubating in tight dark corners of his brain, were finally flushed down the drain of his system. He felt degraded and dirty.

With that thought, he got up and walked round the front of the van and sat in the driver's seat. "Time we went!" he said starting the engine.

Carol squeezed between the seats and sat down. She said nothing, feeling their mutual embarrassment.

Harold drove to the Akrotiri Main Guardroom gate and as Carol went to get out he leaned over and held her arm, "Hang on, I'll take you to your billet," he said quietly.

Carol slumped back in her seat. The MP on gate duty peered at them, checked their 1250s before raising the red and white painted barrier pole.

Parking the van near the WAAFs block Harold did not switch off the engine, but laid his forehead on the back of his folded hands, resting them on the steering wheel. After a minute he spoke, "I'm sorry Carol, not for what I did, or didn't do tonight. No, what I regret is the way I've treated you. I know we agreed to use each other, to make the best use of our bodies for our own personal satisfaction but I was fooling myself all along. I think I grew to love you in my own crazy way. This may sound conceited, it probably is, but I've never stuck with any female, other than Marion, for as long as I've stayed with you. I wanted you both, you and Marion. I wanted to keep the best of both worlds with little thought of Marion's feelings, or yours," he raised his head and looked through the windscreen. "I've never felt so low about myself as I do at this minute. I apologise Carol, for, ahhh," he paused, "for many things. For stealing two years of your life, for treating you the way I have," he nodded his head then looked at her, "I really thought that somehow I could have the two women I cared about to be part of my life ... selfish bastard! For what it's worth, I never wanted to hurt you Carol, but I did really want you, more than I can say. I hope you can forgive me.

"Carol had never heard Harold speak more than ten words when he was melancholy. She was quite choked at his admission and, most unusual for this outspoken young woman, momentarily lost for words. Leaning over she planted a motherly kiss on his lips, then composing herself said, "I'll never forget you Harry, and now that we are in confessional mood, I think I loved you too. Maybe I was fooling myself before, but tonight I don't know you, I don't know this person sitting here beside me. I think you've just grown up, shed your adolescent skin and ... if things were different, I know I could really love the person you are now. But ..." she patted his knee, "we won't start that ball rolling again, will we, you big bastard." Carol opened the door and got out as the handsome head turned and followed her, the smile she knew and loved breaking across his face. Leaning in through the open door she said, "Don't you go hogging all the fucking blame yourself Harry shitface Ross, I was in there doing my bit, remember? And for what it's worth ..." she echoed his parting words, "tonight was a non event so we'll just ignore that, but prior to tonight I enjoyed ... every ... fucking ... minute of it ... while it lasted. Goodnight and good-bye Harry." Firmly and resolutely she closed the van door.

~~~

Chapter 19

The army base at Dhekelia was holding one of its extremely popular and well attended Fetes. As it was the third Saturday in December one might be excused due to the close proximity of Christmas, the day was being held in honour of that most holy of days, but in fact it was not.

Due to army exercises held in the early days of November that year, the annual festival held on the fifth of that month was postponed. The nearest available Saturday thereafter was a week before Christmas so that year's Fete was renamed, 'Guy Fawkes and Christmas Fete of 1966.'

All roads to the garrison were jam packed as thousands of visitors converged on the already packed grounds and stands. The British army had gone a long way to make the day a success. Home-made 'Olde English' pork and meat pies were on sale as were toffee apples, candy floss and sticky candy rock walking sticks among the many stall items surrounding the sports field.

Brass and pipe bands marched in regal order, gymnasts spring heeled through a complicated routine, and the dog handling team were putting their animals through their paces in the centre of the sports field.

Invitations sent to the RAF stations on the island requested representation of five-a-side soccer teams and tug-of-war teams from their respective bases. The open soccer competition was a long established affair but the tug-of-war event was for a new trophy, the Colonel Cuthbert Invitation Cup. The organisers were hoping to entice the all conquering 103 MU team to make an appearance. Not only for the crowd attraction the men from the MU inevitably created, but to see how the most recent arrivals into the Dhekelia base, the Paratroop Regiment, would fare against the island champions. The 103 Maintenance Unit had of course accepted along with two more Akrotiri teams, the Aircrafts Servicing Flight and the Ground Engineering Flight under their new fire breathing coach, Chief Technician Bernard Kowaleski.

The 'Red Berets' were the most recent side to go under in the relentless march of the RAF men from St. Athens in Wales. Only four months had elapsed since the 'Paras' lost in a titanic final by two ends to one at the Royal Highland gathering in Braemar, Scotland. With such solid form they were confident of ending the long unbeaten MU run.

The final whistle shrilled ending the five-a-side soccer final, which the Paratroop Regiment won fairly easily against an RAF five from Episkopi. Callum McAlpine, sitting with his team in the shade of the surprisingly warm winter sun, received a nod from the umpire. With little fuss he gathered his men and led them out for the first semi-final.

The organisers had seeded the tournament, placing the team from 103 Maintenance Unit in one side of the draw and the Paratroop Regiment in the other. They wanted to ensure if both teams were up to scratch in their early rounds, they would meet in the final. Callum felt his team had got the easier side of the draw for his men had not been tested in the early rounds. Stiff resistance was expected against 33 Field Sqd. Engineers in the semi-final but even this was denied the RAF men. They won easily against a lack lustre army side.

Carol Cook and her friend, another WAAF from Akrotiri, sat near the front of the stand clapping the two teams off the field. "The team from the MU, they make it look so easy, don't they?" said Carol's friend.

Carol nodded abstractly. She was watching the slim figure with the red hair lead his team towards a shaded area where they would await the final. 'Why hasn't he phoned?' she pondered. Carol had heard Scots were renowned for being canny but surely this one was cannier than most! Or was he just not interested! 'Could that be possible?' she wondered fretfully. That would be an unwelcome first!

It was three weeks since the darts night, a long time for a girl like Carol Cook to wait. Maybe he was one of those characters who needed a little Dutch courage to help him talk to girls. Somehow she didn't think so. She watched curiously as Callum talked to Harry Ross as the latter prepared to take the field. Harry's GEF team had been a revelation. She had chatted to him for a few minutes before their first match and found him strangely excited about his team's chances. The new coach appeared to have brainwashed Harry and the rest of his mates into thinking they could actually win the competition. She had to agree that might be a possibility now. There was certainly nothing wrong with the way they had easily won their first three matches with their over excited coach swinging his right arm in a circular clockwise motion whenever his team was taking rope.

The girl she was with left to buy drinks and Carol for a moment was distracted as she looked around the packed stands. Suddenly she felt someone move into her friends seat.

"I'm sorry that seat's taken ...." she turned and was surprised to look into the grinning face of Callum McAlpine.

"It is now," he laughed

"Where did you spring from?"

"You should know, you've been watchin' me all day!" His face was so angular it was almost ugly, but Carol felt her innards flutter. She had always been attracted to good looking men so it was a genuine surprise to find she was fascinated by the looks of this man. But it was more than just fascination, she loved his looks. She gazed into the two most beautiful things; his light blue eyes. "Well if you know that, you must have been watching me!" Carol countered.

"Oh shit, caught out again."

He was looking at her for a spell with a sceptical expression when they started to speak at the same time, "Was I supposed ...?" "Why didn't you ...?" Both stopped and laughed, "Go on," Callum offered.

"No, no, please," she said placing a fist under her chin, grinning at him.

Callum felt strangely inhibited with this girl. He felt again he did not want to make a fool of himself, at least no more than he must have done on the darts night. This girl threw his rarely used overtures and even less chat up lines all out of step. For some reason he imagined because of her good looks, she was unattainable.

"Look, I'm sorry, I know I spoke ... we spoke that night in the White Rose but ..." he looked into her beguiling blue eyes, "I don't remember much. You might find that hard to believe, and quite frankly lookin' at you now, I find it unbelievable ... but it's

396

true! Champagne is like a curtain, a black curtain bein' drawn across my eyes. It's like 'Lights out' minutes after I drink it, especially after brandy an' coupla beers." He could not drag his smitten eyes away. She was a magnet.

Carol didn't care if he had forgotten about her. What mattered was he was apologising now and she would make sure he would never forget her again. "I thought that's what happened. You went down so fast. But your friend, didn't he remind you to ring me ... Josh, the bloke sitting next to you that night?"

"Josh!" he frowned, "You told Josh?"

"Yes, him with the number six on his shirt," she pointed to the criminal sitting with the rest of his team.

"I'll kill him," Callum hissed vehemently. "What did you tell him?" he asked, intrigued.

"To remind you to phone me the next day. If he didn't tell you I'll kill him!" she laughed.

"You'll have to wait your turn," Callum grinned. "Look, ahh, can we start again Carol, wipe the slate clean? There's too many blank patches for me. About the darts night. I try never to make statements or promises I can't keep, at least not when I'm sober, an' I don't know if I made any to you." He nodded his head, "And believe it or not, apart from a few teenage experiments and a certain night in the White Rose bar three weeks ago, I seldom get inebriated. Really, not whitewashed anyway. With that out of the way and without the help ... or hindrance of a third party," he inclined his head towards Josh, "I'd like to apologise for the condition I was in when we first met and the chance to know you better, so can I ..." The blaring of the tannoy system cut harshly across Callum's voice.

"Contestants for the second tug-of-war semi-final please. Would the Paratroop Regiment and the Ground Equipment Flight, Akrotiri take the field."

Carol's friend arrived with the cool drinks and catching Carol's frown, tactfully retreated.

"You were saying?" the blonde girl was not to be side tracked by a simple tug-of-war match.

Callum, distracted by the two teams from which his eventual opponents would emerge said. "Aye, that tannoy's untimely and awfu' bad mannered. I was gonna ask you out, that's all. What do you think?"

"What do I think? Are you asking me for my opinion on whether you should ask me out?" If he was making his move, Carol wanted to be asked properly.

"Oh sorry," he snapped his head back to her, "It's important I watch this, the winners'll be our opponents in the final, but," he turned to face her, "I'm an idiot to put them before you."

'That's better,' she beamed inwardly.

Callum went on, "Look, ah, I'd really," he sighed, "like to take you out sometime ... soon"

"That's nice, and have you any idea exactly how soon you would like to take me out?"

"The sooner the better," his face creased into a grin, "what about tonight, after this lot?" Callum nodded towards the field where the teams were lining up.

"And where would you take me Callum, after this lot?" she asked playfully.

"I don't know, someplace nice I suppose. I've no' had time to give the venue any thought. Now can we just watch this first, we'll come back to 'where' later?" Everything had its place for Callum and the match was imminent.

Typically the Parachute Regiment looked menacing dressed all in red. Their incongruous black polished boots enhanced their outfit. At the other end Bernard glowered at his men who in their light blue shirts and dark blue shorts did not bear the same visual impact. However visible impact was the last thing on the mind of the slightly limping coach as he moved along the line issuing guttural instructions.

The army umpire got the match started quickly, both teams adopting the square pulling mode. The Paratroopers were similar to the MU in style, comfortable and relaxed, with the GEF team going about their business with an air of quiet confidence. Callum stared intently at this team which the new coach had shaped in only three weeks. They were rocking and swaying with the considerable pressure applied by the soldiers but the men in light blue looked incredibly insouciant. The minutes passed slowly, the pressure of the supremely fit Paras began to tell and Callum saw the build up of pain on the faces of Harry Ross and the others. After four long hard minutes they lost six feet, fighting grimly as the coach growled his commands. His gyrating arm swinging in circles as they lost ground, but could do nothing as the marker crept over the line.

The Paratrooper's coach looked disdainfully down the rope at his opposite number loudly berating his men. He was unashamedly and blatantly informing his team they had not given their all, they were not trying. The man was grossly over reacting to losing the first end.

For his part Callum was surprised the army lads had taken so long to win the end. He checked his stopwatch but it was functioning perfectly; five minutes and nine seconds. Unconsciously he scratched his chin. Either the soldiers were not the team they were cracked up to be, or this new Chief Tech. had, as Harry Ross promised, improved the GEF team beyond all measure.

Carol whispered in his ear, "Callum, are you going to win today?"

Her words broke his train of thoughts, "Och aye, you can put money on that."

She could see he was engrossed so Carol said no more as the teams changed ends. Her shorts felt they were strangling her so she stood up to ease them down. For a distracting moment Callum's eyes flicked from the field to the tanned legs and well rounded bottom. She smiled secretly as she gave a final tug before sitting again. "What makes you so sure?" she whispered.

"I just know," he answered forcing his concentration on the second end that had started. He had missed the drop due to his lecherous glance at this very distracting female's legs. They were quiet for a minute when he repeated, "You can put money on it!"

"Do you see a bookmaker anywhere?" she taunted. "Just as well for I don't think you will win! If I was to have a bet, I would bet on Harry's team!" She stuck her tongue out at him, "So there!" she added tauntingly.

"GEF," Callum scoffed, "They've got a battle on their hands here. They're down an end already." Just as Callum spoke the team in red did not look so comfortable.

"I think Harry's going to win," Carol sang in his ear.

The side view Carol had of the face staring onto the field, swung slowly round to gaze into hers. She smiled and fluttered her eyelids, "Yes?"

"You fancy GEF?"

"Well yes, but ... not all at once," her eyelids were still fluttering.

Callum looked at the pretty face. He liked her frank attitude, often directing jokes at herself, something pretty girls normally detested. "You know what I mean," he went on at Carol's attempt at a coy nod. He could not ignore the effect this girl was conjuring up inside him, as unashamedly he noted every detail of the smirking face. Her laughing clear blue eyes, the pert turned up nose, the peach tinted skin. He had no idea how long he lingered on her full lips but the shrill whistle snapped both their heads back to the field.

Callum frowned. GEF had taken the second five minute end. The frown grew deeper, "I never imagined they could take an end off the Paras." His mutterings were not low enough for Carol not to hear, "Told you," she sang in his ear.

Determined not to miss a second of the third end, he said, "Listen Carol I have a proposition to make ...."

"Oh goody gumdrops!" she clapped her hands.

Her buffoonery was delicious but distracting, "If we win, there may be some after match piss up which I'm obliged to attend. I may not get back in time to take you out tonight so are we on for tomorrow night?"

His words brought a frown, "And if GEF win?"

"Even better," he answered solemnly. "In the highly unlikely event GEF or the Paras beat us, I will allow you to take me out tonight. How does that sound?"

They both laughed as Carol said, "I lose both ways. You're the last of the big time gamblers."

He looked serious for a moment before saying, "This is one bet I do not intend to lose!"

"Take the strain," the words arrested Callum's meandering thoughts.

The drop was equal, both teams rocking, settling into footholds. Callum watched both teams carefully, swinging from one to the other. With each glance at the GEF team he grew more impressed until eventually he stopped looking at the soldiers, concentrating on the RAF side. Their coach was like a man demented! He was moving up the rope talking to each man, talking through bared teeth and glowering black eyes that could barely be seen under a straight line of black eyebrows. Callum was fascinated, was he threatening his men? It certainly appeared so, but whatever he was doing it was working, and working well. The men in light blue were taking rope, ever so deliberately slowly, devouring each morsel of sweetly won ground.

"They've taken them halfway," Callum mumbled. Four minutes, this was turning into one hell of a match. Nearly fifteen minutes of pulling over the three ends and still at it!

With an inward sigh of relief, Callum realised no matter who won this match, his own team would win the competition. The two teams out on the field were killing themselves. It mattered little which eight faced the MU in the final, they could never be expected to beat his relatively fresh eight that had never been put to the test all afternoon. Neither team out there had any cohesion left, they were pulling by instinct; heads down, eyes closed, everything that was happening was happening through their hands, their movements mechanical. "How did he manage to get them so fit in only three weeks?" Callum wondered staring at the arm swinging coach. He may have been the butt of many jokes but somehow he had inspired this team to reach phenomenal physical heights.

The whistle blew and sixteen men collapsed into heaps. The victorious GEF coach clenched his fists and shook them at the paratroopers. This outrageous action was met with angry glares from the soldiers and a contemptuous down the nose stare from the coach.

"That wasn't very nice," said a small voice at Callum's side. He turned to see the concerned face of Carol watching Kowaleski.

"No it certainly was not," he agreed. Momentarily Carol had been forgotten. Following her gaze he was amazed to see the GEF coach was leading his team away from the paratroopers. He was ignoring the courteous after match practice of walking his team along the rope to shake hands. The snubbed coach watched with knitted eyebrows the departing RAF team with thinly disguised disgust.

Before Callum realised what he was doing, he stood up. "Look Carol I have to go now but I'll see you after we beat that lot." Leaving a frowning Carol he jumped the low rope barrier and ran onto the field where he approached the Paratroop Regiment coach.

"Magnificent. Such a pity there has to be a loser after such a contest. Corporal McAlpine, 103 MU coach," he held out a hand.

He was met at first with a penetrating stare then the man blinked and shook the extended hand, "I appreciate what you are doing Corporal McAlpine but that man should not be allowed to grace the domain of a sports environment. I have never seen anything so diabolical or ungentlemanly to disgrace the good name of sport. Such downright bad manners, who is he?"

"Let me apologise on behalf of the Royal Air Force. I agree his behaviour is grossly out of order. Sorry I don't know the man, he's new, arrived on the island about a month ago."

"I see, he may be new, but he cannot be unaware of the finer points of gentlemanly conduct. I swear when you arrived I was on the point of going after him to inform him precisely what I thought. However ... forgive me Corporal, the man's ignorance is infectious. Lieutenant McAllister, pleased to meet you, and thank you for your thoughtful intervention." The army officer dragged his eyes back to Callum, "That man may be uninformed in the finer points of conduct but he has a fine team there, rather surprised us."

"Me too sir, amazin' what he's done with those lads in only three weeks."

Again the stare from the officer, "You mean ... three weeks!" The words were said in a tone of hostile shock, "I don't ... no, no, I can't believe that."

"It's true. A little over three weeks ago he gathered and hand-picked a team and started trainin' them virtually from the first day he arrived for work. There's a few new faces in the team we beat in June but he's worked wonders wi' them."

The officer looked again at the group of light blue shirts resting under the trees, mingling with the blue and white hooped men from the Maintenance Unit. The coach was nowhere to be seen.

"Corporal, I find that ... incredible, and hate to say this but, rather commendable too."

"You lost to St. Athens in August sir, that's not the same eight you've got here today, is it?"

"More or less, two of my lads could not make it, my anchor man and No.3, but in all honesty I did not expect to lose today. As a matter of fact I thought we would win the competition. I was told that your lot might provide a rather stiff hurdle, yet here we are, beaten by beginners. Must be losing my touch."

"They're not exactly beginners sir but definitely transformed."

"Yes, if what you say is true. You must do what I failed to achieve Corporal. Rub that man's nose in the dirt, teach him a lesson. He cannot be allowed to go on like that."

"I have every confidence of doin' that sir, you've drawn their sting. We will win, as I've said already, you can put money on it!"

Callum was crossing toward his group when he saw Chief Tech. Kowaleski making his way towards the two teams gathered together under the trees. "What do you think this is a bloody tea party!" he barked, "if you must fraternize with the opposition leave it until after we've won. You're not here to amuse yourselves, may I remind you, you are here to WIN! Come away Akrotiri GEF, NOW, all of you, away from these bloody MU people."

Frowns and muttered oaths greeted the words but Harold and his team mates slowly rose. They followed their coach as he stormed off to a spot void of competitors.

Callum shook his head at this bizarre situation where the man seemed hell bent on making himself highly unpopular. He looked for Carol and found her eyes were watching him. With a nod and a wink towards his team, she returned the nod. Settling back in her seat, Carol found for the first time in her life she was tingling in anticipation over of all things, a tug-of-war final.

Forty-five minutes later a steward informed Callum they would be called in fifteen minutes to take the field. He gathered his team in a circle round him. "There's no need to tell you the team we have to beat have gone a long way towards makin' it easy for us. The job still has to be done of course, they're no' gonna lie back and give it to us. Just try to imagine how you lot would feel if, less than an hour ago you'd just come off after three five minute ends! You'd all be knackered, right! And they are not supermen. They might have recovered a wee bit after this break so treat them with respect for two minutes with heavy pressure. Take rope if it comes don't worry if it doesn't. After two minutes pressure listen to me. Now relax completely, we're on in ten minutes." The thought crossed Callum's mind what the position might have been had the positions been reversed, if the MU had met the Paratroopers in the semi-final?

The tannoy blared and the finalists summoned. The next few minutes were a blur of colour, of organising calls, heeding of commands and the excitement of preparation. It all came to an abrupt end when the teams dropped on the rope and suddenly locked in solid confrontation.

All movement and speech ceased as the men at each end of the rope, solid as a bar of steel, sought to feel each other out. Each coach moving along his team looking for flaws to correct. Neither found any.

Callum started his stopwatch and waited patiently as two minutes crawled by, then, "Wind it on lads, give them a warnin' let them respond. I want to see what they've got."

There was little response and soon the GEF team were being pulled deeper into the squat position. They had no answer to the applied pressure from the untapped power of the MU and forced to jump forward to gain new positions. This was repeated as the MU turned the screw.

Chief Tech. Bernard Kowaleski was reduced to screaming and threatening again but no amount of threats could inject energy and fresh resolution into exhausted muscles. The powerful and experienced team from the MU knew they had the advantage and were not about to relinquish it. The whistle blew.

After much haranguing from the GEF coach at his dispirited men, the umpire finally got the second end started. The end was only a minute old when it became obvious Callum's words were well founded. The men who battled grimly against the Paratroop Regiment had drawn every ounce of energy from the bottom of their reservoirs. They had nothing left and knew it. Nevertheless they gave everything in futile resistance. This was demonstrated by exhibiting their torture with facial expressions wrapped in agony. Only one person believed he could still win; Bernard Kowaleski was red faced and hoarse as he moved rapidly from one man to the next inducing, goading, encouraging, demanding extra effort. Every team member was breaking his heart for this dominant man, fighting the inexorable power that was drawing them, pulling them ever nearer the line. The swinging arm of Bernard was gyrating in vicious circles trying to inject his own energy into the straining men.

Callum glanced along the rope and saw only three feet remained. Then he stole a glance at the opposing coach. The man was like a demented dervish, hopping and dancing along the line of men, his right arm scything in circles. He could not touch the rope but was mentally forcing his physically beaten team into a last dying effort. Callum for a moment felt a pang of admiration at the way this coach was driving himself and his men, gesticulating and shouting though his language was unusual for a sporting event.

"You lazy bastards," he bent over and roared into the faces of the Nos.3 and 4 men, glaring wildly, his face puce, arms straight out behind him. Suddenly his right arm, in what looked like the start of another arching swing, pivoted into what turned out to be a perfect uppercut punch which landed square on the jaw of Harold Ross.

Like a line of falling dominoes the MU team toppled backwards hauling slack rope as the resistant pressure was suddenly released. The umpire blew only dimly aware an incident had taken place with the team on his right, his eyes firmly locked on the central markers.

Strangely it seemed no one saw the punch! There was no doubt in Callum's mind the coach struck someone in the middle of the team corroborated by Harry Ross falling away from the rope. Therefore it was the big No.4 man who was on the receiving end to the arching blow but Callum had not actually seen the punch. The heads of the three men in front of Harry obstructed his view. The side judge saw something, possibly a blow had been struck but he was uncertain.

The air of uncertainty quelled the immediate celebrations as the men of the MU looked at the opposition who were lying in untidy heaps. Callum muttered to Josh, "That bastard's crazy ye know, he lashed out at someone. It looks like Harry Ross was the one who caught it."

The side judge was speaking to the umpire as Akrotiri GEF struggled to their feet. The umpire nodded then the two judges approached the prone figure lying on the ground. Kneeling down the umpire turned a groggy Harold Ross over. "This man has been struck!" the official called seeing the bloody split on the stricken man's chin "What happened here?" he demanded glaring at the curiously detached coach.

Nothing brought Bernard Kowaleski back to his senses quicker than officialdom. As his innards burned after losing to the despised 103 MU alarm bells were ringing in his befuddled brain. Through the haze clouding his vision he saw Ross semi conscious on the ground. A blonde girl and young man with fair hair had arrived from somewhere were attending to him.

"What happened here?" It was the umpire, the voice of officialdom again and with his words the haze melted. "I think I am responsible for that." There was no other path available. He adopted a downcast attitude. "I must apologise for my over robust methods, It was an accident, I wanted so badly to win I sometimes get carried away with my own enthusiasm."

"You most certainly do. I am Captain Wood, may I have your name and rank please!"

"Of course sir, I am Chief Technician Kowaleski, Royal Air Force, I am truly ..."

"You could be in a serious situation here, Chief, my side judge seem to think you lashed out at this man," the officer nodded curtly at the stirring Harold Ross. The couple attending him were wiping the stricken man's face with a sponge produced from a bag with the hated words ' 103 Maintenance Unit' emblazoned along the side. The same words were on the back of the track suit worn by the man.

"There's no doubt that is how my action must have appeared but I assure you! I did not and could never strike anyone intentionally. What happened, happened in the heat of the moment." Bernard could barely remember the last seconds of the end, and certainly could not recall striking Ross, something he was not likely to attempt in front of hundreds of people. Help for Bernard arrived from a most unexpected source.

"Sir, I saw the whole incident," volunteered the man attending Ross, who was now sitting up moving his head and jaw around. "I was watching this team. The coach was trying all through the final end to stop his team from losing. He simply got too close, that's all. With that unfortunate swinging arm it was no surprise to me he could possibly strike someone. Ross here happened to be the luckless recipient. It was an accident sir, there's no doubt about that!"

"I see," said the umpire, "and who, may I ask, are you?"

"SAC Cantwell sir, Utility man for 103 Maintenance Unit."

"Utility man, my God, whatever will they think of next?" Captain Wood squatted down and spoke to the airman on the receiving end of the full blooded blow. Thankfully he seemed to have fully recovered, "And what about you young man, did you see anything?"

"No, I saw nothing,!" Harold mumbled rubbing his forehead.

"Can you walk or shall I send for a stretcher?"

"I think I can walk," Harold answered rising unsteadily whilst also being assisted to his feet.

"Cantwell, there is a marquee specifically for this purpose behind the stand facing us. Would you and the young lady," he indicated Carol, "take him there?" Without waiting for an answer the officer turned to Bernard, "Chief, a word if you please." He marched off about a dozen paces then stopped, impatient for Bernard to join him.

Bernard, his patience wearing thin was struggling to keep up the pretence of his downcast appearance. Keeping the pounding blood behind his eyes in check with a tight squeeze of his lids, he joined the army captain.

"I am not entirely satisfied with the explanations I have heard. I intend to send a report to your commanding officer at Akrotiri. Is there anything you would like to add?"

The officer was pushing his head forward belligerently and Bernard's urge to butt his own forehead into the rigid face was overwhelming. "Sir," Bernard's voice was shaking with anger but fortunately mistaken for wretchedness, "this contest meant a lot, a heck of a lot, to my team and myself. We have only been training solidly together for three weeks and desperately wanted to beat the Maintenance Unit, we'd set our hearts on it. Maybe I ruined it for my lads, I'll never know but yes I got carried away, over enthusiastic, and this swinging arm, it's something I started to do at training. Makes me feel part of the team, like I'm actually involved you know?" Bernard lowered his head meekly in what he hoped resembled an act of contrition.

The captain looked closely at the Chief Technician, uncertain of the best course of action. This was certainly a different man from the roaring, prancing personage urging his team on a few minutes ago. He made up his mind. "All right, I do not wish to order you Chief, but I strongly recommend you to present yourself to your Medical Officer. I want you to request a full medical examination. Do you understand, a FULL medical examination. It will be for your own good. Will you do that?"

"On my word sir, I will!" Bernard grated.

"I would give up coaching until the MO has cleared you, certainly stop that swinging arm action of yours, you could really hurt someone you know, least of all yourself."

"You're probably right sir, this afternoon's incident has given me a lot to think about."

"I hope so. Meantime I will withhold my report but I have your name," he wagged a little booklet. "Nothing personal you understand, but I sincerely hope I never hear your name again!"

Bernard joined his men in the changing tent and drew Harold Ross aside, "I care nothing about striking you or your feelings towards me but I want you to know what happened was unintentional."

"Don't worry ab-" Harold started to speak but Bernard Kowaleski was not waiting for any response. The Chief had turned away as he finished speaking. Harold looked around the others and shook his head, "That is one of the queerest bastards I've ever come across!"

Alf Austen who was behind Harold on the rope spoke out for the first time on the incident,

"Harry, I hope that army captain reports him."

"Why is that Alf?"

"Because although we were right in the middle of the action I saw him take careful aim and land that haymaker on your chin. He was so fucking wound up at us losing he took it out on the poor mug nearest him ... you. Honestly Harry, his eyes were glowing, like burning coals, the fucker's a lunatic!"

Harold screwed his eyes until they were almost closed, "Wha ... You saw him deliberately hit me. Why the fuck did you not tell the army captain, he asked if anyone saw what happened?"

"Listen Harry, he might be crazy but I'm not. What do you think my life would be like if I put up my hand and said, 'Me sir, I saw that nutter belt poor Harry on the jaw,' eh? You got an uppercut for trying to please him breaking your balls on the rope, what do you think he would give me for shopping him? No thanks Harry, I never saw a fucking thing!"

Later that evening a function was given by the army in a large hall. Trophies were presented to winners and runners-up, to soccer and tug-of-war teams, to dog handlers and bands. Victories were toasted and losers drowned their sorrows. There were no social losers that evening. All competitors for their contribution in helping to stage an extremely successful day could eat and drink their fill at the army's expense.

Bernard stood at the bar drinking alone. In a room crowded with dozens of people it was strange how a man could stand apart, generally unnoticed by the milling boisterous swell of the human herd. One man in that room of a hundred and fifty people did notice Bernard; one man watched his perfect isolation that struck a chord deep inside him. Julian Cantwell felt sorry for the figure at the bar, strangely isolated although surrounded by happy laughing faces. Bernard might have been a ghost, no one saw or spoke or ordered a drink for him. The fair haired young man found himself wondering why he had lied. That afternoon suddenly and spontaneously he said the coach had accidentally struck Harold Ross. Julian bit his lip as he recalled the black ferocious glare of the GEF coach. How he sighted his stare on the oblivious face of his No.4 man, swung like a pendulum his massive fist and the big frame of Ross had shot off the rope and lay still. Such vicious power! How he wanted to approach, speak to the lonely figure.

At eleven o'clock buses arrived to transport the merrymakers back to their various camps.

Last drinks were forced down, new friends hastily exchanged addresses and long visits to the toilets taking place.

Callum had dragged Carol into the prize giving ceremony. She was not keen on these normally long drawn out boring events but as she had lost her friend chatting with an army chap, she agreed with her victorious coach's request to accompany him. There had been plenty to eat and drink but had it not been the growing warmth between herself and Callum, the night would have been, at best, boring! Together they boarded the Akrotiri bus and settled in the back corner seat. It was going to be a rowdy run back to Akrotiri.

Twenty minutes into the journey, the boisterous singing was interrupted with shouts of 'Stop the bus,' from the weak bladder brigade. Not only did it stop the bus, it also brought an end to Carol getting to know Callum. He was a very unusual man this Scotsman. She was in the process of discovering another facet to his nature that appealed to her; he did not try to paw or lower her dignity by making use of her quite blatant sexuality. Yet paradoxically, Carol being the girl she was, wanted his approaches and feel his hands caress her. She was sitting on his knee, their heads buried in each other's necks with his arms wrapped around her when the call came for those who needed to go, to go now. The driver would not stop again.

Callum unravelled himself from the soft warmth of blonde hair,

"Think I better go."

"Don't pee on the side of the bus," she hissed back, "if you try you'll pee all over the roof!" she giggled squirming her bottom into his groin.

"Ouch, careful you'll damage some very special equipment," he said standing up and sliding her on to her own seat, "I'll no' be long," he whispered.

He followed Josh and the others as they wandered into the nearby bushes where a line of men could dimly be seen directing steaming jets into the dark depths.

"Dis must be dah place," Ray Buckley commented as he, Callum and others joined the end of the line. Soon their arcs of water were hissing into the bushes, "It's like I always said," Callum added his comment to the general host of remarks, "drink a pint, piss a gall - what the fuck? " Callum nearly fell as he stepped away from what he knew was warm urine splashing on the back of his trouser legs. "Ya blind bastard, can ye no' see us standin' here. Ye've pissed all over me ya fuckin' idiot."

"Sorry, oh sorry mate, I'm so drunk I don't know where I am," said the very steady voice of an unconvincing drunk. The head lifted and the man looked into Callum's eyes.

"It's you ya twisted bastard, I might have fuckin' known!" Callum's temper was broadening his accent again. He was a pubic hair away from driving his knee into the exposed genitals of Bernard Kowaleski. Josh saw the situation and pushed the grinning Chief heavily to one side. "He's not worth it Callum, come away now."

The Scot growling with frustrated temper followed Josh with Frank and Ray behind him. All the while he gingerly tried to keep his wet trouser legs away from his skin. Snickering laughter followed them as they neared the bus and the group, each of them knowing they shouldn't but couldn't resist the urge, to turn round.

Kowaleski was holding his left hand up at Ray, the last man in the line, wagging a V-sign in his face, his right hand was engaged in trying to masturbate a flaccid penis.

"You sick bastard," Ray said then coughed phlegm from the back of his throat and spat it at the offending organ. To his chagrin the missile passed harmlessly between the man's legs.
Callum went to the back of the bus explaining loudly that he was not responsible for 'peeing his trousers, that honour belonged to the misguided Chief Tech. Kowaleski who could neither see straight nor pee straight.' The explanation brought laughs and comments but the hilarity and playful banter died as Bernard clambered aboard.

Julian handed over a track suit as Callum emptied his pockets then quite unashamedly dropped the offending trousers. Kicking them under a seat he declared loudly, "I'll never wear those trousers again, they've been pissed on by a very sick and dirty dog, they stink like him too, like a rotten sewer." The comment brought only a thin ripple of uncertain laughter.

The rest of the journey passed in subdued silence, the joviality dampened by the incident.

A collective mental sigh of relief could almost be audibly heard as the bus pulled into the Akrotiri car park outside the main gate.

Those that had driven to camp to catch the RAF transport made for their cars. The next stop for the bus driver was the MT section so those who lived near the MT section stayed on the bus, the rest got out at the car park.

The bus pulled away and within minutes only a handful of passengers and one car remained..

The car, a Hillman Minx, belonged to Chief Tech. Kowaleski. He was waiting for his only passenger, apparently taking no interest in the conversation of three people standing a fair distance from him. But the night was quiet and sounds carried clearly.

"I meant to ask you earlier Harry, how is Marion?" Carol asked.

"Great, she's actually blooming ... look I'd love to chat but you know who's waiting for me."

"You should've bummed a lift back with Ray or Frank, I'd hate to be dependent on that shithouse." Callum said, not in a quiet voice.

"He's my coach and offered to pick me up, so ...." Harold shrugged.

"Still got your van?" Carol laughed, "That's seen a few ... oh sorry Cal. But you don't mind do you ma wee Scottish flower?" Her attempt at the Scottish accent was atrocious.

If Callum lived on the moon there was a slight chance he may not have heard of Carol's fling with Harry. He knew of course and was adult enough to accept their meetings were not entirely innocent, "Course I mind, so I might just kick your bonny wee bum all the way back to your billet, ya wanton wench!" Callum threatened.

"When you're finished with that tart, maybe you can kick her arse over here, I could make good use of it!" The laconic voice floated across the car park space from where Bernard sat on the bonnet of his car .

"Hey you." Carol turned to the detestable grinning man.

"Leave it Carol, I don't want you takin' advantage of a drunken shit," Callum took her arm.

"Run away you spineless skinny little twat! I want you to know Corporal McAlpine, we are going to beat you. We are going to beat you corporal!" The words were said in a high pitched aggravating tone.

"Listen pal, you're a disgrace to the Royal Air Force, a disgrace to sport in general and a disgrace to yourself which to an arsehole like you is neither here nor there. As for beating us, if today's match was any indication of your abilities then it's time you stopped trainin' wi' the girl guides, that final was embarrassing to a team such as 103 MU."

"You did not meet opposition like the Paratroopers," Bernard shouted, stung by the insult.

"That would've been even more embarrassing. I spoke to their coach after your match. He said he was surprised it took you so long. Told me he'd grabbed eight men from the cookhouse, eight fat cooks to make up a team. Aye an' how you battled to beat eight fat cooks!"

"Lying bastard McAlpine, that was their best team, I got that straight from a squaddie." Bernard was still trying to shout but his voice was beginning to crack.

"Straight?" Callum shot back, "straight?" he sang the word theatrically. "You wouldn't know the meanin' o' the word. You'd corrupt a laser beam up your arse!"

Carol could not suppress a giggle, which did not help Bernard's mood. "Very clever," he said, "oh very clever, but I have something straight to tell you, straight from the horse's mouth."

"Here we fuckin' go," Callum was warming up in this verbal battle, cut in. "You're now about to tell us what comes out of your mouth should be used to grow tomatoes, is that right?" He prodded, niggling now and at his prickly best, "Come away then, let's have it straight from the horse's arse mouth? Aye, an' I've heard horse's wet farts produce better noises than the gaggin' splurges you're producin'." Callum barely paused before he went on, "An' while we're on the subject of bein' straight, I've seen a wee five year old pee straighter than you did tonight. Mind you, a five year old laddie is a lot better endowed that the wee wart you have between your legs. Go on Chiefy, give us an exhibition, show us how straight ye can pee!"

Callum's tirade halted suddenly. For a second Bernard felt a series of blows had stopped pounding his face and ears. He blinked rapidly, feeling his sight was dimming, his lungs were starved of air. He had stopped or somehow forgotten to breathe when the part of his body responsible switched back on, forcing him to hurriedly suck in air. As his vision partially cleared the red swirling mist enveloped the central tormentor who was still spitting obscenities at him. Bernard felt energy surge through him, he had to catch this throbbing antagonist who was poking, prodding, stinging him with poisonous words.

"You better stop Callum. Look at his eyes," Harold cried but with his intervention, Bernard took his chance, "You are a woman McAlpine, you fight with your mouth, like a whore!"

"Aye, an' you'll have first hand experience in that department."

Callum taunted, "and I take it, from your remark Chief Tech. Polack, you'd like to exchange blows with my person?"

The black eyes of the older man were glittering with evil fire, "I want to fuck you up, I want to fuck you up so bad you haggis heathen," came the growled answer.

"Well well, he wants to fuck me up," Callum started to hop and jerk, shadow boxing, moving quickly. "Can you believe that, a Chief Tech wants to fuck up a corporal." Callum stepped up his jabbing at shadows.

Bernard could barely contain himself, he wanted to grab the prancing figure, tear it to pieces,

"There's no rank here," he roared, making a move towards Callum.

"Everybody hear that?" Callum danced away. "From the mouth of the beast itself, 'there's no rank here.'"

Harold stepped between the pair, it had gone far enough, "Cool it Callum. Bernie, let it be, there's nothing to be gained from this. You're both pissed, you'll regret it tomorrow." He stood between the pair with arms straight out, fending them off.

"He's no' drunk Harry, an' neither am I. He's been spoilin' for this since we thumped him this afternoon, he clobbered you Harry, he's as mad as a fuckin ..."

"CALLUM!" Carol's voice shrilled out a warning but it came a fraction late. Callum's gaze had for a split second switched to Harold. It was the gap Bernard was waiting for. He quickly closed the short distance swinging a clubbing roundhouse fist on to the side of Callum's face. Due to Carol's warning, it was only at the last fraction of a second the Scot started to pull away in reactionary shock. Not much but it was enough to prevent him from being knocked unconscious. The blow carried every ounce of Bernard's considerable strength.

Callum staggered away hovering on the brink of a yawning abyss, dimly aware he must at all costs stay on his feet. The scuffles and fights that were part of his upbringing in the rougher parts of Edinburgh's slum areas saved him from further telling blows as Bernard stepped in for the kill. To gain seconds of recovery time and with the impulse of sheer preservation, Callum's hands folded around the back of his head. His elbows closed across his face as the first blows started to rain on the protective cage of limbs. He needed precious time to shake free of the cloying fog and weightlessness caused by the first unguarded blow. Struggling to get his bearings he could not pin down where his adversary was.

Amazingly it was Bernard who gave his reeling victim the respite he so badly needed.

"Not so full of talk now you cocky bastard," Bernard was puffed, punching into the cowered rib cage and protected head of the bent over man. The out of condition Chief Tech. had thrown around twenty blows and paused momentarily. He knew most of his punches were landing on the protective arms surrounding the head he so ardently wanted to smash his bleeding fists into. But there were many ways of opening an oyster.

Bernard stood back to aim a kick at the groin of his grovelling sitting target. "Where's all the fancy shit slinging now corporal, cat got your tongue?" A final taunt before the delicious gut crushing kick.

Callum blinking rapidly trying hard to focus when he saw the legs of the Chief Tech. not two feet away. He knew instinctively the man was angling to land a kick. Even as Bernard drew back his foot, Callum's cat like reflexes launched him forward and swung his right fist hard to land in the area of the abdomen just under the centre of the rib cage. The air whooshed out of Bernard's lungs, and now he doubled over, tottering backwards. Callum followed, he had opened up like a flower and throwing dozens of blows. Though his punches carried less power, they were telling blows, peppering vulnerable areas.

Bernard bewildered by the reversal was driven back. The anger and ire within him with no escape vent was building up. With his impotency to end the continued and stinging persistent assault, he was reaching the limits of his pressure valve. The second he uncovered his eyes, vicious punches rained in on them. He covered his eyes and thumping clouts landed on his body. He tried charging forward trying to grab the elusive bludgeoning phantom but all he caught was shadows and even more blows.

Mercifully after some minutes of perpetual consistent thumping Bernard began to lose consciousness. The smacking thuds seemed now to be losing their sting if not their persistency. Somewhere in the deepest caverns of his brain he was forcing himself to stay conscious. He could not lose again to the MU, not again! But he was in a hornet's nest, being stung met at every turn. There was no way of stopping them. The pressure valve went into the red mist and blew! Ignoring the blows Bernard stood up with his arms stiff at his sides, "NOOooooo!" he screamed at the heavens.

Callum jumped back, somewhat surprised at the outburst from what was now little more than a large punching bag. But he too had had enough of his expert cat and mouse tactics. At that precise moment, Callum had no feelings for this man. The numbness tended to cloud positive thinking. He had simply switched from defensive mode into attack when the opportunity presented itself with a great deal of success. Now it was time to finish the attacker off.

He stepped forward intending to place a weighty punch on the unguarded jaw. Whether it was Carol who broke through his self protecting shell with a screamed "NO," or the helplessness of his victim. It mattered little. Something froze Callum from applying the coup de grace.

Bernard stood head down, like a dejected oxen awaiting the executioner's slicing swing. Slowly when he realised the blows had stopped, his battered eyes opened slowly and sought his tormentor. "I ... am ... going ... to ... beat ... you." The words hissed through broken lips, the corners of his mouth tried to lift in erratic jerks as they battled to rise in a grotesque smile. "I ... am ... going ... to ... beat ... you ... corporal."

"You're crazy Chief. I feel nothin' in havin' beaten you twice on the same day, you're as nutty as a fruitcake an' shouldn't be in the Air Force." Callum stepped closer and peered deep into eyes that were searing into his. He saw, there was no doubt about it, dozens of tiny red neon worms dancing, zigzagging in the dark depths of those blazing orbs. Shaking his head, Callum stepped back, "You'd better get him home Harry, I swear to God, I really think he's demented." Turning to Carol he said with a worried frown, "Come away lass, I'm sorry. I wish I'd never got involved here."

The couple walked away and Harold took Bernard's arm, "Give me your keys Chief," he said leading him off towards the Hillman. There was no answer as Bernard sat on the boot, then, "Leave me a minute," the smitten man moaned. Harold took out a pack of cigarettes and glad of the break, went for a short walk.

Ten minutes later as Harold did his favourite butt flicking trick, he heard the car engine cranking noisily, trying but failing to start. Returning to the car he asked, "Having problems?"

"It does this," Bernard grunted. He was sitting behind the wheel, "A couple of teeth missing from ring gear. A starting handle ... in the boot, give it a crank, it'll start."

"Are you sure you can drive Chief?"

"I can drive my own car Ross. The skinny prick hits like a woman. Don't worry, I'd let you drive if I was not capable. Get the handle."

Harry opened the boot and found the long sturdy handle lying loose. Inserting it through the aperture provided for the tool he engaged the lugs. "Are you switched on?" he asked.

A tired nod from Bernard. Harold gave the handle a hefty clockwise crank. It took a second crank before the engine kicked into life. Pleased with the reassuring purr Harold was on his way to return the handle when Bernard said, "Gimme it here, I'll stash it under my seat. Could be using it a lot 'til I get that ring gear sorted."

They drove back to Limassol in silence. Not far from Harold's home Bernard suddenly asked,

"Does the wife drive?"

"What ... my wife?" the question caught Harold by surprise, "No. No, she doesn't."

"My bitch doesn't either but she wanted something to get her back and forward to the Naafi shop here in town, and other shops. Day after I bought this heap of shit she wanted a scooter. One of those eyetie jobs. I hope she breaks her fucking neck on it, and that brat of hers too!"

For a moment Harold thought Kowaleski had begun to sound fairly rational; happy at having bought something for his wife, then he'd resorted back to normal.

"That's my house Chief," Harold called, still wondering at the complexity of this man. The car stopped and Harold got out. "Thanks Chief." Momentarily lost for words he stood on the narrow pavement and noticed the nearside red lamp. "Your rear light on this side's very dim, probably got the wrong bulb in there Chief. I'll see if I can find you one in the section stores."

"You'll do no such thing! I buy my own spares Ross. I don't steal from Her Majesty's stores and don't let me catch you or

417

your mates at it either!" Bernard drove off scattering small stones and dust in his wake.

Harold watched the car with one bright rear light and the other trying bravely to overcome the darkness. "How the fuck can anybody get friendly with a prickly bastard like that?" he muttered into the quiet night.

Ten minutes later Bernard drove into his garage missing 'that stupid cow's scooter' by inches. He went to the rear of the house and entered by the kitchen door as he usually did. It was nearly midnight but he made no effort to be quiet. Switching on every light he made towards his bar in the lounge and proceeded to pour brandy into a tumbler, half filling it. Without pausing he took the glass with him to the bathroom intermittently shedding an item of clothing, supping from the glass as he went. He reached the bathroom naked and staggered as he pulled the cord light switch. The effects of the alcohol he had consumed earlier, the beating, and now this large brandy was catching up on him. He slumped heavily onto the toilet seat.

"My God Bernie, what happened to your face?" Yvonne appeared at the open bathroom door.

"Never you mind. Find the first aid box and boil water, I'm going to take a shower."

Completing his toilet Bernard entered the shower cubicle. He washed all over his hard body leaving his head until last. When he started on his face he rubbed soap into the cloth and proceeded to rub his cheeks and nose, then ears and forehead as hard as he could. Every part in fact where Callum might have touched. He soaped the cloth again and again and rubbed the broken skin until he was stinging with burning pain. Satisfied he had cleansed every grain of McAlpine filth from his pores he stepped from the shower snapping off the water supply then grabbed a towel. In the bedroom he rubbed the towel quickly over his body in a token effort to dry himself then lay down sighing heavily.

Yvonne, prepared for him in the kitchen, followed him into the bedroom. "Bernie!" she cried seeing him on the bed, "I can tend you better in the kitchen, I'm all prepared through there."

"Tend me here, and bring the bottle with you."

Yvonne frowned but as he was injured perhaps he was right.

"Who the hell did this?" she asked dabbing the cuts and abrasions all over his head, "your face is so swollen, what a mess."

"Get on with it and shut the fuck up!" he barked. Her words stirred tortuous barbs of memory and razor wire twisted in his gut. He was cringing inside with painful embarrassment.

Yvonne hated his course words but she could understand his injured feelings. She hurried to get the jar of mild salving cream bought for Allan's forever scraped knees.

Applying the cream gently, she covered Bernard's face and ears then bandaged both elbows. She was about to start on his torn knuckles when to her surprise he slipped his right hand under her nightgown and around her bottom. Yvonne tried to look into his eyes but could see little other than two cream covered slots. The pressure on her bottom grew stronger and she laughed. "You're joking Bernie, surely?" Then glancing down, she noticed his erect manhood, "You're not joking, are you." Pulling back she laughed, "You must be daft, in your condition and you want to screw, no way Charlie!"

His unoccupied hand, lying limp on the bed, swung in an arc and crashed against the woman's face. "Who the fuck is Charlie?" he shouted rising off the bed.

Yvonne although dazed was still capable of putting up a modicum of defence though it was paltry as Bernard had her by the throat. His left hand reached over to the jar of cream and plunged his fingers into it. Forcing her back until she was against the wall he jammed his knee painfully between her thighs forcing them apart. Yvonne was gasping for air as he sought her opening and harshly entered her, painfully driving himself deep into her.

"You scum!" Yvonne managed to grate through bared teeth, hate burning in her eyes.

Bernard was smiling but the condition of his face made it appear like a grimace as he pushed his left hand, cupping the cream behind her and down the cleavage of her bottom. He opened his closed hand and forced the cream into and around her anus.

Yvonne's eyes opened wide. What she tried to say was, "Oh no, not with me you don't." but it poured from her mouth in an incongruous gurgle. Her left hand stopped pummelling his rib cage and came up with raking nails that went for the cream covered but grossly swollen eyes.

Bernard tried to grab the marauding hand but in so doing let go of her throat. Free from the choking grip, without thinking, she thumped her forehead forward as hard as she could. It smacked into the bloody creamy mess and he suddenly stepped back, pulling out of her. Dazed he staggered back taken by surprise at the vicious double pronged attack.

Yvonne was elated at yet another escape. She stepped forward with one sole intention. That of driving her knee into his upright organ, "Die you twisted bastard," she screamed into the gross cream and blood streaked mask. Never had she meant anything more in her life. If Yvonne could have defined the feeling, she would have at that point, recognised the flush of sadistic pleasure she experienced at the thought of permanently damaging this creature's manhood. Her eagerness to hurt him was her undoing. She did not see the clubbing right hand, folded into a hammering fist that came from nowhere and crashed into the side of her head.

Bernard caught the melting body before Yvonne fell senseless to the floor. Hefting her up he turned back and laid the soft oblivious creature face down on the bed, drooling through his broken lips in anticipated pleasure.

~~~

Yvonne soaked in the bath for an hour. She could not recall much about the previous night but the evidence that her body had been depraved, debauched and used was only too plain. Her body shuddered in the cooling bath water as she recalled the last seconds of being attacked. She did not know if she had simply awakened, or regained consciousness from Bernard's blow as the first yellow glimmers of dawn streaked across the dark blue sky. Bernard was sound asleep beside her as she slipped from the bed and staggered down the hall into Allan's room. Once there enveloped in the sanctity of her sleeping son she clambered in beside him all the while holding her pounding head. When Bernard left for work she lay quietly cursing. 'Sick bastard, should have known, I should've known!' A full pot of tea laced with whiskey and a long soak in a hot bath could not alleviate nauseous gut feeling. Yvonne's thoughts were diverted when she heard Allan and the landlady's young son arguing. Daria, her landlady, lived with her husband and three year old Myron in a small house in the back garden. Yvonne saw a lot of the Greek-Cypriot family as Myron and Allan formed an instant friendship. Inevitably due to the children the women met frequently and a bond naturally formed between them too. Neither Allan nor Myron could speak the other's language but were having a real go at each other so Yvonne reluctantly rose from the bath and dressed quickly. She was buttoning her blouse when Daria put an end to the threatening war between the children. She gave them each a sticky syrupy doughnut in a saucer and the two made instant peace, settling down to devour the sweet before the ants did it for them.

Yvonne waved her thanks to Daria then retreated to her kitchen. Apart from Allan's breakfast dishes, medical accoutrements for Bernard's injuries were still on the table top. Resisting the urge to side swipe the lot, she gathered and hurriedly replaced them in the first aid box. The December sun was warming up and on impulse the bitter young woman took a canvas chair to the front veranda, "Maybe a little warmth will help burn out that bent bastard's dirt!" she muttered grabbing a magazine.

The sun was glorious at this time of year for the sunshine deprived British, never getting too hot for fair English skins. Yvonne basking in its healing rays at last began to feel the cold lump of anger melt in the pit of her stomach. She closed her eyes and drifted into a light sleep.

A Mercedes taxi stopped and a blonde girl in her early twenties got out. She glanced at Yvonne before reaching inside and withdrew two heavy bags of groceries "Hi!" she called.

Yvonne fluttered her eyes and looked towards the sound.

"Sorry did I wake you? I thought you were reading," said the girl nodding at the magazine on Yvonne's lap. Before Yvonne could gather her thoughts the pert little blonde went on, "I'm your neighbour. Fancy a cuppa? I do, I'm desperate for one as a matter of fact. Give me five minutes to get the kettle on then come through, I'm dying to meet you!" She paid the taxi driver then the girl bobbed away and using her backside pushed open the gate of the house next door.

Initially Yvonne was vexed by the brash interruption of a lovely nap. As she became more awake however, the idea of female company grew more appealing. Due to the narrow minded community of Kirkcross, she had been starved of female company since Allan was born.

In the bathroom she freshened up then with a final pat on her hair, went next door to see what charitable alms the girl could offer in the way of friendship. The house lay-out was similar to her own with the same frontage, even down to the white glass ball that shaded the veranda light.

"Come on in, I won't be a minute," came the call to Yvonne's knock. "There's ciggies on the table, help yourself." The owner of the voice almost followed her words into the room as the blonde girl minced along carrying a laden tray. She had changed into a pair of tight blue shorts and halter top.

Setting the tray on a table beside the cigarettes the girl straightened up. "Right, let's do this properly. My name is Mrs. Patricia Parrot, and who, may I ask, are you?" The girl was enjoying herself and it was contagious. She was short, five feet one or two inches but in that small frame, every ounce of bone and muscle was packed delightfully into every round curve. To round it all off she wore a wide welcoming smile

"I'm Yvonne Kowaleski, pleased to meet you Patricia, oh, you're like a breath of fresh air."

"Thanks Pet, and it's Pat," the smile grew wider, "now that's the posh stuff over, just help yourself to the tea and bickies, and when you're ready you can tell me all about yourself."

Yvonne felt comfortable with this girl. Within minutes the pair were chatting like old friends.

"How long have you been out here Pat?"

"Too bloody long. No, I'm not joking," Pat said when she saw her visitor look doubtful, "Seriously I am beginning to get a little fed up now. We go home in four, or is it five months? Whatever, but the first thing I'm going to do in dear old blighty is split from this prick I'm married to." The pretty face had for the first time lost its smile.

"Why? Oh sorry, that's too personal." Yvonne stumbled.

"No, not at all," Pat laughed, "You obviously have not met Fred. I feel quite ashamed of him, honestly, he is the nearest thing to a human weasel you're ever likely to meet. I was fifteen when I met him at the dancing and the same night he weaselled his way into my pants," she laughed. "Mind you I didn't mind that part so much. To be honest to God truthful if you shut your eyes he fucks really well," Pat looked at Yvonne to catch any reaction. There was none, she carried on, "We fucked for four hours that first night, I swear! And Geeezuss was I sore! Then as a result I thought I must be pregnant. Oh and in love! Yeah, can you imagine? Me and Fred, it was like Frankenstein and the Virgin Mary." They both giggled "Anyway, he never said he was using condoms, how was I to know that for God's sake I was fifteen! Anyway I don't know why but I missed a period, the shit hit the fan and we got married double quick. I was happy, pregnant and in love, a month later I found I was neither. What I was, was stupid, young and fucking impressionable. My hero, Fred, he was twenty five, should've been locked up for what he did! That was six years ago, and yes I am twenty one and I'm 'fucked up, fed up and far from home' as they say."

Yvonne was shaking, holding a hand to her mouth through which filtered restrained laughter.

Pat went on, "You might as well know it, we have a bit of a reputation, Fred and me, we live together but go our separate ways." She shrugged, "Sometimes, I bring a bloke back here, well no, to be brutally honest I've brought many a bloke back here, and Fred when he hits a rich vein of luck, like when he manages to get some girl drunk enough, carries her back here, and I mean that. Three times he's walked in here literally carrying a woman, once over his shoulder."

"My God!" Yvonne muttered, "You surely can't go on like that ... can you?"

"No, but you know what Yvonne, we get on great, Fred and me. I know by conventional standards we lead a peculiar life but it works! At least it does for us. We get on better now than we did when we conformed to the accepted way of married life!" Pat shook her head ironically. "But ah, it's like you say, we can't go on like this, that's why when we go home I'm leaving him and giving going 'straight' a try," she laughed, "I know it's arse about face but I couldn't live a straight life with Fred, and I couldn't lead this life back in dear old blighty, no straight guy would put up with me, so ...." she spread her hands.

"I don't know whether to congratulate or commiserate with

you," Yvonne said sadly.

"I'll settle for a little of both. Enough of me, how's your set up? I see you've got a little boy."

"Yeah, Allan, he's the light of my life, I had him before I met ..." Yvonne stopped, "before I met Bernard." Without thinking she gingerly lifted her hand to the left side of her head.

"I didn't like to say but was that him, gave you that?" Pat indicated the swelling bruise.

Yvonne nodded.

"Look, it's none of my business but for once we came home together last night, me and Fred. We heard the commotion coming from your bedroom then suddenly it just went quiet."

"When it went quiet, that's when I got this," Yvonne gently massaged around the swelling.

"Oooh, I see, I'm sorry Yvonne." She paused then, "Men are funny creatures aren't they! Fred made a peculiar comment when I said maybe something had happened to you after it went quiet. For you had been certainly letting your man know what you thought of him! Anyway Fred said, 'It may be right, it may be wrong, but funny things turn funny people on.'"

"Fred was right, funny things were going on, and I'm worried," Yvonne said quietly.

"I'd worry too," Pat said yet she did not fully understand what her new friend meant.

Yvonne stared out the window, "There's more to his beating me!" she said quietly.

"More, what else is there? I mean if he's beating you what else is ... Oh ... he's not kinky?"

"I think he is. There's two places in my body he can ... use, they're only an inch apart. One's the right place, the other, as far as I'm concerned is the wrong place. He's only interested in the wrong place."

"Well that's not so bad, oh sorry," Pat shrugged. "When you've been with as many men as I have nothing surprises you about what they want to try next. Some actually prefer ..." she stopped then carried on in a more sober tone. "So, Yvonne, you don't like this ... wrong place?"

Yvonne shuddered, "No I don't," she trembled more violently a second time, "but to top that I think he may be ... I don't know how to say this ... I think he's mental, you know,

424

deranged."

"Oh my God!" Pat threw a hand over her mouth. "How can he be ... that? I mean he's in the RAF. I know they're all a bit daft, but, well, deranged, that's big time stuff isn't it, like ... crazy?"

Yvonne went silent thinking perhaps she had made a mistake saying too much about Bernard. Pat picked up on her thoughts.

"Yvonne love, my lips are sealed, whatever you tell me goes no farther. I go on a bit at times but, I'll help if I can, there must be something I can do. You can't go on living with someone who's nuts, especially someone who's dangerous nuts for Christ's sake! Your boy, will he be all right?"

"Thanks Pat, for the offer. Look, this only happened for the first time last night," she lied. "Yesterday someone gave him a terrible hiding, his face was all smashed up. Maybe I just caught the rebound, I don't know. I haven't had time to put my thoughts into any semblance of order. But yes, Allan, he's my big worry, I'd really like to send him to my sister in Manchester but I haven't got the money."

Pat looked thoughtful for a moment, "How much ... to send him home?"

"Haven't a clue but if you're thinking of helping out, forget it, I ..."

"Perish the thought ... me!" Pat cut in, "No, we spend it faster than Fred can bring it home on payday. But," she said mysteriously, "there might be a way."

Yvonne said nothing other than shifting uncomfortably.
Pat clucked her tongue against the roof of her mouth repeatedly before going on, "This is a secret that not even Fred knows, it wouldn't matter if he did mind you but I've never told him. I needed some cash not so long ago, about £35, and I made it in double quick time." Pat sat back and smiled impishly, lifting her eyebrows and tilting her head to one side.

"Made it?" Yvonne was not quite sure what was meant but had the faintest suspicion.

"Yes Love, 'Made it' in more ways than one!" Pat answered, confirming Yvonne's suspicion.

"You mean ... you mean?"

"Yep," Pat nodded emphatically, "I started charging for something I was giving away for nowt, £3 or £4 a time. I got a fiver once from a very appreciative Greek," she declared proudly.

There was a time such words would have shocked Yvonne, but with maturity came another layer of hardness, another ring to her young tree of life. With a brittle edge to her voice tinged with an air of acceptability she said, "I wouldn't know how to go about anything like that."

Pat for a moment was quiet, unsure if she should push this girl down the road she herself had found necessary, but easy to travel a year ago. Her squalid past, even lower than her present seedy life was water under the bridge and she had enjoyed the short lived experiences. It was something to tell her grandchildren about, which would shake the little bastards! Her version of Snow-White and the seven dwarfs would be quite different! She smiled at the thought then snapped back when she saw the uncertain look on her visitor's face. "Look Yvonne, I'm not saying this is the way you should go, but ... you need cash, this is one way of getting it. If you want to try, I'll show you the ropes, it's easy after all," she laughed. "We're only doing what comes naturally."

Yvonne had never in her life spoken so openly to anyone. This girl was confident, bright and cheerfully open, someone she would dearly like to make friends and spend time with. Then she recalled Pat was going home in the summer, four or five months she said. Realistically that was all the time she needed, maybe more than enough to send Allan home. "All right Pat, show me the ropes!"

"Okay, but it's winter now, maybe not too many men about - johns, must be professional," Pat laughed, "but we'll give it a try in two or three weeks, get Christmas and new year parties over. Well have to be very careful Yvey love, the RAF don't like this sort of thing and we'll need some sort of plan. I think it might be best to work only one night a week to start with, see how it goes. So, start watching your man. Make a note of any night when he goes out regular."

~~~

Chapter 20

To make space for his car Bernard had to stop and move the damn scooter closer to the garage wall. The stupid woman was forever leaving the dumpy two wheeled conveyance in the centre of the garage floor no matter how many times he complained. One day he would run over the machine preferably with her under it.

It was after seven in the evening, he was two hours late. One of his section sergeants had put up the beers due to his imminent return to the UK and Bernard, as the senior NCO, was obliged to attend. With three pints and four double brandy sours warming his innards he arrived in an unusually affable mood, despite the hiccup of the infernal scooter.

Three weeks had passed since the night he knocked Yvonne unconscious and the atmosphere inside the Kowaleski home still had ten degrees to rise before it reached freezing. Talk between the pair was stilted and she still slept with her bastard son. Bernard couldn't care less. Sex in any form with her comatose was more preferable than her non responsive conscious body. He couldn't care less because exploratory visits to bars and brothels in and around the older parts of Limassol had paid dividends. Especially in the out of bounds Turkish quarter.

"You're late," Yvonne greeted him as he entered through the back kitchen door. "Your dinner's probably a little dry now, it's been in the oven nearly two hours." She was standing at the sink washing dishes, and surprisingly her tone was not quite so hostile. Bernard edged nearer. She had not spoken half a dozen words to him since that night and he misread her light tone. Maybe, he thought, she was coming round, maybe she needed him, it was after all three weeks? He slipped his arms round her waist and pulled her against his body, nuzzling his mouth into her neck.

Had Bernard approached Yvonne differently, if he had turned her round to face him in his approach, gently attempting to repair

427

the broken bridges between them, what happened next could have been vastly different.

Yvonne initially was surprised by what was for Bernard, an unusual but warm approach to make up, then she felt his hardness push against her buttocks. Reacting as most violated woman would, she swung round and her open wet hand cracked across his cheek. The stinging smack surprised and stung Bernard both emotionally and physically. Vulnerable and open as he was, in the middle of demonstrating a tender side that surprised even him, his survival mechanism raised his defensive shields back into place. Too late, he had already been stung by this viper bitch. Bernard growled menacingly and as she had reacted instinctively, so did he. His forehead jerked forward in a vicious head butt, luckily only catching Yvonne a glancing blow to the side of her head as she squirmed free of his grip. She staggered and nearly fell as Bernard shot out his left hand catching her upper arm. Pointing his right bent elbow at her face he swung the same hand round in an arc and backhanded Yvonne across her mouth, knocking her sprawling backwards to, fall through the open lounge door.

She squealed in pain tasting the blood from her burst lip, and was rolling over when he grabbed her again. Intuitively she pulled her head to one side just missing the clubbing fist that painfully grazed past her cheek. Survival at all costs was blasting through all her intuitive systems as she pulled away and fell, rolling into a ball with her arms covering her head. Kicks and punches were raining down on her from all sides. Bernard lathered into frenzy as he tried to inflict pain and damage on this tight ball of humanity. Yvonne knew if he got one telling blow on her head, there was only one way she would end up, all the while bewildered at the viciousness and fever of his frenzied attack. Determined to hurt her he punched and kicked with more strength than he needed to use, knocking side tables and ornaments over he was grunting like an animal in his efforts then mercifully, he paused briefly in his barrage.

Peering timidly under her forearm at the break in the bone crushing kicks, her eyes opened wide in terror. Not consciously afraid at that moment, her mind bent only on survival, but when she looked up into Bernard's face she experienced a deep gut chilling fear for the first time in her life. His eyes were burning red coals set in a demon face black with rage. White teeth were bared in a growling snarl and he was prowling round her like an animal. She saw him take deliberate aim again and his crunching fist was driving straight at her arm protected face. At the last fraction of a second she pulled round and away. Had she not done so her forearms would surely have snapped under the sheer power of the blow. Lying on her left side the blow caught her shoulder and sent her into a backward spin, her right leg straightening out at the knee with the force of the spin. Her ankle caught Bernard unawares, knocking him off balance, toppling backwards he fell over the settee. It was the only chance she was likely to get and groggily fighting through a haze of bewilderment she staggered to the front door, across the veranda and onto the street. Reeling and confused her thoughts flashed to Allan, her young son. Thankfully she recalled, he was in Daria's house and safe for the moment, she had only her own safety to worry about.

Bernard followed her out then stopped as she ran into the neighbouring house. "All right you bastard cow!" he roared. He was breathless and blowing heavily, everything shrouded in the now familiar rolling red haze. His cheek still smarted from the wet open handed crack, his eye twitching fearfully with both soap and pain. Pacing to the bedroom with a stride born from anger, frustration and hate, he changed into civilian clothes then remarkably, considering his mood, carefully hung up his discarded working blue uniform. Back in the kitchen he opened the oven and lifted out a plate of meat stew and potatoes. Approaching the sink that was full of warm water and dishes, he placed the plate on the soapy water surface and watched it sink slowly, the soapy suds invading the gravy surrounded meal.

The thin film of domestic bliss that initially showed only minor snags and flaws, had given way to great rents and tears between the Kowalski's. Getting married had not been the answer to Bernard's problems. What figment of his imagination has driven him into this situation. Whatever he hoped to gain from a permanent union with this woman had not materialised. If he, as a married man, Bernard thought bitterly, was supposed to present a more stable element in the unwritten laws of the Royal Air Force, it certainly had not worked in his case. His five, nearly six years, at Kirkcross after a stuttering start had been as steady as a blockhouse. Little did Bernard suspect his quiet spell at the camp near Blackpool had simply been the dormant calm before the invading storm.

He threw on a leather jacket and stormed out to the garage feeling his anger melt in an anticipatory excitement buzz. The previous Wednesday night he had ventured into the 'Out of Bounds' Turkish quarter of Limassol. Sitting at a table outside a bar, a twelve year old boy pimping for his sixteen year old sister, had led him to the girl. The Turks knew how to make a man like Bernard happy.

Yvonne watched from Pat's window as the Hillman Minx scudded backwards across the road from the driveway. It progressed into a crabbing turn trying to obtain an impossible grip in skidding bounding leaps before finally wagging its tail and squealing away down Christos Street. "I swear the bastard's beyond help," she muttered through a face cloth, given to her by Pat. The cloth growing more blood sodden by the minute.

Yvonne had fell into a surprised Fred Parrott's arms when he opened the door. Her face was covered in blood and caring little for the sight of the red viscid fluid he nearly fainted. "Pat, PAT!" Fred roared. His wife responded and eased the girl into the kitchen. "My God Yve, what's he done? That bastard!" she screamed, "Go and sort that nutter out Fred!"

With raised eyebrows Fred nodded vacantly. He had seen the size of the Chief Technician next door and no way was he was about to get involved with that raving head case. He busied himself putting the kettle on, poured a large drink and disappeared with it into the back yard.

After Bernard's irrational departure, Pat fussed and carefully washed Yvonne's face, then armed with two large brandies she sat beside the trembling girl. "Here Yve, drink this, make you feel better." She eased the glass between the trembling lips.

The fiery liquid burned the lacerations inside and around her mouth. Yvonne pulled away then snuffled painfully before swallowing a burning mouthful. Her sobbing eased. Pat came back from the fridge with ice blocks wrapped in a tea towel and placed it behind the shaken girl's neck. Within minutes Yvonne's nose stopped bleeding and both women sighed. For the moment at least, the worst was over.

"Pat, I swear on my son's life, he's the devil incarnate I

actually saw for myself, he is MAD!" Sobs were hovering around the edges of her speech as she sipped at the fiery amber drink.

"Do you want to tell me what happened Yve?"

"He tried it on me again Pat! Fuck!" Yvonne seldom swore but on this occasion she put every ounce of feeling into the word. "I can't ... I hate the thought of ... FUCK!" she roared at the floor.

"Yeah all right Yvey, all right, it's not everybody's cup of tea. But some blokes ..." Pat gulped her drink to stop rambling. After a gap, "So what d'you want to do?"

"Can Allan and I sleep here tonight? It might be safe enough in our own bed for when he comes home from the brothels he never comes near us. But I don't want us to be anywhere near him ... just in case."

"Brothels?" Pat raised her eyebrows, "He visits brothels, how do you know?"

Yvonne nodded as she licked delicately around the split in her lip. "From his clothes these past two Wednesday nights. I can smell him, he stinks. Cheap perfume and that sickening stink of stale sex!"

"Hmn ... so?"

"So I want to start making money now, get Allan home, soon as possible."

Pat smiled, "Lovey, it's going to take a week at least for your face to heal, we don't want our customers to think you're into the sadistic stuff or that you like hidings. You might find some of them like to hand out the odd bloodletting. Give it a week then we'll talk about it."

Yvonne sighed heavily, "I suppose you're right, but if he gets violent again, my main worry, apart from him killing me," Yvonne snickered nervously, "is Allan. I'm dead scared he'll turn on my boy. Could he stay here for a few nights to see how all this turns out?"

"Of course, it may cramp my style a little I'll have you know. Although you may be out of business ... temporarily ... I sometimes fancy, you know ... Not often you understand," Pat laughed, "but problem is we only have the one spare bedroom. Fred goes in there when I bring a friend home or he uses it when he gets lucky. But all right, we'll put our love life on hold for the next week or two. Fred might think it's his birthday if I get randy enough, Ha!"

Their temporary guest did not interrupt the Parrott's normal routine. Indeed they had been invited to a 'Key Party.' the following Saturday and Pat wondered for a moment if she should invite Yvonne along for 'experience'. She could always go as an 'extra' with the lucky man who drew Pat's keys, as a sort of bonus. There was no doubt her neighbour was capable but was she mature enough to handle casual sex with total strangers? Pat decided in the meantime it might be better not to ask her along. There were too many problems with her brute of a husband.

Key Parties were fun and Pat loved them. When the party warmed up, when all the games had been played and everyone was randy and excited enough to go home with a partner other than their spouses, the men placed their car or house keys into a black bag. The ladies dipped a hand in. She would fish out a bunch then claim the key owner to be their slave until next morning. The game was extremely popular in tight clandestine circles, and especially for the men when Pat Parrott was one of the prizes. No woman of course wanted Fred, which only added to the spice of the game.

Most of the type of men who attended these parties yearned for a spell with the delicious and inventive Mrs. Parrott. For the women however, it was quite the reverse, the game was akin to Russian roulette, dreading the awful moment if Fred Parrott claimed the keys the unlucky lady pulled from the bag. However, surprisingly, some of Fred's victims were pleasantly surprised. The man's demeanour may be rattish and unwholesome but few could perform in the sack as well as the nose twitching Londoner.

Time crept slowly for Yvonne. With each passing day she grew more determined to find the cash that would send Allan home. As she waited for her face to heal she began to prepare and wrote to her sister Jean in Manchester. Yvonne warned Jean she may have to put her son on a plane, if so, would she meet Allan at the airport at some future date. She enquired at a travel agent and discovered unaccompanied children often travelled alone and well chaperoned on route. The only criterion being a responsible agent must meet the child at journey's end.

Yvonne had to wait until the end of February before she and

Pat could knit their preparations into a workable pattern; healing of bruises, periods and unforeseen barriers hindering progress.

But their opportunity arrived one Wednesday night. Ten minutes after Bernard left on his jaunt to the older part of Limassol where he was gaining a reputation, a cheerful Pat Parrott knocked on Yvonne's door. She was looking forward to the escapade and had ordered a taxi driver friend to pick them up. "Put your veranda light on Hon, so Stavros knows it's okay to collect us," she said on entering, "it's the signal he knows."

Yvonne flicked on the homely white bowl. It was silhouetted with the bodies of dead insects but illuminated the veranda adequately. She then poured two huge brandies, handing one to Pat.

"Hell's teeth Yve, we'll be bombed out of our tiny skulls before we get our first fuck. I'll be enjoying myself so much I'll be giving it away for nowt! Here gimme that." Pat took the glasses and poured most back into the bottle.

"I'm just so nervous Pat, God I don't want to bump into him!"

"No chance. You said your dick of a husband goes to brothels, where we're going we'll be meeting a classier set of pricks than your old man."

Twenty minutes later Stavros in his Mercedes taxi with the standard horizontal nine inch painted yellow band encircling the car, deposited the girls outside a plush modern hotel near the beach at the extreme eastern end of Limassol. They clicked their way over the tiled entrance where Pat led her protégé to the lounge. "This is a good place Yve, the guys who come here don't use brothels. The few girls that are here, that's us in case you haven't noticed, we're better class, yeah, don't you agree?"

It was fairly quiet and the pair sat warming their brandies for an hour before two newly arrived Greek men sent them a drink. Pat raised her glass and flashed a wide smile, crossing her legs in their direction as she did so. One of the men beamed and made his way to their table.

Yvonne did her best to act both sexy and uncaring as instructed. Pat did the negotiations. She was surprised however when the man returned to his table. "What's going on?" she hissed.

"He refuses to pay a fiver. He wants it for nowt but hey, we're worth it. We'll hang on a bit."

Two slightly drunk men entered the lounge. Dressed in casual clothes and on looking around, the darker of the two spotted the girls sitting alone. He said something to his friend before approaching their table. He addressed Pat, "Are you available, if not I'm in big trouble?"

Pat smiled, his accent was obviously English. She guessed they were Army officers out on the town. "That depends." She answered cautiously, loath to lose a hooked fish a second time.

"From that, I gather, you might be ... if we can meet your price, am I correct?"

Pat showed the tip of her pink tongue and gave a light nod, "Five pounds!" she said quietly.

The smile faded slightly and the second man stepped forward. "My little blonde beauty, just so we do not waste each other's time, we have been out celebrating and are pretty well skint, Colin and I. But I do appreciate you have a living to make, so ..." The man rummaged in his pocket, "I have three pounds and change, for what will no doubt be a very short time but ..."

"Sorry this is not Happy Hour at La Ronde," Pat mentioned one of the lower class brothels. "Come back when you have the necessary."

Colin smiled at Pat's caustic wit, "I can pay five, Bob has three, that, by my calculations is eight pounds! Not enough to meet your price but enough I sincerely hope for you both? If not then I'm afraid you commit us to seek our comforts elsewhere! In evils of drink and eventually happy oblivion ... I fear."

Bob meanwhile with a small smile was running his half open eyes over the shapely Pat and breathing heavily through his nose. He leaned over, "Look, I have no doubt you are worth a lot more than we have, but I desperately want your body, you gorgeous little creature. On that score, I will be brutally honest with you. We could up the price by another pound, but then we really would be penniless, with no taxi fare or even one round of drinks after our little sortie. Don't, please don't refuse our very kind offer of nine pounds and if you are very good, we will escort you back to these premises where you can buy us a drink afterwards."

Pat smiled at the two swaying men, "Okay you lucky sods, let's go, we haven't got all night!"

434

Yvonne's stomach took a somersault but outwardly remained calm. As all four left the hotel she wanted to go to the 'Ladies,' just to sit and calm her fluttering nerves. She resisted the urge.

Pat crossed the road to the beach and removing her shoes, led the little group to a secluded spot behind some rocks. Here she turned and wordlessly held out her hand.

In the luminescent darkness the men gathered their money and handed it to Pat. She in turn handed a five pound note to Yvonne, "There you go, a quid extra to a good cause."

Yvonne accepted with her head down, too embarrassed to talk about money. In a daze she followed Pat, stripping off her blouse, skirt and underwear then lay down in the sand. She tried to deaden her mind from what was going on yet at the same time attempted to keep part of her brain sentient to fool the man she was enjoying what he was doing. She got Colin and at first he had difficulty in having an erection. When he requested help this was eventually achieved, then he had trouble finishing. Yvonne had no idea how long he took having switched off her immediate surroundings but was brought back with Bob and Pat laughing. They had finished and were watching Colin hump erratically as he at last approached a climax. With his last painful thrusts he moaned loudly then slumped heavily over Yvonne, covering her to lie as if dead. Little contented sounds confirmed however he was still alive.

A few minutes later all four were retracing their steps back to the hotel, Yvonne with mixed feelings. She was disgusted that she had actually gone through with it, but had to admit it was an easy way to make money. The worst part was when he asked her to perform oral sex. The request embarrassed her and declined by a demure shake of her head. She could not do that with a total stranger. The one and only man she had ever done that with was Allan's father, her first, and who she blithely imagined was the only love she would ever have. However she did what was necessary with her hands and what happened after was routine, although the image of her lying there under him sickened her too. The episode required constant reminders she was in this business only to send her son home.

"Thanks girls, maybe the same time next week?"

"Certainly, but that was only a taster, the full fee next week,"

Pat laughed, "and bring your friends, we do special prices

on block bookings!"

"Just as a matter of interest, doesn't your friend speak?" Colin asked Pat.

Yvonne looked at him in surprise. This man had lain with her, fondled and been intimate with the most secret parts of her body, and she with his, yet she had not uttered a word since before the two men approached their table.

"Sorry," Yvonne said quietly, "I've never done this before. Not for money anyway"

Colin nodded; he seemed to have sobered up. "Thought so, see you next week then?"

"Why not."

"We won't trouble you for that drink you promised us girls," Bob smiled, "by the way, what are your names?" he asked as he waved a cruising taxi.

Pat hesitated then called, "I'm Candy, she's Mandy and we're both randy! What difference does it make? We'll be here next week!" She waved as the taxi pulled away then turned to Yvonne, "Come on Mandy, I'll buy you a drink on your first kill, it's still early yet."

"No you won't Candy." Yvone giggled, "You gave me the extra pound. My round!"

They had just sat down and before the waiter could reach them, the two Greeks who had shown interest earlier, joined them. "We have been conseedering and eet is amazing how some nass dreenks can make a man feel reecher. And you lovely gels to grow een value for what you selling." The tall one smiled.

"Do you have five pounds ... each?" Pat asked recklessly, not too keen on the pair.

"Of course, yes but we most go now, my friend and me have appointment so we be queeck!"

That sounded better to Pat, a quick fiver. She turned to Yvonne and raised her eyebrows. Her friend nodded and soon both girls were following the men outside. This time the girls were led to a big American car parked under the trees. "A Dodge, very nice,!" Pat said impressed and ran her hands over the wing. The car seemed more chrome than paint. "Get een back of car please." They were told.

Both girls sank into the soft comfortable seats. Yvonne unsure watching Pat for guidance when Pat said, "Before we take your money, where are you taking us?"

"Oh no my leettle Aphrodite, we not take you anywhere! It is you who most take us some place, not so? You beautiful gels you take us to heaven, justa for few minutes out of our sheet humdrum lives."

"Yes, well the return fare to heaven is five pounds, paid in advance," Pat held out her hand.

Five singles and a five pound note were passed to Pat who transferred the notes to her jacket pocket. The men clambered in beside the girls and again panties were removed, this time more roughly than their previous detachment. Skirts were hurriedly hiked up high around hips as the pace suddenly picked up. It appeared their spell in the back of the car would indeed be brief. Yvonne was surprised how everything could be turned upside down with the exchange of money. A part of her body that not so long ago she regarded with a great wealth of respect, self-esteem and mystery. The very heart of where her love for the man she adored years ago, who had given her so much pleasure from the centre of her being and the first to breach this citadel she once guarded so carefully. Was it possible the same place was now being used as a trough of pleasure for another stranger to draw gratification, yet she could feel nothing? No, not quite nothing, not this time. This man was making his presence felt and despite her mental aversion, she was forcibly being made aware of how big, how painfully big he was. This man was hurting her, splitting her apart. His breath reeked of garlic and with each heavy almost measured lunge her left knee was being rammed against something hard on the door.

After ten minutes of this agony the men without warning quickly changed over. "Hey! what's going on?" Pat shouted, "Both of us is extra!"

The men ignored her and moved around on their knees like rutting pigs. "Hold it right ...."

Pat was struggling with Garlic Breath when he said, "You hold it my pretty leettle one, you jost hold it. For ten pounds we taste two Eenglish conts! You ask too much for one leettle crack, now jost shut up ... enjoy and you no get hurt."

Pat went very quiet and Yvonne sensed the situation might turn ugly. Ten more minutes passed in silence other than the sounds of fornication and protesting springs. Then in a flurry of quiet bedlam both men turned into demons for some seconds as they thrashed and flayed in what seemed fits of agony. Mercifully at last, both fell in heaps gasping on the girls.

"So, what you theenk Nando?" asked Garlic Breath as he pulled himself free of Pat.

"Not good, not bad. Not so good as the Greekie gels eh, what you theenk?"

"I theenk was waste of good fock, these Eenglish!" Garlic breath shook his head, "I'm sorry, you no worth five pound!" Without warning he drove his hand into Pat's jacket pocket and pulled out the money. Picking out the five pound note, he threw the five singles at Pat's face. "Go please, and be happy we give sometheeng, queeckly - GO!"

Pat snatched up the notes and her underwear, nearly falling out of the car in her urgency to get out, followed by a frightened Yvonne. The man named Nando threw Yvonne's panties out after her. "Maybe you don wear these t'ings too often dahling but I don want them in car, my wife she keel me!" Raucous laughter followed as the car revved powerfully then drove off.

As Pat wriggled into her wispy underwear she noticed Yvonne's face, "You okay?"

Yvonne retrieving her underwear answered as she gingerly pulled them on, "I suppose but Jesus that guy was massive, I'm bloody sore!"

Pat stared wistfully after the car then handed the five notes to Yvonne. "Here," she said."

"No ways, we split it!" Yvonne said firmly.

Pat shook her head, "No really, you keep it," she was still staring after the car. "If I'd known that Greek bastard was so big, he could have had me for nowt ... and to hell with his bad breath."

Yvonne stared at the smiling impish face then both erupted in fits of laughter.

Staggering back to the hotel Yvonne said, "I insist we split the fiver, two quid each. The other will buy us that well earned drink and a taxi home, but no more guys, I can hardly walk."

For a third time that night they entered the lounge bar and sat this time in one of the more secluded alcoves around the edge of the room. The waiter eventually brought their ordered drinks and

Yvonne sighed, settling back in the chair. Pat sipped her drink and glanced at her friend. She looked tired. "What did you think of your first foray with the paying public?"

Yvonne considered for a moment, "Not as bad as I imagined it might be, but I was wary of those Greeks. I thought they were going to turn nasty."

"Nah, I've never heard of them hurting anyone but as you saw, they can duck out of paying, that sort of thing. They're bloody funny; they either cut your money or pay over the top but seldom pay the asking price! In future we'll cut out the locals. There's plenty servicemen and the odd tourist around this area, we'll stick to them."

"Okay, you're the boss," Yvonne smiled, relaxing now, beginning to enjoy her surroundings. She went on, "It's a pity we couldn't do this more than one night in the week. At this rate I could soon have enough cash for both Allan and me."

"Ask your old man for another night, tell him you're just off to town to screw a few blokes. I'm sure he wouldn't mind, would he?" Pat smirked.

Yvonne smiled and nodded wistfully, "Mind? I really think he would kill me ... and Allan. Unfortunately Wednesday is the only night the Mad Hatter goes looking for his Queen of Hearts. He goes out other nights but not regular." She looked around, " I like it here, are we using this place next week?"

"Oh yeah, if for no other reason than to see the two nice chappies we had earlier, I think they were army guys, unmarried officers probably."

"What makes you say that? Neither wore rings but they could've been removed."

"Guys prepared to pay don't worry their empty heads about little things like rings. No Yvey, married blokes don't give out names. Bob and Colin couldn't care less about us knowing their names and they were too natural with each other for their names to be false, anyway ..." Pat took a long drink and sighed, "We'll do this place next week then move on before the management ask us to. We'll circulate a little, spread our charms around. The easiest way to get blokes ... johns" she flicked her eyebrows, "I like to use that word, is through a reliable taxi driver. Remember Stavros who brought us here? He used to do it for me and was rather pissed off when I packed it in. There's no hassle that way.

We sit at home and he delivers a long line of clients to our door for a percentage."

"I think Daria my landlady might cotton on very quickly to what was going on if I did that," Yvonne said slowly, "Besides I couldn't with Allan in the house."

"Then we use my place, I've used it before and my landlady didn't notice - or care! She never complained anyway. I just used to leave my veranda light on a couple of nights in the week then Stavros knew my legs were open for business," she giggled. "He would deliver the john then collect him an hour later. I've seen me do five johns from Stavros in the one night, pretty exhausting. When we've had enough, switch off the veranda light. Then he won't bring any more clients - johns!" Pat giggled again.

"How much does Stavros charge?" Yvonne could see the possibilities.

"Forty per cent, some fifty, but like I said no hassle, like we had with those two."

Yvonne whistled softly but the idea was sound. "Would Stavros do it for us on Wednesdays?"

"Sure, he'd be happy to. I'd have to speak to him, arrange it for Wednesdays only, between the hours of 8 and 12, okay? And for the signal; both our veranda lights on mean we're both available, one light means only one of us, you know like time of the month etc. No lights mean piss off Stavros."

A smile spread across Yvonne's face, "Yeah, it might be fun. When can we start?"

"We won't find him tonight so I'll set it up tomorrow morning. You can take me down to Hero's Square on that little putt-putt of yours and I'll speak to Stavros. He can farm us out to others if he likes, it won't cost us any more. By the way, is there anything you won't do? Stavros has to inform prospective clients what we will and won't do."

Yvonne demurred. "I know it will narrow the field but I will not do it with my mouth, and you know how I feel about my bum."

"Well Hon, that as you say will cut half of the Greek gents from our clientele but okay, only your front door is open to the public. Blow jobs and back door strictly forbidden."

"Right, good, and make sure he knows it's only for, let's say a couple of months. As soon as I've gathered enough, Allan and I are out of here."

"A couple of months, that'll be at the end of April. I go home on the seventh of May so yeah, we'll hit the UK almost together. Maybe we can take up our business over there, lots of money in this old game gel!"

"Don't think I could do it for a living Pat, maybe, if I was desperate enough, like now. On the other hand I never thought it would be so easy and quick. I'm disgusted really yet I can accept it. Can't understand it." Yvonne shrugged, "You never know what's round the corner."

"Men, they're around the corner, me anyway, round every corner, men, men and more fucking men. Thank God Yve, I couldn't live without them, honest, life would be so dull without men!"

Yvonne giggled at her so open friend. She was of loose morals and low in virtuous character, of that there was no doubt. However, the enlightening fact and delightful thing about the girl was she cared less than a hoot for the world or opinions. But most of all, and strangest of all, her heart was of solid gold.

"Let me buy you another drink Pat, for opening my half open eyes a little more on the facts of life. We still have time but I don't want to leave it too late. Daria is baby-sitting and I must find a place to hide this money, this hard earned, yet so easy money before my dear sick husband gets home."

~~~

Chapter 21

The Inter Services tug-of-war league matches started in March 1967, two months earlier than usual. The Army organisers in Dhekalia made the change hoping the league would finish in September and not run on, for whatever reason into October and even December.

The team from the 103 Maintenance Unit opened their season as usual in commanding style, winning their first four matches. Their coach, Cpl. Callum McAlpine although pleased with his team, was not counting his chickens this year. His attention was drawn to the latest pretender to their crown, an extremely powerful combination hovering very close.

It was common knowledge the Chief Tech down at Station Ground Engineering Flight had his men training all though the winter months and it showed. Callum had watched the rising team under their demonic coach on two occasions. They were exceptional and Callum knew from the way they wiped aside two very good army teams that in this campaign real opposition awaited the MU. It would not be long before the two teams clashed. Their first fixture was due to take place the following Tuesday afternoon.

On the Sunday prior to the match the Connolly's, the Ross's and Julian Cantwell were relaxing. The men were seated in Frank's garden around the dying charcoal fire where Frank had earlier tried out his practised barbecue skills on his visitors. Both the afternoon and the barbecued meat proved an unqualified success but with the approaching dusk, the sun warmed air of the day was turning cool. The two women, whose whole conversation centred around Marion's pregnancy, and the Connolly children drifted into the house, which conveniently left the men to discuss a much more important topic - tug-of-war.

"You must be worried, even a fraction, we can beat you on Tuesday?" Harold asked Frank.

"The MU, worried!" Frank laughed, "C'mon we've nothin' to prove. Sure you lot are hungry for success but do you know how many hungry teams we've seen off in the past? We get them comin' after us all the time. I'm not sayin' it won't be close with that 'hell bent on beatin' us' coach you've got, but there can only be one result Harry!"

"You know, you lot have been floating on that cloud too long now. Skee's a nutter, no doubt about that but for all his antics he has managed to install into our team the will to win. You and I both know whoever wins on Tuesday, wins the league!"

"Skee?" Julian asked.

"Yeah, everybody calls him that. Behind his back of course, Kowale - skeee!"

Julian nodded, "Yes, I suppose it was inevitable he would be tagged with a nickname."

Harold peered at Julian, "You sound like you feel sorry for the old nutcase, Julie?"

"No no, that's not true, but no one can deny his arrival has injected a new lease of life into the sport." Julian felt strangely uncomfortable and wanted to change the subject, "So you really believe you can win on Tuesday, Harold? It is possible of course, you have an excellent team. Intriguing situation isn't it. I have been involved with the MU for over two years now so it follows that I've been a close observer of our teams in that time." Julian picked his words carefully, "It is with no flaunting or ludicrous boast that I say this, Harold, but I honestly feel the present eight probably form the best team we've had since Errol gave me the Utility man job."

"So you've seen us in action Julie?"

"I was coming to that. Yes I've watched you twice and it is impossible to separate one team from the other." Julian looked away thoughtfully, "The fact he has brought your team up to the standard of a great, in my opinion, MU team, then your 'Skee' has indeed worked wonders. It should be quite a match."

"Julie," Frank cried, "this guy's the enemy, remember? Now he'll be boastin' to his mates they've got us worried!"

"Don't be daft Frank," Harold laughed heartily, more than pleased with Julian's endorsement. "I don't have to tell the guys anything, they know! We're on the verge of doing something nobody has managed since El Adam in the Nee-Af games two years ago!"

"I'll throw you this crumb Harry. If by some miracle you do manage to win on Tuesday, then you will be the better team - on the day! We approach every match the same way, never underestimate the opposition. Even the guys stuck at the bottom of the league who turn up week in week out, have never won an end against anybody, we treat with the same respect as we'll treat you."

"So do we!" Harold said indignantly.

"Aye Harry, but you're not one-oh-three Maintenance Unit!" Frank leaned forward, his eyes gleaming, "We're the ones that every man jack of the opposition gives that wee bit extra when they meet. An' we're only human, so it's only a matter of time, some team will beat us sooner or later. It might be your GEF mob with your nutter of a coach. But you won't be allowed to sit on your laurels pal! You'd replace us as the team everyone is gunnin' for, includin' us. Then you'd get a taste of what we go through every week!"

Harold nodded in noncommittal agreement.

"One other thing," Julian added. "You may well win on Tuesday but if I may I'd like to refer to the old adage, 'One battle does not win the war.' If you look back over the records you'll see in the past ten years the MU have participated in literally hundreds of matches. Yes, of course we occasionally lose, but somehow we always manage to come back. Tug-of-war is not just a sport on 103 MU it's a tradition! When they suffer the odd defeat, like the true champions they are, they come back stronger than ever as they did after El Adam surprised us all. That was as you say, two years ago, but since that defeat, the MU haven't lost a match or an end since! That record speaks for itself." He sat back and smiled, smugly content.

"That was quite a speech Julie, there's no doubt where your heart lies." Harold said, "You're right of course, no one can argue with your record, but it's precisely that, strangely enough, that seems to be Skee's prime aim. He lets it slip every now and again that his prime interest is not just to get a good team, but a team that's going to murder 'them bastards from the MU.' He's shoved it down our throats he wants the Nee-Af title this year. We want it too, naturally, but all our blokes, me included have commented on this commitment he has about beating the MU. It's like no other team exists. He doesn't give a shit about winning the league ,or anything else for that matter except Nee-Af, just as long as we can beat you lot along the way."

"Well he's got that right hasn't he, to win at Happy Valley you're goin' to have to beat us, in fact you'll have to beat us twice!" said Frank.

"Twice? Why is that?"

"Let's cross that bridge if we ever come to it. We still have this minor clash on Tuesday that will make this season very interestin' for us both." Frank winked to emphasize his point.

"Frank, you might as well get used to the fact that we are going to be nipping at your bums all season, and it doesn't matter how many times we meet. I really think GEF are going to beat you in two days time!" Harold leaned over, returning an exaggerated wink.

"Hey you two," Julian complained, "I'm feeling neglected, why is nobody winking at me?"

~~~

The following Tuesday afternoon the first match was won by the Royal Corps of Transport who struggled but eventually beat the Hawks, the 103 MU 'B' team.

The spectators who gathered as always when the celebrated team from the tiny Maintenance Unit were on show licked their lips in anticipation. The next encounter was the mouth watering clash between the unbeaten champions and the team who openly boasted they were about to remove the crown from the badge on the MU crest.

Bernard Kowaleski kept his team apart from the rest of the competitors. They looked smart clad in light blue shirts and dark blue shorts but the opposition didn't have to be too far away to see he was ominously warning his men. "If we lose today, not one of you will have a moments respite from my attentions. I will haunt you for the rest of your time on this island. You cannot lose, you are fitter than they are, stronger than they are, you are better than they are! Believe that for it is true!"

Harold watched the coach's dark features as he glowered from face to face, punching his fist into his palm. Old Skee was angry yet there was no reason for his anger. In the Workshops when the Chief went on his daily rounds he was a normal

445

rational man going about his daily duties. There was no doubt he was recognised as a hard no nonsense boss but he was fair and carried the respect of everyone around him, including his superiors. On the sports field he was transmogrified.

But today as the teams took to the field he was at his worst! Why? His intense hate puzzled Harold, it darkened his features, his whole attitude was ultra aggressive and Harold who would normally never back down on eye to eye contact with any man, looked away when Bernard stopped in front of him. "Ross, I struck you once, accidentally, it will not be accidental today if I feel you're not giving your all. You will die for me on that rope today - won't you Ross?"

"Chief," Harold muttered.

"Was that a 'Yes' Ross? Look at me man!"

"Yes, Chief," Harold turned his head and peered under the hooded black brows. Slivers of fear streaked across Harold's consciousness as he saw two dancing bleeps deep in the depths of the black eyes. "Yes it was, Chief." He found himself repeating.

Three short blasts of a whistle interrupted Bernard. "Good!" he said then about to turn away, he lowered his voice and muttered, "I need your strength in this match Ross. If we don't win today, it will not be you that will die, it will be me!"

Harold stared after the coach, 'Jesus, what a character. One minute you want the bastard to drop dead, then he says something like that and you'd jump into a bottomless pit for him.'

The umpire, a Royal Corp of Transport sergeant, tossed for ends. The MU coach called correctly. "That's all you'll win today corporal," Bernard said pleasantly retrieving the umpire's coin from where it had fallen.

Callum ignored him and went to his chosen end. The teams were nervous and it showed. On taking the strain the rope markers wandered back and forth before some firm words from the umpire settled them.

"PULL!" the official bent his knees and dropped his upraised arms in a physical effort to inject emphasis into his call. There was no lateral movement on the rope but it did drop from the horizontal of four feet above the ground to one foot. There was an 'Oooh' from the spectators as the sixteen men, a mirror reflection of eight athletes on each end of the rope, steadied into position.

It was stalemate. For the first time in many a pull, Frank felt the other end of the rope was tied to a tree it was so solid. He settled down, it was nothing new to feel strong opposition. It was just going to take a little longer to beat them.

"How do they feel?" Callum asked after a motionless three minutes.

"Solid, don't do anything," answered Frank. His experience had evolved to such an extent he could tell precisely how a team was feeling or reacting at the other end of the rope. He could tell when someone took a new foothold, or weakening or struggling. The rope was a live transferral link to the opposition for the No.3 man.

"That's four minutes Frank," It was normal for something to start happening around that time. "Anything?"

"Solid Cal, hold steady," Frank muttered. He was beginning to feel the pressure and as such it was difficult to talk. Against a training bucket, the team could hold it suspended for nine, even ten minutes, but holding time was drastically cut when pressure was applied.

Callum was pacing up and down his team now. He was seeing definite creaking signs. Robbie Stone the No.1 had dropped his head between his straight arms and Callum could see bared teeth from others in flagging effort. "Frank, it's five minutes son, anything yet?"

Frank had not yet reached the end of his tether but his stamina reserves were being tapped. Callum just managed to hear the muted whisper "Solid Cal, swear to God!"

The MU coach sucked in air. If Frank Connolly was weakening, the rest of his team were not too good. He went to each man getting as near as he could without touching them.

"They're feelin' it worse than you lads, just a wee bit longer, hold on!"

Ray even in the face of dire exhaustion managed to hiss, "If they're feeling worse than me they must be fucking masochists!"

Callum hurried back to the No.3 position, "Frank?"

"They're feelin' us but you've no choice, our lot are crackin'. You'll have to try them!"

"Okay lads, stalemate's over, give us some pressure, wind it

447

on!"

Callum went along the line. His team might be cracking as Frank said but they were not showing it now! The rope came a foot. Not enough to take a new foothold but suddenly the hard won foot was lost, this was followed by another ... and another! Suddenly his men were struggling.

The MU were forced to take new footholds and hauled a foot back but this too eased away from them. Frank knew the GEF team had the edge, only the smallest ounce but that tiny weight was making the difference between the two finely balanced teams. There was nothing Callum, or Frank or the team could do. The marker came perilously close, abruptly the whistle blew and the crowd applauded.

"Shit and corruption, that was over seven minutes!" Callum exclaimed. He looked down the rope. Some of the GEF men were on the ground, others staggering around as Chief Kowaleski pummelled their backs. Callum shook his head, was Skee actually showing emotion?

The teams changed ends walking on unsteady legs, shaking their feet and flexing stiff hands, forcing blood into tired muscles. "Get into them right away," Callum whispered tersely. "Don't let them settle this time, hit them with the old fast drop!" He urged his men as the umpire called the commands.

"PULL!" The MU dropped a shade faster and were immediately straightening their backs taking rope, nibbling the ground, digging in their heels five or six inches at a time, inching back quickly until back in the crouched position. Straightening up, nibbling back repeated again and again. GEF team were stumbling, unbalanced, and not allowed the time to take good position. The blessed whistle blew. Callum looked at his watch, "That's more like it," he shouted, "thirty seconds! Well done lads, well done. Now let's get this third end and stop this messin' around." Callum was shouting for a reason, he wanted the demoralised GEF team to hear.

Bernard was talking animatedly to the rear end members of his team when the order came to change ends. There was no good natured jibes or threats this time as the teams silently crossed.

The MU again caught their opponents with a fast drop and straightening backs, chopping heels reeled in rope against more stern resistance. They took seven hard fought feet and although it was heavy going, their pressure was inexorable. Callum looked at the markers; eight feet, nine, ten, eleven feet, one last supreme effort and the MU hauled the GEF rope marker into line with that of their ground line. The umpire raised his whistle. Screaming hoarse shouts were spewing from the dark tall coach and the official paused. The marker had stopped.

Callum was doing everything but grip the rope as he tried to force his eight straining men to pull the marker over the line.

"C'mon lads, an inch, one fuckin' inch that's all!" He glanced at the marker for the hundredth time, "They're in line, half an inch, one good effort! Altogether now ... HEAVE!"

The marker was frozen. The umpire stared hard at the white rope marker to his extreme right. It aligned perfectly with the first ground line to his extreme left. He lowered his whistle and glanced at the team who were fighting to the last. Their coach was a man demented, yelling and threatening, punching his fist and roaring into the faces of his men. It may not be the recognised method of extracting the last ounce of energy but it was working. Somehow the light blues that were so close to losing were miraculously holding. And in good positions. The MU were throwing everything, trying to drag the marker over, but it stayed obstinately in line.

Callum steadied his team. They were growing erratic and disjointed in their frantic efforts. "Settle down, wait, wait, steady up, we've got this won just gather yourselves."

Incredibly, as he spoke he saw Frank and the others start to bend forward. The rope was creeping back. "HOLD IT!" The frenzied shout engendered enough strength to stop any more movement. Callum sighed heavily, "Shit, now I know what it must be like to pull against us. These bastards won't admit defeat."

All was maddeningly static for another two minutes. Sixteen men appeared beaten and lifeless but as soon as any movement threatened they stirred and grew firm, heads lifted and painful eyes searched.

Callum felt as drained as any one of his exhausted men and began to wonder if either team would have enough strength to drag the other over the line. He glanced at the man who injected this new life into a team that had always been troublesome but never the same class as the MU.

Chief Tech. Bernard Kowaleski or 'Skee,' was unaware how he must appear to spectators. He was on his toes, a maestro conducting an orchestra, waving his batonless right arm in sweeping circles, hips rolling, swaying to music only he could hear.

For a brief moment in one of those sweeping scything movements, Callum thought he saw the men cringing under that arm, actually respond! He glanced at Frank. His No.3 was bending forward again at the waist. "Fuck sake Frank, hang on man, another few seconds."

Frank could not answer; he could only roll his head from left to right. Every ounce he could muster was going into resisting. One foot of ground was lost agonisingly slowly, then two, then three, four, all the grinding way back to the starting point where at last the MU dogged resistance halted all movement with a 'Jump' call from Callum. The end was well into its fifth minute. At that point eight healthy schoolgirls could have pulled either of the teams over the line. All pockets of resistance were now empty as the men gathered their last granules of strength but it was the hungrier of the two groups who were finding the bigger grains. The screaming, raging coach was squeezing the life out of his team but they were starting to respond. For the first time in this monumental end the red MU marker passed over the central line into the GEF half. Six minutes and the reserves of both teams were gone. Seven minutes and the GEF team, because they had the momentum, if the slow creeping of the rope could be called momentum, pulled the MU marker over the third ground line.

The whistle blew and sixteen men fell into lifeless heaps. Bernard Kowaleski somehow had the strength to leap in the air then turned to the vanquished blue and white hooped team. With both hands he gave hard upward thrusted V-signs, repeating the action again and again.

The RCT sergeant strode across to Bernard. "Coach, you will stop that immediately. Your actions are uncalled for and vulgar. Persist and I will have no hesitation in disqualifying you."

"No you won't Sergeant, you cannot take away something I have waited years to achieve. I show only pent up emotion and no words you say can bitter the pill of sweetness I feel at this moment. I have beaten 103 Maintenance Unit fair and square Sergeant, FAIR AND SQUARE!" He roared the last words. "Allow me to savour the moment I have dreamed about." Bernard paused then said proudly, "You may if you so wish report my actions Sergeant, That is your prerogative. I am Chief Technician Bernard Cornelius Kowaleski."

"I can understand your elation Chief," said a surprisingly abashed umpire, "but please, I'm asking you to consider the ladies watching, tone down your actions. Oh and eh, congratulations, apart from beating the MU that match in my book must rate as some sort of a record."

Callum watched Chief Kowaleski and the umpire talking. Although brisling at the V-sign insult, he decided to demonstrate his team could, even in defeat, perform as true champions.

"Congratulations Chief, your team performed brilliantly." Callum held out a hand.

Ignoring the outstretched hand Bernard sneered, "I told you didn't I? This is only the beginning corporal. We have broken you now and like a tamed stallion you will dance to the new master's tune in future." The sneer turned into a wide grin.

Callum controlled himself; he felt his fist curl into a ball as the grinning face leered. With an effort he turned to the umpire who was staring somewhat bewildered at the GEF coach, "Thank you Sergeant, I'm Corporal McAlpine, That must be among the longest ends you have ever officiated?"

The umpire dragged his eyes from an obviously very bitter man and focused on the red haired young man who addressed him with a soft Scottish accent. "Corporal, I seem to be caught in the middle of a rather malignant situation here. I'm appalled to see such bitter feelings should arise in what is after all, only a low key sporting contest. As for the length of each end, yes, it is certainly the longest match I have ever been associated with. That is taking part, officiating or even watching! Your team lost nothing in defeat, they performed magnificently."

"Not magnificently enough!" Bernard growled before stomping over to his team.

"Most unusual," the sergeant watched the departing rigid figure, "Is he always like this?"

"This is one of his good days Sarge, you should see him when

451

he gets beat!" Callum was thinking about Harry Ross back in the November.

"No I wouldn't. I did hear a coach clouted one of his men in Dhekelia, same man?"

Callum nodded, "There was talk about him being reported but it never came to anything."

"Well he struck no one today, that must be an improvement, excuse me corporal."

They shook hands and Callum went to his team who were showing some signs of returning to the land of the living. "Well done lads," he called, "they only just shaded us. Just shows we're only human after all and as we all knew, it had to come sooner or later. Now then there's nobody here seen us beaten before so let's show them we are as gallant in defeat as we are in winning. Walk up the rope and shake their hands."

Groans and mutterings met Callum's words as seven men struggled to their feet. Robbie Stone the No.1 made no effort to rise. Callum crouched beside him, "You OK Robbie?"

"Sorry Cal, It was me that let the team down," Robbie said dejectedly.

"Don't talk fuckin' daft man, nobody let the team down. We were fuckin' great! We could never have lasted as long as we did if there was a weak link. I won't have talk like that!"

Stone looked up at Callum then looked away, "My missus has been in the U.K. for three weeks now. Her mother died so she went home to organise the funeral an' sort out what needed sorting out."

"So?"

"So I've been looking after myself, eating all sorts of shit and drinking more than normal. Over the weekend one of the girls who lives up the road came in to cook me a decent meal and..."

"Don't want to hear any more. They were the better team on the day Robbie, that's all there is to it. Get yourself fit for the return match wi' them in six or seven weeks I'll need you fit for that one. Now c'mon, they're waitin' for you to lead them down the rope!" Whatever it was that happened with Stone was a one off. It was typical of Callum not to allow the burden of defeat to rest on the shoulders of one man.

There were lots of 'Well dones' and 'Congratulations' from the vanquished to the victors but Bernard stood back disassociating himself from the mingling teams. After a few minutes the GEF coach called, "My team, my winning team, pay attention. To celebrate our easy victory, I want you all in the Peninsula Club tonight. Bring your wives, girlfriends and your bits on the side if you like. We'll have a party, drinks are on me!"

Derisive laughs from the MU team and support greeted the words. The man was determined to demonstrate his hate for the Unit. Since the Peninsula Club opened, the lounge bar was the traditional celebratory stomping ground of 103 MU.

Callum removed his team from the celebrating winners and waited for them to settle down. "Can I have your attention please," he called. Signs of frustration, staring into the distance and plucking grass shoots were the only movement as heads turned to their coach.

"We have another crack at them in the return match you know," Callum opened, "in a month or two, so don't look so despondent. We only lost 2-1, so they lead us by a single point!" Some faces were showing more interest, He went on, "All we have to do is beat them 2-0, and we still win the league, assumin' of course nobody else beats us in the meantime."

"That'll be easy then, ha, just beat them two nowt!"

Callum let the jibe slide away. He had to build their spirits up.

"It won't be easy, I know that! But when has it ever been easy for us? That's what we thrive on, isn't it? The fact everybody's after us, that's what makes us a wee bit sharper, more competitive! But we will do it! The MUs. been beaten before, we're no' supermen, but it's our first defeat as a team! The last time the MU suffered a defeat, we come back stronger, we haven't lost since, in two and a half years! So don't worry about today's result. It was long overdue and better we lose in a league match than a knock out competition. Don't you lot see? This way we can get back at them, and when we beat them in the return match it will taste, believe me, that much sweeter." Callum swept his eyes over the faces and most were returning to normality. "Now that we have that out of the way, I don't want this man to think he has beaten us out of our social circle with that result so, all of you, I want to see every one 'in the Peninsula Club tonight!'" He tried in his last few words to mimic Chief

Kowaleski before going on, "If this bastard thinks he's goin' to beat us psychologically as well as physically, he doesn't know what we're made of." Reverting back to his poor impersonation Callum went on, "And I want you there with your wives and girlfriends, we'll have a party!" He nodded his head vigorously, "But that is where the miming ends folks, I am but a poor corporal, you buy your own drinks!"

Later that evening Callum and Josh crossed the veranda and approached the old Skoda the latter had bought a year ago from a UK bound airman. He had paid the princely sum of £35 for this truly magnificent machine. Magnificent only in the sense that it was still running. The Skoda had actually been bought new by a sergeant in 1950, but deciding against taking the car back to Britain at the end of his tour, the sergeant sold it to another airman. This was to be the repeated pattern of the car's life; when the current owner reached the end of his tour, the Skoda was sold on and on, until eventually Josh acquired it. It had seen lot's of service and more airmen had serviced its working parts and been in and out of its interior than customers in the entire entourage in the working life of a 50 year old prostitute.

Like the prostitute, spare parts were largely unavailable for the model and very little under the bonnet was original. Engine spares, pipes, clamps, nuts and bolts had been pirated and modified to fit, and any part that refused to fit or screw together in the recognised manner was simply welded or bonded. It was a simple arrangement that worked and when a welded seam cracked or a glued part split, they were simply re-welded or glue renewed. The amazing thing was the car ran - after a fashion - and could lick along at a fair speed when Josh felt so inclined to give the old biddy its head. It would never win a London to Brighton rally but got Josh and his passengers from point A to point B - eventually.

"Jesus, Josh," Callum said, trying to settle in the front of the old car. He was squirming awkwardly hoping to find a position without doing himself an injury among the lumps and broken springs. "You better not get Carol sittin' on this," he shifted from one lump to another, "If she takes a fancy to one of these bumps you'll never get her out of the fuckin' car!"

They were on their way to the WAAF block to pick up Carol before going on to the Peninsula Club. Josh had lain in the bath for an hour trying to ease the agony from his muscles and bones. He suffered every known pain and torture in the match and although the hot water had eased him, he felt drained and not particularly looking forward to the night ahead. Carol had asked Josh if she could organise a blind date, to make up a foursome for the evening but he had declined gracefully - she was determined to fix Callum's best friend the 'uninterested in women' Josh with a girl.

Carol, in contrast to Josh's feelings, was looking as fresh as a daisy when the car shuddered to a halt almost beside her. Dressed in a white blouse with a dark tartan mini skirt, which she had tailor made to please Callum. It did the trick. When he first saw her as they swept majestically round the bend, his face broke into a wide smile, "What a woman Josh eh? I swear I might just be beginnin' to go under wi that wee bitch," was his very colloquial accolade as he ran his eyes over her petite but perfect figure.

"I thought it was a bloody tractor coming down the road," Carol complained climbing into the back seat before smirking at Callum then Josh in the cracked driving mirror.

"Aye, the Rolls is being serviced madam, which is more than you'll get if you don't stop complainin'," said Callum grinning as he turned reaching out to squeeze her knee. "I was gonna be the gentleman an' get in the back with you, but I don't want to shock the driver here, You look good enough to eat lass." He ran his eyes over her again, then, "Jesus wept Carol, how many times have I told you? Wear a bloody bra' when we go out. I don't mind the blokes lookin' at ye but draw the line at them seein' you half naked!"

"You love it," Carol taunted, pushing her breasts up. "What do you think Josh?"

"You want me to drive off the road?" Josh countered keeping his eyes firmly ahead.

The good natured banter went on throughout the short drive to the Peninsula Club. It ended when Carol said "Don't park too near the door Josh, I don't want anyone to see me getting out of this heap."

"Right that's it! You're walking home tonight." Josh tried to sound affronted.

"Promises, promises!" she laughed.

455

The car park was packed. Callum noticed Chief Kowaleski's white Hillman Minx near the entrance. 'The arse hole must've got here early,' he thought climbing the stairs of the club. Callum caught his friend's arm, "Josh, I don't want to get involved wi' that madman tonight. If you see a situation developin', for God's sake nip it in the bud, will you? I know it's a lot to ask but he gets right up my ..."

"I'll try, but I can't do it on my own, you'll have to listen to me, I mean, really listen!"

"You're not on your own Josh," Carol cut in, "I swear if that clown starts anything I promise I'll ... I'll kick him in the goolies."

"Charmin'," Callum shook his head as the couple followed Josh into the main lounge.

Josh stopped suddenly causing Callum to bump into him. "What ..." he said then followed Josh's gaze. He was staring at Chief Kowaleski in what could only be described as disbelief.

Every seat and table around the GEF coach was occupied. He was seated in the hallowed MU corner holding court like a prophet among his disciples. Annoying Callum thought but not entirely unexpected. He looked again at Josh whose face still registered something more than shock. His troubled frown was deep. This reaction was away beyond the depth of surprise to what was going on.

"Josh, we expected him to be sittin' in our corner, it's part o' the bastard's game. Don't let him see you're upset." Callum warned the frozen figure.

"Eh? What? Oh sorry," Josh blinked but still he stared towards Bernard Kowaleski.

Callum glanced curiously at Carol, "And you thought it was me that was about to get into trouble," he gave a light nod towards Josh then ran his eyes over the crowd. Because the room was fairly busy his group of around forty were merging round the extremes of the noisy GEF crowd. "That's our lot over there Josh," he said.

Josh dragged his eyes away, looked with what was almost a glare at Callum and Carol then blinked, glanced back at the boisterous GEF party, with frown firmly in place, walked quickly towards the relatively quiet MU group.

The abandoned couple exchanged further puzzled looks then followed Josh who found a table quickly and sat down. "Aye right, you've got us guessin' Josh, what is it?" Callum asked.

There was no doubt Josh was troubled. Frowning and blinking rapidly, as if trying to focus.

"Josh?"

"I'm not sure but I think I've just seen a ghost from the past!" The words were barely audible.

"A ghost?" echoed Carol, a smile playing round the her mouth and eyes. "Oh tell me more."

Ignoring her Josh spoke to Callum, "Remember a long time ago Cal, when we first met, you asked me if I was married? I told you, truthfully, I was not."

"Aye, I remember."

"You and lots of others thought I was queer because I never showed an interest in females. Well I was at one time, interested in a girl I mean. I was at Kirkcross for five months on a General Fitters course, that's where I first met Kowaleski. He was my instructor and a nicer bloke you could never hope to meet. He was quiet, didn't mix but a helluva good tutor. Anyway on my first visit to the village, I met a girl and we hit it off, right away, soon as we saw each other. We started going out, at first it was only one or two nights a week, then it was three or four until eventually we had to see each other every night ... but nothing happened!" Josh looked from Callum to Carol, then back to the Scot, "Not at first anyway."

"Oh!" Callum said quietly, nodding his head.

"What?" Carol looked at the face of the suddenly dour Scot then at Josh, "What Josh? Did I miss something? For Christ sake!" she said in frustration.

"Carol!" Callum reprimanded harshly.

"We were both rookies at the game," Josh carried on only dimly aware of Carol's impatience and Callum's rebuke. "I wanted her, God knows I wanted her but I didn't mean to, didn't want to ... make her pregnant. But that's what happened!" He sighed glancing again towards the singing GEF crowd and Kowaleski.

"It was the first time she had ever done it, and my previous grand total was one or two fumbles in the dark. We were both so immature. She told me a week before I finished the course she

457

was pregnant. It was like being hit with a ton of bricks. I felt cheated ... trapped? I don't know, but I was certainly confused. I took the only way out. The coward's way. I told her I'd write when I got settled in my next camp and we could get married, all that crap, anything just to get away to think it all out. Then I listened to other older, so called wiser blokes after that, experienced men who were supposed to know better than me, ha! Anyway, I listened and allowed the 'out of sight' thing to kick in, you know, until I fooled myself into thinking she was 'out of mind.' But every day that passed I grew more guilty and angry at myself. The time gap widened and with each day I found it more difficult to contact her, until it became impossible."

"You should have written to her," Carol said sadly.

"You don't know how many times I said those words, Carol."

"You're not helpin'," Callum reprimanded his girl friend a second time. "He feels guilty enough, can you no' see that?"

Carol mouthed an 'Oh,' then leaned over and took Josh's hand.

"I'm sorry Josh, you've gone all white, as white as that ghost you were talking about. And what about that 'ghost' Josh?"

"She's here!" Josh said simply.

"What, here," Carol gasped in surprise, "in the club?" The irrepressible girl tittered, "I don't mean that club, not again!" She had to place a hand over her mouth to stifle her giggles.

"Carol, shut up you cold hearted bitch!" Callum hissed, then to Josh, "She's in here, now?"

Josh nodded and Callum suddenly dreaded the answer, recalling the direction Josh had been staring. "Where, where is she sittin'?"

"Over there. Her name is Yvonne Preston, or it was Preston. She's sitting with the renowned clown prince himself, so," he paused, "I suppose it's Mrs. Yvonne Kowaleski now."

Carol was craning round to catch a glimpse of the young woman sitting on Bernard's right. "Oh, she's a pretty little thing Josh, she ..."

"Christ almighty Carol, you'll be standin' on the table next, wavin' your arms about. Behave yourself!" said an agitated Callum.

"I'm not doing any harm, they're not even looking this way," Carol responded, tiring of so many scoldings.

"Makes no difference. If that nutcase catches you looking God only knows what he'll make of it." Turning back to Josh, Callum went on, "So what do we do, are you gonna hide here all night or slink away?" For the first time since they met, Callum had never seen Josh so bewildered. Callum did not wait for an answer to his question. "Tell you what, just play it by ear and see what happens. Right, we'll wait all night for a waiter, I'll get us somethin' to drink."

Callum wended his way through the crowded tables to the bar. Near the bar he detoured slightly to saunter into the midst of a rather tranquil MU crew. He ruffled a few heads of his team and the action had the desired effect. Smiles and good natured banter was hurled in the direction of the popular coach and he responded with equally spiked repartee. Within a few minutes he was encircled in guffawing uproar.

From the other side of the room Bernard watched Callum with growing hatred. Why were they in such good humour, why so many of them? Why indeed were they here at all? They had been beaten, had lost their precious record, yet the idiots were performing as if they had won!

While Bernard glowered at Callum, Yvonne watched her husband. She was thinking how he had come home earlier that evening in the highest of good spirits, raving of his win. He grabbed her and whirled her around, nearly letting her go when his knee clicked and almost buckled under him. But the cursed knee inflicted on him by the hated 103 Maintenance Unit was not going to spoil his plans tonight. She was told to get dressed up. He was taking her to meet 'His boys, his team, his champions!' Although Yvonne did not foresee a good time with the usually subdued Bernard, tonight he was in a mood, a high almost ecstatic mood she had never seen before. The invitation carried with it a visit to the classy Peninsula Club on the Akrotiri base. She had heard about the club from Pat Parrott but never expected to see the place, not with Bernard anyway! In his present frame of mind she could perhaps dig deep and reclaim the feelings she once thought were just under the surface - never love, never! But something, hopefully, possibly akin to that feeling? And having arrived here in this lavish club she was enjoying herself for the first time in months. The members of Bernard's team had her laughing and smiling so much her jaw and sides were sore. Why was he so miserable and bad tempered now? The evening was going wonderfully well until the tall and very thin red haired man appeared on the far side of the room. He had got the people over there laughing and by his very presence, was making that group come alive. When Bernard first saw the new arrival, his face darkened and his mood changed completely. Yvonne, anxious to preserve the happy atmosphere tugged at her husband's sleeve, "What's wrong Bernie?" she asked.

Bernard appeared not to hear. Yvonne was about to repeat her question when a man, sitting nearby leaned over, "That's the MU coach Yve, he and the Chief are sworn enemies."

She smiled her thanks, slightly embarrassed she could not remember the man's name. Bernie had introduced her earlier, both he and his wife, but she had met so many people, the names of Harold and Marion Ross escaped her. Determined however to gain Bernard's attention, she tugged again at his sleeve, "Bernie, I'd like a drink."

Bernard at that moment was seeking a reason to go to the bar. "A drink? Sure, what was it, a brandy, brandy lemon wasn't it, anyone else?" he asked expansively, running his eyes around the surrounding tables. One or two others called for refills and Bernard nodded agreeably. "Help me with this, will you Ross? I might need some back up here."

Harold frowned at the phraseology. What sort of 'back up' was needed to get a round of drinks? Perhaps it was innocent enough but Harold caught the glare of hate directed at Callum McAlpine. Surely this was not a repeat of the night in the car park. With little choice in the matter however, Harold resignedly followed a departing Bernard.

Yvonne leaned over to the pretty dark haired girl, "I'm sorry, I've met so many people ...."

"Marion, Marion Ross," the girl obviously understood, "and that's Harry, my lovely man."

"He certainly is!" Yvonne laughed, "Marion, it's my first time here, where are the toilets?"

The girl's face broke into her ready smile, "They're over there," she nodded to a corner beyond the now boisterous and noisy MU party. "Do you mind if I come with you?"

"Course not, I may need some 'back up,'" Yvonne rolled her eyes as she mimicked her husband. "If we are to fight our way through the screaming hordes of those terrible Maintenance Unit heathens, I think it best we attack in numbers."

"They should be so lucky!" Marion said mischievously.

At the bar Bernard tapped Callum on the shoulder. "Piss off Chief!" was the latter's comment on turning, "We're here for a quiet drink and I don't want to get involved wi' the likes o' you!"

"Why so bitter McAlpine, as today's victors, I was hoping to buy your group a drink!"

"Buy us a drink?" Callum laughed, "does this mean when we meet in future, the winners buy the losers a drink, are you tryin' to set a precedent?"

"Why not? I would be happy to go along with that." answered a grinning Bernard.

"Listen Chief Kowaleski, if I were to agree to that I'd need to take out a bank loan for I'd be buyin' your lot drinks for the rest of my time on the island. And another thing, I'm a Scot and we Scots have some funny traditions. One of them is that we have never been known to refuse a drink, especially when it's free. Some of us have been known to take a drink from our worst enemies, even from the devil himself. I myself have lowered my standards in the past and admit to have once accepted a drink from a sworn enemy. In truth and to my knowledge, I have never met the devil face to face so I cannot say wi' any degree of certainty that I would refuse a drink from him. Which brings me to my belaboured point Chief Tech Kowaleski, I'm about to break an old Scottish tradition here and have millions of dead Scots writhin' in their graves. I might accept a drink from my worst enemy, even from the devil himself - but you?" Callum shook his head, "I hope I never sink that low. No thanks, I don't want your fuckin' drink, fuck off!"

Harold listening to the conversation acted quickly. He stepped between the pair and faced a glowering Bernard. "Let's get the drinks Chief. Listen to me, we don't want trouble in here!" Harold could see the coals glowing deep in the older man's eyes, "Fuck sake, listen to me! The barman can phone the guardroom and snowdrops will be all over this place in seconds. They're only round the corner for Christ sake!"

The derogative name for the white capped RAF police poured coolant over Bernard's burning hot coals. He reluctantly settled back on his heels, "It's a pity the Maintenance Unit cannot take their defeat like gentlemen," he called loudly, which brought an eruption of jeering from the nearby tables.

Callum wrapped both hands round his drinks and lifted them. Before walking away he pushed his face towards Bernard, "I don't know what your deep rooted problem with us is Chief but it's sick whatever it is. So you won a match today, so what! You'll have to beat us again to win the league, you know that don't you?" He stared unflinchingly into the smouldering black eyes.

"Let it go Callum, leave it," Harold appealed in a soothing tone.

"Aye, okay Harry, but in future be careful where and when you let that thing off its leash."

Both groups heaved a sigh of relief when Callum turned and walked back to his table.

Yvonne and Marion reached the toilets but had paused at the door watching the events at the bar. When the man with the golden red hair turned away, both girls raised their eyebrows at each other in relief. Once inside the sanctuary of the toilets Yvonne said, "It's a good thing Harry went with him Marion, he got between them just in time."

"Yes, Harry's quietened down a lot." Marion replied proudly, "He's the one who used to swing first then ask questions later."

First to complete her toilet Marion sat at the dressing table repairing what little damage to the tiny amount of make-up she wore. Yvonne emerged from her cubicle cursing, "Damn!" she muttered at the wash hand basin. "What a time to come on. That's my little friend come to pay his monthly visit!"

"Oh," Marion blinked, "are you all right?"

"Yes, yes. I knew I was about due so I came prepared." Yvonne held up her handbag.

"Oh thank goodness for I couldn't have helped you. I won't need anything like that for a few months yet." Marion said dropping a lipstick tube into her bag.

Yvonne stared at Marion's stomach, "You're pregnant?"

Marion nodded and smiled, "Yes, I'm due in July."

"But that's only four months away, where are you hiding it?"

Yvonne exclaimed.

"Oh he's here all right," Marion said happily patting her abdomen.

Yvonne tried to recall her own plump image at five months. She was convinced she was massive, then again, perhaps it was her guilty conscience that made her imagine she was big. "Are you pleased, I mean are you happy about being pregnant?"

"Oh yes, Yvonne," Marion gazed down at her midriff, "I can't wait for him to arrive. We're both so excited and it's made Harry change, he's so domesticated now I can't believe it!" she giggled happily.

"You've decided it's a 'he,' then, you've placed your order, have you?" laughed Yvonne.

"He has to be, no doubt about that at all!" Marion answered firmly as they left the toilets.

The fickle finger of Fate was about to interfere at this point, poking itself painfully into the future of the girls. Had they exited the Ladies a minute before or after the time they actually did, chances are both their lives could have taken so vastly different routes.

Marion was carefully picking her way between tables and chairs when she overheard a young airman, talking loudly through drink. The sullen, dark featured man was in fact giving a very good impression of being drunk, but Senior Aircraftsman Jimmy Walsh may have swallowed a few whiskies but was a long way from being inebriated.

Walsh had waited a long time to get back at 'Strong Arm Harry fucking Ross.' The opportunity had presented itself when he heard the two top tug-of-war parties were meeting in the Peninsula Club that night. An event that promised a little action. And as his old friend Harry Ross was a member of one of the teams there was just the possibility a chance might pop up where he could get back at the big stud. Jimmy's hackles had never really settled after the night on cinema Fire Picket duty. He had actually caught Ross with his pants down screwing that Cookie wench in the women's toilet. And he, not known for doing favours for anyone, had gone to the trouble of warning the big bastard about the cow's boyfriend. What did he get for his good deed? Jimmy had received a back handed battering! Well now was comeuppance time Harry my boy! Walsh had seen Ross sitting with a beautiful dark haired girl in the GEF group. He made inquiries and discovered the lady was indeed Mrs. Ross. Harry my boy, revenge is sweet, here is where you get yours!

Walsh watched as the two women stepped carefully between the crowded tables, retracing the path they had taken as the despicable young man had hoped they would. Mrs. Ross, the dark girl was leading the way. Just as she reached the table where Walsh and his friends were sitting, some twenty feet away Carol Cook, in all innocence, added her own poison to the dart that was to embed itself in Marion's heart.

The tartan skirt had ridden up Carol's thighs and now resembled a broad belt across her hips Normally she would have ignored this, for a while anyway enjoying the open stares and covert glances her shapely legs and tight bottom usually received. Tonight however as Fate sharpened her finger nail, Callum brusquely told his girl friend to 'stop showin' off tomorrow's washin'.'

Carol reluctantly obeyed but made the most of it. She stood up and wiggled her hips, in the process tugging the tight wayward skirt back into place. Just as Carol stood up, Jimmy timed his dart to perfection.

"That's Carol Cook, just look at her the randy bitch! She's flashing big Harry Ross! He's been knocking the arse offa that little blonde tart for years, the lucky bastard!"

Marion stopped as if she had walked into a stone wall. Over two years ago Harry had called her by that name in a drunken love making stupor, 'Carol, Carol, Oh Carol.' The words jangled painfully in her head. Almost guiltily she followed the direction in which the grinning speaker was gazing.

A young blonde girl was in the process of sliding her hands voluptuously over her bottom before sitting down, keeping her errant skirt in place as best she could. Oh dear God, she was so sexy. And gorgeous! Marion could not help but stare and felt a lump grow in her throat.

Yvonne nearly bumped into her friend who had stopped then Marion's hand rose to cover her mouth and throat.

"Marion ... are you all right? Marion?"

Blinking, breathless trying to keep her vision clear, Marion could not answer. Her eyes were somehow locked on the beautiful girl sitting between the MU coach and another man.

464

Yvonne shook the rigid figure gently, "Marion?" she cried softly, feeling the first flutters of panic. Then unsure of her next move, Yvonne abstractly followed Marion's intent stare. A blonde girl turned her head slightly and looked directly into Yvonne's eyes. A look of sombre surprise quickly replaced the laughing smile on the pretty face. The blonde girl turned away, almost guiltily. Then the guilt melted, replaced with despondency as she looked at the man on her left. Yvonne wondered mildly why this girl reacted the way she did, for Yvonne certainly did not know her. She followed the direction the girl was looking.

Yvonne lurched and reached out, grabbing the nearest person on her left. Her eyes did not wander however, they were locked into the flaky brown eyes of Josh Munroe!

"Josh?" she muttered in amazement. "Josh!" this time her voice shook with incredibility. She did not know she was falling but her knees had given way and though clasping someone with her left hand it was not enough to keep her upright. With her right hand she hastily grabbed Marion's sleeve and staggered in the effort to stay on her feet.

With the sudden grasping grip on her arm Marion tore her gaze away from the blonde girl faced as she was with this new crisis. "Yvonne, what's wrong? Oh Yvonne don't faint on me," wailed Marion seeing the glassy sheen in her friend's eyes.

The man on her left took a firm grip of Yvonne's elbow and stopped her falling. Grateful for the assistance for she could not hope to keep Yvonne on her feet by herself. She grasped the hand that was clinging to her sleeve. "Yvonne, oh, talk to me, Yvonne please."

Yvonne fluttered her eyes, trying desperately to clear this damned fuzziness. "Yes yes," she uttered and turned to the fair haired young man supporting her. "I'm fine now, thank you."

Marion momentarily had forgotten her own dilemma in the face of Yvonne's plight. "Gee, Yvonne," seeing her friend had recovered slightly, "you know I'm the one who is pregnant, I'm the one who's supposed to faint. What happened?"

"I don't know," lied Yvonne, not daring to look in the direction to where Josh was sitting.

"What's going on here?" a concerned male voice asked. It was Harold and behind him bulldozing his way through was Bernard Kowaleski. "You all right?" asked Harold, then "What's going on?" he added looking around, wondering why the girls had stopped and both seemed in some distress.

Marion was looking at Harold with a frowning questioning look then her eyes slid away to her left seeking something. Harold at a loss, followed her look and saw the blonde head of Carol Cook turn quickly and guiltily away. He felt his stomach drop.

"Do you know that girl?" Marion asked simply.

"What girl?" Harold was desperately trying to think.

"That blonde girl, that very pretty blonde girl who is doing her best to ignore us, do you know her? I believe her name is Carol. Is that the girl from your Orderly Room, the one you dreamed about?" Marion referred to the girl Harold had indeed dreamed up to get him out of the dreadful situation he dropped himself in at the Kyrenia hotel. Marion's face was sad, her voice low as she looked up at him, waiting.

"No!" he said stiffly, then in direct contrast, he said hesitantly, "I don't know that girl."

Marion continued to look at him. Harold took her arm and led her firmly back to their table for once completely nonplussed as to what to do or what to say.

While the Ross's were talking, Bernard pushed past the couple to where a fair haired man was supporting Yvonne. "I don't think she's quite steady on her feet Chief, I'm loathe to let her go."

Bernard recognized the man. He was Julian Cantwell, the MU so called Utility man. "She'll be all right now, thank you." Bernard reached to take Yvonne's arm, the same arm Julian was holding when their hands touched. In less than a second Bernard looked into Julian's clear blue eyes and took in the wonderfully effeminate features at close range. Julian unashamedly returned the look, staring openly into the black depths under those jet eyebrows. Bernard under the hypnotic gaze, momentarily lost in spinning images, had to resist a sudden but burning impulse to reach forward, over the few inches separating them and kiss those soft lips.

"I'm all right," Yvonne said, catching a glimpse of the two men, sensing something. She tugged free from the young man noting as she did so, his soft handsome features. 'Oh dear God!' she thought inwardly.

Bernard took her arm, in so doing placed his hand over Julian's upper arm and gave it an intense squeeze. "Thank you, thank you very much," he said, trying to impart a thousand messages into those senseless empty words. Reluctantly he led Yvonne back to their group.

Yvonne sat down and took a gulp from her drink. She noticed Marion sitting on the edge of her seat. She too was looking bemused and for a moment her own confusing situation was forgotten. "Marion," she said. Her friend looked up slowly, "What's up, it's not the baby is it?"

Her question was greeted with a warm smile that somehow did not light the room as it had done earlier. A slow shake of the head, "No, I'm fine, but I thought you were about to faint."

"I may have blacked out for a second or two, and would've fallen if that quite gorgeous looking bloke hadn't caught my arm. Bernie knows him," she turned to Bernie, "don't you?"

"Yes," he answered guardedly, "from an incident that happened in Dhekelia. Funny he came to my assistance that day too. Julian something or other, the 103 Utility man."

"Julian?" echoed Marion, recalling the moment when Yvonne was about to faint and she caught a glimpse of Julian supporting Yvonne. In the confusion she had forgotten. "Yes of course it was Julian! That beautiful young man is Julian Cantwell, a really decent bloke. He stays weekends at the Connollys and sometimes comes with them to eat with us." Marion intentionally used the word 'beautiful' to describe Julian, it fitted him so well. What did not occur to her was she never used that word to describe any other man. The welcome diversion caused by the mention of Julian's name was only temporary however. Her mind could not wipe out the comment she had so sickeningly overheard. Harold had not uttered a word since bringing her back to the table. He looked shaken.

Marion quickly glanced towards the table where the MU coach was seated. Perhaps hoping the blonde girl had been an apparition, a figment of a pregnant women's imagination. But infantile optimism and longing did not work in the real world. The blonde head stood out like a fire beacon. Even at that precise moment the fickle finger twisted in the wound in the young girl's soul, by allowing Carol to turn her head and look directly into Marion's eyes. Neither one nor the other could tear their locked gaze away with the look on the English girl's face a written page. All Marion had to do was read. It was full of remorse, apologies and guilt.

"I want to go home!" Marion declared.

"What?" Harold said sitting forward.

Marion repeated the words in a flat monotone. Harold felt a huge rock had been dropped on his stomach. He knew what was troubling Marion and dreaded any confrontation for Carol truly was a thing of the past with him as were other women. But the charging ogre of his wanton association with the WAAF it seemed, had finally caught up with him. He leaned over and made his apologies to his coach who seemed preoccupied. Bernard merely nodded. The Ross's rose and quietly left the club.

Bernard could not get Julian out of his mind. Marion Ross had called him a 'beautiful young man'. That summed him up precisely. He had to make some plan to meet him but the bloody MU crowd surrounded Julian. He must find a way, and it had to be tonight.

The party was noisy as the drink and laughter blended the moods of the group around the Kowalskis but it no longer affected Bernard or Yvonne. She still had that block of ice sitting behind her rib cage. Her breathing felt restricted, but desperately wanted to look towards the table where Josh was sitting. If she did, would the ice block freeze the rest of her body? She shivered. Yvonne had hated every fibre of his being, cursed him every time his image crossed her mind. All the warmth and understanding they had shared, and wonderful tender love making, and the promises! Yes, he was going to get in touch with her when he got back to his base camp. At first she fooled herself thinking he had lost her address, but he knew where she lived! If not the street name and number, he knew the village, county and country! He could always catch a bus or a train. She shook her head. He had let her down, 'deserted her.' She smiled ironically at the Victorian term. And with the passing of time, it became clear he did not want her or her child. It had all been a fling for him and she had built a burning pedestal of hate with him at the top of the pyre. That effigy proved to be a worthy leaning post for her to rest on - until a few minutes ago! That oh so lovely mound of smouldering hate had all too easily been brushed aside. Her crutch had snapped and with its sudden removal she had so nearly keeled over with the strong surge of love and feelings she felt for that man.

The edges of everything around her started to merge together again, losing their definition. Too much noise and smoke. "I'm going out to the car a minute Bernie, I'm choking in here."

Bernard was preoccupied. He had seen Julian rise and make his way towards the toilets. "Huh! What?" he stammered.

"I'm going outside, some fresh air." Yvonne's voice penetrated the cacophony of merriment.

"Okay, I understand. I'll come out in a few minutes." he said abstractly, then stood up.

"Don't bother, I just want to clear my head. I'll come back when I'm ready."

The gallant Bernard did not help his wife cut a path through the happy jostling crowd, but as soon as she was on her way, he quickly went off at a tangent towards the toilets.

Across the room Josh had hardly taken his eyes off Yvonne. When she stood up and walked towards the exit, Carol, always the one for stating the obvious, leaned over, "Josh, she's leaving, get your bum into gear."

Josh ignored her, he was watching Bernard. He was not following Yvonne; Bernard was going to the toilets! "I have to talk to her," he hissed and hurriedly pushed through the crowd. At the exit he paused at the top of the stairs and scanned the car park. The slim figure was leaning against the white Hillman and suddenly he wanted to hold her. Running down the steps he slowed at the bottom, controlling his eagerness. He could not expect the best of welcomes.

Yvonne looked up as he contritely took the last steps to stop in front of her. Her right hand flashed in an arc and the resultant crack ricocheted across the car park. It stung and hurt for it was full blooded and tears sprung to his eyes. Then another blur and her left hand cracked against his right cheek. Her right hand was halfway through another swing when Josh caught her wrist. It shook her, wrenching her shoulder for every ounce of her strength had gone into the blow. She tried with her free left hand but this too was caught in a vice like grip.

Holding both wrists and blinking back tears, Josh stared into two eyes that were bewildered and angry, her lips quivering in rage. Surprising himself Josh leaned down and covered that trembling mouth with his own. He did not know what to expect with his action but was not surprised when her captive hands turned into claws. With renewed strength he only just missed losing an eye as twisting a hand free she drove her nails at his face and curled over to try and rip his strong retaining hands. She was like a lithesome cat, wriggling, turning, trying to tear free, accompanied with each effort by small whinnies of exertion. Josh naturally was much stronger and could easily hold the wild twisting woman. He was aware however, in his present position he had a weak point. She could almost at any time knee him in the groin. He would then be helpless against these talons only inches from his face. He had to defend that vulnerable area. It was not sexual, it happened in a naturally defensive action when pressing his body against hers, pinning her against the car. Nothing happened suddenly. The frantic movements of her writhing body and clawing hands slowly, very slowly grew calm and still, until he leaned against her limp body. He kissed her again, and slowly, very cautiously she kissed back until the kissing grew frantic and again her body writhed against his but with a much altered fervour.

"Oh God!" Yvonne gasped as they wrapped their arms around each other and held on tight, almost to the point of pain. "What happened," she snuffled into his neck, "why, why, why?"

He breathed in the warm, long remembered fragrance from the base of her neck. "I wanted to write, I wanted to get in touch but I was weak and the longer it went on, the weaker I got. It grew into weeks then months and fooled myself into thinking you wouldn't want me anymore."

"Want you? Mother of God, there was never a night passed I wasn't thinking of you, oh Josh!" They kissed hurriedly as if parting was threatening again but after some minutes Yvonne pushed him away and looked into his worried eyes. "Oh Josh, why didn't you at least write?"

"I swear to God Yvonne, I swear on everything that's holy, I really don't understand how it happened. I wanted to write, but I was worried, immature I suppose, a family worried me and I listened to others. Maturity doesn't come overnight and when it did I thought it was too late ...." He stared into her sad face and saw the lines of worry that had not been there four years ago.

"I thought I hated you," she whispered, returning his look.

Josh stepped slightly away from her. He took hold of her hands and paused, feeling awkward, "The baby," he paused again, "was it all right, did you ... what did you have?"

"You mean 'what did WE have?'" she countered, "I had a baby yes, what did you think I was going to have?" She was feeling defiance return after her feelings had run amok, the onslaught of emotion and, dare she admit it, was it love she felt? What else could it be - relief at having found Allan's father? No, who was she fooling? She loved this man. Her love overturned every other emotion burning inside her, above all, hate. Yet, on seeing him, only love rose to the surface.

"I don't deserve to know, the way I've treated you, but I need to know."

She wanted to keep him in pain longer but the words poured out, "His name is Allan."

"A boy! And he's all right?" Josh said, his face brightening.

"Yes, Josh, a boy. It's a damn funny name for a girl, he's just turned four, he's perfect but there's something else you should know. I married a bastard just to give your bastard a name!" It hurt to say that, to call Allan, her own son a bastard, but she was trying to hurt Josh a little more for all the pain he caused.

The smile was wiped from his face and she immediately wanted to put it back, regretting the moment her tongue had lashed out in petty spite. "Don't talk like that." Josh said simply.

"Don't talk like that!" she spat back, "Huh, where have you been for the past four, nearly five years?" She peered at him, "I married that crazy maniac to give us a home. Oh he was nice to begin with, but lately, Christ, he's begun to reveal what a really nice person he can be."

"What do you mean?"

Yvonne pulled back the hair from her forehead. "See this!" She revealed a newly healed scar. "And this, and this." pointing other scars under her ear and chin.

"Christ, Yvie," Josh shivered as a chill trickled down his backbone.

"Oh there are others a lady doesn't show strangers," she paused then added in a quiet sad voice, "but some strangers know where they are."

"What do you mean?"

471

Yvonne searched him with a look, then almost angrily said, "Josh, I'm going to tell you something but before I do, I want you to understand why. It was you who deserted me so you have no right to condemn anything I do or have done. Now if you do, you won't see me ever again. I swear, ever again!" Yvonne spoke defiantly and firmly. He nodded slowly just once.

"I am, what is termed in men's circles," she paused and looked defiant, "on the game!"

"You're what?" he croaked.

Yvonne said nothing, allowing the time to pass in stony silence. Josh was first to break it. "But why?" he choked, his head turned away near to tears.

"Josh I had no money, I've never had any money! I did it for the first time after Bernie started to beat and abuse me. I got worried about Allan ...." she stopped abruptly and as she did, looked off into the distance, then with a deep sigh went on, "He's bent Josh, he likes bums!" She paused finding it difficult. "And I was worried how long it would take him to get round to Allan."

"Christ almighty!" Josh exploded and Yvonne carried on, "Yeah! Well that's why I wanted money, needed money to send Allan home to my sister in Manchester so ..."

"You stop it now. Right now. Right fucking now!" he roared. Sucking in air like he had just surfaced from deep water. Josh, controlling himself went on, "Promise me you won't do that again, Christ I'll give you money to get Allan away from him, as much as you want but you stop that NOW! Oh Jesus!" He sobbed and pulled her roughly to him, "What have I done?"

They held each other lost in their thoughts when Yvonne whispered, "I better get back, he's bound to be looking for me. We mustn't be caught like this."

Josh hugged and kissed her then asked, "Have you any transport?"

Yvonne was puzzled, "Bernie has ..."

"No, I mean you, have you any transport?"

"Yes," she said flustered, "I've got is a little scooter."

"Good, a scooter's fine. Tomorrow at, say 12.30, meet me at the main Post Office in the old town, I think it's off St. Andrews street, meet me there, I'll have the money. I'll get a couple of hours off work. We're going to plan our way out of this. I lost you once, I'm not going to lose you again. Ever!"

"But I don't ..."

A sharp whistle cut through the air. Nobby Clarke stood on the stairs at the entrance of the club. He was pointing a thumb over his shoulder, a clear indication for Josh to get back inside.

"Have you got transport for tomorrow?" Yvonne suddenly asked.

"Yeah, that's my Skoda over there!"

"Skoda? what's a Skoda?

"That grey car, at the end of the line, that's mine!" Josh said with a tinge of pride.

"What, that square - tank?"

Josh frowned, "Yeah all right, but that 'tank' goes well, it'll take us anywhere on this island."

"That's because it's not a big island. I won't have any problem picking you out in that."

"Go on, get inside. I get enough cracks about my old bus without you adding your tuppence worth. Get inside, I'll see you tomorrow, now beat it." She turned to go when he called, "Yvonne!"

"Yes?"

"I love you ... it'll be all right. From now everything'll be good."

She smiled, blew a kiss then hurried towards Nobby. He in turn, on seeing at least one of the pair returning to the club, disappeared inside, returning to stand by his table. Lorna and Frank Connolly were in his group as was Babs and Ray Buckley, and Julian Cantwell. The latter had only just sat down after twenty minutes in the toilets. Nobby only a few minutes ago had actually been on his way to the toilets to see if Julian was all right when the errant airman emerged looking flushed. Whilst Nobby watched the blushing Julian cross the crowded room, Callum came up to him. "Do me a favour Nobby," the coach hissed, "Josh is out in the car park with Kowaleski's wife. Tell him it's time he got back in here!" When Callum saw the look on the big Indian's face he added, "Don't worry, they're only talkin' ... I hope! I'd fetch him myself but I may have to distract the twisted twat if he goes lookin' for his missus."

"Where is he?" Nobby asked.

Callum nodded towards the toilets, "Been in there for ages, but even if he's constipated to his eyeballs, he must come out soon."

Nobby did as Callum asked. He had warned Josh and now back at his table, he was troubled at the length of time Julian and Kowaleski had spent in the toilets. He glanced over at Julian. His flushed cheeks were all that remained from his flustered appearance when emerging from the 'Gents.' A wry shake of the dark head was all Nobby was prepared to commit himself to, for the moment. He excused himself and went to complete his diverted mission to the toilet.

Julian, unaware he wore the tiniest of frowns was very quiet. The others noticed but then Julian was often serene and tranquil so no one noted any difference in his more than usual serenity. Julian could not help thinking about what had happened! Bernard had approached him in the toilets. Even when using the toilets to urinate, Julian did not stand at the bowls like other men. He used the booths and sat. It was simply more comfortable. After Julian exited the booth and washing his hands Bernard was also washing up and had struck up a conversation. Initially thanking him for supporting his wife when she had so nearly fallen. Also it was the first time he had the opportunity to thank him for the support he had shown in the Dhekelia final.

Julian had been attracted to Bernard the first time he laid eyes on him and had lied in Dhekelia. He knew the coach deliberately punched Harold Ross in frustrated anger, but everyone was ganging up on the man so Julian had lied. Intentionally. Why? Because of the animal magnetism he felt. Julian was mesmerised by this powerful figure. For the first time in his unstable life, he felt here was someone ... someone ... what was the word? 'Connect with' didn't go far enough, 'marry up with ' too strong. Perhaps the word didn't exist as according to the laws of the land, neither did he sexually. Gel? Was that a word? Perhaps not but it was close. Therefore the isolated Bernard was someone he felt he could gel with! Not just another potential friend who accepted him but a man who understood him. This man, this real man did not feel superior or bitter towards him because he was different from the accepted norm. And what Julian found so exhilarating, he felt, no it was stronger that feeling - he knew their attraction was mutual!

They had talked about tug-of-war and how he, Bernard should find someone to do the magnificent job Julian was performing for the Maintenance Unit. They had spoken what seemed a long time and when the toilets were at last empty and found themselves alone, Bernard thanked Julian again, reaching out to shake his hand. As the hands clasped, Bernard's left hand reached over to grip Julian's right elbow and while they shook hands Bernard slowly slid his hand down Julian's arm, squeezing and caressing as he did so until he reached their clasped hands. With both hands Bernard slid them slowly over Julian's trapped hand, stroking, caressing each finger, rubbing his palm and sensuously entwining his own, sliding them through those soft fingers of a now perspiring Julian.

Julian's eyes closed with pleasure and his breath grew short. The sensual feelings from a simple caressing of hands was overwhelming.

Bernard felt himself go hard and gently placed the soft unyielding hand against his upright organ. He watched the lovely blue eyes snap open suddenly, then slowly, uncontrollably, the pupils began to roll upwards. For the first time in his muddled life, Bernard felt a surge of warmth and gratitude and ... love? Could it be love he felt towards this most beautiful ...?

With something utterly foreign driving him, he leaned forward and kissed the soft cheek of the unresisting Julian. 'He even smells like a fucking woman,' Bernard thought catching the merest hint of Julian's perspiration. His total arousal made him forget for the moment where they were, as he placed his lips over Julian's then drove his tongue deep inside the opening mouth.

The toilet door started to open and hurriedly they pulled apart, turning to the sinks. Julian was breathless. It was the first time he had been kissed, truly kissed and but for the door opening - it was all he could do to pull away. Bernard had been the strong one, he had pushed Julian off and turned away the instant the door moved.

Julian smiled as the cold water ran through his fingers, if it had been up to him, he would have carried on kissing that hard tearing mouth and go on holding that hot burning bar of iron. He felt strangely elated in a befuddled and intoxicated way and sighed. The cold water was cooling his pumping blood.

Bernard at the next sink was mouthing the words 'We must meet.' Julian nodded slowly, sadly, yet happily. The last doors within him that had remained stubbornly closed, were now opening and he caught a glimpse of a whole new world. The last cringing ramparts in his forts of masculinity were being overrun. Forced into accepting the finality of the dominant female genes, rampaging around in his system like a victorious army. Everything inside his body was screaming the war was over. Peace reigned and he was for the first time ever, deliriously happy. The battle that had for years raged within, was now lost, or was it won? Won! It had to be won for now he knew for certain he was in control. At long last he knew where his life was going.

~~~

Chapter 22

Mid April, eight days after the 103 MU team had tasted defeat for the first time in 22 months. A rather young Sergeant Peter Skaw, the new NCO i\c Machine Shop was feeling his way having taken over from Tom Sawyer, the latter enjoying a promotion and new job in St. Athens in sunny south Wales. As with all new senior NCOs, if there were any shirkers around they would always chance their hands to see if they could squeeze a few hours off work. This was the sergeant's first time abroad and the bright pink Peter Skaw, exposed for only a week to the Mediterranean sun and his new job, had been approached with, 'I've an appointment with the hygienist Sarge,' or the well used, 'they're screaming up in the library to get this book back, won't be long Sarge'. Excuses such as these added a page in the very thin book of Sgt. Skaw's experience, so with an enlightened nod he proceeded to screw the lid down tight on anyone skiving off, for any reason. Peter Skaw, an amiable chap, accepted with a smile, the quick uptake on his own vulnerability, but these young lads were still trying. Here was SAC Josh Munroe begging time off. He had been sent through from the Ground Equipment section as their senior NCO was on leave.

"You're taking someone up to Nicosia airport?" he asked sceptically.

"Yeah, seriously Sarge. A cousin of mine, she's a civilian. Been here on holiday with her little boy and she's stuck for a lift." Josh lied.

"Jesus wept, she must be stuck even to consider travelling in that heap of yours!"

The sergeant received a withering look, "You didn't mind when you were stuck the other day." Josh retorted. Sgt. Skaw had begged a lift down to Limassol the day after he started work.

"Yeah but nobody warned me about your death trap. I've been tasting petrol ever since!"

"It's not as bad as that," Josh groaned, "I've tried to find that tiny leak but I stop short of taking the carburettor off. There are so many parts glued and fixed on to it."

"It's bloody dangerous as it is Munroe, and I wouldn't trust it to reach Nicosia in one run."

"Balls," retorted Josh, "it's only a tiny leak." His patience was wearing thin with everyone continuing to exaggerate the problem in his beloved Skoda. In spite of the welding, bonded glue, brazing and wire holding everything together, the car was surprising reliable considering the vehicle had never felt the trained hands of a car mechanic nor seen the inside of a proper servicing garage.

"Are you coming back?" Peter asked, "I mean today?" he laughed.

"I really don't know Sarge, I'll try but you yourself know it's dangerous to push that old heap too hard." Josh grinned, now taking advantage of the car's condition.

"You take your time Munroe, never let it be said your demise was caused by my good self." Sgt. Skaw may have been caught in the past with skivers but decided the Senior Aircraftsman's reasons were genuine. No one in his sane mind would travel all the way to Nicosia in that death trap of a car unless the journey was absolutely necessary.

Josh hurriedly changed out of his denims into working blue, the change over to the well loved KD was still a week away. Returning to his billet he changed again into civilian clothes. He had arranged to pick up Yvonne and Allan by 11 o'clock then drive to the island's capitol and only International airport.

A lot of planning and scheming had gone on over the past fortnight between Yvonne and Josh. They had bought Allan's one-way ticket and arranged for him to be chaperoned on the journey. In Manchester Allan would be met by Yvonne's sister Jean and husband Joe Morton.

Josh drove up Platonos street then turned into Christos where he stopped outside No. 327. He noted the house next door was identical to the one from which Yvonne immediately appeared on the veranda. She carried a small suitcase as Allan walked ahead of her. In his eagerness to help, Josh nearly fell out of the car then scooping up his son, plucked the case from Yvonne. He hurried back to the car where he got the lad seated in the back.

Yvonne was locking the door when a girl appeared and stopped beside the car.

"Hi, I'm Pat Parrott, Yvonne's neighbour." The bright cheery girl introduced herself, "You look after that little boy now won't you!" she greeted him with a wink.

Before Josh could answer Yvonne arrived and both girls were suddenly engaged in a huddle of arms mutually patting the other's back. "Don't worry, Lovey," the pretty girl said, "I'll see you when you get back. I've still got plenty of time on this lahvelly island, an' it won't be long before we're back in dear old Blighty. I'm not about to lose a good friend like you, now am I?"

"I'll be lost when you go, Pat but as you say, I won't be long after you. Now what have you got here?" She peered in a paper bag Pat was trying to give Allan. "He'll be as sick as a dog if he eats all that rubbish Pat," Yvonne smiled warmly at the girl dressed seductively as always in very tight hot pants and halter top.

"No he won't!" Pat ignored her friend and pushed the bag onto the quiet child sitting in the back. In the process she bumped her breasts against the arm Josh was holding the door with. "Like I was saying, you look after that little boy, or I won't be your friend anymore." With that she jiggled her breasts under his nose.

"Pat!" Yvonne admonished her neighbour, "and you haven't been introduced." she laughed.

"Oh I don't hang about Yvie, and besides I know who you are don't I. You're Josh Munroe, the big daddy and saviour of my best friend."

Josh nodded. He wanted to get on his way and this little sex bomb of whom he had heard many harrowing tales was holding them up. "We haven't got a lot of time," he said simply.

The blue eyes fluttered, there was a nod, hugs all round then seconds later they drove off.

For the next hour the much maligned engine never missed a beat and they arrived in good time for the flight. At the ticket counter a stewardess with flaming red hair came to collect Allan. Yvonne crouched down to her son, "Darling, this nice lady will look after you for the rest of the day, and when the lovely air plane lands in London, she will take you to meet Auntie Jean and Uncle Joe. You'll like that, won't you?"

"Yes Mum, but when will you come?" he asked for the hundredth time.

"Pet," Yvonne looked into the dark brown eyes, "do you like Josh?"

"Yes Mum," he answered, "I like uncle Josh, but when are you coming home?"

"Allan, I've got a big surprise for you. It's something I couldn't tell you before 'cause I was afraid you might say something to Bernie. Now this man, Josh, this nice man standing beside us, the man who took us to the ice cream parlour the other day and brought us here in his car ...."

"His smelly car mum ...."

"Yes sweetheart," she laughed, "in his smelly car. Allan ... Josh is not your uncle, he is your real dad, your REAL daddy!"

"Yes Mum I know but ..." Allan stopped and looked into her eyes unbelievably. "My real daddy?" His eyes swung round and stared at Josh with a furrowed puzzled frown. "You're my real daddy?" he asked quietly.

Josh scooped him up and hugged him, something he had wanted to do since the first moment he laid eyes on the child. "Yes son, I'm your dad." He felt peculiar, "and we'll have a great time when we, your mum and me, come home ... soon, to fetch you from your Auntie's house."

Allan for the moment was speechless and could only stare at his father with wide eyes.

"Darling, we'll have to be quick now for the lady's waiting just for you. Do you remember that fat envelope I put in your case?"

Allan nodded solemnly.

"Remember what I told you? You must give that to Auntie Jean. There's a letter explaining everything about Josh and me, and some money, oh darling it's very important you ..."

"Mum, you've told me that a million zillion times!" the boy said in feigned disgust.

"I know my little sweetheart, I just don't want you to forget." smiled Yvonne.

"My mum thinks I'm stupid," declared Allan, looking up at Josh.

"No she doesn't, she thinks you are very clever, trusting you with that very important envelope, and she loves you very much, as I do." said Josh, aching to crush the round innocent face into his own.

"Can I call you Dad?" the boy asked with all the blitheness of a child, never realising the earth tremors such a question caused for the recipient.

"Oh yes, Allan," Josh could hardly speak. "You can call me dad." He could say no more, his throat had closed. Yvonne came to his rescue. "We'll have to go sweetheart, the lady and the air plane's waiting. You'll soon be with Auntie Jean and if I know my sister she'll have you spoilt rotten by the time we get home."

Allan gave an emphatic nod then he was being hugged by both parents, smothered in kisses by a mother who could not hold back her tears as she reluctantly handed him over.

As the stewardess led him by the hand, the boy had taken only a few steps when he stopped. "Wait a minute!" he called in a haughty tone then turned for a last time.

"Good-bye mum, good-bye ... dad?" he called. Then having gained the confidence he obviously needed, he yelled, "Good-bye DAD!" He turned and satisfied it seemed, allowed the lady to lead him away.

He never looked back again before vanishing into the Departure Hall. "Oh I hope he's all right," Yvonne murmured, "I'm getting the most awful feeling I'll never see him again!"

"Don't be daft woman! Course he'll be all right, and we'll see him in July!"

"July," she repeated,, "you'll have no problems getting leave?"

"I'll tell you all about it on the way back. Let's see if we can catch a glimpse of Allan."

They watched buses leave for the aircraft but because the vehicles stopped on the far side of the Viscount and obstructions on the runway, they could not see the boy. "He's probably chatting up that red head by now, glad to be away from his mother's watchful eye. He's all right Yve, don't worry." Josh tried to console a fretting mother. "Little sod," she sobbed, "you'd think he'd at least look for us."

In the Skoda Josh said little until he got clear of the Nicosia traffic. Back on the Limassol road he said, "I spoke to my CO, told him the whole story about us. I left out the fact that you're married of course. I told him you found I was stationed over here, you came out, got in touch with me and told me about Allan. The rest was easy. I asked if I could have a couple of weeks leave in July, ostensibly to make preliminary plans for our wedding at the end of the year when I finish my tour," Josh glanced at her. "Whereas in truth I take you home in July, leave you with your sister then I'll see you at the end of the year!"

"Huh, that would be nice!" Yvonne said sarcastically, "Us getting married. You're forgetting I'm lumbered with a husband and divorces cost lots of money!"

"Yvonne!" Josh glanced at her again, "I've already told you, I've got £3000. That's plenty to get us started and cover the cost of a divorce. Allan's ticket cost next to nothing, I could have got you a ticket too, you could have been on that flight with him."

"Yes I know, such a decision to make Josh. But getting Allan away from that house was top of my list, and finding you again, oh Josh, I couldn't bear to leave you, or lose you, not again."

"You'll have a hard job doing that Yve, we are going to be together for the rest of our lives."

Yvonne laid a hand on his thigh, "I hope so and thanks Josh, for doing all you've done. I'm just so glad I found you. My life's taken on a whole new meaning again. I can't wait for us to be together, live together whether we're married or not, doesn't matter, I love you so much!"

Josh smiled happily as the Skoda thundered along, "And I love you pet." Staring ahead he went on, "It's only since I met you again, all the running around we've done. Since that night in the Pen Club, it's brought it home to me how empty life has been without you. I used to think of you before but now, I can think of nothing else but you."

Yvonne felt a surge of love and squeezed his iron hard thigh, "Can't you find ...?" She paused and he gave yet another quick glance. "Can't you find some place to turn off?"

This was the first time they had been alone since the night in the Peninsula Club car park and Josh could not control his mind as it raced ahead. He knew their eventual lovemaking was inevitable but hoped to arrange something better than stolen moments writhing in the grass, trying to fill five missing years into only a few minutes. She squeezed his thigh hard.

Josh felt himself harden. She was the last woman he had lain with. Her image had filled his every dream. He was not going to do her or himself justice but that did not matter, he wanted Yvonne badly, as bad it seemed as she wanted him. There was a dirt track a hundred yards ahead. Josh ran his eyes down it, following the straggly fence that ran alongside the track, and saw the fence disappear into a small cluster of trees. He slowed down and turned into the rutted track that was not kind to the springs of the hardy old Skoda. "I've not ... I haven't come ... you know, I'm not prepared," he stammered above the rattling car and engine noise.

"Who cares, when we get married at the end of the year or whenever, a bun in the oven won't chase you off again. Not this time." She smiled, confident her life was at last taking shape.
Her words warmed Josh. He did not mind at all if she ended up pregnant. This time he would be around to support her.

The fence stopped when it met the knot of trees and the little secluded spot could have been made for lovers. He eased the car under the sheltering trees, dappled blades of sun welcoming them into perfect isolation. All was suddenly breathtakingly quiet when Josh switched off the engine and in a sweep of emotion, reached for her.

"There won't be any running away by either of us. Wherever I go with the RAF, we go together or not at all. I swear. I will never lose you again." He spoke the words into her hair and she nuzzled into him. His words were so beautiful; she knew in her heart he meant every word. He would never leave her again.
Later that day Bernard drove his Hillman Minx into the coolness of the small garage. He was in his usual blistering bad mood after training. He treated the men in his team like so many robots and when they performed like human beings, his mood degenerated to new depths, as low as their training performance that afternoon. Stomping into the kitchen he tore off his working blue tunic. Yvonne had just placed a pot on the stove and lit the gas when Bernard looked around suspiciously. There was no cooking smell and the house was strangely quiet.

"What's up?" he asked, staring at Yvonne, not quite sure what he suspected but he had an inkling, a feeling something was different.

"What do you mean, 'What's up.' I'm late with dinner, that's all!" Attempting to hide her fear she tried to sound aggressive, fussing around the sink area.

Bernard was no fool. She was moving around a lot but achieving nothing. "What the fuck are you playing at?" he

483

roared, his temper rekindling, trying to stop his vision from blurring.

Yvonne placed her hands on the edge of the sink with her head lowered. After some seconds in this position she swung round, "I've sent Allan home!" she stated defiantly.

"Ha!" he roared, "that's the best fucking news I've had all day, is that why my meal's not ready?"

"Yes!" she shouted. Her defiant mood rising she went on, "and I'm following him in July!"

"A second piece of good news! Things are not so bad after all," he stormed back but as the words were uttered, inevitably a doubt crossed his mind. The bitch and her brat could leave him in peace any time, that must be considered a bonus, but how had she managed to do it? Where did she get the money, was there a man involved? Deceptions of any description could not, would not be tolerated. The strange peculiarities in Bernard's twisted mind were he cared less than a penny whistle if his wife was being laid by every man on the base, as long as he was aware, and condoned what was going on! He drew a line against even his best friend, if he had one, of using or taking advantage of anything that belonged to him, if he was not aware of it! His suspicions floated to the surface, "Why? Why send him home?" he asked.

"Why? Why not? He hasn't got a life here and he's due to start school. I want him in an English school." 'That wasn't clever,' she thought. There were very good English schools in Limassol. He was not interested in schools.

"Where did you get the money?"

"My sister sent it!" Yvonne had prepared for this line of questioning.

He looked at her warily. All forces mail was sent through the British Forces Post Office, and every letter Yvonne received, Bernard had brought from the Akrotiri BFPO. "How come I don't remember bringing a letter that you have not opened in my presence. There was no money in any of them."

"I asked her to send it to the local Post Office off Leontiou, I collected it myself."

"And you sent your letters from there too, I suppose?" he grated.

"Yes!"

Bernard raised his voice, realising he was getting nowhere,

"You can fuck off as soon as you like, the sooner the better, I mean that. The quicker you go the better it will suit me!"

"Then give me the money, I'll go now." She stared defiantly at him.

"You my dear, can go and get fucked!" he said, staring and wagging his head at her.

How she wanted to scream into that face, how she yearned to shout, "I got well and truly fucked for hours a little while ago, I can hardly fucking walk!" She would love to see his reaction. Josh had lasted all of five seconds on their first attempt, but the second time had gone on - and on - and on. She daren't tell this eye popping crazy man but the temptation was strong. Yvonne stared back at him, trying to convey the message through her eyes of her recent fornication with the man she loved.

Perhaps he read something in her contumacious glare for he was the first to snap his head away. "Don't bother to cook anything for me. I could no doubt find something more palatable in a slop house bin."

Yvonne smiled as he stomped off to the bedroom. Feeling strangely relaxed she rested her behind against the sink top and called after him, "Bring me back a bag of puke then will you? There's nothing else in this house to eat." Her remark was not so far from the truth. Potatoes were in the pot and there were a few sausages in the fridge, which was to have been the evening meal. Apart from that the cupboard was bare. She had put every note she earned through foul means and doubtfully fair into the envelope she placed in Allan's case. Slipping her hand into her pocket she felt the £10 note Josh had given her. It had not been 'for services rendered,' No, no, she grinned. Just something from the man she loved in case she needed money. He had slipped it into her pocket at the front door. A now familiar rush of warmth washed through her. "Roll on July, oh God please, roll on."

Bernard had to crank the engine with the starting handle, cursing the fault for the hundredth time. He screeched off towards town in his usual manner, his bitter mood transferred from his useless team to Yvonne. He meant what he said about the 'quicker she went home the better,' for he could still keep the house. The RAF wouldn't know she had pissed off! The more he thought about this aspect, the more it appealed to him. He could invite anyone to spend the night. Carnal scenes invaded his mind, memories of Singapore flooded back. And there was Julian! She could not go quick enough.

He was approaching the Bypass, or Archbishop Makarios 111 Avenue, as the street had eventually been named. He slowed the car turning his mind to the more mundane matters of his stomach. Spoilt for choice with so many restaurants and kebab bars for something to eat, and later the ladies from the cabarets and bistros around Hero's Square beckoned. But the lure of female flesh was somehow not so attractive tonight. Something to do with that stinking cow of a wife no doubt. At the lights at the bottom of the hill he turned onto the Bypass and cruised along in the light traffic. The Twiga Bar loomed on his left and on his right the Soho Take-Away. Blue smoke was belching from the outdoor cooking grills and the welcome odours of grilled goat meat made him pull over. He bought a huge chapatti from the Soho Take-Away and returned to the car. The meal, wrapped in grease proof paper was placed on the passenger seat and Bernard warily pressed the starter button. The engine caught immediately causing him to grunt in relief before pulling back into the traffic. He drove west, towards the end of the Bypass and passed the point where the checkpoints until a year ago, had been situated on the outskirts of town. Casually he glanced at an abandoned blue UN shed with those huge letters in white painted on the side. Coughing up a ball of phlegm he spat it towards the shed through his open window. The blue and white of the UN were the same colours as the hooped shirts sported by the reigning Akrotiri champions, the gut churning detestable 103 Maintenance Unit.

Driving slowly, looking for somewhere to stop and whilst eating nurse his most current hatred for Yvonne - she having been elevated for the moment to the top of his hate list. When it occurred to him he had not bought a drink. Cursing at his stupidity, for he had to have at least water with his meal, he abandoned the package of food after trying unsuccessfully to delve into its innards with one hand. Flooring the accelerator in frustration the powerful car screeched forward towards Akrotiri and his final choice of watering hole, the Peninsula Club.

Fifteen minutes later he parked a discreet distance from the entrance and opened the grease proof parcel. There was far too much stuffing in the chapatti. It bulged with meat, lettuce, onions, peppers and a myriad of cut and spiced vegetables. He would eat what he could, dump the rest then go inside for a drink. Breaking of a sizable piece he started to eat. Even in his present mood Bernard could not fault the meal. It was delicious and it helped to know the oasis was only a few yards away. His brooding and the pungently garnished meal held his attention but this was arrested as a man crossed his line of vision. Almost reactionary he pipped the horn.

Julian Cantwell looked up startled. Peering under a shading hand for in the reflective glare it was impossible to see, but Julian knew the car. He hoped Bernard was alone.

The Chief Tech. leaned over and opened the passenger door.

"Julian!" he called.

Julian went limp. He had thought about nothing or no one else since that night in the toilets in this same club. Something about this man, his power, brutality, his sheer dedication in everything he did, added to the tenderness and understanding he showed Julian. It had been overwhelming. The airman had never known such sensations or feelings. As a result, his whole attitude towards what he wanted in life had changed. If he was unsure before, he was certain now! He wanted Bernard. That's why he was here! Julian heard a whisper that occasionally the fire eating coach sometimes drank in the Peninsula Club. As indeed Bernard did, especially on his philandering Wednesday nights. He'd kill the first hour in the Club before descending to his unsavoury debaucheries in the seedier regions of Limassol.

On that whisper alone, Julian had walked from his billet and spent a lonely two hour vigil every night since his joust with Bernard over a week ago, hoping to bump into the Chief. Tonight his perseverance paid off. Bernard was here and he was alone.

Inside the car Bernard was not surprised to feel himself harden. The very posture stirred the older man's innards.

"Julian," he called again, "Come and have a chat, share this chapatti with me."

Julian looked in through the open door, "Hello Bernard," he said simply.

"Nice to see you again Julian. Here, let me move this." Bernard picked up the package from the passenger seat. "Have a seat, I won't eat you," he smiled encouragingly, 'but I think you might do me that honour." his grisly thoughts pushed up the rate of his heartbeat.

Julian got into the seat as a woman would enter a car. He placed his bottom on the seat first then swung his head and legs inside in one fluid movement. He turned and looked at Bernard.

Bernard was for a moment confused. The beautiful action of Julian getting into the car had both sickened Bernard and yet turned him on. For a crazy few seconds he wanted to push the effeminate bastard out, yet he wanted to hold him, caress him, kiss him, all at the same time! The clash of opposing feelings were confusing "What you doing here?" he asked breathlessly.

"I've been having a drink," answered Julian, then without prompting, as if his feelings had just boiled over, he went on, "Bernard, I don't know what is happening to me. Since that night last week, I've been upset. No, perhaps that's too strong a word. I'm not upset, confused maybe, bewildered even. I simply have never had feelings like this before. For anything, or anyone."
Bernard took Julian's hand, "Me too! Feelings are carousing around inside me I can't explain. I want you badly yet repulsed at my own feelings." Bernard felt like a tongue tied schoolboy. "Look, try to understand, I've fucked many a man, but I don't like men! But you, you're different Julian, you're not a man, you're not a woman. But that's how you come over to me ... and I want whatever you are." He caressed the limp hand, "My longing for you is stronger than whatever the accepted modes are of what's right and what's wrong. I want you."

Julian listened to the strange words coming from a man's mouth. Similar words had been said to him in jokes and friendly banter, but never had he heard them spoken in the same tone.

Bernard said them. Again this man was conjuring up the feelings that washed down the back of his neck in tingling icy yet warm sensations. "Please," said Julian feeling weak, "I want this, don't misunderstand me, I truly want this. I have been looking for you, searching for something but have no idea what it is! And though I want it, I have this feeling I'm rushing headlong and about to fall. I must have a little time." He looked down at their clasped hands, "Strange, I have wanted something to happen for years, something like this, and now that it has, I feel I might be pushing it away." He raised his head and looked into the burning coals of Bernard's eyes.

"Please, just a little more time, for I think in here, I love you." he placed a hand on his chest. Bernard looked into the sad blue eyes and leaning over, placed his mouth over the unresisting lips.

Julian's eyelids closed but his eyes rolled back into his head and felt he had been plunged into a void. He was lost in a world of dizzying sensations. His body no longer existed, he let himself float to be pushed and guided.

Julian was not aware Bernard was unbuttoning his fly. In one practised movement Bernard placed the limp hand on his exposed upright penis. Julian blinked as he tried to stay on the same level of consciousness, feeling this disconcerting motion of movement, of floatation yet he was perfectly still. With a tight grip the bewildered youngster held on to what was keeping him anchored in his seat. Bernard's hand slipped behind his thick fair hair and he was being kissed again, deeper and longer. Then he was falling, falling, his head being guided into the dark warm depths. In order to stop himself floating off into space Julian clung to the solid warm bar of reality in his hand. It was only when he placed his mouth over it, which seemed the most natural thing to do, did he realise what it was.

Bernard heard his own small gasp of pleasure. His groin area was glowing with soft sliding sensations as the movement and caressing fired his tender nerve ends. In this state of elevated liquid mass, when all flesh melts into the ether yet blends and sends the finest and strongest of sensations back into the body, Julian and Bernard stayed in this suspended fluid state for many minutes. Bernard began to rise above even this level of sensorial levity when he felt the stirring of molten fire begin in a circular motion deep in the melting pot of his groin. It was hot and instinctively he began to push upward, away from the fire.

An old Skoda thundered past the white Minx, the very distinctive engine roar blasting its arrival. Julian stirred and went to pull away from this wondrous scene of sensation when a hand pushed his head forcibly back. The sudden foreign action dispersed the cloying clouds of wonder, the noise rousing him back to reality. He twisted his head, pushed and rolled until the restraining hand fell away. He sat up.

"I've got to go, we mustn't be caught like this!" Julian said, "That's Josh and the others. I cannot allow them to see me getting out of this car."

"Are you going to leave me like this?" Bernard looked at his groin.

"Oh I'm sorry," Julian cried seeing the rampant white shape in the dim reflected light.

The Skoda was negotiating to reverse park. Bernard hurried on, "Never mind, this'll keep for another time. Julian listen, I must ask you this, my wife's leaving soon, she's returning to England. When she goes will you move in with me?"

"Move in with you?" Julian asked in surprise then thought for moment, "What excuse, what do I tell the others?"

"Tell them anything ... you're moving in with a friend. You don't have to say who!"

Josh, Carol and Callum were crossing towards the club entrance. Julian ducked under the dash. "They'll expect to find me inside. They knew I was coming up here. Oh dear, Yes, yes all right I'll do it Bernard,!" He brought his head up when the clatter of feet on the steps died away. "When do you expect your wife to go home?"

"Wonderful. My wife? Oh yes, soon, a month maybe less," he lied but there was hope.

"It will take me that time to make up some sort of story." Julian mused.

Bernard started to reach for his hand again but Julian pulled away, "I'm going, I have to. But one very important thing Bernard. If anything comes of this, if what we have started grows into relationship ... it must remain a secret. We'll be kicked out if we are ever found out!"

"That goes without saying Julian, but they'll never find out, not from me anyway."

"Nor me, we'll have no option" Julian shook his head and opened the door, "Look, I don't want to but I am going. I don't know when we can meet but I must see you. Let me work on it."

"Don't leave it too long, phone me when you come up with something." Bernard hissed.

"And you me when your wife has her return date." Julian stepped outside. "Good night, Bernard," His stomach taught with worry about being seen with of all people, the GEF coach.

490

"Good night," Bernard called as Julian looked nervously around, then with a tight smile the young man trotted towards the entrance. Bernard groaned and dropped his hand on to his still painfully erect manhood.

~~~

Two weeks later on a Thursday morning Lorna Connolly in what was now a routine weekly run, picked up first Babs Buckley then on to Pappachristos street for Marion Ross.

Thursday mornings over the years had developed into a social gathering for the wives of British servicemen It started simply as these things tend to do when a group of wives visited the Soldiers Sailors and Airmen's Family Association to report faults in their hirings, exchange faulty items, or replace broken crockery etc. When finished with their business at the SSAFA someone suggested coffee at the very convenient Twiga Bar, next door to the SSAFA building. And so it began. Social Mornings at the bar restaurant every Thursday was an outlet for these women, a place to meet and verbally murder their husbands or someone else's.

It was only minutes after 10am when the threesome arrived and as usual on these mornings the Twiga Bar was crowded. Probably a little more than usual as there were no vacant tables anywhere, even those outside the bar were occupied. At a loss Lorna asked "What now girls?"

"Marion!" someone called from a table near the jukebox. All three turned to see Yvonne beckoning them to join her. She was sitting with a blonde girl Marion found vaguely familiar.
Seats were found and introductions made. The blonde girl was Pat Parrott and Marion could not recall where she had seen the girl. Cool drinks and coffees were ordered and Michael the perennial waiter placed the drinks and inevitable bowl of salted nuts on the table. The girls settled into their seats.

"I don't know if we should mix with people like you," Lorna said, smiling at Yvonne.

"What do you mean, 'people like us?'" bristled a lightly ruffled Pat.

"Sorry Pat," said Lorna, "It's a sort of 'in' joke between us. My Frank and Babs's Ray are both in the MU tug-of-war team,

Yvonne's husband coaches the opposition, and ..." she went on in a growling voice, "they're sworn enemies!"

"Oh!" said Pat, surprised the mistaken slur was not intended for her but to teams in some sport of other. "I thought ... never mind what I thought," she giggled.

"Just a minute Lorna," said Babs, "you forgot little reserved Marion here. Her husband's probably the biggest bestest hunk of beef in both the teams!"

"Oh I don't know about that ..." Lorna began defensively, then after a pause, "On reflection, if we're talking about sexy men, my old man is obviously far and away the sexiest," she preened happily. "But if we have to select another, I think ... I quite fancy Nobby our Indian anchor man."

They laughed but the thin flat chuckle from Marion did not go unnoticed. Sitting next to Babs the London girl grew aware as time passed midst the good-natured banter, Marion was not her usual self. "You all right love?" she asked lightly, "You're very quiet."

Marion looked quickly at the girl she had got to know through these Thursday meetings. "Yes," she tried to sound convincing, "I'm fine!" she lied. But Marion was not 'fine,' and had not been in that contented state since the overheard comment about her husband and the girl Carol. The heaviness that sat astride her heart would not budge. She had made attempts to shake off what amounted to a stray comment from a drunken airman, but the gash was deep.

Lorna had also noticed the difference in Marion, she reminded her of a clockwork toy in need of winding up. The Scottish girl put it down to the obvious reason. "Our little dove IS pregnant Babs," and decided at this point to make her own announcement, "as I am!" She smiled into Marion's eyes, "There now, we're both in the same club. Doesn't that make you feel just a wee bit better?"

Marion stared, "Are you sure?" she asked timidly, glancing at Lorna's midriff, "Since when?"

"Oh I know exactly when," Lorna laughed remembering one particular night of unbridled passion. "But I only found out this morning for certain. I'm two months already." She looked into the fretting face, "So WE, Marion dear, are ALLOWED!

Allowed to have as many quiet, or any other kind of mood WE please!"

"Pregnancies and kids are the worst possible diseases," Pat said, "haven't got any myself but love to practice making them."

They laughed again and Marion at last gave one of her warm smiles allowing them to believe her condition was the reason for her depression.

"Maybe you need a break?" suggested Lorna, "Why don't you and Harry take yourselves up into the mountains in that little wee love nest he drives around in." The statement was said in all innocence but in Marion's paranoid brain, the piercing words drove harshly into the suppurating wound of doubt. She had to concentrate to hear Babs repeat something. "Marion lovey, you really don't look too well, you're very pale."

"I'm fine Babs, really," Marion said, "but yes I am tired, all I want to do these days is sleep."

"I went through that spell too, it'll pass pet," offered a concerned Babs. Changing the subject she went on, "Marion, Ray and I ... Ray's my hubby, Ray and I ... and of course the kids unfortunately," a smile and a wink, "have booked a chalet in a little holiday resort near Troodos for the weekend. Why don't you and your Harry join us? It sleeps six, there's only the four of us. It'll do you the world of good to get away for a few days. Don't you think?"

"That sounds really nice but I don't know if Harry has anything planned this weekend. If he hasn't, then yes, maybe we could join you." Marion tried to sound pleasant, but a trip to the mountains was not all that attractive to her at the present time.

"Look, if you mean that," Babs said perhaps catching a negative note in Marion's voice, "I'll take a walk down to your place tomorrow morning, it's not too far, only a two or three streets along from me I think, you can let me know what Harry says. The reason I say that is we're hoping to get away, soon as possible after Ray gets home after work tomorrow, around 1.30."

"Oh Babs, don't put yourself out for us. If we decide to come, we can always drive up a little later," Marion felt she was allowing herself to slip too deeply into this situation.

"Okay, whatever you feel like doing, but I'll pop down around 9.30 anyway. You can let me know what he says." Babs decided to drop the subject. She could sense the tiniest resistance.

"That'll be nice, I'll have the kettle on."

Normally Marion would welcome anyone being so friendly but everything was out of kilter, she was not sure if she wanted or needed an invasion of her privacy. The overbearing burden of Harold and the image of the girl was on her mind, dragging her down.

The women prattled and laughed their way through another hour, Marion suffering quietly. She had hoped, by joining Lorna and Babs in a visit to the SSAFA and Twiga Bar, her problem might be pushed to the rear of her thoughts, or washed away in good natured banter. It had not worked, she should not have come. Now all she wanted was to get home, to take one of the taxi's hovering outside. However, Lorna who brought her and always took her home, may feel slighted. That would never do. Marion could never knowingly hurt anyone. As Marion again tuned into the conversation she smiled for like a rising bubble in her brain she remembered where she had seen the bubbly blonde girl.

"So you're off back home on Saturday Pat," Yvonne was saying to her friend, "there'll be a few broken hearts that day when you wing your way out of here."

Never the one to hide her background or her liking for men, Pat had kept the girls entertained with stories of her escapades over the past three years. She made no attempt to hide the fact she had often been the prime mover in a liaison if she fancied a man. Marion felt another of her natural, rather than forced smiles grow wide when Babs asked Pat if she had ever slept with a black man.

"Black man, yeah of course, but the daftest was a couple of years ago," Pat dropped an eyebrow as she tried to recall the episode. "When I met this bloke, black as the ace of spades he was - Oh God, that's terrible! I've only realised this minute where the term 'spade' comes from!" she giggled. "Met him in the old 'Gold Fish Bowl' like I said, a couple of years ago, what a dump that place was. He was a really nice bloke he was, bought us drinks you know, the usual thing. We danced real close but my God, I remember thinking, 'This guy's trying to fool me, he's got a roll of salami down his trousers.'" The girls burst into spontaneous laughter at the vivid description. Marion recalled the picture of the gyrating hips pressed together on the dance floor.

"I couldn't wait to get him home but what a disappointment! Oh he was big all right, huge I'd say, not that I've seen all that many you understand!" A round of titters from her captive audience. "But I swear we hadn't been at it two minutes when he finished, nearly blew my little bum out of bed. But that was it, kaput, game over, when I say finished, I MEAN finished. He rolls over onto his back and falls asleep. I belted him, jerked him off, gave him a blow job, everything but no good. Everything about him was dead, shut up shop and I hadn't even got started. Next morning, Fred my man comes home, he's been in a fight and sat with a friend in hospital all night. Fred wanders into the kitchen, makes tea, shouts and asks if I want a cup and I shout back, 'Two please.' Five minutes later he brings in two mugs. My one night short, very short stand, ducks under the covers not knowing what to expect from my Fred, and gets the shock of his life when Fred says, 'Sorry mate, hope you don't take milk, there's none left for the tea.' so I tell Fred, 'The night's been a flipping disaster, there's no milk left in this bastard either,' at which Fred pulls back the covers and sees my paramour's wide staring eyes. 'Oh, morning' mate,' says Fred, ''ere, you're lookin' a bit off colour! Here's a nice hot cuppa black tea, that'll put some colour back into your cheeks it will. Get it down ya before it goes cold!' Fred winks at me and buggers off back to the kitchen."

Smiles, howls of laughter, and shaking heads greeted the end of Pat's colourful tale. The storyteller more than pleased at the response to one of her adventures.

"Ladies, I hate to break up the party but I have to get home and start preparing my hungry man's dinner, so I must love you and leave you," Lorna said downing the last of her cool drink.

"I wish I had ten bob for every time I heard that line," Pat said reminiscently.

"You'd be a millionaire and you're terrible," Lorna laughed as Pat nodded enthusiastically. Lorna went on, "It was nice meeting you ... and enlightening, very enlightening. Bon voyage lass and when you get home, try to keep it down to one man a day."

"That might be difficult," Pat replied, "but I'll try," she said shaking Lorna's hand.

The women broke up outside the bar in a noisy laughing group with Pat waving wildly from the back of Yvonne's scooter. Lorna took Marion home first dropping her at her gate. With waves and kisses she then drove off towards the Bypass.

Marion opened her gate and paused to look at the green Ford van. Could Harry possibly have been using it for something else? What was the title she had heard vans described as in other people's lives? So distant from her own she herself had laughed when she heard the name, 'Passion wagons!' That's what these things were christened, 'Passion Wagons,' or perhaps as Lorna described it, a 'Love Nest!'. With a choked cry she fumbled with the house keys.

Entering the cool hallway Marion sat in one of the cast iron chairs. She felt faint. The fickle finger of Fate it seemed had not yet finished with Marion and Harold. The previous night Harold had dropped his van keys into the bowl on the hall table. Usually he picked them up on his way out in the morning. But that morning he was a little late as the transport beeped its horn and in haste, hurried out to the waiting bus. Marion's eyes were drawn to the keys as inevitably as a compass needle is pulled north. She stared at them resignedly, almost accepting they would be in the bowl on this day. She did not want to look inside the van, yet mechanically her hand reached out and picked them up. Continuing to stare at the glinting chromed pieces of steel, she wondered idly what sights they had witnessed as they hung from the ignition, perhaps swinging in time to the pelvic driving lunges. Another small cry escaped her lips as she shook the images away and like fragments of ice-cold glass shards they settled and prickled on her fluttering shoulders and back. Breathing deeply she composed herself then went to the van.

Unlocking the double rear doors she opened them and looked inside. The mattress was still there covered with the quilt. Scatter cushions lay all around giving the interior a homely look. Marion ran her eyes around the sparse bodywork hoping against hope she would find nothing, but her body was like a robot. She could not stop reaching inside and pulling out the cushions, dropping them on the driveway to be followed by the quilt. The thin sponge rubber mattress would have taken the same route but it snagged somewhere. Climbing laboriously inside she peered down the side of the mattress and saw the carrying handles had been tied to the ribs of the van. Untying these she saw a chewing gum wrapper, which struck her as strange for Harry rarely if ever chewed gum. Deciding not to lift the mattress out as it was too heavy and awkward, she lifted the edge and looked underneath. There was nothing in the right side of the van, nothing at all apart from the gum wrapper.

Starting behind the passenger seat she forced up the mattress and saw a hairgrip. This she was prepared to ignore, as it could have been her own. She had not slept in the van for a while but nevertheless it COULD have been hers. Had Harold never cleaned out the van? Something else caught her attention. Something red was caught under the bars of the driver's seat. Marion felt her eyes widen and her breath shorten. She should stop here, she should throw everything back and go back into the house. But like a gear engaged in her brain she methodically carried on. Easing the object carefully out from the entanglement of bars and springs under the seat, she felt her heart drop as the item pulled free. Marked with a little black grease from the seat mechanism, Marion held up a pair of skimpy female briefs.

No, not this time. Marion could not claim these as her own for she had never owned red underwear and certainly never panties so minuscule. Suddenly she felt the blood drain from her and her arms dropped weakly into her lap. When Fate is dealing the cards she can be a real bastard, and she was a proper bastard that morning.

Something else was bugging Marion as it has a habit of doing when all the pieces do not quite fall into place. Picking up the briefs, she turned to leave. She did not want to find anything else but there was something she had already seen that was part of the pattern! And she was being nagged for her brain had not fitted the given piece into place. It would forever haunt her like a bad dream. Puzzled the troubled young woman looked around. There was absolutely nothing else other than the gum wrapper. Reaching over she picked it up. Staring at it fearfully, almost afraid it might strike her, Marion forced herself to look at the wrapper more closely. It had been torn nearly in half but she saw the letter 'r' at the end of the one half. Bringing up the other half she aligned the letters and although there were other words, she saw only the word 'Durex'. The word was embossed very prettily in blue on a silver background. Sadly she flattened the foil as best she could, trying to keep her brain from thinking, pushing the fleeting images back.

She did not push away the image of the hairgrip that indeed could have been her own. The fact it might be hers offered a sole crumb of comfort. But she could not tear her eyes away as mechanically she watched her thumbs go on endlessly flattening the foil sachet. 'No Harry, this is not mine, not this little package, nor what had been inside this little package. Why Harry? The contents of this little silver envelope with your help has pushed up the insides of another woman and it caught your seed. The same seed that started this little chap inside me. Why Harry? You never used these on me, never with me, no not with me Harry, not with me.'

Marion replaced everything back in the van, locked it, replaced the keys in the bowl, locked the house and started to walk up Pappachristos Street.

When Harold arrived home he was surprised to find the front door locked. Frowning, as he did not have his keys, he went to the back of the house where he found Nina. "Have you seen Marion?" he asked.

"I see Mareeyon walking on Bypass when bus bring home from school trip," she smiled at Harold, hoping she could rekindle another fiery afternoon with the gorgeous Englishman.

Harold was much too pre-occupied to notice. "What do you mean, walking on the Bypass?"

'These Eengleesh, they were like the Chinese. How could they say the same word and yet make a different meaning?' "Walking!" she shrugged,, "walking with the feet. I don' know. She is eh? nearby to the Danish butcher shop ... walking like thees." Nina illustrated a walking action with her fingers.

This was very confusing! Where would she be going so far along the Bypass. It was well past the Connolly's where conceivably she might venture to, but to walk there. In her condition? And at a time when she would normally be preparing lunch! Something was wrong. Airman's houses normally did not have the luxury of a telephone so instant communication was impossible. Confused he left Nina and went into the house through the permanently unlocked back door. He looked around. Nothing unusual, no note, nothing ... what the hell was going on?

Slivers of panic began to prick viciously. Trying to think rationally he opened a can of beer and sat at the kitchen table. He lit a cigarette and inhaled deeply, trying to settle his scrambled thoughts. It wouldn't be anything serious, no, not a miscarriage or anything. Someone would have phoned the camp if it were anything like that. Fifteen minutes, he decided, in fifteen if she had not returned he would start driving around friends' homes.

Thoughts, unrestrained and wild started to run riot through Harold's head. Marion had been extremely cool since the night she pointed Carol out to him. It was obvious she did not believe his denials of knowing the girl. What was he supposed to tell her, 'Yes Marion, I've been fucking that sexy bitch for years, every chance I get!' Words like that would kill her, yet he knew lying was almost as bad. She had not spoken half a dozen decent words since. 'There's too many skeletons in my cupboard,' Harold thought as the demons of panic probed to be let loose. Fifteen painful minutes later he dropped the dead butt into the empty beer can, crushed it and dropped both into the bucket under the sink. With a feeling of resignation and inevitability he stormed through to the hall and retrieved the keys he had stupidly left in the bowl. He could not get into his locker or toolbox at work today because of his forgotten keys.

The roar of the powerful engine made him sigh with relief. The car with the fitted Cotsworth engine belonged to Ray Buckley and Ray was the only person Harold knew who stayed beyond the Danish butcher shop. He opened his front door as the green Riley pulled up at his gate.

Harold knew the Buckleys as friends of Frank and Lorna Connolly, Also Ray as a member of the MU tug-of-war team. They had chatted on a number of occasions, especially about the beautiful green Riley Ray had acquired.

Harold met them at the gate, and Ray who was very elegantly holding Marion's arm lending support, passed her over to Harold. "See you tomorrow then," he said then caught the look on Harold's face. "Look Harry, I don't know what's going on. She arrived at our place in a terrible state, walked all that way to tell us she wants to come with us over the weekend!"

"She's what?" Harold exploded in frustration.

Ray showed the palms of his hands, "Speak to Marion, Harry."

"Yes, speak to Marion Harry. Don't talk about me as if I wasn't here!" Marion cut in bitterly.

Harold looked at her in surprise. He had never heard that tone of voice. She spun on her heel and walked into the house. Harold turned back to Ray, his eyebrows furrowed.

"Look, for what it's worth, when I got home I found Marion sitting with Babs. Seemingly this morning at the Twiga, Babs invited both you and Marion to spend the weekend with us at a resort up in Troodos. When the party broke up Lorna Connolly dropped Marion off here. An hour and a half later she appears at our door! She's walked all the way, only to tell us she wants to come with us, SHE wants to come with us ... but not with you Harry. Didn't say why or anything else just she wants to come with us tomorrow. She's dead sober. I thought she might have been tippling, the state she was in but ..." Ray shrugged, "anyway like I say, I don't know what's going on, you'll have to sort it out. I've arranged to pick my lot up after work, around 1.30 tomorrow, if you want to come you'll be welcome, but be ready. I like to get up there in time to watch the sun go down." Ray did not relish any sort of domestic problem. Back in the car he started the engine, nodded and drove off.

Climbing the steps slowly Harold found Marion in the lounge. She was sitting at the table crying, sobbing heavily but quietly. He sat opposite and waited for the sobs to subside. It took a few minutes for her to snuffle and go quiet but the silence that followed reigned for even longer. Neither of the miserable pair wanted to break the serenity knowing once broken, harsh words would probably follow. Marion was the first to speak. She suddenly asked, "Do you love me Harry?" her tone low but firm.

"With all my heart," he answered truthfully.

"Then how can you make love to another woman?"

Harold wanted to answer as truthfully as possible and hopefully without hurting her but the directness of her question caught him off guard, "I don't ... "

"You DO ... please Harry," she shouted, "if you love me don't lie to me anymore! If we have any chance of ever picking up the pieces, don't LIE to me." Her voice was strained and hard.

"I was about to say I don't anymore," he spoke humbly.

"When was the last time?" she fired at him.

"When you told me you were pregnant."

"And when did it start?"

"Marion Sweetheart I don't want ..."

"WHEN DID IT START?" Tears were flowing down her face although staring hard at him.

"January," he hesitated but knew it was pointless holding back, "1965."

The answer came like a kick in her lower belly. Her brain tried to count back but she couldn't come up with the precise time period. "How long was that Harry, two years? This is April 1967 so you can tell me ... it's been going on for a very long time, hasn't it ... MY GOD."

Harold walked round the table and went to place a hand on her shoulder. "Don't touch me," she pulled away. "I have to hear every sordid detail before I can ever think straight again. Why Harry? Wasn't I enough for your needs? Did this Carol give you something different from what I give you, oh please say yes ... so I can have something ... a crumb of something to forgive you."

"I love you Mari, I swear I love you with all my heart." He wanted to reach out, take her in his arms but she had wedged herself firmly between chair and table.

"Then why? WHY Harry?" she shouted again, "If you love me ... WHY?"

"I thought I had feelings for her Mari, but I only realised when you told me you were pregnant that I loved you, and only you, I swear to God. I feel so ashamed." Harold was now in abject fear of losing the only woman he had ever had so many deep and wonderful feelings for.

"What were you doing, playing one of us against the other, seeing which one of us you could get pregnant first?" She threw something at him and it fluttered down on the table. He stared at the torn sachet and grasped the last straw. "I've lent the van out to a couple of mates you know," he spoke quietly.

"And do your mates wear red panties?" Marion again threw something, this time with much more accuracy. The object draped itself over Harold's head.

He caught the faintest whiff of body odour and a familiar perfume as he clawed the wisp of material from his face. He stared at them and recalled the one and only time Carol had lost a pair of panties she claimed she really liked. They had both searched inside and around the van fruitlessly for them. 'Well,' Harold thought as he gazed at the excruciatingly damning evidence in his hand, 'they've certainly been found now.' He could not speak.

Marion sucked in air, "Harry, I'm going away with the Buckleys tomorrow for the weekend. I want time to think, to sort things out in my mind."

"I want to come with you." Harold said as firmly as he could muster.

"If you don't let me go alone this one time, I will go home to Scotland as soon as I can!" It was Marion who was now speaking in a sad low tone. "I need time on my own, away from you. I have to think this out, allow it to filter through my system and cleanse all these terrible images running through my head."

Harold sat quiet then after a lengthy pause said, "Okay." It came out like a grunt but she heard and understood. She was about to stand when Harold said, "Mari, never lose sight that whatever I did wrong, I did it believing it was all right to do it. I thought I loved her, I thought I could love you both. Of course I was wrong, very wrong. But it's over and finished. I love you Mari, there will never be anyone else. I swear on the head of our unborn child, I will never EVER do anything to hurt you again."

Marion looked at Harold for a long moment then stood and walked to the door where she stopped and turned, "Harry, I want to sleep alone tonight, would you mind sleeping in the spare room?" Without waiting for an answer she left the lounge and Harold heard their bedroom door close softly. It was barely 4 o'clock in the afternoon. They had not eaten but it was certain neither of them could swallow a morsel between them. The drink cabinet beckoned and Harold reached inside. He pulled out a bottle of brandy and a glass. Harold was about to considerably shorten the miserable night ahead.

Many hours later, Harold heard a door close and with great difficulty raised his head from the arm on which it had been resting. The first thing that registered was the brandy bottle. It was lying on its side and he vaguely recalled trying desperately to place the bottle upright but it insisted on falling over. Maybe it was falling over because it was empty. He laughed ironically for he had drunk the contents, therefore he must be full, yet he couldn't stand up either! There was no justice.

He turned his head away from the recumbent bottle. The second thing to register was her silhouette in the doorway. It was dark but the hall light was on and framed in the entrance was the slim figure of Marion swathed in a thin lace nightgown. "Harry," she said softly. Harold peered at her, drinking in her exotic beauty. "Mari," he said struggling to rise. Once on his rubbery legs he worked his way round the table then staggered towards her. They fell into each other's arms and Harold pushed his face into her thick freshly washed hair. "Oh Mari, Mari I'm sorry." He kissed her and felt himself harden immediately against her soft slim body. She reciprocated, pushing against him as his hands roamed round her waist, hips and buttocks. She was lovely and soft yet firm.

A pin prick of a pick axe was picking away in his brain. This silken waist was wonderfully firm and slim, too slim! Was this a dream? Marion was pregnant! He frowned and pulled his head from the luscious smelling hair and looked down into the beautiful oval face.

"Nina?" he said in surprise, then tried to pull away but her arms were firm around him, supporting him as he would surely have fallen.

"Ssh." She placed four fingers across his lips. "Ssh, ssh Harry, your keetchen door, she open, I hear the trahbel with you and your wife. Early, early before the dark come. I wahry because eet so quiet, I t'ink maybe you do somet'ing bad Harry, I come see. You dreenk too mach, no Harry, you must not be alone, not tonight." Nina took his hand and led him slowly and quietly like a floating apparition to the second bedroom.

~~~

Marion sat at the solid wooden table outside the chalet and watched Babs, Ray and their two little girls climb up the hill. No sound came from their feet as they walked over the mattress of pine needles. The setting was idyllic as she remembered when Harold brought her to this resort two years ago. How different it had all been then, how different she thought it had all been. 'He was actually seeing that girl then ... when we were curled up in front of a roaring log fire in No.9 chalet making plans for our future, he was making love to Carol even then ... oh how could he?'

Natalie, aged five and youngest of the two Buckley girls interrupted Marion's thoughts. She had stopped a few feet away and was holding her arms out. Marion did likewise and the child ran forward to clamber on to her knee.

"You be careful you don't hurt your auntie Marion Natalie, you know she's expecting a baby." Babs believed in keeping an open mind with her children regarding the facts of life.

"She's all right Babs, you won't hurt me, will you pet?" Marion gave the child a hug.

It was Sunday evening. The weekend had flown in a whirl of relaxation for Marion. For her part, most of the time she just sat in the warm spring sunshine which was very pleasant up here in the mountains. She had tried ... and enjoyed short walks through the glorious pines but the weight of her child was beginning to bear heavily on her. The resting was wonderful, the peace and tranquillity therapeutic so the ache caused by Harold's philandering had eased, a fraction.

The hurt would never go away, that was much too deep. It would leave a scar and for the moment, the wound was painful, raw and obvious. The best she could hope for was it might in time heal over and blend into the background of her life. However, one firm resolution had settled in her mind over the weekend. There was no doubt she could never stop loving Harold, but was still finding it difficult to forgive him, and wondered if she ever could.

Babs climbing the steps up to the chalet asked, "Marion, we're going to get tidied up then have a meal in the bar, just to finish off our holiday. Feel up to it?"

"That'll be nice, yes all right." They had spent their two evenings in the pleasant little bar where Ray in his inimitable style had entertained not only Marion and his family but also the other bar occupants. "Can I help with the kids?" Marion asked.

"Not really Mari, they're going to get a wash then change out of those clothes they've been tearing round in all day, then come with us. Are you all packed?"

"Yes, for the little I brought, it took me two minutes."

"Good, then you've probably noticed Ray's already disappeared into the bar so why don't you join him? He knows what we want and he'll order for us. Go on, we'll join you soon." Marion looked round uncertainly. There was nothing in the chalet left to do so it was a good idea to order the food as it took a while to prepare. "Okay Babs, see you in the bar then."

Babs wanted Marion to do anything as long as it took her out of that faraway mood she seemed to spend most of her time in. She had not pried into Marion's closed almost meditative monk like state she seemed happy to lock herself away in. Now as watching the lovely girl cross the area towards the bar, although beginning to show her pregnancy, she had a style in that slow wonderful walk. And her head had lifted, just a little, but it was a sign. Babs did think the weekend had worked a minor miracle, for the gentle girl had begun to smile again. And Marion's smile was in itself, a minor miracle.

"I thought you were never coming," said Ray, then under his breath for only the barmaid to hear, "said the actress to the bishop." He was at the bar collecting his second pint when Babs and the children entered. Marion who had kept Ray company for fifteen minutes was seated at a table by the window festooned with bright coloured napkins and candles. For the next few minutes Ray was busy buying and taking drinks over to the table. Just as he sat down, he got the signal the food was ready. There was no waiter service so meals had to be collected at the bar. "No, no," Ray held Babs in her seat, "I do the fetching and carrying tonight, it's not often I get the chance to service you my dear," he leered wickedly at her.

"Please, I'd prefer not to discuss our sex life in front of the children," Babs said quietly, out of earshot of the two girls who were completely wrapped in their own conversation anyway.

"Right, and it's not often I get the chance to fall down cleavage like Marilyn's got. Hold me back ...." Ray rushed off back to the barmaid with the Marilyn Monroe cleavage and name.

"He's harmless," Babs said watching the tight little smile play around Marion's mouth as she in turn watched Bab's husband who never seemed to be in any other mood. Ray's cheeriness rubbed off on the others and he had helped the weekend to fly pleasantly by.

An hour later Ray insisted on taking the empty dishes back to the bar and as he collected the last napkin, Babs leaned over, "Go and chat up the barmaid, for a few minutes."

Ray turned his head but said nothing as he peered into his wife's eyes.

"Just for five minutes," Babs said marginally inclining her head towards Marion.

"Excuse me Marion," Ray leaned over the table, "I'm just going over to the bar, I fear I'm about to break the heart of that young lady's over there. You see she is totally unaware I am about to leave this oasis of love she has created for me. It seems I just cannot help but make lasting impression on women, forgive me."

His two daughters covered their mouths tittering gleefully at their fun loving father.

"I'll make a lasting impression on your face in a minute, bugger off Ray." Babs hissed.

When her husband had shook his fair hair back into its ruffled and windswept state, he sauntered away. "Thank God for that, he can be a right ars- ... idiot at times." Babs said as she watched Ray approach the barmaid yet again. The buxom girl smiled her greeting at the effervescent Ray at which point Babs turned to her friend. "Marion," she spoke quietly, "it's none of my business, but I'd like to help any way I can."

"I know Babs, you're very sweet and you've been like a mother hen over me all weekend. I appreciate everything you've done ... and not done." Marion knew Babs had been at great pains to help but had never mentioned until now, her problem. "I know I've been a damp squid, not participating in anything but I've had a lot to think about."

"I know you have,"

"You know I have?" Marion looked up, "You know, don't you?"

Babs looked away then back into Marion's eyes and saw clearly the hurt deep within. "Yes, I think I know, but it doesn't matter how I know." She had no wish to hurt this girl any more than she was already aching. How could she tell her Harold's affair had at one time, been the base of the women circle's jokes. Marion started to talk, slowly at first, starting with the night in Kyrenia when Harold called Carol's name at the peak of

506

intercourse. She told Babs everything; about her feelings, about her love for Harold, and her doubts if she could continue her marriage under this black cloud.

"Do you think Ray and I are happy Marion?" Babs asked.

"Oh yes, very."

"Would you believe for a year after we got married, I was seeing ... and sleeping with a boyfriend? I just could not give up. I thought I loved him. Ray found out and it nearly killed the poor bugger. I'm convinced he deliberately crashed his car in a rally." Babs paused watching her girls play at the window "It was then I realised it was Ray I really loved. I've been making it up to him ever since. I really hurt him, but I'll never hurt him again."

Similar words had been said to Marion as recently as Friday afternoon. Harold's beautiful but broken face floated across her vision. "Did you ever have regrets Babs, about the other bloke?"

"Yes and no! That chap was someone I simply had to get out of my system, but once I made the break, got clear of him, the love for Ray got stronger, beautiful and most of all ... uncluttered. I love the daft bastard with all my heart."

The smile on the London girl's face was not wide, but it bore the stamp of contentment and happiness. Impulsively Marion half stood and leaned over the table. She hugged Babs in an awkward embrace. "Thank you, oh thank you thank you."

"Listen you two, why is it when I do that, I get a belt round the ear?" Ray had stood back for a minute as the two girls hugged but the position could not have been comfortable for a pregnant woman. He cut it short. "I don't know what's been going on, but I wish I was caught up in the middle of you two."

"Oh if you weren't so happily married I would kiss you Ray" The smile was back, lighting the room. Marion looked into Babs face, "Thank you again, I can never thank you enough ... I'm just desperate now to get home."

Ray gave his wife a quizzical look tinged with new respect. She'd somehow worked the oracle. Ray never one to lose the chance at making a crack, said to Marion, "Listen, we've spent a lovely weekend together, you and me, but don't let a little thing like marriage stop you from doing whatever takes your fancy with me. I guarantee you won't get pregnant again."

Babs could not speak. She was so choked with her own emotions at the unheralded show of love from the lovely girl and desperately wanted to return the hug. She turned to Shirley who stood looking blankly at all these silly adults. "Right girls, time to go, give us a hug Shirl!"

Ray shook his head; all this show of unbridled affection was beyond him. "Maralyn I want a gallon of the stuff these two have been drinking," he called to the laughing barmaid. The two women and children had only ordered fruit drinks. The bat eared comedian was the only one to have beer.

"I'll see you lot outside," Ray said, "I'll pack the car and hand in the keys. Don't be long."

In the chalet he found the luggage by the door. After a quick check for toothbrushes or pyjamas under the children's pillows, he gave Babs a mental pat on the back before carrying everything out to the car.

It was such a joy to drive this car. A little over a year ago a friend had been looking around the car showrooms in Nicosia. The friend, knowing Ray had a love for certain cars and his background of rally driving, told him he had seen a Riley 4/72 saloon. Ray was interested. But when he phoned the showroom and learned the car had a Cotsworth 2 litre engine, he got into his three-month-old Simca and drove to Nicosia. Returning home in the throbbing Riley Babs had just shook her head at her irrepressible husband.

Starting and revelling at the growl as the engine fired up he sat back and listened for a moment with pleasure to its throaty purr, then clicking into gear, and not without a tingling chill of immense pride, rolled the car over to the building which housed the bar, restaurant and reception. Leaving the engine ticking over he pushed the chalet keys through the reception letterbox, then returned to the car. Settling into the leather seat, he was looking forward to the run back to Limassol. He would take it easy down the mountain for there had been a lot of rain the previous night but once let loose on the level he would open her up, clear her tubes a little.

The noisy chatter of happy females warned him his wife had at last condoned to join him. He looked at the Smiths clock on the dash and nodded. Darkness had fallen but they would be home comfortably by 8.30. "Home James and don't spare the horses," he declared as Babs and the others arrived.

"No you don't Ray Stirling Moss Buckley, you take very good care of them horses under that bonnet. You take it nice and easy until we get down and off this mountain, do what you like after that." Babs showed uncharacteristic signs of nervousness. The mountain road frightened her even in daytime.

"Precisely what I had planned madam," Ray droned. "Settle down and enjoy the scenery."

Which of course was impossible as the night was as black as jet under the trees. He meandered out of the resort and down out of the forest. Once clear of the trees, the stars and moon enveloped everything in a silky silver sheen. Marion settled as Ray, driving expertly was if anything driving slower than normal. She was sitting between the two girls and both snuggled into her. They were tired and wanted only to close their eyes and open them outside their own house. Marion, situated as she was in the middle of the rear seat had an unobstructed view of the road ahead. She was fascinated by the strong beams of light thrusting out into the darkness framing the two silhouettes of Ray on the right and Babs on the left, their heads pitch black against the bright illuminated background. The throbbing of the engine, the piercing arrow point of the twin poles of penetrating light contributed to the hypnotic effect on Marion and her mind raced ahead in a dreamlike trance. She envisaged the meeting with Harry and knew in her heart she had forgiven him. The one off affair had tested her feelings but they had survived and she felt Harry would be a better person for his perilously close brush to losing her. She really believed what he told her, 'He loved her and there could never be anyone else.' Marion smiled and with an arm round each girl on either side of her, hugged them both. Harry, like all men were just kids. They needed controlling ... and loving ... and looking after ... and sometimes ... they slipped up. She fell asleep.

The faintest squeals of the rear tyres made her blink her eyes into wakefulness. Ray was driving carefully as he snaked the big car round the sharp bends but the tyres were complaining a little as he twisted the car weight from right to left. Marion again started to watch the twin beams as they fell into a pattern. The harsh ragged rock face of the cliff would light up dead ahead only to go sliding past on her left and the beams into black space. Then as the sharp frightening wall of rock reappeared and was about to swallow them again, Ray turned the wheel in a clockwise direction and the beams would shoot off into nothingness, into space again. Marion found the lights snaking off into the void exhilarating as the seconds passed in silence, then suddenly the rock face appeared again then the whole cycle would start over.

Every passenger who travelled up or down this road at night experienced what Marion was going through, but not the driver. Ray's eyes were fixed on his side of the well maintained centre line. There were no on coming lights climbing the mountain so it was safe to assume he had the road to himself, but Ray took nothing for granted. He stuck safely to his side of the line.

Marion was just nodding off again when something broke through her dozing slumber. A man appeared at the point where the beams of light met on a short piece of straight road. He was standing on the middle white line waving a red flag.

"Shit!" Ray exclaimed and Marion blinked awake at his outburst. "It's those bloody terrorists again." He cast his mind back to when he and his friends had been stopped near here on the Whitsun weekend two years before. It had been a complete waste of time that night and he never discovered what these people wanted. A flush of misgiving slithered over his mind. What if those terrorists had found women in the car that night two years ago? There had only been four men but what if it had been four women? And there were four females in this car tonight! It didn't matter to these people what ages they were or if one was pregnant. They were female! Questions of all sorts suddenly bombarded Ray as he applied the brake and the car slowed. The man with the flag, an evil looking bastard, on seeing the car slow down walked to the side of the road and nodded to someone. A man stepped from a cleft in the cliff face and approached the car. On impulse Ray floored the accelerator. "I'm not stopping," he yelled causing Babs to scream in alarm.

"They're Turkish terrorists Babs, God knows what they want but they're not getting it here."

The engine roared and the Riley sat back on its springs as it shot past the surprised and furious flag waving man. But Ray had made the bend and expertly skated round it, the back end skidding away under him but under perfect control. Ray sighed, he had expected to hear some sort of shooting but his unexpected quick take off had probably caught them off guard. Easing back slightly for he still wanted to put some distance between himself and the terrorists, but not kill himself in the process. He could see the road ahead was again perfectly clear and congratulated himself on his clear quick thinking.

Without warning an object appeared on the next bend. The image was barely discernible and it was only as he approached, now only thirty feet from the car, could the object be identified. Piles of fallen rock were all over the road! In that flashing fleeting second there was no time to think. Ray saw a gap between the solid mass of rocks and edge of the road. It was a risk but the space was wide enough to get the car through. Ray had to make a split second decision; no matter how hard he braked he would crash into the rock pile, That in itself was not life threatening but at the present fifty mph speed, even getting down twenty, crashing into the angled rock pile would probably bounce the car off the narrow road and over the drop to his right. The only alternative left was to go for the gap. So be it! Hitting the brakes as hard as possible and hauling on the hand brake, he skilfully managed to steer for the gap.

Marion held her breath as the beams of light shot out into darkness but Ray was skidding and manoeuvring expertly through and round the breach to the right of the rock pile, miraculously missing the jutting fallen rocks as they flew past narrowly missing the left side of the car.

Ray thankfully pumped the brakes to stop the skid but the air was sucked from his lungs when the road, clear and passing so uncannily quiet under the edge of the bonnet, disappeared!

There was no more road. The heavy rains the previous night had caused the massive rock fall and the bludgeoning weight had sheared a short stretch of road from the face of the mountain.

The Riley shot out into space, the weightlessness causing Ray's feet to slide and lift off the brake pedal. The wheels, liberated from the curbing effect of both road and brakes, spun free allowing the engine noise to grow into a growl, then quickly to a roar, and finally like a dying aircraft into a screaming whine.

Marion positioned as she was in the back, could not see the road disappear and searched for the rock face to light up again as Ray grappled with the wheel which seemed to have come loose in his hands. There was something drastically wrong, she could not understand precisely what but there was nothing she could do about it anyway. She slumped back in her seat as Babs and Ray, abandoning the wheel, threw their arms around each other. Ray was crying into his wife's neck, "I'm sorry - I thought - oh I'm so sorry."

There was a wonderful sensation of floating, of weightlessness as Marion calmly looked round. She didn't hear the whining roar of the engine. The young woman was aware only of a deep sadness that she would never see her unborn child, or her lovely Harry again.

She placed a hand on the head of Natalie, the sleeping child on her right. The other arm she linked with Shirley on her left who was awake but bravely silent. Her free left hand she pressed against her swollen belly. The headlights were still on, brighter if anything, arcing out into space but meeting nothing to illustrate their brilliance. Then slowly into view as the car nose dipped, the lights settled on a brilliant silver green carpet of tree tops. They were rushing towards her.

Marion smiled ironically and sighed. It all looked so beautiful, it looked so very, very nice.

~~~

Chapter 23

The news of the accident swept through RAF Akrotiri base but nowhere did it cause bigger shock waves than in the yard of the General Engineering Flight of 103 Maintenance Unit.

Chief Tech. Jock McKinley on hearing the news shook his head sadly. He initially assumed, 'Aye, young Buckley's paid the ultimate penalty for his drinkin'.' This was followed by severe remorse when he learned the accident was caused by a rock fall shearing away part of the mountain road. "Sorry son, jumpin' the gun a wee bit there," muttered the old Chief under his breath. "That could have happened to any o' us. God rest a' yer souls."

A pall of gloom hung over the Machine Shop. Frank Connolly and his family had been close friends with the Buckleys but the biggest shock and surprise was when Frank heard Marion Ross had also been killed in the accident. He was stunned and overwhelmed with the news, which filtered through the grapevine shortly after starting work. He refused to believe the early morning rumour but confirmation came when the official order for coffin plates arrived in the Machine shop at 10 am. How could Frank possibly explain this to his family? Apart from the sad loss of the entire Buckley family, the young lass from Kirkaldy had particularly endeared herself to Lorna and the Connolly children.

Mustapha the machine shop labourer immediately broke down in tears. The little Turk and the Londoner had shared a similar sense of crazy humour. Ray on one of his many visits to the Machine Shop had caught Mustapha beautifully one morning, although it must be said, Mustapha loved to be 'caught.' The Englishman had manoeuvred the bare-labourer into placing a glass of water on his forehead. This of course was a simple task for Mustapha, who often danced in his village with a glass of ouzo on his head in a display of dancing ability and balance. When Ray had finally got Mustapha bent over backwards with the glass balanced firmly on the dark forehead, Ray produced a jug of ice-cold water and poured it down inside the front of the unfortunate Turk's trousers.

Down at the other end of Akrotiri in Station Workshops, no words in any language can explain Harold Ross's devastation. When Marion had not arrived home on the Sunday night Harold assumed she would arrive early next morning. He waited until the last minute, waving his pick-up bus on, before leaving for work in his van as 6-55 a.m. Shards of broken glass begun to dance in his innards as the morning wore on. He consoled himself with blithe inner messages such as 'no news is good news,' etc., but at 9 o'clock when he saw some of his mates start to cast covert glances in his direction, he decided to phone Chief Tech. McKinley at the 103 Armoury. The gnarled old Scot told him simply, "SAC Buckley has not arrived for duty."

The Riley had broken down. Harold grasped on the excuse. That was the only logical reason they were late. Why was he getting himself so uptight? There was some rational reason why they were not back and he would hear soon enough. If that was true, why was his gut twisting, his breath coming in short gasps, and his mates avoiding him?

At 10 o'clock the Commanding Officer Technical Wing telephoned Workshops and asked if SAC Ross might report to the COs office on a personal matter. This was the confirmation Harold needed! He knew now there was something wrong but did not expect by the longest stretch of his wildest imagination to receive the news he did.

"Stand easy Ross," said Wing Commander Hollier as the obviously worried young airman marched into his office.

'Oh sweet Jesus,' thought Hollier, 'what appalling news to pass on to such a young chap.' The officer looked up, "Ross, I'm afraid I have some rather bad news."

The airman tottered slightly. "Perhaps you better sit down," the CO said gently.

Harold could hardly breathe. The walls had started to close in on him. He shook his head.

Wing Commander Hollier detested these duties. He had performed similar in the past, but this one was particularly horrendous. "I believe your wife travelled with a family named Buckley to a resort in the Troodos Mountains over the weekend?" He stated in a flat monotone.

Harold's throat closed. He was gagging and could only stare at the Wing Commander.

"You must prepare yourself for a shock Ross. Please, won't you sit down." The man was decidedly rocky on his feet and for some seconds stared wide-eyed, then startling his CO the airman suddenly exploded, "FOR CHRIST'S SAKE SIR ... TELL ME WHAT HAPPENED!"

"Of course, yes of course, I'm terribly sorry." Hollier gathered himself, "It is my unfortunate duty to pass on some terrible news. ... Senior Aircraftsman Ross, at twenty-twenty five hours yesterday evening, your wife, along with an SAC Buckley, his wife and their two children were travelling by car on the Troodos mountain road. Due to a rock fall a small section of the road had broken away. It grieves me to tell you Ross, the car ran off the road. Unfortunately ..." the officer looked up apologetically but in a firm voice continued, "there were no survivors."

There was a look of non-comprehension on the airman's face. The words had penetrated Harold's brain with the touch of a steam hammer pounding every nerve end in his body. A bright white light was washing through his consciousness, washing out the words. The words were unacceptable, unwanted and being beaten into nothingness by the pounding hammer.

"Are you all right Ross?" The officer asked. A glazed look had swept over the man's eyes.

"I'm ... all right ... sir, thank you ... sir!" Harold replied, unaware he was shouting at the top of his voice.

"Ross, sit down!" the Wing Commander ordered as he himself stood up.

"I'm all right sir." The voice had adopted a new tone, like the man was being strangled.

"I said sit down Ross ... please!"

Harold fell into a straight-backed chair, wide eyed and bewildered.

"Sergeant!" Hollier called to his NCO who sat at a desk in the main office. The man quickly appeared at the door. "Sir?"

"Telephone the Medical Officer sergeant, we have a case of severe shock on our hands."

The sergeant glanced at Harold and saw the wide staring, but sightless eyes. "Right away sir!" Harold started to sob. Strange he had no idea why he was sobbing for all conscious thought had been plugged when a door slammed closed in his head. A part of

515

him was dimly aware the sobs were progressively developing from little more than sharp intakes of breath into harsh racking wails of sound, tearing painfully at his throat and chest. All the time the tiny part of his brain that still retained enough clarity to think, was asking why was he crying. The nonstop nagging question was slowly, very slowly, prying open the door so harshly shut. He caught only a glimpse but what he saw through the partially opened aperture induced Harold to stand on his feet and stare blindly at the Wing Commander. Nonplussed as to why Ross was glaring at him, the officer was about to call again for his sergeant when the airman screamed at the top of his voice, "NO ... NOO ... NOOOooo!" As the door of comprehension in Harold's brain opened wide, he dropped to the floor at the officer's feet in a dead faint.

The Medical Officer placed Harold in the Princess Margaret Rose hospital. On admittance, the nurses assumed he was speaking gibberish when they heard him muttering over and over, 'Provydinskilderurmeuckinina!' In Harold's head the words were very clear; 'Providence killed her for me fucking Nina.' The unpronounceable word tumbled out hour after hour, even in sedative induced sleep, the same mumblings dribbled from his inert mouth. The MO kept him in for rest and observation initially for three days. But another week of convalescence passed unnoticed by Harold. Back on his feet on the tenth day, he sat on the balcony of the ward staring out over the Mediterranean, eating little, while his body and mind reluctantly returned to a world of reality he did not want to be part of.

When the MO hinted he might be sent back to the UK Harold shook his head. "I feel lost in this environment without her sir but I have friends here. In England I would surely kill myself. Give me a few days leave, I'll be all right after that."

The atmosphere in the house in Pappachristos street hung over Harold in a smothering cloak of memories. Helena fussed and busied herself around him. Giga and Nina tried to comfort him but he cut them both dead, holding a deep resentment towards Nina. To get away he drove off to anywhere his thoughts and mind led him, sleeping rough and eventually to Kyrenia where he slept in a bar, the owner kindly providing accommodation. Harold could not face Demetria's Bar or the Bristol hotel.

Three weeks after the accident Harold reported back to work. Chief Kowaleski sent for him and warned the big No.4 he must put all his troubles behind him and get fit for the return match with the MU the following week. The GEF team had not lost during Harold's enforced absence but had not shone either. On leaving the coach's office Harold shook his head balefully but turned out later that morning for training, as 'requested' by his coach. He might as well have stayed in the section. As Bernard watched hoping to see something of the old Harold Ross, he was disappointed. The stuffing had been knocked out of the man and no amount of threats could inject any fire into him.

One hundred and fifty yards down the road on the MU Callum McAlpine slotted the genial giant Irishman Sam Haire from the 'B' team into Ray's position. He proved a capable replacement, lacking only Ray's staying power, but that would come in time. However, stamina was not required in the long awaited return match on the Wednesday afternoon at Akrotiri. The contest turned out to be a damp squib. The MU took the first end after a short stiff struggle, then won the second end fairly easily. Whether this was due to the induction of Sam Haire into one team, or the exclusion of Harold Ross from the other was anyone's guess. Chief Kowaleski swore and threatened but the MU were back on top of the league. The result was heartening for the MU with the League virtually won with Station Sports and another possible clash with Kowaleski's GEF team only two weeks away.

After the final whistle the GEF team sat on the ground in a despondent heap. Bernard surveyed them in disgust, hawked and spat in the grass then turned and stomped off towards his car. He got in, slammed the door, then seconds later clambered out bearing a long starting handle. One hefty crank and the engine started. Without a glance in any direction, he got back in and screeched onto the road in a skidding turn.

"Isn't he a bloody charmer," exclaimed Callum to no one in particular, then became aware of Josh at his elbow. His friend was staring with a worried expression after the departing Minx.

"Yes Callum, that man has a massive grudge against life for some reason."

Callum was the only person Josh had only recently taken into his confidence. The Scot knew all about Yvonne and their son

Allan now safe with relatives in Manchester. He also knew of arrangements made by the couple for later this very evening when Josh intended to secretly drive Yvonne to Nicosia airport. Mrs. Kowaleski was booked on the 2300 hours UK flight.

Both men watched the dissimilar brake lights gleam as the disgruntled GEF coach slowed to take the bend leading to the camp gate. "Will Yvonne be all right?" Callum asked.

"God, I hope so!" Josh muttered. "She used to duck into Pat Parrott's when he came home in a foul mood, but they're back home so it'll be her landlady's house for refuge now I suppose. She's bound to see he's totally lost it today."

"Aye, she better stay out of his road, that crazy bastard's capable of anythin' after that result," Callum turned to look at the two teams. He was happy to see they were mingling freely.

"She'll stay clear of him don't worry and by the time he gets home later tonight after screwing his whores, Yvonne'll be on her way." Josh smiled. Their plans were taking shape.

Callum placed an arm around his friend's shoulders, "C'mon, we still have to shake hands wi' the losers. D'you like that ... losers? We made them look sick today Josh, didn't we?"

Josh nodded, "We did that, we most certainly did!"

Callum went serious again, "That car o' yours Josh, you sure it'll get you to Nicosia?"

"Ye of so little faith! Has it ever let us down, really? Think about it, it never has! Only this morning I put fresh epoxy glue around the carb, no smell of petrol now." Josh nodded firmly.

"You'll be tellin' me next you've changed the elastic bands on her drive shaft."

"You've been looking under her bonnet Corporal McAlpine, and that's no place for strangers. I'm the only one allowed to fiddle around in her delicate areas. Keep your hands off!"

Someone else had watched Bernard stomp away from his scene of disappointment. He watched Bernard throw himself into the driver's seat after starting the car with the cranked handle and drive off like a cat with its tail on fire. Julian felt so sorry for Bernard. Why had the two coaches become such bitter enemies? As soon as Bernard left the scene of battle, the sworn foes of both sides proved their bitterness lived on the sports field, but died as soon as the final whistle sounded. Afterwards they could mingle, joke, and laugh together. But not Bernard.

518

Julian felt for the man who made it so obvious how desperate he was to beat the team from the Maintenance Unit. He wanted to offer his condolences, or just speak to the man, to comfort him. Didn't Bernard understand the immense mountain he was tackling? To remove the crown from the MU had been tried many times in the past. Had he not already gained a splendid victory and with it a massive slice of tug-of-war glory? Surely he could not expect to claim the whole cake. "Oh," Julian sighed, "if only I could comfort you."

~~~

Yvonne heard the squeal of tyres followed by the crunch of gravel. Every evening without fail, Bernard announced his frame of mind by the way he entered the driveway. This evening Yvonne heeded the screech of tormented rubber indicating tonight's mood was bad. She learned from Josh the top two teams were due to meet this afternoon and her dear husband's arrival declared without doubt the result. If she was correct in her assumption, then it was prudent to be well clear of him. She hurried out back to Daria's house and entered her kitchen.

Yvonne was ecstatic about returning home but miserable at the prospect of not seeing Josh until the end of the year. She was more or less packed although nothing was in her suitcase, not yet! Once Bernard went off on his usual Wednesday night pilgrimage to the town's bars and brothels, she would quickly lift her pre-arranged bundles of clothes into her case. Although Bernard often stated he would be happy to be rid of her, she did not trust him. He was very possessive with everything and dreaded to think what his reaction would be if he discovered her short spell at prostitution, or her involvement with Josh. With Pam and Fred Parrott returning to the UK her last link with friendship and normality had gone. There were minor links with others like Lorna Connolly but nobody close. Only Josh remained and she could not see him as often as she wanted. Their plans were she would return to England and try, with her sister Jean's help to set up a home for Josh when his tour finished at the end of the year. Plans had been well thought out; the first step was to take place that night. With Bernard off whoring, Josh would pick Yvonne up at 8.30, in plenty time for booking in at 10 o'clock.

Bernard came round the side of the house like a marauding bull and saw Yvonne with Daria just inside the door of the Greek-Cypriot woman's kitchen. "Haven't you got anything better to do than stand gossiping to wogs all day. Is my meal ready?" he roared.

Yvonne glared defiantly at him, "There's stew and potatoes on the stove, help yourself!"

Bernard stopped at the back door, "You bitch! You do fuck all all day and you can't take the time to serve my meals!" he shouted across the small yard.

"You're lucky I cook for you, you sick sod." Yvonne sounded bold but inwardly wary of this man who was blatantly mad and getting worse every day. Why did the RAF not throw him out? Yvonne apologised to Daria although the woman had already formed her own opinion. She felt sad Yvonne, or any woman should have to live with such a man.

Bernard banged the door behind him, rattling the glass in the upper half to the point of shattering. With a disdainful stare at the door, Daria took the English woman's arm. "Kom Eefawn, you take the Toorkish caffee weeth Daria. Maybe he goes quiet when he eets."

The two women sat at a small kitchen table, sipping the strong black brew. Amazingly, considering her initial disgust to her first tasting the drink, Yvonne had grown to like the thick acrid drink. She must sup it the way Daria had shown her; sucking noisily the froth and coffee from the surface, making very unladylike noises in the process. Her feelings for the Greek-Cypriot woman had grown to border kinship. Daria had bathed Yvonne's wounds on occasion when the English girl had run from the house to her second port of refuge when neither Pat or Fred Parrott were at home. Now the time was at hand for Yvonne to leave and perhaps never see Daria again. On impulse she pulled a £5 note from her pocket and held it out.

"What?" the olive skinned woman said, staring at the money but made no move to take it.

"I'm going to tell you a secret, but you must tell no one until after I've gone. Here take it."

"Secret?" repeated Daria puzzled, then "gone?" Her eyebrows shot up into her hairline.

"I'm going home to England, tonight. You know Josh who comes here sometimes?"

"Yes, I sometime see heem." Daria answered vaguely.

"Josh is the father of my son, not that crazy bastard in there."

Daria tittered but said nothing. Yvonne went on, "Josh told me to tell no one I was leaving. His motto is you can't be too careful. But I trust you Daria." She paused as her landlady leaned over and held both her hands in a warm gesture.

"Josh is taking me to the Nicosia airport tonight. I'm leaving Mr. Kowaleski."

"T'is good!" Daria nodded towards the house, "Thees man, he crazee, better you go. No' come back?"

"One day I would like to return, to visit you, if I may, but somehow I fear I never will."

"Neh, you will come, of course, stay here and we dreenk Toorkish caffee, like now!"

"I will, I will," Yvonne smiled and in turn clasped the hands that had been holding hers. Daria was only a few years older yet perhaps because of her isolation, Yvonne felt the warmth of a new depth to friendship.

They sat together and talked until Yvonne began to grow anxious. The clock on Daria's sideboard was moving inexorably on. It was 7.15 and Bernard had not yet left the house. Just as she glanced again at the clock, as if on cue Bernard emerged from the kitchen and without a glance at Daria's kitchen, went to the garage. They heard the starter whirl, mumbled curses and the clatter of the starter handle being inserted. The engine caught on the second crank and soon he was reversing down the driveway to roar off down the hill into town.

Feel really excited now, Yvonne received a hugging farewell from Daria, slipping the forgotten £5 note, the equivalent of two weeks wages for her husband, into her apron pocket.

Tearfully the English girl returned to the deserted house.

The first thing she had to do was switch on the veranda light above the front door, a pre-arranged signal to let Josh know Bernard was not at home. They had used this signal the previous Wednesday when Bernard was off whoring. Next, she rushed through to the bedroom, hurrying not because she needed to, but budding excitement was goading her. She had over an hour before Josh was due to pick her up so everything must be packed and nothing forgotten. She would not be coming back here.

~~~

Bernard parked across the road from the taxi rank near Hero's Square, and walked to the first brothel bar he was acquainted with. He was anxious to pour some brandy down his throat and steady the nervously ticking mouth. Lately his eyelids had started to act in a peculiar fashion also, flickering very quickly especially when he was angry or upset. 'A few brandies will put that right,' he thought, walking past tables and up to the bar. "Double brandy, no triple, make it a triple Leo," he called to the swarthy Greek barman.

Bernard was halfway into his drink before he felt the cheap harsh liquid start to snip off the jangling feathery fingers that were tugging at his innards making them jump and dance. He sighed contentedly.

Petra, a prostitute who knew Bernard intimately, approached her occasional Wednesday night customer. It was hard-earned money with this man but the middle of the week was the poorest time for trade, as this man knew exploiting to the full the lack of clientele. "Hello lova boy," she smiled an ice-cold teeth exposing grimace that ten years ago had beguiled many a man. "Buy an old friend a dreenk?"

Bernard downed the rest of his brandy, looked the woman over from head to toe, then swung back to the bar. "Same again Leo, and give this bitch an ouzo ... a straight ouzo and I'm going to taste it. When I pay for drink, I want the booze, not water, yeah?"

The comment was not well received by a resentful Leo who hated the British. This one he could cheerfully have killed, as he had done on three occasions in his EOKA guerilla days. Those days were past unfortunately; the best he could hope for now was for this man to catch the 'clap' or worse from one of his girls. But he would catch nothing from Petra, she was clean then Leo saw a glint in the Arab woman's black eyes. He smiled, Petra's temper could be a joy to behold.

"Why you call me the beetch?" asked the raven-haired woman, piqued but not yet prepared to toss away a hated but valuable customer. This man was big and painful but he paid the elevated prices she reserved for him, and sometimes he paid over the top, the only good thing about him.

"Because that is what you are, a dirty little fucking bitch!" Bernard said in a conversational tone glowering into her face, his equally black eyes boring into hers.

"Oh yes!" Her expression showed a tight grin, but there was no humour in her face. Her building anger was similar to a runaway train, once out of control, it became dangerous. "And you?" she spat, "You like to fack the derty little facking beetch ... neh? You kinky man you, eh? You ... you a kinky facking bastard, neh? NEH?" She was shouting now as Leo placed the drinks on the bar.

"Keep it down Petra," Leo called knowing he was adding fuel to Petra's fire. He was used to outbursts and squabbles in his bar, and Petra could at times like these, be the main attraction.

"Whaht?" she rounded on Leo who tried to keep the grin from his face, "You know what thees wan he call me ... ME? He call me derty, DERTY And whaht heem eh? He no derty? Heem, who like to fack in the bams, heh?" Petra was off on a foul mouthed tirade of Bernard that seemed endless.

Bernard felt the bile rise in his throat and wanted to spit it into the face of this raving slut. He tried to ignore her and picked up his drink, downing half the triple brandy.

"Shatup Petra," he shouted and pushed the ouzo towards her, "Drink, forget I spoke."

Petra had been out of sorts all day but if Petra was anything, she was not dirty. She bathed twice a day and hated the feel of the dirty sweaty men she put up with. The ouzo looked inviting and she picked it up but there was no way she was about to drink it. With a flick of the wrist, she whipped the clear fluid into Bernard's face. "You dreenk an you wahsh, you derty bastard. You never get Petra no facking more, you hear me, you hear me good! No more facking in thees leetle bam," she patted her behind. "you derty facking bastard you!"

Bernard wiped a hand over his face, one last fragment of common sense stopping him from lunging at the spitting witch. He vaguely knew that by attacking Petra he would present the two bouncers an open license to give him a good hiding then deposit him in the local clanger. Leo allowed his dogs to beat up British servicemen if they were proving troublesome and Bernard was not about to allow them that privilege, not for a cow like Petra. He picked up his drink and swallowed it, then taking two one-pound notes from his pocket tossed them on the counter.

"Keep the change," he called as calmly as he could muster.

"One minute, sorry friend, five pounds please ... for the drinks." Leo's face was set flint hard.

Bernard looked round and two beefy individuals were close by, grinning at him.

"Pay you derty bastard, you pay for my dreenk ... now!" Petra stopped her nonstop slanging and latched on to this new baiting game. Five pounds was enough money to buy everyone in the place a triple whiskey twice over but Bernard went into his pocket counted and tossed three crumpled notes on the bar top.

Leo picked them up, "There is only three sir, I ask five."

"I already gave you two, I'm going." Bernard turned but found his way blocked.

"I do not see this man's two pounds, do you Petra?" Leo asked the grinning woman.

Petra tugged at something in her cleavage. The two notes could clearly be seen, "No Leo, I no see thees derty bam facking bastard hees money." She laughed raucously.

Bernard was fighting to hold his temper but there was no way out for him. Frustrated and angry at his self-imposed detention, he dug into his pocket and threw the money on the counter, then turned and stormed past the bouncers. He gained the street with derisive calls from Petra and her supporters ringing in his ears. He was unsteady on his feet as an angry red mist clouded his vision. Standing uneasily under the course neon lights from the bar, blinking rapidly in the wash of the verbal abuse, he staggered across the road. He may have looked inebriated but it was not the hastily swallowed alcohol making him stagger. This was due to a mixture of his slight limp, exasperation, hate and frustration at his inability to strike back at the Arab bitch who started it all.

Holding on to a railing, breathing deeply Bernard cleared his vision before looking around. Hero's Square held the same traps as the bar he had just escaped from. Despite his mauling from

Petra, his need and drive had not waned, if anything they were heightened. Perhaps he should direct his attentions to the Turkish quarter where an element of risk existed but only as the area was still out of bounds, enforced nowadays with patrols of RAF snowdrops or army redcaps. But the seed for sexual exploitation was planted and the need to find something new was strong! There were many ways to find a woman in Limassol.

After a few minutes, his eyes focused on the taxi rank across the square from his car. He had heard some taxis ferried customers to amateur prostitutes in the Turkish and Greek quarters. Maybe they could find something to whet his appetite. He felt himself nodding, 'Yes, that's what I need tonight, a nice Turkish belly dancer, or Greek goddess.' Feeling his spirits rise fractionally he went to a Mercedes taxi at the top of the line. Without preamble, he said to the driver, "Can you find me a woman?"

The driver eyed the burly figure framed in the street light. "I don' know you sir."

For a moment, Bernard was stumped then he wondered if perhaps the driver thought he was some sort of undercover policeman. He reached for his wallet and produced his RAF 1250.

The driver looked at the photograph on the identity card. Obviously satisfied he said, "Maybe I can help. Any particular lady you like?"

Bernard had a fleeting vision of Petra, "White, she must be white, no fucking wogs tonight."

Eyes glittered at the insult but there was money to be made. "I take you. Two pounds."

"Two pounds ... for what?"

"I take you. Very nice ... young, seventeen, eighteen. Not been in business long."

Bernard had heard that story before, particularly a young girl on his first visit to the Turkish part of Limassol. She had obviously never heard of the Turkish sexual preference and Bernard was forcing his attentions on the girl when King Kong crashed through the door and forcibly ejected the Englishman into the street. "I don't want any bouncers interrupting the action. It's happened before," he growled.

"No one will interrupt you sir, this girl delivers, anything you want. Two pounds please." A hand came out of the window and lay, palm up in the dim light.

"How much does she charge?"

"Six, maybe five, I don know. Depends what you wan, you must speak for yourself."

"Six pounds and two for you. Very fucking expensive." Bernard grumbled. He hated taking his wallet out in the street but his supply of intentionally placed crumpled notes in his pockets had all taken up new residence in Leo's bar. Two between the breasts of the delightful Petra. "I'll follow you in my car." he indicated the Hillman. The driver looked at the white car and saw another two pounds disappear with the cancelled return trip. "Wait!" he called to Bernard as he fished around under the dash. "Give this to the girl."

Bernard took the card and saw 'ACE taxis.' "Is this an introduction card?" asked Bernard.

"Yeah, yeah," said the driver not bothering to explain the card claimed his commission for providing a customer. It was a nice little sideline.

The Englishman was having trouble starting his car, but no, it had started. 'Now where to take him?' thought Stavros. Pity Mrs. Parrott was gone; she was always ready to fuck his customers.

Bernard watched the Mercedes pull away and he fell in behind not wishing to lose the greasy little shit who pimped as a sideline. Despite his mood, he was beginning to feel as he always felt on these occasions. The excitement built up slowly, spreading deep down in his groin he felt the bitter anger being pushed aside. He was concentrating on the back of the Mercedes, paying little attention to where they were going. Then he noticed they were travelling along the Bypass, away from the old Greek and Turkish quarters. They stopped at traffic lights and the taxi was indicating to turn right, up Platonos, which led to an area where vast amounts of British servicemen and their families lived. Bernard knew some British women were 'on the game' and the thought excited him further. His hands grew clammy as he followed the taxi up Platonos and it turned into ....

Bernard's eyes glittered as he watched unbelievingly but there was no doubt the Mercedes was turning into Christos Street. The taxi slowed without braking as the driver searched for something, then found what he was looking for as the brake lights lit up. He had stopped across the road from No. 327. The man got out and walked back to the Minx. "This house sir," he pointed across the road. "Just give the lady my card, she will give you what you want."

The back of his throat was closing as the thin red mist filtered down again, slowly blanketing his vision. Bernard stared up at the taxi driver, "Which house?" he croaked.

The man pointed again and nodded with his head, "That one sir."

"That house is empty, they've gone home."

"Not that house, ha! So you know the Mrs. Parrott, neh? Very nice lady, I bring plenty." He grinned conspiratorially "No sir, the one next, with the veranda light. It is signal she open for the business."

Bernard could not accept what he was seeing and hearing. He cared not a fig for Yvonne, nor what she was doing, but there was a sickly feeling in his gut that men were invading his home, stealing personal effects, taking what he had bought and paid for. Unknown men were helping themselves to his possessions! It was much worse than being burgled. Floods of shivers were running through Bernard, "I'll park in the driveway," he mumbled

"Awright, but make sure you get out before the old man come home," snickered the driver. "Enjoy yourself sir. You have one hour, maybe I breeng someone when you feenish."

Bernard drove slowly up the driveway and in through the permanently open door of the garage, keeping the noise down to a minimum. He was not going to the back kitchen door tonight! For tonight he was a customer. Bernard walked round to the front door and knocked.

Yvonne opened it and stood there with a bright expectant smile, which froze for a second then her expression turned to shocked surprise.

"The driver told me to give you this." Bernard held out the business card.

Yvonne stared at the card, then up to Bernard's face before flicking back to the card.

"He said I've got to be finished by ..." Bernard looked at his watch, "9.15, in one hour. There was something else, oh yes, he may bring another customer, and ... he said I must enjoy myself."

"You don't understand," cried Yvonne finding her voice and backing away, "Pat told a taxi driver to bring men here ... not here, next door, I mean next door ... to Pat's place, but that's finished now, she's gone home. He's made a mistake." Inwardly Yvonne was cursing. Pat had promised she would speak to Stavros and cancel all the arrangements. It had been weeks, before she met Josh, since Stavros last brought a man to her door. She was backing away looking for an avenue of escape having recovered somewhat from the shock of seeing Bernard and not Josh standing in the doorway.

"He made no mistake my dear, I know now where you got the money to send your bastard home. You wanted money and that is why you are doing this, selling your little twat. I understand perfectly. What I cannot understand is that anyone could be desperate enough to pay good money for a skinny little crack such as you posses." Bernard was surprising himself at how cool he was, having caught his wife in the act of prostitution. He pulled out his wallet and threw a £10 note on a table. "There you are, that is twice going rate, wouldn't you say? And my driver reliably informs me that you 'deliver.'"

Yvonne was still shuffling backwards but there was nowhere to go. Bernard had moved over to block the exit to the kitchen and her usual escape. He was inching nearer the kitchen when he saw the suitcase. "What is that, you planning on going somewhere?" His voice rose.

Yvonne was cornered but growing angry and anger was overtaking her fear. What was he doing here anyway when he should be screwing some little tart in a stinking brothel. He was ruining her precious plans, her and Josh's plans. She was worried Josh would arrive as he was due any minute and detested this trapped feeling. Yvonne reacted the only way she knew how, she retaliated, "I'm leaving you, you crazy sick maniac, now get out of my way!" She shouted her words in angry panic feeling the desperate need to be clear of him. Her eyes searched frantically for an escape route.

Bernard had taken enough insults from whores tonight. Petra with her screaming and derogatory remarks, now from this, his cow of a wife! On another night he may have laughed at her then dragged her screaming and kicking, off to the bedroom. That he would have enjoyed, but this insult-spitting bitch? He had done nothing to warrant her cutting insinuations, and her stinging words proved to be the proverbial straw. Bernard snapped. His hand came up from a long way and it smashed, back handed across the soft face.

Yvonne staggered then blinked in shock and pain. Trying to gain her composure, she steadied her trembling body against a chair then stared defiantly through tears and blurred vision.

"Now come on little lady, this is a business transaction," Bernard purred. "There on the table is your money. You can leave me afterwards if you so wish, I don't care, but not before I've had my money's worth."

The sting in her cheek was forcing her to blink more than she wanted, letting him know she was hurting. "Over my dead body!" she hissed.

"Necrophilia, mmnn," he mused, "well, if that's what it takes."

Yvonne stared in disbelief, "You are crazy, Josh'll be here any minute, he's ..."

Bernard darted forward and grabbed her hair hard, twisting his fist into the rich brown mass so she could not move. For a moment he was unsure how to handle this squirming she cat but knew precisely what he wanted to do. Pulling her face up, twisting his hand painfully in her hair, he glared into her wild eyes. "I am going to take you to the bedroom where I shall punch you and kick you until you beg me to fuck every hole in your body. If you do not beg me I shall continue to punch you and kick you until you are unconscious, then I will fuck every hole in your body. Either way, I will have my way with you. After all, this is what you get paid for, what I have paid you for, therefore I am only taking my dues."

Yvonne spat into the smirking face only inches from her own. This action was the last foul insult. Holding her head firmly he drew his fist back and in a downward blow, smashed it into the centre of the girl's face, feeling a thrill of delight as his knuckles crushed the bones of her nose. He quickly released her thick hair, stepped back and surveyed the damage. Yvonne, only grasping the verges of consciousness was swaying and moaning.

The word 'gosh' or 'josh' escaping from her slack mouth. Bernard was on a sexual high and he unleashed as powerful a punch as he could possibly muster. His knuckles connected perfectly on the point of the young woman's jaw and her feet left the floor. With the impetus of the horrendous blow, her body catapulted six or seven feet backwards landing on its back, skidding across the parquet floor. Yvonne came to a sudden stop when her head cracked against the corner of the kitchen and lounge doorjamb. Her body twitched and jerked for a few seconds then lay still.

Bernard stared. He was not afraid but was held in total fascination of her spasmodic jerking as if she was in the throes of a sexual climax. There was nothing sexual in what was happening to Yvonne, but it certainly was a climax. Her skull had cracked open and her life juices were draining onto the polished wooden parquet blocks. By the time Bernard walked over and looked down at her, she was dead. He could not believe it, not that there were any regrets, but that life could be snuffed out so easily. He knelt and felt for a pulse; there was nothing. What a night this had turned out to be ... and still no woman to fuck. For a calculating moment, he reflected on his next move and looked down at the still body. The brown skirt had ridden up over white panties and he reached forward. 'What would it be like?' he wondered slipping his fingers under the rim. "She's not cold yet." There were few variations Bernard had not tried in life and tonight's search had indeed thrown up something interesting after all. Death. Or to be more precise, dead meat was something new in his category.

Something was distractingly annoying him which stayed his hand, something she had said. His eyes went to the suitcase. Yes, she had said someone, he had not caught the name, was due any minute. Reluctantly he got back on his feet and opened the suitcase. Clothes, all her clothes. On the cabinet lay her handbag, he snatched it up. There it was, an airline ticket. His mind raced on, 'But how was she to get to Nicosia, the island's only international civil airport?' Suddenly his brain clicked into its thinking mode, away from sex and its deviations. This someone who was due any minute was obviously taking her to the airport. What if this pick up person was the boyfriend? He recalled the surprised look on Yvonne's face when she opened the door. And hadn't she shouted 'someone would be here any minute!' For a fleeting second Bernard panicked as he glanced at the door then down at Yvonne. "We'll have to postpone our little union until later dearest," he muttered. Slipping his hands under the shoulders he dragged the body up the passageway into the departed brat's bedroom. 'Now the two of them have departed,' he grinned maliciously. The suitcase and handbag were also thrown into the room.

Quickly he mopped up the bloody mess, went to the drinks cabinet, his nerves on a razors edge but the bottle of his favourite brandy contained no more than a thimbleful. "Bastard!" he cursed, "what a fucking night!" Swallowing the dregs he remembered the bottle he always kept in the glove compartment in the car. Hurrying quickly out to the garage and leaning over the driver's seat, he withdrew the bottle from the recess in the dashboard. His foot kicked against a metallic object on the floor and leaning down he picked up the starting handle. Tucking it under his arm as a possible weapon he was about to retrace his steps when he heard a throbbing car engine pull up outside the house then switch off. Bernard scrambled back into the kitchen in time to hear a knock on the front door. He was two strides into the short passageway leading to the lounge when he saw the front door handle begin to turn. This was not what he expected. Bernard wanted to welcome the person at the door and fob him off with some excuse or other. The man must be sure of himself to enter the house. Bernard stood frozen for a second before taking the nearest escape route available. He sidestepped into the bedroom where the body lay. Standing behind the door, he could peer between the tiny gap of door and door jamb.

Josh walked into the lounge, "Yve," he called. Strange, the place was very quiet, too quiet! Josh felt peculiar; he sensed there was something wrong yet the veranda light was on. Yvonne would only put that light on if Bernard was out on the town. "Yvonne!" he called, louder. Perhaps she was in the toilet. He entered the passageway, the open toilet door was in darkness. He passed the spare bedroom but in doing so, something caught his eye through the partially open door. Yvonne's handbag was on the floor. Josh pushed the door and stepped inside.

"My God Yve!" In the half-light, the first impression Josh had was Yvonne had fallen and banged her head, perhaps tripping over the case lying beside her. He bent down and turned her on to her back. She slumped flat and lifeless. A cold shiver ran through him. "Yvonne, for Christ sake, Yvonne!" It was only then in what little light there was, he saw blood on the floor. The tiniest sound made Josh turn back of the door. Surprise and shock froze him only for a moment when he saw Yvonne's husband towering above him like a giant colossus. His legs were spread and he was holding something above his head with both hands. Josh started to rise but the object above the man's head was already swinging in an ark with great force. Josh threw up his right arm across his head successfully blocking the blow, but the immense power behind the swing caused a loud crack to be heard. There was a degree of sharp pain but Josh was nevertheless surprised to see his hand and wrist swing loose from his lower arm. His arm was broken midway between wrist and elbow. Realising his desperate position Josh tried to get to his feet as another blow rained down and instinctively he dodged to his left. It was a physical impossibility to move fast enough and avoid the blow completely as the bar hit him painfully but harmlessly on his left shoulder. The bar was being raised again so Josh desperately threw everything into a roundhouse swing with his remaining good arm. The punch was off the mark very slightly, connecting with only the tip of his attackers chin. Not enough to thwart the blow that landed heavily on his shoulder again, this time breaking the left collarbone. He tried to swing again but it was hopelessly off the mark. His swing only spun him off balance, his own impetus twisted his body round and he fell, toppling over the body of Yvonne.

The first blow with the iron bar to the back of his exposed head was not completely flush and did not bring unconsciousness, but with rueful resignation, Josh knew it was the end. His broken right arm was trapped painfully under his chest and he could not push on his left to raise himself. Yvonne's tousled head was only a foot away. Though his body was screaming in agony Josh nudged over the small gap to the familiar smelling tress's and pushing aside the brown hair from her face with his nose, kissed her slack lips.

"Now isn't that a touching sight?" called Bernard paused before taking careful aim with the handle poised above his head. There was no need to rush this time for his adversary was down, nor his swing to be so hurried. Then with every ounce of his strength, he brought the handle down onto the back of the unprotected head.

~~~

Bernard drove the Skoda carefully. He was afraid the old heap would break down before he could complete his plan. He was on the Nicosia road, and had been for twenty minutes. The thin beam of the car headlights did little to lift the darkness from the black road. The engine of the car resembled that of a tractor but it kept going and that was all Bernard asked of it. He glanced over into the well between the rear and front passenger seats and saw the knees of Yvonne spread wide to accommodate the rear wheel of her scooter, which was jammed between her thighs, the front wheel rested against her head. Underneath Yvonne lay the body of Josh, also lying on his back with bent and knees spread.

Bernard had struggled to get both bodies into the car then to a lesser degree, the little scooter. Methodically in line with his hastily devised plan, he placed on the floor beside the bodies; a gallon can of petrol Yvonne kept for topping up the scooter, her hand bag, an old newspaper, and lastly, a roll of nylon line from his toolbox. The suitcase he placed in the boot.

The petrol gauge on the dash showed the tank was three quarters full. If the instrument was reading correct, there was more than enough for Bernard's needs. Keeping well to the left, he was scanning the road for a 'Dangerous bend' road sign. He had seen many bad bends from his regular use of this road on duty runs to Nicosia and trips to away matches with his team. The more hazardous bends were on slopes and hills and the one he knew to be by far the most perilous could not be far now.

The Skoda with its morbid cargo roared on through the night, the driver congratulating himself how, after a bad start, how nicely things had turned out for him after all. He had got rid of a particularly annoying and troublesome wife plus her boyfriend. There was the added bonus the boyfriend had turned out to be one of the main men from the 103 MU team. He smiled into the darkness. Life had a funny way of levelling things out.

Driving up an incline for what seemed miles when at last on cresting the hill top, Bernard saw the 'Dangerous bend' sign, followed by another indicating a steep incline. He slowed as the headlights picked out the white painted guard rail. He knew the road ran steeply downhill for fifty yards from this point then curved sharply to the right protected by a heavy corrugated steel rail. The rail followed the worst part of the bend for another fifty yards and finished as the road straightened up. This was the perfect spot. He stopped the car and the engine whined heavily as he reversed back up the precipitous hill to a point where he could still see the beginning of the rail on the bend. Manoeuvring the car as precisely as he would aim a rifle, he checked and rechecked until he was satisfied he had the bonnet perfectly lined up with the open gap to the left of the guardrail. This done, he switched off the engine.

The petrol can then the scooter was unloaded. Having previously checked the vehicle for petrol, he started the motor that fired and ran sweetly. Switching it off he wheeled the little machine under nearby trees. Next, he wrestled with the body of Yvonne cursing her all the time for being so heavy before dropping her onto the lumpy passenger seat where the springs had almost broken through. "Enjoy the hard lumps you cow, they're the last thrill you'll ever get," he muttered arranging her into a sitting position. Josh was heavier and much more of a struggle. By the time he had the dead airman in the seat behind the wheel he was sweating profusely but the hardest of his work was over.

Two cars passed while he was working, the second slowed down. Bernard stepped into the road and waved, "We're all right thank you." He received a hoot and a wave. The car drove on.

After checking both front wheels were perfectly straight, he looped the nylon line half a dozen times around Josh's left hand and the rim m of the steering wheel. From there he tied it securely to the stem of the quarter light window on the far passenger door, keeping the line taught. The flaccid right hand he also tied to the steering wheel then secured the line to an air control outlet on the right side of the steering column. Bernard tied and secured the steering wheel in three other places before he was satisfied it could not move before proceeding with his next task. Again using only the nylon line, he tied the accelerator to Josh's right shoe pushing the pedal flat to the floor. When he finished the pedal eased back to approximately half way, which was more or less, what Bernard wanted. The Chief Tech.

checked everything time and again. Nothing could be left to chance here. Yvonne's handbag he placed on the floor at her feet, her case was already in the boot and the wheel was locked and aimed to the left of the guard rail. Bernard nodded, satisfied. He unscrewed the lid of the petrol can, dipped the rolled up newspaper into the fluid then calmly poured the petrol over the two bodies before dousing the back and front seats. Cautiously he started the engine. It roared into life, running fast as the accelerator pedal was half depressed, thanks to Josh and the dead weight of his foot. Standing to the right of the driver's seat with the door open, Bernard pushed his left foot onto the clutch and leaning over Josh, selected top gear on the column gear change. He released the hand brake. The Skoda, as if reluctant to go on to its own end, hesitated to move down the steep hill, but with Bernard shaking and rocking, the great weight, unfettered by brakes or gears, eased then started to roll.

Trapping the petrol soaked newspaper between windscreen wipers and windscreen, and jamming himself between the open driver's door and the body of the car, he brought out and flipped open the cap of his Zippo lighter with his right hand. The car was rolling down the slope at around 5 mph so the wind protected lighter had no problem igniting with one turn of the serrated wheel. He leaned round and touched the flame to the petrol soaked newspaper. As the flame caught, he flicked the lighter shut transferring it to his shirt pocket. Grabbing the dry bottom part of the newspaper quickly he slid it free from the wiper and held it aloft, as far out to his right as he could reach like a torchbearer in a political rally. The Skoda was nearing the beginning of the guard rail and had picked up speed to 15 mph. Bernard did two things at this point simultaneously; he jumped from the car thus releasing the clutch and threw the paper torch inside the car.

He only just escaped the WHOOF of jetting flame that shot out the open front door and passenger window. He had a brief glimpse of Yvonne's hair erupting in a ball of thick smoke and flame as he rolled over on the road, feeling his knee twist as he landed. The car's speed picked up dramatically with the top gear engaging to the fast engine speed. The kernel of roaring inferno with sheets of flame flying in its wake swept past only just clearing the left side of the barrier. It carried on bumping down the hill very erratically, flames shooting out at every bump, then suddenly the old Skoda crunched noisily to an abrupt halt. The old car had obviously ended its days against a rock and with the sudden jarring stop, the roaring ball of flames shot onwards, rolling momentarily skyward, leaving the source of fire behind.

Bernard hopped as best he could to the guardrail and watched for a moment as the car burned. Then in a blinding flash of white and purple light that momentarily lit the surrounding hills, the Skoda exploded, burning petrol leaping into the night sky in rolling fingers of belching flame.

The Chief Tech limped gleefully back to the scooter congratulating himself on the wonderful fireworks display and how flawlessly his plan had worked out. The engine of the scooter caught and suddenly he loved this little machine, cursed so often for blocking his path in the garage. He turned the switch on top of the headlight and the beam of light lanced off into the darkness. Bernard smiled, not only would the purring motor provide the power to transport him home but it would also illuminate his path along the way. He relaxed into the comfortable seat, clicked into gear, released the clutch and swung round, steering the little front wheel and beam of light up the hill towards Limassol.

~~~

Chapter 24

"Oh, no! God almighty!" Frank Connolly exclaimed after Callum McAlpine told him the news. The latter's eyes were red rimmed and obviously very distressed, "That fuckin' car, Frankie," Callum groaned, "why the fuck did he insist on usin' that heap to take her to the airport? I warned him but he trusted that fuckin' death trap. Jesus Christ!"

Callum looked at Frank with shocked eyes, "The fuckin' thing blew up Frank ...."

The other airmen in the machine shop turned when Frank asked incredulously "It blew up?"

"Aye, it fuckin' well blew up! Oh, kerrrrighst !" Callum mangled his maker's name in heartfelt agony, spun on his heel then the lank figure stomped across the machine shop, ducking out quickly through the small wicket door.

Frank watched the wretched figure leave. Josh was well liked but no one would feel his loss keener than Callum. Since they first met the two men had been the closest of friends. Frank shook his head. What was happening with this run of tragedies? First poor Marion with Ray and his family. Now Josh who only recently was reviving the vibrant person everyone knew lurked under his reserved exterior. His life clicking together at last due to his finding the missing link in Yvonne. Gazing at the door through which Callum had been swallowed by the bright sunlight, it suddenly opened again and two figures entered. Nobby was first followed by Julian. The obviously upset Indian was first to speak, "We just heard. It can't be true, this rumour about Josh?"

"I don't think it's a rumour, Callum's just told me. God knows where he got it from but he wouldn't go round sayin' things like that unless it was true."

Julian's hand covered his mouth, staring at Frank with incredulous eyes. Tears that threatened suddenly formed and ran unashamedly down his cheeks. He moved close to Frank, placed his head on his friend's shoulder, and sobbed. Frank looked at Nobby sadly, both understanding Julian's open display of grief. The other machine shop airmen looked at Frank and Julian and for once there were no jeers or remarks.

Sgt. Peter Skaw, working on the engraving machine nearby heard everything. He stepped forward. "Come lad," he took Julian's arm. "Have a cup of tea." Skaw jerked his head towards the steaming tea urn at the same time flicking his eyebrows at Frank. Nobby said nothing and left to return to his section as the Scot attended to the tea then took it to the office where Skaw had left the shaken Julian.

Julian was silent as he sipped the brew then, "What's happening Frank?" he whispered.

"Fuck knows!" Frank answered miserably.

Julian spoke again voicing Frank's earlier thoughts, "First Marion with Ray and Babs and their two children, now Josh and that young wife of poor Chief Kowaleski."

Frank's head turned slowly, a mildly puzzled frown on his face. "I'm sorry about Mrs. Kowaleski Julie, but I feel nothin' towards that nutcase she was married to. They weren't exactly gettin' along you know! She was known to have sported the odd 'keeker,' or black eye in your language. Josh was takin' the poor bloody woman up to the airport last night."

"She was leaving ..." Julian stopped. He almost said 'Bernard.' He went on lamely "... him?"

"Aye she was man! What the fuck's wrong with you? You're more concerned wi' that crazy bastard than you are wi' the two that were bloody killed. Och I'm sorry Julie ..." Frank stopped when he saw the two penetratingly blue eyes look painfully up into his own. "I'm really broken up over Josh, sorry pal."

Julian nodded but said nothing. As Frank excused himself and returned to his lathe Julian was surprised at his own feelings. The news of Bernard's wife was actually leaving him the previous night was the only bright spot in a black morning. It had a warm yearning yet disturbing effect on him. The primary sad news regarding Josh was terrible of course, but he was momentarily forgotten. He had to speak to Bernard soon, very soon.

~~~

538

What was left of the Skoda was winched back up the slope to the road. What was left of the occupants had previously been removed, and the RAF Medical Officer signed the necessary paperwork. The owner and driver (still to be confirmed) was a Senior Aircraftsman Joshua Arnold Munroe who, the officer concluded had in all likelihood lost control for the car had obviously run off the road with disastrous results. What was left of the suitcase in the boot provided adequate proof it belonged to the passenger a Mrs. Yvonne Shirley Kowaleski, nee Preston, (still to be confirmed) who was booked on the 23.00 Nicosia/Manchester flight. According to the time of the accident, provided by a witness who arrived minutes after it happened, the car ran off the road at approximately 21.55 hours. This would suggest, as they were running a little late, the driver was perhaps attempting to make up lost time. Verdict: Accidental death; Automobile accident.

Bernard kept a low profile for the next week. He had declined the Medical Officer's offer of compassionate leave, explaining he preferred to be at work. There was also the other reason; he was overjoyed at the prospect of a life away from the cloying glutinous embrace of living the sham life of a married man. The very considerate MO told him he quite understood the settling of family affairs could take months so he need not rush to give up his Limassol house. When Bernard was good and ready, he could move into the Sergeant's Mess.

Bernard's bubbling effervescence at having got so cleanly away with the murders saw him once more in Hero's Square a week after the 'accident.' To celebrate his freedom he picked up two prostitutes and took them back to his unfettered home. All three performed admirably but strangely, there was a certain element missing in the action, so the night did not gel the way Bernard hoped it would. During the course of the evening he found the image of Julian Cantwell flitting across his vision, interrupting his thoughts and deeds. This ghost of the young airman eventually sickened Bernard of the women's bodies, and it was this element he found most disturbing. The female form had fascinated Bernard, from the day he escaped the cloistering clutches of boys' homes. They were beautiful objects and the more he could hurt and debase these creatures of soft

539

vulnerability, the more sexual satisfaction he gleaned from the encounter. For the first time in his life Bernard was at a loss; he could not fully understand why he wanted Julian so badly, for he was after all a man, though it must be said, a beautiful man. Sexual relief or exploitation did not enter into the brief, he really wanted Julian. His innards were being stirred by this spectre and proved to be the eventual downfall of Bernard's usually dependable puissance. The two women were suddenly shown the door. He had emptied his love sack but gained little from the encounter. A large meal had been consumed but he was still hungry.

The next morning Bernard sat in his office trying to make a dent in the growing mound of paperwork when the phone rang. He snatched it up angrily, "Workshops, Chief Tech Kowaleski," he growled.

"I was hoping you would phone me." The soft words eased into Bernard's ear.

"Julian!" his surprise tempered his mood with expectancy.

"Yes, why haven't you telephoned me? You said you would."

"The accident ... it was a terrible shock," Bernard lied, surprising himself. Why was he lying?

"Oh yes, of course, it must have been terrible for you Bernard." The voice was low, afraid of being overheard but the tone was stimulating, like warm oil caressing the inside of Bernard's ear. He remembered the night they had kissed in the darkness of his car. His breath grew short, "It was," he lied again. Feelings were running deep and making him uncomfortable. He wanted to see this person, to embrace him, kiss him ... to love him? Bernard grunted in disgust when the word skitted across his mind. He felt vulnerable and unsure, yet he had never experienced feelings like this for anyone, male or female.

"You still there?"

"Yes," Bernard snapped, frowning as he realised he could not ignore his feelings.

"I'm sorry Bernard, I shouldn't have done this," the quiet purring went on, "I'll phone you in a week or two when you're feeling better. I just wanted you to know I go home next month."

"What, in July?" Bernard spat out the words, "I had no idea you were so near repatriation." He paused then as Julian started to speak, Bernard cut him off, "Julian, will you move in with me?"

He was surprised at his sudden words yet his burning groin and the deep urge to reach out and hold the person at the other end of the line was tremendous. Suddenly everything was clear, this is what he needed, what he wanted most.

The instrument was dead in his hand, "Julian?" he hissed, afraid now of all the implications.

"Yes," said the quiet voice, "I mean, yes ... I will move in with you."

Bernard sighed heavily and shakily, "When?"

"As soon as possible, tomorrow?" Julian answered tentatively, "tomorrow after work?"

Bernard thought for a confused moment, so soon? Then, "Okay, I'll pick you up outside the Guardroom in the car park, 8 o'clock. Bring all the gear you'll need, we'll sort out the details when I get you home."

"Wonderful," breathed Julian, the word 'Home' strummed a gentle chord. "Tomorrow then."

"If anyone asks where you're going, tell them you're staying with friends for the weekend."

"I usually do," Julian reflected regretfully that his visits to the Connolly's were now a thing of the past. Frank being the man he was would understand his needs, though Julian doubted if he, or anyone, would approve his chosen partner.

Next day after work, Frank Connolly climbed aboard the No.32 bus. Removing his RAF issue sunglasses, he looked around expectantly for Julian. He was usually one of the first aboard, sitting in the most sought after seat, the one nearest the open door. Another airman had claimed the coolest seat today as Frank scanned the bus. There was no sign of the gentle Julian .

It was nearly time for the bus to leave. The driver started his engine and Frank leaned over, "Would you mind hangin' on a minute, I think my mate's maybe got on the wrong bus." Frank skipped out into the bright sunlight after a weary nod from the driver. Replacing the glasses for the afternoon sun was dazzling, Frank went round the other buses but there was no sign of his friend. 'Strange,' he thought re-boarding his bus. For Julian to miss a weekend at the Connolly's was most unusual. 'Strange,' the word repeated itself again in Frank's head. He sat down and gazed out at the swirling dust as the buses churned up the powdered white dust cloaking the ancient vehicles. Carol and Dawn would be disappointed for they loved the quiet spoken Julian who tirelessly read stories or sang to them at bedtime. The groaning and crunching of gears brought Frank back to reality as the vertical gate poles allowed the convoy of vehicles to roar through. These noises died away gradually as the drivers climbed the gears, replacing the roars with whining purrs as the train of old buses rolled and bumped on tired springs on the downhill slope towards Limassol.

Back in the ablutions of his Block, Julian bathed slowly, taking a great deal of time and effort to ensure he washed and cleansed every corner and crevice of his entire body. The time in his life had finally arrived where he was faced with the actuality that with each passing day, he was slipping deeper into a void. Time was empty, passing so quickly, leaving in its wake a grieving sense of loss. There was no rest from the nervous twitching in his frame. Every second of solitude, particularly when he closed his eyes, hoping to wrest blissful sleep from the chirping cricket night, came the same gut tearing feelings. He needed someone. The pain was not physical yet it would coil him from lying on his back into the foetal position until eventually his brain locked his muscles followed by cramp which jerked him back into the original straight position. Then the cycle would start all over again

Julian knew Chief Tech. Bernard Kowaleski was not a pleasant
man. If anything he was hard and bitter, yet perversely these qualities attracted Julian. He needed someone strong, someone to force him into taking this first hesitant step. The step he wanted to take but never before had the nerve nor the person to help initiate it.

He looked down at his girlish body. The rounded curve of his hips, the hairless thighs and legs any female would be proud of, but there tucked at the apex of his groin, lay his curse. His eyes flickered distastefully as he looked at the underdeveloped penis and scrotum. This tiny, but absolute major part of his body that belied his true sex. Breasts had begun to form. These he kept discreetly hidden, not parading his body as he once did in the veiled hope of being noticed. He would be noticed now, there

542

was no doubt about that, therefore drastic changes in his immediate plans must be adopted. To openly declare this latest physical change would surely see him quietly ejected from the Royal Air Force. That path of course was inevitable now, and he must go soon. But where? He was unsure but Bernard, thank God, had arrived in time and was now a major player in Julian's plans. Because of Bernard, the quietly harboured thoughts of self destruction were cast aside. Julian had at last found his long sought niche in the hard rock face of bitter humanity.

He towelled his body dry adding various lotions and sprays then dressed in clean underwear, he walked slowly and languidly back to the empty billet room. The day had at last arrived when he was on the verge of a new life.

Most of his belongings were packed into his large RAF holdall and Julian dressed slowly into the clothes he left out.

Nobby Clarke walked in draped in a towel having just showered. He glanced at Julian's bag on the floor and frowned. No airman used their large holdall, the modern replacement for the old kit bag, unless they were about to leave the billet for any number of reasons such as, getting married, about to live out, detached for a lengthy period, or posted.

"Going somewhere Julie?"

Julian was prepared, "A couple I used to know in England asked me if I would like to live out permanently at their house. I'd have to apply for permission of course but I don't see any problem. Thought I'd give it a try as I've only a few weeks left on the island." He busied himself throwing the last of his toiletries into the bag. His words did not sound as convincing as when he rehearsed them.

"Anybody I know?" Nobby asked, wondering about Julian's usual visit to the Connolly's.

"Don't think so," mumbled Julian rooting in his locker avoiding further conversation.

In the car park outside the Main Guardroom, Bernard sat in his car and watched the slim figure under the security lights struggle through the gate with a holdall. As Julian approached, Bernard got out quickly and opened the boot. "Give us it here and get in," he growled snatching the blue grip and tossing it into the boot. He was nervous and it showed when crunching the gears to get free of the camp's shadow. He glanced at his passenger, "I didn't want to be seen with you," he said ungraciously.

Julian nodded his understanding, accepting without question Bernard's brusque attitude. He sat back and relaxed allowing his tired hands to rest in his lap

Nothing was said as last minute doubts flitted across both their minds while insects and large moths determinedly committed suicide against the car windscreen. The headlights luring them into oblivion. Bernard glanced to his left and saw the pale image of Julian reclining in the seat. In the luminescent light his passenger looked beautiful and the suffocating feeling returned to the back in Bernard's throat. He wanted to reach over and kiss the soft bewitching figure. He was so like a girl it was hard to believe this was a male, yet therein lay the contradiction and attraction. The fair angelic image scorched his vision and he had to blink hurriedly, concentrating on keeping the car on the road. Suddenly perversely and without warning his feelings reversed! He wanted desperately to hurt Julian, really hurt this abomination. He glared again at the reclining figure, totally without comprehension as to why he wanted to harm this person and yet love him at the same time. He wanted Julian more than he ever wanted a woman, yet was repulsed by such an effeminate man and yearned to hurt him. Bernard gagged at the gorge of frustration. Feeling more confused than he had ever felt in his entire life he spat a ball of phlegm out the open window, then turned yet again to look at Julian. This time he looked into a face that had noticed his discomfort and moved towards him, concerned. Two smoky blue eyes were looking into his, openly, invitingly.

Bernard pulled over to the side of the road skidding to a halt in the soft shoulder. He reached over and pulled Julian towards him roughly, hurriedly. Julian felt himself lifted half out of the seat as two strong hands held his head then he was being kissed. Rough stubble of Bernard's chin scrubbed coarsely around his mouth and a tongue probed deep and harsh but lovingly around his own. For the first time in his life Julian felt his mortal being lift off into a world of new sensation. His heart was beating at the base of his throat, almost choking him as he struggled for air. Hands caressed his body as he soared to dizzying heights then plunged steeply, worryingly into dark bottomless pits.

Bernard grew uncomfortable. Something in his pocket due to his awkward position was grinding agonizingly into his thigh. The pain breaking the enchantment. He pulled away and dug into his pocket to remove the object. His hand closed around the rule knife he always carried. Sitting back in his seat he looked at Julian and singularly glowered at him. "You bastard," he growled. "You fucking bastard!"

"Wh- ... what's wrong?" cried Julian taken aback, in heaven one moment, hell the next.

Bernard could not answer; his conflicting feelings were in total confusion. He could not understand the strong attraction he had for this soft attractive person where sex for once was not the ultimate but certainly partial attraction. Moreover, he was troubled by what he was doing - why? He'd fucked many a male posterior but never actually kissed a man, yet here he was kissing this man/woman! His inner feelings in wild turmoil he wanted to be away from this, yet still the strong magnetic urge to continue. The conflicting pulses of his impulsive feelings were causing his stomach muscles to dance uncontrollably and painfully. Abruptly his mood inverted again, his reserves melted when the concerned face of Julian broke again into his vision. "What's wrong?" Julian repeated, rubbing Bernard's hand. Slowly the twisting muscles in his tight stomach unravelled and relaxed.

"I'm all right, I'm all right now," Bernard said breathlessly placing a hand on Julian's cheek. For a brief moment in time all seemed right in the world. "I don't ... I can't control what comes over me," he said, "I want you so bad then when we kissed something fucked around inside." He shook his head, "It felt like the sharp edge of a knife cutting across the edge of another, grating, squeaking, hurting, cutting me up."

"Oh Bernard, that sounds so painful," Julian gazed into the smouldering black eyes. "But I, too, feel something so vastly different to what I've ever felt before. I'm so nervous I feel so ... so brittle, as if I'm going to break."

Julian was rubbing his hand up and down the hard thigh and the simple action revived the hunger lurking under the surface. Bernard hurriedly unbuttoned his fly and stared into the eyes inches from his own. Nothing was said, messages transmitted and Julian lowered his head into Bernard's groin. Bernard collapsed back into his seat, groaning and twisting in pleasure.

Minutes later bright lights pierced the older man's semi consciousness as a car passed the Minx. Bernard opened his eyes and his spirits sank. Brake lights glowed as the car had stopped.

Julian raised his head to look through the windscreen.

"We've got to go," Bernard said gruffly arranging his clothing.

The driver of the car got out but stopped when Bernard started the engine which fortunately caught first time, then flashed his lights. The driver waved, returned to his car and drove off.

"We can't stay here, I should've pushed on home," Bernard said easing back on to the road.

Julian nodded, "Yes, but while we're here, let's go to the beach," he surprisingly declared, straining his eyes to reach beyond the beam of lights. "It's not far, there's a road just ahead that branches off to the southerly end of Ladies Mile, please let's go there."

"We can go to my house Julian, there's no need to go to the beach."

Julian smiled, "I know," he said quietly continuing to look through the windscreen. "It's just one of my whims. I've always had this feeling, you know, like walking on the beach with someone close, someone you love. I can't explain properly but let's do it just this once, then we can go home."

Once again the effeminacy that exuded from this person; the whim for a walk on the beach and the declaration of love softened Bernard. The undeniable fact that physically Julian was a man, yet sitting close to him was the epitome of being with a girl. This was the yeast that caused the fermentation in the older man's brewing vessel of a body. He wanted to kick him out of the car yet love him all at the same time. The frustration of these extreme emotions was the base attraction. Bernard was surprised to hear himself say, "Okay, if that's what you want, let's go to the beach." It was a new feeling, akin to excitement. He was a boy again. Or rather a youth prepared to do anything to please his first girlfriend.

He was rewarded with a wide smile from the young entrapped girl. Julian had thrown off the last vestiges of masculinity. He now accepted he loved Bernard and would do anything for him. His love was precisely the same as any female felt for her man and wanted to prove it. "Turn here, it's a sand road that leads directly to the beach." Julian cried spotting the turning. He reached over and moved his hand along the inside of Bernard's thigh, at last confident and free to show his emotions.

It was not long before the lights picked out the small dunes. Bernard stayed on the sorry excuse for a road that turned and followed the line of dunes parallel to the sea. "Stop Bernard, please we can walk from here. It's so wonderfully beautiful."

The Chief did not want to get trapped in soft sand so careful to keep the car on a patch of solid road, stopped and switched off the engine and lights. Julian jumped out and was already climbing. He disappeared into one of the many valleys before Bernard saw him climb another only to vanish again. Following the deep footprints Bernard slowly and thoughtfully walked in the wake of this person. This prospective lover that he knew for certain was about to change his life. When he topped the last dune before the beach levelled, he saw Julian standing facing the sea, a lonely figure on a wide stretch of limitless glistening sand. Bernard felt his heart lift.

Neither figure moved for a few minutes then Julian turned and waved for Bernard to join him, his white teeth gleaming even in the silvery half-light of the moon. Bernard walked down and stood beside the obviously overjoyed Julian who slipped a delicate hand into his huge fist. They walked slowly and the magic of Julian's presence plus the glistening night began to permeate through the iron crust of the hardened Chief. He began to respond to the squeeze and caresses of this wondrous person that had at last come into his life.

They strolled on, skirting the lazy wash of the almost non-existent Mediterranean tide. Linked together now both lost in their thoughts of what lay ahead. Bernard was experiencing a deep peace. It was warm, soothing calming. Something completely foreign to him and in that serene moment, he made a decision. Their life together could not go undetected and with Julian due to go home soon, Bernard realised he did not want a life without this wonderful person. But the RAF would never condone what he wanted therefore he had to act! He would buy himself out of his beloved Royal Air Force and try to carve a life in the granite face of normality with Julian.

They turned to retrace their steps when Bernard suddenly, conversely, had the feeling he would find it hard to resign. No, he did not want to leave his vocation. His job had protected him since he was a boy, had given him a wonderful living, been everything to him. Despite his glowing mounting happiness, Bernard could not stop his conscience from informing another part of his brain that he was walking hand in hand with a man! These images were sprinkling coolant on flames that were kindling with new life. It caused him to self-consciously glance round at the deserted beach. In those few seconds his feelings faltered falling from hot to cold. Suddenly, without recollection of his tender thoughts, he hated Julian, the instigator of this turmoil. He had to resist the irrational urge to smash his fist into the serene beauty of this person so blissfully unaware of the turbulence tearing his partner's insides.

Julian was ecstatic. His true self was on the crest of each wave washing in on the beach. He was sailing, this sensation of light, the pure night air, this new feeling of life was ecstatic. He sighed but as he did so, Bernard stopped abruptly, pulled his hand away and walked on ahead.

Julian watched him go, recognising the mental battle raging through the Chief's head. To make love to someone was vastly different from loving someone of the same sex, as it was with someone of the opposite sex. But now confronted with the deepest of all feelings being offered to Bernard perhaps for the first time from either sex, it was proving difficult to accept or even to understand. There was no doubt in Julian's mind where his own future lay. Bernard was all the man he could ever want so there was no choice to be made. The fact remained however tonight Bernard must make his final decision otherwise there may be regrets later.

Julian was surprised at himself as he slowly traced Bernard's footsteps in the sand. How he had accepted the situation so readily. He had only been waiting for the right moment, and the right person to come along. The magical moment had happened that day in Dhekelia when his eyes locked with Bernard's. Something reached out from inside Julian that particular day, some unknown element had connected with all his unattached going nowhere wires and he had suddenly lit up, come alive! The message that came through was unequivocally clear.

Bernard stopped not far from the car in the shadow of the dunes and waited for Julian to catch up. He turned and watched the dark silhouette against the shimmering backdrop of sand and sea, stepping silkily and lightly. A soft groan, not unlike a growl escaped his throat and all doubts and resistance that had been melting as he walked along the water's edge, left him yet again. Julian was a woman, how could this girl coming towards him be otherwise? Bernard reached for the soft figure and roughly pulled him into an embrace. Staring down into the calm blue eyes Bernard kissed the half-open lips harshly, then suddenly breathless in his urgency he fumbled with the buckle of Julian's belt. The clasp proved a complete puzzle as Julian whispered, "Hold the right side and tug the strap to the left." No jerking to the left or right would free the buckle and for a frenzied minute they both struggled. "It seems to be jammed," Julian whispered calmly then looked up at his prospective lover. "Are you sure about this?"

"Damn your fucking eyes Julian, of course I'm sure," the aroused Chief hissed reaching into his pocket. There was a precise 'click' as the rule knife flicked its gleaming blade and Julian stared at it fearfully. "Careful Bernard," he said but his partner was in no mood to wait. Holding the knife in his right hand, he slipped the blade under the chastising belt and cut it free. With a practiced flick, he turned an unresisting Julian around then in sexual agitation tugged and pulled at his trousers and underpants.

"Bernard, you must be sure, please don't ... if you're ... if you're not sure about us!" Although Julian was breathless almost fainting with anticipatory exultation he worried about Bernard's conviction.

"I'm sure bitch, I'm fucking sure. Now shut up, shut your fucking mouth!" Bending Julian over and supporting him round his middle he fumbled roughly with his own clothing, cursing all the while as his mind in a turmoil raced, he gazed down at the round female rump. No, no, he must not rush this, he didn't want to rush this, but he was a runaway roller coaster and couldn't stop his fumbling. Impatient, a snagging zip now! He had to hurry as his driving body approached ejaculation he at last got rid of his underwear. There was a noise like a roaring waterfall in his ears, struggling for position with his erect manhood he heard Julian gasp, "Bernard careful, no wait, stop, oh stop you still ..."

"You can't stop me now you stupid bastard!" With his right arm supporting the weight Bernard pulled Julian towards his own body and felt immense relief as he eased into Julian.

"Oh ... Bernard, stop Bern- ... Ooh ...." Julian groaned painfully then with a shudder, the full weight of his body went limp.

Bernard stared down at the suddenly very quiet form. Tiny noises and peculiar movements were taking place, noises and movements he had experienced once before. He knew somewhere inside his head warning bells were clanging but some inner mechanism was preventing him from hearing them, then suddenly without warning, he climaxed. As his body took over his sporadic lunging movements he automatically pulled Julian in hard against his groin and for a blinding few moments of exultation all else was forgotten.

Moments afterwards as he returned to reality, the diminishing movements and unnatural noises from Julian made him shudder with recollection. He recalled when they had happened on a previous occasion, and where it had taken place. It was in a dark shop doorway in Singapore when he choked the life out of a wriggling Chinese man. Numbing with apprehension, he stared down at Julian feeling himself go cold as he became aware of the warm sticky mess in his right hand! And that he was holding on to something solid and slippery. Moving his fingers he felt around its contours and his eyes widened in shocked horror and surprise. He jerked his hand away. Julian fell slowly to the sand as Bernard watched in sickened disbelief. It was all too familiar as to the strip of the man in that Singapore doorway flashed across Bernard's vision.

Gleaming darkly in the moonlight a six-inch rule appeared to be protruding from the base of Julian's chest.

"Julian?" Bernard whispered. "Julian!" he repeated with more intensity. He had to stop himself from screaming the name when he spotted the dark patch spreading around the upper part of Julian's body. He wanted to rush forward, do what he could to try and help but he knew instinctively Julian was dead. "You rotten bastard," he cried, his voice thickening with fear, hurt and pain. "You can't be dead? Jesus, just when I find someone I can..." Bernard stopped, cleared his throat and spat in the sand, "Pull yourself together man. Can't go to pieces now," he took a deep breath.. Minutes passed and nothing moved as the tragedy sunk home. His head twitched, slowly vision cleared and torment disappeared. "You fucking thoughtless bastard," he whispered at the corpse, "why Julian? You knew I had the knife in my hand, why didn't you tell me, you stupid cunt! I WANTED YOOOOOOU!" he roared at the corpse. "What the fuck am I going to do with you now?" His voice was rising with his temper. He drew his right foot back and kicked the body, not hard, and had no idea why he did it. Perhaps tucked away in some dark recess he was looking for reaction. Again he kicked, harder this time and again nothing, except the slapping clap of his foot.

Bernard wiped his hands in the sand, adjusted his clothing quickly as pain started again at the base of his head. Walking back to the car he took a pack of Turkish cigarettes from the glove compartment, his hand brushing against another knife, a beautiful long bladed stiletto he had taken a fancy to and bought in the Turkish quarter.

Bernard did not smoke often but the heavy scented tobacco and thick blue smoke he found soothing, especially after sex. But it wasn't helping much tonight as he stared towards the dark mound that was Julian's body, "I should have known! The fucking MU if they don't get me one way, they get me another." He cursed for permitting himself to become emotionally entangled with someone from the Maintenance Unit. Such an encounter could only breed trouble.

Somewhere deep inside he was in shock, grieving terribly at his loss but these feelings would never be allowed to surface. They would fester and burn inside him forever, creating new raw areas to hurt him. Trying to think rationally he realised he must get rid of the body and started to look for something he could use as a spade. There was nothing big enough among his tools in the boot then his skills at improvising saw his eyes alight on the deep chrome bowls of the Minx hubcaps. Prizing one off with a resounding 'tang' in the still night air, he hurried back to where the body lay. Close by was a natural depression between two dunes. In this dip, he started to dig. He never noticed all the while he worked, deep heartfelt sobs and whimpers with the same words over and over "Why Julie," or simply "Why, why, why," escaped unbidden from his mouth.

Half an hour later he had a deep hole approximately six feet by two wide. Sweating profusely Bernard dragged the corpse to the hole and rolled it in, pushing back the warm thoughts of the person the body had once represented. Obligingly in death as he had been in life, Julian's body rolled neatly into the hole settling face upwards, the sightless blue eyes staring heavenwards. "Jesus!" Bernard cursed as he saw the handle of his peculiar knife still protruding from the chest. Stepping into the hole, he stood on the stomach and yanked the handle. The upper half of Julian lifted upwards with the jerk and the eyes stared accusingly into Bernard's. With a cry of disgust and shock, he let the knife slip and the body fell solidly, allowing a small terrifying sound to escape from Julian's mouth. The air trapped in the lungs escaped up Julian's throat and passing over the vocal chords emitted a ghastly "Aargh." Bernard mistaking the sound as a long drawn out incantation of his name, tripped and fell as he tried to escape the hole then grew annoyed when he realised what had created the sound. Glaring at the corpse, he jumped down and stood on the chest. Placing a foot on either side of the knife, he gripped the handle and pulled hard. There was a scraping sound as the steel blade pulled free then Bernard dancing as he lost his balance on the unstable base and ended up sitting astride Julian. Glowering in anger he leaned over and roared into the serene face, "You're still fucking me about, you bastard." Raising the knife and pausing briefly as if taking one last look, the deranged Bernard plunged the blade again and again into every part of the face and body. When at last he tired there was nothing recognisable left of what had once been Julian. Panting heavily Bernard went to the car and returned with Julian's holdall. This was tossed on top of the gory mess then without a pause, he filled the pit. Lastly, he tossed the hubcap over to the car then looked around and congratulated himself. There was no obvious bump only the natural hollow had filled marginally. Feeling slightly better before turning away he gazed at the spot. "Pity," he said at last admitting his immense loss and the heaviness in his heart seeing the effeminate features clearly in his mind's eye. "Why me, why you ... oh Christ," he shook his head, "what a fucking pity."

He was covered in drying blood with a course layer of clinging sand so he walked down to the water's edge. Here he paused looking down at his hands as he rubbed the cloying red fluid between his fingers. All he had left of a person who promised him a new life, the residue from someone who would have taken him away from his nightmare existence. Of someone who loved him and someone he could .... Bernard caught the lump before it could reach his throat and spat out a ball of phlegm into the sand. He gathered his stupid meditations and locked them away in one of a long line of impenetrable compartments of his brain. These melancholy musings were in similar company for in each of the sealed cells lay memories, experiences that would never be allowed to rise to the level of conscious thought. But like any trapped acidic material they would burn and rot their surroundings.

Fully clothed, Bernard calmly waded into the undulating silvery sheen surface until he was waist deep and there washed unhurriedly in the lapping waters of the Mediterranean Sea.

~~~

Chapter 25

A cloud of depression descended over 103 Maintenance Unit as word spread that Josh Munroe, yet another member of the stricken tug-of-war team had died tragically. To add to their woes the sudden disappearance of their favourite son and character of debate, Julian Cantwell, posted AWOL. The departure of such a character left a massive void. A patch was missing from the colourful quilt that surrounded the tiny community of 103 Maintenance Unit.

Work of course continued. Tug-of-war training went on in the dip behind the marquees but the atmosphere was perforated. Personnel all over the unit did what they had to do; arrive at work, perform tasks and duties then return to domestic sites at the end of the working day - but they were robots. The joviality and conviviality that permeated throughout the yard was missing until eventually officers and Senior NCOs took on the same worried expressions. This hapless attitude was even more evident when in the middle of the month their tug-of-war team lost for a second time to the same Akrotiri GEF side that beat them in a league match 2-1 over two months ago. This time the reigning champions lost by the same score in the final of the Inter Services Knock-out cup. There was no backbone in the team. Their fighting spirit had gone, sheer class carrying them through the earlier rounds. It was the first time this particular trophy had been torn loose from its proud resting place in the 103 Maintenance Unit's display cabinet.

The disappearance of SAC Julian Cantwell was a particularly puzzling affair. Apparently Julian told a room-mate he was moving out to live with friends but no trace of these friends could be found. The RAF police quizzed Cpl. Tech. Frank Connolly with whose family Cantwell had spent most weekends but the Turkish bus driver remembered Connolly looking for his friend prior to boarding his bus. Cantwell it seems, took most of his kit and personal gear and simply vanished. The case was handed over to the British CID but having nothing to go on, went through their routine with Special Branch of the military police and continuing investigations. Beneath the flurry of officialdom, it was generally assumed Julian had met and went AWOL with a homosexual lover. The fly in that particular ointment was, if Julian had taken the decision to go Absent Without Leave, in effect leave the Royal Air Force, then why bother to take his RAF kit with him?

"I hope he's okay," Frank muttered as he sat with Nobby in Mustapha's kiosk. The big Indian said nothing morosely staring at his 7 Up.

"I feel I've let him down, Nobby. I once promised if he ever needed help I'd be there for him. He never ever mentioned these phantom friends he told you about. An' he always seemed happy stayin' weekends' wi' us, Jesus! If he had a problem how could I help him if he never told me about it?"

"You can't blame yourself," Nobby said. "I wouldn't say he was happy, more content, but a little secretive last Friday. But, Frank," he paused, "we were all aware Julian must inevitably take this step. He had no choice."

"Aye, Nobby, I know that but it's the abruptness of his goin'! He would've told me, I'm certain sure he would've warned me at least. We were the best of friends. I can't help but feel somehow he ... you'll think I'm fuckin' daft but I really feel he's not around anymore!"

"You don't mean ...?"

"Aye, I do, I mean fuckin' dead and I couldn't do anythin' to help him."

The remark shook Nobby, "That's quite a statement, Frank. What makes you say that?"

"I don't know, fuck's sake I don't know, I just feel it." His voice hardened, "But I swear, Nobby, I swear by all that's holy, on my life, on everything I hold dear. If Julian's come to harm, if he's hurt or ... or dead, I swear I'll somehow repay the bastard, the ..." he searched for the word. "the perpetrator of his pain or demise that I will, or if it's not me, me or mine will do to him what he's done to Julian."

Nobby shivered in spite of the balmy midday heat, "Shouldn't say things like that. Where I come from a sworn vow must be followed to its finish or you or your children are damned."

"Oh I meant it, I just hope it's me that does whatever needs to be done. I have two wee girls after all. Can't see them takin' up the challenge. But hopefully it'll never come to that. I just hope Julian is sittin' somewhere enjoyin' a brandy sour wi' his boyfriend and thumbin' his nose at us." As an afterthought Frank went on, "Maybe I shouldn't have included my wee lassies when I was doin' all that swearin' this an' swearin' that. I just cannot see my two wee lassies kickin' the shit out o' some hairy arsed poofter that's run away wi' their favourite uncle." He tried to lift his mood, "An' I nearly forgot!' There's the wee one in the oven, maybe that's a wee boy so if there's any retribution to be meted out, he might finish the job if I fail."

"That's a hellish thing to implant on your unborn child's head Frank, you must be careful."

"Aw piss off, you and your daft beliefs. If anything has happened to Julian I'll take care of my own vows thank you very much. That's if I can get my hands on the bastard first."

Frank Connolly and Nobby Clarke and everyone connected with 103 Maintenance Unit tug-of-war team, were in for a further shock when the team reached the final of the Akrotiri Station Sports only to have their famous heels dragged through the lush turf in a successive 2-1 defeat. Their Nemesis, the Greek goddess of vengeance had arrived in the male form of an arm swinging foul-mouthed but quite brilliant Chief Tech. Kowaleski as he goaded his team on to another fantastic effort.

The lethargic blanket clouding the entire MU clung even more heavily around the shoulders of the team. Peter Prentice who slotted nicely into the gap left by Josh Munroe seemed a confident and capable replacement and Sam Haire the Irishman was improving with every match. There was nothing physically wrong with the members of the team. The mental spark had simply burned itself out. In a long five-minute first end, the MU took their opponents to the line only to be pulled all the way back. In the second five-minute end, Callum McAlpine had performed miracles to lift his men and level the score, but there was no denying GEF in the third and final end. After four minutes, something happened that had not happened in ten years, the MU lost the Akrotiri Station Sports final, and with it, the right to wear the prized Akrotiri colours of blue and white hoops.

Bernard Kowaleski skipped crookedly down the rope after the final whistle and in full view of the umpire and the Group Captain CO who started the pulls, stuck his face into the sweating MU coach. "I told you your days were numbered you pompous shit! Where's the invincible 103 Maintenance Unit now?" hissed the grinning dark face and staring eyes.

"One thing you can bet on, you mad bastard, it's me that's chasin' now, my turn to get you!" Both coaches glared, each hating the other, and like the match just completed, Bernard had one final and telling arrow to shoot. "You've had your turn and your last chance you haggis eating bastard! It's us!" he thumped a thumb into his chest. "It's my team that will be pulling at the Neeyaf games!"

Callum stared after the departing strutting Chief. The madman was right! Because of this afternoon's defeat, he had not won the right to take his team to the NEAF Championships.

Now, as Akrotiri champions, Kowaleski had just claimed that honour. With a sinking feeling, Callum realised he would never get another chance. This afternoon's defeat was this season's last meeting between the two teams.

The umpire and CO exchanged glances, "He does tend to get a little over excited sir," said the umpire. "But he grinds out results. That's the second consecutive time he's beaten the MU. Something no one has ever achieved. Excitable perhaps, but he has at last managed to build an excellent team from off the station.

The CO watched the slightly limping figure slapping the backs of his team members, "I don't mind exuberance, but I do hope he behaves at the championships," the hawk-eyed Commanding Officer muttered. "We simply cannot have that sort of behaviour with our visitors coming from all over for the games. I believe the tug-of-war final is the last event and we don't want an incident of any sort to sour the afternoon, do we? Perhaps you can have a word, Flight, quieten him down a little?"

"Of course sir," answered the umpire knowing the request was a forlorn hope. This particular Chief Technician had been approached a number of times but when in direct conflict with the Maintenance Unit, it was akin to pouring a gallon of water over a blast furnace.

~~~

The following Monday morning Frank Connolly had polished his tug-of-war boots, something he had never done since his first pull on the island under the watchful eye of Flight Lieutenant Errol Barrymore. Just another little superstition being laid to rest. The matt black boots would never shine again as the leather had sucked the polish as thirstily as blotting paper sucks ink. When Frank tied them together with newly bought white laces carefully fed through the eyelets, they at least looked like boots again. He walked across the Machine shop floor and hung them outside sergeant Skaw's office. "That's it then," he declared to the Machine shop personnel. "We had a good innin's, me and the auld boots, won more than we've lost, haven't we?" Frank addressed to the boots, "So I'm hangin' you up. That's what people do when they're finished wi' a sport, you lot get hung up! Fuck knows why." He tried to sound light and welcomed the chortles from his work mates but he knew he would miss the challenge the sport brought. It was still five minutes to tea break but his mood was heedless of time. He poured a cup of tea from the urn.

"You're a touch early with your tea lad. You'll be getting me into trouble," said Peter Skaw looking at his watch. "Oh I don't know though, it's gone five to, think I'll join you." He poured a cup and joined Connolly at the domino-strewn table. The other machinists took the cue to switch their machines off. "What's up with the team Frankie?" the sergeant asked.

Frank shook his head sadly before sipping his tea, "Don't know Pete. Only thing I can suggest is, no team can lose two of their best men, especially two good ones like Ray and Josh, and hope to beat the pressure the GEF lads are hittin' us with."

Skaw nodded, "So what's the answer, you still have a couple of fixtures to tie up the league, can't you try something new against those teams?"

"They're two of the bottom sides so the league's tied up! We could win those with our 'B' team. It'd prove nothin' tryin'

558

somethin' new against weak opposition. Besides that was our last chance, we'll no' get another crack at GEF this year."

"Oh well there's always next year. So Akrotiri will be represented by one of their own section teams for a change. That's actually good for the station mind you, but it's a pity the MU couldn't get another crack at wiping the smile off that clown's face."

Frank frowned, "What's that?" Something Skaw said rattled the memory banks in his brain.

"I said it's a pity we couldn't wipe the smile off that -"

"No, no, before that," Frank cried excitedly, "you said something about the MU ... 'and it was a pity'," he tried to recall Skaw's words. "Shit what was it?"

A milky white new arrival to the Machine shop and Cyprus sitting on Sgt. Skaw's left said, "Sarge said something about the MU. That is was a pity the MU couldn't get another crack at wiping the smile off somebody's face."

Frank stared at the latest import from the UK. "Aye that was it, that's what he said!" He stood up switching his gaze to the sergeant, "That's right ... fuckin' hell, Pete, you're right!"

Frank ran across the Machine shop floor, caught hold of a surprised Mustapha who was sweeping up, and danced the pleasantly surprised little Turk round in circles. Mustapha's face was creased in smiles that melted away as Frank ended their romance when he ducked out through the small wicket door.

"I think the sun's got him," said the new arrival solemnly then looked back as Frank's head reappeared through the doorway, "Do me a favour," he called. "Take my boots off that nail, I think I might be needin' them!"

The word spread fast. The Maintenance Unit was entitled to enter a team into the NEAF championships. The fact that 103 MU was a base on its own, based within the auspices of Akrotiri had been all but forgotten. Over the years as the MU consistently won the title at the Akrotiri Station championships, they as Akrotiri champions went on to represent Akrotiri in all sporting events. Therefore, through a strange twist of fate, because of their defeat in the Akrotiri final, 103 Maintenance Unit were free to represent themselves at the NEAF games this year and not RAF Akrotiri as in previous years.

Callum was first at the training gantry next morning. He was early and sat under the trees waiting. The previous day Frank Connolly had charged into the toilets looking for him. Bubbling with excitement as Callum washed his hands, Frank suggested they could still legitimately enter the team into the premium games. Their Administrative Officer had confirmed that indeed they could enter 103 Maintenance Unit into the NEAF games. Callum hurried round the sections informing each team member with the news and to be at the training ground next day at 11am.

The air was still and Callum was lulled into reminiscing on the teams and men he had seen come and go. Sadly, this was his last season, the last major competition he would have with the tug-of-war team he had grown to love. The first time he visited this area, he sat more or less where he was now, watching a proud Flt Lt. Barrymore put his team through their paces. The resounding, "Yes - yes - yes" echoed across the valleys of his memory. It was all side pulling and speed then, now square pulling and pressure. Pressure that bled opposition of stamina, strength, ground, and grip on both rope and reality. There was one last and most important element to consider ... heart! When the heart went, or more precisely, resolution, when that went, all was lost. Were his men losing their resolution against Kowaleski's lot?

Robbie Stone the No.1 man was first to arrive and break Callum's nostalgic spell, quickly followed by John 'Cocky' Ennis. Robbie was an old hand but Cocky had come into the team halfway through the previous season. He was a solid twelve stones, a stocky five foot seven inches tall and had been a good addition. His nickname had been bestowed, not as one might imagine, because of any physical endowment. In truth, Cocky was only slightly above average in that department. The responsibility for his name lay squarely on the shoulders of his parents who displayed a magnificent lack of foresight when they had their child christened. As was the pattern of the times, children were given names of existing members of their families. Keeping in step with the custom, his parents took the name 'John' after his father, and 'Thomas' after his mother's brother, and Patrick after their patron saint. Hence, John Thomas Patrick Ennis! Poor John had to go through life with two clubbing fists until he tired of fending off the inevitable nickname 'Cocky.' It was a losing battle he could never hope to win. His initials preceded him whenever and wherever he went. Girls giggled when his name was called out, 'J.T.P. Ennis.' It was years before he realised the significance of his first names 'John Thomas.' No prim little girl wanted her name carved on a tree, 'Mary Smith loves John Thomas P. Ennis.' Thus, 'Cocky' stuck and would no doubt stick with him forever.

A noisy group of four more team members trouped down the slope. Big smiling Sam Haire could be heard for miles as he related some joke or story. He had also been a good addition but extra long pulls could still pose a problem for the big man. Frank Connolly the No.3 walked with Sam. The Scot, dependable as ever, never knew when he was beat and had been since his first pull, the kingpin in the middle of the team. The solid square figure of Nobby Clarke along with George Banks completed the quartet as the last pair clumped down the slope. Callum watched the six mingle, laughing together almost as if it was the first training session of the season. Nervous tension lurked just under the surface for they all knew this unexpected chance was the last curtain call they would ever get as a team, and possibly restore bruised pride. A lifeline to haul back their tattered image that had been tossed overboard by a series of mishaps and accidents. Their physical attributes were as solid as ever but the psychological damage might prove an impossible hill to climb. 'How do I repair that?' Callum wondered.

Last to arrive were two lads who had been in and out of the team for over a year; Ricky Wright and Pete Prentice. Wright weighed only ten and a half stone but like Connolly, would hang on all day. He could pull thirteen stone up the gantry so there was no worry about him pulling his weight.

Pete Prentice, Josh Munroe's replacement grabbed his chance literally with both hands. He had been a 'B' team member for over a year awaiting the opportunity to show his undoubted talent. He was a tall man with an athletic physique and made a smooth transition into the team.

The men milled around and the talk among them dwindled as they waited. The coach seemed to be looking, perhaps even scrutinizing each man individually. Cpl. McAlpine was indeed appraising each man, looking for a weak link that might conceivably be there. He was keenly aware if he lost this competition against the 'Pretenders' from Akrotiri Ground Equipment Flight, the MU and its reputation, built up over many years, would be irretrievable. Just another memory, a name from the past. And his name as the coach would always be associated with the downfall of traditionally, one of the best teams in the British forces. It took a lot to get under the skin of the lean, rawboned Scot but there was no doubt, the recent downturn of events on the MU had penetrated his hide more than he was prepared to show. The recent loss of his close friend Joss Munroe hurt Callum more than even he knew, but Carol Cook provided a steady shoulder. As was his way, Callum said nothing to anyone concerning his plans with Carol. She was UK bound in three weeks so the couple had decided to become engaged shortly before her return date. They planned to throw a party in the Peninsula Club on her last Saturday before repatriation.

Carol told Callum everything about her total infatuation with Harold Ross. She held nothing back on their relationship. Callum for his part accepted her honesty for what was past, was past. Being the man he was, he cared not a hoot what Carol's lifestyle had been prior to having taken up with him. But woe betide her if she stepped out of line now. The couple were surprisingly well suited and loved each other deeply.

Questioning glances were now being openly cast at Callum and the sharpest snapped him out of his reverie. He clapped his hands. "Right lads, as you now know we've got another bite at the cherry thanks to Frank. He remembered something we all missed. So, for the next week, I want you to train with one thing in mind, and one thing only. I don't want you to think about beatin' GEF, and we can beat them all right, they, the team are not the problem! We must concentrate in beating the driving force behind the team. And the drivin' force we've got to beat is that crazy horse Chief Kowaleski."

There was a rumble of laughter and smiles as yet another derogatory title was bestowed upon the GEF coach, but Callum nipped the hilarity immediately. "This is no laughin' matter lads! If we want to beat that crowd, we've got to do everythin' you've ever done in trainin' but do it twice as hard. So no more laughin' or carryin' on. Not this week anyway.

"Sorry Cal," said George Banks who had probably laughedheartiest of all. "It's just the title 'Crazy Horse' suits him so well."

"Aye George, it probably does, but Crazy Horse himself is no laughin' matter anymore is he. Whenever anyone mentions his name, it doesn't matter what name we call him, we laugh! We think he's a clown." Callum paused, "In case you've forgotten, that clown has beaten 103 Maintenance Unit, the pride of the tug-of-war world, in our last two encounters, and ..." he glowered at the ring of serious faces, "he's beaten us three times out of four this season. Some fuckin' clown!"

A few eyes were downcast, others showed resentment. Callum carried on, "If we don't get serious between now and next Wednesday, this clown is goin' to fuck us up a fourth time!" He was shouting into their faces now as he moved round the men slowly. "I want you to picture this ravin' maniac in your heads and remember it's him that's taken away the pride we had, US, the one-oh-three Maintenance Unit, kings of the tug-of-war world! That impenetrable barrier we had when we met teams who were our equal in every department, but when the chips were down, the coin balanced on the edge of a razor blade ... WE would inevitably win. Do you know why we always won these close matches? No? Then I'll tell you." Callum didn't wait for anyone to break his flowing oratory. "When a team of men have given everything they've got and still haven't beaten us, the straw that breaks their backs is the thought, 'Well we've given the MU a good go but we'll never beat that mob, they're the 'MU' That's the impenetrable barrier we had, 'They're the MU!' the psychological barrier that made us that wee bit better! If those teams had adopted one positive thought in their minds, for instance, 'Come on you MU bastards, you're never goin' to beat us,' we may have lost a couple of those close matches in the past, as we have against Kowaleski. He's taken that psychological barrier away. Now we're up for grabs against every half decent team next year. Why? Because he's demonstrated we can be beaten. The MU is not invulnerable after all, all because of that CLOWN!" Callum glared round the faces and was thankfully met with equally defiant stares. "When I started trainin' as a coach under a man some of you will remember, Flt. Lt. Barrymore, he said there was one thing that made the difference between us and all the other teams of eight men out there. Not strength nor balance nor skill or any fancy technique. It was ...

wait, maybe some of the older hands remember what made us a cut above the rest?"

Somebody spoke a word quietly at the front. "What was that? Was that you Frank ... aye? Would you repeat what you just said?" Callum zeroed in on Connolly.

Frank cleared his throat, "Determination!" he called in a strong voice.

"Repeat that for me," Callum said, staring at Robbie Stone and George Banks. When they hesitated Callum shouted angrily, "C'mon, this is no a fuckin' game we're playin' here. Repeat the fuckin' word!"

"Determination," the hesitant twosome chorused.

"All of you, what did Connolly say?" Callum bellowed.

"DETERMINATION!" the word was almost physical as it wafted over the glowering coach.

"I said ALL of you!"

Once more seven men roared the word in raucous chorus. Callum glared at Peter Prentice, the only non-participant.

"Look Pete, I don't give a flyin' fuck if you think this is as daft as your expression indicates, but if you don't join in with the rest of us, you won't be in the team. Everybody in my team does everythin' I tell them to do, an' they do it together. I've no time for individuals."

Pete looked uncertainly as the coach went on, "Okay Pete, what word did Connolly say?"

"Aw come on Callum, this's fucking daft!" Prentice looked away, avoiding Callum's eyes.

There was an awkward contemplative pause before Callum said, "Thanks for comin' down Pete, but I don't need you anymore. Report back to your section."

Pete's head swung back to stare into his coach's face, "You just can't be fucking serious Cal! Jesus sweet Christ, just 'cause I won't say a stupid word, you're bungin' me out?" growled an angry Peter Prentice.

"No. That's no' the reason Pete. The reason is, you're no' a team man. When you're on that rope under pressure, if I said 'Shit!' I'd truly expect you to shit on the spot. You'd be entitled to ask or question the wisdom of the command afterwards, but not when I give it. Sorry Pete." Callum turned away.

There was a moment of deathly silence, then Pete shrugged his shoulders, spat into the dusty soil and with a philosophical shake of his head, walked away and up the slope.

"Cocky," cried Callum. "Would you go to the MT section for me please? Ask Cpl. Tony Debden if he'll join us in his trainin' gear, right away, or better still, like ten minutes ago!"

Cocky jogged up the slope and passed the despondent Prentice then trotted down the road towards the MT yard. The words floated up and overtook Cocky, "What was that word?" he heard Callum shout, soon to be followed by the chorused,

"Determination!"

"Again!" the coach roared. "DETERMINATION!" rolled out of the gully like a warm breeze. Cocky grinned as he turned into the MT section, "I think our man's determined," he said.

Callum had eight days, including Saturday and Sunday to get the team on to a high, to raise their morale. At every opportunity he told them, "You're gettin' better," or "now THAT'S what I'm lookin' for, better than you've ever been." He took the opportunity to drive determination into their every move. Tony Debden was an adequate replacement. He had not managed to hold a permanent place so his surprise recall gave strength to his arm and jumped at Callum's every command having heard of the Prentice dismissal.

Callum varied their training. There was no doubt they knew the gantry well so he took the eight men running. He got them out on the Saturday and Sunday when the camp was quiet, had them jogging round the base carrying the rope, stopping at intervals and have an impromptu pull, four against four. He insisted they did not try to out-pull each other, it was merely an exercise. On one of these occasions he found the answer to the problematic hands of Sam Haire.

After one of these long layouts of four against four, Callum noticed Sam clench then unclench his hands repeatedly as he sat in the grass. He spoke to the Irishman, "Havin' problems Sam?"

"No more than usual Cal," the big man smiled. "I don't know if it's me bloody size but there's a lot o' weight for these to support, look at them." Sam held up his huge ham shank hands. Across both palms the heavy indents of the spiralled rope could clearly be seen.

"Are they always as bad as that Sam?"

565

"Not after short ends you understand, but after long ones of four, five minutes, aye they are."

Callum called Banks over, "Let's see your hands George."

Banks dutifully held out his hands. There were no indentations. "Thanks George." The coach turned back to Sam, "George is almost as big as you Sam, his hands are not marked."

"I saw that," Sam said frowning.

"Tell you what I want you to do for me. We're nearly finished today apart from one or two goes at the gantry. The last pull on the gantry will as usual be a long one. During that pull Sam, I want you to ease your right hand off the rope. Don't remove it or even uncoil your fingers, but ease it a little, then move it, flex your fingers and palm, everythin' as much as you can. Do that for half a minute then reclamp the rope with the hand you've just exercised and repeat the exercise with the left hand. Do that all the time the team are layin' out. Obviously you'll grip the rope with both hands if you have to start seriously pullin' Sam. Use this only in layouts when the pressure's neutralised." Callum was flexing his own hands trying to impress on Sam what he wanted. Sam watched the movement and copied it. "Yeah it could work. It's only the blood not gittin' into me palms that make them feel dead. Aye, it could work."

Callum demonstrated to the others what he had just shown Sam, and asked them to try it if they thought it might help when under pressure.

Back in the dip as the team lined up against the gravity laden bucket, Callum informed them,

"Many of you will be back in the UK next year so this is the last trainin' session we, this eight, will have together ... ever! There's no trainin' tomorrow as the pull-offs are on Tuesday, so make this session somethin' you'll all remember." He neglected to tell them he had increased the weight in the bucket by another eight stones so they were pulling in the region of one hundred and sixteen stones. A formidable weight.

On the first drop surprise registered on their faces as the bucket moved out of the hole by less than a foot. "Let it down," Callum called as he walked down to the bucket them turned to face his men, "Shall I go up to the WAAFs block, maybe get wee Carol and a couple of her pals to help you out here?"

The next attempt was not much better but he continued to work them for two or three minutes warming them up to the new weight. When the bucket dropped into the hole rather heavily again, he allowed them a two minute break. The weight was beating them. After the last failure as the bucket thumped into the hole, Callum shouted, "You're pullin' like a load of fairies round a fuckin' maypole. I've seen more effort goin' into pullin' off a French letter. For Christ's sake, what is wrong wi' you lot?" He spat in disgust.

After the short break, Callum addressed them again, "This is supposed to be your last days trainin' ... right? I swear it won't be if I don't see some effort, you'll be back here tomorrow I promise, and we won't be goin' home today until you make that fuckin' bucket dance. Just to prove I mean business let's put four more stones in the bucket. That'll make you work!

There were groans but the extra weight was duly added and again the team lined up. Callum did not expect miracles but he wanted the extra heavy bucket to reach the top of the gantry and for the team to have at least a three minute layout.

The team dropped and the bucket barely moved. "No, no, NO!" yelled Callum. "Come up, come up, come ON." The men rose and stood shuffling as Callum lambasted them ferociously.

"There's no point in us goin' to the games, Jesus wept, this is diabolical. You're forgettin' who you are! Don't you know you are 103 MU? ONE-OH-THREE MAINTENANCE UNIT! We have a certain reputation, and me? I am ashamed of you. No wonder we're gettin' beat, were you all on the job last night? Listen here to me," he dropped his voice. "I'm fed up wi' you lot, seriously, I mean this. I've decided we will give this one more go, if it doesn't bounce at least one foot, that's twelve tiny little fuckin' inches out of that hole, I'm goin' to cancel our entry. You lot are not goin' t' embarrass me. I mean it! I fuckin' do!" Callum walked away, took a deep breath then rejoined them. "Right then, for the very last time this year and this particular team, once the pride of the Royal Air Force, get on the rope and you better make it good."

There were no smiles as Callum gave the commands, all eight faces fixed on the coach's mouth. "Take the strain," he called, looking down the line for the least sign of distraction. There were none. "PULL!" he shouted willing everything into the word, simultaneously swinging round to see the bucket move. He was too late! The container was eighteen inches out of the hole and moving! Not rapidly but steadily at an even pace skywards. Callum felt a surge of adrenaline and pride mingled with not a little surprise. Each man was pulling at least two stone more than his own weight. Glancing back at the team he saw again the familiar centipede action of the legs on either side of the rope, nibbling along the ground. Tendons and muscles looked like they would cut through skin on arms and thighs, taking three, four inches with each nip.

A tingle ran across the back of Callum's neck. He had felt this way only once, two and a half years ago, when Errol Barrymore had taken great delight in showing off his time honoured team. How magnificent that team had looked then. This eight was every bit as magnificent. A straight edge could be laid along the heads, all staring at the bucket in solid effort and determination. Yes, it was determination that was moving that bucket, sinews and muscles glistening as they rippled under the strain. They were certainly helping but it was determination that was lifting that extra weight. Callum almost laughed in delight. 'Jesus wept, there's one hundred and twenty stones in there an' it's goin' up like a bag o' feathers.' He listened as a connoisseur listens to a good orchestra at the slightly strident rolling noise of a strained cable turning the pulleys.

A clang pulled him out of his euphoric trance and he saw the bucket swing lazily at the peak of its travel ... but it didn't drop, not an inch of rebound. "This is too good to be true," Callum muttered as he dashed up the line of his team in his usual quick crab like scuttle, bending his body to communicate better with the crouched men. "Good ... excellent," was all he could think to say as he collected his thoughts. The ease in which they raised the bucket after their earlier efforts had shocked him but he did not want to ruin it now. "Ease it down lads, slowly, I'm goin' to give you a stop." Like clockwork they clipped forward, cutting heels into the solid ground.

"HOLD!" Callum roared. He had no need to shout or get excited other than in the pleasure he felt in seeing the bucket stop as if it had stopped on an invisible table. "Okay lads, we're goin' for a long layout, last one ever for this team on this gantry. Get comfortable, I want at least six minutes." He glanced at his watch then went up the rope to Sam Haire.

"How's it goin' Sam?"

Sam smiled and winked, opening and manipulating one hand slightly to demonstrate he was already trying out the new method. "Come back ... ten minutes ... ask me then," Sam hissed. The minutes ticked by with no obvious discomfort from anyone. Callum looked at his watch and was surprised to see five minutes had already elapsed. Some of the heads were beginning to dip lower than others but when Callum enquired he got a definite nod to affirm they were coping. "How's the hands Sam?" Pressure was now showing in the Irishman's face.

"This is workin', must be five or six minutes now, they're not bad!" Sam was slightly out for it was nearer eight minutes as Callum looked down the line and saw all the hands working as they opened and closed. All the heads including Nobby at anchor were down between extended arms but the bucket remained rock solid. 'This is fantastic!' he thought then warning bells rang in his head. Shades of an earlier Barrymore? Enough was enough, they had proved their determination which was all he was after.

"Okay lads, let it down slowly now, slowly, slowly."

The round weight came down as if being lowered by a mechanical winch, easing its way into the welcoming coolness of the dark hole in the ground, and here it would remain, until exhumed by mostly new and keen hands the following spring.

There was deep satisfaction of the nine men as they gazed at the slight curl of dust rising from the cavity where the bucket would hibernate for the winter. Callum was first to drag his eyes away and run them over the men as they sat exhausted in the well churned dusty ground. "I want a wee bit better effort than that on Wednesday!" he said nodding his head sagely. The response was eight handfuls of sand and dirt thrown around his head and shoulders. Callum danced and spluttered under the choking attack then stammered, "Right then, you bloody lot, just for that I'm not goin' to tell you now. You lot don't deserve to know there's a hundred and twenty stones in that bucket so you can all get stuffed, I'm goin' t' keep it to myself!"

~~~

Two days later on the Wednesday morning of the Near East Air Force sports day, Callum and his team sat under the trees at the training area doing nothing more than talk shop. They had won their three pull-off matches the previous day to reach yet another NEAF final. In their half of the draw and seeded No.2 for the competition, the opposition proved tough but thankfully not unbeatable. In the other half the GEF team methodically proved their worth as top seeds. They also beat off three teams, including RAF Malta with superlative ease. This surprised the watching spectators as the team from the George Cross island had been touted around as good enough to upset the top Cyprus teams this year. When the GEF team returned to the marquee after their third victory, Bernard Kowaleski leaned over the MU coach and said in a loud voice, "You're next in line for us Cpl. McAlpine." Callum had grimaced up at the dark figure standing in the blinding sunlight then spat in the grass. Kowaleski didn't upset him, the only factor that did annoy Callum, he had lost the right to wear the blue and white hooped jerseys. Once regarded to be the sole property of his MU team. It was bizarre to see eight strangers parading around in those colours. No less strange was it to see his own men wearing the resurrected yellow and black quartered shirts of the Maintenance Unit.

Tactics, mental approach and attitude. Every last detail had been discussed the morning after the pull-offs when Callum said, "Okay lads, I think we've covered the lot except this one last thing. We haven't used it for a while but it used to work well. Connolly shares the middle of the team as you know at No.3. He's our most experienced man so I'm not goin' t' waste time dancin' up and down askin' every one of you. He'll be my link with you all. If we get into a long layout, and that's almost a certainty, I'm gonna ask Frank if he thinks they're ready to be taken. If he says yes, we'll go ... I hope! If he says no, we wait until they are." Some heads nodded whilst others shrugged acceptance. "Okay, see you in the competitors marquee at 3 o'clock. For God's sake, don't forget your kit, Julian's not around to pamper you any more so I hope your new jerseys are nicely washed and pressed after yesterday's exertions."

At Happy Valley a little after 3 o'clock in the competitors' marquee, Callum sighed with relief as Cocky Ennis entered. He was the last of the eight to arrive so now it was just a matter of killing the last gut twisting hour. GEF were gathered at the far end of the tent already changed into their boots and strips. A definite sign of nerves Callum was happy to note. There was at least thirty minutes before the call to change, and boots were not the most comfortable items to wear on a hot afternoon.

It seemed umpires were cast in the same mould. They all adopted exactly the same apparel. There was no set 'uniform' for the officials but obviously somewhere along the lines of communication unwritten laws had been written. The whitest of white shirt, shorts, stockings, shoes and if possible hair to match, seemed to be the adopted standard. For a moment Frank Connolly thought they had the same umpire as the two previous years, The almost painfully clean, starched clad in brilliant white, heavy set figure that called the two teams together into the centre of the marquee could easily be mistaken for Flt Sgt. Flowers. However, Frank realised when the man spoke, this was a more austere person, an officer probably. He was right. "Good afternoon, my name is Squadron Leader Laurel, would the tug-of-war finalists please gather round." He seemed impatient as the men did as he asked.

"I am your umpire," he opened briskly, "I know you are two experienced teams and well aware of the rules, so unless anyone has any questions we will pass on. Anyone?"

When it seemed no one had anything to ask the officer was about to carry on when, "Is it possible to keep an eye on this MU team, they tend to sit in long layouts!"

An imperious eyebrow rose as Sqdn. Ldr. Laurel turned to seek the speaker. When he found him he asked, "You are?

"Chief Tech. Kowaleski, GEF coach." The words were said in a dead monotone.

"First of all Chief Technician Kowaleski, you need have no fear about my side judges or myself doing our job. I have been a sports administrator and official for twenty years. AND ... I am an approved triple 'A' tug-of-war umpire ...."

"That's good, for they tend to cheat."

The officer frowned, "I am going to overlook that Chief. I do not intend to cover the same ground. I was about to make a second point when you intervened. May I continue?"

Bernard twitched his eyebrows and gave a slight shrug.

"I take it by your rank and your being here today, you are one of us Chief, yet although I have informed you of my rank, you continue to address me in a disrespectful manner!"

Bernard stared but made no attempt to speak. The commanding figure of the umpire looked closely at the man. He seemed angry, sullen and somehow distant.

"Chief Technician Kowaleski, are you still with us, are you all right?"

Bernard was statuesque, his eyes fixed on the officer.

"I say ... a simple 'Yes sir' will do, in fact Chief I have reached the point where I insist!"

It may be the heat, or the excitement before the big event, but the officer had a feeling all was not well with this man. "Chief Kowaleski, if you do not answer me ... immediately I will have no hesitation in postponing this final until the Medical Officer has examined you."

A minute passed in stony silence. The umpire turned ostensibly to look for another official when someone in the GEF team called out, "For God's sake Chief, address the officer, we're going to lose this before we get on the field." It was Harold Ross lamenting his utter disgust. Harold's words were enough to break through the hard-headed arrogance.

"YES SIR!" Bernard shouted but continued to glare.

Sqdr. Ldr. Laurel ignored Bernard to search for the airman who had called out.

"Airman, do you have a reserve coach, someone who could take this man's place?"

"No sir, we have a team reserve but no one to take over as coach," Harold replied.

The officer turned back to Bernard, "Tomorrow morning Chief Kowaleski, I want you to report to Sick Quarters. I order you to report to Sqdn. Ldr. McKenzie. He will be expecting you. Now try to pull yourself together man."

"Yes sir," the Chief answered in a more reasonable tone. Inside his head Bernard was puzzled. Why was he baiting the officer, especially as he was also the umpire in this important match. With a lingering look at the dark featured Chief Technician, Sqdn. Ldr. Laurel carried on with his preparations. He tossed for ends, then informed both parties to be at the exit door at three fifty. When the band started to play 'Aces High'

572

each coach would march his team smartly through the flaps onto the field.

Callum quietly implored his men to listen only to him, ignore all and everything going on, listen only to his commands. "Do that lads, and I promise, we will take them!"

The Akrotiri band struck the first bars of Aces High and the teams marched together across the rich green turf. Harold Ross called across to Frank Connolly, "Good luck Frank but I'm sorry mate, we're going to beat you ... again!" He winked.

"No' this time pal, this is the one that counts, an' you'll no' be disappointed wi' the runner's up medal. The cheeky bastards have engraved 'G.E.F.' on them already, I think that's terrible!". Both men grinned giving the other thumbs up as the teams wheeled away to line the rope.

Callum danced up his line of men muttering "Determination," time and time again as the umpire rapped out the commands. Suddenly, both teams had dropped and a sound similar to the crack of a pistol shot rang over the ground as the rope snapped taught.

Sqdn. Ldr. Laurel, his aggravation with the insolent Chief Technician forgotten for the moment, looked at the central rope marker. "Amazing," he muttered. The marker had not moved an inch either way from the central painted line on the grass. He looked left along the rope then right. It was a mirror image. The eight men to his left were in exactly the same positions as those on his right. Only their shirts were different.

Harold was comfortable, his hands gripping the rope between half-bent knees, body coiled and relaxed. Raising his head he looked down the line and groaned inwardly. The 'centipede' legs of the MU team resembled an insect, even more menacing in their yellow and black colours. "We're in for a long one," he called to the man directly in front of him.

"Ross, what are you saying?" Bernard called scrambling over to his No 4 man.

"They're looking good, that's all."

"Save your fucking breath, Ross," snapped the coach but stole a glance at the opposition. He came very close to admitting Ross was right. They did indeed appear to be solid, in perfect formation. Perhaps too comfortable, he had to do something to upset them. "Wind on the pressure, try them, hit them now!"

Nothing happened at first then slowly the backs of the blue and white men began to straighten. Harold Ross and his team were surprised at their coach attacking so early. Certainly they were taking rope but at what price?

Frank felt the expected pressure build. He tried to apply equal power to stop the rope moving away, to stop his hands, tightly clasped on the rope passing slowly between his knees towards his feet. Eight heads dipped in the MU team, chins deep in chests. Their shoulders slowly moving past the central point of gravity.

Callum watched the postures of his men gradually bend under the extreme pressure. A foot was lost already, maybe two. This early onslaught was not entirely expected, it may even be welcome but if he didn't act soon, it could develop into a rout. "New position!" he yelled. Eight men tensed then roared as they carried out the manoeuvre. "One - two!" The left foot quickly followed by the right chopped hard into the turf to gain two strong footholds. They had lost a little rope but were back into solid positions as they were before Bernard's stamina sapping charge to win ground.

Bernard knew now what 'that skinny red headed bastard' was up to.

"He's going for the long layout," he informed his men. "Relax, take it easy, we'll do it his way. We can out stay that lot!"

After three minutes, Robbie Stone in the MU No.1 position felt good. He was back in a regular routine at home again, eating his wife's meals, and celibate for a week before big matches. There was none of that heavy leaded feel about his legs. It was early days but he knew he could last another five, maybe six minutes. 'If this lasts another five minutes,' Robbie thought as he lulled himself into a sort of never-never land where he spent his time during long pulls, 'then that should be around eight minutes. Surely that must be some sort of record for an end in a Neeyaf? But they'll never last another five minutes, not the way they're pulling their hearts out.' Robbie raised his head and looked up the line. "Oh Christ!" he muttered when he saw the opposition had settled in for a layout. "Fuck it, record here we come." He lowered his head between his arms again.

Cocky Ennis knew he was in for another tough match. He had never pulled so hard in his life and still they had lost a couple of feet. Thankfully, thought Cocky, Callum knew what he was doing. That jump forward to gain new footholds and renew good position was really something. He was staring down between his knees at nothing in particular, when he did something he always tried to avoid; he looked up. Staring defiantly back at him along the rope he looked into the half and full faces of the GEF team. "Bloody, bloody hell!" he muttered, lowering his head quickly to its accustomed position and focused at the grass between his thighs. He would not look up again, nor allow any thoughts to enter his head until it was all over.

Callum glanced at Ennis when he heard him mumble something.

This was unusual. His No.2 was one of his quietest men once a pull started. He approached his No.3. "How do they feel Frank?" he asked too casually, belying his taught innards.

"They're strong Cal," Connolly answered.

Frank felt no pain whatsoever. There was pressure certainly, but it was not heavy now and for the young Scot this type of pull was a walk in the park. He calmly stared along the rope at the opposition and the thought crossed his mind, 'Aye, it's goin' t' be a long one, they look as good as I feel'.

The man behind Connolly, Ricky Wright in the No.4 position could hold the weighted bucket on the single gantry for six minutes comfortably. Ricky however was keenly aware his team had actually never won an extended pull over six minutes. Every time he was involved in a long layout they had lost ... that only happened against these bastards at the other end of the rope. At the moment he felt good even though the time since the 'PULL' command must be around the five-minute mark. He forced his mind to think of anything as long as it was away from this energy sapping stupid sport he had got himself involved in. It was so daft he was prepared to die for it. 'I've got to win this,' he half said under his breath. "This'll be something to show the family, them that think I'm no good at sports. Me, that weighs a lick over ten an' a half stone in a championship tug-of-war team, that'll surprise them! God help me ... shit I've got to win this!" He cursed as the first twinges of pain shot across his wrists and hands. "C'mon, work them fucking fingers and hands, c'mon work them."

Callum glanced at Wright, normally rock steady. He was another one talking to himself. Callum continued to go up the rope, reassuring, vocally patting the back of each of them.

Tony Debden at No.5 was calmly picturing in his mind the precise shape of a George Cross medal. He had only recently started to collect medals as a hobby and a George Cross medal would really be a prize. He had found a few first and second world war medals when he was a boy, and these had lain around at home gathering dust before the bug to start a collection bit him. He started to ask other airmen on every camp to which he was posted, if they might have 'any military insignia or old medals' lying around at home. In this way, Tony had received many a pleasant surprise as numerous little prizes had been dug out. The best trophy he had acquired was a pristine Royal Victorian Order medal, which cost him a small fortune. Tony considered that particular decoration to be worth every penny. Pain stabbed through his thoughts so he eased the fingers of his right hand and worked them a little. "I wish they would get on with it, before I'm too knackered to do anything. Now then, somebody told me a cook might have a North African campaign...."

Callum heard Tony grumbling and wondered if he should start applying some pressure against the continual unrelenting tension the GEF team somehow kept constant. He might be forced to do something soon for his men were beginning to hallucinate.

George Banks was fascinated as he watched a little black and yellow ladybird beetle in the grass directly between his knees. It was trying unsuccessfully to climb a blade of grass. 'Funny,' thought George, 'that little bastard's wearin' oor colours. Go wan son!' Suddenly the equation of the beetle's colours and his team took on a whole new meaning. 'Go wan, that blade of grass is not so high, you can make it to the top, go wan now!'

George's blue eyes watched as the beetle awkwardly clambered its ungainly way up the green stalk, then only a few miniature steps from its goal, loose its footing and tumble back into the grass.

"Stupid bastard!" George shouted down between his legs, "you'll 'ave to do bettah than that you little twat! Where have you got to now?" The No.6 scanned through the area where the insect had disappeared.

'Jesus,' Callum muttered as he stopped at Banks who seemed to be suffering most. He kept goading himself into further effort shouting at the ground. Callum whispered words of encouragement in his ear.

'Go 'way Cal, joost tell us when action starts,' George thought. 'Where's the little buggah now?' George's mind switched off completely from the pain and torture of his aching body as he again caught sight of the ladybird. The beetle started yet another ascent on another unwieldy green blade of grass.

"Come on soon," urged George. The black and yellow insect had nearly reached the summit of its climb when it clumsily swung over, hung upside down for a second then dropped again into its green jungle. "Fuck you!" George shouted at the ground, his curse loud enough for Callum to swing round.

'Must be the heat, he's never been like this,' the coach muttered staring at his No 6, 'somethin' better happen soon, big George is crackin' up!'

The end was now well into its eighth minute and though his men were suffering under the severe physical strain, so too was Callum with mental pressure. "How are they Frank?" he shouted into the ear of his No.3 man. It was necessary to shout now for he could barely hear himself above the mounting roar of the crowd sensing something was about to happen. Never had an end lasted so long in a tug-of-war match and the crowd were rising in crescendo, urging on their favourites aware a result was imminent. Callum watched Connolly's head nod, then his hoarse voice confirmed, "They've cracked Cal, somebody up there has just cracked. Take them, they're ready." Frank was near the end of his endurance. "Just now, Frank, just now," Callum cried glancing along the rope at both teams. The GEF team still looked solid. Sam Haire was physically exhausted but far from beaten. His hands were going dead despite exercising. He never imagined he could last this long and without the exercising it was certain he would have fallen off the rope by now. Sam was the only man in the team who could not switch his thoughts elsewhere during torturous long layouts, but no one in the team had the same resolution as Sam Haire. If the never-never land had existed in Sam's mind, he would gladly have entered, but the Irishman was too much of a realist. As a result he physically suffered for his realism. Sam heard Frank Connolly telling the coach to take these persistent buggers at the other end of the rope. The coach had only muttered something and nodded his head. "God's sake Cal, do it soon!" Sam prayed.

Nobby Clarke, at the end of the rope, was making love to Sandra. The beautiful young Indian girl had been selected as a wife for Nobby by the respective sets of parents and Nobby himself could not have chosen better. At the age of twelve in Calcutta, Nobby fell in love the moment he laid eyes on the dark eyed eight year old. When he saw Sandra last, four years ago on a visit to his home country, it was then revealed to him she was to be his wife. Nobby wanted to marry her on the spot, she was so beautiful. In September, only a few months away, the young airman would return to Calcutta for their arranged wedding, but as time grew near so did his burning and untapped manhood near boiling point. He spent most quiet moments dreaming of his lovely bride-to-be, as he was this afternoon. Nothing could ease away the pain of this tortuously long end more completely than a fantasy afternoon with Sandra. The anchorman was jumping the gun in thought if not in deed as he lay between the smooth dark thighs of his beloved. He was completely immersed in the beautiful scene, feeling little of the pain racking his body. They were naked on the bed. Candles and incense were burning on tables on either side. It was the middle of the afternoon, the radio was playing one of the latest love songs and diluted sunbeams played around their slowly moving forms. Nobby smiled as he watched his own bottom move lazily, then suddenly it started to pick up speed as Nobby recognised the tune his own mind had selected as background music. It was Matt Munroe nearing the end of his latest hit, and the words crooned in his ear, "Almost there, I'm almost there -" Nobby could not suppress a bark of laughter.

"Fuck's sake, I'll have to move them now," Callum said when he heard the ever staid Nobby laugh. At that moment George Banks suddenly saw the ladybird crest the blade of grass at last, open its shell like back, spread its purring wings and fly heavily away. George raised his head, "We're flying Callum, go! That's it, go now!"

Callum looked at his watch, ten and a half minutes. "Christ. Okay lads, let's go for it. Wind it on, c'mon now, wind it on." He looked up the rope and said more in hope that certainty, "One good heave will break them, and take them lads, I promise you."

He watched, breath locked in his chest as his team, like a monster slowly uncoiling, tried to straighten their limbs in a pressure building heave. For a frightening few seconds nothing happened as the men at the other end of the rope resisted the force then slowly, slowly the blue and white hooped figures started to bend. Callum had to suck in air, forgetting to breathe, then he saw his eight start to move ... backwards, actually move their feet. The MU began to take rope and ground. Callum hopped alongside all the while keeping up his verbal encouragement.

The whistle blew and only then did the men from either team hear the crowd cheering in a frenzy of noise. Eleven minutes and fifteen seconds was an unbelievable time, and both teams looked as if they had taken part in what was certainly a record NEAF pull. All sixteen were laid out on the ground as the umpire called, without the least sign of concern, "Change ends please."

Sqdn. Ldr. Laurel may have seemed unconcerned but inside he was concerned about these men dredging their last ounces of energy simply to rise in order to walk to opposite ends of the rope. He had never in all his years seen such a pull. The official timekeeper would no doubt have recorded the time but the officer guessed it had to be over ten minutes. Amazing, but he had a job to do and two minutes was the time allowed between ends, no matter how many records were broken. Glancing at the teams he may have to stretch the rule, within reason, on this occasion. "Coaches please, have your teams change ends, quickly now!" He tapped his watch.

"On your feet lads," called Callum. "Get down to the other end, or this keen laddie might disqualify us, move it, c'mon." The totally spent men struggled to obey and somehow managed to line the rope, hands resting on hips, sucking in great volumes of air.

At the other end, had Bernard Kowaleski possessed a whip, he would have used it. He was cursing his men roundly, accusing them of giving up, of not giving their all especially at the finish when it mattered most. He pointed to the MU team, showing his men how exhausted they were. It seemed to have escaped his notice his squad were in precisely the same condition.

Harold Ross had given everything, as he knew his team mates had done. To hear this idiot accuse them of not trying after what must have been ten minutes of solid effort was all Harold could take. He stood up on trembling legs and said breathlessly to the man in front of him, "Norrie, get up! Steve, why are you lying there? Get up or Skee'll accuse you of not trying."

Harold received a black glare from his coach but the slur had the desired effect. The men managed to form an unsteady line and trundled to the opposite end of the rope.

The winning of one end had not won the match and both coaches tried to instil into his glassy eyed troops what was necessary to secure the next end. When the teams dropped at the command "Pull!" pressure again was equal but only for a matter of approximately ten seconds. Frank felt neither fibre nor quality in the resistance normally expected from the GEF team. "Callum!" he called the name quietly and the coach was crouching by his side, "Aye Frank?"

Frank blinked, "I think ... I don't know if we've got anything left but they're ready. There's nothing there!"

"You sure?" asked a cautious Callum glancing at the blue hooped opposition, fully aware one mistake could reverse the advantage that for the moment seemed to lie with the MU.

"Christ's sake Cal I'm tellin' you, go for it! We're about fucked anyway."

Callum needed no further urging when he took in a realistic glance at his own men. They were literally holding on by the skin of their teeth. "Okay lads, this for the championship. Kill them off, show them you've got plenty left. Wind it on, now!"

There were one or two sets of bared teeth and eyes raised in Callum's direction at his choice of words for many were falling back rather than pulling. They had little strength left but the slight tipping of the scales as they applied what little pressure they could was enough to move the rope. Everyone, including Callum was surprised but as ever his wits were sharp. He gathered his team into a steady unit then into a beating metronomic pattern, "One - two - keep it goin' - one - two." punching one hand then the other.

The giant MU centipede taking six inches with every stroke of the coach's call, reduced the eight men at the far end of the rope from chirping cocks to staggering stumbling wretches. When the whistle shrilled, they sank thankfully to the ground.

For a moment Callum remained in a dreamlike state. He saw his men back slapping each other, shaking hands, delighted smiles lighting their faces. All signs of steamy exhaustion apparently evaporating in the heat of victory. He turned to look at the desolate opposition, smiling happily then his eyes locked with those of the staring, hate filled face of Chief Tech Bernard Kowaleski. At that precise moment, his hearing mechanism switched back on and the roaring surging sounds from the crowd filled his ears. Callum could understand the momentary loss of hearing after the excitement, but the shock of it returning as he locked vision with the opposition coach was like a slap across his face. He blinked, disorientated for a moment. Thankfully, his attention was distracted as his ecstatic team surrounded him. Hands were pumping his, others patting his head and shoulders and he was happily jostled around. "You did it Cal you old prick, you fuckin' did it!" someone shouted.

For the next few minutes everyone involved, and quite a number who had nothing at all to do with either team, were immersed in the euphoria of the hard fought victory. Congratulations were still being poured on the team when the umpire blew a long blast on his whistle. Callum looked over the bobbing sea of heads and caught the signal from Sqdn. Ldr. Laurel. The umpire wanted them back to traditionally walk up the rope to shake hands with the losers.

"Okay lads, a wee bit o' decorum, back on the rope," called the MU coach. "Back on the rope now, where's your manners. Shake hands with our worthy opponents, come on!"

The eight men obviously exhausted, nevertheless light heartedly, lined up amid jokes and banter. Then each team shambled down the rope line towards each other, the coaches of each side following in their team's wake. Tired remarks and comments passed between them as hands were clasped as best they could then as Nobby Clarke shook the hand of his opposing anchorman, the coaches came face to face. Bernard grimly

581

extended his hand as Callum did likewise. Their grip was firm and seemed affable to those watching but Bernard was holding Callum. In what appeared to be a friendly congratulatory offering to their win, Bernard leaned over and spoke calmly in his opposite number's ear, "I'm going to kill you!"

Callum pulled back and glared at the face so close to his own. There was no bitterness in the madman's slack grinning face yet the tone implied this was no empty threat. The Scot for once was momentarily stuck for words and could only continue to stare at the now expressionless face. The black unfocused eyes were fixed on a point on Callum's forehead and the head was erratically moving slowly in every direction, as if the motor operating that part of the anatomy was seizing up. There was nothing wrong with his speech however when he said clearly. "I am," the steely black eyes dropped and pierced Callum's, "I am going to kill you ... I swear!"

Callum felt a shiver course down his spine and fought to find his voice, "Aye? You? You and what fuckin' army? Ya brainless bastard. Don't you threaten me or I'll stick your crazy head up your slack arse where you can eat shit as well as talk it."

If Bernard heard the breathless if unrealistic counter threat, he showed no sign as the MU coach watched Bernard walk away. A hand scratched his red hair, a frown on the craggy face.

"My heartfelt congratulations coach, that was an absolutely magnificent match." Sqdn. Ldr. Laurel extended his hand then noticed the scowl on Callum's face. "Something amiss?"   .

Callum hesitated then said, "Sir, I hate to run down a man at any time no matter who he is, but," he paused still looking after the departing Chief Kowaleski, "but I really think that man has just topped sir."

"Topped? He's WHAT?"

"I don't know the medical term sir, but that man's gone round the bend, I'm convinced of it!"

The umpire watched the ambling figure of the troublesome Chief Technician disappear into the crowd. His earlier assumption apparently was accurate. "First of all, you better let me have your number, rank and name. Secondly what makes you say such a thing?"

"Sir, people have threatened to kill me in the past, but this time that bloke really meant it!"

"He threatened you?" Laurel was incredulous, "He actually threatened to kill you, in those precise words?"

Callum was slowly nodding, then after supplying the officer with his details, he went on as the officer scribbled in a notebook, "His name is Kowaleski, a Chief Technician from Ground. Equipment Flight, Akrotiri."

"Yes I recall his rank and name, Is there anything else you can tell me about him?"

Callum told what he could to this very fastidious officer. The fact remained however, despite the dire threat his team had just won the prestigious NEAF tug-of-war final in two straight pulls and Callum wanted to join his team to immerse himself, to wallow in the short and sharp taste of victory. "Sir, with all due respect, I've given you my details, can we talk about this tomorrow? That was our last pull together as a team sir and I'd really like to rejoin my team in this, our magic moment, if I may. Besides, the immediate threat has taken himself off to wherever daft people go."

"Yes, yes of course, but this man's name has been connected with a number of adverse reports, particularly connected to this sport corporal. This threat, this very serious threat, we simply cannot allow to go unheeded can we? I did order this man to report to sick quarters in the morning as you are aware." He gave a little shake of his white head, "It'll be point of interest if the same man that was here today, turns up tomorrow. Look, I'm sorry for keeping you but I will most definitely be sending for you in the morning about this. Off you go then, live your moment, but," he held up his notebook, "please be careful. Enjoy, and once again, well done!"

Harry Ross and Frank Connolly joined Callum. They heard the officer's parting comments.

"What's he talkin' about?" asked Frank.

"Nothin'!" Callum had no intention of allowing the threat to sour the celebrations. Harold was not convinced as he exchanged glances with Frank.

"Callum, I don't know what was said between you and old Skee, but there's no doubt that bloke's a penny or two short of the full shilling. We're all fed up with him on the section, he goes over the top with everything."

"If you're tryin' to tell me he's as nutty as the proverbial fruit cake Harry, don't worry, that's ancient history. Now, can we just forget that clown for I refuse to let him spoil this win or my evening's entertainment. Let's all have a beer and later you and your team are welcome to join us in the club if you fancy it, but no' that daft bastard. If Kowaleski walks into the club, I walk out, and so will my team."

"He'll no' show his face," offered Frank. "If he does, there will probably be a mass walk out." Harold agreed as he turned his head in a sweeping scan, " You know, I don't think he's stuck around to pick up his runners-up prize, he's disappeared!"

"Aye, he went up they steps an' through the crowd, there's no sign of him." Frank confirmed.

"Good bloody riddance," Callum stated, "now let's get into that beer. I think it might just take at least half a dozen of the big ones to wash away that ...." Callum shook his head. He could not find the words to adequately describe his feelings towards the peculiar Bernard Kowaleski.

~~~

Chapter 26

Callum drank the last of his half dozen beers and Happy Valley was the warmest, most pleasant companionable and happiest place on earth. Apart from the content group sitting in the stand, the green valley was deserted when Carol finally managed to drag her fiancée away from his clinging team members. All the men who had taken part in winning the match earlier that afternoon wore comfortable grins as they floated on a surreal atmosphere vainly trying to hold on to a glorious day. A day that would all too soon pass and fade into history. The losers too, although losing, had enjoyed a wonderful season that was sadly over. All bitter sporting feuds would lie dormant for another season. The many long hours of training were over. Now in the aftermath of battle with the beers tasting like milk from the breasts of Aphrodite, and honours more or less even, sanguine feelings of fulfilment reigned supreme. In their five matches, three trophies had been won by GEF whilst two went to the MU. Oddly, over the five contests, the Maintenance team won seven ends against six by the Station men. It could not have been closer, and neither could the men from both camps as the light faded in Happy Valley. All decried the attitude of the thankfully absent coach, but no one could deny his brilliant training accomplishment, which lifted an ordinary team to heights that surprised everyone, none more so than the GEF team themselves.

The babbling group of jocund men, wives and girlfriends had settled in the stand after the presentations. Every second of both ends in the match had been recalled, relived and recounted, over and over. Now, as the sun sank slowly heading for its daily extinction on the distant yellow horizon, the winners were privileged to breathe in the wonderful heady perfume associated with the wafting breezes of victory.

Carol heaved the reluctant Callum to his feet and begged, "Don't drink any more Cal, we still have to put in an appearance at the club tonight. And you have to give your little impromptu speech you've been practicing for a week, remember?" Laughter greeted Carol's remark, and cheers as Callum rose, "Okay Darlin', I'm comin' I'm comin." He smiled and looked around the faces, trying to imprint the warm images on his brain. He must not allow this memory to fade nor forget this day, for never in his life did he ever imagine he could be so content. Grinning he called, "I'll see you all in the Pen Club, in an hour ... or so ... all of you! I know all your faces, so if you're not there, you will be in big ...." he wagged his finger around the faces.

The mixed crowd smiled at the red headed Scot who was both ugly in his craggy looks, and   wonderfully handsome in his happiness. He was obviously enjoying his perfect day. Someone stuck a can into Callum's hand as he turned away. "Oh you shouldn't have given him that," Carol scolded the smiling benefactor. "And you shouldn't have taken it, all that beer on an empty stomach!" she chided the grinning Callum.

"You're beginnin' to sound like a wife already," he leaned over and kissed her cheek, nearly falling over in the process. Carol moved her mouth to his ear, "Listen lover boy, we ARE married already, or haven't you noticed. We just haven't been churched." She could not help nuzzling her nose into his ear, breathing in the warm salty manly smell of him, feeling her love for the man well up inside her. Whatever feelings she thought she had experienced for anyone else, they could not compare to what she felt for her Callum.

"Wanton wench," he whispered back, still wearing that silly smile.

They left the group and walked to the trees where the couple paused and waited for Cocky Ennis. He was giving them a lift back to camp. "I'm fated not to win a bloody tankard Carol," said Callum staring at his latest ubiquitous trophy. It was a small figure of a woman, perhaps Artemis the Greek goddess or perhaps Diana holding a spear. The statuette had her feet firmly implanted on a chrome dome in the centre of a bakelite dish.

"Aye, they're either runnin' out o' cash or ideas. This must've cost as much as what a wee pot would've cost. That's me fucked ... sorry ... had it now, I'm never gonnay win a pot." Callum was trying to stop swearing. Carol vowed if he stopped, she would too.

"You'll win one when you get back to the UK. You've only just started coaching when you think about it and look what you've won already. You should be grateful Cal." Carol scolded.

"Ooh, I'm grateful my little spitfire, Jesus ... sorry ...." he apologised again for his slip of the tongue as he gazed back at the tight circle of people beginning to break up in the stands after his departure. "What a team to get landed into my lap eh? What a fu- ... reputation they ... we've got." He stopped swaying as he picked out Cocky saying his goodbyes, "C'mon Cocky bloody Ennis, you prick" he roared, suddenly feeling the pangs of hunger, "I want to eat tonight, not tomorrow bloody night."

Carol turned her eyes skyward.

Cocky dropped them at the cafe in the heart of Akrotiri where Callum bought chicken and chips for them both. They crossed the road and walked to the hill overlooking Submarine Rock and sat down on the grass. Callum was ravenous and nothing was said as he wolfed down his food. He had not eaten since breakfast and the beers and excitement had honed his appetite. Carol took her time, picking delicately as she looked round with a pang of memory. This must be very close to the spot where she had lain under a blanket with Harry Ross. 'My God! That was two and a half years ago!' she recalled with surprise. A stab of remorse and regret worked through her emotions remembering Harry's wife and her terrible death. Carol often wondered if her alliance with Harry had in any way been connected with the girl's demise. She could not see how, but deep down a strand of guilt tugged painfully at her conscience. Harry never told her why Marion had gone with the Buckley's without him. Indeed Harry hardly spoke to her since he lost his wife, contributing to the guilt Carol harboured.

"Anythin' wrong?" Callum asked, wondering if she had found something amiss with her food.

"I used to come here, with Harry," she answered simply. The beauty of their relationship was they had no secrets. Callum was mature enough to accept he could never have had any control in Carol's life before he became part of it.

"Any regrets?" he asked.

"Regrets? Oh no, Cal, none at all," she gave a small smile, "but I have a nagging worry I might   have been somehow connected with his wife, Marion was it? going off to Troodos without Harry that weekend." She turned to face him, "Do you think she found out about us, Harry and me?"

"Who knows darlin'," Callum answered. 'Could this be the reason for her recent mood swings.' Callum wondered. She was not finished as her blue eyes sought his; "That's really bothered me. I'd hate to think in years to come the damage it might create inside me if I go on like this, you know thinking it was me that caused that girl to die. Why did she go alone, I mean without Harry?"

"It was nothin' to do with you!" Callum said emphatically. He had no idea what caused Marion to go off with Ray and his family to a holiday resort without her husband. But he could not allow this burr of memory to grow into a thorn bush. He had to cut it now. "Harry finally talked about that last week. Told us he couldn't go for he had a streamin' cold that weekend. Marion was lookin' forward to the trip so much he insisted she go with the Buckley's. That's why he felt it even worse than just losin' her. He felt he sent her to her death, that's why he ended up in hospital." When it came to sparing Carol's feelings, Callum found he could lie quite easily.

"Thank God," breathed Carol, "oh thank God," she added fervently. "I know it doesn't pardon me for my part in screwing around with her husband, but at least she didn't know, she didn't die cursing Harry ... or me." Carol had never been the one to thank her Maker for anything but the words helped ease her conscience. Abstractly she picked up a chip and chewed on it then went on, "But it's funny, isn't it Cal, and fucking cruel," she did not apologise for swearing, "when you remember Harry was burning his candle at both ends. We were having the life of Riley the two of us. Sorry Cal," she leaned over and clasped his hand. "But Harry just could not get enough sex. He had to have it every day with me or his missus and not just the once yet ... when she fell pregnant, he broke up with me! He went straight into married man mode, stopped messing around! Sods law took over then I suppose, for it's then he loses the only person he really cared about."

"Aye," Callum muttered, "poor bastard ... sorry, got his fingers badly burnt right enough!"

They sat quiet for a few minutes then Callum said, "You've hardly eaten a thing lass, but if you're ready we'll need to think about movin'. I'm half cut, need a shower before we go to the club." He grinned, "Don't know why but somethin' tells me it's gonna be one helluva night, tonight."

~~~

The MU corner was jam packed full of happy noisy people. It seemed every airman from the little Unit had brought along their wife or girlfriend, and every WAAF, her boyfriend. Their team was back on top having beaten off yet another pretender to their throne. The bad spell was over and personnel from every corner on the MU were paying homage to their heroes. Team members were championed and applauded on arrival. Their backs and hands aching, not only from the marathon pull but from the constant back-slapping and hand-shaking gauntlet they endured just to walk through the boisterous crowd. Following up from their gelling session after the match the numbers were swollen by members and the incumbent following of the GEF team.

Chief Tech. Jock McKinley sat with his wife who was in animated conversation with another lady. Jock was enjoying the hubbub and buzzing atmosphere that reminded him of the days when 'Old Barrymore' had been the coach. 'Aye,' mused Jock, 'Old Barry used to create evenin's like this when he won, an' that was regular as clockwork. Mind you, this team lost a couple o' really good lads earlier in the season, knocked them off their stride for a bit. There was that strong bugger Munroe, takin' somebody's wife up to Nicosia airport, two o' them killed. An' my lad Buckley.' Jock shook his head, 'Sad case that one. Tried to fly his car doon the mountain instead o' stickin' to the road. They reckon the road fell away, but I don' know. He might've been pissed, always seemed to be on the juice that poor bugger. Could be wrong of course.'

Jock always drifted back into the past when half a dozen large whiskies were warming his innards. Life was always much better 'back then' somehow and the whisky always brought 'back then' that much nearer. He had a month left on the island before repatriation then one year to serve in the UK before retiring on a comfortable pension. A cottage anywhere on the coast of Britain beckoned Jock. Just as long as there was a store not too far away where he could purchase a supply of the amber gold he loved but never allowed to dominate. His mellow musing was interrupted when Mrs. McKinley crashed through his thin walls of contemplation

"Are ye gonna fill our glasses or sit there dreamin' a' night?"

Jock's nearest and dearest was certainly sinking them. She didn't go out with him too often so tonight he could just about put up with her demands. 'Can't afford t' tak' her oot too much, the way she knocks them back,' he smiled benignly to himself. "An' whit would ye like?" he asked amiably, "an' maybe yer pal would like a wee somethin?" It was worth getting a drink in for her friend. Anythin' wis worth it, if it keeps her forever waggin' tongue oot o' my ear.' Jock was distracted when a cheer went up as the colourful couple of the red headed Cpl. McAlpine and his blonde girlfriend wended through the tight throng into the MU corner. Chairs had obviously been reserved and were magically produced for the pair at the central table.

Seated at this table were Nobby Clarke, Harold Ross, George Banks with his wife and Frank and Lorna Connolly. Lorna, in her third month of pregnancy avoiding the flowing alcohol was happily sipping fruit juice. The cheering was deafening at the coach's arrival as Frank raised his voice above the din, "Those are yours," he pointed to two pints and two brandy sours. "We were DETERMINED you were not gonna fall behind." He winked, "You're bloody late mate, where've you been?"

Callum nodded towards Carol who was nodding and smiling in light conversation with Harold. "One of her hairs was out of place," he shrugged then asked, "What's the kitty?"

"Ten bob," Frank answered. Callum dropped a pound into the glass then nudged Carol, indicating her drinks. She looked at them enquiringly. "They didn't want us to fall behind," he grinned.

"Cal, you better go easy drinking that stuff," Carol nodded towards the beer. "You're looking pale honestly pet. Please, don't drink too much."

Callum nodded. Despite his high spirits, his stomach was sending 'No Entry' signals.

"Promise?" Carol wanted confirmation. "Aye promise!" Callum duly confirmed and smiled. It was nice having someone look out for him and what's more she was right. He did not feel his usual perky self. Food always tasted better after a few beers and he had allowed his stomach's need to overpower his good sense. Normally his system could handle anything he could throw at it, but the way he tossed the fish and chips from the cafe down his throat was verging on the edges of feeble-mindedness. He'd eaten much too hurriedly and could feel the meal sitting heavily inside. Perhaps all it needed was a good flushing and there's plenty of beer around to carry out that function. Nothing was going to sway his determination to make the most of the celebrations. But within reason! The promise made to the girl who was growing more precious to him by the minute, was made in good heart. He would keep the promise and not drink too much, but he had not promised not to drink! He, Callum McAlpine had coached his tug-of-war team, 103 Maintenance Unit in TWO NEAF finals and won them both. Not a bad record! He picked up a glass and downed half its contents in one swallow, confident his iron clad system, would as it had in the past see him through the night.

No one noticed the white Minx draw into the car park and reverse into a space at the far end of the parking area. No one that is other than Jock McKinley. The Chief who for some strange and paradoxical reason preferred to have a smoke in fresh air rather than in a smoky atmosphere. He was halfway through a cigarette at the entrance of the Peninsula Club and paid scant attention other than notice the odd tail lights on the car as it slotted into the bay. Jock wasn't sure if he knew the car, then the door opened and Kowaleski got out. Jock nodded in recognition. Lots of stories circulated about this so-called 'Crazy' Chief Technician who ran Workshops on the main base. Typically, the old Chief paid little heed to rumours for if half the tales he heard about this man were true, then why was Kowaleski running around on the loose minus a straight jacket? On the odd occasion Jock had seen Bernard in the Sergeants' Mess, the man bothered no one. He was a bit of a loner certainly but that was no crime.

Bernard approached and climbed the steps. He would have passed Jock without a glance had the latter not greeted him, "Come to join your lads Chief?"

Bernard stopped, blinked as if reorienting himself, then looked at McKinley. "My lads?"

"Aye, they're inside, fair enjoyin' themselves wi' our blokes. Havin' a good time they are."

"My lads, with those bastards?" Bernard growled tearing his eyes from the Scot to stare towards the club doorway. "Bastards!" he muttered then resumed his walk and entered the club.

Jock frowned, "Aye, well mebbe there is some credence to what's bein' said aboot that yin."

Bernard crossed the entrance hall and entered the fray in the main lounge. Head down he slipped through the throng to the Gents toilet. No one in the heaving jovial crowd noticed him.

Having gained the sanctity of the toilets, he entered the first cubicle, partially closed the door and sat down. He was prepared for a long wait, or he might get lucky and have only a short stay in the pleasant smelling well-kept cubicles. Either way it did not matter, he would wait all night if necessary. Bernard knew from living in barracks of one sort or another for most of his life, for some strange reason when men felt the need to use the cubicles they avoided the first one in the row. The second, or the third were universally the most popular, even the fourth or whatever was available. But the first toilet was rarely used unless the others were occupied. He first noticed this peculiarity when as a cadet whilst on 'Ablutions duty'. He had to check cubicles for toilet roll replacement. Inevitably the roll of paper in the No.1 cubicle lasted much longer than the others.

"Mixing with our fucking blokes! The bastards, the fucking turncoats!" The two thick eyebrows formed a straight black line as Bernard sat staring at the door. "I'll sort those bastards out!"

In the main lounge things were hotting up in the MU corner. The raucous surrounding group near the central table were chanting, "SPEECH - SPEECH - SPEECH!"

"Go on Cal, they're going to bring the place down if you don't stand up," urged a happy Carol as she laughed, pleased at the attention he was getting.

Callum had been quietly hoping to get off lightly and perhaps escape the speech everyone knew he had to make tonight of all nights. Not allowing himself to falter he rose to his feet quickly and was surprised as he staggered a little, which brought a resounding cheer from the crowd.

"Steady on," Nobby said, reaching out to support the strangely faltering coach.

"Whew!" Callum exclaimed which brought more laughter and cheers. The crowd thought the coach was as inebriated as they were, but quietened when the Scot held out his arms. There was a small solid table nearby and Nobby cleared a space for Callum to stand.

"Whew," the coach said again scanning the sea of faces. "I don't know where to start."

"At the beginning," someone nearby called.

"That might be the best place, but I don't want to stand here for the next three hours," Callum grinned, "and I'm bloody sure you don't want to listen to me awe night either?"

Another cheer rang round the lounge but quickly subsided when Callum again held up his hands. "Before I fall off this table, I want to make an announcement. I want to share my good news with you all. This little bundle of candyfloss sittin' on my left has made me a happy and I must admit, a contented man. She makes me feel somehow, complete! For the life of me I'll never understand why, but SACW, Cook, or Carol, the love of my life, has accepted my offer of marriage!"

The roar that greeted this statement was the loudest and longest of the night. In the first cubicle in the Gents, Bernard Kowaleski cringed imagining the cheers were for the 103 tug-of-war team.

It took Callum longer to quieten them down but after what was probably the best moment of quiet he could hope for he went on, "Now the important things are out of the way, I'm goin' to bend your ears for a minute or two and go back to when I was given this coach's job just over two years ago. I felt privileged then and nothin's changed, I still feel the same way today. To have the undoubted honour that I am connected with such a dedicated and gifted bunch of athletes as the one-oh-three MU tug-of-war team!" He raised his hands to stifle a cheer that threatened, then continued, "Two years ago, almost to the night, my predecessor, Flt. Lt. Errol Barrymore, some may remember him? He gave me the job in this very club. I hope I have fulfilled some of the promise the great man placed on a rookie coach that night."

This time there was more heartfelt hand clapping than drunken cheering as smiles and thumbs held high greeted Callum's words. "This afternoon was my last real competitive match wi' this team, my team so you must forgive me if I indulge myself jist a wee bit here. I won't be here next year so this is the last time I'll get the chance to do that." He glanced down at Carol and winked at her.

'He's beginning to enjoy himself up there,' Carol thought returning the wink.

Callum spoke for another ten minutes about the team and their exploits then as he neared the end of a longer than intended speech, certainly for the usually reserved coach, someone shouted "Any regrets Cal?"

"I was just about to wind up but funny you should say that," Callum smiled as he faced them again. "Only one ... in all our wins, all our competitions, I never won one of those," he pointed to someone who continually raised a pewter tankard at every cheer. "When I started here with this team I thought I would win at least one pot. Every winnin' team was collectin' tankards at one time. Tankards used to be standard prizes for winnin tug-o'-war teams. Typically when I took over, pots for prizes went out of fashion."

"Here, you can have this," the man called offering up his tankard.

Callum smiled, "Thanks, but my pot's got to be won. Oh I'll get one, maybe when I get back to the UK. I'll get involved with another team, but I doubt if I'll ever get involved wi' a team as good as this one." Confirmation from the crowds' boisterous cheers at this last remark rang in his ears as he waved and stepped down from the table. Carol went to hug him as he sat beside her but stopped "Cal, your shirt ... you're sopping wet!" she cried, concern sharpening the edge to her voice.

"Stomach's givin' me a hard time, don' worry it'll settle down." Carol said nothing, she didn't want to nag but it was only minutes later she noticed the tall gangly figure of the slim Scot bend forward, folding arms across his middle. For Callum's digestive system to be upset this was indeed a rare event. Carol recalled how quickly he ate his meal on the hill overlooking Submarine Rock, but he always ate fast. Could it be a touch of food poisoning? Carol weighed each possibility. "Do you feel you want to be sick?" she asked.

"Me ... sick?" Callum raised his eyes and gave Carol a look as if she asked him if he had messed his pants. "Naw, naw, I'll be fine, I'll go outside, get some fresh air, it'll pass." Callum was surprised at himself. He always maintained he had an 'iron constitution'. He could not remember the last time he was physically sick and reluctant to admit his stomach could not handle a few lagers followed by fish and chips! A mere hiccup to his gastronomic consummative capabilities. It was an insult to see his second pint, bought and paid for, placed on the table before his arrival, just lie there untouched. The night he so looked forward to was being governed by his sour stomach. Stubbornly, if chauvinistically, he clung to the hope his, as yet, unbeaten if non gourmet system, would fight off this lethargy and deliberately he leaned over for the glass.

Carol noticed the slow kneading of Callum's hand across his stomach, and his pathetic attempt to make conversation with others around him so when he reached for the second beer, she spoke quietly, "Do you really want that?"

Lorna Connolly like the others had noticed Callum's discomfort and she, being a woman and in tune with Carol, was more than a little concerned. "Callum, you okay? You look hot. They've got the air conditioning on, it's not so warm in here." A look of concern creased her lovely features as her husband Frank leaned over, "For the first time in your life sonny boy, your skin looks like porcelain. What is it Cal?"

Callum sighed finally admitting defeat, "I wasn't very clever earlier on. Bolted some grub down an' it's sittin' like a red hot brick in my gut. It may be that, maybe the beer, don' know." He rubbed a hand over the upper part of his abdominal area as if trying to push the offending pain away. "Thought it would pass but I've got the funniest feelin' I'm gonna pay for my stupidity. Maybe ..." he gave a wan grin, "I am goin' to be sick!"

"C'mon Cal, let's get you to the bogs. Stick yer fingers down yer throat an' ye'll feel much better." Frank said followed by a female chorus of "Oh for God sake Frank," and "Must you?"

"I've heard it put more delicately," Carol said, "but that's exactly what hc needs!"

Frank and Nobby helped Callum to his feet, "Hey wait a minute," the latter complained, "I might be wee bit of colour but I'm no' decrepit. Where do you two think you're goin'?"

"Thought we'd come with you, see you're all right," said Nobby.

"I'm no' a bairn," Callum frowned in mock anger at the

Indian then his expression changed as he felt his stomach roll and his mouth fill with saliva. He was close to vomiting. Not trusting himself to speak again, he shrugged nonchalantly and nodded. Giving Carol a wink, he turned and led the way through the packed tables to the toilets. Despite their rebuff, Frank and Nobby followed in his wake.

Callum tried to hurry yet at the same time did not want to reveal his mounting panic. His gait was unsteady as he felt back slaps and heard comments. He hoped he was not about to embarrass himself bang in the middle of these people who had him on a pedestal. To them he was for this evening's performance only, a divine being, the star of the show, to be held up and admired through beer stained glasses. Tomorrow he would be just be another corporal.

At last he reached the toilets and pushed through the door. The first cubicle was slightly ajar but with the 'engaged' sign showing. 'Probably some drunk honkin' his ring up like I'm about to do,' thought Callum. The second door was wide open, empty and welcoming. He lurched inside. Never had a toilet bowl looked so inviting. He was just in time as the first heavy retch cut painfully up his throat. Despite the guttural and noisy choking sounds he was making, only a little beer came up. The ponderous molten lump, the base of the deep problem however was beginning, with each painful pick axe picking retch, to give notice it intended to make an appearance very shortly.

Frank and Nobby entered the toilets to be greeted with the unusual sight of the slim figure of their team coach retching over a toilet bowl. They both grinned and Frank leaned over the sluggish shape, "Go for it Callum, we'll just pull the door on you a wee bit, don't want anybody comin' in an' seein' our leader's arse to the fore while spewin' his heart out, now do we?"

This was answered by a grunt followed by a rather ragged, "I'll no' be long!"

Frank pulled the door as near to closed as he could manage.

"Take your time, we'll be here when you're ready."

"Fuck off the pair of you!" the embarrassed Scot grunted. He was utterly uncomfortable in such a vulnerable position. "Since when do I need a fuckin' wet nurse? Go on, piss off!" Another choking, strangled cough emanated from behind the door.

His two friends went to the urinal, both grinning, "I know

exactly what he's goin' through," Frank said, remembering his first drink strewn days on the island.

Bernard in the first stall peered through the small gap in the doorway. He was smiling. Just as he thought, every man in the lounge bar that night, at one time or another would visit the toilets and the one man he was waiting for had just entered. Not only was he in the toilets but there was a bonus! The very man he was tarrying for in this female perfumed stink hole was in the next cubicle being as sick as a dog. How very convenient. Initially Bernard planned to wait for the red headed coach to go to the urinal. Whilst engaged in the act of emptying his bladder Bernard would walk up behind him and stick him like the pig he was. Bernard would not care if there were others around, he wanted only to kill that man. The circumstances and penalties of the deed were of secondary value, however the Gods were smiling! They obviously agreed with his plans, therefore it must be the right and proper thing to do, otherwise why deliver the sacrificial swine to his door, or should that be, next door? Again the humourless smile spread across his darker than normal features.

Bernard could hear the sounds from the next cubicle. At last the occupant was being violently sick. No more retching or half-hearted efforts, the outpouring of lumps and fluids was clearly evident as the man emptied his innards. Time to act. The built in computer that precisely controls a madman warned the action part of Bernard's brain; the chance of committing the act would disappear in the next few seconds. The two pricks that come in with the pig were in no hurry to leave as they washed up and laughed at the guttural but nevertheless cleansing and curing noises from the next cubicle. Suddenly the sacrifice was laid on the sacrificial block when one called, "We're goin' Cal. We'll come back in five minutes, give you a chance to clean up."

A grunt from the animal next door, then mercifully the two left. Bernard was about to open his door when a raucous noise filled the toilets and five young lads, worse the wear for drink, rampaged into the room. They were full of high spirits and lined the urinals but as there was only room for four, the fifth staggered over to the cubicles and Bernard heard him push open the door to the next booth. "Oops, sorry mate, nearly pissed all over ya!" Laughter and banging of doors until the man eventually urinated loudly into the water of the bowl which seemed to Bernard, to go on forever.

More horseplay between the five then all at once the place went deadly quiet. Flames in the black eyes burnt fiercely as the occupant from the first cubicle wasted no more time. He moved quickly and opened the door from the where the retching sounds were now reduced to spitting. He saw the familiar slim figure of the MU coach beginning to rise from his crouched position.

The knife was already in the demented Chief's hand as the head began to turn. Bernard grabbed an ear and a handful of the hated red hair and with a high backward underarm swing, put all his weight into punching his fist hard against the exposed back. The knife stuck fast, buried deep in the rib cage. Holding the head firmly, Bernard had to jerk once, then twice before the weapon would pull free.

Callum was trying to twist away from the tight grip his attacker had on his ear and hair. He tried to dig his elbow into the midriff of the man behind him but Bernard caught the blow on his hip. Another underarm arc was greeted again with the sweet feeling of the blade driving deep into the back of his hated enemy. Heavy dark blood was pouring out of the first wound as Callum jerked his body trying to twist away from the knife when there was a dull 'click,'

Bernard stared down in disgust. In his hand lay the rule handle of his precious knife, the broken blade embedded deep in his victim's back. Callum's eyes, already glazing over sought his attacker, "Why ... why this, you crazy, crazy bastard, do you think you've won now?" It was no more than a hissed whisper as the blue eyes closed. Callum went limp.

With only a few millimetres of blade left protruding from the six inch rule handle Bernard tossed it aside. Still holding the handful of red hair he looked at the multi coloured mush in the toilet bowl. With a sickly smile frozen across his face he pushed the head into the glutinous mess, forcing the head and shoulders deep into the bowl.

Bernard stood up and admired his work, then kicking aside Callum's legs, closed the door. Moving quickly now, he rushed to the basins and turning on both taps washed the blood from his hands and wrists. He was wearing a short-sleeved shirt but some bloodstains had splattered over his trousers and shoes. Giving these a perfunctory wipe he realised he could not tempt providence any longer. He had not expected to, but he was actually going to get away with this! A quick check in the mirror then he crossed the tiled floor to the exit, opened the door and without hesitation marched smartly through the crowded room and out to the car park. He was elated and light headed as his feet seemed to glide and float over the ground. The Gods were with him, provided the ideal opportunity for him, that was why no one gave him a second glance crossing that crowded room.

But Bernard was wrong. Chief Tech. McKinley grumbled as he ordered yet another round of drinks from the bar. "She's drinkin' like a bloody fish tonight," He complained to one of the current team members who worked in the Machine shop.

"Wouldn't mind so much but she's got her pal keepin' up wi' her."

Frank had no sooner got back to his table with Nobby when Lorna asked him if he would get her, of all things a glass of water. He joined the Armoury Chief at the bar and chuckled at the comment old McKinley made about his wife. The Armoury Chief, one of the best liked characters in the MU yard went on, "That was a nice wee speech yer man gave t'night."

"It was Chief, pity he's goin'" Frank agreed.

"I don't agree with that," said the tall good looking lad joining the pair. "He cannot go quick enough for us," smiled Harold Ross, also on a return visit to the bar.

"For us?" asked Jock, then "Oh aye, now I've got ye. You'll be one o' the GEF lads, right?

Harold nodded.

"Haven't see yer coach havin' a drink wi' his team, what's happened to him?" Jock asked.

"No, he decided not to grace us with his presence. He's a bad loser," answered Harold.

"Didn't grace you wi' ...?" Jock screwed his face into a huge frown, "Oh but you're wrong laddie, I spoke to your man over an hour ago, outside on the steps. He came in here ... in fact," Jock paused and looked towards the toilets, "As I was comin' over to the bar just now, only a minute ago, I saw him leavin' the shithouse in a bit of a hurry, on his way oot!"

Immediately alarm bells started to clang in Frank's head.

"You saw Kowaleski leavin' the toilets a minute ago?"

599

"Maybe your hearin's damaged workin' in that machine shop son, but aye, that's what -"

"Fuckin' hell, Harry!" Frank exploded cutting off the older man's words, "Callum's bein' sick in there. Oh God, c'mon."

The two left Jock looking after them in bewilderment but the seasoned airman was long enough in the tooth not to remain in that condition. Obviously something was wrong. He had no idea what it might be but by the reaction of the two men cutting a swathe through the crowd towards the toilets, it was something serious. Jock turned to two sturdy young men at the bar, "You two, come wi' me!"

"And who might you be?" asked one.

"I'm a Chief Technician, that's all you need know. I want you to accompany me immediately." The voice bore all the power of easy command and the two hurried after the hardy older man as he pushed through the thick mass packing the bar.

Frank was first into the toilets where he stopped suddenly. An airman was standing ashen faced staring into the first booth. He looked to be on the point of fainting but when first Frank then Harold charged in, he turned to the pair, eyes wide, then pointed wordlessly at cubicle one.

Frank pushed past him, skidded and grabbed the sides of the booth. "Oh my God!" he breathed. Callum had slipped down the outside of the toilet bowl. His upper half was covered in vomit, his clothes saturated in blood, which was spreading across the floor and out of the booth. It was this that caused Frank to slip. "He's done it Harry," he shouted, "Aw Jesus, the madman's done it!"

Frank leaned over and gripped Callum's belt. Gently pulling he eased the injured coach out from the cramped position, jammed between the left side of the bowl and wall. Then he saw what he thought was a six inch rule. He picked it up just as Jock McKinley arrived and immediately took charge. The experienced Chief had seen similar situations in his time and knew the drill.

"Don't move him, just get him comfortable." Jock turned to one of the two airmen trailing him, "You, get to the nearest phone, tell the hospital what's happened here. We need an ambulance, immediately ... immediately ye hear! Tell them there's been a stabbin' at the Peninsula Club." Turning to Harold, Jock said, "It might have been the Chief Technician from your section who did this lad, you're familiar wi' the man so I want you to get after him." Jock looked at Frank, "You go wi' yer mate here but don't make any move to apprehend this man, he's dangerous, extremely so but we need to know where he's goin', that's all, we don' want him runnin' amok. Take every -"

"Aye okay Chief," Frank cut in. "We'll go in my car, it's a white Simca in case you have to come lookin' for us."

"Right, but don't make this a personal vendetta now, if that man can do this," McKinley nodded at Callum, "he's capable o' anythin'. Now if you find him, try somehow to get back, maybe one of ye get in touch wi' any guardroom, but keep yer distance, that's an order, d'you understand?"

Before Frank could answer, everyone in the room heard a female voice fighting its way through the crowd blocking the doorway, "Stabbed? STABBED?" the voice screamed. The rising panic could be heard as she went on, "Who is it, TELL ME, OH CHRIST WHO IS IT?" Carol's blonde head appeared as she tumbled and fought her way through the crowded doorway. Her lovely face blanched as she stopped when seeing the blood on the floor and every apprehensive eye turn towards her. At the angle where Carol was standing, she could not see Callum but she could see his feet, where Jock was kneeling. Carol stared at the older man she had met socially with Callum, "Tell me ... tell me it's not him, Jock ... oh, Jock please ... tell me it's not ... it's not my Callum!" She was taking timid steps towards the Chief who for the moment could not answer her. She knew of course, deep inside. She recognised the trousers, then as she rounded the end of the cubicles, the shirt, the heavily blood stained shirt, and finally the red hair messed up with slime. "Oh dear God," she said quietly. Then, "Oh the fucking bastards, what have they done to you, oh I'm sorry Callum darling, I didn't mean to swear ... oh don't lie in that mess Callum, get him out." She would have hugged the prone figure had Chief Mckinley not grabbed her.

"Come now lass, come, come, come! We daren't touch him for fear of doin' more damage." Jock could just see the silver end of a blade protruding from Callum's back, and blood was pumping weakly from the wound. "He's still alive lass and I need you to help me clean him up and stop the bleedin'. The ambulance'll be here any minute."

Someone suddenly appeared with bundles of clean towels. Carol blinked rapidly and seemed to gain her self-control. "He's still alive?" she blinked owlishly, wisps of mascara raking her cheeks. "Oh ...." she said, then grabbing some towels started to gently clean the mess from her loved one's face.

Frank's brain was in turmoil but he pushed his way through the crowd and found a worried Lorna with other women standing back, away from the crowd around the toilet door. "Darlin' it looks like Kowaleski stabbed Callum. Harry and I are goin' to see if we can find him, just to see where he's goin'. We won't get involved wi' him, don't worry. Get a taxi home or go to the hospital wi' Callum. I'll see you later." Lorna biting her knuckle, nodding dumbly.

Ten minutes earlier when Bernard Kowaleski walked out of the toilets, no one had given him a second glance. Which was strange for Bernard felt he was like a glowing beacon, alight with pleasure and if not exactly covered, certainly splattered in blood, yet no one noticed! He almost exploded with laughter and had to stifle the impulse placing a hand over his mouth. He had just scored a   major victory over 103 Maintenance Unit and no one had seen him do it. The result of his action   tonight would stain the name of the MU for years. He felt elated as he bounded down the steps into the car park feeling a delicious stab of pain in his knee. The pain reminded him he had gone a long way to recuperating some of his lost glory days denied him by the despised MU. This would wipe the smiles off all the faces at their celebration party.

Hurrying to his car he paused and then surprisingly relaxed, turning to deliciously lean his hot back against the cool car door and gaze up at the stars. He had never noticed how close they were before, proving once again the gods were smiling down on him. They were closer tonight because they had guided him, cleared the way for him, and fulfilled their wishes, that was why he was so ecstatically fulfilled. There was a burning need in his groin to savour again the moment of feeling the knife drive into the hated body. He almost climaxed with pleasure, had he had more time there was no doubt he would have, the gratification was so intense. Pity about the knife, it had such a beautiful blade and in retrospect, wished he had not discarded the intricate mechanised handle. There was always the chance of having a new blade fitted. Too late now. He got into the car and sat back in the seat with a long comfortable sigh. On impulse he reached for the pack of Turkish cigarettes and lit one, allowing the acrid smoke to linger round his nostrils. Closing his eyes he watched himself committing the brutal act again and again, relishing the "Ugh!" from his victim the first time the knife grated through the ribs. He had hoped to cut the throat as his final achievement but the damn knife .... Tossing the cigarette pack into the open recess in the dash, he dipped his hand into the well and pulled out the long dagger. The one he bought in the Turkish quarter but never had it moved from its glove box residence except for the occasional inspection. It was another beautifully made weapon, though designed more for decorative purposes. When the ornate silver handle was pulled it exposed from its elaborate sheath a fine blade of nine inches and only half an inch in width. The keen stiletto type hollow ground edges were sharp enough to shave the toughest beard. Bernard's face creased into a smile as the night reflections danced along the glittering steel. "You are my source of pleasure now, you can effortlessly pare the skins for me, from all the fruits of the world."

He replaced the knife into the sheath then solemnly tucked the weapon deep in the dash recess. Activity elsewhere sparked his brain back to reality. Noises were erupting from the building he had just left and it occurred to Bernard he had been dawdling and dreaming. Somewhere under the surface of Bernard's unbalanced medulla oblongata warnings were being issued, he must be away from this place. Without questioning his built in alarm system, he switched on the ignition then pressed the starter button. There was a whirring noise as the starting gear failed to engage. "Bastard, bastard!" Bernard complained and slapped the dash in disgust. Something was niggling away at the back of his mind, urging him to retire from this place. Then he caught a whiff of drying blood from his shirt. "Oh yes of course, now I suppose they'll be looking for the culprit." He pulled the handle out from under the seat.

Pushing the pinned handle into the slotted nozzle, he cranked only once and the engine caught. Movement at the club entrance snagged Bernard's attention. A member of the MU team whose name he could not recall and his own SAC Ross were framed in the club's doorway. Both were looking left and right when Ross pointed. "There! Jesus can you believe it, he's still here!"

Bernard scuttled up the side of his car, threw the handle inside and scrambled behind the wheel. Gunning the engine he immediately skidded into a tight turn and roared out of the car park. 'Idiots,' the demented Chief thought, 'they want retribution for what I did to their precious coach,' his eyes grew hard, 'but it is me! I claim compensation for what they did to ME!'

"Where's your car?" Harold called as he watched the odd taillights of the Minx race off.

Frank was already running towards a relatively new Simca. Harold followed and threw himself through the open door just as Frank drove off. Within minutes they skidded to a halt as the MP stopped them at the main gate. "Now then, what's all the hurry?" he asked amiably.

The corporal's slow approach destroyed Frank's patience "For Christ's sake lift the bar, that madman you've just let through in the white car just knifed someone in the Pen club, hurry man!"

The policeman scrutinised the pair in the car, "The chap in a white car, the Minx, you say he knifed someone?" The policeman thought the driver of the Simca appeared drunk, his eyes were wide and staring. "The chap you claim to have just knifed someone, a Chief Technician, appeared to be in a much more lucid condition than you are. He certainly was not drunk! 1250s please and switch off the engine."

A guardroom window opened and a sergeant appeared waving a piece of paper towards his colleague on the gate.

Undecided for a moment the white capped MP glanced from the car to the sergeant, "Switch off your engine please while I speak to my sergeant. I won't move until you do!"

With a cry of disgust Frank switched off and sat back. The young 'snowdrop' marched the twenty paces to the guardroom. In less time than it took Frank to realise what was happening, Harold jumped out of the car and pressed the lever to lift the red and white painted bar blocking their way.

"Move Frank, we can't wait for these guys, Skee will be out of sight soon"

Frank started the engine and with a shout ringing in his ears slowing barely enough to allow Harold back in, went hell for leather down the moonlit strip of road.

"Oh Lord!" the Military Policeman exclaimed as he read the note, 'Airman attacked in Peninsula Club. Attacker suspected to be Chief Tech. Kowaleski. Apprehend at guardroom main security gate. Approach with caution, suspect may be armed and is extremely dangerous.'

"Why don't they give us reasonable warning?" the policeman complained.

Two sets of eyes were straining into the darkness ahead. Five minutes hard driving had produced nothing. Frank and Harold were beginning to despair of catching the Minx. Suddenly, a splash of lights flashed in the distance, "There he is!" the occupants of the Simca shouted simultaneously and both unconsciously leaned nearer the windscreen. Frank daren't look at the speedometer, aware only that his driving abilities were stretched to their extreme limit.

Harold did glance however, 'Shit!' he said inwardly, '95 miles an hour!'

They were fast catching and eventually passed the first set of car lights. It proved to be a cruising Saab. Minutes later they saw a second set of tail lights, odd taillights! There was no doubt about these. Kowaleski was licking along around the 80 mark.

"We've got him Harry," Frank said gratefully easing back on the pedal, "I don't want to get too near the bastard and ..." he glanced at the fuel gauge, "we can follow him all night."

A road sign indicating the Episkopi turn off flashed past then a few hundred yards preceding the junction, Bernard's car lights went out. "What!" Frank exclaimed, "what's he playin' at?"

All the lights from the white Minx had vanished as Frank skidded to a screeching halt at the Episkopi-Limassol junction. They got out. There was no indication which way the deranged Chief had taken. "Crafty bastard, where is he?" 'Frank muttered as they peered in both directions for any sign of the lights.

"All right, he's worked a flanker, but think about it," said Harold. "He must be going to Limassol. Where else would he be going at this time of night, I mean, where else is there to go?"

Both men jumped back inside and Frank's answer was to take a skidding right turn onto the Limassol road. Within seconds they crested a rise and an empty moonlit road stretched straight ahead. There were no vehicles of any sort on the road. "Unless he's had a jet engine fitted there is no way he could have got clear over that stretch Frank. He's taken the Episkopi road!" As Harold spoke, Frank shouted. "Harry, I just saw twin beams in my mirror, surely he's not flashing us?"

Frank had not practiced a skidding hand brake turn for years. The last time he tried and mastered the manoeuvre fairly successfully was between two hangers in Leuchars. Tonight he did it without thinking. With the accelerator flat to the floor, he spun the wheel and simultaneously jerked hard on the hand brake. In a heartbeat the rear of the car swung round majestically in a long U-turn and Frank on releasing the hand brake, was suddenly battling to control the vehicle which was now facing the road they had just come down. The Simca did a couple of tail wags then with blue smoking tyres, Frank gained traction and was soon racing back to the junction.

Harold was dumbstruck, "Fucksake!" he roared. "Give me some warning if you're going to do that again. I thought you'd lost it!"

"So did I," Frank muttered, "but it turned out fine though it's burnt a year's wear off my tyres! Harry, what's goin' on, he was in front of us, how did he get behind us? now he's in front again? Don't know if it is him. Look ... och they're gone, I think I just caught a blink of his taillights!"

"There's no other cars is there? Just keep going, this has be the road he's on."

The Episkopi road was full of bends as it curved through the hills. Frank's confidence rose with each passing mile as he rediscovered his driving skills. They had been allowed to submerge over the years under a protective screen of marriage and family. Screeching round bends, braking and using gears to suit the conditions, he felt absolutely in control. "Ray would've been proud of me," he muttered remembering the driving skills of his dead friend.

"Down there!" Harold suddenly shouted. "There he goes Frank!" Harold was pointing downwards through the passenger window on his left. "No don't you look for Christ's sake," Harold cried, "but it's him all right. Can't mistake those bloody taillights. He's taken the road into Happy Valley."

Frank's eyebrows knitted together, "Happy Valley, what the hell for ... this time o' night, why?"

"Simple, he's flipped, Who knows what he's thinking?"

Bernard had initially tried to lose any pursuers, but found he could not outrun this maniac who obviously had a much faster car than his supposed speedster. Lack of a decent service and tune up had clipped the performance of the Hillman Minx engine and 85 mph was the best he could force from the badly maintained car. Minutes earlier as Bernard passed the road sign warning of the Episkopi Limassol T-junction one mile ahead, he saw in the glimmer of moonlight, the imposing square shape of Kolossi castle loom in the moonlight on his left. Impulsively he took a massive gamble for he could not brake without warning those behind of his intentions. To lose speed he quickly crash changed down the gears, the gearbox screaming in agony as he dropped to around 25mph. To kill the brake lights, he switched off his ignition and braked as hard as his non-responsive system would allow. The car careered off the road, skidded down an angled incline, side slipping crazily for dozens of yards. At the last seconds after what seemed long minutes of steering with one hand and hauling on the hand brake, Bernard managed to skid steer into a gap between side buildings of the castle. Miraculously, he finished inches away from an ancient but very solid looking wall.

Unperturbed at his close call he quickly tried the starter. It whirred in space but he wasn't too perturbed. He had time. Jumping out and with one crank, the engine caught. While he was doing this he watched the other car race past the point he had skidded from the road. Their car braked skidding to a halt at the junction. They got out and in the silvery half-light he picked out the crazy driver. It was Connolly, yes, yes, suddenly he recalled the name. With the recollection of the name other information filtered into Bernard's brain. Wasn't Connolly regarded as their top man? Had he not learned from some source the MU team revolved around their No.3? He was the MUs top dog! Bernard sat back and stared in wonderment at the stars. The gods were being kind to him tonight.

He reversed out from the shielding buildings and regained the road. At last they were filling his long empty good luck sack with all his sworn enemies. To repay the gods it was simply a matter for him to reap their bountiful benefits and to reverse his role from hunted to hunter.

Bernard turned at the junction and followed the Simca as it roared off towards Limassol, He instinctively knew Limassol had too many people, too many bright lights, was much too busy for him to inflict any damage on Connolly without interruption. He had to get this man to a quiet spot, somewhere where he would not be interrupted. And he knew of just such a place! But first he must inform the driver in front he was going the wrong way. They were so gullible these idiots. With his foot on the headlight dip button on the floor he flashed his main beam up and down twice. Although he was at least a mile behind the Simca, the gods proved their worth again as they as good as delivered his next victim into his hands. Bernard did a quick reverse turn when saw Connolly perform his fancy U-turn.

Bernard had a feeling as he drove up the silver strip of moonlit, a warm gut feeling. It was out of his hands now. A matter of destiny, their karma. This was meant to happen. The top two agents from each camp had to meet at their appointed meeting place. And where else could sworn enemies clash but at the chosen point of all worthwhile conflicts, Happy Valley?

Bernard drove towards the green playing field where earlier that day he had been let down. The field was bare, only the marquees to his right remained to show a major sports meeting had recently taken place. He smirked when he saw the lights of a car rounding the bend far up to his left. They must see him now and slowly he drove to the marquee. Looking across the green field in the swathe of light cut in the darkness from his headlight beam, he drove on to the grass and followed the route he had so proudly led his team only a few hours earlier. Carefully approaching the stand he was looking for something, keeping his headlights low, and soon spotted what he was searching for. He stopped and stared at the three painted lines six feet apart. He emitted a huge sigh. Those lines were all that remained of the tug-of-war final. He could pick out some of the deep gouges in the turf where he vainly tried to stop the MU taking the honour he so badly wanted. 'No, no,' he corrected himself. There were two details wrong with that train of thought. Firstly, the MU had not won today, they had not WON the final, no, no! His men had given it up! They had presented the match to the MU. He was there. He had seen it! Secondly, he, Chief Technician Bernard Kowaleski, did not want to win the NEAF tug-of-war final. No, no, no, that was not the case at all. His aim had been to STOP the MU from winning! And this he achieved for had his team not given up? Had they not presented his enemies with the title? Therefore, something presented or donated could not be construed to have been won! So how could the MU be winners?

The befuddled and constant questioning and contradicting of Bernard's brain made the hate he harboured akin to an old friend supplying fuel to a caustic active ulcer. The resultant acid burned and tore at his innards sending in return poisonous gasses to his thinking grey matter. He felt his eyes smart and his distorted view of the world saw the lights of the car delivering his enemy to him.

"They have taken away the rope Connolly, but we are nothing if we are not resourceful. We must find another game where we can decide who fucks who!"

"What's he playin' at Harry?" asked Frank as he saw the white car parked in the middle of the field, its headlights blazing, lighting the empty stand.

"God only knows what the clown's thinking about Frank. We best be careful. Let's not forget what Chief McKinley said about keeping our distance." Harold was very apprehensive.

Frank parked at the edge of the field and switched everything off. Minutes ticked uneventfully by. The watching airmen saw the occasional glow of a cigarette and heard the purring engine as Bernard smoked one of his Turkish cigarettes glaring at them all the while. Harold grew uneasy, "I think you should switch on your engine Frank, I don't trust him, he could try anything and with your engine off we might be caught flat footed!"

Suddenly the stillness of the night was shattered when the ticking engine of the Minx revved high and the white car reversed at speed throwing up clods of turf and earth. "I think he heard you," Frank shouted, starting his engine, "He's makin' a run for it!"

Kowaleski turned hard right and drove straight for an access track to the right of the stand. The tight track, used as a service lane, ran all the way round the rear of the stand to connect to the main entrance road. If he got there, there was nothing to stop him reaching the main road where the 'catch me if you can' game would start all over again.

"That's what he's doin'" Frank yelled gunning the Simca into a tight circle and driving back the way they had come in. He reached the track's exit point and skidded round trying to block both the main exit road and the service track. He overshot a little ending up facing the track as Bernard's lights appeared. Frank was playing this game 'by ear'. He had no idea what Kowaleski was doing. All he was concerned about was to keep this madman in his sights until the RAF police arrived. They would certainly be out looking for him by now.

The Minx slowed to a stop and for a second time in as many minutes they faced each other like two angry bulls, the headlights glaring head-on fifty yards apart. "What now, Harry?" Frank was uneasy for there no way to out-think Kowaleski.

Bernard did not pause for long. He revved up and drove straight at the Simca. The not unexpected forward move still surprised Frank and for a breathless second he sat on the sore point of indecision. It was pointless reversing for in slow reverse gear Bernard could easily ram Frank. There was no alternative but to drive forward, try to dodge the Minx but then the exit road would be open. The latter had to be the lesser of two evils! Frank floored the accelerator steering into the blinding lights of the advancing Minx. Both car occupants cringed awaiting the crash of tearing metal as the Simca raced past the blinding lights, into darkness! Missing the light source by inches. Steering right and racing back into the ground, Frank was about to spin into a U-turn to follow Bernard, who he assumed was back on the main road, but was amazed to see headlights in his mirror. Bernard had not left! He had turned and was right behind Frank!

"He doesn't want to escape!" Harold shouted looking through the rear window, "he's playin' with us, he could have gone right up that road but he's turned back. He's chasing us!"

Frank scowled. Kowaleski had lured them into Happy Valley and like it or not, they were caught up in some sort of lethal dodgem car game. "Hang tight, Harry, he's tryin' to ram us." Frank tried to think as he drove hard, zig zagging over the grass, skidding and tearing great lumps of the soft green turf. Frank had no intention of allowing this bampot the doubtful pleasure of ramming his lovely new Simca. Racing towards the sheer rock face at the far end of the ground he executed yet another U-turn. The dew wet grass allowed a slewing sliding half moon skid, then a waggle and a bounce before Frank regained control. Convinced he had gained enough room with his manoeuvre, he steered straight back on a clear run for the exit road.

Unfortunately for Frank, Bernard had out-thought him. He had seen the manoeuvre performed by the Scot minutes earlier on the Limassol road and suspected, no expected Connolly as he raced towards the rock wall, to try it again. As they raced over the length of the field, Bernard knew the only way to avoid crashing into the wall of rock at the south end of the ground at the speed they were travelling, was a U-turn! Seconds before Frank swung his wheel, Bernard had turned in a tight skidding half circle emerging slightly ahead and to the right of the Simca completing its U-turn.

Concentrating on the manoeuvre, Frank was surprised to see the lights racing in on his right. Too late he tried to wrench the wheel into an evading turn but no vehicle on earth could react quickly enough. The screeching screaming tear as the charging Minx tore into the rear of the Simca was all Frank heard. The wheel was ripped out of his grasp. The car went into a circular skid as the back end swung away, then the bonnet went into what seemed a fast dizzying circular spin. Another thumping crash followed as the spinning cars collided again. Frank was picked up bodily and thrown into space. There was a dreamy sensation of flying, revolving at great speed then oblivion.

It could not have been too long before Frank opened his eyes. Fifty yards away he saw Lorna's pride and joy on its side, one wheel lazily performing its last dying spin. He was utterly winded, trying to drag air into flattened lungs. Someone was lying next to him on his left side. He could feel the person's arm and hand by his hip, brushing his left hand. Frank moved his hand gingerly to touch the one beside his own, at the same time turning his head cautiously to the left. There was no one by his side! He suppressed a scream rising in his throat when he realised the hand he was gently touching was his own!

His right arm was dislocated at the shoulder and broken above the elbow. It was trapped by his own body weight under his back. He tried to roll his weight off the arm but stopped immediately when a dozen hot pokers lanced across his chest.

The pain was so terrible, excruciating did not come near to describing it when he moved. 'Harry, where was Harry?' Frank turned his head again to the car and searched more carefully around the smoking creaking wreck. Then he saw him. Harold Ross was a bloody mess. His head and upper body was a mass of blood. Harold's head and shoulders had smashed through the windscreen, his chest and arms halfway through the frame of the windscreen. His hips and legs were meshed darkly over the dash. The majority of the blood flowed from a deep gouged wound that ran over the top and down the back of Harold's head and neck and into his shoulder. The wound had been caused by the rear mirror stem situated at the top part of the windscreen. There was no sign of life, not from Harold.

Bernard on the other hand was displaying an abundance of life. He was slightly dizzy and muddled but there was no doubt of his intentions. He limped splay footed over to where Frank lay. "You lose friend," he shouted as he reached then stood astride the prostrate Scot. "You ... fucking ... lose ... don't you?" he screamed, dragging out the words, bending low over Frank's face.

Bernard's attention was snagged by an object that lay at the side of Frank's head. Frowning he picked it up. Frank recognised it to be the rule handle of the knife used in the stabbing. He meant to give it to Chief McKinley, but in the confusion unconsciously placed it in his shirt pocket.

"You're a thief too!" Bernard shouted, "This is mine! Why do you take things that do not belong to you? This is mine!" He thrust his fist enclosing the handle into Frank's chin. "You people from the MU always take things you have no right to take, always fucking things up aren't you?" He glowered at Frank who was frantically trying to collect his scattered thoughts. The raving went on, "You fucked me up, YOU! You fucked me up good all those years ago but you are not having it all your own way now. I'm paying you back good now, aren't I?" He was waving the handle across Frank's face, "Your coach broke this, but we have a standby. I'm not finished with you, not yet."

All the time Bernard was raving he had kept his right hand behind his back and Frank bore the light hope perhaps the crazy Chief had damaged it in the crash. It was a forlorn hope.

Drawing his hand from behind his back Bernard produced something Frank could not at first identify but as the preening madman held it high and waved it around, Frank recognised it to be a car starting handle. Calmly Bernard placed the broken knife handle in his pocket. Still standing astride Frank gripping the angled piece of steel with two hands raised it high above his head. "If you haven't guessed, I'll tell you what I hope to achieve here, Number three man Connolly from 103 Maintenance Unit. I want to see if I can split the centre of your forehead open all the way down to your chin in one blow. Like the axe men of medieval times when they were considered to have done a good job if they lopped the heads off in one clean chop of their axe. Of course, like the axe men, I could do it in two or three swings but my bell will ring if I can do it in one. From your forehead down to your chin. Close your eyes Connolly, you really won't want to see this. And I don't want you moving spoiling my aim. Or you can watch, I really don't care, but unless you want me to really hurt you, I ask one last time, do not move!" Bernard spoke conversationally as he wound up his considerable strength in his shoulders. The handle started its swing.

Again Bernard's concentration was broken and swung the handle away harmlessly. There was something peculiar about his victim's posture he only just noticed. He scowled when he realised Mr. Connolly had two left hands! "Ha, HA," he roared, "I have heard of two left feet, but never hands. What have you done to yourself, you silly stupid man?" In the bright moonlight lying alongside Frank's left arm, his right hand could clearly be seen, plus a portion of wrist protruding from under the body. From the angle the right hand was lying it was obvious the arm was broken.

"You've broken your arm?" Bernard asked lightly, enquiringly. Frank could but stare defiantly at his tormentor. "You have! You've broken your fucking arm," Bernard roared into the night and went into a fit of laughing, which degenerated into a coughing spluttering spasm causing him to stagger away and roll around like a drunk tossing the starting handle away to one side. After some minutes, the wild eyed Chief recovered, and returned to survey his victim, his eyes glittering like a cat watching an immobile helpless mouse. Then, as if to assure himself of the damage, he stepped forward and adopting his astride stance over Frank again, leaning over him to get a closer look.

In that split second Frank, immobile certainly, but his brain racing saw and grasped the only chance he was ever likely to get and swung his left fist as hard as he could into the jaw of the man bending over him. It landed square on the point and on impact, the worst agony Frank had ever experienced seared through his body almost causing him to faint. The pain was almost worth it!

Bernard grunted and dropped heavily to Frank's right thudding into the turf. Job done, he knew he had to get to his feet before this madman recovered. Scrabbling for some sort of a grip, he pushed down on his left arm in an attempt to raise his upper body. Blinding pain like molten fire shot through his upper body. Frank bit his lip, cutting off the scream that so nearly reached his mouth, afraid his shriek might revive the unconscious Kowaleski.

He slumped on his back again, the pain exhausted him but he daren't waste time. His only hope lay in getting to his feet and somehow immobilize this unpredictable man lying by his side. Building up a resistance barrier against the agony he knew would come, Frank shut his eyes. He pushed with his left leg on the ground and with his left hand, tried to roll over to his right, hoping to ease his weight off the broken arm. A blast furnace of searing torture burnt through his flimsy barrier but he kept on, forcing the screaming all too heavy weight of his torso on to his side. But he made it! He may be gasping, sucking air like a landed fish, but he was on his side and the pain had eased to simple agony. The next step was to roll over onto his front, bring his knees up to his chest and get up on to his knees. After that it would be relatively easy.

"So you are not beaten yet Jock? You do indeed make a worthwhile opponent." Bernard was kneeling, fingering his jaw tenderly. "But worthwhile opponents only provide extra pleasure for me when I want to play ... and to win."

Frank was desperately trying to get to his knees but a kick sent him crashing back into the pit of searing agony. Again he nearly fainted but retained enough clarity to watch the stumbling Chief go to the edge of the running track and return carrying something. He placed the object which was round and heavy ... a rock? ... under Frank's good left arm, stand on the hand then calmly but heavily stamp down on the exposed limb near the elbow. There was a loud crack. Frank fainted.

It must have been weeks later Frank opened his eyes. He wanted to stretch but his inner brain warned him not to move.

"So you return to the land of the living Corporal Connolly. I am very pleased to see that you have, I was becoming impatient."

Frank's heart, which for a moment had taken flight from this dire situation, plummeted. Bernard was sitting in the grass at his feet smiling benignly like a priest who just heard a particularly spicy confession. For the past ten minutes the Chief had felt his emotions begin to boil as his victim seemed to sleep in comfortable repose. Then it would be his last mortal rest, for Bernard was going through each different style, the one that might prove best to dispatch into eternity this central figure of the MU tug-of-war team.

Bernard stood up, his decision made. The starting handle had figured in the majority of his weird methods to send Frank into the next world but the handle was too crude. He needed something more refined. Bernard went to his car.

Frank was desperate to come up with some solution to at least delay whatever the Chief had in mind. He knew Chief Tech. Jock McKinley must have got the RAF police and probably the civil police out looking for them by now. He had to stall this man somehow, but with two broken arms he could not physically resist. He had nothing else to pit against this man but to use his head.

Bernard returned holding something, then took up position between Frank's kicked wide splayed legs. In his hand he held up what looked to Frank like a maestro's baton. Then he saw it glimmer in the moonlight. It was a long thin blade and unwittingly he jerked his head back. Bernard's teeth glistened as he saw the look of recoil.

"I was undecided between my useful starting handle, and this. Bought this lovely little tool in the Turkish quarter. Amazing what they sell down there. Had no idea how I might make use of it, but thanks to you, I do now. You are NOT going to like this," Bernard said quietly.

"I'm gonna fuckin' love it you bent bastard!" Frank tried to roar but it came out as a hiss.

"You're going to love it, are you?" sang Bernard as he lowered and ground his rump into the nether regions of his victim. "Don't get any ideas lover boy," taunted the smiling Chief drawing the flat of the blade across Frank's face, "for if I feel so much as a bump, I will slice it off, I promise."

Never taking his eyes from Frank, Bernard cut through the trouser belt. "I am going to slice you up a little, my Scottish sausage." He smiled widely as he remembered something, "I used to like that peculiar Scottish sliced sausage they serve at Kinloss, I was detached there you know?" he spoke conversationally popping the buttons off Frank's shirt with the knife.

"Chief!" Frank said, not knowing what he was going to say, merely trying to buy time. Bernard raised his wide pre-occupied eyes, "Yes?" he answered pausing.

Frank searched his jangled thoughts trying to pin one down. Anything to get this man to stop what he was doing. "Your wife, what happened to her?" the stricken airman managed to blurt out.

The dark eyes could clearly be seen to glitter in the depths of those hooded brows, then they flickered as they focused on the face below him. "That was a shame, that was really sad because it was so brilliant. I should have been allowed to boast to the world how I committed the perfect crime because it was so absolutely brilliant! I did a good job there, eh Jock? They didn't even connect me with that, did they? Tied them up in nylon. Soaked the car with petrol I did, then BOOOOM! Nylon melted, it was beautiful. I mean that, everything about it was beautiful!"

Frank despite his position stared at the man sitting on him,

"You killed them?" he asked shakily.

"'Course I did, beat their fucking brains in didn't I, then set their little two timing bums on fire." He chuckled, then methodically carried on cutting. He opened the shirt wide and exposed the finely muscled chest. Holding the knife vertically by the handle with two fingers he danced the point over the chest, the honed point causing pinpricks of blood, then dropped it on a nipple. "Useless things these, aren't' they?" he said drawing the point round the taut nipple. Raising his eyes again, he looked into Frank's smouldering orbs, "I'm going to kill you, I want you to know that Corporal, you do know I-am-going-to-kill-you?" he said spacing the last words in his favourite way.

"And-you're-a-crazy-bastard! You do know that too, don't you?" fumed Frank, frustrated and helpless.

Bernard with a benign smile, held the knife up firmly in his right hand. Holding the weapon up in front of his waxen face as if in offering to some god, Bernard placed the pad of his left thumb at the base of the blade. Slowly he lowered the weapon to lay it flat on Frank's chest with the point at the central inverted 'V' where the rib cage meets. "I hope this hurts you a little more than the intense pleasure I shall experience doing it," Bernard said in a soft contented voice.

Applying only a little pressure the point eased under the skin and disappeared as Bernard pushed gently upwards. Up under the skin the razor-sharp blade eased, on and on upwards towards Frank's chin. Warm blood ran down over Bernard's fingers and with its touch, thrills coursed through his body as he watched the man under him try to disguise the pain he was feeling. But this joy had to be extended, to make it last. At this rate his bleeding adversary would be dead in minutes.

"I am going to repeat this at five points along your rib cage, Connolly," he spoke like a doctor performing a series of injections. Withdrawing the steel shaft slowly he allowed blood to drip on selected points he intended to pierce next. Moving down the lower right side, he again slipped the knife under the skin, resting on the bones, keeping it parallel to the body, cutting up, keeping the blade against the upper side of the ribs.

"Bastard, mad bastard," Frank whispered hoarsely as he tried not to twist away from the probing blade. These words only brought a wider smile to the face of Frank's tormentor as he moved the blade in a level arc like a windscreen wiper blade.

The smile was reduced to flickering grimaces across Bernard's mouth as he worked carefully now, withdrawing the knife from the second incision, "As I was saying, I will now do, let me see, is it four, there is so much blood, no three more little incisions, then I will dispatch you - another loss to the MU. I will do that by carrying out the same action I am performing to your chest, to your throat. You will feel this delicate tool push up alongside your windpipe, then through your chin, up into your mouth, then finally through your tongue. That I think will be the coup de grace, for there is little to stop me going up into your brain from that point, is there? You will be happy to know I was thinking of cutting off your penis and testicles, but then you would die on me very quickly. I don't want that." Working all the while he was talking, the blade was inserted under the lower left side of Frank's rib cage. The maniacal half sneer softened when he spoke again, "And your little poofter, him too! Ah, but I didn't want to hurt Julian." For a moment Bernard stopped cutting. He sat back on solid hips and sighed heavily. The words, although softly spoken penetrated through the pain and mists of his victim's consciousness. Frank's brain fought through folds of coherence that were as cobwebs as he reached for support. "You killed Julian?" he whispered.

Bernard blinked as he heard the hissed question but was happy at the fact this current subject of his hate was still conscious, still able to feel the pain he intended to inflict. "What did you say, what did you say, Connolly?" he croaked at the blood splattered face.

"You ... killed ... Julian?" Frank could barely resist floating off into the realms of welcoming wallowing clouds of comfort. "You ... hurt Julian?" he repeated. Frank was dimly aware if he fought to speak he might stay conscious long enough to hear the answer.

"Your fucking Julian?" Bernard's tone carried a mixture of hate, jealousy and strangely something approaching love, as he glared at Frank. "Your precious little girlfriend, Julian? Yes I did! I cut him and stuck him like the sow he was. I fucked your little girlfriend, Connolly and I cut his heart. I cut his heart and he died in these hands, I felt the life drain out." Bernard stopped when he saw Frank's lips move but the voice was faint.

"... dead ... you're dead Chief ... signed your own death warrant." The words came with each expiration of breath. "I swore I'd get the one who hurt Julian, you're dead Chief, somehow I'll get ...."

The idiotic grin widened. The blinking eyes of the mindless Bernard loved this resistance being shown by this lump of gibbering meat under him. "Oh YES," he roared into the face where the only part that was moving were the lips as they continued to swear vengeance at the self confessed killer. But even as he roared into the face, Bernard knew the game was nearly over, the fun was fading from this game. If he did not end this soon the man would die under him then, he would feel nothing. He began to itch at the determination of this half dead, half conscious but stout hearted body he sat on and growled as he pushed upwards, missing vital organs with the slim knife. The movement was meant only to instil pain but he could see this man was losing his grip on the world and feeling little of the pain he was trying to inflict. Time to send this almost lifeless 103 MU team member on his way otherwise he was going to slip off the edge of the world gently. He could not allow that, he had to pay!

"Now Jock my boy, all your gibbering about gaining revenge for Julian is sadly over." Bernard slapped the face trying to revive Frank back to awareness. "This is where I get into a delicious sticky mess," he garbled in his excitement. The deranged Chief placed the knife flat on Frank's throat and upper chest with the point one inch below the Adam's apple, "But I am looking forward to showering in your blood, so be a good boy Scottie and say, bye-bye." Bernard pushed the blade gently upwards. The point pierced under the skin of Frank's neck, grating against the windpipe and delighted Bernard when he saw the dark arterial blood run along the bright steel.

"Don't be like that now, when you've been so good," Bernard said, when he saw the eyes open and Frank's last stare glowering hatefully up at the sick man sitting astride his body. The drooling smile widened as he re-applied the pressure and pushed the handle of the knife slowly upwards towards the chin.

"What a lovely feeling, ooh," he groaned, "better than entering any woman. Come now Scottie, before you depart, say bye-b-"

There was a dull but ringing 'TUNG,' and Bernard's head shook, the words and smile frozen. Only the eyes widened and blinked once, twice, then his pupils tried vainly to force their way up under the suddenly heavy eyelids. There was another similar noise, 'TUNG,' then another, and another. The fourth blow saw Bernard drop his chin onto his chest, then slowly, as if reluctant to do it, toppled to one side and slumped heavily alongside Frank.

Harold swayed with the effort, doing his best to stay upright. He held the starting handle with both hands and was raising it

619

again when he realised Bernard had fallen unconscious.

"My God!" muttered Harold as he again nearly lost his balance at the pitiful sight of Frank. "My God," he repeated, surveying the whole scene, seeing for the first time the carnage of cars, blood and bodies. He looked from Frank to the face of the Chief Technician, calm now and rather elegant in repose. Harold raised the starting handle as high as he could reach, and scythed it down with every ounce he could muster on to the dark featured but handsome relaxed face.

As the handle struck, it bounced free of his grip, then slowly like a sand castle crumbling in the wash of the waves, Harold toppled first to his knees then over the prone bodies and lay still.

~~~

Chapter 27

Nobby Clarke sat outside the Main Guardroom at RAF Akrotiri. On his knee was a cardboard box on which his hands were resting as he waited for Flt. Sgt. Terry Grieg. It was seven o'clock in the evening and the mood of the solid Indian was morose as he stared out across the salt flats where flamingos in great numbers wintered annually. It was too early for the long necked graceful creatures as it was still high summer and the salt flats were precisely that: hard baked beds of raw salt.

Two days had passed since the knifing in the Peninsula Club. Two stunned days since Callum McAlpine suffered such grievous injuries, and later that same night, the terrible incident at Happy Valley where Frank Connolly and Harold Ross had come so near to losing their lives. Nobby's great head rocked slowly from side to side as he thought of the carnage caused by the man everyone joked about being mad. 'Well,' he mused sighing heavily, 'it's no joke now.' Callum, the inspired tug-of-war coach had died from the madman's frenzied attack in the Peninsula Club. A team of doctors and Callum had fought for the life that was so reluctant to die but in the end the fiery haired Scot succumbed and passed away peacefully four hours after they got him up to the Princess Margaret Rose hospital.

The instigator of all the turmoil, Chief Tech. Bernard Kowaleski had been flown back to England trussed in a straight jacket. When they found him on that terrible night they got the unconscious Chief back to the same ward, ironically only a few beds away from where his victim lay dying. On regaining consciousness he had tried to strangle the nurse tending his facial injuries. A male nurse who came to the girl's aid received a bloody head butt for his trouble and eventually it took five male nurses to overpower the immensely powerful Chief Technician. A hastily applied sedative ultimately brought the bleeding Chief to his knees snarling like a wild animal.

The MU was still reeling from the shock of yet another death, this time a murder. The question now being asked was had the killing of their coach been the only murder in recent times? If one cast an ear into the wind that soughed across the entire base, the whispers were there probably had been others.

Many insinuations, half facts, hints, rumours, sightings and anything else that may ostensibly contribute to the stew of the whole mishmash of information, had been tossed into the melting pot. After boiling, mixing and masticating for two days it seemed there might be, after all, a case that the illegal taking of lives in recent times had indeed taken place. The most damning of these was the rumour that rose to the top of the witch's brew after the two day distillation period. It was said the mass ramblings from the mouth of an initially delirious Cpl. Connolly were being investigated. It seemed the badly injured young man was making enough sense to indicate the deranged Kowaleski was responsible for amongst others, the recent disappearance and murder of another airman, SAC Julian Cantwell.

Nobby jumped, scattering his thoughts like sparks in a fireworks display when a car horn sounded. Terry's Austin Cambridge was wheeling into a turn before rolling to a gentle stop beside the square set anchorman. Before climbing into the back, Nobby stared out again over the serenity of the salt flats and sighed heavily. The inner serene, reserved nature of the man had taken a brutal shock and could not come to terms with the harsh reality of recent events. He sighed again, the cool evening air smoothing the ruffled silk of his cramped lungs. Robbie Stone glanced at him but said nothing as the bulky Indian sat beside him, gently for a big man in the spacious back seat. Beside Terry in the front Sam Haire sat staring silently ahead. The mood inside the car matched the universal anguish.

"How do you feel, lad?" Terry asked, having noted his last passenger's melancholy expression.

Tears rimmed his eyes as Nobby answered quickly, before his voice broke, "I'm okay, Terry."

"I hear Carol Cook's in a bad way, poor lass," Sam spoke woodenly to the windscreen.

"So I hear. They've got her in dock too. What you got there?" Robbie changed the subject. He was referring to the square box on Nobby's knee.

If Nobby heard the question he didn't answer and Robbie decided not to push. The four fell silent as Terry drove down the main road for a spell then took the turn off for the hospital.

The car occupants were on their way to pay their last respects to Callum. The casket was to be sealed at 8 o'clock that night followed by a short service. It would then be flown to Scotland where relatives had claimed the body for private burial.

The imposing building of the military hospital rose from the rocks as the Austin Cambridge rolled down the narrow road. Terry parked and as the others made for the entrance of the small chapel, Nobby stopped. "I have to find the padre Flight," he spoke to Terry, "I'll join you in a minute or two."

Terry nodded as he, Sam and Robbie entered the vestibule of the stone building. Peering past the trio deeper inside the church, Nobby caught a glimpse of an open topped coffin in a small recess. There was only one door at one side of the entrance, which was unmarked. Assuming this to be the vestry he rapped it gently.

A be-speckled young officer, suitably dog collared and looking slightly startled, appeared in the dimness of the interior.

"Can I help you?" he asked, in an unexpectedly deep fruity voice.

"Can I come in for a few minutes sir, I have a rather unusual request."

The padre peered closely at Nobby, took a step out and glanced into the chapel. "I was just on my way out actually but, yes, all right." He turned back into the anteroom, "Please, do come inside, let us see what we can do for you. Unusual requests are as rare as prostitutes in a vicarage!" he laughed heartily. "Not unheard of mind you!" he laughed again. "Oh I'm so sorry, so sorry, do forgive me, I shouldn't be in this job." He cleared his throat noisily, "I don't have a leg to stand on after that little outburst do I. Yes, now what is this request that is so unusual?"

Nobby taken aback at this unusual officer of both church and Air Force, closed the door and placed his box on a leather topped desk. He introduced himself giving for some unknown reason his full name and rank, then went on, "Sir, the man in the coffin next door, Cpl. Callum McAlpine, was a very dear friend of mine," he paused and looked up at the bare stone walls gathering himself.

His normal deep voice was even more resonant in the small room.

"Yes, yes I'm sure he was," the padre said in a more understanding compassionate tone.

"Well sir, the reason I'm here is," Nobby paused, aware his request might sound ridiculous but never the less, he was desperate to be taken serious, "I promised him, Corporal McAlpine, that one day he would win a tankard and ... well, he's dead now."

The officer looked nonplussed, "I'm sorry Clarke. Oh, look under the circumstances let's dispense with rank here, Rowland was it? Rowland, I'm afraid I don't understand?"

Nobby nodded realising the ambiguity of his words. He went on to explain how Callum had lost the only tankard he ever won back in Stradishall and how the two friends had made a pact. They would present each other with a tankard if neither of them had managed to win a pewter drinking vessel for their efforts in the sport of tug-of-war.

"You and the deceased, you were both in the MU team? Surely you must have won a pot of some sort in all your conquests?" the padre stared aghast. The startled look was back.

"Strangely enough sir, we won everything else but ... no tankard. At least, not at tug-of-war." Nobby picked up the box and opened it. He withdrew the beautiful gold plated tankard evoking memories of happier times. "I was fortunate enough to win this trophy sir, but strangely, I won this playing darts! It's such a beautiful cup, I think I would like to give it to Callum." A large bulbous tear ran down the smooth brown cheek though neither of the men seemed to notice.

The padre looked pensively at his hands, "And ah, how do you intend to do that, may I ask?"

"I was hoping you might be able to help me there sir, I was hoping you might allow me to place this," Nobby held up the tankard, "in his coffin."

The blue eyes of the officer opened wide in surprise, "Ah, the light begins to glow," he began, "but wouldn't it be better to send that lovely cup to his relatives? I could arrange ..."

"That's decent of you sir, but I have to give it to Callum, and that too presents a problem. He always said any trophy he received had to be won. It wouldn't be the same just to be given a pot, it had to be won!" Nobby was finding it increasingly difficult to talk about Callum and stop the lump growing in his throat. Both he and the padre sought the source of the light flowing in the only window high above them avoiding each other's eyes. The padre cleared his throat, "Look, let me put it this way. If a gift such as that lovely gold tankard somehow ended up beside your friend, I don't want to know how it got there, do we understand each other? I cannot for the life of me see what damage it might do. Since time immemorial all sorts of vessels accompany the dead. On the other hand if as you say your friend had to win the tankard, how do you propose he can do that now?" The hint of a smile played around the corners of the officer's mouth, a glint of sunlight from the solitary beam flashed off his rimless glasses.

The Indian looked at the tankard and gave a slight shake of his head, "I don't know, maybe he'll like the cup anyway and understand there was no way he could win it, now that he's ...."

"Sometimes," the officer cried in his fruity voice, "the light shines on me ... as now," he smiled into the ray of fading light, "and I receive such a clear message why I'm in this job! Occasionally my boss blesses me with the working of his miracles!"

Nobby was not given to staring but at that moment he came close, "Sir?" he said doubtfully.

The padre fished in his pocket and pulled out a Victorian half crown. "I always use this whenever I am called to toss up for anything important, be it to referee a rugby or soccer match, or sometimes to decide amongst my colleagues whose turn it is to make the tea."

Nobby looked at the coin, "Toss up, sir?" he asked blankly.

"Yes of course. We're about to decide if you must keep the trophy or if your friend wins it away from you." He held up the coin and showed both its sides, "Okay heads or tails, which do you choose?" The padre asked holding the silver coin on his thumbnail.

"Just a minute sir, what if I call it right?"

"Oh ye of so little faith," the officer mocked with a smile. "If that happens, which I very much doubt knowing my boss as I do. But if by some unforeseen sleight of hand you do manage to call correctly, then we will go for the best of three of course!" The padre laughed and pushed his glasses up to where he was regarding his bewildered visitor through the centre of his lenses again. He went on, "But don't worry. If you have the same belief as I, and you firmly believe what we are doing here is right and most of all, good, then have no fear, you will call it wrong the first time, you'll see! Now, for the winning of this magnificent gold tankard, what do you say, heads or tails?" With no further ado he spun the coin high above the desk.

"Tails!" Nobby cried hurriedly.

The half crown landed on the desk and spun upright in a whirring quiet circle round its top. It carried on spinning almost as if the divine powers were undecided on which side to fall. Nobby looked at the young face of the padre who smiled benignly back at him, nodding his head. The coin fell showing the head of the old queen.

The officer smiled, lifting his eyes from the coin to look up at the high window, then into the surprised black orbs of his visitor. "Told you!" he said simply, picking up his coin, "your friend wins the pot. I must go into the hospital for a few minutes, I suggest you make the presentation in my absence." He turned then stopped at the door, "Do you know Rowland, it is on such pillars as your unusual request today, that contributes to the bricks and mortar of my job?" With a smile the padre walked out.

Nobby looked at the door and wondered if a man of the cloth could cheat and if so how? Nobby had free choice in the call and there was no doubt the half crown had the queen's head on one side and four shields on the other. Nobby saw them when the padre showed both sides of the coin. If he had called "Heads," they could have been spinning the coin all night; 'Best of three, Best of five, Best of seven." With a flick of his eyebrows Nobby happily accepted his wrong call. "So, there's no doubt about it, Callum, you win!" he smiled. Leaving the box on the desk he tucked the tankard inside his shirt and left the room.

In the small chapel his three friends were sitting in one of the pews. The chapel was beginning to fill with twenty minutes remaining before a small ceremony and sealing of the coffin. Nobby entered the small recess where the casket lay and waited as two GEF team members paid their respects.

When the two airmen left, Nobby stepped up close to the waist high coffin. Two thirds of the casket was closed with only the upper flap open. Nobby looked down upon the face of his well loved friend. Callum seemed to be asleep. He was pale and the craggy lines of his features had softened, also the red of his hair seemed a shade lighter. The waxen sheen of his appearance was the only evidence that Callum, as Nobby had known him, was not present in this husk that remained. Nobby had to choke back a sob as the thought crossed his mind.

The genial Indian forced the rising desolation back as he reached inside his shirt. Leaning over slightly he pushed the golden trophy into the gap down the right side of the body. "Here my very dear friend, you finally won your tankard, and yes, you truly won it, fair and square!" Remembering he might be addressing a power that knew the circumstances of the 'win' process, Nobby added, "Under the eyes of a padre and his own half crown Callum." Swallowing hard as emotions again threatened to overcome his hard held calm, he laid a hand on the cold crossed hands and stood for another minute. "Rest in peace old friend!" he whispered, then withdrawing his hand, turned away as the tears at last flowed. He nearly bumping into a beautiful blonde girl dressed in black. She was deathly pale and the black colour emphasised her natural beauty. A uniformed WAAF was supporting her. "Sorry, Carol," Nobby murmured.

Nobby eased his way into the pew as Sam pushed up to make room. The small chapel had filled quickly and was crowded now with people standing at the back, waiting respectfully for the service to begin.

"Hey, Nobby," said Sam in his rich voice, "isn't it a pity poor old Callum never won that tankard he always hankered over?" he directed a deliberate gaze to look under Nobby's arm.

Nobby's mouth lifted slightly at the corners as the Irishman went on, "Yeah shore, maybe he never managed to win one before he died, but I'm almost certain shore he's not goin' out of this world empty handed. What do you t'ink Nobby?"

~~~

EPILOGUE

The man dressed in a the dark suit with the shock of white hair was tired of sitting. He uncrossed his legs for the hundredth time, leaned forward and cupped his chin on his upturned palms. So many visions, so many memories and so many regrets. Many people had flashed across the inner screen of his mind in the seven hours he had sat in the old stand. He'd been so deeply engrossed, so drawn back into the past he had actually heard voices, commands, songs, shouts and whistles. His hands were sore as he unclenched them yet again, never tiring of the feeling the harsh hemp rope gave as it creaked and responded in his grip like a live thing. He had been the central figure in the team and relished that responsibility. It had been really good then, back in the fifties on the old MU, before the bad time started.

A deep sigh escaped the man's lips as he stood and stretched, glancing round the scenery as he did so. These surroundings had changed so very little as far as he could tell. A few trees may have grown, a few had died but basically everything was as he remembered this place all those years ago.

The man turned and made his way stiffly down the stairs to ground level and looked for the toilet where it had once been. Yes, it was still there, exactly as he remembered and he noted, the door was not locked. That was nice. Vandalism it seemed was unheard of here, not yet anyway, that was nice too. He smiled recalling the happy carefree island, untouched by commercialism on both his postings to Cyprus.

The toilets were cool and clean smelling, reminding him of his days in the RAF when aircraft and ablutions smelled like this, like the essence of pine nuts and lemons.

He stood at the urinal, slowly, reluctantly allowing his mind to return to the present. Rinsing his hands under sun warmed water running from the cold tap, he raised his head and gazed in the small mirror above the basin. He looked again for the millionth time at the long healed scars on his nose, across his forehead and right cheek where the starting handle had bitten deep all those years ago. Thankfully the wielder of that old starting handle was surely only semi conscious otherwise the strongest man in his team would surely have cracked his skull. He must have made a marvellous recovery for he certainly appeared to be dead with that hideous head wound, his head and upper body through the frame of the windscreen, spread out over the bonnet of the car. Yet, the 'dead' man, one of his own, had miraculously recovered and struck down his own coach! Another quirk in his sad life. Why? Why had he done it, was it Ross? Yes, SAC Ross, one of his best men, why should he attack him? All he was doing was seeing Connors? No! Not Connors ... Connolly ... yes, Connolly a sworn enemy from the cursed MU.

A twisted smile spread across the face in the mirror. Strange, after all these years he still felt the sadistic kick it gave him to revive the hate that burned as bright as ever deep in his soul. He had come so near to killing Connolly, and in turn he himself had come close to being killed by Ross. Fingering the long deep scar on his cheek he stared into the black eyes boring back at him.

"You were a crazy bastard in those days," he muttered, "a crazy, dangerous bastard!"

Bernard Kowaleski had been an uncontrollable basket case for two years after the night he killed the MU coach and had come so near to repeating the act with Connolly. Slowly, ever so slowly the RAF had cared for him, drawing him back into the world of sanity and over the years in different institutions had patiently tried to purge the poison from his system.

Five years ago in 1985 apparently they were satisfied. At last! As far as they were concerned, after seventeen years in their care, the last dozen in exemplary normality, he was normal. His diligence in his work, his level headedness in abnormal circumstances had raised the bar high enough to convince the white coated moles with their pads and pencils that he was no longer a threat. However, Bernard could never be slotted back in the maelstrom of everyday life. He still needed care and medication, but the straight jacket would, hopefully, never be required again. They even placed him in the equivalent of an old age home. An old age home of sorts! Surrounded as it was by a tall fence, with loose security and it was never made clear to the inmates whether the fence was to keep people on the outside from getting in, or those inside from getting out!

All the people living inside the old age home had at one time suffered ... in the past ... from some mental illness or other. However, the staff were very good and treated them well. He took his medicine regularly like a good little boy and his temper was a thing of the past. In his quiet surroundings there was nothing to trigger him off! The odd little bug could periodically make his skin crawl but that bug would always remain under his skin to nip and annoy him whenever the name came up. Which fortunately was rare nowadays. They could shovel barrels of pills, pour gallons of medication down his throat, but nothing could ever free him from the biting, stinging burr of the 103 Maintenance Unit. The doctors had tried to eliminate his problem with their wishy-washy methods, medicines and programmes. Left him vegetating in a bland room at one time, for years. When he had settled down they allowed him to mix with a gentler mix of people in the home. Bernard discovered his new friends were not really criminals. Their only crimes were they sometimes set fire to buildings or took orders from spacemen to kill their relatives! The problem with Bernard was he didn't have a problem! Sadly he had to admit there were some who were not quite right! No doubt about that but he, Bernard Cornelius Kowaleski was as sane as, as sane as ... the next man in the next room for instance, whose only crime was he wanted to cremate his father. Unfortunately, his insignificant sin was the man lacked the patience to wait until his father died.

All those wasted years. The entire span of all that time he had wanted, no lusted to return here, to this sports field when the NEAF championships were being held. To see again the team from the MU in action. It was a paradoxical urge. He longed to see them, to see their brilliance yet see them beaten, to lose emphatically. But the aching beauty of watching their poetic majesty in the sport they excelled in was the irresistible pull he had yearned for all those years. He had no idea if the present MU tug-of-war team still held court here in Cyprus, or indeed if 103 Maintenance Unit still existed!

Mr. Kowaleski was out of touch. Over twenty years out of touch with military sporting events taking place in Cyprus. Although, remarkably little had changed in that time. When he was last on the island, the major sports meeting was held on the second Wednesday in June. It was still early June so only two days ago he decided on impulse to pay Cyprus a visit! It had all been so childishly easy to escape from the complex where people like him were subjected to live. One night he complained of pains in his chest to the resident nurse, and she, always wary of chest pains with any of her aging residents had packed a small case the patient gave her. This case had been previously modified by Bernard's own hands, and fitted with a false bottom. Inside the false bottom was his bankbook, which he could claim at any time for inspection, along with all his cash savings over the years and an old out of date passport with a few other bits and pieces from his past they allowed him to keep. The nurse sent the ailing Mr. Kowaleski and his male nurse escort off in an ambulance. At the clinic in south London, they gave him the usual round of ECG and blood tests but finding nothing, decided to keep him in for observation for a few days. The next night Bernard having taken note of the set-up, waited until the night sister passed on her rounds then slipped out of bed, dressed quickly and simply walked out of the building.

Next morning Bernard made his way to an area in London where at one time with the passing of a few notes, one could buy anything. The place had changed little, other than the ridiculously high amount of pounds he had to hand over to secure a current passport, which miraculously was produced in the space of one day.

He travelled to Cyprus under his new passport name of Charles Cowan, a supposedly born and bred Londoner. In a much changed Limassol he booked into the 'Miramar Hotel.' After a pleasant night and breakfast he asked at reception if they could check through their forthcoming events to see if they had information on the NEAF sports meeting due to be held at Happy Valley. A call to RAF Akrotiri confirmed that indeed, the sports meeting was to be held the following Wednesday. He asked the efficient receptionist if she could arrange for the hire of a car, which she smilingly did, and received a generous ten pound note for her trouble.

The black eyes stared defiantly back at him from the mirror and he blinked quickly when his seeing vision returned. Screwing off the still running tap, he was surprised to hear a car pull up close to the toilets. Stepping outside he was even more surprised to see the WAAF corporal who spoke to him earlier that day.

"Ah there you are Mr. Cowan," she greeted him. "I was on my way home when I saw your car still parked here. I have to admit sir, I've been a little concerned about you all day. Hope you don't mind but I decided again to check, just to see if you enjoyed your day? I must seem to you like a terribly nosey Miss busybody "

Bernard Kowaleski studied the fair haired police woman for the first time. She was young, in her early twenties, tall, slender, good looking and he noted, did the uniform proud.

"Not at all my dear," he answered, "Indeed I have spent a most pleasant melancholy day, reminiscing, you know. This place holds many memories." Despite his outward calm he was troubled, trying to keep his voice in the same even tone, he asked, "May I ask how do you know my name?"

The girl turned her pretty head and pointed to his car, "I took the liberty of noting your car number this morning and phoned around the hotels and car hire companies. A very helpful young lady in the Miramar told me she hired the car for you from 'Hercules Hire,' and your name." The girl could not help beaming at the man whose brows were raised in surprise, or was it anger?

When he spoke she could not tell, "You have done your homework young lady. Now as you have the advantage on me, may I have your name?"

"Certainly sir, my name is corporal ..." she dropped her head coyly then looked up. "Sorry, there's no rank here is there? My name is Connolly, Gina Connolly, sir."

"Connolly?" Bernard repeated. The name ricocheted across the ravines and crevices of his memory banks. Words imprinted in those fissures of time hissed in his ears as he recalled the night he sat only a few yards from this spot carving someone up with the same name. Could that Connolly possibly be related? The hissing words buried deep in his head took on some clarity and he again heard, 'You're dead Chief ... swore I'd get you for hurtin' Julian, I'll get you ....'

"Yes Connolly sir, my father Warrant Officer Connolly only recently retired from the RAF. He lives, or more precisely, my parents and I, live in the village of Episkopi now. Dad loved the RAF life as I do. I was very fortunate to get a posting out here where I can live-out with my parents for the duration of my tour. Incidentally, I was born here, in the hospital on the base."

"Very interesting," Bernard's mind was racing. 'Could it be ... could it possibly be?'

"Would it be wrong of me to assume, you were in the Royal Air Force sir?" The question was asked suddenly but politely.

"Perhaps," he answered after a pause, "perhaps ... a long time ago," he added slowly.

"The reason I ask Mr. Cowan, you made reference to something about the playing field this morning." She turned her head delicately and looked towards the sports field. "You spoke as if you had intimate connections with it ... perhaps a long time ago?" The girl also stretched out the last few words.

"Why do you ask me that corporal ... I mean," he tried to ease his sharp words with a light chuckle. "Why specifically do you want to know?" He could not help feeling uneasy.

"Well Mr. Cowan sir, my father was posted here in the sixties, and he became a member of an excellent tug-of-war team from the Maintenance Unit. He's quite proud of the fact that many people connected with those teams come back here over the years, reminiscing, just as you said, reviving memories. I wondered if you were connected with one of those teams in some way?"

The man's eyes took on a faraway look, "Oh yes, corporal, I was, but they ... a lot of things happened ...." Bernard stopped, he could not possibly tell this girl any more.

"Please go on. I'm fascinated with that era. I suspected you were part of the sporting scene, for you pin pointed the precise location of the athletes' marquee. You must be familiar with the layout of the meetings. Please Mr. Cowan," she smiled invitingly, "you've been connected in some way with the NEAF games. The receptionist in your hotel told me you made inquiries about our upcoming meeting here?"

The annoying questions, this nosey woman prying, probing into his private affairs and the mention of the team from the Maintenance Unit. They were hurting Bernard but she persisted.

"There was a huge scandal around that time, you may have heard about it? A deranged man tried to kill my father! It was all tied in somehow with the team. This all happened a few months before I was born, perhaps that's why I'm so interested in what happened." She smiled prettily, "Do you know anything at all about that time, sir?"

Bernard's vision was beginning to cloud over, as if a misty red haze was descending over the valley, and the hellish crow was back pecking at the festering sore inside. The girl would not stop. "... 103 MU were unbeaten for years, sir. Fantastic they were. They still have photographs all over the station library and gym showing scenes from that time. They just went on forever, winning - winning - winning." She smiled happily, "It seems nobody could beat them, my father talks about the team ...."

The voice droned on but Bernard could not listen any more. He felt hot and swayed slightly as he tried desperately to clear his vision. He wished he could block his ears, there was no stopping the girl's voice, "... when he was posted back here in the seventies he took over the coaching of the team and they just carried on winning!"

Mercifully the voice stopped abruptly. He glanced up and the pretty girl was peering intently at him, "Are you all right, sir?" she asked.

Bernard staggered turning towards the toilets. "Water," he muttered, "I'd like some water."

"Of course, you've been sitting here all day and probably never had anything to eat or drink in all the time. How bloody stupid of me!" The girl exclaimed hurrying past him. "Here let me."

She entered the cool toilets and quickly held her handkerchief under the running water. Squeezing the excess from the wisp of cotton she went on, "I'm sorry sir, churtling on and on about my father and his team, I just tho- "

She was in the act of turning away from the basin, otherwise the blow would have caught her cleanly on the back of the neck. As it was it glanced painfully off her shoulder.

"Ogh!" she grunted in surprise, turning to stare at the man. His terrible black eyes were boring into her, and disconcertingly were not focused on her eyes, more to the centre of her forehead.

"What gives you the right to call me deranged? You, you stupid woman. You don't know what happened to me! I was an original member of that team! I was a brilliant athlete ... their best man, but they were jealous, jealous of me! They set me up! My own team mates, didn't like me, I was far too good for them, too good for them all so the bastards set me up, ended my sporting career, they broke my knee." Bernard pointed at his leg but continued to glare at her.

The woman had her back to the basin now, gripping it with both hands as she stared at the suddenly very angry face only inches from her own.

"They wanted to hurt me you see, like my father, he wanted to hurt me too and he did. I could never be a man, a proper man not after that, not after he turned me into a woman." His eyes drifted from her face to the trees outside, "When those bastards hurt me, broke my body, I could never be the athlete I could have been, just as I could never be a man! Sport was my only escape, do you understand me?" he raised his voice, "Sport was my only escape into the real world, I could have had it all!" The man seemed to have aged many years, was near to crying, "It was my way of getting back to normality, where I could regain my self respect but they took it away from me, the fucking MU that everyone was talking about. It was me that gave them their start yet they wanted rid of me, and to do so they removed the only link I had with the real world. They're responsible, they made me like this," he sobbed, "made me do the things I did!"

The woman could only watch the man as he rambled on bitterly. Though his attitude was threatening she sensed a heavy tinge of dolour in his bitter words. She cursed herself for lighting the spark, opening the vent to this man's inner inferno. Her training told her to wait for the tormented verbal flushing to diminish before she dare speak again. He continued unabated, then her attention was snagged when he hissed, "Your father was one of them, one of those bastards who set me up and I so nearly got him!" The black eyes again drifted out of the open toilet door again to gaze at the sports field. In Bernard's confused brain he was mixing his years, seeing Frank Connolly as one of the airmen who had supposedly 'fixed' the small gantry that caused his accident. "I so nearly skewered your father that night, over there," He pointed through the door to the field of green grass.

"But I took too long, enjoying myself you see." Slowly he turned from the open door and looked at the girl.

She had not moved from her original position. Her rump was still hard against the wash hand basin. "I enjoyed spiking your father that night, maybe today I can skewer his daughter. What do you think, are you a match for me?"

"Sir, I bear you no malice and I don't know who you are referring to. My father hurt no one! He never hurt anyone in his life." Gina Connolly spoke firmly but her words went unheeded.

"I nearly got your father that night ... no, it's true I didn't actually get him, but I certainly got his mate, the red headed bastard of a coach everyone thought was invincible, I got him!"

The corporal's eyes widened at the mention of the coach. Her father when pressed had reluctantly told her of that terrible night and of the insane person who had come so close to killing him. The man had murdered his friend, the MU coach that same night. The woman felt her body go cold. Realising she was in a tight spot, self-preservation urged her to get out of the enclosed confines of the toilets. If this man were to turn violent she would have a better chance to defend herself in the open. Just as she went to move, the man pulled something from his pocket and threw it at her. Instinctively she pulled to one side. The object flew past her head and sailed through the open door, skidding away in the gravel near her car. "Have a look at that young lady, go on," inadvertently he presented her with the opportunity to leave the toilets. "Show your precious father that! If the blade had not broken inside the swine of your coach, you would have been born minus a parent. That was my pet pig sticker and I would not have wasted time indulging myself with a new toy pin pricking your father's rib cage. If that little beauty had still been intact I would have happily and very quickly cut your father's throat."

Gina Connolly turned and moved quickly. With the words ringing in her ears she ran from the building over to the object that had come so close to hitting her head. It looked like a six inch rule - but no, it wasn't? It was too bulky to be a rule yet it had all the markings. Picking the object up she nearly dropped it as inadvertently she pressed the sides. There was an audible click and a short piece of steel pushed out along with two brass guards. The object was a cleverly disguised knife with only two or three millimetres of the broken blade remaining.

636

The crunching of the gravel made her look round. The man was already on her and had her firmly by the shoulders.

"You may not know it my girl but it's years since I've had a woman, and what better woman could I hope to violate than the daughter of an old enemy?" He was trying to drag her back to the toilets and for a man of his years he was surprisingly strong.

"Please don't do this, let me go and no one will get hurt. Nothing will be said about this if you let me go now!" The young woman was desperately trying to gather her wits; desperately trying to recall her training to handle such situations, yet still reluctant to hurt the older man.

"Hah, me, me get hurt?" he scoffed, "But it is you who are about to feel some pain my little wench, unless of course you like, or even prefer, the kinky methods I employ in fucking."

His crude and threatening words had a dramatic effect on the Air Force police woman. His words in a few seconds clicked her switch, turning her from a befuddled young girl into the mode of what her training had moulded into her second nature. Corporal Connolly took stock of her situation in that short space of time and sized up her options. The man was behind her holding her shoulders in a bone crushing grip. From his mutterings there was no doubt he intended to rape her, irrespective of what method he intended to use. She could not allow him any further scope.

The man was pushing her. Digging her heels struggling and skidding through the gravel as he propelled her towards the open toilet door she called, "Let me go sir, let me go NOW! If you persist I have no option other than defend myself!"

Bernard stopped and shook the surprisingly strong shoulders.

"Don't talk wet bitch. I intend to have my way with you! Who knows, you may even enjoy it!" Bernard again went to push the resistant girl but this time when he pushed her shoulders, the woman buckled at the knees. As she did so, her right elbow jack-knifed backwards into the unsuspecting groin. There was a gasp of pain as he released his grip and started to topple forward. She, knowing precisely how her attack would affect the man, turned quickly and caught his falling body. Taking a firm grip of the man's lapels, dropping her bottom onto the gravel to use as a fulcrum, she pushed her right foot into Bernard's stomach. Using his falling weight she dragged him with her. Her rolling rump and spine hit the ground and she

637

carried the momentum on at speed and pushed up as hard as she could with both her legs, ejecting his body effortlessly away. The man disappeared from view as he somersaulted across the short distance to crash heavily into the wall of the toilet building. It was a move Gina Connolly had learned well during her hand to hand combat training and it had reversed her situation in a matter of seconds.

The corporal rose to her feet knowing full well the man would not rise quickly. The sickening thud all to evident as the man hit the solid brick wall very hard. Sucking in one deep breath to steady herself she crossed to where he lay. "I'm sorry I had to do that, but you really gave me no choice.

There was no response from the man lying awkwardly on his side on the ground. He was quiet and very still. "Sir!" the woman pushed him with her foot. From his position his face could not be clearly seen. "Sir?" she repeated, her voice rising involuntarily. Leaning over she tugged gently at his shoulder. Without a sound he started to roll over on to his back but stopped, lying midway between on his side and his back, mouth open, head lolling.

Staring at the figure, white hair fluffing in the breeze, she leaned hesitantly forward again and placed her fingers on his neck. "Oh my God!" The words no more than a whisper. Nothing! There was nothing. No pulse, no sign of life! The girl stood up hurriedly backing off, nearly tripping in her haste, gasping as she did so, "Oh dear, I'm sorry Mr. ... sir ... oh, God!" Her eyes felt sore, like they were about to pop from their sockets. She started to cry, "I'm so sorry," she sobbed, "so terribly, terribly sorry Mr. Cowan, I didn't mean to ... oh I didn't want to hurt you."

A hand shot up covering her mouth and nervously she stepped back. Staring hard at the body. It started to move! As if hearing her words. She could not tear her eyes away for it was definitely moving! Slowly yes, but moving.

The girl need not have worried; it was merely the relaxing and dying muscles of Bernard Kowaleski toppling due to the settling spread of body weight. First the arm fell behind his back which dragged the shoulder then the chest rolled over and Bernard settled, snugly and completely onto his back, to at last, lie still.

Gina Connolly was to start one last time. For in the process of settling, from deep inside his chest and out through the open mouth, there emitted a long, satisfying and comfortable sigh.

The End

9496251R00353

Printed in Great Britain
by Amazon.co.uk, Ltd.,
Marston Gate.